Why had Helena Trescott picked Travis McGee to look after her crazy, suicide-bent daughter?

I think slaying oneself is a nasty little private, self-involved habit and, when successful, the residual flavor is a kind of sickly embarrassment rather than a sense of high tragedy. I am not suited to the role of going around selling the life-can-be-beautiful idea.

So why pick me?

Am I supposed to be the kindly old philosopher, and go set on the girl's porch and spit and whittle and pat her on the hand?

Hang around, kid. See what's going to happen next.

JOHN D. MACDONALD

THE GIRL IN THE PLAIN BROWN WRAPPER

A FAWCETT GOLD MEDAL BOOK
Fawcett Publications, Inc., Greenwich, Conn.
Member of American Book Publishers Council, Inc.

1 *IT IS ONE* of the sorry human habits to play the game of: What was I doing when it happened?

After I heard that Helena Pearson had died on Thursday, the third day of October, I had no trouble reconstructing the immediate past.

That Thursday had been the fourth and final day of a legitimate little job of marine salvage. Meyer made a lot of small jokes about Travis McGee, salvage expert, actually doing some straight-arrow salvage. He kept saying it almost made my cover story believable. But he did not say such things for any ears but mine own.

Actually it was not my ball game. Meyer gets himself involved in strange little projects. Somewhere, somehow he had gotten interested in the ideas of a refugee Cuban chemist named Joe Palacio. So he had talked a mutual friend of ours, Bobby Guthrie, a damned good man with pumps and pressures and hydraulics, into listening to Joe's ideas and going to Joe's rooming house in Miami where Joe had set up a miniaturized demonstration in an old bathtub he had scrounged somewhere.

When Bobby got high enough on the idea to quit his regular job, Meyer put in the money and they formed a little partnership and named it Floatation Associates.

Then Meyer, in one of his mother hen moods, sweet-talked me into donating my services, plus my houseboat, *The Busted Flush,* plus my swift little *Muñequita* boat to the first actual salvage operation. So I had to take the *Flush* down to a Miami yard where they winched aboard a big ugly diesel pump with special attachments rigged by Bobby Guthrie, some great lengths of what appeared to be reinforced fire hose, and several 55-gallon drums of special gunk mixed up by Joe Palacio, plus scuba tanks, air compressor, tools, torches, and so on. Once I had topped off the water and fuel tanks and laid aboard the provisions and booze, the old *Flush* was as low in the water as I cared to see her. Even with all her beam, and that big old barge-type hull, she had to react to what Bobby estimated as seven thousand pounds of extra cargo. She seemed a little discouraged about it.

"If she founders," Meyer said pleasantly, "we'll see if we can raise her with Palacio's magic gunk."

So we took off down Biscayne Bay with the *Muñequita* in tow, heading for the lower Keys. We got an early start and kept waddling along, and by last light we were far enough down Big Spanish Channel to edge cautiously over into the shallows off Annette Key, in the lee of a southwest breeze, and drop a couple of hooks.

The immediate forecast was good, but there was an area of suspicion over near the Leeward Islands, and there was an official half month of the whirly-girl season left. Also the girls are known to come screaming up through hurricane alley after the season is over.

Later I learned that Helena Pearson had written the letter to me that same Saturday, September 28th, the day after she guessed she wasn't going to make it, the letter the attorney mailed, still sealed, with his cover letter. And with the certified check.

That evening at anchor aboard *The Busted Flush* the three Floatation associates were edgy. For Meyer it was simple empathy. He knew the risks they were taking. Joe Palacio had a chance to make a new career in his adopted land. Bobby Guthrie had a wife and five kids to worry about. The three of them had periods of contagious enthusiasm, and then they would get the doubts and the glooms and the hollow laughter. If it worked on a very small scale in the scavenged bathtub, that didn't mean it was going to work out in Hawk Channel, in the Straits of Florida, in seventy-five feet of ocean.

In the morning we went south down Big Spanish, past No Name Key, and under the fixed bridge between Bahia

Honda Key and Spanish Harbor Key. Then the overladen *Flush* was out in the deeps, and we had a nine-mile run at about 220 degrees to lonely little Looe Key, across a slow heave of greasy swell. Soon I was able to pick up the red marker on Looe with the glasses. On the way, while on automatic pilot, I had figured out the quickest and best way to run if things blew up too suddenly. I would pour on all the coal and run just a shade east of magnetic north, perhaps 8 degrees, and if I could manage to make eight knots, I could tuck the *Flush* into Newfound Harbor Channel in maybe forty minutes, and find a protected pocket depending on the wind, maybe in Coupon Bight or close offshore by Little Torch Key.

Bobby Guthrie had the coordinates on the sunken pleasure boat. She lay a half mile southwest of Looe Key. She'd been down there for two months. She was the *'Bama Gal,* owned by a Tampa hotelman, about ninety thousand dollars' worth of cabin cruiser, only six months old. Forty-six feet, fiber glass hull, twin diesels. The hotelman and his wife and another couple had been out fishing and the hotelman had keeled over with a heart attack while fighting a billfish. Nobody else aboard knew how to run the ship-to-shore radio. They barely knew how to run the boat. There was a tug with a tow of three barges about a half mile farther out, so they figured that the tug would have a radio they could use to call a Coast Guard helicopter and get the man to a hospital. The guest ran the boat over toward the tug and cut the engines and they all started waving their arms. Maybe they thought that tugs and barges have some kind of braking system. The tug captain tried evasive tactics, but mass and momentum were too much. The forward port corner of the lead barge put a big ugly hole in the cruiser, but the crew launched a skiff and got the people off in good order before she went down. By the time the Coast Guard arrived, the owner was as dead as the other fish they had caught, which had gone down with the cruiser.

The insurance company had paid off on the cruiser, and Meyer had gotten a release from them, so any recovery was going to be profit—if we could bring it up, tow it in, and find something worth money.

So on that Sunday I worked the *Flush* into the most protected water that Looe provides. It is shaped like a backward "J" that has fallen onto its back, and I put the hooks out in shoal water, as close as I could get without risking being hard aground at low tide. We took the *Muñequita* out and located the *'Bama Gal* after about forty minutes of skin diving and looking. We made a bright red buoy fast to her, and then I ran the *Muñequita* up-current, put the anchor down in about seventy feet, and let her come back to the buoy before snubbing her down, almost at the end of my four hundred feet of anchor line. Not enough scope to be sure of holding.

We had just the two sets of tanks aboard the *Muñequita,* so I went down with Joe Palacio to get a good look at what condition she was in. She lay on a little slope, bow higher than the stern, and she was on about a fifteen-degree list to port, making the hole in the starboard side, a little aft of amidships, easy to see. She was picking up new grass and weed and green slime, but it wasn't too bad yet. We had expected to find her picked clean of everything the skin-diver kids could lift, but by some freak of chance they hadn't found her. The big rods with their Finor reels were still in the rod holders. Binoculars, booze, cameras, tackle boxes, rifle, sunglasses—all the toys and gear and gadgets that people take to sea were either stowed or lay on the cockpit, cabin, or flybridge decking. While Joe busied himself with studying the hatches and the interior layout, and measuring interior spaces, I kept assembling bundles of goodies and, with a couple of pulls on the dangling line, sending them up into the sunlight.

When we went up, I found that all the stuff had looked better down in the depths, green and shadowy, than up on the deck of my runabout, all sodden, leaking, and corroded.

Monday we took the *Flush* out and anchored her over the wreck and worked all day, in shifts, beefing up those places where Palacio thought the floatation might

8

come busting out, and also cutting through some interior bulkheads to make a free flow of water through all the belowdecks areas, and fastening some plywood against the inside of the hull where the big hole was. Whenever we came across anything we could tie a line to and lift to the surface, we did so.

The weather held on Tuesday and by noon Joe was satisfied that we were ready to try. We took the reinforced hose down and clamped it securely in place, leading it through the hole we'd cut into the damaged side above the waterline. We had made no attempt to make her watertight. That was the last thing Palacio wanted.

Bobby Guthrie got his funny-looking pump going. It throbbed, smoked, and stank, but it pulled water up through the intake hose dangling over the side and pumped it down and into the wreck and out through dozens of small openings here and there. Palacio was very nervous. His hands shook as he clamped the small hoses that led from three drums of separate kinds of gunk to the brass nipples on a fitting on the big hose that led down to the wreck. He had flow guages and hand pumps on each drum. As Meyer had explained it to me, Gunk One reacted with the water, raising its temperature. Then Gunk Two and Gunk Three interacted with the heated water as they went swirling down, and when they were released inside the hull down below, they separated into big blobs and, in the cooler water, solidified into a very lightweight plastic full of millions of little bubbles full of the gases released through their interaction on each other and the heated water. Palacio had the three of us manning the hand pumps and he hopped back and forth from one flow gauge to the other, speeding one man up, slowing another down. There was, after about ten minutes, a sudden eruption about forty feet down-current, and a batch of irregular yellow-white chunks the size of cantaloupe appeared and, floating very high on the water, went moving swiftly away in the slight breeze.

Palacio stopped us and cut the flow. Guthrie turned off the big pump. We went down and found that the ventilator on the forward deck had blown out. By the time it was secure, it was time to quit. All day Wednesday there was pump trouble of one kind or another. We thought Palacio would break down and start sobbing.

By midday Thursday everything seemed to be working well for about forty minutes. My arm began to feel leaden. Palacio was gnawing his knuckles. Suddenly Guthrie gave a roar of surprise. The hose began to stand up out of the water like a snake and a moment later the big cruiser came porpoising up, so fast and so close that it threw a big wave aboard, drenching us and killing the pump. She rocked back and forth, streaming water, riding high and handsome. We stomped and yelled and laughed like idiots. She was packed full of those lightweight brittle blobs of foam, and I tried not to think of how damn foolish I had been to never even think of what could have happened if she had come up that fast and directly under the *Flush*.

We wasted no time rigging for towing. We were getting more swell and I did not like the feel of the wind. Between periods of dead calm there would come a hot, moist huff, like a gigantic exhalation. I set it up with short towlines, the *Flush* in the lead, of course, the salvaged *'Bama Gal* in the middle, and Bobby Guthrie aboard the *Muñequita* in the rear. I broke out the pair of walkie-talkies because the bulk of the *'Bama Gal* made hand signals to Bobby back there impossible. The system was for him to keep the *Muñequita*'s pair of OMC 120's idling in neutral, and if our tow started to swing, he could give the engines a little touch of reverse and pull it back into line. I knew the inboard-outboards could idle all day without overheating. Also, when I had to stop the *Flush* down for traffic, Bobby could keep it from riding up on our stern.

It was early Saturday afternoon before we got her to Merrill-Stevens at Dinner Key, and we had to work her in during a flat squall, in a hard gray driving rain, the wind gusting and whistling. I'd phoned a friend via the Miami marine operator earlier in the day, so they were waiting for us. We shoved the *'Bama Gal* into the slings and they picked her out of the water and put her on a cradle and ran her along the rails and into one of the big sheds. Palacio wore a permanent, broad, dreaming grin.

The dockmaster assigned me a slip for the *Flush* and space in the small boat area for the *Muñequita*. By the time we were properly moored, hooked into shoreside power, and had showered and shaved and changed, heavy rain was drumming down, and it was very snug in the lounge aboard *The Busted Flush,* lights on, music on, ice in the glasses, Meyer threatening to make his famous beef stew with chili, beans, and eggs, never the same way twice running. Guthrie had phoned his wife and she was going to drive down from Lauderdale to pick him up Sunday morning. They were tapping the Wild Turkey bourbon we'd found aboard the *Gal,* and I was sticking to Plymouth on ice. Meyer kept everybody from going too far overboard in estimating profit. He kept demanding we come up with "the minimum expectation, gentlemen."

So we kept going over what would probably have to be done and came up with a maximum fifteen thousand to put her in shape, and a minimum forty-five thousand return after brokerage commission.

That is the best kind of argument, trying to figure out how much you've made. It is good to hear the thunder of tropic rain, to feel the muscle soreness of hard manual labor when you move, to have a chill glass in your hand, know the beginnings of ravenous hunger, realize that in a few hours even a bunk made of cobblestones would feel deep and soft and inviting.

They wanted me to come into the fledgling partnership, with twenty-five percent of the action. But struggling ventures should not be cut too many ways. Nor did I want the responsibility, that ever-present awareness of people depending on me permanently to make something work. They were too proud—Guthrie and Palacio—to accept my efforts as a straight donation, so after some inverted haggling we agreed that I would take two thousand in the form of a note at six percent, payable in six months. They wanted to put their take back into improved equipment and go after a steel barge sunk in about fifty feet of water just outside Boca Grande Pass.

I was sprawled and daydreaming, no longer hearing their words as they talked excitedly of plans and projects, hearing only the blur of their voices through the music.

"Didn't we make it that time in an hour and a half? Hey! Trav!"

Meyer was snapping his fingers at me. "Make what?" I asked.

"That run from Lauderdale to Bimini."

They had stopped talking business. I could remember that ride all too well. "Just under an hour and a half from the sea buoy at Lauderdale to the first channel marker at Bimini."

"In what?" Guthrie asked.

I told him what it had been, a Bertram 25 rigged for ocean racing with a pair of big hairy three hundreds in it, and enough chop in the Stream so that I had to work the throttles and the wheel every moment, so that when she went off a crest and was airborne, she would come down flat. Time it wrong and hit wrong, and you can trip them over.

"What was the rush?" Bobby asked.

"We were meeting a plane," Meyer said.

And I knew at that moment he too was thinking of Helena Pearson and a very quick and dirty salvage job of several years aback. We were both thinking of her, with no way of knowing she had been dead two days, no way of knowing her letter was at Bahia Mar waiting for me.

Even without the knowledge of her death, Helena was a disturbing memory . . .

2 *FIVE YEARS* ago? Yes. In a winter month, in a cold winter for Florida, Mick Pearson, with his wife Helena and his two daughters, aged twenty and seventeen, crewing for him, had brought his handsome Dutch motor sailer into Bahia Mar, all the way from Bordeaux. The *Likely Lady*. A wiry, seamed, sun-freckled talkative man in his fifties, visibly older than his slender gray-blond wife.

He gave the impression of somebody who had made it early, had retired, and was having the sweet life. He circulated quickly and readily and got to know all the regulars. He gave the impression of talking a lot about himself, not in any bragging or self-important way, but by amusing incident. People found it easy to talk to him.

Finally I began to get the impression that he was focusing on me, as if he had been engaged in some process of selection and I was his best candidate. I realized how very little I knew about him, how little he had actually said. Once we began prying away at each other, showdown was inevitable. I remember how cold his eyes were when he stopped being friendly sociable harmless Mick Pearson.

He wanted a confidential errand done, for a fat fee. He said he had been involved in a little deal abroad. He said it involved options on some old oil tankers, and some surplus, obsolete Turkish military vehicles, and all I needed to know about it was that it was legal, and he wasn't wanted, at least officially, by any government anywhere.

Some other sharpshooters had been trying to make the same deal, he said. They refused to make it a joint effort,

13

as he had suggested, and tried to swing it alone. But Pearson beat them to it and they were very annoyed at his methods. "So they know I've got this bank draft payable to the bearer, for two hundred thirty thousand English pounds, payable *only* at the main branch of the Bank of Nova Scotia in the Bahamas, at Nassau, which is the way I wanted it because I've got a protected account there. I didn't want them to find out how I was going to handle it, but they did. It's enough money so they can put some very professional people to work to take it away from me. Long, long ago I might have taken a shot at slipping by them. But now I've got my three gals to think of, and how thin their future would be if I didn't make it. So I have to have somebody they don't know take it to the bank with my letter of instructions. Then they'll give up."

I asked him what made him so sure I wouldn't just set up my own account and stuff the six hundred and forty thousand into it.

His was a very tough grin. "Because it would screw you all up, McGee. It would bitch your big romance with your own image of yourself. I couldn't do that to anybody. Neither could you. That's what makes us incurably small-time."

"That kind of money isn't exactly small-time."

"Compared to what it could have been by now, it is small, believe me." So he offered me five thousand to be errand boy, and I agreed. Payable in advance, he said. And after he had given me the documents, he would take off in the *Likely Lady* as a kind of decoy, and I was to start the day after he did. He said he would head for the Bahamas but then swing south and go down around the Keys and up the west coast of Florida to the home he and his gals hadn't seen for over a year and missed so badly, a raunchy sun-weathered old cypress house on pilings on the north end of Casey Key.

That was on a Friday. He was going to give me the documents on Sunday and take the *Likely Lady* out to sea on Monday. At about noon on Saturday, while Helena and her daughters were over on the beach, they came aboard and cracked his skull and peeled the stateroom safe open. It would have been perfect had not Mick Pearson wired his air horns in relay with a contact on the safe door, activated by a concealed switch he could turn off when he wanted to open it himself. So too many people saw the pair leaving the *Likely Lady* too hastily. It took me almost two hours to get a line on them, to make certain they hadn't left by air. They had left their rental car over at Pier 66 and had gone off at one o'clock on a charter boat for some Bahamas fishing. I knew the boat, the *Betty Bee,* a 38-foot Merritt, well-kept, Captain Roxy Howard and usually one or the other of his skinny nephews crewing for him.

I phoned Roxy's wife and she said they were going to Bimini and work out from there, trolling the far side of the Stream, starting Sunday. At that time, as I later learned, the neurosurgeons were plucking bone splinters out of Mick Pearson's brain.

I knew that the *Betty Bee* would take four hours to get across, so that would put her in Bimini at five o'clock or later. There was a feeder flight from there to Nassau leaving at seven fifteen. A boat is a very inconspicuous way to leave the country. Both Florida and the Bahamas have such a case of hots for the tourist dollar that petty officialdom must cry themselves to sleep thinking about all the missing red tape.

It was two thirty before, in consultation with Meyer, I figured out how to handle it. If I chartered a flight over, it was going to be a sticky problem coping with the pair on Bahama soil. Meyer remembered that Hollis Gandy's muscular Bertram, the *Baby Beef,* was in racing trim, and that Hollis, as usual, had a bad case of the shorts, brought on by having too many ex-wives with good lawyers.

So it was three when we banged past the sea buoy outside Lauderdale, Bimini-bound. Meyer could not hold the glasses on anything of promising size we spotted, any more than a rodeo contestant could thread a needle while riding a steer. And if I altered course to take closer looks,

I stood the risk of wasting too much time or alerting a couple of nervous people.

We got to the marker west of the Bimini bar at four thirty, and after a quick check inside to make certain the *Betty Bee* hadn't made better than estimated time, we went out and lay in wait five miles offshore. I faked dead engines, got aboard, alerted Roxy Howard, and we took them very quickly. Roxy was easily alerted as he had become increasingly suspicious of the pair. An Englishman and a Greek. It was useful to do it quickly, as the Greek was snake-fast and armed. We trussed them up and I told Roxy what they'd been up to as I went through their luggage and searched their persons. The envelope with the bearer bank draft was in the Greek's suitcase and with it was the signed letter to the bank identifying me, authorizing me to act for Mick Pearson, with a space for my signature, and another space for me to sign again, probably in the presence of a bank officer. The Greek had two thousand dollars in his wallet, and the Englishman about five hundred. The Englishman had an additional eleven thousand plus in a sweaty money belt. It seemed reasonable to assume that that money had come out of Mick's stateroom safe. As far as I knew, Mick had taken a good thump on his hard skull and certainly had no interest in bringing in any kind of law. Roxy was not interested in tangling with the Bahamian police authorities. And I did not think the Englishman or the Greek would lodge any complaints. And it was obvious that trying to get word out of either of them would call for some very messy encouragement, something I have no stomach for. Theirs was a hard, competent, professional silence.

So I gave five hundred to Roxy. He said it was too much, but he didn't argue the point. We off-loaded them into the *Baby Beef,* and Roxy turned the *Betty Bee* and headed for home port. I ran on down to Barnett Harbour, about halfway between South Bimini and Cat Cay, and put them aboard the old concrete ship that has been sitting awash there since 1926, the old *Sapona* that used to be a floating liquor warehouse during prohibition. I knew they'd have a rough night of it, but they would be picked off the next day by the inevitable fishermen or skin divers. They had their gear, their identification papers, and over twenty-five hundred dollars. And they would think of some explanation that wouldn't draw attention to themselves. They had that look.

I ran back outside and into Bimini Harbor and found a place to tie up, where the boat would be safe. We caught the feeder flight to Nassau, and I called old friends at Lyford Cay. They refused to let us go into the city, and as they had what they called a "medium bash" going, they sent one of their cars to bring us over from the airport. We spent most of Sunday sprawling around the pool and telling lies.

Monday morning I borrowed a car and went into the city to the main offices at Bay Street at Rawson Square. The size of the transaction made it something to be handled in a paneled office in the rear. I was given a receipt that gave the date and hour and minute of the deposit, gave the identification number of the bearer draft rather than the amount, and gave the number of the account maintained by Pearson rather than his name. The receipt was embossed with a heavy and ornate seal, and the bank officer scrawled indecipherable initials across it. I did not know then how good my timing had been.

Meyer and I caught a feeder flight back to Bimini in the early afternoon. The day was clear, bright, and cool. The Stream had flattened out, but even so, a two-and-a-half-hour trip was more comfortable than trying to match our time heading over.

The *Likely Lady* was all buttoned up when I walked around to D-109 to give Mick the receipt. The young couple aboard the big ketch parked next door said they had talked to Maureen, the elder daughter, at noon, and she had said that her father's condition was critical.

I told Meyer and went over to the hospital. When finally I had a chance to talk to Helena, I could see that there was no point in trying to give her the bank receipt or talking about the money. The receipt would have meant as much to her at that moment as an old laundry

17

list. She said with a white-lipped, trembling, ghastly smile that Mick was "holding his own."

I remember that I found a nurse I knew and I remember waiting while she went and checked his condition out with the floor nurses and the specials. I remember her little shrug and the way she said, "He's breathing, but he's dead, Trav. I found out they've got the room assigned already to somebody coming in tomorrow for a spinal fusion."

I remember helping Helena with the deadly details, so cumbersome at best, but complicated by dying in an alien place. He died at five minutes past one on Tuesday morning. Had he died, officially, seventy minutes sooner, the whole bank thing would have been almost impossible to ever get straightened out. I remember the gentle persistence of the city police. But she told them repeatedly that the safe had been empty, that she could not imagine who had come aboard and given her husband the fatal blow on the head.

She and the girls packed their belongings, and I assured Helena that I would see to the boat, get the perishables off her, keep an eye on her. I offered to drive them across the state, but she said she could manage. She was keeping herself under rigid and obvious control. When I gave her the cash and the bank receipt, she thanked me politely. They left to go to the funeral home and, from there, follow the hearse across to Sarasota County. A very small caravan. Prim, forlorn, and quite brave.

Yes, I knew that Meyer was remembering her too. I knew he had probably guessed the rest of it, perhaps wondered about it, but would never ask.

The rain came down and Meyer cooked his famous specialty, never-twice-alike. We ate like weary contented wolves, and the yawning began early. Yet once I was in the big bed in the master stateroom, the other memories of Helena became so vivid they held me for a long time at the edge of sleep, unable to let go . . .

3 . . . *THERE HAD* been heavy rains drumming on the overhead deck of the *Likely Lady* in August of that year in that lonely and protected anchorage we found at Shroud Cay in the Exumas, and under the sound of the rain I had made love to the Widow Pearson in that broad, deep bunk she had shared with the man who, by that August, had been almost six months at rest in Florida soil.

She had come back to Lauderdale in July. She had dropped me a note in June asking me to have someone put the *Likely Lady* in shape. I'd had her hauled, bottom scraped and repainted, all lines and rigging checked, power winches greased, blocks freed, both suits of sail checked, auxiliary generator and twin Swedish diesels tuned. She was less a motor sailer in the classic sense than she was a roomy, beamy powerboat rigged to carry a large sail area, so large in fact that she had a drop centerboard operated by a toggle switch on the control panel, and a husky electric motor geared way, way down. There was maybe two tons of lead on that centerboard, so shaped that when, according to the dial next to the toggle switch, the centerboard was all the way up, sliding up into the divider partition in the belowdecks area, the lead fitted snugly into the hull shape. Mick had showed me all her gadgetry one day, from the automatic winching that made sail handling painless, to the surprising capacity of the fuel and water tanks, to the capacity of the air-conditioning system.

I wonder who has her now. I wonder what she's called. Helena came over on a hot July day. She was of that particular breed which has always made me feel inadequate. Tallish, so slender as to be almost, but not quite, gaunt. The bones that happen after a few centuries of careful breeding. Blond-gray hair, sun-streaked, casual, dry-textured, like the face, throat, backs of the hands, by the sun and wind of the games they play. Theirs is not the kind of cool that is an artifice, designed as a challenge. It is natural, impenetrable, and terribly polite. They move well in their simple, unassuming little two-hundred-dollar cotton dresses, because long ago at Miss Somebody's Country Day School they were so thoroughly taught that their grace is automatic and ineradicable. There are no girl-tricks with eyes and mouth. They are merely there, looking out at you, totally composed, in almost exactly the way they look out of the newspaper pictures of social events.

I asked about her daughters, and she told me that they had gone off on a two-month student tour of Italy, Greece and the Greek Islands, conducted by old friends on the faculty of Wellesley.

"Travis, I never thanked you properly for all the help you gave us. It was . . . a most difficult time."

"I'm glad I could help."

"It was more than just . . . helping with the details. Mick told me he had asked you to . . . do a special favor. He told me he thought you had a talent for discretion. I wanted those people . . . caught and punished. But I kept remembering that Mick would not have wanted that kind of international incident and notoriety. To him it was all some kind of . . . gigantic casino. When you won or you lost, it wasn't . . . a personal thing. So I am grateful that you didn't . . . that you had the instinct to keep from . . . making yourself important by giving out any statements about what happened."

"I had to tell you I'd caught up with them, Helena. I was afraid you'd want me to blow the whistle. If you had, I was going to try to talk you out of it. The day I get my name and face all over the newspapers and newscasts, I'd better look for some other line of work."

She made a sour mouth and said, "My people were so

certain that Michael Pearson was some kind of romantic infatuation, we had to go away together to be married. He was too old for me, they said. He was an adventurer. He had no roots. I was too young to know my own mind. The usual thing. They wanted to save me for some nice earnest young man in investment banking." She looked more directly at me, her eyes narrow and bright with anger. "And one of them, after Mick was dead, had the damned blind arrogant gall to try to say: I told you so! After twenty-one years and a bit with Mick! After having our two girls, who loved him so. After sharing a life that . . ."

She stopped herself and said, with a wan smile, "Sorry. I got off the track. I wanted to say thank you and I want to apologize for being stupid about something, Travis. I never asked, before I left, what sort of . . . arrangement you had with Mick. I know he had the habit of paying well for special favors. Had he paid you?"

"No."

"Was an amount agreed upon?"

"For what I had thought I was going to do. Yes."

"Then did you take it out of the cash before you gave me the rest of it, the cash that had been in the safe?"

"No. I took out five hundred for a special expense and two hundred and fifty for a rental of a boat and some incidental expenses."

"What was the agreed amount?"

"Five thousand."

"But you did much much more than what he . . . asked you to do. I am going to give you twenty thousand, and tell you that it isn't as much as it should be."

"No. I did what I did because I wanted to do it. I won't even take the five."

She studied me in silence and finally said, "We are *not* going to have one of those silly squabbles, like over a restaurant check. You *will* take the five because it is a matter of personal honor to me to take on any obligation Mick made to anyone. I do not think that your appreciation of yourself as terribly sentimental and generous about widows and orphans should take priority over my sense of obligation."

"When you put it that way——"

"You will take the five thousand."

"And close the account without any . . . squabbling."

She smiled. "And I planned it so carefully."

"Planned what?"

"You would take the twenty thousand and then I would feel perfectly free to ask you a favor. You see, I have to go to that bank in Nassau. On the transfer of those special accounts there has to be an actual appearance in person, with special identification, as prearranged by the owner of the account. I was going to fly over and see them and fly back, and find someone to help me take the *Likely Lady* around to Naples, Florida. A man wants her, and the price is right, and he would pick her up here, but . . . I can't bear to part with her without . . . some kind of a sentimental journey. So I thought after you took the money, I could ask you, as a favor, to crew for me while we take her over to the Bahamas. Mick and I planned every inch of her. We watched her take shape. She . . . seems to know. And she wouldn't understand if I just turned my back on her. Do you find that grotesque?"

"Not at all."

"Would——?"

"Of course."

So we provisioned the *Likely Lady* and took off in the heat of early July. I had the stateroom Maureen and Bridgit had used. We fell into an equitable division of the chores without having to make lists. I made the navigation checks, kept the charts and the log, took responsibility for fuel, engines, radio and electronic gear, minor repairs and maintenance, topside cleaning, booze, anchoring. She took care of the proper set of the sails, meals, laundry, belowdecks housekeeping, ice, water supply, and we shared the helmsman chore equally.

There was enough room aboard to make personal privacy easy to sustain. We decided that because we were on no schedule and had no deadlines, the most agreeable procedure was to move during the daylight hours and lie at anchor at night. If it was going to take too long to find the next decent anchorage, we would settle for an early stop and then take off at first light.

There were several kinds of silence between us. Sometimes it was the comfortable silence of starlight, a night breeze, swinging slowly at anchor, a mutual tasting of a summer night. Sometimes it was that kind of an awkward silence when I knew she was quite bitterly alone, and saying good-bye to the boat and to the husband and to the plans and promises that would not be filled.

We were a man and a woman alone among the sea and the islands, interdependent, sharing the homely chores of cruising and living, and on that basis there had to be a physical awareness of each other, of maleness and femaleness. But there was a gratuitous triteness about the unconventional association that easily stifled any intensification of awareness.

It was five years back, and she was that inevitable cliché, an older woman, a widow, who had invited the husky younger male to voyage alone with her. I knew she had married young, but I did not know how young. I could guess that she was eleven years older than I, give or take two years. At the start her body was pale, too gaunted, and softened by the lethargy of months of mourning. But as the days passed, the sun darkened her, the exertion firmed the slackened muscles, and as she ate with increasing hunger, she began to gain weight. And, as a result of her increasing feeling of physical well-being, I began to hear her humming to herself as she did her chores.

I suspect that it was precisely because any outsider, given the situation and the two actors on the stage, would have assumed that McGee was dutifully and diligently servicing the widow's physical hungers during the anchored nights that any such relationship became impossible. Not once, by word, gesture, or expression, did she even indicate that she had expected to have to fend me off. She moved youthfully, kept herself tidy and attractive, spent just enough time on her hair so that I knew she was perfectly aware of being a handsome woman and did certainly not require any hard breathing on my part to confirm her opinion. Nor did she play any of those half-innocent, half-contrived games of flirtation that invite misinterpretation.

We had a lot of silences, but we did a lot of talking too. General talk, spiced with old incident, about the shape of the world, the shape of the human heart, good places we had been, good and bad things we had done or had not quite done. We went up around Grand Bahama, down the eastern shore of Abaco, over to the Berry Islands, down to Andros, and at last, after fourteen days, over to New Providence, where we tied up at the Nassau Harbour Club.

She went alone to the bank and when she came back, she was very subdued and thoughtful. When I asked her if anything had gone wrong, she said that it had been quite a good deal more money than she had expected. She said that changed a few things and she would have to think about the future in a different way. We went out to dinner and when I got up the next morning, she was already up, drinking coffee and looking at the *Yachtsman's Guide to the Bahamas*.

She closed the book. "I suppose we should think about heading back," she said. "I hate to."

"Do you have a date to keep?"

"Not really. Somebody I have to see, eventually. A decision to make."

"I'm in no hurry. Let's look at some more places. Exumas. Ragged Islands too, maybe." I explained to her how I take my retirement in small installments, whenever I can afford it, and if it was late August or early September when we got back, I wouldn't mind at all. She was overjoyed.

So we sailed to Spanish Wells, then down the western shore of Eleuthera, and then began to work our way very slowly down the lovely empty chain of the Exumas, staying over wherever we wanted to explore the beaches and the technicolor reefs. We did a lot of swimming and walking. I was suddenly aware that her mood was changing. She seemed remote for a few days, lost in thought, almost morose.

The day she suddenly cheered up I realized that she had begun to deliberately heighten my awareness of her. I had the feeling that it was a very conscious decision, something that she had made up her mind to during those days when she seemed lost in her own thoughts and memories. As she was a tasteful, mature, elegant, and sensitive woman, she was not obvious about it. She merely seemed to focus her physical self at me, enhancing my awareness through her increased awareness of me. Inevitably it would be the male who would make the overt pass. It baffled me. I could not believe she was childish enough or shallow enough to set about enticing a younger man merely to prove that she could. There was more substance to her than that. She had begun something that would have to be finished in bed, because I did not think she would begin it without having recognized its inevitable destination. It was all so unlikely and so deliberate that I had to assume she had some compulsion to prove something or to disprove something. Or maybe it was merely a hunger that came from deprivation. So I stopped worrying myself with wondering about her. She was a desirable and exciting woman.

So when she provided the opportunity, I made the expected pass. Her mouth was eager. When she murmured, "We shouldn't," it meant, "We shall." Her trembling was not faked. She was overly nervous about it, for reasons I could not know until later.

The first time was just at dusk in her big wide double bunk in the master stateroom. Her body was lovely in the fading light, her eyes huge, her flesh still hot with the sun-heat of the long beach day, her shoulder tasting of the salt of the sea and the salt of perspiration. Because she was tense and anxious, I took a long gentling time with her, and then when finally, in full darkness, she was readied, I took her, in that ever-new, ever-the-same, long, sliding, startling moment of penetration and joining, which changes, at once and forever, the relationship of two people. Just as it was happening she pushed with all

25

her might at my chest and tried to writhe away from me, calling out, "No! Oh, please! No!" in a harsh, ugly, gasping voice. But she had been a moment late and it was done. She wrenched her head to the side and lay under me, slack and lifeless.

I could guess what had happened to her. She had arrived at her decision to bring this all about through some purely intellectual exercise, some kind of rationalization that had seemed to her to be perfectly sane and sound. But a coupling cannot be carried out in some kind of abstract form. I could guess from knowing her that she had never been unfaithful to Mick Pearson. All pretty little rationalizations and games of conjecture can be wiped out in an instant by the total and immediate and irrevocable fleshy reality. The ultimate intimacy exists on a different plane than do little testings and tryings. When she made a small whimpering sigh, I began to move apart from her, but she quickly caught at me and kept me with her.

Five years ago, but I had the memories in full textural detail of how often and how desperately Helena struggled to achieve climax. She wore herself into exhaustion. It was ritualistic and ridiculous. It was like some kind of idiotic health club: Orgasm is *good* for you. It was like some dogged kind of therapy. It was completely obvious that she was a healthy, sexually accomplished, passionate woman. But she was so concentrated on what she thought was some sort of severe necessity that she choked up. She would manage to get herself right out to the last grinding panting edge of it and get hung up there and then slowly, slowly fade back and away. And apologize, hopelessly, and plead with me to please be patient with her.

Four or five days later, wooden with fatigue, she confessed what had led her into this grotesque dilemma. Her voice was drab, her sentences short and without color. A man wanted to marry her. A very dear man, she said. The sex part of her marriage to Mick had been very very wonderful, always. During the months since his death, she had felt as if that part of her had died along with him. She did not want to cheat the man who wanted to marry her. She liked him very much. She liked me equally well. So it had seemed reasonable to assume that if she found she could enjoy sex with me, then she could enjoy it with him. Sorry she had used me in such a cynical way. But she had to make up her mind whether or not to marry him. That was one of the factors. Sorry it had turned into such a dismal trying thing. Sorry to be such a dull mess. Sorry. Sorry.

It is no good telling somebody they're trying too hard. It is very much like ordering a child to go stand in a corner for a half hour and never once think about elephants.

So when she said there was no point in going on with such a stupid performance, I agreed. I let one day, one night, and one day pass. She was embarrassed and depressed. That night I began howling and roaring and thrashing at about one in the morning. She came hurrying in and I made it quite an effort for her to shake me awake. I had made certain that it had been such a physical day that she would be weary.

Woke up. Sagged back, deliberately trembling. Said it was an old nightmare that happened once or twice a year, based upon an exceptionally ugly event I could not ever tell anyone, not ever.

Up until then I had been all too competent. Big, knuckly, pale-eyed, trustworthy McGee, who had taken care of things, first for Mick and then for her. Could handle boats, navigation, emergencies. So I had presented her with a flaw. And a built-in way to help. She told me I had to tell someone and then it would stop haunting me. In a tragic tone I said I couldn't. She came into my narrower bunk, all sympathy and gentle comfort, motherly arms to cradle the trembling sufferer. "There is nothing you can't tell me. Please let me help. You've been so good to me, so understanding and patient. Please let me help you."

Five years ago, and back then the scar tissue was still thin and tender over the memories of the lady named Lois. There was enough ugliness in what had happened to her to be suitably persuasive. The world had dimmed a little when she was gone, as if there were a rheostat on the sun and somebody had turned it down, just one notch.

I pretended reluctance and then, with a cynical emotionalism, told her about Lois. It was a cheap way to use an old and lasting grief. I was not very pleased with myself for selecting Lois. It seemed a kind of betrayal. And with one of those ironic and unexpected quirks of the emotions, I suddenly realized that I did not have to pretend to be moved by the telling of it. My voice husked and my eyes burned, and though I tried to control myself, my voice broke. I never *had* told anyone about it. But where does contrivance end and reality begin? I knew she was greatly moved by the story. And out of her full heart and her concern, and her woman's need to hold and to mend, she fumbled with her short robe and laid it open and with gentle kisses and little tugs, with caresses and murmurings, brought us sweetly together and began a slow, long, deep surging, earth-warm and simple, then murmured, "Just for you, darling. Don't think about me. Don't think about anything. Just let me make it good for you."

And it happened, because she was taking a warm, dreamy, pleasurable satisfaction in soothing my nightmared nerves, salving the wound of loss, focusing her woman-self, her softnesses and pungencies and opened-taking on me, believing that she had been too wearied by the energies of the day to even think of her own gratification but unaware of the extent to which she had been sexually stimulated by all the times when she had tried so doggedly and failed. So in her deep sleepy hypnotic giving it built without her being especially aware of herself, built until suddenly she groaned, tautened, became swollen, and then came across the edge and into the great blind and lasting part of it, building and bursting, building and bursting, peak and then diminuendo until it had all been spent and she lay slack as butter, breath whistling, heart cantering, secretions a bitter fragrance in the new stillness of the bed.

I remember how she became, for the whole ten days we remained at anchor in the cove at Shroud Cay, like a kid beginning vacation. A drifting guilt, a sadness about Mick—these made her pleasure the sweeter. There was no cloying kittenishness about her, as that was a style that would not have suited her—or me. She was proud of herself and as bold, jaunty, direct, and demanding as a bawdy young boy, chuckling her pleasures, full of a sweet wildness in the afternoon bunk with the heavy rain roaring on the decks over us, so totally unselfconscious about trying this and that and the other, first this way and that way and the other way, so frankly and uncomplicatedly greedy for joy that in arrangements that could easily have made another woman look vulgarly grotesque she never lost her flavor of grace and elegance.

For that brief time we were totally, compulsively involved with the flesh, pagans whose only clock was that of our revived desires, learning each other so completely that, in consort, we could direct ourselves, joined or unjoined, as though we were a single octopoidal creature with four eyes, twenty fingers, and three famished mouths. When we raised anchor and moved on, the tempo diminished, and the affair became a more sedate and comfortable and cozy arrangement, with ritual supplanting invention, with morning kisses that could be affection without any overtone of demand, with waking in the broad bunk to feel the heated length of her asleep, spoon style, against my back, and be content she was there, and be content to drowse off again.

The last day of August was our last day in the islands and we spent the night anchored wide of the Cat Cay channel, and would cross the Stream the next day. She was solemn and thoughtful at dinner. We made love most gently and tenderly, and afterward when I held her in my arms, both of us on the edge of sleep, she said, "You understood that it was our last time, dear?"

"A way to say good-bye. A good way."

She sighed. "I had twenty-one years with Mick. I'll never be . . . a whole person without him. But you did some mending, Travis. I know that . . . I can stumble through the rest of my life and accept what I've got left, live with less. Make do. I wish I could be in love with you. I would never let you go. I would be your old, old wife. I think I would dye your hair gray and have my

29

face lifted and lie about my age. I'd never let you get away, you know."

I began to tell her a lot of things, very significant and important and memorable things, and when I stopped, waiting for applause, I discovered she was asleep.

When the *Likely Lady* was back in a slip at Bahia Mar, she took one wistful walk around the deck and made a sour little smile and said, "Good-bye to this too. I'll let the man who wants her pick her up here. Will you show him through her and explain everything?"

"Sure. Send him to me."

When I had put her luggage in the trunk of the rental car, and kissed her good-bye, and she had gotten behind the wheel, she looked out at me, frowning, and said, "If you *ever* need *anything,* darling, anything I can give you, even if I have to steal to get it . . ."

"And if you start coming unglued, lady . . ."

"Let's keep in touch," she said, blinked her eyes very rapidly, grinned, gunned the engine, and scratched off with a reckless shriek of rubber, lady in total command of the car, hands high on the wheel, chin up, and I never saw her again.

4 *FORGET THE* Lady Helena and get some sleep. Stop damning Meyer for bringing up that trip to Bimini and thus opening up that particular little corner of the attic in the back of my head.

She had married the sweet guy, had invited me, but I had been away when the invitation came. Then postcards from the Greek Islands, or Spain, or some such honeymoon place. Then nothing until a letter three years ago, a

30

dozen pages at least, apologizing for using me once again as a foil, clarifying her own thoughts by writing to me.

She was divorcing Teddy. He was a sweet, nice, thoughtful man who, quite weak to begin with, had been literally overwhelmed and devoured by her strength. He had diminished, she said, almost to the point of invisibility. All you could see was his pleasant uncertain smile. She admitted that she kept prodding him, pushing at him, hoping for that ultimate masculine reaction that would suddenly fight back and take over the chore of running a marriage. Maybe, she wrote, living with a dutiful creature on an invisible leash was preferable to being alone but not for her. Not when she could see herself becoming more domineering, unpleasant, and more shrill—week by week, month by month. So she was cutting him loose while he could still feed and bathe himself. She was getting the divorce in Nevada. When she had married, she had closed the house on Casey Key, had considered selling it many times, but something had kept her from making a final decision. Now she was glad. She would go back there and see if she could recover what some people had once thought a pleasant disposition.

She said that her elder daughter, Maurie, had been married for six months to a very bright and personable young man in the brokerage business, and seemed deliciously happy. She said they were living in the city of Fort Courtney, Florida, about a hundred miles northeast of Casey Key, and it seemed a workable distance for a mother-in-law to be. She reported that Bridget, known as Biddy—and nineteen at the time she wrote to me three years ago—had transferred from Bryn Mawr to the University of Iowa so she could study with a painter she admired extravagantly, and had changed her major to Fine Arts.

Though it had dealt with personal, family matters, it had not been a particularly intimate letter. No one reading it could have ever guessed at the relationship we'd had on that lazy long cruise of the *Likely Lady* through the Bahamas.

She asked me to stop and see her the next time I was over in the Sarasota area. I never did.

I had thought of her a few times. Something would remind me of her, the look of a boat under sail, or the sound of hard rain, or a scent like that of the small pink flowers that grew out of the stony soil of the Exumas, and she would be in and out of my thoughts for a week or so. Now it had happened again, thanks to Meyer, and I would be remembering Helena Pearson for a few days or a few weeks. It had been one of those relationships you cannot really pin down. To the average outsider it would have been something to smirk about. The older woman, half a year widowed, who sends her daughters away so that she can go cruising with a man young enough to be the son of her dead husband, a new consort of considerable size, obviously fit and durable and competent and discreet, and obviously uninterested in any kind of permanent relationship.

Yet I was quite certain that it had not been a situation she had planned. It had arisen through two sets of rationalizations, hers and mine, and the truth of it was perhaps something quite different from what we suspected. For her perhaps it was the affirmation of being still alive after the intense emotional focus of her life was gone forever. Maybe it had been something the body had created in the mind, just for its own survival, because with her perhaps a sexual continence would have been a progressive thing, parching and drying her, month by month, until all need would have been prematurely ended. My own supercilious little rationalization had been, in the beginning of it, that it would have been both cruel and stuffy to have failed to respond when she began her tentative invitations, to have let her know through my lack of response that the age differential did indeed put me off, and that I felt both clumsy and self-conscious in the role of the available younger man in a kind of floating bedroom farce. The least I could do would be to respond with as much forced enthusiasm as I could manage. But a sweet and immediate reality of the flesh had erased the reasons and the rationalizations. She was all limber girl in the half-light, slenderly, elegantly voluptuous, so consistently determined to never take more pleasure than she was able to give that she made a few intervening women seem dreary indeed.

At last I was able to dim the vivid qualities of the memory and slide away into the earned sleep . . .

Sunday, October sixth, was still and gray and breathlessly muggy. Bobby Guthrie's wife came for him at ten in the morning and they gave Joe Palacio a ride back into Miami. Monday they would get the Merrill-Stevens appraisals and estimates, based on detailed inspections. Meyer and I got the *Flush* out into the channel and headed north for Lauderdale at about eleven, with the *Muñequita* in tow and a pale sun beginning to burn through the overcast. *The Busted Flush* was still burdened with the gear and goop of Floatation Associates. Meyer assured me that as soon as the partnership had turned the *'Bama Gal* into money, they would move their stuff over onto the work boat Bobby had located, which they could buy at the right price.

"Bobby will build special chemical tanks right into the work boat and rig up some automatic pumps with flowmeters so that one man can handle the flow of the stuff down to the job."

"That's nice."

"After another good piece of salvage, we're going to install the same kind of a setup, but smaller, on a truck, and put a good winch on it. It will make it easy to pick automobiles out of the canals."

"That's nice."

"Am I boring you or something, McGee?"

"If I was all hot to get tangled up in a nice profitable little business with three nice people, I'd probably be chuckling and dancing and singing. Lots of luck, Meyer."

He stared at me, shrugged, and went below to start taking the cameras and reels apart to see if the rinsing in fresh water had made them salvageable. He was in one of his mother-hen periods, but this time he was taking care of Guthrie and Palacio instead of McGee. They were in good hands. But Meyer was going to be a bore until the little business was safely launched.

I had no plans. I felt mildly restless. I decided I would help the trio get their work boat set up and then maybe I would round up a batch of amiable folk and cruise on up the waterway, maybe as far as Jax. In another month or so I would have to start looking for a client so whipped-down he would snap at my kind of salvage, at my fifty-percent fee. Meanwhile, some fun and games, a little action, some laughs.

There was a note in my post office box about something I had to sign for, so I didn't get Helena's letter until Monday, a little before noon.

First there was a crisp white envelope with the return address in raised black letters: FOLMER, HARDAHEE, AND KRANZ, ATTORNEYS AT LAW. There was a cashier's check for $25,000 paperclipped to the letter signed by one D. Wintin Hardahee in tiny little purple script. The letter was dated Sept 28th, and the check was dated Sept 27th.

My dear Mr. McGee:

Pursuant to the wishes of Mrs. Helena Trescott . . .

[The Trescot put me off the track for a moment, and then I remembered the wedding I had missed, when she had married a Theodore Trescott.]

I am herewith enclosing a cashier's check in the amount of twenty-five thousand dollars ($25,000.00) along with a letter which Mrs. Trescott asked me to mail with the cashier's check.

She has explained to me that this sum is in payment of an obligation of several years' standing, and because it does not seem probable that she will survive her present critical illness, she wished to save you the trouble of presenting a claim against her estate.

If you have any questions about this matter, you can reach me at the address and telephone number given above.

Yours very truly,

The law firm was in Fort Courtney, Florida. Her letter was thick, sealed in a separate envelope, and addressed to me. I walked back to the *Flush* and put it, unopened, on the desk in the lounge. I took one of the big glasses and laid an impressive belt of Plymouth atop the cubes, and then roamed about, sipping at it, continually catching a glimpse of the letter out of the corner of my eye. The eerie coincidence of not having thought of her for maybe almost a year, then having such vivid memories just one week after the letter had been mailed, gave me a hollow feeling in the middle.

But it had to be read and the gin wasn't going to make it any easier.

Travis, my darling,

I won't bore you with clinical details—but oh I am so sick of being sick it is almost a relief to be able to see in their eyes that they do not expect me to make it . . . sick unto death of being sick—a bad joke I guess. Remember the day at Darby Island when we had a contest to see who could invent the worst joke? And finally declared it a draw? I'm not very brave. I'm scared witless. Dying is so damned absolute—and today I hurt like hell because I made them cut way down on the junk they are giving me so I could have a clear head to write to you . . . Forgive lousy handwriting, dear. Scared, yes, and also quite vain, so vain I would not look forward to walking out of this place—tottering out, a gray little old lady, all bones and parchment.

Up until a year ago, dear, I looked very much as I looked that marvelous summer we had together, and might look almost as well this year too, except for a little problem known familiarly as Big C. A year ago they thought they took it all out, but then they used cobalt, and then they went in again, and everything was supposed to be fine, but it popped up in two more places, and Thursday they are going to do another radical, which they are now building me up for, and I think Dr. Bill Dyckes is actually, though maybe he wouldn't even admit it to him-

35

self, letting me leave this way instead of the long lousy way that I can expect if they don't operate.

I said I wasn't going to bore you! I'm tempted to tear this up and start again, but I think that one letter is about all I can manage. About the check Mr. Hardahee arranged for, and which you will get with this letter, please don't get stuffy about it. Actually, practically by accident, I became medium rich—an old friend of Mick's took over the investment thing shortly after Mick died. He is very clever and in the business of managing money for people. For the last five and a half years he has been buying funny little stocks for my account, things I never heard of before, and some of them are never heard of again, but a lot of them go up and up and up, and he smiles and smiles and smiles. But lately, of course, he has been changing everything around so that it will all be neat for the estate taxes. Don't have strange ideas about you getting money that should go to my girls, because they will be getting enough. Anyway, the money is sort of a fee . . .

It's about my big daughter, Travis. Maureen. She's practically twenty-six. She's been married to Tom Pike for three and a half years now. They have no children. She's had two miscarriages. Maurie is a stunning-looking young woman. When she had her second miscarriage, a year ago, she was quite sick. I would have been able to take care of her, but at about that time I was in the hospital for my first operation—Gad, talk about soap operas! . . . Bridget had come down to help out, and Biddy is still here, because things are a Godawful mess. You see, I always thought that Maurie was the solid-as-a-rock one, and Biddy—she's twenty-three now—would be the one who'd manage to mess herself up because she is sort of dreamy and unreal and not in touch. But Biddy has had to hang around not only on account of me but because Maurie has tried three times to kill herself. It seems even more unreal to me when I see my hand write the words on this paper —kill herself—such a stupid and frightening waste. Tom Pike is a darling. He could not be nicer. He and Biddy are trying as hard as they can to bring Maurie out of it, but she just doesn't seem right to me. As if she can't really be reached. Tom has tried all kinds of professional care and advice, and they have been trying to make me believe that her troubles are over now. But I can't believe it. And I certainly can't get up out of this damned bed and take charge. Let us just say I am not likely to ever get up out of this damned bed.

Remember on our cruise when you told me how you live, what you do? Maybe I am stretching the definition, but in this situation my elder is trying to steal her own life. Do you ever operate on a preventative basis? I want you to try to keep her from stealing her life away. I don't have any idea how you would go about it, or whether anything you could do would be of any use at all. Certainly fifty percent of Maurie's life would be worth far more than twenty-five thousand.

I have been thinking of you these past days, finally deciding there is no one else I could ask this of, and no one else I would trust to be able to do anything to help. You are so darn shrewd and knowing about people, Travis. I know that you put a raggedy widow-lady back together again with great skill and taste and loving kindness. In my memories of that summer you are two people, you know. One was a young man so much younger than I that at times, when we were having fun and you seemed particularly boyish, you made me feel like a depraved and evil old hag. At other times there was something so . . . kind of ancient and knowledgeable about you, you made me feel like a dumb young girl. Had it not been for the time we had together, I might have been able to adjust to spending the rest of my life with Teddy Trescot . . . Anyway, my lasting impression was that there cannot be too many things in this world you would not be able to cope with. And I don't mean just muscle and reflex . . . I mean in the gentle art of maneuvering people, as I think Maurie needs to be maneuvered. Can't she comprehend how valuable life is? I certainly can, right now more than ever.

Believe me, darling, I am very tempted to drop one of those horrid death-bed demands upon you—Save my daughter's life! But I cannot bring myself to the point of such dra-

matic corn. You will if you want to and you won't if you don't. It is that simple.

I just had a couple of bad ones and couldn't keep my jaw shut tight enough and so I humiliated myself by squealing loud enough to bring the nurse scuttling in, and so they gave me a shot and things are beginning to get a little vague and swimmy. I will hang on long enough to sign this and seal it, but it might get to sounding a little drunky before I do . . . I wrote about you being two people to me . . . I am two people to myself . . . Do you know how strangely young the heart stays, no matter what? One of me is this wretched husk here in the electric bed, all tubes and bad smells and hurt and the scars that didn't do much good, except for a little while . . . the other me is caught back there aboard the Lady in Shroud Cay, and the other me is being your bounding, greedy hoyden, romping and teasing in the nakedy bed, such a shameless widow-wench indeed, totally preoccupied with our finding, over and over, that endless endless little time when it was all like deep hot engines running together . . . the heart stays young . . . so damnably yearningly unforgivably young . . . and O·my darling hold that other me back there long ago far away hold her tightly and do not let her fade away, because . . .

Signed with a scrawled "H." They keep emptying out the world. The good ones stand on trap doors so perfectly fitted into the floor you can't see the carpentry. And they keep pulling those lousy trip cords.

So do your blinking, swallowing, sickening, ol' Trav, and phone the place. The girl said that Mr. Hardahee had left for lunch, and then she said he hadn't quite, and maybe she could catch him, and she asked was it important, and I said with a terrible accuracy that it was a matter of life and death. D. Wintin Hardahee had a purry little voice, useful for imparting top-secret information. "Ah, yes. Yes, of course. Ah . . . Mrs. Trescott passed away last Thursday evening . . . ah . . . after the operation . . . in the recovery room. A very gallant woman. Ah . . . I count it a privilege to have made her acquaintance, Mr. McGee."

He said there had been a brief memorial service yesterday, Sunday.

There have been worse Mondays, I am sure.

Name three.

Helena, dammit, this is not one of your better ideas. This Maureen of yours is getting devoted attention from people who love her. Maybe she just doesn't like it here. And anybody could make out a pretty long list of contemporary defects. Am I supposed to be the kindly old philosopher, woman, and go set on her porch, and spit and whittle and pat her on the hand and tell her life can be beautiful? Hang around, kid. See what's going to happen next.

I remember your daughters, but not too distinctly, because it was five years ago. Tallish, both slender-lithe blondes with the long smooth hanging sheath of hair, blunt-featured, a bit impassive with all that necessity for total cool that makes them look and act like aliens observing the quaint rites of earthlings. The infrequent blink is when the gray-blue eyes take pictures with hidden cameras. A considerable length of sea-brown legs and arms protruding from the boat clothes, resort clothes. Reservedly polite, quick-moving to go perform the requested errand or favor, a habit of standing close together and murmuring comments to each other, barely moving the shape of the unmadeup girl mouths.

What the hell makes you think—*made* you think—I could communicate with either of them on any level, Helena Pearson Trescot? I am not as much older than your elder daughter than you were older than I, but it is a large gap. Don't trust anybody over thirty? Hell, I don't trust anybody under thirty or over thirty until events prove otherwise, and some of my best friends are white Anglo-Saxon Protestant beach girls.

Helena, I think slaying oneself is a nasty little private, self-involved habit and, when successful, the residual flavor is a kind of sickly embarrassment rather than a sense of high tragedy. What is it you want of me? I am not suited to the role of going around selling the life-can-be-beautiful idea. It can be, indeed. But you don't buy the concept from your friendly door-to-door lecture salesman.

No thanks. Husband Tommy and sister Biddy can cope. Besides, what in the world would I say to the three of them? Helena sent me?

Besides, dear lady, you left me the out. "You will if you want to and you won't if you don't. It is that simple."

I don't.

Tell you what I *will* do, though. Just to play fair. I'll take a little run up there, for some reason or other I'll dream up, and prove to both of us just how bad your suggestion is. Let's say we'll both sleep better. Okay? Fair to all?

5 *COURTNEY COUNTY:* Pop. 91,312. County Seat: Incorporated municipality of Fort Courtney. Pop. 24,808. Gently rolling country. Acres and acres of citrus groves, so lushly productive the green leaves on the citrus trees look like dark green plastic, the profusion of fruit like decorative wax. Ranchland in the southern part of the county. Black angus. White fences. Horse breeding as a sideline. An industrial park, a couple of nice clean operations making fragments of the computer technology, one a branch of Litton Industries, one spawned by Westinghouse, and one called Bruxtyn Devices, Inc., which had not yet been gobbled up by anybody.

Lakes amid the rolling land, some natural and some created by the horrendous mating dance of bulldozer and land developer. Golf clubs, retirement communities, Mid-Florida Junior College.

No boomland this. No pageants, gator farms, Africalands, shell factories, orchid jungles. Solid, cautious growth, based on third- and fourth-generation money and control—which in Florida is akin to a heritage going back to the fourteenth century.

My afternoon flight on that Thursday a week after Helena's death, wing-dipped into the final leg of the landing pattern, giving me a sweeping look at downtown, half shielded by more trees than usual, at peripheral shopping plazas, at a leafy residential area with curving roads, with the multiple geometry of private swimming pools, and then a hot shimmering winking of acres of cars in a parking area by one of the industrial plants, and then we came down, squeak-bounce-squeak-bounce, and the reverse roar of slowing to taxi speed.

I had decided against arriving in my vivid blue Rolls pickup of ancient vintage. *Miss Agnes* makes one both conspicuous and memorable. I certainly was not on any secret mission, but I did not want to be labeled eccentric. I had a mild and plausible cover story and I was going to be very straight-arrow about the whole thing. I just couldn't barge in and say, "Your mother asked me to see if I could get you to stop killing yourself, kid."

The girls were going to remember me not only because I had been a small part of their lives back when Mick had been killed but also because there are not too many people my size wandering around, particularly ones that have a saltwater tan baked so deeply that it helps, to a certain extent, in concealing visible evidence of many varieties of random damage and ones who tend to move about in a loose and rather sleepy shamble, amiable, undemanding, and apparently ready to believe anything.

Because the girls would remember me, I had to have a simple and believable story. The simple ones are the best anyway. And it is always best to set them up so that they will check out, if anybody wants to take the trouble. The fancy yarns leave you with too much to keep track of.

I walked across the truly staggering heat of the hardpan and into the icy chill of the terminal building. A crisp computerized girl in a company uniform leased me an air-conditioned Chev with impersonal efficiency, then turned from robot into girl when I sought her advice on the most pleasant place to stay for a few days. She arched a brow, bit her lip, and when I said I never had any trouble with my expense accounts, she suggested the Wahini Lodge on Route 30 near the Interchange, go out to the highway and turn left and go about a mile and it would be on my right. It was new, she said, and very nice.

It was of the same Hawaiian fake-up as most of Honolulu, but the unit was spacious and full of gadgetry and smelled clean and fresh. I was able to put the car in shade under a thatched canopy. Out the other side of the unit I could see green lawn, flowering shrubs partially blocking the view of a big swimming pool in the middle of the motel quadrangle. It was about three thirty in the afternoon when I dialed for an outside line and dialed the number for Thomas Pike. The address was 28 Haze Lake Drive.

A female voice answered, hushed and expressionless.

"Mrs. Pike?"

"Who is calling please?"

"Are you Maureen?"

"Please tell me who is calling."

"The name might not mean anything."

"Mrs. Pike is resting. Perhaps I could give her a message."

"Bridget? Biddy?"

"Who is calling, please."

"My name is Travis McGee. We met over five years ago. At Fort Lauderdale. Do you remember me, Biddy?"

". . . Yes, of course. What is it you want?"

"What I want is a chance to talk to you or Maurie, or both of you."

"What about?"

"Look, I'm not selling anything! And I happened to do some small favors for the Pearson women when Mick died. And I heard about Helena last Monday and I'm very sorry. If I've hit you at the wrong time, just say so."

"I . . . I know how I must have sounded. Mr. McGee, this wouldn't be a very good time for you to come here. Maybe I could come and. . . . Are you in town?"

"Yes. I'm at the Wahini Lodge. Room One-0-nine."

"Would it be convenient if I came there at about six o'clock? I have to stay here until Tom gets home from work."

"Thanks. That will be just fine."

I used the free time to brief myself on the geography. The rental had a city-county map in the glove compartment. I never feel comfortable in any strange setting until I know the ways in and the ways out, and where they lead to, and how to find them. I learned it was remarkably easy get lost in the Haze Lake Drive area. The residential roads wound around the little lakes. There was a big dark blue rural mailbox at the entrance to the pebbled driveway of number 28, with aluminum cutout letters in a top slot spelling T. PIKE. Beyond the plantings I saw a slope of cedar-shake roof and a couple of glimpses of sun-bright lake. The house was in one of the better areas but not in one of the best. It was perhaps a mile from the Haze Lake Golf and Tennis Club and about, I would guess, $50,000 less than the homes nearer the club.

On my way back from there toward the city I found a precious, elfin little circle of expensive shops. One of them was a booze shoppe, with enough taste to stock Plymouth, so I acquired a small survival kit for local conditions.

Biddy-Bridget called on the house phone at five after six, and I walked through to the lobby and took her around to the cocktail lounge close to the pool area, separated from the hot outdoors by a thermopane window wall tinted an unpleasant green-blue. She walked nicely in her little white skirt and her little blue blouse, shoulders back and head high. Her greetings had been reserved, proper, subdued.

Sitting across from her at a corner table, I could see both portions of the Helena-Mick heritage. She had Helena's good bones and slenderness, but her face was wide through the cheekbones and asymmetrical, one eye set higher, the smile crooked, as Mick's had been. And she had his clear pale blue eyes.

The years from seventeen to twenty-three cover a long, long time of change and learning. She had crossed that boundary that separates children from people. Her eyes no longer dismissed me with the same glassy and patronizing indifference with which she might stare at a statue in a park. We were now both people, aware of the size of many traps, aware of the narrowing dimensions of choice.

"I remembered you as older, Mr. McGee."

"I remember you as younger, Miss Pearson."

"Terribly young. And I thought I was so grown up about everything. We'd been moved about so much . . . Maurie and me . . . I thought we were terribly competent and Continental and sophisticated. I guess . . . I know a lot less than I thought I knew back then."

After our order was taken, she said, "Sorry I wasn't very cordial on the phone. Maurie gets . . . nuisance calls sometimes. I've gotten pretty good at cooling them."

"Nuisance calls?"

"How did you know where to find us, Mr. McGee?"

"Travis, or Trav, Biddy. Otherwise you make me feel as old as you thought I was going to be. How did I find you? Your mother and I kept in touch. A letter now and then. Family news."

"So you had to hear from her during . . . this past year, or you wouldn't have asked if you were talking to me."

"I got her last letter Monday."

It startled her. "But she'd——"

"I was away when it arrived. It had been mailed back in September."

"Family news?" she said cautiously.

I shrugged. "With her apologies for being so depressing. She knew she'd had it. She said you'd been here ever since Maurie was in bad shape after her second miscarriage."

Her mouth tightened with disapproval. "Why would she write such . . . personal family things to somebody we hardly knew?"

44

"So I could have them published in the paper, maybe."

"I didn't mean it to sound rude. I just didn't know you were such a close friend."

"I wasn't. Mick trusted me. She knew that. Maybe people have to have somebody to talk to or write to. A sounding board. I didn't hear from her at all while she was married to Trescott."

"Poor Teddy," she said. I could see her thinking it over. She nodded to herself. "Yes, I guess it would be nice to be able to just spill everything to somebody who . . . wouldn't talk about it and who'd . . . maybe write back and say everything would be all right." She tilted her head and looked at me with narrowed eyes. "You see, she wasn't ever really a whole person again after Daddy died. They were so very close, in everything, sometimes it would make Maurie and me feel left out. They had so many little jokes we didn't understand. And they could practically talk to each other without saying a word. Alone she was . . . a displaced person. Married to Teddy, she was still alone, really. If being able to write to you made her feel . . . a little less alone . . . then I'm sorry I acted so stupid about it." Her eyes were shiny with tears and she blinked them away and looked down into her glass as she sipped her drink.

"I don't blame you. It's upsetting to have a stranger know the family problems. But I don't exactly go around spreading the word."

"I know you wouldn't. I just can't understand why . . . she had to have such a hellish year. Maybe life evens things up. If you've been happier than most, then . . ." She stopped and widened her eyes as she looked at me with a kind of direct suspicion. "Problems. About Maurie too?"

"Trying to kill herself? Not the details. Just that she was very upset about it and couldn't understand it."

"*Nobody* can understand it!" She spoke too loudly and then she tried to smile. "Honestly, Mr. . . . Travis, this has been such a . . . such a terrible . . ."

I saw that she was beginning to break, so I dropped a bill on the table and took her just above the elbow and walked her out. She walked fragile and I took a short cut across the greenery and through a walkway to 109. I unlocked it and by the time I pulled the door shut behind us, she had located the bath, and went in a blundering half-trot toward it, making big gluey throat-aching sobbing sounds, *"Yah-awr, Yah-awr!"* slammed the door behind her. I could hear the muffled sounds for just a moment and then they ended, and I heard water running.

I went down to the service alcove and scooped the bucket full of miniature cubes and bought three kinds of mix out of the machine. I put some Plymouth on ice for myself, drew the thinner, semiopaque draperie across the big windows, and found Walter Cronkite on a colorcast speaking evenly, steadily, reservedly of unspeakable international disasters. I sat in a chair-thing made of black plastic, walnut, and aluminum, slipped my shoes off, rested crossed ankles on the corner of the bed, and sipped as I watched Walter and listened to doom.

When she came shyly out, I gave her a very brief and indifferent glance and gestured toward the countertop and said, "Help yourself."

She made herself a drink and went over to a straight chair and turned it toward the set. She sat, long legs crossed, holding her glass in both hands, taking small sips and watching Walter.

When he finished, I went over and punched the set off, went back and sat this time on the bed, half-facing her.

"Getting any painting done?"

She shrugged. "I try. I fixed it up over the boathouse into sort of a studio." She made a snuffling hiccupy sound. The flesh around her eyes was pink, a little bit puffed. "Thanks for the rescue job, Trav. Very efficient." Her smile was wan. "So you know about the painting too."

"Just that it was your thing a couple of years ago. I didn't know if you still kept at it."

"From what I'm getting lately, I should give up. I can't really spend as much time on it as I want to. But . . . first things first. By the way, what *did* you want to talk to Maurie about?"

46

"Well, I hated to bother you gals so soon after Helena's death. Especially about something pretty trivial. A friend of mine—his name is Meyer—can't seem to get that custom motor sailer you people used to have out of his mind. The *Likely Lady*. She must be six years old now or a little more. He's been haunting the shipyards and yacht brokers for a long time, looking for something like her, but he can't turn anything up. He wants to try to track her down and see if whoever owns her now will sell. As a matter of fact, I'd already promised him I'd write to Helena when . . . her letter came. I made a phone call and found out she had . . . was gone. I told Meyer this was no time to bother you or Maureen. But then I wondered if . . . well, there was anything at all I could do. I guess that because I was on the scene the last time, I'm kind of a self-appointed uncle."

Her smile was strained. "Don't get me started again. Lately I just can't stand people being nice to me." She put her glass down and went over and stared at herself in the mirrored door of the bathroom, at close range. After a few moments she turned away. "It works. It always has worked. When we were little and couldn't stop crying, Mom would make us go and stand and try to watch ourselves cry. You end up making faces at yourself and laughing . . . if you're a little kid." She was frowning as she came back to her chair and her drink. "You know, I just can't remember the name of the man who bought the *Lady*. I think he was from Punta Gorda, or maybe Naples. But I know how I could find out."

"How?"

"Go down and open up the house at Casey Key and look in Mom's desk. I have to do that anyway, the lawyers say. She was very tidy about business things. File folders and carbon copies and all that kind of thing. It will all be in the folder for that year, the year she sold it. It was such a great boat. I hope your friend finds her and can buy her. Daddy said she was forgiving. He said you could do some absolutely damfool thing and the *Lady* would forgive you and take care of you. If you could give me your address, I could mail you the name and address of the man who bought her."

"Do you plan to go down there soon?"

"We talked about going down Saturday morning and driving back Sunday afternoon. It ought to give us enough time. But it depends on . . . how Maurie is."

"Is she physically ill?"

"In addition to being mentally ill? Is that what you mean?"

"Why the indignation? Trying to knock yourself off isn't exactly normal behavior."

"I get . . . too defensive about her, maybe."

"Just what *is* wrong with her?"

"It depends on who you ask. We've gotten more answers than we can use. And more solutions. Manic depressive. Schizophrenia. Korsakov's Syndrome. Virus infection of a part of the brain. Alcoholism. Name it, and somebody has said she has it."

"Korsa-who?"

"Korsakov. Her memory gets all screwed up. She can remember everything prior to this past year, but the past year is a jumble, with parts missing. I think sometimes she uses it as a . . . convenience. She can really be terribly sly. As if we were against her or something. And she does manage to get terribly stinking drunk, and she does manage to sneak away from us, no matter how careful we both are. We put her in a rest home for two weeks, but she was so upset by it, so confused and baffled by it all, we just couldn't stand it. We had to bring her home. She was like a little kid, she was so pleased to be home. Oh, she's not buggy-acting at all. She's sweet and dear and a lovely person, really. But something has just . . . broken, and nobody knows what it is yet. If I hadn't told you all this, you could come to the house and never know anything was wrong, really."

"But she has tried to kill herself?"

"Three times. And two of them were very close calls. We found her in time the time she took the sleeping pills. And Tom found her in the tub after she cut her wrist. The other time it was just something she'd prepared, a

48

noose thing out of quarter-inch nylon, over a beam in the boathouse. All clumsy knots, but it would have worked."

"Does she say why she keeps trying?"

"She doesn't remember why. She can sort of remember doing it, in a very vague way, but not why. She gets very frightened about it, very weepy and nervous."

"Who's taking care of her now?"

"Tom is home with her. Oh, you mean what doctor? Nobody, actually. You could say we've run out of doctors. There are things Tom and I can do for her. She was doing pretty well until Mom died. Then she had . . . some bad days."

"Would she remember me?"

"Of course! She hasn't turned into some kind of a moron, for heaven's sake!"

"What about those nuisance phone calls you mentioned?"

Her expression was guarded. "Oh, just from people she gets involved with when she . . . manages to sneak out."

"She gets involved with men?"

"She goes out alone. She gets tight. She's very lovely. It's hell on Tom and it isn't any of your business."

"That's no way to speak to your kindly old uncle."

A wan smile. "My nerves are ragged. And that part of it just . . . makes me want to resign from the human race. Those damned oily voices on the phone, like filthy children wondering if Maurie can come out and play. Or like the way you see packs of dogs, following. They don't know she's sick. They don't even give a damn."

"How often does she sneak off?"

"Not often. Maybe three times in the last four months. But that's three times too many. And she never remembers much about it."

I took her empty glass and built her a fresh drink and took it to her, saying, "You must have some kind of a theory. You probably know her as well as anyone in the world. What started all this?"

"When she had the second miscarriage, it was because of some kind of kidney failure. She had convulsions. I thought that could have done something to her brain. But the doctors say no. Then I thought she might have a tumor of the brain, but they did all kinds of tests and there's nothing like that at all. I don't know, Travis. I just don't know. She's the same Maurie, but yet she's not. She's more . . . childlike. She breaks my heart."

"Care if I stop by and say hello?"

"What good would it do?"

"And what harm could it do?"

"Is it just kind of a sick curiosity?"

"I guess that's my bag, going around staring at crazies."

"*Damn* you! I just meant that——"

"She's not on display? Right? Okay. She was twenty. She took that ugly business about Mick with a great deal of class and control. I knew how much she adored her father. Look, I didn't ask to be let in on all the family secrets. But I was. I'd like to see what she's like. Maybe you're too close to it. Maybe she's better than you think she is. Or worse. Can you think of anybody else who hasn't seen her since she was twenty?"

"N-No. Suppose I ask Tom what he thinks. And phone you here either later this evening or in the morning."

When she finished her drink, I walked her out to her little red Falcon wagon. She thanked me for the drinks and apologized for being so tired and cross and edgy, and drove off.

She phoned in the morning and invited me to lunch at the house. She said Maurie was looking forward to seeing me again, and that Tom would join us for lunch if he could get away.

6 *BRIDGET PEARSON* apparently heard the sound of tires on the driveway pebbles and appeared from behind the house, on the lake side. She wore yellow shorts and a white sleeveless top and had her hair tied back with yellow yarn. Her sunglasses were huge and very black.

"So glad you could make it! We're out back. Come along. Tommy fogged the yard before he went to work, and there's hardly a bug. He should be along any minute."

She kept chattering away, slightly nervous, as I followed her out to the slope of lawn overlooking the lakeshore. Tall hedges of closely planted punk trees shielded the area from the neighboring houses. There was a redwood table and benches under a shade tree, a flourishing banyan. The two-story boathouse was an attractive piece of architecture, in keeping with the house. There was a T-shaped dock, iron lawn furniture painted white, a sunfish hauled up onto the grass, a little runabout tethered at the dock. The makings of the picnic lunch were stacked on one end of the redwood table. A charcoal fire was smoking in a hibachi. She pointed out the pitcher of fresh orange juice, the ice bucket, the glasses, the vodka bottle, and told me to make myself a drink while she went to tell Maurie I'd arrived.

In a few moments Maureen came out through the screened door of the patio, moving down across the yard toward me, smiling. Her dead mother had written me that she was stunning. In truth she was magnificent. Her presence dimmed the look of Biddy, as if the younger sister

51

were a poor color print, overexposed and hastily developed. Maurie's blond hair was longer and richer and paler. Her eyes were a deeper, more intense blue. Her skin was flawlessly tanned, an even gold that looked theatrical and implausible. Her figure was far more rich and abundant and had she not stood so tall, she would have seemed overweight. She wore a short open beach robe in broad orange and white stripes over a snug blue swimsuit. She moved toward me without haste, and reached and took my hands. Her grasp was solid and dry and warm.

"Travis McGee. I've thought of you a thousand times." Her voice was slow, like her smile and her walk. "Thank you for coming to see us. You were *so* good to us a long time ago." She turned and looked over her shoulder toward Biddy and said, "You're right. He isn't as old as I thought he'd be either." She stretched up and kissed me lightly on the corner of the mouth and squeezed my hands hard and released them. "Excuse me, Travis dear, while I go do my laps. I've missed them for a few days, and if I stop for any length of time, I get all saggy and soft and nasty."

She walked out to the crossbar of the T and tugged a swimcap on, dropped the robe on the boards and dived in with the abrupt efficiency of the expert. She began to swim back and forth, the length of the crossbar, so concealed by the dock that all we could see were the slow and graceful lift and reach of her tanned arms.

"Well?" Biddy asked, standing at my elbow.

"Pretty overwhelming."

"But different?"

"Yes."

"How? Can you put your finger on it?"

"Maybe she seems as if she's dreaming the whole scene. She sort of . . . floats. Is she on anything?"

"Like drugs? Oh, no. Well, when she gets jumpy, we give her a shot. It's sort of a long-lasting tranquilizer. Tom learned from one of the doctors and taught me how."

I watched the slow and apparently tireless swimming

52

and moved to the table to finish making my drink. "There's nothing vague or dazed about her eyes. But she gives me a funny kind of feeling, Biddy. A kind of caution. As if there's no possible way of guessing just what she might do next."

"Whatever comes into her head. Nothing violent. But she is just . . . as primitive and natural as a small child. Wherever she itches, she'll scratch, no matter where she is. Her table manners are . . . pretty damned direct. They get the job done and in a hurry. And she says whatever she happens to be thinking, and it can get pretty . . . personal. Then if Tom or I jump on her about it, she gets confused and upset. Her face screws up and her hands start shaking and she goes running off to her bedroom usually. But she can talk painting or politics or books . . . just so long as it's things she learned over a year ago. She hasn't added anything new this year."

We heard another car on the pebbles and she went hurrying off around the corner of the house. She reappeared, talking rapidly and earnestly to the man walking slowly beside her. A certain tension seemed to be going out of his posture and expression, and he began to smile. She brought him over and introduced him.

He was tall and wiry, dark hair, dark eyes, a face that had mobility and sensitivity, and might have been too handsome without a certain irregularity about his features, a suggestion of a cowlicky, lumpy, aw shucks, early-jimmy-stewart flavor. His voice did not have the thin country whine of Mr. Stewart, however. It was surprisingly deep, rich, resonant, a *basso* semi-*profundo*. Mr. Tom Pike had exceptional presence. It is a rare attribute. It is not so much the product of strength and drive as it is a kind of quality of attention and awareness. It has always puzzled and intrigued me. People who without any self-conscious posturing, any training in those Be Likable and Make Friends courses, are immediately aware of you, and curious about you, and genuinely anxious to learn your opinions have this special quality of being able to somehow dominate a room, a dinner table, or a backyard. Meyer has it.

He shed his lightweight sports jacket and pulled his tie off, and Biddy took them from him and carried them into the house. With a tired smile he said, "I've been worrying all morning about how Maureen would react to you. It can be very good or very bad, and no way to tell in advance. Biddy says it's been fine so far."

"She looks great."

"Sure. I know. Dammit, it makes me feel . . . so disloyal to have to act as if Biddy and I were keeping some kind of defective chained up in the cellar. But too much exposure to outsiders shakes her up." His quick smile was bitter and inverted. "And when she gets upset, you can be very very sure she's going to upset the outsider, one way or another. She's going to find her way out of the thicket. Someday. Somehow."

"It must be pretty rough in the meanwhile, Tom."

"And there's another reason I feel guilty. Because most of it lands right on Biddy. I'm out of here all day working. We've tried and tried to find somebody to come in and help out, somebody kind and patient and welltrained. We've interviewed dozens. But when they find out the trouble is maybe in some psychiatric area, they back away."

Biddy had returned and was busying herself with the food. I asked what luck they were having with the doctors. He shrugged. "They raise your hopes, then say sorry. One recent diagnosis was that a calcium deposit was diminishing the flow of blood to the brain. A series of tests, and then he says sorry, it isn't that at all. The symptoms just don't fit anything in their books. But I have some people who keep checking, writing letters."

"Excuse a painful question, Tom. Is she deteriorating?"

"I keep wondering about that. I just don't know. All we can do is wait and watch. And hope."

Maurie stopped swimming, put her palms flat on the dock, and came vaulting up, turning in the air to sit on the edge, lithe as a seal. She got up and smiled up the slope at us. She used the short robe to pat her legs dry, then put it on, pulled her swimcap off, and shoved it into the robe pocket, shaking her hair out as she walked. As she approached Tom Pike her slow, floating assurance seemed to desert her. She came to him with downcast eyes, shoulders slightly hunched, her welcome smile nervous, her walk constricted. She made me think of a very good dog aware of having disobeyed her master and hoping to be so engaging and obedient that the infraction will be forgiven and forgotten. He kissed her briefly and casually and patted her shoulder and asked her if she had been a good girl. She said shyly that she had been good. It was a most plausible attitude and reaction. She was the wife and no matter how lost she had become, she could not help knowing that she no longer measured up to what they both expected of her. It seemed more an awareness of inadequacy than a conscious guilt.

Mosquitoes were beginning to regroup under the banyan shade. Tom went and got the little electric fogger and plugged it into a socket on one of the flood lamps and killed them off, commenting to me when he was finished that he hated to use it because it was so unselective. "When I was a kid, we'd sit on the screened porch on a summer evening and see clouds of mosquito hawks—dragonflies—darting and swooping, eating their weight. Then the bats would begin when the sun went down. So we've killed off the mosquito hawks with the spray and we've killed the other bugs the bats ate, and now there's nothing left but billions of mosquitoes and gnats, and we have to keep changing the spray as they get immune."

"You grew up around here?"

"In the general area. Here and there. We moved around a lot. Steaks ready, Bid? Time for one more drink, then, Trav. Let me fix it for you. Maurie, darling, you are supposed to be tossing the salad, not sampling it."

She hunched herself. "I didn't mean . . . I wasn't——"

"It's all right, darling."

At one point while we were eating, one scene, like a frozen frame, like a color still, underlined the strange flavor of the relationships, of the ménage. Maurie and I were on the same bench on one side of the picnic table,

Maurie on my left. Biddy was across from me. Maurie was eating very politely and properly, and I glanced over and saw the two of them watching her. Husband and kid sister, looking at the wife with the same intent, nervous approval, as a couple might watch their only child plodding through a simple piano solo for visiting relatives. Then the frozen frame moved once again as Biddy lifted the poised fork to her lips and as Tom Pike began chewing again.

Later, as Biddy was saying something to me, Tom's low voice in a sound of warning, saying merely "Darling!" made Biddy stop abruptly and look quickly at Maureen. I turned and looked at her and saw that she had hunched herself over her plate, head low, had picked up her steak in a greedy fist, and was tearing and gobbling at it. She dropped it back onto her plate and sat, eyes downcast, while under the shelter of the edge of the table she wiped her greasy fingers on the top of her bare thigh, leaving streaks of sheen across the firm brown.

"You forgot again, dear," Tom said in a gentle voice.

Maurie began to tremble visibly.

"Don't get upset, honey," Biddy said.

But suddenly she wrenched herself up and away, striking the edge of the table so solidly with her hip that drinks and coffee slopped out of the glasses and cups. She ran toward the house, sobbing audibly in her blundering, hopeless flight. Tom called sharply to her, but she did not look back or slow down. Biddy got up quickly and hurried after her.

"Sorry," Tom said. "I guess you can see why we don't . . . Biddy will get her settled down and . . ." He pushed his plate away and said, "Ah, the *hell* with it!" and got up and walked down toward the lake shore.

He was still there when Biddy came walking back out. She sat opposite me. "She's resting now. In a little while she won't remember what happened. I want to have Tom look at her and see if he thinks she needs a shot. Is . . . is he all right?"

"He acted upset."

"It's because she was doing so well."

She stared down toward the silent figure by the shore. I was at an angle to her that gave me a chance to see more than she would have wanted me to see. Her face had a soft and brooding look, lips parted. It was adoration, worship, hopeless helpless yearning love. I knew why she had started to go to pieces in the cocktail lounge. It was a situation nicely calculated to fray her to the breaking point, to have been for a year in this house with the deteriorating wife, the concerned and suffering husband. Loyalty to the big sister. And a humble self-sacrificing love for the husband.

After a little while we all went inside. Tom went up and looked at her and came back and said she was sleeping. He sat for a moment, glancing at his watch.

"Nice to meet you, Travis. Just . . . sorry that it had to be . . . to be . . ." His voice thickened and his mouth twisted, and he suddenly buried his face in his hands. Biddy hurried to him and shyly, hesitantly, put her hand on his shoulder.

"Tom. Please, Tom. It will work out."

He sighed and straightened up and dug in his pocket for a handkerchief. His eyes still streaming, he said in a husky voice, "Sure, honey. It will all be peachy dandy by and by." He mopped his eyes and blew his nose. "I apologize for myself too. See you around." She followed him out and I heard him saying something about getting home late. The car door slammed. He drove out. She came back into the two-level living room. Her eyes looked moist.

"He's . . . quite a guy, Travis."

"Little tough to go back to the office and sell stocks and bonds, I guess."

"What? Oh, he hasn't done that in a long time now. Over two years. He started his own company."

"Doing what?"

"It's called Development Unlimited. It's sort of a promotion company. They do a lot of land-syndication things. I don't really know how it works, but it's supposed to be a wonderful idea for people in high tax brackets, like doctors and so on. They pay a lot of interest in advance when they buy the land, and then they sell it later for capital gains. Tom is very clever at things like that. And they set up shares in apartment houses and do something very clever about depreciation and losses and cash flow and all that. He tried to explain it to me, but I have no head for that kind of thing. I guess he's doing well because he has to go out of town a lot and arrange deals in other places too. To have Maurie the way she is makes . . . his success so kind of hollow. He is really a marvelous human being."

"He seems to be."

She wanted to show me her studio and her paintings. But she was making too obvious an effort to entertain me. The shine had gone out of her day. I said I should be getting along. I wrote out my address for her and told her to send me the name of the man who had bought the *Likely Lady* when she went through her mother's papers.

We stood out by my car and told each other we hoped we'd see each other again someday. Maybe we *did* hope so. Hard to say.

I got back to the Wahini Lodge at three. I stretched out on the bed and told myself that it had to be the end of the obligation, if there was any. I had taken a good look. It was a sorry little situation. Prognosis bad. When you can't identify the disease, the prognosis is always bad. And two nice people, Tom Pike and Bridget Pearson, were stuck with it. Maybe if Maurie could knock herself off in such a way that Tom wouldn't blame Biddy and she wouldn't blame him or herself, they might be able to make a life. A lot of widowers have married kid sisters and enjoyed it.

The restlessness was back in full force. I didn't want to go home to Lauderdale. I didn't want to stay where I was. And I couldn't think of anywhere to go. I felt like a bored kid on a rainy day. Maurie kept sliding into my mind and I kept pushing her out. Go away, woman. Have a nice sleep.

I went into the bathroom. I glanced at my toilet-article kit atop the pale yellow formica of the countertop, and my random restless thoughts were gone in an instant, and I was totally focused, the back of my neck feeling prickly and cool.

Caution is like the seat belt habit. If you are going to use seat belts, then you'd better make it automatic by latching your belt every single time you get into the car. Then you stop thinking about the seat belt and you do not have to make any decisions about seat belts because you are always strapped in.

I have a lot of little rituals that are completely automatic. They are the habits of caution. A lot of these habits are seemingly casual and accidental arrangements of things. When I leave the toilet kit open, the last thing I usually replace in it is the toothbrush. I am a brush-last type. I lay it, bristles-up, across the other items in such a way that it is fairly stable and is on a perfect diagonal, aimed from corner to corner out of the case. When I reach into the case in the morning to take the stuff out, I am not consciously aware of the precise placement of the toothbrush. I am suddenly very aware, however, if it is not in its proper place and alignment.

I reconstructed the morning. By the time I came back from breakfast, the maid had done the room. I had been in the bathroom, and had the brush been in the wrong place, I would have noticed it. I studied the new position of it. No passing truck, no sonic boom, could have moved it so far from its proper position.

All right. So somebody had been messing with my stuff, poking around. Petty thief with a passkey. Very easy to prove. All I had to do to prove it was lift the soap dish. (Only masochists use those sorry little slivers of lilac that motels call soap.) Two twenties, folded twice. I unfolded them. There were still two. A dumb thief would take them both. A slightly less stupid thief would take one.

If you are in a line of work where people can get very emotional about the fact you are still walking around and breathing, a forty-dollar decoy is a cheap method of identifying the visitor. Had the money been gone, it would not have been absolute assurance that it had been a visit by a sneak thief. A professional of enough experience and astuteness would take it anyway, knowing that if I had left any little trap around the place, the missing money would be a false trail.

I went back to the bed, sat on the edge of it and glowered at the carpeting. I had brought nothing with me that could possibly clue anybody about anything. My temporary address was known to Biddy, Tom Pike, the car rental girl, and whoever they might have told or who might have questioned them.

Biddy and Tom knew that I would be away from the motel at lunchtime. Tom would have had time to come to the motel before going home. Looking for what? Helena's letter? Work on that assumption and stay with it until it breaks down. But why? What could be in the letter? Unless Biddy was one hell of an actress, she hadn't known there was a letter until I told her. Seemed doubtful that Helena would mention having written me a letter. It was too highly personal a letter, for one thing. D. Wintin Hardahee had known for sure. And maybe a nurse had known. Forget the why of it, at least for now. Start at a known point or with a known angle, which is the basis of all navigation.

I knew that it could be some foul-up in identification. Maybe I looked like somebody somebody was looking for. Maybe it had been a little once-over by the law. Maybe there was a nut on the loose with a toothbrush fetish.

I phoned Mr. D. Wintin Hardahee, of Folmer, Hardahee, and Krantz, located in the Courtney Bank and Trust Company building on Central Avenue. I got through to his secretary, who said that Mr. Hardahee was in a meeting. She did not know when it would be over. Yes, if I wanted to take a chance on coming in and waiting to see him, that was all right, but if the meeting lasted past five, he would not be able to see me until Monday.

I was going to walk very lightly and keep looking and listening for anything off-key in my immediate area.

And I was no longer restless. Not at all.

7 *AT FOUR THIRTY* Hardahee's matronly secretary came into the paneled waiting room to lead me back to his office. As middle partner in the firm, he had a corner office with big windows. He was round, brown, bald, and looked very fit. He had some tennis trophies atop a bookcase. He spoke in the hushed little voice I remembered from our phone conversation, a voice that did not suit him at all. He leaned across his desk to shake hands and waved me into a deep chair nearby.

"She was a fine woman. Shame to go that way," he said. He seemed to be slightly wary and curious. "Is there any way I can help you, Mr. McGee?"

"I just wanted to ask a couple of questions. If any of them are out of line, just say so."

"I'll tell you what I can. But perhaps you should understand that I was not Mrs. Trescott's personal attorney. Her affairs are handled in New York, legal, tax and estate, and so on. Apparently she telephoned or wrote her people in New York and asked them to recommend someone here to handle a confidential matter for her. A classmate of mine is one of the partners in the firm she had been dealing with up there, so when they gave her my name, she phoned me and I went to see her in the hospital. Perhaps they'll call on me to handle some of the estate details at this end, but I have no way of knowing."

"Then, you didn't tell anyone about the letter and the check?"

"I told you that she wanted it handled as a confidential matter. She wrote a check on her New York account and

I deposited it in our escrow account. When it cleared, I had a cashier's check made out to you, as she requested. She gave me a sealed letter to go with it. If you were not the recipient, I would disclaim knowledge of any such transaction."

"Sorry, Mr. Hardahee. I didn't mean to——"

"Perfectly all right. You couldn't have known how it was handled until I told you."

"I told her younger daughter about getting a letter from her. I had lunch there today, with the Pikes and Miss Pearson. I assumed from Helena's letter that she was staying there before she went into the hospital this last time."

"That is correct."

"Can I establish a confidential relationship too? I guess I could as a client, but I don't know what kind of law you work with, Mr. Hardahee."

"Both the other senior partners are specialists. I'm the utility man. Play almost any position."

"Do you represent Tom Pike directly or indirectly in any way? Or either of the daughters?"

"No one in the firm represents them in any way."

"Very quick and very definite."

He shrugged. "I try to be a good and careful attorney, Mr. McGee. When I got a note from Walter Albany in New York saying Mrs. Trescot might contact me, once I established who she was, and her condition, it struck me that because Tom Pike has many contracts in the legal profession here it might develop into some sort of an inheritance problem. So I checked our shop to make certain we wouldn't be in any conflict of interests if the transaction led eventually into a dogfight."

"And you based that guess on her having gone through New York to find a local attorney instead of asking her son-in-law?"

He ignored the question. "A client has to have a legal problem. What's yours?"

"I'm in One-O-nine at the Wahini Lodge. When I returned this afternoon, after being at the Pike home, I discovered by accident that somebody had gone through the stuff in my room. Forty dollars in cash was untouched. No sign of forcible entry. Nothing missing."

"And thus nothing you can report?"

"That's right."

"What is the legal problem?"

"In her letter Helena Trescot asked me to see what I could do to keep Maureen—Mrs. Tom Pike—from killing herself. It was a confidential request. We're old friends. She has confidence in me. So did her first husband, Mick Pearson. A dying woman can ask for a damfool favor, I guess. So I came up and checked. I had a logical reason for getting in touch. Imaginary but logical. So I looked the scene over and Mrs. Pike is in a pretty spooky condition, but there isn't anything I could do that isn't being done. I had to make sure, because Helena *did* ask me. So I was at the point of deciding I should check out and leave town when I found out somebody had gone through the room."

"Looking for the letter? Because they knew there *had* been a letter, and it made somebody uneasy not to know what was in it?"

"That was one of the things that occurred to me."

"As if somebody might be concerned about an inheritance situation?"

"I didn't think about that."

"Walter Albany said her resources were 'substantial.' "

"Meaning how much?"

"Hmmm. To interpret the trust attorney lingo, taking into account the area where Walter practices, I would say that adequate would mean up to a quarter million, comfortable from there up to a million, and substantial could mean anything from there on up to . . , let's say five or six million. Beyond that I think Walter could say 'impressive.' So you thought it over and you came to see me because you want to know how many people knew there *was* such a letter. Me and my secretary and the deceased. And you, and whoever you may have told."

"And a nurse?"

"Possibly. I wouldn't know."

"I told Miss Pearson, the sister, yesterday when she

came over to the motel to have a drink with me. She had no idea her mother and I had stayed in touch the past five years. I had to account for being fairly up to date. But I said nothing about what Helena asked me to do."

"You brought the letter with you? It was in the room?"

"No."

"If somebody were looking for it, would they look elsewhere? At your home in Fort Lauderdale?"

"They might, but they wouldn't find it."

"Would you know someone had looked for it?"

"Definitely."

He looked at his watch. It was after five. He frowned. "What kind of work do you do, Mr. McGee?"

"Salvage consultant."

"So what you want to find out from me is whether you should trust your initial judgment of Mr. and Mrs. Pike and Miss Pearson or whether the incident at your hotel room is sufficient cause for you to look more closely?"

"Mr. Hardahee, it is a pleasure to deal with someone who does not have to have detailed drawings and specifications."

He stood up. "If you can manage it conveniently, you might join me for a drink at the Haze Lake Club at seven fifteen. If I'm not in the men's bar, tell Simon, the bartender, that you are my guest. I have a date to play doubles in . . . just twenty minutes."

When I walked in, I saw that D. Wintin Hardahee had finished. He was at the bar with a group of other players, standing with tall drink in hand in such a way that he could keep an eye on the door. When I appeared, he excused himself and came over to meet me and took me over to a far corner by a window that looked out at the eighteenth green. In the fading light the last foursomes were finishing.

Hardahee was in white shorts and a white knit shirt, with a sweat-damp towel hung around his neck. I was correct about his fit look. His legs were brown, solid, muscular, and fuzzed with sun-bleached hair. The waiter came over and Hardahee said the planter's punch was exceptional, so I ordered one without sugar and he asked for a refill.

"Win your match?"

"The secret of winning in doubles is to carefully select and train your partner. That blond boy over there is mine. He is constructed of rawhide, steel wire, and apparently has concealed oxygen tanks. He's keeping my name fresh and new on the old trophies and making all the other players hate me."

"Everybody hates a winner."

"Mr. McGee, since talking to you, I have been synthesizing all the bits and pieces of information I have concerning Tom Pike. Here is my subjective summary. He is energetic, with considerable fiscal imagination, a great drive. He has personal charm with magnetism. A lot of people are rabidly and warmly loyal to him, people who from time to time have been on his team, or connected with his team in one way or another, and who have made out very well and had some fun doing it. They think he can do no wrong. He has the traits and talents of the born entrepreneur, meaning he is elusive, fast-moving, and very hard-nosed, as well as being something of a born salesman. So there are people who have necessarily been in the way of the deals he has assembled from time to time and they have been bruised and are eager to claim they were tricked, and quite obviously they hate him. I know of no successful legal action brought against him. As you said, everybody hates a winner. It is a mistake to confuse shrewdness, misdirection, and opportunism with illegality. I can think of no one who knows Tom who is indifferent to him. He polarizes emotions. My guess would be this. If he knew you had a letter his mother-in-law wrote before her death and if he thought there was any information in it of any use to him, he would have come to you and sooner or later you would have found yourself telling or showing him the part or parts he wanted to know about."

"How would he manage that?"

"By studying you to find out what you want and then offering it to you in such a way you would feel grateful toward him. Money or excitement or advance knowledge or whatever happens to be your choice of private vices. If he had to have something, I think he would go after it his own way first."

"And if that didn't work?"

"He'd probably turn the problem over to one of the many people aching to do him a favor, no matter what it might be."

"And you don't like him."

He pursed his lips. ". . . No. I think I like Tom. But I would be uneasy about getting into any kind of business association with him. I'm quite sure I'd make out very well, as have many others, but the inner circle seems to become . . . a group of faceless men. In any kind of speculation tight security is imperative. They seem to become very . . . submissive? No. That isn't accurate. Retiring, discreet, and slightly patronizing toward the rest of the working world. I guess I am not a herd animal, Mr. McGee. Even if it would fatten my purse."

"So if it wasn't Pike or one of his admirers, how come I had a visitor, then?"

"My considered opinion is that it beats the hell out of me."

"Well, if somebody was looking for something they think I have, and wants it badly enough to take a chance of getting caught going in or out of a motel room, the next place to look is in my pockets."

"If it's smaller than a bread box."

"I think I'll hang around and do a little trolling."

"Keep in touch."

"I will indeed."

I drove back to the Lodge and ate one of the fake-Hawaiian special dinners, then went from the dining room into the cocktail lounge and stood at the bar. Business was very light. Some young couples were sploshing around outside in the big lighted pool. The bar was a half rectangle and I became aware of a girl alone at an end stool, by the wall, under a display of ancient fake Hawaiian weapons. She wore a weight of red-gold wig that dwindled her quite pretty and rather sharp-featured face. She wore a white dress, which seemed in better taste than the wig and the heavy eye makeup. She had a cluster of gold chain bracelets on one arm, smoked a cigarette in a long gold and white holder, and was drinking something wine-red out of a rocks glass, a measured sip at a time, as self-consciously slow and controlled as her drags at the cigarette.

I became aware of her because she wanted me to be aware of her. It was puzzling because I had appraised the motel as no hangout for hookers. Also, though she was apparently dressed and prepared for the part, her technique was spotty and inept. There are the ones who operate on the mark of their choice with the long, wide-eyed, arrogant-insolent-challenging stare, then properly leave it up to him to make the next move. There is the jolly-girl approach, the ones who say to the barkeep in a voice just loud enough to carry to the ears of the mark, "Geez, Charlie, like I always say, if the guy doesn't show, the hell with him. I'm not going to cry my eyes out, right? Gimme another one of the same, huh." Then there's the fake prim, the sly sidelong half-shy inquisitive glance, and the quick turn of the head, like a timid doe. Or the problem approach, troubled frown, gesture to have the mark come over, and then the dreary little set piece: Excuse me, mister, this may sound like a crazy kind of thing, but a girl friend of mine, she asked me to be here and tell the guy she had a date with she can't make it, and I was wondering if you're George Wilson. Or: Would you mind, mister, doing me a crazy kind of favor? I got to wait here to get a phone call, and there's some nut that was bugging me before and said he was coming back, and if you'd sit next to me, then he won't give me any problems, okay?

But this one didn't have any routine to depend on. Her infrequent glance was one of a puzzled uncertainty. I decided that it was another instance of the courage of The Pill bringing the bored young wife out hunting for some action while hubby was up in Atlanta at another damned sales meeting. I wondered how she'd manage if I gave her no help at all.

What she did was get up and head for the women's room. She had to walk behind me. So she dropped her lighter and it clinked off the tile and slid under my feet. I backed away so I could stoop and pick it up, but my heel came down on her sandaled toes. I recovered in time to keep from coming down with all my weight, but I came down hard enough to make her yelp with anguish. I turned around and she limped around in a little circle, saying, "Oh, dear God!" while I made apologetic sounds. Then we compounded it by both bending at the same instant to pick up the lighter. It was a solid, stinging impact, bone against bone, hard enough to unfocus her eyes and unhinge her knees. I caught her by the arms, moved her gently over, and propped her against the bar.

"Now I will bend over and pick up the lighter."

"Please do," she said in a small voice. She grasped the edge of the bar, head bowed, eyes shut.

I wiped the lighter off with the paper napkin from under my drink and placed it in front of her. "Are you all right?"

"I guess so. For a minute there my toes didn't hurt at all."

She straightened, picked the lighter off the bar, and made a rather wide circle around me and headed for the women's room. I motioned the bartender over and said, "Amateur night?"

"New to me, sir. You got each other's attention anyways."

"House rules?"

"They say to me, they say, Jake, use your judgment."

"So what do you say to me?"

"Well . . . how about bon voyage?"

"How was she doing before I showed, Jake?"

"There were two tried to move in on her, but she laid such a cool on them I cased her for strictly no action, that is, until she began to throw it at you."

"She's in the house?"

"I don't know. I'd guess not, but I don't know."

When I heard the tack-tack of her heels on tile returning, I smiled at her and said, "I have liability coverage. Like for broken toes, concussion, lacerations."

She stopped and looked up at me, head tilted. "I think it was a truck, but I didn't get the license number. I could settle my claim for some medication, maybe. On the rocks."

So I followed her and took the bar stool beside her and asked Jake for more of the same for two, and winked at him with the eye farther from her. Ritual of introduction, first names only. Trav and Penny. Ritual handshake. Her hand was very small and slender, fine-boned, long fingers. Faint pattern of freckles across nose and cheekbones. Perfume too musky-heavy for her, too liberally applied. I could detect no evidence of a removed ring on third finger left, no pale line or indentation of flesh.

We made the casual talk that is on one level, while we made speculative, sensual communication on the second level. Humid looks from the lady. Pressure of round knee against the side of my thigh when she turned to talk more directly to me. Parting of lips and the tongue tip moistening. But she was too edgy, somehow, too fumbly with cigarettes and purse and lighter and drink. And her component parts did not add up to a specific identity. Wig, makeup, and perfume were garishly obvious. Dress, manicure, diction were not.

So Trav was in town to see a man interested in putting some money in a little company called Floatation Associates, and Penny was a receptionist-bookkeeper in a doctor's office. Trav wasn't married, and Penny had been, four years ago, for a year, and it didn't take. And it sure had been a rainy summer and fall. Too much humidity. And the big thing about Simon and Garfunkel was the words to the songs, *reely*. If you read the lyrics right along with the songs while the record was on, you know, the lyrics right on the record case, it could really turn you on, like that thing about Silence especially. Don't you think, honest now, that when people like the same things and have enjoyed the same things, like before they ever met, Trav, it is sort of as if they had known each other a long time, instead of just meeting? And people don't have enough chance to just talk. People don't communicate anymore somehow, and so everybody goes around kind of lonesome and out of touch, sort of.

So I played out the charade and walked her out, her elbow socketed in the palm of my hand, and she was thinking out loud of maybe some other place we could go, and rejecting each one for one reason or another as soon as she mentioned it, and I drew her into a dark alcove near the grinding roar of the central air conditioning, and after a sudden and startled rigidity and instinctive defensive tactics, she somewhat hesitantly made a presentation of her mouth, which somehow imitated avidity yet tasted prim, then she let herself be guided to 109 and ushered in, her voice getting too shrill and tight in her effort to stay loose.

"Gin?" she said. "That's your drink, isn't it? I *adore* it, but I don't like to drink it in public because I get too wildly happy and loud and everything. But could we have some, darling?"

There was a double handful of melting cubes afloat in ice water in the bottom of the ice bucket. She decided she did not want any mix with hers either. We clinked glasses and she smilingly fluttered her long plastic eyelashes at me. She took a hummingbird sip and sat and put the drink down on the rug and slipped her left shoe off and tenderly squeezed her bruised toes.

I had taken a mouthful of the Plymouth. I am a taster when I like the taste. But it was subtly wrong, just wrong enough so I knew that the hunch had been right. A bad Penny. Under pretext of taking a second swallow, I let the first slide back into the glass. It left me with an astringent prickling of the membranes of the mouth and a slight aftertaste of dust.

"Excuse," I said, and went into the bath. There, behind the closed door, I dumped the drink into a pocket I made in a face towel. It saved the ice. I rinsed glass and ice and made myself some tap water on the rocks. I flushed the toilet and stood for a few moments assembling the pieces of the procedure before I went back out. She

70

hadn't been near the opened bottle of Plymouth, at least on this visit to my quarters.

So she or some associate had done the doctoring. Then she was there to make sure I had a drink, to take the chain off the door if necessary, assuming there was an associate in their venture. And unless you wanted to risk putting somebody so far under they might not make it back up again, it was efficient to be there to know when it took effect.

I went back out and noticed that two thirds of her drink was gone. Back among the melting cubes, I assumed. She had both her shoes off. She was sitting with her legs crossed. The hem of the white dress was hiked to midthigh. She was a little long-waisted girl. Her legs could have been called chunky had they not been beautifully shaped.

"Am I supposed to drink alone?" she asked, pouting.

"Never compete with a gulper," I said, and drained the tap water potion. I went over to the counter where the bottle and ice were and said, "In fact, I will have another one down the hatch before you finish that little piece of gin you've got left, angel."

She came over in considerable haste and came up behind me and wrapped her arms around me. "Darling, let's not drink *too* much, huh? It can spoil things for people, you know. I think we've both had . . . just exactly the right amount."

It was a helpful clue. If the idea of my having two alarmed her, then it had to be fast-acting. But I thought I might quite plausibly give her a little lesson in anxiety before I faked being overcome. So, instead of making the drink, I turned and began chuckling and wrapped my arms around her. She stood very small in her stocking feet. She tried to seem cooperative until I found the zipper at the nape of her neck and opened it in one tug all the way down to the coccyx. Chuckling blandly, I peeled the dress forward off her shoulders, and she became nervously agitated, hopping and struggling, saying, "No! No, darling! Let's be . . . Hey! More leisurely . . . Hey! . . . Please!" I pulled the dress sleeves down her arms, inhibiting her struggles. She wore a pale yellow bra with white lace. "You'll tear my . . . Wait! Don't . . ." I found the bra snap and got the edge of a thumbnail under it and popped it open, and the bra straps slid down her arms. "No! Dammit! Hey! Please!"

She got one arm out of the sleeve and tried to pull her dress back up, but as she did so I pulled the other arm free, then caught both wrists in one hand, put the other around her waist, and lifted her off the floor. When I shook her a little, still chuckling, the dress and bra slid off her and fell to the floor, and I swung her in the air and caught her, an arm around her shoulders, the other under her knees, and chuckling inanely, toted her over to the bed. She had begun a silent battle, in deadly earnest, to retain the little yellow matching panties, and finally I took pity on her and groaned as hollowly as I could and toppled heavily across her, my chest across her sturdy agitated thighs.

She was breathing hard. She pushed at me. "Hey! Wake up!" I did not move. She caught a fold of flesh on the side of my throat under the ear and gave a painful, twisting pinch. Then she pulled my hand toward her and put her fingertips on my pulse. Satisfied, she pushed at me and wormed her legs out from under me. She grunted with the effort. I kept my eyes closed. The bed shifted as she got off it. In a few moments I heard the little clicking snap of the bra catch and soon the almost inaudible purr of the nylon zipper, the rezipping divided into three segments, as it was hard to reach. Then a faint thudding of her footsteps became audible and I knew she had put her shoes back on.

She picked up the phone on the bedside stand and dialed for an outside line. She dialed a number. She waited a few moments, then said, "Okay," and hung up. Clack of her lighter. Huff of exhalation. Smell of cigarette. I identified the next move as her unlatching the door, probably to leave it ajar for whoever had the word that things were now okay in 109. The edge of the bed had caught me across the lower belly. My toes rested on the rug.

"Come *on!*" she whispered. "Come *on,* Rick darling."

Make it six or seven minutes from phone call to arrival. Male voice, after the door was gently closed. "Everything okay, honey?"

"No problems."

"Nice work. I hated the idea of you coming to his room. I was afraid maybe he'd decide he didn't want a drink, and then he's such a big, rough-looking son of a bitch, I was afraid——"

"Just like I hate the idea of your sleeping with your dear wife Janice every damned night, darling?" Her voice was bitter.

"And you know why it has to be that way."

"Do I?"

"No time to open the same damned old can of worms, Penny. Let's see if we're going to do any good."

He took me by the belt and pulled me back off the bed. I let myself tumble, completely slack. I ended up on my side, knees bent, cheek against the bristle of the rug. He pulled at my shoulder and I rolled slowly onto my back. He rolled me another half turn, face down, and I felt him work the wallet out of my hip pocket, heard the distinctive sound as he sat on the bed. Sizable, I guessed. Young voice. Physically powerful.

"Anything?" she asked.

"Not in this. Pockets of his jacket?"

"Just this stuff. Nothing."

"I better check the side pockets of his pants."

"Would there be anything in . . . in the lining of anything, or in his shoes?"

"I don't know. I'll check it if we draw a blank. The thing that bothers me is that this son of a bitch doesn't have enough on him."

"What do you mean, dear?"

"The average guy has pieces of paper on him. Notebook, notes, addresses, letters, junk like that. McGee here has got car rental papers, a plane ticket to Lauderdale, keys, drivers license, and a half dozen credit cards and . . . a little over eight hundred in cash. Here. Take these two fifties."

"I don't *want* the money!"

"We want him to think he had a ball. Here, dammit!"

"All right. But I can't see why he'd———"

"Win, lose, or draw, we rumple the hell out of that bed, rub lipstick on the pillow, squirt some of your perfume on him, undress him, and leave him in the bed. And dump the rest of that bottle into the john."

"Okay. But you know, he didn't *seem* like somebody who'd———"

"For chrissake, Penny!"

"All right. I'm sorry."

"We knew it was a big man. We know he was from out of town. We know he went to see Pike."

He checked the other pockets. Then the girl asked about the shirt pocket. He rolled me onto my back again. She was standing close. I opened my eyes just far enough to make out the shape and distance of his head as he bent over me. I hit him solidly in the side of the throat with my right fist, rolling my body to the left as I did so to give it more leverage, and then swung my legs in a wide arc at floor level. I clipped her right at the ankles and she landed flat on her back with a very large thud for a girl that size. Her friend had rolled over onto his back and back up onto his knees. He got up just as I did. He was making gagging, strangling sounds. Eyes bulged. Mouth hung open. Sandy-blond with a lot of neck, shoulders, and jaw. Look of the college lineman six years later, twenty pounds heavier, and a lot softer.

But as he got his back against the wall, he pulled a blue-black and very efficient-looking revolver out of somewhere and aimed it at my middle. I stopped very suddenly and took a cautious step backward, and raised my arms, and said, "Easy now. Easy does it, friend."

He coughed and gagged and massaged his throat. He spoke in a rasping, traumatic whisper. "Back up and sit on the edge of the bed, smartass. And hold the back of your neck with both hands."

I obeyed, slowly and carefully. Penny was still on her back on the floor. She was making a horrid articulated sound with each inhalation. She had hiked her knees up.

Her clenched fists were against her breast. The fall had knocked all the wind out of her.

He went over and looked down at her. Her breathing eased. He gave her his hand and he pulled her up to a sitting position, but she shook her head violently and pulled her hand away. That was as far as she wanted to go for the moment. She hugged her legs, forehead on her knees.

"Two hours you said," he whispered. "Or three."

"He . . . he must be resistant to it. He had enough for . . . a full-grown horse."

With his eyes on me, he moved the straight chair over and placed it about five feet from me, the back toward me. He straddled it and rested the short barrel on the back of the chair, centered on my chest. "We'll have a nice little talk, smartass."

"About what? This lousy setup? I've got eight hundred on me, so take it. Wear it in good health. Leave."

She got to her feet, took one step, and nearly went down again. She hobbled over toward the head of the bed, her face twisted with pain.

"My ankle," she said. She was having a clumsy evening.

"We are going to have a little talk about Doctor Stewart Sherman, smartass."

I frowned at him, my bafflement entirely genuine. "I never heard of the man in my life. If this is some variation of the badger game, friend, you are making it too complicated."

"And we are going to talk about how you are putting the squeeze on Tom Pike. Want to deny seeing him today?"

"I went to see Maurie and Biddy, the two daughters of Mick Pearson, a friend of mine who died five years, nearly six years ago, not that it is any of your business."

There was a look of uncertainty in his eyes for just a moment. But I needed more advantage than that and, remembering their very personal little squabble, and remembering how she had reported having no trouble at all with me, I thought of an evil way to improve the odds.

"Like I said. Take the eight hundred and leave. Your broad was pretty good, but she wasn't worth eight hundred, but if that's the going rate, let me pay."

"Now, don't get cute," he said. His voice was coming back.

"Man, the very last thing I am going to be is cute. My head hurts from whatever she loaded my drink with. We had this nice little romp and then, instead of settling down, she wants to go out to some saloon. She said we could come back afterward. So I get dressed and she wants a drink, so I fix two drinks and I drink mine, and the last thing I remember is seeing her watching me in a funny way as she's putting her clothes on. Then the lights went out."

"He's making it up! It wasn't like that at all, darling!"

I raised my eyebrows in surprise and tried to look as though a slow understanding was dawning on me. I nodded. "All right. If she's all yours, buddy, then I'm making it up and it wasn't like that at all. Never happened."

The shape of his mouth was uglier. Without taking his watchful stare off me, he said to her, "How could you figure he'd wake up? How could you figure he'd tell me? A little fun on the side, darling?"

"Please!" she said. "Please, you can't believe him. He's trying to——"

"I'm trying to be a nice guy," I said. "It never happened. Okay, Penny?"

"Stop it!" she cried.

"Maybe the only way you can keep me from using this gun is by proving it did happen. Tell me . . . some things you couldn't know otherwise, smartass."

"Pale yellow bra and panties with white lace. Freckles, very faint and small but lots of them, across the tops of her breasts. A brown mole, about the size of a dime, maybe a little smaller, two inches below her left nipple and toward the middle of her, like maybe at seven o'clock. And when she was making out, she called me Rick. If you're not Rick, you've got more problems."

The blood had gone out of his face. Instead of turning his eyes, he turned his whole head toward her.

In a breathy dog-whistle squeak she said, "But he knows because . . . I never . . . when he was . . ."

"You cheap little bum," he said in a pebbly voice. "You dirty little hot-pants slut. You . . ."

And by then his head was turned far enough, and I made the long reach for the kick and put a lot of energy and hope and anxiety in it, because there was so little barrel jutting out over the back of the chair. But I hit it hard enough to numb my toes and hard enough to kick it out of his hand and over his head. It hit the wall and bounded back, spinning along the rug. He pounced very well and even came up with it, but I was moving then, adjusting stride and balance as I moved, and got my turn and my pivot at the right place and, keeping my wrist locked, put my right fist into the perfect middle of that triangle formed by the horizontal line of the belt and the two descending curves of the rib cage. He said a mighty *hawff* and sat solidly on the floor about four feet behind where he had been standing, rolled his eyes back into his head and slumped like Raggedy Andy. I scooped up the revolver and knelt beside him and checked heart and breathing. It is a mighty nerve center, and fright had added lots and lots of adrenalin to my reaction time, and it can so shock the nervous system that the breathing will stop and the heart go into fibrillation.

I saw a movement out of the corner of my eye and I lunged for the girl and caught her just as she got her hand on the door. I spun her back into the room, forgetting her bad ankle. She fell and rolled and started to get up, then lay there curled on the floor, making little smothered hopeless sounds of weeping.

Her Rick was too big to fool with, and I found a couple of wire hangers in the closet, leftovers hung in with the wooden kind that fit into nasty little metal slots so you won't steal them. I straightened one into a straight piece of wire, then held his wrists close together by grasping both his arms just above the wrist in the long fingers of my left hand. I put the end of the wire under my left thumb and then quickly and firmly wrapped it around his wrists as many times as it would go, then bent and tucked

77

the two ends under the encircling strands. It is a wickedly effective device. And quick.

I went over to her and picked her up and sat her on the edge of the bed. She sat blubbering like a defeated child. I squatted and examined her ankle. It was solid and shapely, and beginning to puff on the outside, just below the anklebone.

"I l-l-love him!" she said. "That was a . . . a wicked . . . a wicked evil thing for you to do. That was . . . a wicked evil lie."

Her wig was askew and I reached and plucked it off. She was a sandy redhead with a casual scissor cut. Without the wig her face was in better proportion, but the eye makeup, particularly with much of it making black gutters down her cheeks, look ridiculous.

"Wick-wick-wicked!" she moaned.

"But there's nothing wicked and evil about picking me up and knocking me out with a Mickey? Go wash that goop off your face, girl. Besides, if I busted it up, maybe I did you a favor. He'll never leave Janice and marry you."

I helped her up. She went limping toward the bathroom. She stopped suddenly and stood quite still, then turned and stared at me. "That was right aft-after he came in, that about Jan-Janice! Then you were never . . . Then you just pretended . . . all along you *knew?*"

"Go wash your dirty face, honey."

When she closed the door, I emptied Rick's pockets and took the stuff over to the desk and looked at it under the light.

The identification startled and alarmed me. I had thumped and wired up one Richard Haslo Holton, Attorney at Law. He was a county Democratic committeeman, an honorary Florida sheriff, past president of the Junior Chamber, holder of many credit cards, member of practically everything from Civitan to Sertoma, from the Quarterback Club to the Baseball Boosters League, from the Civic Symphony Association to the Prosecuting Attorneys' Association.

He carried a batch of color prints of a smiling slender

dark-haired woman and two boys at various ages from about one year to six years. One does not go about needlessly irritating any member in good standing of any local power structure. I had the feeling he was going to wake up in a state of irritation.

Penny came out of the bathroom with her face scrubbed clean and with the big black lashes peeled off and stuffed away somewhere. She had stopped streaming, but she was tragic and snuffly.

Just then Mister Attorney made a sound of growling and an effort to sit up. It seemed useful to leave a small but lasting impression on both of them. So I went over and scooped him up, slung him, and dropped him in a sitting position in the black armchair. It shocked and surprised him. He was meaty and sizable. I had done it effortlessly, of course. It had given me an ache in all my back teeth, ground my vertebrae together, pulled my arms out of the sockets, and started a double hernia. But, by God, I made it *look* easy.

"Now let's all have a nice little chat," I said.

"———— your ———— ———— ———— in ————
————!" he said.

I smiled amiably. "I can phone Mrs. Holton and ask her to come over and join us. Maybe she can help us all communicate."

So we all had a nice little chat.

8 SEEMS THAT Miss Penny Woertz was the loyal devoted office nurse for one Dr. Stewart Sherman, a man in the general practice of medicine. He was inclined, however, to get so involved in special fields of interest that he often neglected his general practice.

In early July, three months ago, Dr. Sherman had gone down to his office on a Saturday evening. Penny knew that he had been anxious to get his notes in shape so that he could finish a draft of a paper he was writing on the effects of induced sleep in curing barbiturate addiction.

He was a widower, a man in his middle fifties, with grown children married and living in other states. He lived alone in a small apartment and did some of his research work there and did the rest of it in one of the back rooms of his small suite of offices. The body was not discovered until Penny came to work on Monday morning at ten, as was her customary time.

The body was on the table in the treatment room. The left sleeve of the white shirt had been rolled up. A length of rubber tubing that had apparently been knotted around the left arm above the elbow to make the vein more accessible was unfastened but held there by the weight of the arm upon it. Over the countertop was an empty container and an empty syringe with injection needle attached. Both the small bottle with the rubber diaphragm top and the syringe showed traces of morphine. The drug safe was unlocked. The key was in his pocket. His fragmentary prints were found on the syringe and the bottle. Beside the empty bottle was a small wad of surgical cotton with a streak of blood diluted by alcohol on it. The autopsy conducted by the county medical examiner showed that the death, to a reasonable medical certainty, was due to a massive overdose of morphine. According to Penny, nothing else was missing from the drug safe, or from the other stocks of drugs used in the treatment of patients. But she could not tell whether anything was missing from the back room stocks especially ordered by Dr. Stewart Sherman and used in his experimentations.

She had unlocked the door when she arrived.

By then I had unwired Rick Holton. His attitude was a lot better and the wire had been painful.

He said, "At one time I was the assistant state attorney here in Courtney County. The way it works, the state attorney has a whole judicial district, five counties, so he has an assistant prosecutor in each county. It's elective. I'd decided not to run again. The state attorney is still the same guy. Ben Gaffner. The day I heard that Stew Sherman was supposed to have killed himself, I told Ben that I would just never believe it. Well, dammit, they had the autopsy, and Sheriff Turk investigated and he turned the file over to Ben Gaffner, and Ben said there was no reason in the world why he should make a jackass of himself by trying to present it to the grand jury as something other than suicide, which it damn well was—according to him."

"The doctor *couldn't* have killed himself!" Penny said.

"That's what I felt," Rick said. "So because they were closing the file, I thought what I'd do was use what time I could spare to do some digging. Ben gave me his unofficial blessing. The first time I interviewed Penny, I found out she felt exactly the same way."

So that was how their affair had started. From what I had heard while pretending to be unconscious, I knew it was going sour. And now they were very stiff with each other, harboring delicious resentments.

As I thought the tensions between them might inhibit their communicating with me, I tried to take them off the hook. I told Holton that when the taste of the gin had clued me, I decided to give her some real reason to be jumpy and maybe teach her that pretending to be a hooker could be a messy little game, so I had peeled her out of her dress and bra. "She put up a good fight," I said.

He looked a little happier. "I see. So you made me so goddamn mad at her, I gave you an opening. You're pretty good, McGee."

"If I'd known you were a member of the bar and every lunch club in town, I wouldn't have tried you. It was a very small opening and you carry a very damaging caliber. If you'd had the hammer back, I wouldn't have tried you. But why me? Like I told you, I never heard of the doctor."

He summarized what he had been able to dig up. He had an orderly mind and professional knowledge of the rules of evidence. With Penny's help he had located two people who had seen a very tall man let himself out of Dr. Sherman's offices late Saturday night. One guessed eleven thirty. The other guessed a little after midnight. Penny knew that when the doctor was working on his research projects, he would not answer the office phone. The answering service had recorded no calls for the doctor that evening. One witness said that the man had gotten into a dark blue or black car parked diagonally across the street, a new-looking car, and had driven away. That witness had the impression that the car bore Florida plates but had a single digit before the hyphen rather than the double digit designating Courtney County. He had taken affidavits and put them in his private file on the case.

"But how does Tom Pike come into the picture?" I asked.

"I was looking for motive. I heard a couple of people saying that Stew had died at one hell of an inconvenient time as far as Tom was concerned, and he might take a real bath on some of his deals. So I wondered if maybe somebody had killed the doctor just to put the screws on Tom. You see, Stew Sherman was the Pike family doctor, and when Tom started Development Unlimited two years ago, Stew invested with him in a big way. He'd always made pretty good money in his practice and on top of that he had the money his wife left when she died three years ago. Tom had put together some marvelous opportunities for Stew and the others who went in on the first deals he made. They stood to make really fantastic capital gains. Money is always a good motive. So I had a long talk with Tom. At first he didn't want to tell me anything. He said everything was fine. But when he saw what I was driving at, he got very upset and he opened up. The doctor had been fully committed on three big parcels of land east of town. Tom had put together a fourth deal, and Stew had made preliminary arrangements to borrow a large sum of money from the bank, using his equity in the first three parcels as collateral. Based on the bank's preliminary approval, Tom had gone ahead and committed the group on the fourth deal. Now not only was he going to be badly squeezed on the fourth deal, but the Internal Revenue Service had come in on an estate tax basis and froze the doctor's equities in the other three parcels, and actually could order sale of those equities in order to meet the estate tax bite. Tom told me that Doctor Sherman couldn't have died at a worse time, not only for the sake of his own estate, but also because of what it could do to the others who were in on all four syndicates. He told me that he was going to have to do one hell of a lot of scrambling to keep the whole thing from falling apart."

"I assume he made out all right."

"The word is that he squeaked through, but that it cost him. As a matter of fact, Stew's sons tried to bring some kind of action against Tom because there was a lot less left than they thought there ought to be. But there was no basis for action. I asked Tom if anybody could have killed the doctor in order to mess up the deals he had on the fire. The idea shocked hell out of him. He said he could think of some people who might have wanted to, but they would have had no way of knowing how badly it would pinch him. He agreed that it seemed very, very strange that the doctor should kill himself, but he couldn't offer any alternative."

"But some tall man has been putting the squeeze on Tom Pike?"

"That's one of those funny breaks you get, the kind that may mean something or nothing. In late August, Tom Pike drew twenty thousand in cash out of one of his accounts. A lot of real estate deals are cash deals, so it wasn't anything unusual. I found out how much by checking back, quietly, through a friend, after I heard what happened. One of my law partners mail ordered a big reflector telescope for his twelve-year-old kid's birthday and had it sent to the office. He set it up, tripod and all, and was fooling around putting the different eyepieces on and aiming it out the office window at the shopping plaza a block away. He had it at two hundred and forty power, meaning that something two hundred and forty yards away looks like one yard away. He focused it on a car parked all alone in an empty part of the lot and when he got it sharp and clear, he found he was looking at Tom Pike standing and leaning against the car. He wondered what he was waiting for. Just then another car pulled up and a tall man got out. My partner said he had never seen him before. He had a lot of tan and looked rugged and wore a white sport shirt and khakis. Tom gave the stranger a brown envelope. The stranger opened it and took out a sheaf of bills and riffled the end of the sheaf with his thumb. My partner said he could damned near see the denomination. He then put the brown envelope into his car and took out a white envelope or package and gave it to Tom Pike, who stuffed it away so quickly my partner didn't get much of a look at it. They got into their cars and took off. He mentioned it to me a couple of days later. We were talking about a divorce action we're handling and he said maybe we should invest in a telescope and told me about spying on Tom. There could be a lot of answers. Maybe it was a cash option on ranchland or groveland. Maybe he was buying advance highway information from a road engineer. But maybe it was the tall man who was in Stew's office that night and got into the act somehow."

"So just how did you come up with me?"

"I was at the bar with a client last night when you came in with Tom's sister-in-law. She started crying and you took her out. I told my client I'd be right back. I saw you unlock One-O-nine and took a look at your plate and saw it was a rental number. I got your name at the desk. I have a cop friend I give some work to when he's off duty and he tailed you today and phoned me when you pulled into the Pike house. I met him here and he went through your room while I hung around the house phone to give him a warning call if you got back too soon. He didn't find a thing that would give us a clue. I don't have any official status, of course. And even if I did, I could still get in real trouble taking you in for a shakedown. Penny and I worked out the idea of her seeing if she could pick you up. I knew about the opened bottle from what my cop friend told me. Penny had something she thought would work fast. While you were eating I spiked your bottle."

"How did you get in?"

"With the passkey from my cop friend. He's got a master key for every big motel in the area."

I looked at them. "You people are very diligent and so on. And damned stupid. So if I didn't want to get picked up? So I wanted to come back here all by myself and kill the bottle?"

"I was five minutes away. She was going to phone me and I was going to come over, use the phone, and get you out of the room on some pretext. She was going to use the passkey and dump the bottle or steal it."

"Because," she said in a small voice, "to make one drink strong enough, I had to put enough in so that all of it would have killed you, through suppression of the sympathetic nervous system."

"Why *did* Pike give you the twenty thousand?" Holton asked.

"Amateur to the end," I said. "I never met him until today. Can I prove it? No, sir. I can't prove it. Do I want to try to prove it? No. I can't be bothered. Do you want to try to prove it? Go ahead, Holton." I spun the cylinder of his Police Positive. Full load. I handed it to him. "The doctor was probably a nice guy. And you are probably fairly nice people yourselves. But you two are a nurse and a joiner and if you found somebody who really killed the doctor, he'd probably kill the two of you also. You belong on serial television. If I had killed the doctor, I would rap your skulls, put you in the trunk of the car, and drop you into one of the biggest sinkholes I could find and cave some of the limestone sides down onto you."

He was flushed as he got to his feet, stuffing the revolver into his belt. "I don't need lectures from some damned drifter."

"Stay busier. Join more clubs."

"Do I have your permission to go, *Mister* McGee!"

"Nothing could give me more piercing delight."

"Come on, Pen."

"Go home to Janice," she said. "You've been out enough nights."

"Look, I'm *sorry* I blew my stack when he said . . . uh——"

"You were so *ready,* darling. You were just *aching* to believe something like that, something nasty. You want to think that because you got to first, second, third base, and home, anybody can. Anytime. Go to hell, Rick. You are a mean lousy little human being and you have a dirty little mind."

"Are you coming with me or aren't you?"

"I'm going to stay right here for a little while, thank you."

"Either you come with me——"

"Or you'll never forgive me, and we're through, and so on. Oh, baby, are we ever through! If there's no trust, there's no nothing at all. Good-bye, Rickie dear. All the way home to Janice you can dwell on all the nasty things you think are probably going on right here on this bed."

He spun around, marched out, and slammed the door viciously.

Her attempt to smile at me was truly ghastly. Her mouth wouldn't hold together. "Hope you didn't mind me . . . hope it was all right to . . ." Then the mouth broke and she sprang up and went, *"Waw! Hoo Oh waw,"* as she hobbled into the bathroom.

Fort Courtney was nice enough if you didn't mind it being full of sobbing women trotting into your bathroom, fifty percent of them running with a limp. I took the ice bucket outside and dumped the water out of it and scooped more cubes out of the machine. I thought of dumping out the spiked gin, then changed my mind, capped it, and put the bottle in a back corner of the closet alcove. I unwrapped a fresh glass and opened the second bottle of Plymouth and fixed myself a drink. When she finally came out, slumped, small and dispirited, I offered her a drink.

"Thanks, I guess not. I'd better be going."

"Got a car here?"

"No. Rick dropped me off. My car is over at my place. I can phone for a cab from the office."

"Sit down for a minute while I work on this. Then I'll drive you home."

"Okay." She wandered over and got a cigarette from her purse and lit it. She picked up the thick red-blond wig between thumb and finger like somebody picking up a large dead bug. She dropped it back onto the countertop and said, "Fifteen ninety-eight, plus tax, to try to look like a sexpot."

"You didn't do badly."

"Forget it. I've got freckles, straw hair, short fat legs, and a big behinder. And I'm clumsy. I keep falling over things. And people. Lucky little old me, falling for Rick Holton." She hesitated. "Maybe I'll change my mind about the drink. Okay?"

I unwrapped the last glass and fixed her one, turned, and handed it to her. She took it over to the chair. "Thanks. Why should you do me favors, though? After what I tried to do to you."

"Guilt syndrome. I clobbered your romance."

She frowned. "It hurts. I know. I walked into it expecting to get hurt. You didn't do it, really. You just brought it to a head a little quicker. He's been beginning to want out. I could feel it. He was looking for a great big reason. Jesus, you made him mad!"

"I think I was a little irritated too. I couldn't find out what your plans were unless I faked you out."

She looked into her glass. "You know something? I think I ought to get smashed. I don't have to drive. And from the way this one is making me feel numb around the mouth already, it shouldn't take much."

"Be my guest. Just don't sing." I started to get her glass but she waved me off and went over and fixed her own.

"You sure you don't mind, McGee? Drunk females are horrid. I learned that from working the emergency ward."

"Look, how can you two be so sure that the doctor didn't kill himself?"

"Perfect health. Loved his work and his little projects.

He had enthusiasm about things. Like a kid. And I know how he felt about the attempted suicides. Well, like Tom Pike's wife. It just baffled him. He couldn't understand how anybody could take their own life."

"He treated her?"

"Both times. And it was close both times. If Tom hadn't been on the ball, she would have bought it. He phoned the doctor when he couldn't wake her up, and the doctor told him to rush her down to the emergency room. He met them there and pumped her out and gave her stimulants and they kept walking her and slapping her awake until she was out of danger. The other time Tom had to break the bathroom door down. She'd lost a lot of blood. There were two of those . . . hesitation marks, they call them, on her left wrist, where she couldn't make herself cut deep enough. Then she cut deep enough the third time. It's slower bleeding from a vein, of course. She's a nice standard type, and Doctor Sherman put four pints back into her and did such a good job on her wrist I'll bet that by now the scar is almost invisible."

"Reported to the authorities?"

"Oh, yes. You have to. It's the law."

"Did you have any idea anything at all might have been bugging the doctor?"

"Gee, it's hard to say. I mean he wasn't one of those always-the-same people. When he'd get involved in some project, he'd get sort of remote, especially when things wouldn't be going well. And he wouldn't want to talk about it. So . . . *maybe* something was bothering him, because he'd been acting the way he usually did when things weren't going the way he expected. But I just *know* he wouldn't kill himself."

"Anything questionable in the autopsy?"

"Like maybe he was knocked out first? No. No sign of it and no trace of anything but morphine, and that was more than a trace."

I was slouched deep in the armchair, legs resting on a round formica table. After the silence had lasted a little while, I looked over at her. She was staring at me. She had one eye a third closed and the other half closed. She had one brow arched and she had her lips pulled back away from her rather pretty teeth. It was a strange, fixed grimace, not quite smirk and not quite sneer.

"Hi!" she said in a husky voice, and I suddenly realized that the stare had been meant to be erotic and inviting. It startled me.

"Oh, come *on,* Penny!"

"Well . . . listen. You're cute. You know that? Pretty damn cute. What I was thinking, that sumbitch was so ready to think I cheated, right? I was thinking like they say about having the name and the game too. Whoose going anyplace anyways? Friday night, iznit? Dowanna waysh . . . *waste* the li'l pill I took this morning, do I?"

"Time to take you home."

"Yah, yah, yah. Thanks a lot. You must find me real attractive, McGee. Freckles turn you off? Doan like dumpy-legged women?"

"I like them just fine, nurse. Settle down."

She came around toward me and stood and gave me that fixed buggy stare again, put her glass on the table, then did a kind of half spin and tumbled solidly onto my lap, managing to give me a pretty good chop in the eye with her elbow as she did so. It hit some kind of nerve that started my eye weeping. She snuggled into me, cheek against my chest, and gave me another breathy "Hi!"

"Penny-friend, it is a lousy way to try to get even with good old Rick. You're bold with booze. You'd hate yourself."

"D'wanna take d'vantage of a girl?"

"Sure. Glad to. You think it over and come back tomorrow night and scratch on the door."

She gave a long, weary exhalation and for a moment I wondered if she was suddenly passing out. But then in a level and perfectly articulated voice she said, "I have a good head for booze."

"Hmmm. Why the act?"

"It ain't easy, McGee, for a cold-sober girl to offer her all to the passing stranger. Maybe for some, but not for Penny Woertz. No! Don't push me up. I can tell you easier if I'm not looked at."

"Tell me what?"

"It's a bad hang-up for me. With Rick. He really *is* mean. Do you know how a guy can be mean? Cruel little things. Know why he can get away with being like that?"

"Because you're the only one with the hang-up?"

"Right. You're pretty smart. Know what I'll do now?"

"What will you do?"

"Get very firm with myself. Tell myself it was a no-good thing. Chin up, tummy in, walk straight, girl. Think of him every three minutes of every waking hour for two or three or four days, and then dial the private line in his office and humble myself and whimper and beg and apologize for things I didn't do. And be ashamed of myself and kind of sick-joyful at the same time."

"No character, hey?"

"I used to think I had lots. He got to me in . . . a kind of physical way. I think of him and get to wanting him so bad my head hums and my ears roar and the world gets tilty."

"Hmm. Humiliating?"

"That's the word. I want out. I want free. So while I was in your bathroom blubbering because he walked out, I had this idea of how to get loose, if I could work up enough nerve."

"Use me to solve your problem?"

"I thought you'd jump at the chance. Not because I'm so astonishingly lovely, something that turns all the heads when I walk by. But I've had to learn that there is some damn thing about me that seems to work pretty good. I mean if I was in some saloon with Miss International Asparagus Patch, and a man moved in on us because he drew a bead on her, a lot of the time he'd switch targets, and I've never known why it happens, but it does. That's why I was so sure I could pick you up in the bar."

"You *do* project a message."

"Wish I knew what the message reads."

"I think it says, 'Here I am!' "

"Darn it. I *like* men. As men. Six brothers. I was the only girl. I've never been able to really be a girl-girl, luncheons and girl talk and all that. But I don't go shacking around. I love to make love, sure. But it never seemed to be any kind of real necessity, you know? Except now I'm hung up that way with Rick, and I don't even *like* him very much. I don't even know if . . . it would be any good at all with another man nowadays. I thought you'd be a good way to find out. I thought, once I'd pumped up the nerve, one little opening and Pow. Easier to play drunk. Hardly know you. Won't see you again. So you come on with these scruples. Or maybe my mysterious whatzit isn't on your wavelength, dear. Oh, Christ! I feel so awkward and timid and dumb. I never tried to promote a stranger before, honest."

"So if nothing much happened, wouldn't you be hung up worse than ever?"

"No. Because it would keep me from having the guts to phone him. After sleeping with you—win, lose, or draw—I'd feel too guilty. And that would give me the time to finally get over it. You see, I always have to go crawling to him. If when he doesn't hear from me, he comes after me, I don't know if I can stay in the clear. But . . . it would give me a pretty good chance."

She gave that deep long sigh once more. Strange little freckled lady, radiating something indefinable, something lusty and gutsy. Something playtime. So the world is a wide shadowy place, with just a few times, a few corners, where strangers touch. And she could be a partial cure for the random restlessness of the past weeks. Ol' Doctor McGee. Home therapy. The laying on of hands. Therapeutic manipulation. The hunger that isn't a damned bit interested in names or faces is always there, needing only a proper fragment of rationalization to emerge. So I drifted my fingertips along the sad curl of her back and found the same old zipper tab and slowly pulled it from nape to stern. She pushed up, swarmy-eyed, hair-tousled, to make the opening gift of her mouth in her acceptance.

But stopped and focused, frowned. "It's a sad story, okay. But it isn't *that* sad! It shouldn't make a strong man cry."

"I'm not. You got me in the eye with your elbow a while back."

Hers was a good laugh, belly laugh, total surrender to laughter, enough for tears, but with no edge of hysteria. While I got the lights, she hung her dress on a hanger and turned the bed down. We left the bathroom door ajar, a strip of light angling across the foot of the bed. She was constricted and muscle-taut and nervous for a time but not for long. And after more unmeasured time had gone by, I found out just what that mysterious aura was. It was clean, solid, healthy, joyous, inexhaustible girl, all clovery oils and pungencies, long limber waist and torso sophisticating the rhythmic counterpoint of solid, heated, thirsty hips, creating somehow along with release the small awarenesses of new hunger soon to rebuild.

I awakened slowly to the morning sound of her shower and drifted off again, and was awakened a little later by sun-brightness shining into the darkened room, and saw her naked by the double draperies, holding the edge away from the window while she peered out at the day. With her other hand she was foamily scrubbing away at her teeth with my toothbrush and toothpaste.

She turned away from the window and, seeing that my eyes were open, she roamed over to the bed, still scrubbing. ". . . ood oring, arley."

"And good morning to you too, tiger."

"O you O eye."

"What?"

Removed brush. "I said I hope you don't mind. Me using your toothbrush. I mean invasions of privacy are sort of relative, huh?"

"Like the old joke, it's been the equivalent of a social introduction."

When she started brushing again, I reached and caught her by the free wrist, pulled her closer. She removed brush, stared thoughtfully at me. "Really? You're serious?" She smiled. "Well sure! Let me go rench." She went into the bathroom. The water ran. The sound of spitting was *p-too, p-tooey,* like a small child. She came trotting back, beaming, launched herself into the bed, landing solidly, reaching greedily, and saying an anticipatory "Yum" with utmost comfortable satisfaction. In her own special field of expertise she was the least clumsy thing in probably the entire county.

After we were dressed, she began to be increasingly nervous about leaving a motel room at high noon on Saturday. She was almost certain Rick was out there, waiting in murderous patience. Or that a group of her friends would be strolling by the room, for some unknown reason. She put the wig on as a partial disguise. She had me go out and start the motor in the rental, open the door on her side, and tap the horn ring when I was certain the coast was clear.

She came out at a hunched-over half gallop and while scrambling into the car she gave her knee such a hell of a whack on the edge of the door that she spent the first three blocks all scrooched down, hugging her knee and moaning. Then from time to time she would stick her head up just far enough to see where we were and give me directions. She had an apartment in a little garden apartment development called Ridge Lane. After she insisted I drive around two blocks twice to make certain Rick's red convertible wasn't parked in the area, I drove into her short, narrow drive behind the redwood privacy fence and stopped a few inches behind the rear bumper of her faded blue Volkswagen in the carport. She spelled Woertz for me and said she was in the book. But I had the feeling she did not want me to call her. I had performed the required service. She did not want to trade one entanglement for another.

I remembered a question I had forgotten to ask. "By the way, what were you people hoping to find on my person, Penny?"

She shrugged. "We didn't know, really. Anything that would tie you in somehow. Papers or money or letters or notes or something. When you come to a blind alley, you're ready to try almost anything."

We sat there and suddenly both yawned at once, great luxurious shuddering jaw-creakers. Then laughed at ourselves. She kissed me, got out, and gave a squeak of pain when she put her weight on her leg. She bent and rubbed her sore knee, then limped to her door. When she had unlocked it and opened it, she smiled and waved and I backed out.

On the way back I stopped at a place as clean as any operating theater and had fresh juice, hot fresh doughnuts, surprisingly good coffee. Then, feeling a little bit ridiculous at being overly prim and fastidious, I walked a half block and bought a toothbrush before driving back to the motel. Yes, there are different degrees of personal privacy, and a toothbrush seems to be on some special level all its own, a notch above a hairbrush.

The room had been made up. Though checkout time was eleven, I was certain they would not clip me for the ensuing night, as they just weren't that busy.

But I sat and yawned and sighed, feeling too pleasantly wearied to make any decisions. The episode, I told myself, had changed nothing. A dead doctor, no matter how he died, had nothing to do with a damaged young wife who seemed to want to die.

Nothing new had been added except . . .

Except something she had said in the middle of the night after that time that had been unmistakably the most complete one for her, not any kind of thrashing wildness, or spasmodic yelping, but just very lasting and very strong, fading very slowly for her, slowly and gently. It was one of those fragmented drowsy conversations as we lay in a night tangle of contentment, sheet and blanket shoved down to the foot of the bed, the flesh drying and cooling after the moist of effort. Her deep and slowing breath was humid against the base of my throat. Round knee against my belly, her slow, affectionate fingertips tracing over and over the line of my jaw from earlobe to chin. In down-glance I could see, against the light that lay in a crisp diagonal line across the foot of the bed, a round height of her hip, semiluminous, and a steep descent to the waist where rested, in dark contrast, my large hand with fingers splayed.

"Mmmmm," she said, "so now I know."

"Search for guilt?"

"Too soon for that, darling. Feel too delicious for that. Later maybe. But . . . damn it all anyway."

"Problem?"

"I don't know. Girl finds she can get turned way, way on, big as can be, with a nice guy that comes along. So she's kind of a lousy person."

"Glandular type, eh?"

"A lousy nympho, maybe."

"Then, I'd have to be number eight hundred and fifty-six or something."

She lay in thought for a moment and then giggled. "Counting Rick, you got one figure right. The six. The other four, I was married to one and engaged to two and head over heels with the other. Compared to some of the R.N.'s I work with and was in training with, I'm practically a nun. But my old grandma would faint dead away."

"Nymphs are concerned only with self, honey. They lose track of who the guy is. Don't know or care. A robot would suit them fine."

"I knew you were you, all along. Even more so when it got to the best part. What does that make me?"

"Serendipitous."

"Is that dirty?"

"No. That's a clean."

She stretched, yawned, shifted closer. "I keep wanting to say I love you, darling. That's for my conscience, I guess. Anyway, I like the hell out of you."

"Same here. It's the afterglow that proves it worked right."

She pushed herself up and knee-walked down and sorted out sheet and blanket and pulled them up over us, straightening and tucking and neatening, and then curled again, shivering once, fists and forehead against my chest, knees in my belly, her cheek resting on my undercrarm, with my other arm around her, palm against her back, fingertips wedged under the relaxed weight of her rib cage against the undersheet.

I moved back and forth across the edge of sleep, thinking of that afterglow, trying to explain it to myself. With the mink, the musk ox, the chimpanzee, and the human, the proper friction at the proper places if continued for x minutes will cause the nerve ends to trigger the small glandular-muscular explosive mechanics of climax. And afterward there is no more urge to caress the causative flesh than there would be to stroke the shaker that contained the pepper that caused a satisfying series of sneezes.

So in the sensual-sexual-emotional areas each man and each woman has, maybe, a series of little flaws and foibles, hang-ups, neural and emotional memory pattern and superstition, and if there is no fit between their complex subjective patterns, then the only product you can expect is the little frictional explosion, but when there is that mysterious fit, then maybe there are bigger and better explosions down in the ancient black meat of the hidden brain, down in the membraned secret rooms of the heart, so that what happens within the rocking clamp of the loins at that same time is only a grace note, and then it is the afterglow of affection and contentment that celebrates the far more significant climax in brain and heart.

Her voice came from far off with an echo chamber quality, pulling me back across the edge of sleep. ". . . like they say female moths give off some kind of mating signal. Gees, I don't bat my eyes and wiggle my behind and moisten my lips. But the bed patients make grabs at me. And the deliveryman from the dry cleaner. And Mr. Tom Pike, last spring."

"Pike?"

"While his wife was in the hospital for a couple of days of observation after she emptied the pill bottle. It was in the office while she was waiting for Dr. Sherman to come back from an emergency. There was nothing crude about the pass, you understand. Tom Pike is a very tasty and very careful guy. And I felt so darn sorry for him, and I respect him so much for the way he's handling the whole mess with Maureen . . . I almost got involved just out of pity."

"When was all that?"

"March, I guess. Maybe April. One thing, I knew he'd be very careful and cautious and secretive and he wouldn't go around bragging about his loving little nurse friend. I guess he'd have been a good thing, because then I wouldn't have gotten messed up with Rick."

"Think he found some other recruit?"

"I sort of hope so. Somebody sweet and nice and loving. But who would know? Somehow Mr. Pike gets to know everything about everybody, and nobody finds out much about him. It's probably even more important he should have found a friend now that Mrs. Trescot is dead."

"Why?"

"Now there's just the three of them, and kid sister has a terrible yen for him, and nobody could really blame him for giving her some very long second looks, either. And that would be as messy a triangle as you could find."

She yawned and sighed. " 'Night, sweetheart," she said.

I slid almost back into sleep and stopped on the dreaming edge of it. Little by little I became ever more aware of every single place where flesh touched flesh. She had achieved such a honeyed and luxuriant completion that in some bewitched way it seemed to mark the spent flesh with a kind of sensuous continuity, as though it had not ended at all but was still continuing in some hidden manner. I was increasingly aware of the resting engines of our bodies, our slow thump of hearts, blood pulse, suck and sag of the bellows of four lungs, breathing commingled in the cozy bed, all the incredible complexity of cells and nourishments and energy transformation and secretions and heat balance going on and on. I wondered if she slept, but at my first tentative and stealthy caress she took a deep, quick breath that caught and she arched and stretched herself, made a purr of acceptance and luxurious anticipations.

So into the tempos and climates of it again, bodies familiarized now. Fragments. Like things glimpsed at night from a moving train. Dragging whisper-sound of palm on flesh. Deep, deep, slow-thick into the clench of honey, clovery oils, nipples pebbled, lift-clamp of thigh, arythmic flesh-clap fading into tempo reattained, held long and longer and longest, then beginning quivorous hesitation at the end of deepening, richening beat, a shifting of her, mouth agape, furnace breath, tongue curl, grit of tooth against tooth, hands then cup and pull the rubberous buttocky pumping, her bellows breath whistling exploding the words against my mouth—"*Love* you. *Love* you. *Love* you." Then somehow opening more, taking deeper, pulling, demanding, a final grinding moaning agony of her, requiring me to drive, batter, cleave without mercy. Then slow toppling. The long slope. Hearts trying to leap from chests. Gagging gasps from the long run up the far side. Tumbling into the meadow. Tall grass. Clover and grass. Sag into sleep, still coupled, fall into sleep while still feeling in her depths the gentle residual claspings, small infrequent tightenings like that of a small sleeping hand when the brain dreams.

Then in the morning, as I lay watching her get dressed and knowing that soon I had to stir myself too, she looked so frowning-thoughtful, I asked her if she was still working at that lousy-person syndrome of hers.

She put her arms into the sleeves of the white dress after she had stepped into it and pulled it up. "You didn't get to me all the way, Travis, because you're some kind of fantastic lover."

"Thanks a lot."

"I mean, you know, none of that sort of tricky stuff."

She came over and turned around to be zipped. I sat up and swung my legs out and, before zipping her, kissed the crease of her back about two inches south of her bra strap.

"See?" she said.

"See what?"

"Well, that was just nice, honey. So I'm in love with you, sort of. And I wasn't in love with you that first time we made it, and so it wasn't so much, and then when I liked you more, then it got to be something else. So I've got a new philosophy about the bed bit."

"Pray tell," I had said, zipping her up, giving her a pat on the rear.

She moved away and turned, hitching at the white dress and smoothing it across her hips with the backs of

98

her hands. "It isn't all set yet. It's sort of in bits and pieces. I'm going to live as if freckled girls have more fun. And to hell with all the whining and bleeding and gnashing my fool teeth about R. H. Holton, boy attorney. And if I've discovered that I just happen to love to make love with men I could fall in love with . . . people have to put up with a lot worse problems. Darling! *Are* you going to get up and drive me home? It gets later and later and later."

So I had taken her home. End of brief affair. You could staple all the wrong tags on it. One-night stand. Pickup. Handy little shack job for the travelin' man. Hell, Charlie, you know how them nurses are.

So maybe the only adventures that don't look trivial and tawdry are one's own.

It had been my impression that while deep in thought I had been packing up to get out of there and go back to Lauderdale. But I discovered I hadn't packed a thing. I was atop the bedspread, shoes off, practicing deep breathing. And the next I knew it was eight o'clock on that Saturday night, and I wanted two quick drinks and two pounds of rare sirloin.

9 *IT WAS NOT* two pounds of steak, but it was rare enough, and I had it in the Luau Room of the Wahini Lodge at about nine, after a long shower, shave, two long-lasting Plymouths on ice.

The mood was the old yin-yang balance of conflicting emotions. There was the fatuous he-male satisfaction and self-approval after having roundly and soundly tumbled the hot-bodied she-thing, with her approvals registered by the reactive flutterings and choke-throated gasps. Satisfaction in the sense of emptied ease and relaxation, with texture memories of the responsive body imprinted for a time on the touching-parts of the hands and mouth. The other half was the drifting elusive postcoital sadness. Perhaps it comes from the constant buried need for a closeness that will eliminate that loneliness of the spirit we all know. And for just a few moments the need is almost eased, the deeply coupled bodies serving as a sort of symbol of that far greater need to stop being totally alone. But then it is over, the illusion gone, and once again there are two strangers in a rumpled bed who, despite any affectionate embrace, are as essentially unknown to each other as two passengers in the same bus seat who have happened to purchase tickets to the same destination. Maybe that is why there is always sadness mingled with the aftertastes of pleasure, because once again, as so many times before, you have proven that the fleeting closeness only underlines the essential apartness of people, makes it uncomfortably evident for a little while. We had fitted each other's needs and could have no way of knowing how much of our willingness was honest and how much was the flood of excuses the loins project so brilliantly on the front screen of the mind.

The loins tell you it is always bigger than both of anybody.

Suddenly, I remembered the hundred dollars that Holton had made Penny stuff into her purse, and smiled. I would hear from her sooner than expected, because when she came across it and remembered, she would be in a horrid haste to get it back to me, as it would make a very sordid footnote to the swarmy night.

And so when I went back to my room at ten thirty something and saw the red light on the phone winking, I was certain it would be Penny Woertz. But it was a very agitated Biddy, expressing surprise that I was still in Fort Courtney and asking me if I had seen or heard from Maureen. She had somehow sneaked down the stairs and out through the back of the house while Tom was in the living room working at the desk, and while Bridget had been out picking up odds and ends at one of the Stop 'n' Shop outlets. She had been gone since a little before seven. "Tom has been out hunting her ever since. I phoned everyplace I could think of and then I left too, about quarter to eight. Right now I'm at a place out near the airport and I happened to think she might come there to the motel, because she knew you were staying there."

"Police looking too?"

"Well, not specifically. But they know she is around and if they see her, they'll take her in. Travis, she's wearing a pink chambray jumper with big black pockets and she's probably barefoot."

"Driving a car?"

"No, thank God. Or maybe it would be better if she did. I don't know. She probably did the same as last time, walked over to Route Thirty and hitched a ride. She doesn't have any trouble getting a lift, as you can imagine. But I am so afraid that some . . . sick person might pick her up."

"Can I help?"

"I can't think of anything you could do. If she does show up there, you could call nine-three-four, two-six-six-one. That's Tom's answering service. We keep calling in every fifteen minutes or so to see if there's word of her."

"Are you with him?"

"No. We can cover more places this way. I usually run across him sooner or later."

"Will you let me know when you find her?"

"If you wish. Yes. I'll phone you."

I hung up wondering why they didn't think about the bottom of the lake. She's had a try at about everything else except jumping out a high window. What was the word? Self-defenestration. Out the window I must go, I must go, I must go . . .

Then some fragment of old knowledge began to nudge at the back of my mind. After I had the eleven o'clock news on the television, I couldn't pay attention because I was too busy roaming around the room trying to unearth what was trying to attract my attention.

Then a name surfaced, along with a man's sallow face, bitter mouth, knowing eyes. Harry Simmons. A long talk, long ago, after a friend of a friend had died. He'd added a large chunk onto an existing insurance policy about five months before they found him afloat, face-down, in Biscayne Bay.

I sat on the bed and slowly reconstructed the pattern of part of his conversation. My thought about the lake and the high window had opened a small door to an old memory.

"With the jumpers and the drowners, McGee, you don't pick up a pattern. That's because a jumper damned near always makes it the first time, and a drowner is usually almost as successful, about the same rate as hangers. They get cut down maybe as rarely as the drowners get pulled out. So the patterns mostly come from the bleeders and the pill-takers and the shooters. Funny how many people survive a self-shooting. But if they don't destroy a chunk of their brain, they get a chance at a second try. Like the bleeders cut themselves again, and the pill-takers keep trying. It's always patterns. Never change. They pick the way that they want to go and keep after it until they make it. A pill-taker doesn't turn into a jumper, and a drowner won't shoot himself. Like they've got one picture of dying and that's it and there's no other way of going."

All right, then say that Harry Simmons might *probably* admit a very rare exception. But Maurie Pearson Pike had opted for the pills, the razor, and the rope. Three methods.

I felt a prickling of the flesh on the backs of my hands. But it was a clumsy fit, no matter how you looked at it. The suffering husband making a narrow save each time. Or the kid sister? Was there a third party who could get close enough to Maurie?

What about motive? The big ones are love and money. The estate was "substantial." What are the terms? Check it out through soft-voiced D. Wintin Hardahee. And noble suffering Tommy *had* made the discreet pass at Freckle-Girl. So on top of that we have a dead family physician labeled suicide, and he had treated Maureen, and does that make any sense or any fit? Penny believed with all her sturdy heart that Dr. Stewart Sherman could not have killed himself.

The tap at my door had to be Penny bringing back the two fifty-dollar bills, and as I went toward the door I was uncomfortably aware of a hollow feeling in the belly that was a lustful anticipation that maybe she could be induced to stay awhile.

But there were two men there, and they both stared at me with that mild, bland, skeptical curiosity of the experienced lawman. It must be very like the first inspection of new specimens brought back to the base camp by museum expeditions. The specimen might be rare or damaged or poisonous. But you check it over and soon you are able to catalog it based on the experience of cataloging thousands of others over the years, and then it is a very ordinary job from then on, the one you are paid for.

The big, hard-boned, young one wore khakis, a white fishing cap with a peak, blue and white sneakers, and a white sport shirt with a pattern of red pelicans on it. It was worn outside the belt, doubtless to hide the miniature revolver that seems to be more and more of a fad with Florida local law. The smaller older one wore a pale tan suit, a white shirt with no tie. He had a balding head, liver spots, little dusty brown eyes, and a virulent halitosis that almost concealed the news that his young partner had been wearing the same shirt too long.

"Name McGee?"

"That's right. What can I do for you?" I was stripped to my underwear shorts and barefoot.

"Well, for a starter, just turn around real slow with your arms out, then you can go stand by the window." He flipped his wallet open and gave me the glimpse of the little gold badge. "I'm Stanger," he said, and, indicating the younger one, "he's Nudenbarger. City."

"And for a starter," I said, "search warrant?"

"Not unless I have to have one, McGee. But you make

103

us go through the motions, everybody gets pissed off, and it's a hot night, and it all adds up the same way anyway. So you—if you want to—you can like invite us to just poke around."

"Poke around, Mr. Stanger. You too, Mr. Nudenbarger."

He checked my wallet on the countertop while Nudenbarger checked the closet, the suitcase, the bathroom. Stanger wrote down some bits of information copied off credit cards into a blue pocket notebook, dime-sized. He couldn't write without sticking his tongue out of the corner of his mouth. Credit cards hearten them. The confetti of the power structure.

"Plenty cash, Mr. McGee."

Cash and credit had earned me the "mister." I moved over and sat on the bed without permission. "Seven hundred and something. Let me see . . . and thirty-eight. It's sort of a bad habit I'm trying to break, Mr. Stanger. It's stupid to carry cash. Probably the result of some kind of insecurity in my childhood. It's my blue blanket."

He looked at me impassively. "I guess that's pretty funny."

"Funny peculiar?"

"No. Being funny like jokes. Being witty with stupid cops."

"No. The thing about the blue blanket——"

"I keep track of Beethoven's birthday, and the dog flies a DeHavilland Moth."

"What's that?" Nudenbarger asked. "What's that?"

"Forget it, Lew," Stanger said in a weary voice.

"You always say that," Nudenbarger said, accusingly indignant.

It is like a marriage, of course. They are teamed up and they work on each other's nerves, and some of the gutsy ones who have gone into the dark warehouse have been shot in the back by the partner/wife who just couldn't stand any more.

Stanger perched a tired buttock on the countertop,

other leg braced with knee locked, licked his thumb, and leafed back through some pages in the blue notebook.

"Done any time at all, Mr. McGee?"

"No."

"Arrests?"

"Here and there. No charges."

"Suspicion of what?"

"Faked-up things. Impersonation, conspiracy, extortion. Somebody gets a great idea, but the first little investigation and it all falls down."

"Often?"

"What's often? Five times in a lifetime? About that."

"And you wouldn't mention it except if I checked it would show up someplace."

"If you say so."

"You have been here and there, McGee, because for me there is something missing. Right. What do you storm troopers want? What makes you think you can come in here, et cetera, et cetera, et cetera. But you don't object at all."

"Would it work with you, Stanger?"

"Not lately. So okay. Would you say you left about noon and got back a little after one today?"

"Close enough."

"And sacked out?"

"Slept like death until maybe eight o'clock."

"When you make a will, Mr. McGee, leave a little something to Mrs. Imber."

"Who is she?"

"Sort of the housekeeper. Checking on the job the maids do. Opened your door with her passkey at four o'clock, give or take ten minutes. You were snoring on the bed."

"Which sounds as if it was the right place to be."

"A nice place to be. Let me read you a little note. I copied this off the original, which is at the lab. It goes like this: . . . By the way, it was sealed in an envelope and on the outside it said Mr. T. McGee, One-O-nine. So we check some places and find a place with a One-O-nine with a McGee in it. Which is here, and you. It says: 'Dear Honey, What do I say about the wages of sin? Anyway, it was one of his lousy ideas and overlooked, so here it is back. Woke up and couldn't get back to sleep and went into the purse for a cigarette and found this. Reason I couldn't get back to sleep? Well, hell. Reasons. Plural. Memories of you and me . . . getting me a little too worked up for sleepy-bye. And something maybe we should talk over. It's about something SS said about memory and digital skills. Have to go do a trick as a Special at eight, filling in for a friend. I'll drop this off on the way. No man in his right mind would pick a girl up in the hospital lot at four fifteen on Sunday morning, would he? Would he? Would he?' "

Stanger read badly. He said, "It's signed with an initial. P. Nobody you ever heard of?"

"Penny Woertz."

"The hundred bucks was the wages of sin, McGee?"

"Just a not very funny joke. Private and personal."

Nudenbarger stood looking me over, a butcher selecting a side of beef. "Get chopped up in the service?"

"Some of it."

Nudenbarger's smirk, locker-room variety, didn't charm me. "How was she, McGee? Pretty good piece of ass?"

"Shut up, Lew," Stanger said with weary patience. "How long did you know Miss Woertz, McGee?"

"Since we met in the bar last night. You can ask the man who was working the bar. His name is Jake."

"The room maid said you must have had a woman in here last night. So you confirm that it was the nurse. Then you took her back to her apartment at about noon. Did you go in with her?"

I did not like the shape of the little cloud forming on the horizon in the back of my head. "Let's stop the games," I said.

"She mention anybody she thought might be checking up on her?" Stanger asked.

"I'll give you that name after we stop playing games."

Stanger reached into the inside pocket of his soiled tan suitcoat, took an envelope out, took some color Polaroids out of it. As he handed them to me he said, "These aren't official record. Just something I do for my own personal file."

He had used a flash. She was on a kitchen floor, left shoulder braced against the base of the cabinet under the sink, head lolled back. She wore a blue and white checked robe, still belted, but the two sides had separated, the right side pulled away to expose one breast and expose the right hip and thigh. The closed blades of a pair of blue-handled kitchen shears had been driven deep into the socket of her throat. Blood had spread wide under her. Her bloodless face looked pallid and smaller than my memory of her, the freckles more apparent against the pallor. There were four shots from four different angles. I swallowed a heaviness that had collected in my throat and handed them back to him.

"Report came in at eight thirty," he said. "She was going to give another nurse a ride in, and the other nurse had a key to her place because she'd oversleep sometimes. The other nurse lives in one of those garden apartments around on the other side. According to the county medical examiner, time of death was four thirty, give or take twenty minutes. Bases it on coagulation, body temperature, lividity in the lower limbs, and the beginning of *rigor* in the jaws and neck."

I swallowed again. "It's . . . unpleasant."

"I looked in a saucepan on the stove to see if she was cooking something. I picked up the lid and looked in and the sealed-up note to you was in there, half wadded up, like she had hidden it in a hurry the first place she could think of. That part about remembering you and getting all worked up would be something she wouldn't want a boyfriend to read. Think the boyfriend knew she spent the night here in this room?"

"Maybe. I don't know."

"She worried about him?"

"Some."

"Just in case there was two of them, suppose you give me the name you know."

"Richard Holton, Attorney at Law."

"The only name?"

"The only boyfriend, I'd say."

Stanger sighed and looked discouraged. "Same name we've got, dammit. And he drove his wife over to Vero Beach to visit her sister today. Left about nine this morning. Put through a call over there about an hour and a half ago, and they had left about eight to drive back. Should be home by now. This is still a pretty small town, McGee. Mr. Holton and this nurse had been kicking up a fuss about Doc Sherman's death being called suicide. That's the SS in the note, I guess?"

"Yes. She talked to me about the doctor."

"What's this about . . . let me find it here . . . here it is, 'memory and digital skills'?"

"It doesn't mean a thing to me."

"Would it have anything to do with the doctor *not* killing himself?"

"I haven't any idea."

"Pictures make you feel sick?" Nudenbarger asked.

"Shut up, Lew," Stanger said.

It was past midnight. I looked at my watch when the phone rang. Stanger motioned to me to take it and moved over and leaned close to me to hear the other end of the conversation.

"Travis? This is Biddy. I just got home. Tom found her about twenty minutes ago."

"Is she all right?"

"I guess so. After looking practically all over the county, he found her wandering around not over a mile from here. The poor darling has been bitten a billion times. She's swelling up and going out of her mind with the itching. Tom is bathing her now, and then we'll use the Dormed. Sleep will be the best thing in the world for her."

"Use the what?"

"It's electrotherapy. She responds well to it. And . . . thanks for being concerned, Travis. We both . . . all appreciate it."

I hung up and Stanger said with mild surprise, "You know the Pikes too?"

"The wife and her sister, from a long time ago. And their mother."

"Didn't she die just a while back?"

"That's right."

"They find that kook wife?" Nudenbarger asked.

"Tom Pike found her."

Nudenbarger shook his head slowly. "Now, that one is really something, I swear to God! Al, I'll just never forget how she looked that time last spring she was missing for two days, and those three Telaferro brothers had kept her the whole time in that little bitty storeroom out to the truck depot, keeping her boozed up and bangin' that poor flippy woman day and night until I swear she was so plain wore-down pooped that Mike and Sandy had to use a stretcher to tote her out to——"

"Shut your goddamn mouth, Lew!" Stanger roared.

Nudenbarger stared blankly at him. "*Now* what in the world is eating you, anyway."

"Go out and check in and see if there's anything new and if there is, come get me, and if there isn't, stay the hell out there in the car!"

"Sure. Okay."

After the door had closed gently behind the younger man, Stanger sighed and sat down and felt around in the side pocket of his jacket and found a half cigar and lit the ash end thoroughly and carefully. "Mr. Tom Pike should send that wife off someplace. Or watch her a little more close. She's going to go out some night and meet up with some bug who'll maybe kill her."

"Before she kills herself?"

"Seems like if a man has good luck in one direction, McGee, it runs real bad some other way. When she lost the second kid, something went wrong in her head. I say it would be a blessing if she had made a good job of it when she tried. Mr. McGee, I think it would be a good thing if you stayed right in town for a few days."

"I want to help if I can. I didn't know Penny Woertz very long. But . . . I liked her a lot."

He pulled on the cigar. "Amateur help? Run around in circles and get everything all confused?"

"Let's just say it wouldn't be quite as amateur as th help you're running around with right now, Stanger."

"It like to broke Lew's heart when they picked him o his motor-sickel and give him to me. What you might do if it wouldn't put you out any, is see if Rick Holton mad the trip he said he made. It's unhealthy for me to chec up on a man in Holton's position. I think maybe Janic Holton would be easy to talk with, easier for you tha me."

Once again I remembered Harry Simmons, and I said "If she phones you to check on me, confirm the fact tha I'm an insurance investigator looking into a death clain on Dr. Sherman."

"Going to her instead of to Holton himself?"

"Just to see if she thinks he's sincere in believing it was murder or if he's been faking it in order to snuggle up to Nurse Woertz."

He whistled softly. "You could lose some hide off your face."

"Depending on how I work up to it."

"If they'd both been in town, both Rick Holton and his wife, and they weren't together, I'd want to make sure I knew where she was at the time that girl got stuck with the shears."

"She capable of it?"

He stood up. "Who knows what anybody will do or won't do, when the moon is right? All I know is that she was Janice Nocera before she married the lawyer, and her folks have always had a habit of taking care of their own problems in their own way."

I remembered the pictures of her and the kids, the ones I had taken out of Holton's wallet. Handsome, lean, dark, with a mop of black hair and more than her share of both nose and mouth, and a jaunty defiance in the way she stared smiling into the lens.

"And I'll be checking you out a little more too," he said, and gave me a small, tired smile and went out.

10 *PAGE ONE* of the Fort Courtney *Sunday Register* bannered LOCAL NURSE SLAIN. They had a sunshiny smiling picture of her that pinched my heart in a sly and painful way.

Very few facts had been furnished by the law—just the way the body had been discovered, the murder weapon, and the estimated time of death. As usual, an arrest was expected momentarily.

It was almost noon on Sunday when I phoned Biddy. She sounded tired and listless. She said Tom had flown up to Atlanta for a business meeting and would be home, he thought, by about midnight. Yes, it was a terrible thing about Penny Woertz. She had always been so obliging and helpful when Maurie had been Dr. Sherman's patient. Such a really marvelous disposition, never snippy or officious.

"Suppose I come out there and see if I can cheer you up, girl?"

"With songs and jokes and parlor tricks? I don't think anything would work today. But . . . come along if you want to."

I pressed the door chime button three times before she finally came to the door and let me in.

"Sorry to keep you standing out here, Trav. I was putting her back to sleep."

She led the way back into the big living room, long-legged in yellow denim shorts with brass buttons on the hip pockets, and a faded blue short-sleeved work shirt. She had piled her long straight blond hair atop her head and anchored it in place with a yellow comb, but casual

111

tendrils escaped, and when she turned and gave me a crooked smile of self-mockery, she brushed some silky strands away from her forehead with her fingertips. "I'm the total mess of the month, Travis. Would you like a drink? Bloody Mary? Gin and tonic? Beer?"

"What are you having?"

"Maybe a Bloody would be therapeutic. Want to come help?"

The big kitchen was bright and cheerful, decorated in blue and white. The windows looked across the back lawn toward the lake.

She got out the ice and ingredients and I made them. She leaned against the countertop, ankles crossed, sipped and said, "If I suddenly fall on my face, don't be alarmed. I did a damfool thing last night after we got her settled down. I had to get my mind off . . . everything and I went out to the boathouse and painted a fool thing I'll probably paint out. It was five before I went to bed and Tom woke me up at eight when he left."

"Can I have a look at it?"

"Well . . . why not? But it isn't anything like what I usually do."

We carried our drinks. There was an outside staircase to the big room over the boathouse, which she had fixed up as a studio. A window air-conditioner was humming. She turned on a second one, then went over and turned on an intercom and turned the volume up until I could hear a slow rhythmic sound I suddenly identified as the deep and somewhat guttural breathing of someone in deep sleep.

She said, "Maurie can't wake up, actually, but I just feel better if I can hear her." The studio had a composite smell of pigments and oils and thinner. The work stacked against the walls and the few that were hung were semiabstract. Obviously she had taken her themes from nature, from stones, earth, bark, leaves. The colors were powerful. Some of the areas were almost representational.

She waved toward them. "These are the usual me. Kind of old hat. No op and pop. No structures and lumps and walk-throughs."

"But," I said, "one hell of a lot of overpainting and glazes, so you can see down into those colors."

She looked surprised and pleased. "Member of the club?"

"Hell, woman, I even know the trick words that mean absolutely nothing. Like dynamic symmetry."

"Tonal integrity?"

"Sure. Structural perceptions. Compositionally iconoclastic."

She laughed aloud and it was a good laugh. "It's such terrible crap, isn't it? The language of gallery people and critics, and insecure painters. What are *your* words, Professor McGee?"

"Does a painting always look the same or will it change according to the light and how I happen to feel? And after it has been hung for a month, will it disappear so completely the only time I might notice it would be if it fell off the wall?"

She nodded thoughtfully. "So I'll buy that. Anyway . . . I seldom do the figure. But here is my night work."

It was on an easel, a horizontal rectangle, maybe thirty inches by four feet. At dead center was a small clearing, a naked female figure sitting, jackknifed, huddled, arms around her legs, face buried against her knees, blond hair spilling down. Around her was angry jungle, slashes of sharp spears of leaf, vine tangle, visceral roots, hints of black water, fleshy tropic blooms against black-green. It had a flavor of great silence, stillness, waiting.

We studied it and could hear the deep sonorous breathing of the sleeping sister. Biddy coughed, sipped her drink, said, "I think it's too dramatic and sentimental and . . . narrative."

"I say let it sit. You'll know more about it later."

She put her drink down, lifted it off the easel, and placed it against the wall, the back of the canvas toward the room. She backed off. "Where I can't see it, I guess."

She showed me more of her work and then she turned the intercom off and one of the air-conditioners. We walked back to the house. "Another drink and maybe a sandwich?"

"On one condition."

"Such as?"

"Quick drink and simple sandwich and then you go fall into the sack. I am reliable, dependable, conscientious, and so on. If you're needed for anything, I'll wake you up."

"I couldn't let you do——"

"Hot shower, clean sheets, blinds closed, and McGee taking care."

She covered her yawn with the back of her fist. "Bless you, bless you. I'm sold."

After we ate, she led me upstairs and down the carpeted hallway to Maureen's room. Maureen slept on her back in the middle of a double bed. The room was air-conditioned to coolness. She wore a quilted bed jacket. The sheets and pillowcases were blue with a white flower pattern. The blanket was a darker blue. Her face and throat were puffed, red-blotched. There was a mixture of small odors in the silence, calamine and rubbing alcohol and perfume. Flavors of illness and of girl. She wore opaque sleep-glasses in spite of the room being darkened.

Biddy startled me by speaking in a normal conversational tone. "I'm going to keep her asleep until at least six o'clock. Oh, she can't hear us. Not while the Dormed is on."

As she took me over to the bed to show me what she meant, I saw the small electric cord that led from the heavy pair of glasses to a piece of equipment on the bedside stand. It looked like a small ham radio receiver. There were three dials. A tiny orange light winked constantly. She explained that it was an electrosleep device invented in Germany and distributed in England and the United States by one of the medical supply houses. There were electrodes in the headset, covered with a foam plastic, two which rested on the eyelids, and one at the end of each earpiece where they made contact with the mastoid bone behind each ear. She said that you moistened the foam rubber pads with a salt solution and put the headset on the patient. The control unit was a pulse generator that sent an extremely weak electrical impulse—in fact a thousand times weaker than the current a flashlight bulb requires—through the sleep centers in the thalamus and hypothalamus.

"It's perfectly safe," she said. "It's been used on thousands and thousands of patients. You just adjust the strength and the frequency with these two dials. The other is the on and off switch. Dr. Sherman got it for us and trained me in how to use it. You see, he was afraid of the side effects of making her sleep with medication, in her condition, whatever it is. We do have to give her shots when she gets too upset, but this is usually enough."

"What does it feel like?"

"Very . . . odd. No discomfort at all. All I felt was a kind of flickering in my eyes. Not unpleasant, really. I was trying to fight it. I was telling myself that this certainly wouldn't put me to sleep. And then there wasn't the flickering sensation anymore, and kind of . . . a slow warm delicious feeling all over me, like sinking slowly in a hot sudsy perfumed tub. And I was gone! It is marvelous sleep, really. Deep and sweet and refreshing. Once she's asleep, you can take them off and the Dormed sleep will just turn into absolutely natural sleep. Or like now, I'm leaving it on at very low strength, and she will sleep on and on until I take them off. You could parade a brass band through here, and she'd sleep like a baby. It's a marvelous invention. It's a portable unit, with a neat little gray suitcase thing it fits into, with a place for the salt solution and all."

"Is there anything I have to do about it while you sleep?"

"Nothing. Well . . . what I do isn't necessary. I just come in and look at her and see if that little light is going on and off. It hasn't ever stopped or anything. And only once did she ever move her head enough to move the headset out of place."

"But you'd feel better if I did the same thing?"

"I guess so. Yes."

"Off with you, then."

We went into the hall and she pointed out her door. "Just knock until I answer. Don't settle for a mumble.

Get a real answer." She looked at her watch. "And don't let me sleep past five o'clock. Okay?"

"Five o'clock."

"If you get hungry or thirsty or anything——"

"I know where things are. Bug off, Bridget. Sleep tight."

In thirty minutes the house was filled with that special silence of Sunday sleep. Little relays and servo devices made faint tickings and hummings. Refrigerator, deep freeze, air-conditioning, thermostats, electric clocks. Kids water-skied the lake, outboards droning, a faint sound through the closed windows.

Where do you look when you have no idea what you are looking for? An alcove off the living room apparently served as a small home office for Tom Pike. The top of the antique desk was clean. The drawers were locked, and the locks were splendid modern intricate devices, unpickable, except in television drama. On a hallway phone table I found a black and white photograph in a silver frame. Helena, Maureen, and Bridget on the foredeck of the *Likely Lady*. Boat clothes, sweaters for cool sailing. Mick Pearson's girls, all slender, smiling, assured, and with the loving look that could only mean that it had been Mick's eye at the finder, Mick's finger on the shutter release.

So roam the silence and up the padded stairs, long slow steps, two at a time. A closed door at the back of the house, unlocked, opening into a master bedroom. Draperied window-wall facing the lake. One end was sitting room, fireplace, bookshelves. An oversized custom bed dominated the other end. It seemed too sybaritic, a bit out of key with the rest of the house. Two baths, two dressing rooms. His and hers. Sunken dark blue tub in hers, square, with clear glass in the shower-stall arrangement. Strategic mirroring there, as on the walls nearest the oversized bed.

The big bed was neatly made, so on Sunday, at least, Biddy was maid, cook, and housekeeper. Maureen's bath had been cleared of the daily personal things. Winter clothing in her dressing room closets. Bottles of perfume and lotion on her dressing table just a little bit dusty. But he lived here, very neatly. Sport shirts here, dress shirts there. Jackets, slacks on one bar. Suits hanging from another. The shoe-treed shoes on a built-in rack. Silk, cashmere, linen, Irish tweed, English wool, Italian shoes. Labeling from Worth Avenue, New York, St. Thomas, Palm Springs, Montreal. Taste, cost, and quality. Impersonal, remote, correct, and somehow sterile. Apparently no sentiment about an ancient sweater, crumpled old moccasins, baggy elderly slacks, or a gummy old bathrobe. When anything showed enough evident signs of wear, it was eliminated.

I searched for more clues to him. Apparently he did not have anything wrong with him that could not be fixed by an aspirin or an Alka Seltzer. He did not leave random notes to himself in the pockets of his suits and jackets. He did not seem to have a single hobby or a weapon or a book not devoted to economics, law, securities, or real estate.

So I gave up on Tom Pike and walked quietly down the hall and into Maureen's room. The deep breathing was just the same. She had not moved. The little orange light on the face of the control unit of the Dormed went off and on as before. I went to the side of the bed. Her arms rested at her sides, atop the blanket. I cautiously picked her left hand up. It was warm and dry, and complete relaxation gave it a heaviness, like the hand of a fresh corpse. The back of the hand was scratched, and welted with insect bites. I turned the inside of the wrist toward what light there was and, bending close to it, I could make out the white line of scar tissue across the pattern of the blue veins under the sensitive skin. I placed the hand the way it had been and looked down at her. The heavy glasses made her look as if both eyes had been bandaged. I could see the slow, steady beat of a tiny pulse in her throat. Even welted and mottled, dappled with the dry orange-white spots of lotion, she was a cushioned and luxurious and sweetly sensuous animal.

Sweet outcast. All the lovely, wifely tumbling in that outsized bed, mirrored hoyden, romping in sweet excitements with the lean and beloved husband. But then paradise is warped and the image becomes grotesque. Instead of babies, two sudden agonies, and two little bloody wads of tissue expelled too soon from the warm black safety of the womb. Then a world gone strange, like something half dreamed and soon forgotten. Exchange the springy bed for the sacking on the floor of the little storage room at the truck depot where, booze-blind, lamed, and sprung, you are kept at the rough service of the Telaferro brothers. Excuse me, my dear, while I pry around your outcast room looking for answers to questions I haven't thought of. Or one I have: Would you really rather be dead?

But there was nothing. There was a steel cabinet in the bathroom, resting on a bench, securely locked. Medicines, no doubt. There seemed to be nothing left in the bedroom or bath that she could hurt herself with. There was a rattling purr at the end of each exhalation. Her diaphragm rose and fell with the deep breathing of deep sleep.

I was glad to leave her room and leave the sound of breathing. Somehow it was like the coma that precedes death. I went down and found a cold beer, turned on the television set with the volume low, and watched twenty-two very large young men knocking one another down while thousands cheered. I watched and yet did not watch. It was merely a busy pattern of color, motion, and sound.

Blue handles of kitchen shears. Helena climbing naked in the red light of the Exuma sun, rising to teeter on the rail, then find her balance, then dive into the black-gray water of the cove at Shroud Cay and then surface, seal-sleek, hair water-pasted flat to the delicate skull contours. Penny Woertz snuggling against me in the night, her back and shoulders moist with exertion, making little umming sounds of content as her breath was slowing. Biddy sobbing aloud as she trotted into my bathroom, her running a humble, awkward, clumsy, bovine, knock-kneed gait. Memory and digital skills. The bleeders don't jump, and the hangers don't bleed. Twenty thousand to a tall man. Jake saying "Bon voyage." The 'Bama Gal erupting into the sunlight after all the weeks on the murky bottom.

Tom Pike lifting his face from his hands, eyes streaming. Mick thumping the cabin trim with a solid fist as he showed me the honest way the *Likely Lady* had been built. Substantial means more than comfortable and less than impressive. Maurie streaking greasy fingers across the rounded, pneumatic, porcelain-gold of her thigh. Rick Holton flexing and rubbing his wrists after I'd unwound the tight bite of the hanger wire. Blue handles of kitchen shears. Penny's clovery scents. Five dozen silk ties with good labels. Orange light winking. An umber-orange mole, not as big as a dime. Huddled nude in a Gauguin jungle.

The mind is a cauldron and things bubble up and show for a moment, then slip back into the brew. You can't reach down and find anything by touch. You wait for some order, some relationship in the order in which they appear. Then yell Eureka! and believe that it was a process of cold, pure logic.

Finally, on my fourth visit to the electrosleep bedside, it was exactly six o'clock, so I gently removed the headset, put it aside, and turned the Dormed off. I watched her, ready to go awaken Biddy if Maureen woke up. For several minutes she did not move. Then she rolled her head over to one side, made a murmurous sound, then rolled all the way over onto her side, pulled her knees up, put her two hands, palms together, under her cheek, and soon was breathing as deeply as before.

As the room got darker I turned on a low lamp on the other side of the room. I sat in a Boston rocker near the bed, watching the sleeping woman and thinking that this was probably where Biddy sat and watched her, while she thought about the marriage and thought about her own life.

At a little after eight I knocked on Biddy's door. After the second attempt I heard a groggy, querulous mutter. I waited and knocked again and suddenly she pulled the door open. She had a robe around her shoulders and she held it closed with a concealed hand. Her hair was in wild disarray and her face was swollen with sleep.

"What time is it!"

I told her it was a little after eight, that I had un-hooked Maurie from her machine at six, and that she was still sleeping. She yawned and combed her hair back with her free hand. "The poor thing must have been really exhausted. I won't be a minute."

When she was dressed, she sent me downstairs, saying she'd bring Maurie down in a little while. I found the light switches. As I was making a drink the phone rang. It was just one ring. No more. And so I decided Biddy had probably answered it upstairs. As I was carrying my drink into the living room it rang again, and once again it was just one ring.

Soon they came down. Maurie wore a navy blue floor-length robe with long sleeves and white buttons and white trim. She was scratching her shoulder with one hand and the opposite hip with the other, and complaining in a sour little voice. "Just about eaten to pieces. How do they get in with the house all closed up?"

"You'll just make them worse by scratching, dear."

"I can't help it."

"Say hello to Travis, dear."

She stopped at the foot of the stairs and smiled at me, still scratching, and said, "Hello, Travis McGee! How are you? I had a very good nap today."

"Good for you."

"But I itch something awful. Biddy?"

"Yes, honey."

"Is he here?" Her tone and expression were apprehensive.

"Tom went on a trip."

"Can I have peanut butter sandwiches, Biddy, please?"

"But your diet, dear. You're almost up to a hundred and fifty again."

Her tone was wheedling, sympathy-seeking. "But I'm real tall, Biddy. And I'm *starving*. And I had a good nap and I itch something awful!"

"Well . . ."

"Please? *He* isn't here anyway. *He* won't know about it. You know something? Some son of a bitch must have kicked me or something. I'm so sore right——"

120

"Maureen!"

She stopped, gulped, looked humble. "I didn't mean to."

"Please try to speak nicely, dear."

"You won't tell *him?*"

Biddy took my glass and they went out into the kitchen. In a little while Maureen came walking in very slowly and carefully, carrying my fresh drink. I thanked her and she beamed at me. Somehow she had managed to get a little wad of peanut butter stuck on the end of her nose, possibly from licking the top off the jar. She went back. I heard them talking out there but could not hear the words, just the tone, and it was like a conversation between child and mother.

When they came back in, Maureen pulled a hassock over in front of the television set. Biddy plugged a set of earphones into a jack in the rear of the set and Maureen put them on eagerly and then was lost in the images and the sound, expression rapt, as she ate her sandwiches.

Biddy said, "She loves to watch things Tom can't stand."

"Does she remember running away last night?"

"No. It's all gone now. Slate wiped clean."

"She won't say Tom's name?"

"Sometimes she will. She's so terribly anxious to please him, to have him approve of her. She just gets . . . all tightened up when he's here. Really, he's wonderfully kind and patient with her. But I guess that . . . a child-wife isn't what a man of Tom's intelligence can adjust to."

"If you think of her just as a child, she's a good child."

"Oh, yes. She's happy, or seems happy, and she likes to help, but she forgets how to do things."

"It doesn't seem consistent with suicide attempts, does it?"

She frowned. "No. But it's more complex than that, Travis. There's another kind of child involved, a sly and naughty child. And the times she's tried, she's gotten into the liquor and gotten drunk first. It's almost as if alcohol creates some kind of awareness of self and her condition, removes some block or something. We keep it all locked up, of course, ever since the first time. But the time she locked herself in the bathroom and cut her wrist, I'd forgotten and left a half quart of gin on the countertop with the bottles of mix. I just didn't see it, somehow. And she sneaked it upstairs, I guess. Anyway, the empty bottle was under her bed. Then the time Tom found the noose, we know she got into something, but we don't know what it was or how. Vanilla extract or shaving lotion or something. Maybe even rubbing alcohol. But of course she couldn't remember. It's quite late. Can I fix you something to eat?"

"I think I'll be moving along, Biddy. Thanks."

"I owe you, my friend. I was irritated you let me sleep so long. But I guess you knew better than I how badly I needed it. I was getting ragged around the edges. The very least I can do is feed you."

"No thanks, I . . ."

She straightened, head tilted, listening, and then relaxed. "Sorry. I thought it was that damned phone again. I think something's wrong with the line. For the last two or three months every once in a while it will give one ring or part of a ring and then stop, and there won't be anybody there. Just the dial tone when you pick it up. Did you say you would stay?"

"I'd better not, thanks just the same."

Maureen's good-night was a smile and a bob of the head and a hasty return to the color screen where a vivid-faced girl was leaning over a wire fence amid a throng, cheering a racehorse toward the finish line. The only sound was the insectile buzzing that escaped from Maureen's padded earphones.

As I walked to the car in the drive I heard the clack behind me as Biddy relocked the heavy front door.

11   *SUNDAY DINNER* was finished by the time I got to the motel dining room, but they could provide steak sandwiches. There was one whispering couple on the far side of the room and one lonely fat man slumped at the bar. Both the couple and the fat man were gone when I went to the bar for a nightcap. I sat on the far stool by the wall, where Penny had been sitting when I had first seen her.

Jake, the bartender, wore an odd expression as he approached me. "Evening, sir. Look, if I got you in any kind of jam——"

"I told Stanger he could check it out with you, that I met her right here Friday night."

He looked relieved. "What happened, he mouse-trapped me. He came up with this thing about we let them come in and hustle, we could lose the license. And one thing and another, he worked it around to you and that girl, and I thought he had been tipped and I couldn't exactly deny it, so I said sure, they left together, but how could I know they weren't friends or something already. Honest to God, sir, I didn't know it was the same one in the paper this morning until he said so. Then I'm left hanging, wondering if you were some kind of crazy that took her home and . . . there are some very ordinary looking guys who are very weird about hustlers. But I couldn't imagine you doing . . . Anyway, when I saw you come in, I felt better, I don't know why."

"I think maybe some Black Jack on one rock."

"Yes, sir, Mr. McGee." When he served it with a proper flourish, he said, "Jesus, I've felt half sick ever

123

since. And . . . I guess you've got a right to feel a lot sicker than me." The implied question was very clear.

"Jake, we walked out of here and shook hands and sang one small hymn and said good-night."

He flushed. "I'm sorry. It's none of my business. I was just thinking she didn't have the right moves, you know? So what she is doing is trying to get even with a boyfriend who's cheating on her by doing some swinging herself, so she takes you home and the next day she tells him how she got even, and he can't stand it. She's laughing at him. He grabs the first thing and——"

"Stares in horror at what he's done and, sobbing his heart out, dials the cops."

"It's just that you try to figure out what happened."

"I know, Jake. I'm sorry. Everybody plays that particular game. That's because we always want to know why. Not so much how and who and when. But why."

"Can I ask you something? Did you stop in your room before you came in to eat?"

"No. I parked in front. The question implies I've been away from the place. So somebody has been trying to get me."

He looked uneasy. "Well, it's Mr. Holton. He comes in off and on and he's never any trouble. He's a lawyer. He was here about five o'clock looking for you. He had two quick ones and he came back about quarter to six. He'd have some and then go looking for you and come back. I let him have more than I would somebody else, on account of he's local and a good customer and he's always treated me good. Well, he finally got mean and loud and I finally had to cut him off. From the way he walked out . . . maybe a half hour before you came in to eat . . . he could have passed out in his car by now. Or maybe he's still on his feet and waiting for you by your room. He began telling me, toward the end, that he was going to whip your ass. Looking at you, I think maybe it wouldn't be so easy to do, unless he sucker-punched you, which he acted mad enough to do. I thought you might want to keep your eyes open on your way back to the room."

It earned him the change from a five for the one drink.

I decided to walk around to 109 rather than drive, as I had planned. I went the long way around and moved onto the grass and kept out of the lights. I stopped and listened and looked and finally discerned a burly shadow standing near a tall shrub and leaning against the white motel wall. I reconstructed the memory of what he had done with the revolver when he got it back. He had shoved it into his belt on the left side, under his jacket, well over toward his hip, grip toward the middle, where he could reach it easily with his right hand. I squatted and figured out a plausible route and then pulled my shoes off and circled and ducked quickly and silently through two areas of light, and then crawled slowly and carefully on hands and knees into the shelter of the foliage just behind him and to his right. As I neared him I heard his bad case of hiccups, a steady solid rhythmic case, each one a strangled, muffled sound due to his effort to stay quiet enough to ambush me. From then on I made each move on the hiccup, a jerky progress as in the most ancient motion pictures. At last, unheard, I was on my hands and knees right behind him and slightly to his right, just where a large and obedient dog would be. I inched my knees closer and put my weight back and lifted both hands. On the next hiccup I snapped my hands out and grasped his heavy ankles and yanked his legs out from under him, giving enough of a twist so that he would land on his left side. As he landed I scrambled onto him, felt the checkered wooden grip, and yanked the revolver free and rolled across the grass with it and stood up.

He pushed himself slowly to a sitting position, rolled up onto his knees, put his hands on the wall, and slowly stood up. He turned and put his back against the wall and shook his thick head.

"Bassard," he said thickly. "Dirry stud bassard."

"Settle down, Richard. I cured your hiccups."

He grunted and launched himself at me, swinging wildly while he was still too far away to punish anything but the humid night air. I ducked to the side and stuck a leg out and he went down heavily onto his face. And once again, with the painful slowness of a large damaged bug, he got himself up onto his feet, using a small tree as a prop.

He turned around and located me. "Wages of sin," he mumbled. "My lousy ideas. Memories. All worked up. I read it, you bassard. Made her sore at me, you tricky bassard. Kept her here and soft-talked her an' pronged her, you lousy smartass."

And with a big effortful grunt he came at me again. As he got to me I dropped, squatting, fingertips on the grass. As he tripped and spilled over my back I came up swiftly and he did a half turn in the air and landed flat on his back. He stared at the sky, breathing hard. He coughed in a shallow gagging way.

"Sick," he said. "Gonna be sick."

I helped him roll over. He got onto hands and knees, crawled slowly and then stopped, braced, vomited in dreadful spasms.

"So sick," he moaned.

I got him onto his feet, and with one arm across my shoulders, my arm around his clumsy waist, I got him into the room. Once in the bathroom he was sick again. I held his stupid head, then sat him on the closed lid of the toilet and swabbed the mud and vomit off him with a wet towel. He swayed, eyes half closed. "Loved that girl. Loved her. Lousy thing. I can't stand it." He opened his eyes and looked up at me. "Honest to God, I can't *stand* it!"

"We better get you home, Rick."

He thought that over and nodded. "Best thing. Bad shape. Who cares anymore? Janice doesn't give a shit. Penny the only one cared. Gone. Some sumbitch killed her. Some crazy. Know it wasn't you. Wish it had been you. Fix you good."

"Where do you live, Holton?"

"Twenny-eight twenny, Forest Drive."

I got his car keys from him and the description of his car, and went around to the front and drove it back to the room. I went in and brought him out and helped him

126

into the red convertible, and got behind the wheel. He muttered directions.

When I had to stop for a light, he said, "Sorry I had to smack you around, McGee. You know how it is."

"Sure. I know how it is."

"Get it out of my system. Hated you. Shouldna layed my girl, my wonnerful freckly nurse-girl. But man to man, shit, if she wanned it, she wanned it, and why should you turn it down, huh? Great kid. Greatest piece of ass in the worl'. You're a nice guy, McGee. I doan wanna like you, you sumbitch, but I do. Hear that? I do."

I had to shake him awake to get more directions. When I turned into the asphalt drive, he was asleep again. It was a cement-block house, one story, white with pink trim, a scraggly yard, house lights on, a gray Plymouth station wagon in one half of the carport.

I turned away from the carport and stopped near the front door. The outside light went on and the door opened and a lean, dark-haired woman looked out through the screen door.

I got out and came around the car. "Mrs. Holton?"

She came out and looked at her sleeping husband. She wore dark orange slacks, a yellow blouse, and she had a bright red kerchief tied around her slender, dusky throat. Gypsy colors.

"Unfortunately, yes. Who are you?"

"My name is McGee."

I had the feeling that it startled her slightly and I could think of no reason why.

"I'll help you get him in."

She reached and took hold of his jaw and turned his head slightly. She raised the other hand, held it poised for a moment, and then whip-cracked her lean palm across his face twice, very quickly and with great force. It brought him struggling up out of the mists, gasping and looking around.

"Hey! Hey there, Janice doll! This here is Travis McGee, my ver' good buddy. He's going to come in and have a li'l drink. We're all going to have a drink. Right?"

As he struggled to get out of the car I took him by the

127

arm and levered him out. We supported him, one on either side, and after we got him through the door, she gave directions in a voice strained with effort. She turned on the light of what was obviously a guest room. We sat him on the bed and he sat with his eyes closed, mumbling something we could not understand. When he started to topple over backward, I grabbed him by the shoulders and turned him so that he landed on the pillow. She knelt and unlaced his shoes and pulled them off. I picked his legs up and swung them onto the bed. She loosened his belt. When he gave a long, ragged snore, she looked at me and made a mouth of distaste. I followed her as she walked out. She turned the lights off and closed the guest room door.

I followed her into the living room. She turned, standing more erect, and said, "Thanks for your help. This doesn't happen often. That is not an excuse or an apology. Just a statement of fact."

I worked the revolver out of my trouser pocket and gave it to her. "If it happens at all, he shouldn't run around with this thing."

"I'll put it away and tell him he must have lost it. Thank you again."

"May I use your phone to call a cab?"

She stepped to the front window and looked across the street. "My friend is still up. She'll come over and listen for the kids while I take you in."

"I don't want to trouble you, Mrs. Holton."

"I'd like some air. And you've been to a lot of trouble."

She went to the phone in the foyer and dialed, then had a brief low-voiced conversation. We went out and got into the car. She asked me to wait for a moment. When the door opened in the house across the street and a woman came out and started across, she told me to start up. She waved and called, "Thanks a lot, Meg."

"Perfectly okay, Jan. Take your time, honey."

Janice Holton untied the kerchief and put it over her dark hair and fastened it under her chin. From her manner it was going to be a swift and silent trip.

"I guess what racked your husband up was having some person or persons unknown kill his girl friend."

Out of the corner of my eye I could see that she had turned quickly and was staring at me. "I couldn't care less what . . . racks him up, Mr. McGee. I feel sorry for the girl. As a matter of fact I regret never having had a chance to thank her."

"Thank her?"

"For letting me out of bondage, let's say."

"Unlocked your chains?"

"You're not *really* interested in the sordid details of my happy marriage, are you?"

"It just seemed like a strange way to put it."

"I find myself saying some very strange things lately."

"Right at the bottom of the certificate, Mrs. Holton, there's the fine print that says you live happily ever after."

I suppose that you could call it role-playing, maybe in the same sense that the psychologists who use group therapy use the term. Or you could call it, as Meyer does, my con-man instinct. Okay, call it a trace of chameleon blood. But the best way to relate to people is to fake their same hang-ups, and when you relate to people, you open them up. So I lie a little. Instant empathy. To crack her facade I had to make out like an ex-married, so I spoke with the maximum male bitterness.

"You sound like you had the tour too, Mr. McGee?"

"Ride the rolly-coaster. Find your way through the fun house. Float through the tunnel of love. Sure. I had a carnival trip, Mrs. Holton. But the setup tends to do a pretty good job of gutting the husband. I believed the fine print. But she turned out to be a bum. So I end up paying her so much a month so she can keep on being a bum. So I'm a little bitter about the way the system works."

"For a girl married to a lawyer, it doesn't exactly work out that way. I believed the fine print too, Mr. McGee. I considered it an honorable estate, an honorable contract. And, by God, I worked at it. I knew after the first year it wasn't going to be the way . . . you hope it will be. So I tried to understand him. I think Rick feels

129

that he is . . . unworthy of being loved. So he can't ever believe anyone loves him, really. So he has a thousand mean snide little ways of spoiling things. He loves the boys, I know. But any kind of . . . family ceremony, something for warmth and love and fun—oh, can he ever clobber everybody. Tears and shambles and nastiness, and everything you try to plan . . . birthdays, anniversaries, he has such a cruel way of making things turn sour. But I was stuck with it. I *thought* I was stuck with it. You know, if you're a grownup, you add up the ledger. A successful man, a faithful man, not a drunk or a chaser. But then . . . the sneaky business with Miss Woertz changed the ledger."

"And let you out of bondage?"

"Kept me from agonizing over . . . making the marriage work. Sort of . . . canceled all my vows."

"Did you find out about her quite recently?"

"Oh, no. I found out practically as soon as it started. He started that crusade about finding out what *really* happened to Doctor Sherman. You know about that?"

"He told me about it. Was that just to help cover up the affair with the nurse?"

"Oh, no. He's sincere about it. But when it threw them together, he sure put in a lot of hours in so-called investigation. Somebody called me up and told me about it, in a very nasty whisper. I couldn't tell if it was a man or a woman. I didn't want to believe it, but I knew it was true, somehow. Then I saw all the little clues." She gave a mirthless laugh. "The most convincing one was the way he became so much sweeter to me and the boys."

"So are you going to divorce him?"

"I don't know. I don't love him anymore. But I haven't got a dime of my own. And I just don't know if I could get enough alimony and child support if I bring suit."

I turned in at the Wahini Lodge and parked away from the entrance lights, over near the architectured waterfall and the flaming gas torches.

"You're too darned easy to talk to, Mr. McGee."

"Maybe because we just wear the same kind of battle

scars. I had to get out of my setup just as fast as I could."

"Any kids?"

"No. She kept saying later, later."

"It makes a difference, you know. It's a pretty nice house, nice neighborhood, good school. There's medicine and dental work and shoes and savings accounts. It's an arrangement, right now. I do my part of the job of keeping the house going. But I won't ever let him touch me again. It would turn my stomach. He can find himself another playmate. I don't give a damn. And we don't have to socialize, particularly."

"Can you live the rest of your life like that?"

"No! I don't intend to. But I have a friend who says that we . . . says that I had better just sort of go along with it as is for the time being. He is a dear, gentle, wise, understanding man. We've been very close ever since I found out about Rick. His marriage is as hopeless as mine but in a different way. I'm not having an affair with him. We see each other and we have to be terribly careful and discreet because I wouldn't want to give Rick any kind of ammunition he could use if and when I try to get a divorce. We don't even have any kind of special understanding about the future. It's just that we both . . . have to endure things the way they are for a while."

"Then, I guess the family outing Rick told me about, the trip to Vero Beach yesterday, must have been pretty grim."

She had turned in the bucket seat to face me, her back against the door, legs pulled up. "Was it ever! Like that old thing about what a tangled web we weave. I didn't have any idea he'd want to spend any part of Saturday with his wife and children. I'd told him I was going to drive over and see June and leave the boys off with my best friend on the way. She lives twenty miles east of here. Her boys are just the same ages, practically. I'd fixed it with June to cover for me in case Rick phoned me there for some stupid reason. And I was going to drive to . . . another place close by and spend the day with my friend. But out of the clear blue Rick decided to come too! I didn't see how in the world he could have found out anything. But he was so ugly I decided he must have had a little lovers' spat with his girl friend. When I left the boys at my friend's place, I had a chance to phone my sister and warn her, while Rick was out in the car, but I couldn't get hold of my friend to call the date off. Rick was in a foul mood all day." Again the mirthless laugh. "What a lousy soap-opera!"

I could not leave at that moment because it would give her the aftertaste of having been pumped, of having talked too much. So I invented a gaudy confrontation between me and the boyfriend of a wife I never had. I spun it out and when I was through, she said, "It's wretched that people have to be put through things like that just because a wife or a husband is too immature to . . . to be plain everyday faithful. Do you ever run into her? Is she still in Lauderdale?"

"No. She moved away. I have no idea where she is now. I send the money to a Jacksonville bank. If I want to find out where she is, all I'd have to do is stop making payments. Look, do you want to come in for a nightcap?"

"Golly, where did the time go? Meg is a good neighbor, but I don't want to take too much advantage. Mr. McGee?"

"Travis."

"Travis, I didn't mean to sound like a long cry of woe, but it's made me feel better somehow, comparing bruises with somebody."

"Good luck to you, Janice."

"And to you too." I had gotten out. She clambered over to the driver's seat, snapped the belt on, and pulled it back to her slender dimension. "Night, now," she called, and backed out and swung around and out onto the divided highway, upshifting skillfully as she went.

I projected a telepathic suggestion to her unknown friend. Grab that one, man. Richard Haslo Holton was too blind to see what he had. She's got fire, integrity, courage, restraint. And she is a very handsome lively creature. Grab her if you can, because even though there are quite a few of them around, hardly any of them ever get loose.

No messages, no blinking red light on the phone. The maid had turned the bed down. Small hours of the morning. When I put the light out, a freckled ghost roamed the room. I said good night to her. "We'll find out, Miss Penny," I told her. "Somehow we'll find out and you can stop this wandering around motel rooms at night."

12   *I HAD A* hell of a night. Hundreds of dreams and from what little I could remember of them, they all had the same pattern. Either somebody was running after me to tell me something important and I could not stop running from them or understand why I couldn't stop, or I was running headlong after somebody else who was slowly moving away no matter how hard I ran, moving away in a car or a bus or a train. Sometimes it was Penny, sometimes Helena. I woke with an aching tiredness of bone, a mouth like a cricket cage, grainy eyes, and skin that seemed to have stretched so that it was too big for me and wanted to hang in tired, draped folds.

After endless toothbrushing and a shower that did no good I phoned the Fort Courtney Police Department and left word for Stanger that I had called.

My breakfast had just been served when he settled into the chair across the table from me and told the waitress to bring him some hot tea.

"You look poorly, McGee."

"Slept poorly, feel poorly."

"That's my story, every morning of my life. You get yourself a swing and a miss with Janice Holton?"

"They took the trip to Vero Beach together. And you could confirm it by finding out who she left the kids with, an old friend twenty miles from here, in the direction of Vero Beach. And Holton is serious about believing somebody killed Doctor Sherman. The Holton marriage has bombed out. She knew about the nurse. She's going through the motions for the sake of the kids until she can find some way to land on her feet. And I think she will, sooner or later."

He blew on his hot tea and took a sip and stared at me and shook his head slowly. "Now, aren't you the one! By God, she cozies up pretty good to some damn insurance investigator."

"I didn't have to use it. You gave me a better approach."

He aimed his little dusty brown eyes at me. "I did?"

I put my fork down and smiled across at him. "Yes, indeed you did, you silly half-ass fumbling excuse for a cop."

"Now, don't you get your——"

"You *knew* Holton was screwing her, Stanger. You *knew* that the note you found made it clear to anybody who can read simple words that she and I had something going for us. So what did you think Holton would do after he saw the note or a copy of it? Chuckle and say, Well, well, well, how about that? You probably know even that the ex-assistant state attorney carries a gun. But did you make any effort to tip me so I wouldn't get shot? Not good old Stanger, the lawman. Thanks, Stanger. Anytime I can do any little thing for you, look me up."

"Now, wait a minute, goddamn it! What makes you think he read the note?"

"Some direct quotes sort of stuck in his mind. He recited them."

He drank more of his tea. He found a third of a cigar on his person, thumbnailed the remains of the ash off it, held a match to it.

"He try to use the gun?"

"He didn't get the chance. I was tipped. I found him staked out and waiting, so I sneaked up on him and took it away. I don't know whether he was going to use it or not. Give him the benefit of the argument and say he wouldn't. He knew I hadn't put the shears in her neck. He knew I was cleared of that. Let's say he resented the rest of it, though. Incidentally, I gave the gun to his wife and she seemed to think it would be a good idea to tuck it away. Maybe there shouldn't be a gun in that happy household."

"So you took the gun away from him and?"

"I yanked his legs out from under him to get it. Then I had to trip him onto his face, and then I had to block him and somersault him onto his back. The last one took it out of him. He'd been drinking. It made him sick. I drove him home in his car. We became dear old buddies somehow. Drunks are changeable. He was passed out by the time I got him home. I helped get him to bed. She had a neighbor watch the kids while she drove me back. She's known about the affair since it started. He sleeps in the guest room. I like her."

He held up the hand with the cigar in it. He held it up, palm toward me, and said, "I swear on the grave of my dear old mother who loved me so much she didn't even mind me becoming a cop that I just can't figure out how the hell Rick Holton got hold of that note. Look, as an ex-prosecutor he's got a little leverage. Not too much but some. I think he would know where to look, who to bug, *if* he knew there *was* a note. But *how* could he know? Look, now. The Woertz woman knew because she wrote it. I knew because I found it. Jackass Nudenbarger knew because he was with me when I found it. You knew because I read it to you. And down at the store, two men. Tad Unger did the lab work and made photocopies. Bill Samuels acts as a sort of clerk-coordinator. He sets up the file and keeps it neat and tidy and complete to turn over to the state attorney if need be. He protects the chain of evidence, makes the autopsy request, and so on."

Had I thought for a moment, I would have realized there had to be an autopsy. They would want to know if

135

a murdered unmarried woman was pregnant, if there was any sign of a blow that had not left any surface bruises, contusions, or abrasions, if she was under the influence of alcohol or narcotics, if she had been raped or had had intercourse recently enough to be able to type the semen. And the painstaking, inch-by-inch examination of the epidermis would disclose any scratches, puncture wounds, minor bruises, bite marks. And there would be a chemical analysis of the contents of the stomach, as death stops the normal digestive processes.

"You all right?" Stanger asked softly.

"I'm just perfect. When did they do the autopsy?"

"They must have been starting on it when I was talking to you in your room Saturday night."

"And those two men, Unger and . . ."

"Samuels."

"They wouldn't volunteer any information about the note?"

"Hell no. The days of volunteering any information to anybody about anything are long gone. Order yourself more coffee. Don't go away. Be right back."

It took him ten minutes. He sat down wearily, mopped his forehead on a soiled handkerchief. "Well, Bill Samuels was off yesterday and Holton came in about eleven in the morning. A clerk named Foster was on duty and Holton told him that the state attorney, Ben Gaffner, had asked him to take a look at the note that had been found in the Woertz girl's apartment. So Foster unlocked the file and let him read the photocopy. It still doesn't answer the question."

"Can I give it a try?"

"Go ahead."

"Would Holton know you were on the case?"

"Sure."

"Would he know he wouldn't be able to get much out of you?"

"He'd know that."

"Would he know who's working with you?"

"I guess he'd know . . . Oh, goddamn that motor-sickel idiot!"

He told me that as long as I'd had the grief of it, I might as well have the pleasure of seeing the chewing process. I signed the check for my breakfast and his tea and followed him out.

The car was parked in the shade. Nudenbarger, now in a sport shirt with green and white vertical stripes, was leaning against it smiling and talking to a pair of brown hefty little teen-age girls in shorts. He saw us coming and said something. The kids turned and looked at us, then walked slowly away, looking back from time to time.

"All set?" he asked, opening the car door.

Stanger kicked it shut. "Maybe on the side you could rent that mouth. People could store stuff in it. Bicycles, broken rocking chairs, footlockers. Nice little income on the side."

"Now just a minute, Al, I——"

"Shut up. Close that big empty stupid cave fastened to the front of your stupid face, Nudenbarger. Stop holding the car up. I just want to know how stupid you are. Every day you become the new world's champion stupid. How did you get mousetrapped into talking about the note the nurse left?"

"Mousetrapped? I wasn't mousetrapped."

"But you talked about it, didn't you?"

"Well . . . as a mattter of fact——"

"After I told you you had never heard of any note?"

"But this was different, Al."

"He just walked up and asked you what we found in the apartment?"

"No. What he said was that he was upset about her being killed. He was out to the place real early yesterday. I'd just got up and I was walking around calling the dog. He said he and his wife were very fond of her and grateful to her. He said he didn't want to get out of line or step on any toes, but he wondered if maybe outside investigators ought to be brought in, and he thought he might be able to arrange it. Al, I know how you feel about anything like that, so I told him it looked like we could make it. He asked if we had much of anything to go on, and I said we had that note and told him what I could remember of it and said that the fellow she wrote it to, meaning you, McGee, had checked out okay."

"What kept you from falling down laughing?"

"About what, Al?"

"That line about him and his wife being fond of the little nurse. And grateful to her? Jesus!"

"What's wrong with that?"

"Why in the world would Janice Holton be grateful to Penny Woertz?"

"Who said anything about Janice Holton?"

"Didn't you say Holton told you that———"

"Holton! It was Mr. Tom Pike that stopped at the place. I haven't said one damn word to Mr. Holton. Mr. Tom Pike only had a couple of minutes. He was on his way to the airport and he was taking the shortcut, the back road past my place, and saw me and stopped because, like he said, he was upset about the girl getting killed. Now you agree it was different? Do you?"

The anger sagged out of Stanger. "Okay. It was different. He's the kind of guy who'd want to help any way he can. And the nurse helped take care of Mrs. Pike. Now, dammit, Lew, did you say one word to anybody else about any note?"

"Never did. Not once. And I won't, Al."

"You shouldn't have told Pike either."

Stanger turned to me. "Back where we started. Look, I'll get it out of Holton and if I think you ought to know, I'll let you know, McGee."

I motioned to him and took him out of earshot of Nudenbarger. "Any more little errands on the side, as long as I'm stuck here?"

He scowled, spat, scuffed his foot. "I've got men ringing every doorbell in the whole area around that Ridge Lane place. Somebody had to arrive and kill her and leave in broad daylight. Somebody had to see something on Saturday afternoon. I've got men going through the office files of Doc Sherman that went into storage when he died, and the files that were taken over by the doctor who took over Sherman's practice, Doctor John Wayne. Hell of a name, eh? Little fat fellow. Sherman treated

138

some crazies when he was researching barbiturate addiction. So we don't want to rule out the chance of an ex-patient going after the office nurse. She'd been working as a special-duty nurse, so I got hold of the list of patients she took care of ever since the doctor died, and we're going through those. On top of that I've got a good man digging into her private life, every damned thing he can find, the ex-husband, previous boyfriends. Nothing was stolen from the apartment. She lived alone. Those are good solid front doors and good locks on the kitchen doors. I think she would have to know somebody to let them in. No sign of forcible entry. From the condition of the bed, she was sleeping and got up and put the robe on and let somebody in. No makeup. A man or woman could have shoved those shears into her throat. We've got a blood pattern, a spatter pattern. Whoever did it could have gotten some on them from the knees down. To reconstruct it, she put both hands to her throat, staggered back, fell to her knees, then rolled over onto her back. She hadn't been sexually molested. There were indications she'd had intercourse within from four to six hours from the time of death. She wasn't pregnant. She was going to start her period in about three days. She had a slightly sprained ankle, based on some edema and discoloration. There was a small contusion just above the hairline at the center of her forehead and a contusion on her right knee, but these three injuries had occurred a considerable time before death. We're processing a court order to get into her checking account records and her safety deposit box. Now if you can come up with something I just haven't happened to think of, McGee . . ."

It was a challenge, of course. And I was supposed to be overwhelmed by the diligence and thoroughness of the law.

"What about delivery and service people? Dry cleaners, laundry, TV repairs, phone, plumber, electrician? What about the apartment superintendent, if any?"

He sighed heavily. He was upwind of me and even outdoors he had breath like a cannibal bat. "Son of a gun.

Would you believe me if I told you that was all in the works, but I just forgot to mention it?"

"I'd believe you, Stanger. I think you might be pretty good at your job."

"I'll write that in my diary tonight."

"What about the nurses' day room at the hospital? She'd probably have a locker there. There might be some personal stuff in it."

He sighed again and took out his blue notebook and wrote it down. "One for you."

"Maybe there's another one too. If there is, can I check it out? I have . . . a personal interest in this, you know."

"If there's another one, you can check it out."

"I don't think a registered nurse would be doing the billing and the bookkeeping and keeping the appointment book. So there probably had to be another girl working for Sherman, part time or full time."

He squinted at the bright sky. He nodded. "And she was on vacation when he killed himself. Just now remembered. Okay, go ahead, dammit. Can't recall her name. But Doctor Wayne's office girl would know. Just don't try to carry the ball if you come up with anything. Report to me first."

"And you tell me what you find out from Holton."

"Deal."

He trudged toward the waiting car. I went back inside and used a pay phone in the lobby to call Dr. Wayne's office. The answering service told me they opened the office at noon on Mondays.

I went back to 109. The cart was outside the door, the maid just finishing up. She was a brawny, handsome black woman. Her skin tone was a flawless coppery brown, and across the cheekbones she looked as if she had an admixture of Indian blood.

"Be through here in a minute," she said.

"Take your time."

She was making up the bed. I sat on the straight chair by the desk module that was part of the long formica countertop. I found the phone number for D. Wintin

Hardahee and as I wrote it down I saw the maid out of the corner of my eye and for a moment thought she was dancing. When I turned and looked at her, I saw that she was swaying, feet planted, chin on her chest, eyes closed. She lifted her head and gave me a distant smile and said, "Feeling kind of . . . kind of . . ." Then she closed her eyes and toppled forward. Her head and shoulders landed facedown on the bed and she slipped and bounded loosely off and landed on the floor, rolling onto her back.

Suddenly I knew what must have happened. I went to the closet alcove and bent and picked the doctored bottle of gin out of the corner where I had put it and, stupidly, forgotten it. There were a couple of fresh drops of colorless liquid on the outside of the bottle, on the shoulder of it. Any moisture would have long since dried up in the dehumidifying effect of the air conditioning. I licked a drop off with my tongue tip. Plain water. So she had taken a nice little morning pickup out of the bottle and replaced it with tap water.

I went to her and knelt beside her. Her pulse was strong and good, and she was breathing deeply and regularly. She wore a pale blue uniform trimmed with white. Over the blouse pocket was embroidered, in red, "Cathy."

After weighing pros and cons and cursing my idiocy for leaving the gin where somebody might find it, I went looking for another maid. There was a cart on the long balcony overhead, in front of an open door to one of the second-floor units. I went up the iron stairs and rapped on the open door and went in. The maid came out of the bathroom. She was younger than Cathy, small and lean, with matte skin the shade of a cup of coffee, double on the cream. She wore orange lipstick, had two white streaks bleached into her dark hair, and a projection of astonishingly large breasts. Her embroidery said "Lorette."

"Sir, I just now started in here. I can come back if——"

"It isn't my room. Are you a friend of Cathy's?"

"You looking for her, great big strong girl, she's working the downstairs wing right under here, mister."

"I know where she is. I asked you if you're a friend of hers."

"Why you asking me, mister?"

"She might need a friend to do her a favor."

"She and me, we get along pretty good."

"Would you come down to Room One-O-nine?"

She looked very skeptical. "What she wants to do and what I want are a couple of different things, mister. I do maid work, period. I don't hold it against her, but she ought to know by now if she wants a girl for anything else, she can go call that fat Annabelle or that crazy kid they got working in the kitchen."

"I got back to my room a couple of minutes ago, Lorette. Your friend Cathy tapped one of my bottles. She thought it was gin. It was sleeping medicine. She's down there passed out. Now, if you don't give a damn, say so."

Her eyes were round and wide. "Cold stone passed out? You go on down, please, and I'll come right along quick."

Ten seconds after I was back in the room, she pushed the door open and stood on the threshold, staring in at Cathy.

"It's like you said?" she asked. "You didn't mess with her any kind of way, did you?"

"There's the bottle over there. Go take a slug and in a little while you can lie down right beside her."

She made up her mind and pulled the door almost closed as she came in. She dropped to her knees and laid her ear against Cathy's chest. Then she shook her and slapped her. Cathy's sleeping head lolled and Cathy made a little whine of irritation and complaint.

"Can you cover for her?" I asked.

She sat back on her heels and nibbled a thumb knuckle. "Best thing is get Jase to bring a laundry cart and he'p load her in and put a couple sheets over her and put her in an empty." She stared suspiciously up at me. "That's no kind of poison, is it? She'll come out of it okay?"

"In two to three hours, probably."

She stood up and stared at me, head tilted. "How come you don't just call the desk?"

"Would they fire her?"

"They sure to hell would."

"Lorette, if I'd had that bottle locked up in my suitcase and she'd gone digging around in there and tapped it, then I might have called the desk. Maybe I would have called anyway if she'd been giving me sloppy service since I've been here. But she's kept this place bright as a button, and I plain forgot that bottle and left it on the closet floor over there where any maid would find it. So I share the blame."

"And maybe you don't want to have to tell a lot of folks how come you keep your sleeping medicine in with the gin?"

"I think you're a nice bright girl and you can cover for her without any trouble at all."

"Because it's slack right now I can do hers and mine both, what rooms we got left. But one more thing. If you turned her in, could she rightly say that you've been messing with her some?"

"No. She couldn't say that."

"Then, I'll be back in just a little while."

It was five minutes before she came back. She held the door open for a tall young boy with enormous shoulders, who pushed a laundry hamper on wheels into the room. He parked it beside Cathy and picked her up easily and lowered her into it. Lorette covered her with a couple of rumpled sheets and said, "Now Annabelle will be waiting right there in Two eighty-eight, Jase. You just put Cathy on the bed there and let Annabelle tend to her, hear?"

"Yump," said Jase, and wheeled her out.

"Finish up fixing your bed for you, mister."

"Thanks."

As she was finishing she giggled. She had a lot of lovely white teeth. She shook her head. "That ol' girl is sure going to wonder what in the world happened to her."

"Explain the situation, will you?"

"Surely. If you're not checking out, she'll be coming by to say thank you tomorrow, I expect." She paused at the door, fists in the pockets of her uniform skirt. "It's important Cathy shouldn't get fired, mister. She needs the job. She lives with her old mother, and that old woman is mean as a snake. All crippled up with arthritis. She about drove Cathy's man away, I guess. There's three little kids, and Cathy could manage all right on the job money, but she'll see a dress and keep thinking about it until she just has to have it, no matter what, and she'll put it on layaway, and then she'll have to use the money for other things at home, and she'll be afraid she'll lose the dress and what she paid on it, and then, well, she'll take chances she wouldn't otherwise and do things she wouldn't otherwise. She's older than me but lots of ways she's like a kid. This place does a lot of commercial trade, and what she does, when you unlock a number and it's a single in there, he's maybe just waking up or he's getting dressed, she gives a big smile and says something like good morning, sir, sure sorry if I disturbed you. And he looks her over and says, Honey, you come on right in here, and, well, she does. Then it's ten dollars or twenty to keep from losing the dress, but she's going to get caught someday and lose this good job. The reason I'm telling you all this is on account of from what I said about her messing around, I didn't want you thinking she was nothing but a hustler. It's only sometimes with her, and even if I wouldn't go down that road, it doesn't mean she isn't no friend of mine. She's my friend. She used to let me hold her first baby. I was ten years old and she was fifteen. And . . . thanks for coming and telling one of us."

She left and I screwed the bottle cap tight and put the doctored—and watered—gin in my carry-on suitcase, wondering all the while if it wouldn't be a sounder idea to pour it out.

D. Wintin Hardahee was with a client. I left the motel number and room number. He called back ten minutes later, at eleven o'clock.

"I was wondering if maybe I could scrounge a little more information from you, Mr. Hardahee."

"I am very sorry, Mr. McGee, but my work load is very heavy." The soft voice had a flat and dead sound.

"Maybe we could have a chat after you get through work."

"I am not taking on any new clients at this time."

"Is something the matter? Is something wrong?"

"Sorry I can't be more cooperative. Good-bye, Mr. McGee." Click.

I paced around, cursing. This nice orderly prosperous community was getting on my nerves. A big ball of tangled string. But when you found a loose end and pulled, all you got was a batch of loose ends. It seemed like at least a month ago that I had thought to check out Helena's estate arrangements. I thought maybe Hardahee could work it through his New York classmate. But Hardahee wasn't going to work out anything for me. So what could turn him off so quickly and so completely? Lies? Fear?

I stretched out on the bed and let the confusing cauldron bubble away, giving me glimpses of Penny, Janice, Biddy, Maureen, Tom Pike, Rick, Stanger, Tom Pike, Helena, Hardahee, Nudenbarger, Tom Pike.

Pike was getting pretty damned ubiquitous. And little bits of conversation kept coming back. I heard parts of the night talk with Janice Holton and something bothered me and I went back over it and found what bothered me, then slowly sat up.

She had asked about my imaginary wife. "Do you ever run into her? Is she still in Lauderdale?"

Review. I had not said one damned word about Lauderdale. Holton had checked the registration. So he knew. But was there any reason for him to have said word one about it to his wife? "Look, darling, my girl friend wanted to stay in the motel room with some jerk from Lauderdale named McGee."

Not likely.

Backtrack. A little look of surprise at hearing my name. Surprise to find me with her husband.

Possibility: Friend of Biddy's. Had met her in supermarket or somewhere. Biddy spoke of an old friend named McGee from Lauderdale.

Or: In the process of checking me out Saturday evening, and checking Holton out, Stanger made some mention of me to Janice Holton. "Do you know, or do you know if your husband knows, anybody named Travis McGee from Fort Lauderdale?"

Possible, but I didn't like the fit. They were like limericks that do not quite scan, that have one syllable too much or one missing. My brain was a pudding. I walked across to a shopping plaza, bought some swim pants in a chain store, came back and put them on and padded out to the big motel pool. There was a separate wading pool full of three- and four-year-olds, shrieking, choking, throwing rubber animals, and belting each other under the casually benign stare of four well-greased young mothers. So I dived and did some slow lengths of the main pool and then gradually let it out, reaching farther, changing the kick beat, stretching and punishing the long muscles of arms, shoulders, back, thighs, and belly, sucking air and blowing out the little layers of sedentary staleness in the bottoms of my lungs. I held it just below that pace at which I begin to get too much side roll and begin to thrash and slap, and then brutalized myself by saying, Just one more. And one more. And one more. Finally I lumbered out, totally whipped, heart way up there close to a hundred and a half, lungs straining, arms and legs weak as canvas tubes full of old wet feathers. I dried my face on the bath towel I'd brought from the room and then stretched out on it to let the sunshine do the rest.

Meyer calls it my "instant I.Q." In a sense it is. You oxygenate the blood to the maximum and you stimulate the heart into pumping it around at a breakneck pace. That enriched blood goes churning through the brain at the same time that it is nourishing the overworked muscle tissues. Sometimes it even works.

But I put my fat, newly enriched, humming head to work on the Janice-Lauderdale problem, and its final report was, "Damned if I know, fella."

So I went back to 109 and before I dressed, I tried the

office of the fat little John Wayne, M.D., got hold of a cheery, cooperative lady who told me that Dr. Stewart Sherman's receptionist and bookkeeper was Miss Helen Boughmer, and she did not know if she was working or not, but I could reach her through the phone listed for Mrs. Robert M. Boughmer. She asked me to wait a moment and gave me the number to write down.

Mrs. Robert M. Boughmer was very firm about things. "I'm sorry, but I couldn't possibly call my daughter to the phone. She is not well today. She is in bed. Does she know you? What is this all about?"

"I'd like a chance to ask her some questions about an insurance matter, Mrs. Boughmer."

"I can definitely say that she is not interested in buying any insurance and neither am I. Good-day."

"Wait!" I missed her and had to call again. "Mrs. Boughmer, I am an insurance investigator. I am investigating a policy claim."

"But we haven't had any accidents with the car. Not for years."

"It's some information on a death claim."

"Oh?"

"On Doctor Sherman. Just a few routine questions, ma'am."

"Well . . . if you'll promise not to tire Helen, I think you might be able to talk to her at about four o'clock, if you'll come here to the house." I said I would. It was at 90 Rose Street, and she told me how to find it. "It's a little white frame house with yellow trim, on the right, on the second corner, with two big live oak trees in the front yard."

After I hung up, I phoned the Pike place and Biddy answered.

"Well, hello!" she said. "Yes, Maurie is doing just fine, thank you. We were just about to have a swim before lunch."

"I wondered if I could come out and talk to you about something after lunch."

"Why not? What time is it? Why don't you make it

about two thirty or quarter to three? She'll be having her nap then. Will that be okay?"

I said it was just fine. I dressed and had lunch at the motel and then went strolling through the rear areas looking for Lorette. There was a service alley behind the kitchen. When I walked along it, past a neat row of garbage cans, I came to an open door to a linen storage room. I looked in and saw Lorette, still in uniform, sitting on a table laughing and talking and swinging her legs. There were two older black women in there, not in uniform. The rubber-tired maid carts were aligned against the wall near a battered Coke machine and a row of green metal lockers.

She saw me and the talk and laughter stopped. She slid off the old wooden table and came and stood in the doorway, her face impassive, her eyes down-slanted. "You want something, sir?"

"To ask you something," I said, and walked on to a place where the roof overhang shaded a portion of the alley and a flame vine was curling up a post that supported the overhang. She had not followed me. I looked back and she shrugged and came slowly toward me. She put her hands in her skirt pockets and leaned against the wall.

"Ask me what?"

"I didn't know if you could talk in front of those other women. I wanted to know how Cathy is."

"Jes fine." Her face was blank and she let her mouth hang slightly open. It made her look adenoidally stupid.

"She come out of it okay?"

"She gone on home."

It was all too familiar and all too frustrating. It is the black armor, a kind of listless vacuity, stubborn as an acre of mules. They go that route or they become all teeth and giggles and forelock. Okay, so they have had more than their share of grief from men of my outward stamp, big and white and muscular, sun-darkened and visibly battered in small personal wars. My outward type had knotted a lot of black skulls, tupped a plenitude of black ewes, burned crosses and people in season. They
148

see just the outward look and they classify on that basis. Some of them you can't ever reach in any way, just as you can't teach most women to handle snakes and cherish spiders. But I knew I could reach her because for a little time with me she had been disarmed, had put her guard down, and I had seen behind it a shrewd and understanding mind, a quick and unschooled intelligence.

I had to find my way past that black armor. Funny how it used to be easier. Suspicion used to be on an individual basis. Now each one of us, black or white, is a symbol. The war is out in the open and the skin color is a uniform. All the deep and basic similarities of the human condition are forgotten so that we can exaggerate the few differences that exist.

"What's wrong with you?" I asked her.

"Nothin' wrong."

"You could talk to me before. Now you've slammed the door."

"Door? What door, mister? I got to get back to work."

Suddenly I realized what it might be. "Lorette, have you slammed the door because you know that this morning I stood out in front of this place talking to a couple of cops?"

There was a sidelong glance, quick, vivid with suspicion, before she dropped her eyes again. "Don't matter who you talkin' to."

"Looked like a nice friendly little chat, I suppose."

"Mister, I got to go to work."

"That housekeeper here, Mrs. Imber? If she hadn't happened to look into 109 on Saturday afternoon and saw me there sacked out, it wouldn't have been any nice friendly conversation with the law. And it wouldn't have happened out in front of this place. It would have been in one of their little rooms, with nobody smiling. They would have been trying to nail me for killing that nurse."

She turned and leaned against the shady wall, arms folded, her face no longer slack with the defensive tactic of improvised imbecility. She wore a thoughtful frown, white teeth biting the fullness of her underlip. "Then it was that nurse girl with you in the room Friday night, Mr. McGee?"

"That's how I got acquainted with the law, with Stanger and Nudenbarger."

"The way I know you had a woman with you, Cathy she told me Stanger asked her if when she did the room she saw any sign you'd had a woman in there. That was before you helped her some. No reason to try to save any white from the law anytime. She said you surely had a party. So it was a lucky thing about Miz Imber checking the room, I guess."

"Yes, indeed."

Her brown-eyed stare was narrow and suspicious. "Then, what call have you got to fool around with those two law?"

"I liked the nurse. If I can help find out who killed her, I'd buddy up to a leper or a rattlesnake. It's a personal matter."

Her eyes softened. "I guess being with someone you like, being in the bed with them, and they're dead the next day, it could be a sorrowful thing."

It struck me that this was the first sympathetic and understanding response I'd had from anyone. "It's a sorrowful thing."

With a sudden thin smile she said, "Now, if she was so nice and all, how come she was giving it away to such a mean honk lawyer like that Mr. Holton? Surprised I know? Man, we keep good track of everybody like Holton."

"What's your beef with him?"

"When he was prosecutor, he got his kicks from busting every black that come to trial, busting him big as he could manage. Ever'time he could send a black to Raiford State Prison, it was a big holiday for him, grinning and struttin' around and shaking hands. The ones like that, they can't get anybody for yard work or housework, at least nobody worth a damn or a day's pay."

"She didn't like Holton, Lorette. She was trying to break loose. Being with me was part of the try. Didn't
150

you ever hear of any woman with a hang-up on a sorry man?"

There had been antagonism toward me when she had talked of Holton. I was on Holton's team because of my color. But by telling her how it was between Penny and Rick, I had swung it all back to that familiar lonely confusing country of the human heart, the shared thing rather than the difference.

"It happens. It surely happens," she said. "And the other way around too. Well, yes, I heard you was with those two this morning. Lieutenant Stanger, he isn't so bad. Fair as maybe they let him be. But the one called Lew, he likes to whip heads. Don't care whose, long as it's a black skull. Stanger don't stop him, so the day they go down, they both go down like there was no difference at all."

"I wanted to ask you how Cathy made out. I had no way of knowing how much she drank out of that bottle."

Her stare was wise, timeless, sardonic. "Why, now, that big ol' gal is just fine. Big strong healthy gal. On account of you didn't get her fired, she might be real thankful to you. How thankful do you want she should be, man?"

"Dammit, why do you think that's what I've got in mind?"

She laughed, a rich, raw little sound, full of derision. "Because what the hell else could you want from black motel maids? Sweepin' and cleanin' lessons? A walk in the park? A Bible lesson? Those women back in that room, now. I know exactly what they're thinking. They got it all figured that finally, somehow a whitey got to me, and probably tomorrow I switch with Cathy, one of mine for her One-O-nine, because I decided to be motel tail and pick up some extra bread. Those women know there's not another damn thing in the world about me or Cathy you could be after. And that's how it is."

"And that is exactly what you believe about me?"

"Mister, I don't know *what* to believe about you, and that's the truth."

"I hunted you up because I wanted to see how Cathy made it. And I wanted to ask a favor."

"Like what?"

"I've seen a lot of towns like this one. Enough to know that the black community knows everything that happens in the white community. Maids and cooks and yard men make one of the best intelligence apparatuses in the world."

"Sneaky niggers listening to everything, huh?"

"If I happened to be black, you can damn well bet I'd keep track, Mrs. Walker. Just to keep from getting caught in the middle of anything. I would have to be just that much faster on my feet, just to get a job and keep a job. I'd listen and I'd know."

She tilted her head as she looked up at me. "You almost know where it is, don't you, man? If you were black, now, wouldn't you be too smart to be a yard man?"

"Exactly the same way that if you were white, you're too smart to be a motel maid."

"So what makes you think I'm so stupid I'd get myself messed up in some white killing by coming to you with anything I hear about it?"

"Because I liked that nurse. Because without special help the cops might plumber this one. Because you can follow your hunch, which tells you I'd never make any attempt to bring you into it at all. But the big reason you'll do it is because it's one of the last things in the world you ever thought you'd do."

She snickered. "My grandma kept telling me, she'd say, 'Lorrie, when you got your haid in the lion's mouth, just you lay quiet. You keep forgetting and it's gone get you in bad trouble.' "

"So?"

"Mr. McGee, I got to do the late checkouts. Cathy wasn't all as fine as I said. She said she felt far off. She worked slow and her tongue sounded thick and she said she felt like her skull was cracked open up on top. So Jase drove her on home, and I got two of her late rooms and three of my own to do up."

"Will you think about it, at least?"

With an enigmatic smile she walked away slowly. She had her hands in the pockets of the uniform skirt. She scuffed her heels and went a dozen steps, then stopped and looked back at me over her shoulder, her smile merry and impudent.

"I might see if there's a thing worth knowing. But if there was and I told you and you told somebody I told you, if they come to me about it, they're going to come up onto the dumbest black girl south of George Wallace."

Nobody looks far enough down the road we're going. Someday one man at a big button board can do all the industrial production for the whole country by operating the machines that make the machines that design and make the rest of the machines. Then where is the myth about anybody who wants a job being able to find it?

And if the black man demands that Big Uncle take care of him in the style the hucksters render so desirable, then it's a sideways return to slavery.

Whitey wants law and order, meaning a head-knocker like Alabama George. No black is going to grieve about some nice sweet dedicated unprejudiced liberal being yanked out of his Buick and beaten to death, because there have been a great many nice humble ingratiating hardworking blacks beaten to death too. In all such cases the unforgivable sin was to be born black or white, just as in some ancient cultures if you were foolish enough to be born female, they took you by your baby heels, whapped your fuzzy skull on a tree, and tossed the newborn to the crocs.

And so, Mrs. Lorette Walker, no solutions for me or thee, not from your leaders be they passive or militant, nor from the politicians or the liberals or the head-knockers or the educators. No answer but time. And if the law and the courts can be induced to become color-blind, we'll have a good answer, after both of us are dead. And a bloody answer otherwise.

13   *I STOPPED* in the driveway at 28 Haze Lake Drive at ten of three. As I got out of the car motion caught my eye and I saw Biddy waving to me from the window of the studio over the boathouse.

She opened the door as I got to the top of the outside staircase. She seemed to be in very good spirits. She wore baggy white denim shorts and a man's blue work shirt with the sleeves scissored off at the shoulder seam. The seams came about four inches down her upper arms. She had a little smear of pale blue pigment along the left side of her jaw and a little pattern of yellow spatter on her forehead. The familiar slow heavy breathing was coming over the intercom.

"Maybe it's the extra sleep you let me have, Travis. Or maybe because it's a lovely day. Or maybe because Maurie seems so *much* better."

"Electrosleep?" I asked, gesturing at the speaker.

"Oh, no. Just to get her to sleep and then I took it off. It's more natural that way, even though I don't really think she gets quite as much rest out of it."

I looked at the canvas she was working on. "Seascape?"

"Well, sort of. It's from the sea oats that used to grow in front of the Casey Key place, the way you could see the blue water through the stems and the way they waved in the breeze. It's coming along the way I want it. We can keep talking while I work."

"So she's much better?"

"I'm sure of it. Strange how maybe something changed for her when she was lost and we were trying to find her.

At least she didn't go off and let somebody buy her too many drinks and get into some kind of nasty situation. I guess she must have been wandering around in the brush. But she doesn't remember anything about it. She just seems to . . . have a better grip on herself. Tom is terribly pleased about it. I even think it might be all right to take her to the opening tomorrow night, but Tom is dubious."

"Opening of what?"

"Maybe you noticed that big new building at the corner of Grove Boulevard and Lake Street? Twelve stories? Lots of windows? Well, anyway, it's there and it's new, and it's a project Tom has been working on for almost a year now. He organized the investment group and got the land lease. The Courtney Bank and Trust will move into the first four floors next week, or start moving next week. Almost all the space is rented already. Tom is moving his offices to the top floor. It's really a lovely suite of offices, and the decorators have been working like madmen to get it done in time. So tomorrow night it's sort of a preview of the new offices of Development Unlimited, a party with bartender and caterer and all, beginning just at sundown. He thinks it will be too much for her, but if she is as good tomorrow as she is today, I really think we ought to try it. If she begins to act as if she can't handle it, I can always bring her home. She is sleeping well now, because I made her swim and swim and swim."

I looked down into the back lawn and saw a chin-whiskered man in overalls and Mennonite hat guiding a power mower.

"What did you want to ask me about, Trav?"

"Nothing of any importance. I wondered if you know a Mrs. Holton. Janice Holton?"

"Is she sort of . . . dark and vivid?"

"Yes."

"I was introduced to her once, I think. But I really don't know her. I mean I would speak to her if I saw her, but I haven't seen her in weeks and weeks. Why?"

"Nothing. I met her Sunday night after I left here, and she looks like somebody I used to know. I didn't get to ask her. I thought you might know something about her, like where she's from, so I could figure out if she's the same one."

"I really don't know a thing about her except she seems nice. She must have had quite an impact on you, if you came all the way out here to ask me that."

"I didn't. I just had some odds and ends. That's one of them. I wondered about something else. I don't mean to pry. But remember, I'm sort of an unofficial uncle. Did your mother leave you enough to get along on?"

She rolled her eyes. "Enough! Heavens. When she knew she needed the first operation, back before Maurie became so sick with that miscarriage, she told each of us how she had set things up and asked us if we wanted anything changed while she still had time. Some enormously clever man handled her finances after Daddy died, and made her a lot of money. There are two trust accounts, one for me and one for Maurie. After estate taxes and legal costs and probate costs and all that, there'll be some fantastic amount in trust for each of us, close to seven hundred thousand dollars! So as soon as it's settled and the Casey Key house is sold and all, we'll start getting some idiotic amount like forty thousand a year each. I had no idea! It's tied up in trust until each of us reach forty-five, or until our oldest child gets to be twenty-one. If we have no children, then of course we just have access to the whole amount when we're forty-five. But if we do, then each child gets a hundred-thousand-dollar trust fund when it gets to be twenty-one, and because, by the time you're forty-five, you certainly know there aren't going to be any more kids, the same amount is sequestered—is that the word?—for your kids, like if you have five all under twenty-one, then a hundred thousand would be set aside for each one for their trust funds, and you would get what's left over."

"What happens if either of you die?"

"All the money would be left in trust for the kids, if I was married and had any. And if not, the trust would just sort of end and Maurie would get the amount that's in trust. God, Travis, it is such a horrid feeling thinking these past weeks what would happen if Maurie did manage to kill herself. Hundreds of thousands of dollars directly to me, and all that income from the trust. It's spooky, because I never knew and I never thought of myself that way. I knew there would be some, of course. But past a certain point it just gets ridiculous." She turned from the painting, brush in hand, and smiled at me. "Dear Uncle, you do not have to worry about my finances." Her face saddened abruptly. "Mother just didn't have much of a life, the last six years of it. After we got back to the Key, after my father died, we'd take long walks on the beach, the three of us, every morning. She talked to us. She made us understand that Mick Pearson just could not have ever accepted a neat, tidy, orderly, well-regulated little life. He had to bet it all, every time. And I remember that she said to us that if she'd only had five years of him, or ten, or fifteen instead of twenty-one, she would still have settled for that much life with him instead of forty years with any other man she'd ever met. She said that was what marriage was all about and she hoped we'd both find something just half as perfect."

"Did she have her first operation here?"

"Yes. You see, Maurie was almost five months pregnant and she'd lost the first baby at six months. It was an absolutely stupid accident the first time. She drove down to pick up a cake she'd ordered for Tom's birthday and it was in July two years ago, and she was driving back in a heavy rain and she started to put on the brakes and the cake started to slide off the seat, and she grabbed for it and when she did, she stomped harder on the brake and the car slid and she went up over the curb and hit a palm tree, and the steering wheel hit her in the stomach, and about three hours later, in the hospital, she aborted and the baby was alive, actually, a preemie, but less than two pounds, and she just didn't make it. It was very sad and all, but Maurie told me on long distance there was no point in my coming down. She recovered very quickly. So I guess mother thought she'd better come over and keep Maurie from running into any palm trees so she would have her first grandchild. After she was here a week or so, she noticed some bleeding and had a checkup and they decided they'd better operate. She had Doctor William Dyckes, and he is fabulously good. When we knew she was going to be operated on, I came down to be with her and do what I could. Then, three days after she was operated on, Maurie went into some kind of kidney failure and had convulsions and lost her second baby, and hasn't been right since. While they were both in there, I flew up and packed and closed my apartment and put stuff in storage and had the rest shipped down."

"When was all that?"

"A year ago last month. Or a lifetime ago. Take your pick. Doctor Bill operated on Mother again last March. And then she died on the third of this month." She frowned. "Only eleven days ago, Trav! But it seems much longer ago. And it was, of course. They kept her so doped, trying to build her up at the same time, for the operation. She was so tiny and shrunken. She looked seventy years old. You'd never have known her. And she was so . . . damn brave. I'm sorry. Excuse me. What the hell good is bravery in her situation?"

"Was there any chance?"

"Not the faintest. Bill explained it to Tom and me. I had to give permission. He said he thought it might help her to do another radical, take out more of the bowel, cut some nerve trunks to ease the pain. He wasn't kidding me. I know he didn't give her much chance of surviving it. But . . . he liked Mom. And she might have lasted for another two months, even more, before it killed her."

I sat and made casual talk for a little while, watching her at work. She asked me to come to the party Tuesday evening. I said I might if I didn't have to leave town before then. She said that if Tom wasn't tied up, the three of them were going to drive down to Casey Key next Sunday, and she would look for that information about the *Likely Lady*.

I found the Boughmer house at 90 Rose Street without difficulty, but it was twenty after four when I walked up the porch steps and rang the bell. The blinds were closed against the afternoon heat. A broad doughy woman appeared out of the gloom and looked out at me through the screen. She wore a cotton print with a large floral design. She had brass-gold hair so rigidly coiffed it looked as if it had been forged from a single piece of metal.

"Well?"

"My name is McGee, Mrs. Boughmer. I called about talking to your daughter on that insurance matter?"

"You're not very businesslike about arriving on time. You don't look like a business person to me. Do you have any identification?"

I had found three of the old cards and moved them into the front of the wallet before I got out of my car. Engraved, fancy, chocolate on buff. D. Travis McGee. Field Director. Associated Adjusters, Inc. And a complex Miami address, two phone numbers, and a cable address.

She opened the door just far enough for me to slip the card through. She studied it, ran the ball of her thumb over the lettering, opened the door, and gave it back to me.

"In here, please, Mr. McGee. You might try the wing chair. It's very comfortable. My late husband said it was the best chair he ever sat in. I will go see about my daughter."

She went away. It was a small room with enough furniture and knickknacks in it for two large rooms. The broad blades of a ceiling fan turned slowly overhead, humming and whispering. I counted lamps. Nine. Four floor and five table. Tables. Seven. Two big, four small, one very small.

She came marching back in, straight as a drill sergeant. A younger woman followed her. I stood up and was introduced to Helen Boughmer. Thirty-three, maybe. Tall. Bad posture. Fussy, frilly, green silk blouse. Pale pleated skirt. Sallow skin. Very thin arms and legs fastened to a curious figure. It was broad but thin. Wide across the shoulders, wide across the pelvis. But with imperceptible breasts and a fanny that looked as if it had been flattened by a blow with a one-by-ten plank. Pointed nose. Mouse hair, so fine the fan kept stirring it. Glasses with gold metal frames, distorting lenses. Nervous mannerisms with hands and mouth. Self-effacing. She sat tentatively on the couch, facing me. Mom sat at the other end of the couch.

"Miss Boughmer, I'm sorry to bother you when you're not feeling well. But this is a final report on some insurance carried by Doctor Stewart Sherman."

"What policy? I knew all his policies. I was with him over five years. I made all the payments."

"I don't have those details, Miss Boughmer. We do adjustment work on contract for other companies. I was just asked to come up here and conduct interviews and write a report to my home office on whether or not, in my best opinion, the doctor's death was suicide."

"She was on her vacation," Mom said.

"Well, I was spending it right here, wasn't I?"

"And is there anything wrong with having a nice rest in your comfortable home, Helen?" She turned toward me. "It's a good thing she didn't spend her hard-earned money going around to a lot of tourist traps, because she certainly hasn't worked a day since her precious doctor died. She doesn't even seem to want to look for work. And I can tell you that *I* certainly believe in insurance, because we wouldn't be living here right now the way we are if Robert hadn't been thoughtful enough to protect his family in the event of his death."

Helen said, "I just don't know what insurance it could be. He cashed in the big policies because he wanted the money to invest with Mr. Pike. And the ones he kept, they'd be so old I guess they'd be past the suicide clause waiting period, wouldn't they?"

I had to take a wild shot at it. "I'm not sure of this, Miss Boughmer, but I have the feeling that this could have been some sort of group policy."

"Oh! I bet it's Physicians' General. That's a term policy and he had no value to cash in, so he kept it. And I guess there could be a suicide clause for the life of the policy. Do you think so?"

"I would say it's possible." I smiled at her. "There has

to be *some* policy where the problem exists, or I wouldn't be here, would I?"

"I guess that's right," the receptionist-bookkeeper said.

"There was no note left by the deceased and no apparent reason for suicide. And the company is apparently not interested in taking refuge in a technicality if the claim should be paid to the heirs. Would you say it was suicide, Miss Boughmer?"

"Yes!"

Her tone had been so wan the sudden emphasis startled me.

"Why do you think so?"

"It's just like I told the police. He was depressed, and he was moody, and I think he killed himself. They interviewed me and typed it out and I signed it."

"I've interviewed Mr. Richard Holton and, prior to the tragic murder of Miss Woertz last Saturday, I talked to her about it too. They were both most vehement in saying that it could not possibly have been suicide."

"Like you said at first," her mother said, "crying and raving and ranting around here, making a fuss like you didn't make when your poor father died. You told me fifty times your wonderful doctor couldn't have ever killed himself. You were going to find out what happened to him if it took the rest of your life, remember? And not two days later you decided all of a sudden that he *had* killed himself."

She sat with her hands clasped on her lap, fingers interlaced and rigid, head downcast. She looked like a child praying in Sunday school.

"After I thought it over I changed my mind," she said, and I found myself leaning forward to hear her.

"But Miss Woertz didn't change *her* mind."

"That's got nothing to do with me."

"Is it your impression that Miss Woertz was a stable, rational human being, Miss Boughmer?"

She looked up swiftly and down again. "She was a very sweet person. I'm sorry she's dead."

"Hah!" said Mom. "To this child *everybody* is a very sweet person. She's easily led. She'll believe anybody.

Anybody with half an eye could see that Penny Woertz was a cheap, obvious, little thing. Why, she couldn't have cared one way or another whether Doctor Sherman killed himself or was murdered."

"Mom!"

"Hush up, Helen. All the little Woertz person wanted to do was dramatize. One of the ladies in my garden club, a very reliable lady, and she's never had to wear glasses a day in her life, saw that nurse and Mr. Holton, a married man, embracing and kissing each other in a parked car in the lot at the hospital just over three weeks ago, practically under one of the streetlights in the parking lot. Do you call that rational and stable, Mr. McGee? I call it sinful and wicked and cheap."

"Mom, please!"

"Did she ever try to take any of that work off your shoulders? Did she? Not once did she ever——"

"But that wasn't her *job!* I did my job and she did hers."

"I *bet* she did. I bet she did more than her job. I bet there was more going on between her and your marvelous doctor than you could ever see, the way you think she was so sweet and wonderful."

The girl stood up quickly and wavered for a moment, dizzy. "I don't feel so good. I'm sorry. I don't want to talk about it any more."

"Then, you go to bed, dear. Mr. McGee didn't mean to tire you. I'll be up in a little while to see if there's anything you need."

She stopped in the doorway and looked toward me, not quite at me. "Nobody can ever make me say anything else about the doctor. I think he killed himself because he was moody and depressed."

She disappeared. "I'm sorry," Mrs. Boughmer said. "Helen just isn't herself these days. She's been a changed girl ever since that doctor died. She worshipped the man, God knows why. I thought he was a little on the foolish side. He could have had a marvelous practice if he'd had any energy or ambition. He was all right until his wife died three years ago. Then he sort of slacked off. She wouldn't have put up with all those stupid projects of his. Research, he called it. Why, he wasn't even a specialist. And I think the drug companies are doing all the research anybody needs."

"Your daughter hasn't looked for work since?"

"Not after she got through straightening out all the files for Dr. Wayne to pick up and trying to collect the final bills. But there doesn't seem to be much point in people paying doctor bills to a dead doctor, does there? No, she just seems to feel weak. She doesn't seem to have the will or the energy to go out and find another job. She's a good hard worker too. And she was a very good student in school. But she's always been a quiet girl. She always liked being by herself. Thank the Lord we have enough to live on. I have to scrimp and cut corners with her not working, but we get by."

"She seemed certain that the doctor hadn't killed himself?"

"Positive. She was like a maniac. I hardly knew my own daughter. Her eyes were wild. But I think it was the second day she was at the office, cleaning things up, she just came home late and went to bed and didn't want anything to eat. She hardly said a word for days. She lost a lot of weight. Well, maybe she'll start to perk up soon."

"I hope so."

14 *NINE THIRTY* Monday evening. Stanger was suddenly standing at my elbow at the bar at the motel and suggested it might be better if we talked in my room. I gulped the final third of my drink and walked around with him. The air was very close and muggy. He said a storm would help, and we might get one in the night.

Once we were in the room, I remembered something I kept forgetting to ask him. "Holton has some buddy on the force who opens motel doors for him and such like. Who is that?"

"Not on the city force. That's Dave Broon. Special investigator for the Sheriff's Department. Slippery little son of a bitch for sure. The sheriff, Amos Turk, didn't want to take him on in the first place. That was about seven years back. But there was political pressure on Amos. Dave Broon has a lot of things going for him all the time. You want a nice little favor done, like maybe some chick starts putting the pressure on you threatening to go to your wife, Dave is your boy. He'll check her out, scare her to death, and put the roust on her, but then when Dave wants something out of you, he's got the names, dates, and photostats of the motel register, so you do him a favor. He's built up a lot of political clout around this part of the state. Lot of the lawyers use him on special little jobs because he's careful and he keeps his mouth shut."

"Next question. Is D. Wintin Hardahee his own man?"

"God, you do get around some, McGee. Far as I know, he is. Soft voice, but don't mess with him. Hardnosed and honest. Nobody tells him what to do."

"And what about Holton and the note?"

"Don't I get to ask any questions?"

"And you'll get answers. What about Holton?"

"That boy was so bad hung this morning he couldn't move his eyeballs. Had to turn his whole head. Kept sweating a lot. Cut his face all up shaving it. What happened was they got in from Vero Beach Saturday night after ten. Car radio was busted. He had a beer and went right to bed and he said he hadn't had much sleep Friday night. Drove around for a long time after he left here. Parked by the Woertz apartment for a while, but she didn't come home. Got in at three, he thinks. So he slept heavy Saturday night. Got up about ten thirty Sunday morning. His wife was already up. He was sitting on the edge of the bed when the phone rang. Picked it up and said hello. No answer for a moment and he thought it was the same kind of trouble they've been having with the line. Ring once and no more. Then he said somebody whispered to him. He didn't get it at first. They repeated it and hung up. Couldn't tell if it was a man or a woman. It made no sense to him. The whisper said, 'The police found a note she left for her new lover.' Some damfool prank, he thought. Then he saw the front page of the paper, and without breakfast or a word to anybody he came downtown and conned Foster into letting him see the note. Hunted around for you. Got ugly drunk. Might have shot you. Told me he'd given it some serious thought."

He stared over at me. "What the hell is wrong with you?"

"It goes clunk, Stanger. Things float around loose in your head and then there is a clunk, and they've lined up and make sense."

"Let me in on this clunk."

"Did you mention to Janice Holton anything about a certain McGee from Fort Lauderdale?"

"Not word one."

"Phone rings once and that's all. In the Holton house and in the Pike house too."

"Slow and steady, man. Try speaking American."

"Janice has a nice warm wonderful tender man she sees on the sly. Nothing physical about the relationship, she says. She found out about Holton and Penny from somebody who whispered the news to her over the phone."

"Do tell!"

"Lover's code, Stanger. The sneak play. You have a place you meet. A nice safe place. So you call up and let the phone ring once and you hang up. The other party looks at his or her watch. Five minutes later it rings again. Meet me at five o'clock at the usual place if you can, honey. Or eight minutes later, or two minutes later, or twelve minutes later for noon or midnight. So Tom Pike told her about me, some casual thing about a man named McGee who'd known his wife, sister-in-law, and mother-in-law in Lauderdale nearly six years ago, and who came to lunch. Maybe my coming to lunch busted up a tryst. She let it slip casually without thinking."

"So who whispers? Tom Pike for chrissake?"

"It doesn't make much sense."

"When Holton got his call from the whisperer, Tom Pike was flying to Jacksonville. Okay, so Nudenbarger told him about the note, but what would be the point? I mean even if he could make the call. Get Holton all jammed up? What for? Tom Pike isn't the kind to walk out on his marriage, fouled up as it is. And if he's got Janice Holton on the string, what is he proving or accomplishing?"

"Janice was supposed to have a big date with him Saturday, out of town, I guess. But Rick fouled it up by going along, and she couldn't get word to Tom that she was stuck with her husband and would actually have to go see her sister over in Vero Beach."

Stanger said thoughtfully, "I'm not going to fault those two, not for one minute, McGee. Janice is a hell of a lot of woman. Two sorry marriages, and they weren't the ones who made the marriages sorry. Jesus! It's a lot better than if he got involved with the kid sister."

"Who happens to be in love with him."

"Think so?"

"Sure of it."

"Then, Janice could be a kind of escape valve. Well, Tom Pike would step slow and careful, and if we hadn't . . . *you* hadn't added it up, I'll bet a dime nobody would have ever found out about it. I'd say one thing, if it isn't like you say physical, it must be a pretty good strain on them. That Janice is more than something ready. It's going to *get* physical, friend. What have we got? Some damn whisperer trying to make trouble for people."

"Al, out of the whole town, who would you pick as the whisperer? Not by any process of logic. Just by hunch."

"I guess the one I told you about. Dave Broon."

"On somebody's orders?"

"Or playing a personal angle. Turk puts him on a case, he's cute. He's got good moves. He comes up with things. And he's lucky. That's a help in cop work. But he doesn't give a goddamn about whether anything is right or wrong, anybody is legal or illegal. It isn't his business to find new work for the sheriff. If he spotted the mayor's wife shoplifting, he'd follow her home and invite himself in for a drink and a little chat. That kind."

"Could he have found out about that note without you knowing he found out about it?"

"Oh, hell yes. Far as I know he might have the leverage on somebody so that he gets a dupe of every photocopy of any evidence they run through our shop. This whole city and county is a big piece of truck garden to Dave Broon. He goes around plowing and planting and fertilizing, and harvesting everything ripe."

"How is he with bugs?"

"Not an expert but maybe better than average. He has good contacts. If it was something tricky, he'd bring in one of the experts from Miami. He can afford it."

"So we could be bugged?"

"It's possible," he said. "But not likely."

"He isn't too bright, Stanger. Not bright enough to be alarming."

"Dave alarms me, friend."

I showed him the toilet kit and the toothbrush, and the two twenties under the soap dish, and explained the situation. At first it bothered Stanger that if Broon was reasonably sure he had not left any traces, why should he advertise by taking the money? I finally made him see that taking it was the lesser of the two risks, because if I did have some way of learning that my room had been gone over carefully, finding the money untouched would alert me that it was not just petty theft.

"Broon has a family?"

"Never has. Lives alone. Lives pretty good. Recently moved to a penthouse apartment on a new high-rise out by Lake Azure. Usually got some broad living there with him. Big convertible, speedboat, big wardrobe. But on the job he dresses cheap and drives a crummy car. I've worked with him sometimes. He has a way of making the suspect choke up and then get in a big hurry to tell all."

"Description?"

"Five seven, maybe a hundred and forty pounds. Knocking fifty but does a good job of looking thirty-five. Blond, and I think it's a dye job and a hairpiece. Keeps himself in good shape. Works out a lot. Manicures, massages, sunlamp in the winter. Either his teeth are capped or it's a hell of a good set of plates. Gets good mileage out of the accents he uses. All the way from British to redneck. He's in so solid with the party, he just about sets his own work week, and there's not a damned thing Amos Turk can do about it. Couple of years ago one of Turk's big deputies took a dislike to the way Dave was goofing off and making him do the work. Dave was giving away fifty pounds, better than six inches in height and reach, and at least twenty years. They went out into the parking lot. I guess it took six minutes. Didn't even muss up Dave's hair. Then they picked the deputy up and put him in a county car and took him over to the hospital. He never has looked exactly the same and he calls Dave by the name of Mr. Broon, sir. Just say he's tough and he's careful and he's smart enough. The odd job he's best at is if somebody needs a little extra leverage to use on somebody else. Then they get hold of Dave Broon and tell him to see what he can come up with. And it's a rare human person there isn't something about that you can put to use, if you know what it is."

Then I gave him a complete rundown on my talk with Helen Boughmer. He said it sounded as if something or somebody had scared her, and I did not tell him that his appraisal seemed to belabor the obvious.

He reported no progress to speak of on the murder of the nurse. He said, "Trouble with that damned place, the architect laid out those garden apartments for privacy. They kind of back up to little open courts, and there's so many redwood fences it's like a maze back in there. If whoever killed her came to the back door, which might be the way it was because of her being found in the kitchen, I might as well give up on shucking my way through the neighborhood. No fingerprints, but come to think of it, in thirty-one years of police work I've never been on a case yet where there was a single fingerprint that ever did anybody any good or any harm in the courtroom."

He sat in moody silence until I said, "It seems to be tied in to the death of Doctor Sherman."

"Please don't tell me that. I've got a file on him that you can't hardly lift. And there's nothing to go on."

"Maybe Penny Woertz had some casual little piece of information and she didn't know it was important."

"You're reaching, McGee."

"Maybe she'd even told it to Rick Holton and it didn't mean anything to him either, yet. If somebody could play on his jealousy and get him to shoot me after she'd been killed, that puts the two of them out of circulation. Maybe Helen Boughmer knows something too, but somebody has done such a good job of closing her mouth, I don't think she'll be any good to you."

"Thanks. You try to give me a motive for one murder by hooking it up to another one last July. I am going to keep right on thinking the doc injected himself in the arm."

"Got any reason why he did that?"

"Conscience."

"Had he been a bad boy?"

"Nobody is ever going to prove anything on him, and it wouldn't do much good now anyway. But let me tell you something. I have lived a long time and I have seen a lot of things and I have seen a lot of women, but I *never* saw a worse woman in my life than Joan Sherman. Honest to Christ, she was a horror. She made every day of that doctor's life pure hell on earth. Damn voice onto her like a blue heron. She was the drill instructor and he was the buckass private. Treated him like he was a moron. One of those great big loud virtuous churchgoing ladies with a disposition like a pit viper. Full of good works. She was a diabetic. Had it pretty bad too but kept in balance. I forget how many units of insulin she had to shoot herself with in the morning. Wouldn't let the doctor shoot her. Said he was too damned clumsy with a needle. Three years ago she went into diabetic coma and died."

"He arrange it?"

Stanger shrugged. "If he did, he took such a long time to figure it out, he didn't miss a trick."

"Want me to beg? Okay. I'm begging."

"Back then the Shermans lived about six miles out, pretty nice house right in the middle of ten acres of groveland. We were having a telephone strike and things got pretty nasty. They were cutting underground cables and so on. She'd had her car picked up on a Friday to be serviced, and they were going to bring it back Monday. Because of the phones out that way being out, he thought he'd better drive in Sunday morning and see to some patients he had in the hospital. Besides, he had to pick up some insulin for her, he told us later, because she used the last ampule she had that morning. He'd pick up a month's supply at a time for her. He made his rounds and then he went to his office and worked awhile. Nobody would think that was strange. He stayed away from her as much as he dared and nobody blamed him. He said he was supposed to get back by five because a couple was coming for drinks and dinner. But he lost track of the time. The couple came and rang the bell and the woman went and looked in the window and saw her on the couch. She looked funny, the woman said. The husband broke in. No phone working. They put her in the car and headed for the hospital. They met Doc Sherman on his way out and honked and waved him down. She was DOA. They say he was a mighty upset man. There was a fresh needlemark in her thigh from her morning shot, so she hadn't forgotten. He said she never forgot. They did an autopsy, but there wasn't much point in it. I don't remember the biochemistry of it, but there just aren't any tests that will show whether you did or did not take insulin. It breaks down or disappears or something. County law checked the house. The needle had been rinsed and put in the sterilizer. The ampule was in the bathroom wastebasket. There was a drop or so left in it. That tested out full strength. The doctors decided there had been a sudden change in her condition and so the dose she was used to taking just wasn't enough. Also, they'd had pancakes and maple syrup and sweet rolls for breakfast. He said she kept to her diet pretty well, but Sunday breakfast was her single exception all week. Now, tell me how he did it. That is, if he did it."

After a few minutes of thought, I had a solution, but I had been smartass too often with Stanger, so I gave up.

It pleased him. "He brought home an identical ampule of distilled water, maybe making the switch of the contents in his office. Gets up in the night and switches the water for the insulin. She gets up in the morning and shoots water into her leg. Before he goes to the hospital, he goes into the bathroom, fishes the water ampule out of the wastebasket, takes the needle out of the sterilizer, draws the insulin out of the one he filched and shoots it down the sink, puts the genuine ampule in the wastebasket, rinses the needle and syringe, and puts it back into the sterilizer. On the way into town he could have stopped, crushed the ampule under his heel, and kicked the powdered glass into the dirt if he wanted to be real careful. I think he was careful, and patient. I think maybe he waited for a lot of years until the situation was just exactly right. I mean maybe you could stand living with a terrible old broad like that if you knew that someday, somehow, you were going to do it just right. Nice?"

"Lovely. And doesn't leave you anyplace to go."

"It's the reason I was willing to lean a little bit toward suicide. Stew Sherman was a pretty right guy. And killing is sort of against everything a doctor learns in school and in his practice."

"And what if somebody else figured it out too and trapped the doctor somehow into admitting it?"

"Strengthens the suicide solution."

"Sure does."

"And I couldn't come up with a single motive for murder. His dying didn't benefit anybody in any way, McGee."

"Right back where we started?"

"I don't know. Sure like to know why that Boughmer

girl changed her mind so fast. Or who changed it for her. Isn't she one sorry thing though? Just imagine what she'd look like if you stripped her down to the buff."

"Please, Al."

He chuckled. "When I was little, we had a scrawny little old female cat out at the place. Had some Persian in her, so she looked pretty good. Picked up some kind of mange one spring, and in maybe ten days every last living hair fell off that poor beast. Honest to God, you'd look at her and you wouldn't know whether to laugh or cry. McGee, now I know that Helen is a sad, ugly, nervous woman, and I'm ashamed of myself, but if I can get to her when her mother can't pull out of the line and block for her, I think I could scare that Helen so bad she just wouldn't know what in the world she was telling me. Suppose I just do that. Tomorrow, if I can. What are you figuring on doing?"

"I might try to have a talk with Janice Holton and see if I guessed right about the boyfriend."

"So what if you did?"

"It will prove it wasn't somebody else instead of Tom Pike. So we can mark that part of the file closed."

"Anything else?"

"Find out if I can why Hardahee brushed me off."

"If he doesn't want to see you, you're not going to see him."

"I can give it a try. By the way, how are your contacts in Southtown?"

"As good as anybody's, which doesn't mean much. You think there's some Negra mixed up in this mess?"

"No. But Southtown supplies this city with cooks and maids and housekeepers and yard men. Waiters, waitresses, all kinds of manual labor. There can't be much going on among the white middle classes that they don't know about."

"You know, I think about that a lot. If I could ever tap that source, I think I'd have fifty percent of my job licked. They hear a hell of a lot, see a lot, and guess the rest. Sometimes I get a little help. But not lately. Sure God not lately. Those movies that have Southren law officers in them give us a pretty bad smell, regardless of how you handle yourself. I try to level with them, but shit, they know as well as I do there's two kinds of law here, two kinds of law practically everyplace. One of them kills a white man, they open the book to a different place from where a white man kills a Negra. Rape is a different kind of word there in Southtown too. Put it this way. A neighborhood where you got lots of garbage collection, good pavement, good water, good mail service, good streetlights, nice parks and playgrounds, rape and murder are great big dirty ugly scary words. Sorry, friend. None of them are on my side and I can't think of a way to change it one bit."

It was late. We had talked a long time. He leaned and rubbed the final sodden inch of cigar out in the glass motel ashtray. We were quiet. He was a strange one, I thought. A man softened and souring in his years, looking used up, but he wasn't. There are many kinds of cop. This one was a good kind. Flavor of cynical tolerance, grasp of all the unchanging human motivations, respect for the rules and procedures of cop work.

He laughed softly. "Just thinking about Southtown, one Christmastime long back. Maybe nineteen forty-eight, forty-nine. I'd been three years in the paratroopers, so I got appointed Sanny Claus by the City Council, jump into the park a day or two before Christmas, and the toys would come down on the next swing around, in a cargo chute. Kids swarming all over."

It gave me a grotesque mental picture of Santa Stanger lifting some little blond supplicant onto his red velvet knee, and with one Ho Ho Ho of that venomous breath turning her crisp and sere as a little autumn leaf.

"One year Sid dropped me too damn high. Maybe seven thousand. Supposed to make it last longer. Wind started gusting strong and I tried to spill some air to get down far enough so I could use the shrouds to steer me into the park. But I could see right away I couldn't even come close. So I rode the wind and it carried me all the way to Southtown. Sid made his next swing around pretty low and dumped the chute with the toys upwind of the park and put them right where I was supposed to already be. But I was by then steering myself into a field right behind Lincoln School right in the heart of Southtown. Landed good and collapsed the chute and balled it up and slipped out of the harness, and then I looked around and standing around me in a big silent circle there's more dang colored kids than I ever seen in one place before. All big-eyed, just looking. There I am saying Merry Christmas! ! ! and saying Well, Well, Well! and saying You been good little boys and girls? and they just look. All of a sudden I can hear old Boyd coming to get me— he's been dead for years—with that siren on high scream all the way, the gusty wind blowing the sound of it around. Ten seconds later I could see just a few of those colored kids way in the distance, just the ones too little to run so fast, and twelve seconds later there wasn't a kid in sight, and I was all alone in that field when Boyd came showboating up to me, making a skid turn that stopped him where I could reach out and touch the door handle. Took me back to the park and I spread that sack of toys so fast they didn't get the pictures for the paper. They took a toy away from a pretty little girl and gave it to me to give back to her, so they got their picture, and that was the last time. The next year I said I had a bad ankle, and they didn't have anybody wanted to jump, so from then on they didn't do it anymore. I used to wonder what those little colored kids thought, hiding behind things and under things, and seeing the cop car pick up Sanny Claus. Maybe it didn't puzzle them at all, them thinking anybody can get arrested anytime."

He stood up and yawned. "Be getting along."

I walked out into the night with him and said, "Al, I have one little ice-cold patch on my back, the size of fifty cents, just under the left shoulderblade. It seems to happen when there are things I should know and don't know, and find out later."

"With me, the back of my neck gets a kind of cool feel."

"I didn't bring a handgun."

He thought that over and said, "The check I ran on
174

you, nobody said you were about to become a director of any kind of bank, but nobody could say you should have been busted if they'd had more evidence either. How do I know you wouldn't be a problem to yourself and anybody who happened to come along?"

"You'd have to make a guess."

He took me to his car and unlocked the trunk. He said, "You took this off Holton and gave it to his wife and told me and I took it off her, so we'll leave it that you took it off him and you'll get around to turning it in to me later on, because I haven't talked about it or filled out the forms yet, and not having to fill out forms is a blessing these days."

"Remember, I phoned you about it and you said bring it in as soon as I had a chance?"

"Remember clear as day, McGee." He watched me as I turned toward the light, swung the cylinder out and checked the full load, used the ejector to spill the six rounds into my hand, snapped the cylinder back, checked the knurled safety to be certain it would not fire either double action or with the hammer back while on safe, then dry-fired it four times into the turf, twice on double action, twice with hammer back, to check the amount of trigger pull and trigger play, swung the cylinder out, reloaded, put it on safe, and thrust it inside my shirt and inside the waistband of my slacks, metal cool against the bellyflesh.

He got into the car and drove away. I saw pink lightning, a pale competition for city neon, then heard deep, fumbling thunder, a hesitant counterpoint to the truck sounds. There was just a hint of rain freshness in the wind.

Third time I'd gotten my hands on this same .38. Forgive me, Miss Penny, for tricking you and then bad-mouthing you that first time to get it away from your lover. You see, I didn't know you then, knew nothing about your silly honest earnest heart. Who were you staring at when you fell to your knees on the kitchen floor, putting your hands in disbelief to the blue handle of the shears? Did you think it some monstrous mistake and wanted only a chance to explain? But no chance. Tumbled and bled and died. Always tripping, falling, hurting yourself. Freckled clumsy girl.

Two portly tourists, male and female, she in a slack suit that matched his sport shirt, came plodding down the walk. They were in the floodlight pattern and did not see me in the shadows.

She was speaking in a thin and suffering voice. ". . . but no, you can't stand it to have anybody think for one stinking minute that you aren't rolling in money and so you have to tip every grubby little waitress like she was some kind of queen bee, and all it is, Fred, is just currying favor, trying to be a big shot, just showing off with the money we both saved to take this vacation, but if you have your way, the way you throw it around, we'll have to go home——"

"Shaddap!"

"They laugh at you when you tip too much. They think you're a fool. You lose all respect when you——"

"Shaddap!"

She began again, but they were too far away from me to hear her words. The tune was the same, however.

15 UP EARLY ON Tuesday. Fifteenth day of October. Pull the cords and slide the draperies away, feel crisp pile of miracle motel rug under the toes. Wonder who the hell I am. That is the blessing of morning routines—soap, brush, towel, lather, paste, razor. Each morning you wake up a slightly different person. Not significantly. But the dreams and the sleep-time rearrange the patterns inside your head. So what you see in the mirror is almost all you, and three percent stranger. It takes the comfort of routine to fit yourself back into total familiarity.

Even the little concerns are therapeutic. Does that tooth feel a little bit hollow? Seems like a lot of hair coming out. Little twinge in the shoulder when you move the arm just so. Sudden sideways unexpected glimpse in the mirrored door. Belly a little soft? Pat yourself, wash the hide, scrape the beard, brush teeth and hair. Little comforting attentions. Recognition symbols. Here I am. Now then. Me. The only me in existence.

Came walking slowly back from breakfast, marveling at how this tidy prosperous community of Fort Courtney kept producing more and more unknowns, making all its secret equations ever more insoluble. The doctor's wife, slick little Dave Broon, Hardahee's change of attitude, the strangeness of Helen Boughmer, the whisperer, and all the other little fragments of this and that. The diffusion was too wide. No new fact, no sudden inspiration, was going to link everything together into any pattern I could understand. So find one chunk of it, break it down, find out all the why and the who and the what-for.

There was a maid cart outside 109. The door was open. I went in and found Cathy doing the bathroom, Lorette Walker making up the bed.

" 'Mawnin', suh," they said. I sat in the armchair and waited and watched. Brisk work, sidelong downcast glances, a kind of humble knowing arrogance. Two to a room, one of the classic defensive maneuvers of the Negro motel maids across twenty states, where, as an indigenous morning recreational device, they are, when young enough and handsome enough, fair game for paper salesman, touring musician, minor league ballplayer, golf pro, stock car driver, mutual fund salesman.

After all, it is the only situation where white male and black female meet in the context of bedroom, and the quarry cannot exactly go running to the management to complain about a guest. Other defensive devices are the switchblade in the apron pocket, the kitchen knife taped to the inside of the chocolate thigh, the icepick inside the fold of the uniform blouse. Some, after getting tricked, trapped, overwhelmed by a few shrewd, knowing, determined white men, become part-time hustlers. Others cannot accept or adjust. Classic tragedy is the inevitable unavoidable tumble from some high place, where the victim has no place to turn, toppled by some instrument of indifferent fate. A high place is a relative thing. Pride of any kind is a high place, and any fall can kill.

"I see you didn't get fired, Cathy," I said as she came out of the bathroom with the towels.

She cast a swift and wary look at Lorette and then said, "No, suh. Thank you kindly."

There was a silence. I saw that they had begun to dust areas already dusted and were making other busy movements without improving anything. Lorette Walker, her back to me, said, "I can take off now, and this here girl can finish up."

"You look finished. You can both take off."

Lorette straightened and turned to face me, swinging that stupefying bosom around. "You want us both leaving, after I went to all the trouble of telling this here girl she should leastway give you the chance to collect on that favor you did her?"

Cathy stood at semiattention, staring at the wall beyond me, Indian face impassive. She was a big brawny woman, wide through the shoulders and hips, nipped narrow at the waist, with strong dark column of throat, husky shapely legs planted, her body looking deep and powerful through the belly and loins.

"Cathy?" I said.

"Yassa."

"There's no point in Mrs. Walker making us both uncomfortable. So why don't you just take off?"

Cathy looked toward Lorette, eyebrows raised in question. Lorette said something to her in a slurred tone. Cathy scooped up the sheets and towels and with one swift and unreadable glance at me, went out and pulled the door shut. I heard the fading jingle of the service cart as she trundled it away.

Lorette came over and sat on the bottom corner of the

bed, facing me, studying me. Small and pretty brown face, coffee with double cream, with no highlights at all on the smooth matte skin, with eyes so dark the pupils and irises merged. She fished cigarettes and matches from her skirt pocket, lit one, crossed slender legs as she exhaled a long plume. There was challenge and appraisal in her stare.

"Black turn you off, man?"

"Not at all. Suspicion does, though. It's an ugly emotion."

"And ugly living with it or having to live with it. Maybe you don't want it from Cathy on account of it would hurt your chance of making it with me, you think."

"How did you ever guess? I forced poor Cathy to drink that doctored gin, and I arranged to have the nurse killed, just so you and I could meet right here and arrange the whole thing. Take a choice of places, honey. Guatemala City? Paris? Montevideo? Where do I send your ticket?"

She was simultaneously angry and amused. Amusement won. Finally she said, "There's just one last thing I got to be sure of. Tell me, are you any kind of law at all? Any kind?"

"Not any kind at all, Lorette."

She shrugged, sighed, and said, "Well, here I go. Out where the nurse lived there's a white woman in number sixty, pretty close by. She's got her a Monday-Thursday cleaning woman, half days. Last Monday the cleaning woman got there and found a note from the woman she'd be away a week, don't come Thursday. The woman works in an office job. The cleaning woman didn't work Thursday and went there yesterday, Monday, like always. She can tell the woman that lives there isn't back yet, but somebody has been in there. Friend, maybe. Somebody lay on the bed a time. One person. Left a head mark in the pillow, wrinkled the spread. Something was spilled, and somebody used her mop, pail, things like that, and didn't put them back exactly the same. Scrubbed up part of the kitchen floor, part of the bathroom floor, and burned up something in the little fireplace those apartments have got, and she said to her it looked like ashes

179

from burning cloth, and she couldn't find some of her cleaning rags anyplace. Don't know what good it is to you. Maybe something or nothing."

"I suppose she cleaned the place as usual and swept out the fireplace?"

"That's what she did. She told me the name of that woman, but I plain dumb forgot it."

"Never mind. I can find out."

"The cleaning woman, she said it's not far from the kitchen door of that place to the kitchen door of the nurse place. Down the walk and around a corner, behind a fence the whole way, a big high pretty fence with little gates in it to little private yards."

"Thanks. Did you get anything else?"

"There's a lot of people in Southtown who plain wouldn't tell anybody anything, black or white. Or they tell a little and hold back some if they think you want to know bad enough to lay a little bread on them. It isn't on account of being mean. Somehow there's never enough money to even get by on. Maybe if . . ."

I worked my wallet out of my hip pocket and flipped it over onto the bed by her hip. With the half-cigarette dangling from the corner of her mouth, head aslant to keep the smoke out of her eyes, she opened it and thumbed the corners of the bills. "Take what you think you might need."

"And if I just take it all, man?"

"It would be because you need it."

Bright animosity again. "Never come into your mind I was cheating you?"

"Mrs. Walker, there's seven hundred and something in there. I've got to go along with the value you put on yourself, and you've got to go along with the value I put on myself."

She stared at me, then shook her head. "You some kind of other thing for sure. Look. I got two hundred. Okay? Bring you change, prob'ly."

She started to get up, undoubtedly to bring the wallet back to me, but then out of some prideful and defiant impulse, she settled back and flipped it at me. I picked it
180

out of the air about six inches in front of my nose, and slipped it back into the hip pocket. She folded the bills and undid one button of the high-collared uniform blouse and tucked the money down into the invisible, creamy, compacted cleft between those outsized breasts. She re-buttoned and gave herself a little pat.

She made a rueful mouth. "Talk to you so long out in the back, and now I've been in here with the door shut too long, and I tell you that everybody working here keeps close track."

She got up and took the ashtray she had used into the bathroom and brought it back, shining clean, and put it on the bedside table.

"Going to make me some nice problem," she muttered.

"Problem?"

"Nothing I can't handle. I'm kind of boss girl, right after Miz Imber. Up to me to keep them all working right. Lot of them may be older, but nobody can match me for mean. Can't tell them why I spent all this time in here with you alone. So they're going to slack off on me, thinking that on account of I suddenly start banging white, I lost my place. Oh, they'll try me for sure. But they'll find out they're going to get more mean than they can handle from ol' Fifty Pound."

"Fifty pound?"

Even with that dusky skin her sudden furious blush was apparent. "It's nothing, mister. Anyplace like this, sooner or later somebody'll give the boss gal some kind of special name. The one they give me, it comes from the way I'm built, that's all. Somebody saw me walk by and said, 'There she go. Ninety pound of mean. Forty pound of gal and fifty pound of boobs.' So it's Fifty Pound. Used to fuss me, but I don't mind now."

"See what you can find out, Lorette, about a man who works for the sheriff. Dave Broon."

She looked as if she wanted to spit. "Now, that one is all mean. Mr. Holton, he's part-time mean. Mr. Broon, he wants to know something, maybe a deputy picks up some boy out in Southtown and then Mr. Broon visits with him. When they bring the boy back, he walks old

181

and he talks old, and he keeps his head down. But he doesn't say a thing about Mr. Broon. One thing I know, he's rich. Big rich. It's in other names but he owns maybe forty houses in Southtown. Rains through the roof. Porch steps fall off. Three families drawing water from one spigot, but the rent never goes down. It goes up. Cardboard paper on the busted windows. Tax goes up on other places, never goes up on Mr. Broon's houses."

"You told me that the Holtons couldn't get domestic help because of Holton's attitude toward your people. I know that Mr. Pike and Miss Pearson have been trying to get somebody to look after Mrs. Pike. I noticed they have the yard work done by a white man. Any special reason for that?"

She stood by the door and all expression had left her face. "It's something went on long ago, three years, maybe more, just after that house was built and him new married. Had a live-in couple quartered over the boathouse. Young couple. Good pay. They drank some kind of poison stuff that you spray on the groves. Para . . . para . . ."

"Parathion?"

"Sounds right. Both died in the hospital. Mr. Pike paid for a nice funeral."

"Accident?"

"Not with the bag right there on the floor next to the table and the powder still stuck to the spoon. Put it in red wine and drank it. Must have seen it in the movies, because they busted the glasses, threw them at the wall."

"So?"

"So the man had been in Southtown three days before. Quiet boy. Got stinking smashed pig drunk. Cried and cried and cried. So drunk nobody could hardly understand him. Something about signing a paper so they wouldn't have to go to jail. Something about some nasty thing somebody was making his wife do on account of they signed the paper. And about not being able to stand it. Nobody knows the right and wrong of it. Nobody knows what happened."

"But the Pikes can't get any help out there?"

"They maybe could have. People were thinking on it. Then just before they let Mr. Pike get out of the broker business instead of putting the law on him, he was trying to learn to play golf, and he hit a colored caddy with a golf stick. Laid his head open. Mr. Pike give up trying the game after that. Gave Danny a hundred dollars and paid the hospital. Nobody else seen it. Mr. Pike said Danny walked the wrong way at the wrong time."

"Into his backswing?"

"That's what it was, the way they said it. Danny said he had a cold and he sneezed and Mr. Pike missed the ball entire and come at him with his eyes bugged out, making crazy little crying sounds, and Danny turned to run and he knows Mr. Pike couldn't run that fast, so he figures Mr. Pike threw it at him. Then those that had any idea of working out there, they decided against it."

"Why were they going to put the law on him when he was in the brokerage house?"

She looked astonished. "Why, for stealing! How else you going to get in trouble in that kind of job? Mr. McGee, I've *got* to get back on the job. See you tomorrow I guess. You don't see me, it'll mean I didn't get anything much tonight out home."

I could get in touch with neither Janice Holton nor D. Wintin Hardahee, so I backtracked to pick up a loose end that would probably turn into nothing. I placed a call to Dr. Bill Dyckes, the surgeon who had operated on Helena Pearson Trescott. A girl in his office told me he was operating but would probably phone in when he was through, so I did not leave a message but drove over to the hospital to see if I could make contact with him there.

A very obliging switchboard girl put a call through to the doctors' lounge on the third floor in the surgical wing and caught him there and motioned me to a phone. I said I was an old friend of Helena Trescott and just wanted to ask him a couple of questions about her. He hesitated and then told me to come on up, and gave me directions.

He came out of the lounge and we walked down the corridor to a small waiting room. He wore a green cotton smock and trousers and a green skullcap. There was a spray of drying blood across the belly of the smock, and he smelled of disinfectants. He was squat and broad and younger than I had expected. His hands were thick, with short, strong-looking fingers, curly reddish hair on his wrists, backs of his hands, and down to the first knuckle of the fingers.

He dropped heavily onto a sofa in the waiting room, sighing, stretching, then pinching the bridge of his nose. He looked up at the wall clock. "Next one'll be all prepped by eleven fifteen, and please God it will be nice, straight, clean, and simple because I'm scheduled for a son of a bitch this afternoon. What'd you want to know about Mrs. Trescott, Mr. McGee?"

"Did she ever have any chance at all?"

"Not by the time I went in the first time. Big juicy metastasized carcinoma right on the large bowel with filaments going out in every direction. Got the main mass of it and as much more as I could. Left some radioactive pellets in there to slow it some."

"Did you tell her she wouldn't make it?"

"I tell each one as much as I think they can safely take, when it's bad news. I realized later I could have told her the works. But I didn't know her well enough then to know how gutsy and staunch she was. So I said I thought I'd gotten it all, but I couldn't be sure, so we'd go into some other treatment to make sure. I didn't tell the daughters because I figured she could read them loud and clear. Told Tom Pike so that he could help cushion it for the girls when the time came."

"Then, how was she the second time?"

"Downhill. Had to go in to clear a stoppage. Damned jungle in there by then. Nothing like the anatomy books. Malignant is quite a word. Turned a good experienced operating-room nurse queasy. Then by the last time there wasn't anything about her that wasn't changed by it, in one way or another, except her eyes. Great eyes on that woman. Like the eyes of a young girl."

"Too bad that Maureen is in such condition now."

"I didn't get in on that. It isn't something you go after

with a knife. But just about everybody else has had a piece of the action. She's had every test anybody around here has ever heard of, and some I think they made up. It would take two men to lift her lab files."

"Does it boil down to some specific area?"

"If by that you mean her head, yes. If you mean neurology, yes. No physical trauma, no tumor, no inhibition of nourishment. Something is screwing up the little circuits in there, the synapses. Tissue deterioration? Rare virus infection? Some new kind of withdrawal that's psychologically oriented? Some deficiency from birth that didn't show until now? Secretion imbalance? Rare allergy? My personal guess, which nobody will listen to because it's not my field, is that the trouble is in some psychiatric area. That fits the suicide impulse. But the shrinkers have gone through that and out the other side, they say. Series of shock treatments, no dice. Sodium Pentothal, no dice. Conversation on the couch, nothing. I thought you were interested in Mrs. Trescott."

"In the whole family, Doctor Dyckes."

"And I just sit here and open up like the family Bible, eh? And you take it all in, just like it was the most ordinary thing in the world to listen to a doctor violate the ethics of his profession."

"I . . . I thought you were responding to an expression of friendly interest and concern, Doctor, and——"

"Bullshit, McGee. Wanted to see if you handled yourself with any kind of sense at all. You do. Know why I'm talking to you about a patient . . . and the patient's family?"

"I guess you want to tell me why."

He brooded for a long time, eyes half closed. "Trying to find the words for what she did for me. Even when there wasn't anything left of her but the pain and her eyes, I'd go sit by her bed when things went wrong for me, like when I lost a young one that I'd prayed I wouldn't lose. Dammit, I was borrowing guts from Helena Trescott. Leaning on her. We talked a lot, up until the time I had to keep her too far under. One night she told me about a man named Travis McGee. She said that you might show up someday and you might ask a lot of questions. 'Tell him how it was, Bill. Don't pretty it up. Trust him. Tell him what you know about my girls. I'm going to ask him to help Maureen, I think.' So, friend, she's the one who made it easy for you. Not your persuasive charm. Okay?"

"Okay. Thanks."

"So where were we?"

"The next thing I was going to try to do was to get you to give me your opinion of Doctor Sherman."

"Too bad about Stew. Good man. Vague spots here and there but generally solid. I mean in the medical knowledge sense. Damned fool about money, like most doctors. We're the prize pigeons of the modern world. Gold bricks, uranium mines in Uganda, you hold it up and we'll buy it."

"I understood he invested in Development Unlimited."

"Which may be as good as gold. The guys who have gone in swear by Tom Pike. Maybe they're getting rich. Good luck to them. I turned down my golden opportunity. I was pretty interested there for a while."

"What put you off it?"

"My brother. He and his wife were down visiting us. He's a big brain in financial circles in New York. Taught economics at Columbia, then got into securities analysis and real estate investment with a couple of the banks. Then he started a no-load mutual fund a few years ago. A hedge fund. They watch him like eagles up there, trying to figure out which way he's going to jump next. I was invited to one of those little get-in-on-the-ground-floor dinners Tom puts on from time to time. Stag. Took my brother along. Tom made quite an impressive talk, I thought. Had me about to grab for my checkbook. When we got home, Dewey told me what was wrong with the things Tom said. It boiled down to this. Tom used some wonderful terms, some very tricky ideas, a lot of explanations of tax shelters and so on. But my brother explained that it didn't hang together. As if he'd memorized things that wouldn't work in the way he said he was using them. Dewey said it was like a ten-year-old kid explaining Einstein to a roomful of relatives who never got past the tenth grade. The words were so big that, by God, it had to be good and had to be right. Dewey told me to stay out. Any spare change I have, I put in his mutual fund. And little by little he's going to make me rich. He promises me he will. You know, I hope he was wrong about Tom Pike. Because if Tom is goofing, a lot of men in Fort Courtney are going to get very, very badly hurt. Look, I better go scrub. Nice to talk to you. She was one very special woman, that Mrs. Trescott."

I tried Hardahee again and struck out. But Janice Holton was home and said sure, I could stop by if I wanted to. I parked in front on the circular drive and went up and rang the doorbell. As I was waiting she came around the side of the house and said, "Oh. It's you. I'm fixing some stuff around in the back. Want to come around? I don't want to leave it half done."

She had newspapers spread on the grass, under a metal chaise, a piece of lawn furniture originally pale blue. The blue paint had been chipped off by hard use. She was giving it a spray coat of flat black DeRusto from a spray can. She wore very brief and very tight fawn-colored stretch shorts, and a faded green blouse with a sun back, and ragged old blue boat shoes. I stood in the shade within comfortable conversation range. She had a deep tan. She moved swiftly and to good effect, limber as a dancer when she bent and turned, and able to sit comfortable as a Hindu, fawn rear propped on the uptilted backs of the boat shoes. She was sweaty with sun and effort, her back glossy, accenting the play of small hard muscles under her hide as she moved.

She turned, tossing her black hair back, and said, "I ran off at the mouth Sunday night. It isn't like me. I must have been lonely."

"Funny. I had the feeling I talked too much. Had the feeling I'd bored you, Janice."

"Excuse me, but I forgot your first name."

"Travis."

"Okay, Travis. So we were a couple of refugees or

something. And excuse me for something else. Meg got a glimpse of you and thought you looked *very* interesting. You know, she *has* been covering for me, but she doesn't know who I've been seeing. She decided it had to be you, so I didn't say yes and I didn't say no. She thinks it is awfully sophisticated for you to bring my husband home drunk so we can put him to bed and go out together. Hmmm. Have I missed anything?"

"That brace over there on the left, under the seat."

"Where? Oh, I see it. Thanks."

She covered the last blue neatly and precisely and straightened up, cocked her head to the side, shook the paint bomb. The marble rattled around inside. "Just about completely gone. I *love* to have something be just enough instead of too much or too little. Want a drink or a cold beer or anything? I've been promising myself a beer."

She led me into the cool house and the cheerful kitchen. She tried to thrust a glass upon me, then admitted that she too preferred it right from the bottle. She leaned against the sink, elegant ankles crossed, uptilted the bottle, and drank until her eyes watered.

"Hah!" she said. "Meg probably saw you drive up. She'll think this is terribly *soigné* too, a little visit just before lunch. She's probably lurking about in the shrubbery, panting."

"As long as I'm nominated, don't you think I ought to know where we've kept all these other assignations?"

"Not assignations. Just to be together. And talk. Talk about everything under the sun. Hold hands like school kids. Cry a little sometimes. Hell! Why shouldn't a man be allowed to cry?"

"They do, from time to time."

"Not enough. Not nearly enough. Well, we had to meet where there would be absolutely no chance of anyone seeing us together."

"Pretty good trick."

"Not terribly difficult, really. We'd arrange a time and both drive to the huge parking lot at the Courtney Plaza and once we had spotted each other, you'd drive out and

I would follow you and you would find a place where we could park both cars and then sit together in one of them and not be seen. Out in one of the groves, or on a dark residential street, or out near the airport, someplace he . . . you thought we'd be safe."

"How would we arrange the date in the first place?"

"You won't have to know that."

"Is that what we were going to do last Saturday? Spend the whole day, or most of it, sitting around in some damned automobile holding hands and crying?"

"Please don't make cheap fun of it."

"Sorry."

"Saturday it might have become something else. Second phase of the affair, or something. Maybe it's just as well Rick spoiled it. I keep yearning for someplace where we could be really alone, really safe. Someplace with walls around us and a roof over us, and a door that will lock. But not a motel, for God's sake. I don't think I could stand a motel. And that would be a risk. You see he . . . he's in a position where a lot depends upon people having total confidence in him. It would be more than just . . . the appearance of infidelity."

"He's a banker?"

"You may call him a banker if you wish. He found a place for us for Saturday. He couldn't get away until about noon. So I was going to drive back and wait for him in the parking lot of a small shopping center north of town, then follow him to the place. He said it was safe and private and nobody would know. He said that not even the person who lived there would ever know we'd been there. So I guess we both knew that if we were ever alone together in a place like that, nothing could help us or save us."

"But good old Rick decided to make the Vero Beach trip."

"He was in horrible shape Monday morning, so stiff and sore and lame he could hardly get out of bed. And terribly hung over, of course. When I told him I'd taken his friend, McGee, back to the Wahini Lodge, he stared at me and then laughed in the most ghastly way. We're not speaking, of course. Just the absolute essentials."

She came and took my empty bottle and dropped the two of them into the tilt-lid kitchen can. "Again I'm doing all the talking, Travis. You have a bad effect on my mouth. Was there something you wanted to see me about, particularly?"

"I guess I've had you on my mind, Janice."

She stared at me, and her frown made two vertical clefts between her dark brows, over the generous nose. She shook her head slowly. "Uh-uh, my friend. If you're thinking what I think you're thinking. Help the embittered lady get her own back? Eye for an eye, and all that? What's the next part of the gambit? Healthy young woman deprived of a sex life, et cetera, et cetera? No, my dear. Not even to keep Meg happy by confirming her suspicions."

"Now that you bring it up, the idea has some merit, I guess. I've had you on my mind for a different reason."

"Such as?"

"Suppose I named your boyfriend by name. The dear, kind, tender, sensitive, wonderful and so on."

"You can't, of course. What are you getting at?"

"But if I did, would you feel you had to go to him and tell him that somebody knows?"

"On a hypothetical basis? Let me see. If you did name him, what would be your point, really, in wanting to be certain? What would you be after?"

"A clue to what kind of man he is."

"He is a marvelous man!"

"Does everybody think so?"

"Of *course* not! Don't be so dense! Any man who has strength and drive and opinions of his own will make enemies."

"Who'll badmouth him."

"Of course."

"Okay, his name is . . . Tompestuous K. Fliggle, Banker."

"Travis, you *are* an idiot."

"These are idiotic times we live in, my dear."

190

And the little inadvertent muscles around her eyes had clued me when I hit the first syllable of the invented name, which was as far as I cared to go.

At a few minutes past noon I read the nameplate on the mailbox at 60 Ridge Lane. Miss Hulda Wennersehn. The name of the real estate firm that managed the garden apartments was on a small sign at the corner. From the first drugstore phone I came to, I called the real estate offices and was switched to a Miss Forrestal. I told her I was with the credit bureau and would appreciate some information on Hulda Wennersehn. She pulled the card and said that Miss Wennersehn, age fifty-one, had been in number sixty for four years and had never been in arrears. I asked if Miss Wennersehn was employed by an insurance company and she said, "Oh, no, unless she changed jobs and didn't inform us. Of course, she'd have no reason to inform us, actually. But we have her as working for Kinder, Noyes, and Strauss. That's a brokerage firm. She works as a cashier." So thank you, my dear.

So I phoned the brokerage house and the switchboard girl told me that, my goodness, it had been at least two years since Miss Wennersehn had worked there. She was working for a real estate company. She gave me the phone number. On a hunch I asked her if a Mr. Tom Pike had ever been with the firm, and she said that he had, but that had been some time ago. The number she gave me turned out to be Development Unlimited.

"Miss Wennersehn? I'll transfer you to . . . oh, excuse me, sir. She is still up at our Jacksonville office. Shall I see if I can find out when she'll be returning?"

I thanked her and told her not to bother.

I went back to the motel to see if there were any messages. Stanger was waiting for me.

16 *SOMETHING HAD* changed Stanger, tautened him, given him nervous mannerisms I had not noticed before. We went to 109. He moved restlessly about. I phoned for sandwiches and coffee.

When I asked him what was wrong, he told me to let him think. He paused at the big window and stood with his hands locked behind him, teetering from heel to toe, looking out at people playing in the pool.

"I could maybe go with one of those security outfits," he said. "Gate guard. Watchman work."

"You get busted?"

"Not yet. But maybe that's what they'll want to do."

"Why?"

"That Mrs. Boughmer was off on some kind of garden club tour. I finally got the daughter to let me in. Went into my act. Want to warn you you're in serious trouble. Withholding information about a capital crime. Maybe I can help you if you level with me now. And so on and so on. Until she split open."

"What was her problem?"

He turned and walked over and sat heavily in the armchair. "She was bellering and squeaking and sobbing. Spraying spit. Words all jammed together she was trying to say them so fast. Grabbing at my hands. Begging. Confessing. Jesus!"

"Confessing what?"

"That poor dim ugly girl was in love with Doc Sherman. Not so much romance and poetry. Passion. Hot pants. You saw her. Any man ever going to lay a hand on her? So there was something she was doing, God only knows what. Last to leave. Lock the doors. Leave the office lights on. Go into the dark treatment room. Do something in there. She wouldn't say what. Something, according to her, that was nasty and evil. Went on for years, I guess. Some kind of release. No idea what Broon was after or how he got in. She was working on the files after Sherman had died, a few days later. She was in the treatment room and the lights suddenly went on and Broon is in the doorway watching her. Told her to put her clothes back on and he'd talk to her in the office. Apparently, McGee, he convinced that poor sick sad homely woman that there was some law, crime against nature, jail her as a degenerate or some damned thing. Told her that if she ever tried to tell anybody Sherman didn't kill himself, he'd have her picked up and taken in right away. He took some kind of 'evidence' away with him. How the hell was I supposed to know she was so close to the edge? All of a sudden she went rigid as a board, bit right through her lip, started whooping and snapping around, eyes out of sight. Followed the ambulance in. Some kind of breakdown. Left a neighbor woman on the lookout for Mrs. Boughmer. Probably Dave Broon slipped the lock on the rear door that night and came easing in."

"That won't be anything to bust you for, Al."

"It isn't that. It's what comes next. Maybe."

"Which is?"

"Dave Broon. I've come right up to it with him. Too many years, too many things. No way to nail him according to the rules I'm supposed to follow. We're supposed to be on the same ball club. He gives the whole thing a bad smell. Maybe there's a time when you don't go by the book. Look, I've got to have somebody with me. The things I'm thinking scare me. I've got to have somebody stop me if I can't stop myself."

"Maybe you'd better think it over."

"Meaning you don't want any part of it."

"If you want me with you, okay. But just for the hell of it, before we see him, can you get a decent check on where he was the night Sherman died, and where he was the afternoon Penny Woertz died?"

"I don't know about last Saturday, but I remember he was up in Birmingham to bring a prisoner back when Sherman died. Anyway, let me see where that fancy little scut might be."

He moved to the bed and used the bedside phone. He would mumble greetings, ask about Broon, listen, hang up, dial another number. He made at least eight calls. He got up and said, "Guess I'll have some time to think it over. He's been here and there, but nobody's got a fix on him in the past hour or so. Might be hanging around the courthouse. He's got cronies over there who feed him little bits of information, probably for cash on the line. Or he could be at city hall for the same reason. Or he could be holed up in that so-called penthouse with a new playmate. Hasn't had one around for a while, so he's due."

He left, saying he would get in touch and pick me up so I could go with him to talk to Dave Broon. After he had gone, I put the lunch tray outside the door so no one would have any reason to come in after it. And before I left, I used one of the oldest and simplest tricks to warn me if anyone came into the room by way of the door while I was gone. I wadded up a sheet of the motel stationery and, as I left, I leaned over and reached back through the opening and placed it on the rug, close to the door, a precise placement because I could measure it by the length of my forearm, from the crook of elbow to the thumb and finger in which I held it. The door opened inward. Anyone entering would brush it away with the door. Even if they had the wit to try to replace it, they could never put it in the same identifiable position as before. When a door opens outward, it is easiest to close it against a bit of matchstick or toothpick inserted at some precise spot and broken off so that it is barely visible from outside the door. But a careful workman can defeat this protection, or the hair and chewing gum device, or the carbon-paper gimmick.

The day blackened, the sky cracked open, and the rain came down, storm gusts whipping the spray of the rebound and the mist of the hot streets, tearing brown fronds off the cabbage palms, shredding the broadleaf

194

plantings, swinging signs and traffic lights. Same kind of storm wind that had made the *Likely Lady* rock her weight against the anchor lines, creaking and grunting. It had been cozy below.

I tried Hardahee. She said he had left for the day, and I could not tell if she was lying. I found Rick Holton's law office. The girl took my name and disappeared. She came back and led me down a paneled corridor. He had a big desk with a window wall behind it that looked out onto a little enclosed court paved with Japanese river stones and with some stunted trees in big white pots. Rain ran down the window wall. He had a lot of framed scrolls on the persimmon paneling of his walls, and framed photographs of politicians, warmly inscribed.

He tried the big confident junior chamber smile, but it had sagged into nothing before the girl had closed the office door.

"Sit down, McGee. Told Sally I didn't want to see anybody. Supposed to be getting through all this damned desk work. Jesus! I read things three times and don't know what I've read. Know where they're getting with the investigation? Noplace. I think it was some crazy. Hell, Penny would have opened the door to anybody. They panicked and ran. One of those lousy meaningless things. They'll pick him up for something else someday, and he'll start talking and hand them this one."

"It might open up. Stanger might come across something."

"He's good."

"Better than your friend Dave Broon?"

He shrugged. "Dave is handy for odd jobs."

"Can I get your opinion on a few things, Holton? Not legal opinion. Personal."

"For what it's worth, which isn't much lately. Everything seems to be going sour. You know, the deal with Penny was going sour. We were about ready to close the books. So why do I miss her so damn much?"

"She was pretty special."

"So Janice was very special. Past tense. I blew the whole bit. For a roll in the hay with Penny Woertz. Nowhere near as good-looking a girl as Janice. What was I trying to prove? With Janice you don't just make a sincere apology and go on from there. Done is done. Total loyalty, given and expected. I've lost her. Funny thing, driving back from Vero Beach, when I had no idea in the world Penny was already dead, I tried to tell Jan that it was something that had just sort of happened. I said it was over. I wasn't *sure* it was over, but I had the feeling that if I told Jan it was, then I'd have to make sure I kept on feeling just the way I felt when she wouldn't leave your room Friday night when I did. That was before we picked up the kids at Citrusdale. She let me talk. I thought she was really thinking it over, giving me a chance. I reached over and put my hand on her arm. You know, she actually shuddered? And she said in a polite voice to please not touch her, it made her stomach turn over. That was the end of it, right there."

"When you were waiting for me Sunday night, did you have any idea of shooting me, Holton?"

He tilted his chair back and looked up at the sound-proofed ceiling, eyes narrowed. "That was pretty dim. Jesus, I don't know. I'd read a stat of that note she wrote you. It made it pretty clear about you two. I was aware of the gun. I had the feeling that my whole life was so messed up nothing mattered too much. And you'd hit me harder than anybody ever hit me in my life. I'm still sore from it. Four days and I still hurt when I take a deep breath. I've got a lousy temper. Maybe, McGee. All things considered, I just might have. Scares me to think of it. Without Janice and without Penny, things aren't all that bad. I've got a lot of friends. I do a good job for my clients. I made a good record as an assistant state attorney and I've got a good chance of becoming county attorney next year, and that's worth a minimum forty thousand, plus other business it brings in. They say money won't buy happiness, but you can sure rent yourself some. I'm grateful to you for suckering me. And thanks for taking me home. Where's the gun anyway?"

"I turned it over to Stanger and he gave it back to me."

He was puzzled. "Why'd he do that?"

"It's just sort of a temporary loan, just a little delay in officially turning it over to him."

"When you give it back to him, tell him to hang on to it. I don't think I ought to have one around. Not for a while. Maybe not ever. But why does Al Stanger think you need a gun?"

"Just a whim, maybe."

"You mean you'd rather not say? Okay. Yesterday morning I checked out what you said about yourself. I phoned Tom Pike and he said you were an old friend of Mrs. Trescott and her daughters."

"If you could check that easily, why didn't you check before you and Penny pulled that stupid deal, that grade C melodrama?"

He blushed. "So now it seems wild and stupid. We sort of talked each other into it. If it had worked—and you have to admit it came close—then I would have maybe found out from whatever papers you were carrying on your person, the missing piece. We'd narrowed it down to one theory that looked better and better. The tall man could have been in some kind of drug traffic."

"Oh, come *on!*"

"Wait a minute now! I held back a little on you when we talked in your room. Penny followed my lead. The man seen leaving Sherman's office was carrying a case of some kind, light-colored and heavy. No controlled drugs were missing, according to the office records. But there was no control on the stuff he ordered for his experimentations. He did some animal experimentations along with the other stuff. He could have been ordering experimental compounds, couldn't he?"

"Aren't you reaching?"

"I talked to Helen Boughmer the day after he died. She was convinced that a lot of stuff might be missing from the room in back, and she was going to check the file of special orders against the inventory of what was left. *She* believed he'd been killed. And two days later, she'd changed completely. She said she had changed her mind. She said she believed he'd killed himself. She said she had checked the special orders and nothing was missing. I asked her to produce the file. She claimed she couldn't find it. And she never did find it. Now somebody, dammit, had to get to her. If Sherman had killed himself, why would anybody take the time and trouble to shut her mouth. She was a changed woman. She acted terrified."

"Then, why would I come back here, if I was the one who killed Doctor Sherman? What would there be here for me?"

"Now you can say I'm reaching. Why would Tom Pike pay you twenty thousand in cash? It was one of those crazy breaks you get sometimes that one of my partners here saw him giving the money to a man who matches your description. Let's say Sherman stepped out of line when Maureen Pike was so critically ill at the time of her miscarriage, and gave her something not authorized for use on patients. Suppose he did this with Tom's knowledge and consent, and whatever it was, the side effect was some kind of brain damage? Hell, it kind of dwindles off because it doesn't seem as if it would give anybody enough leverage to pry money out of Tom Pike. But you'd seen Tom, and even if we didn't find a thing except a heavy piece of money on you, that would mean some kind of confirmation."

"Personal opinion again, please. Do you think Doctor Sherman killed his wife?"

"Ben Gaffney and I—he's the state attorney—went up one side of that and down the other. Going after him with a circumstantial case just didn't add up. We could show motive and opportunity, but there was absolutely no way to prove the cause of death. Do I think he did? Yes. So does Ben. The specialists we talked to said it was highly unlikely there could have been such a sudden deterioration in her condition that she could go into deep coma after the amount of insulin she had apparently taken. But 'highly unlikely' isn't enough to go to court with. So we closed out the investigation finally."

"Who was handling it?"

"The death occurred in county jurisdiction. Dave

Broon was handling it, under joint direction of my office and the sheriff. If Dave could have come up with something that strengthened the case, it would still have been a pretty unpopular indictment."

"Now, to get back to Sherman's death, do you have the feeling that Penny had any kind of lead at all that she hadn't told you about yet?"

He looked startled and then grim. "I see where *that* one is aimed. I don't really . . . wait a minute. Let me think." He leaned back and ground at his eyes with the heels of his hands. "I don't know if this is anything. It would have been . . . a week ago. Last Tuesday. She was working an eleven-to-six-in-the-morning shift, a postoperative case, and that was the last time she was on that one. I pulled out of here early. About quarter to four and went over to see her. She'd just gotten up. She had dreamed about Doctor Sherman. She was telling me about it. I wasn't paying much attention. She stopped all of a sudden and she had a funny expression. I asked her what the trouble was and she said she'd just thought of something, that the dream had reminded her of something. She wouldn't tell me. She said she had to ask somebody a question first, and maybe it was nothing at all, but maybe it meant something. Very mysterious about it."

"Can you remember anything about the dream?"

"Not much. Nutty stuff. Something about him opening a door in his forehead and making her look in and count the times a little orange light in there was blinking."

"But you don't know if she asked anyone that question?"

"She never brought it up again."

"While you were . . . conducting this unofficial investigation of Sherman's death, were you telling Janice about it, about things like the file the Boughmer woman wouldn't produce?"

"I guess I was telling her more than I usually would. Hell, I was trying to cover for the time I was spending with Penny. But Janice was turning ice cold, and fast. She wasn't buying it. I kept trying, but she wasn't buying it. She found out, I guess."

"Somebody told her about it practically as soon as it began."

"No kidding! Some real pal."

"Do you think she's found some other man?"

"I keep trying not to think about that. What's it to you?"

"Let's say it isn't just a case of big-nose, Holton."

"I get home and that damned Meg is either over at the house with her kids, or the kids are over at Meg's house. No note from Janice. No message, nothing. So she comes home and I say where have you been, and she says out. Looks so damned smug. But I keep telling myself that when she comes home, she doesn't have that look. You know? Something about the mouth and the hair and the way they walk. A woman who's been laid looks laid. Their eyes are different too. If she's got somebody, he's not playing his cards right. If she likes him and she's sore at me, and I know she's known about Penny, all he'd have to do would be lay one hand on her to get her going, and she'd take over from there. A lousy way to talk about the wife, I guess. But I know her. And she's no wife now. Not anymore. Never again, not for me."

"Does she think Sherman was murdered?"

"She was fond of him. She's sure of it. Not from anything I dug up or any chain of logic I explained. She operates on instinct. She says he couldn't have and to her that's it."

"So she wanted to have you find out who did it?"

"Not because she was hot to have somebody punished, but more because it would clear his name."

"What do you know about the trouble Tom Pike got into at Kinder, Noyes, and Strauss?"

"What? You jump around pretty fast. All I know is the shop talk I heard about it. He was a very hot floor man. He had people swearing by him. He went in there and built up one hell of a personal following. High fliers, discretionary accounts, a lot of trading in and out, accounts fully margined. And he's a very persuasive guy. He made a lot of money for a lot of people in this town, in a very short time. But there was one old boy who came down to

200

retire, and he had a portfolio of blue chips. He had Telephone and General Motors and Union Carbide. He signed an agreement to have Tom Pike handle his holdings on a discretionary basis. As I understand it, Tom cashed in all the old boy's blues and started swinging with the proceeds. Fairchild Camera, Texas Instrument, Teledyne, Litton. At the end of three months the total value of the old boy's holdings was down by about twelve thousand. And Tom had made about forty trades, and the total commissions came to eight grand. The old boy blew the whistle on Tom, claiming that the agreement was that Tom would commit only twenty percent of his holdings in high-risk investments, that Tom had ignored the understanding and put the whole amount in high fliers, and had churned the account to build up his commissions. He had his lawyer send the complaint directly to the president of the firm in New York. They sent down a couple of lawyers and a senior partner to investigate. Brokerage houses are very sensitive about that kind of thing. Big conference, as I understand it. Complete audit of all trades. Tom Pike claimed that the man had told him that he was after maximum capital gains in high-risk issues and that he had other resources and could afford the risk. The man denied it. It looked as if Tom was in serious trouble. But one of the female employees was able to back up Tom's story. She said the man had phoned her to get verification of the status of his account and his buying power, and that when he had been twenty-five thousand ahead of the game, he had told her over the phone that getting out of the tired old blue chips and letting Mr. Pike handle his account was the smartest move he had ever made. The old man denied ever saying that."

"What was her name?"

"Hilda something. Long last name. The cashier."

"Hulda Wennersehn?"

"If you know about it, why are you asking me?"

"I *don't* know about it. What happened?"

"They decided that in view of Tom's knowing the man was retired and needed security, he had used bad judgment. They slapped his wrist by giving him a sixty-day

201

suspension. And they busted a couple of the more recent trades and absorbed the loss in order to build the old man's equity back to almost what he started with. That's when Tom said the hell with it and started Development Unlimited."

"And Miss Wennersehn now works for him."

"So?"

"So nothing. Just a comment. How did the business community react to Pike's problem?"

"The way these things go, at first everybody was ready to believe the worst. People pulled their accounts. They said that while he was looking good with their money, he was piling up commissions. They said he'd been lucky instead of smart. Then it swang right around the other way when he was pretty well cleared. He was out of the brokerage business, and so what he did was move his big customers right out of the market, off-the-record advice, and put them into land syndication deals. Better for him because you can build some very fancy pyramids, using equities from one as security for loans on the next, and he can cut himself in for a piece by putting the deals together. He's moved very fast."

"Credit good?"

"He got past that iffy place when Doc Sherman's death fouled up some moves he was going to make. His credit has to be good."

"What do you mean?"

"He's got bankers tied into the deals, savings and loan, contractors, accountants, realtors. Hell, if he ever screwed up, the whole city would come tumbling down."

"Along with the new building?"

"All four and a half million worth of it. Land lease in one syndicate, construction loans and building leases in another."

"Very quick for a very young man."

"How old are the fellows running the big go-go funds? How old are the executives in some of the great big conglomerates? He's quick and tough and bold, and you don't know what his next move is going to be until it's all sewed up."

202

"Last item. How well do you know Hardahee?"

"More professionally than socially. Wint is very solid. Happens to be under the weather right now. Scheduled this morning at ten on an estate case where I represent one of the parties at interest and Stan Krantz appeared and asked for a postponement because Wint is ill and nobody else over there is up on the case. It's pretty complex. Jesus! All this work to do and I just can't seem to make my mind work. McGee, what are you after? What's this all about?"

"I guess it's about a dead nurse."

"That mean that much to you?"

"She was very alive and it was a dingy way to die."

"So you're sentimental? You're carried away because she was so sore at me she took you on? All she was, McGee, was——"

"Don't say it."

"You mean that, don't you?"

"Say it then, if you're sure you want to find out."

He looked at me and rubbed the back of his hand across his lips. "I think I'll take your word for it."

"You're mean in a curious way, Holton. Small mean. Like some kind of a dirty little kid."

"Go to hell," he said with no emphasis at all. He swiveled his chair. He was looking out at his little oriental garden patio as I walked out. The rain had stopped.

17   *IT WAS FIVE* when I got back to 109. I unlocked the door and leaned over and reached around it. No wad of paper anywhere near where it should be. I opened the door the rest of the way. The balled-up piece of stationery was five feet from the door, where it had rolled when somebody had opened the door.

It seemed a fair guess that if it had been a maid or a housekeeper, I would have found it in the wastebasket. I checked the phones first. I took the base plate off the one by the bed and found that my visitor was going first class. He'd put a Continental 0011 in there, more commonly known as a two-headed bug. It would pick up anything in the room and also over the phone and transmit it on an FM frequency. Effective maximum range probably three hundred feet. Battery good for five days or so, when fresh. It goes for around five hundred dollars. So he could be within range, listening on an FM receiver, or he could have a voice-activated tape recorder doing his listening for him. Or he could have a pickup and relay receiver-transmitter plugged into an AC outlet within range, and be reading me from a much greater distance. One thing was quite certain. The sounds of my taking the screws out of the base plate with the little screwdriver blade on the pocket knife would either have alerted him at once or would when he played the tape back.

So I said, "Come to the room and we'll have a little talk. Otherwise you're out five hundred bucks worth of playtoy." I took it out and thumbed the little microswitch to off. I then made a fairly thorough check of the under-side of all the furniture and any other place I thought a backup mike and transmitter might be effectively con-cealed. The professional approach is to plant two. Then the pigeon finds one and struts around congratulating himself, but he's still on the air. If the same person, Broon, had checked me over the first time, then I had two more reasons to believe he wasn't much more than moderately competent.

I was finding a good place for the gun when Stanger phoned me. He said he hadn't been able to get a line on Broon as yet. He said the continuing investigation on the murder of Penny Woertz hadn't turned up a thing as yet. He had checked on Helen Boughmer and found they had her under heavy sedation.

I told him I had no progress to report.

I didn't actually. All I had was a lot more unanswered questions than before. I stretched out on the bed to ask them all over again.

Assume that Tom Pike had arranged that he and Janice Holton have their first assignation, in the full meaning of the word, in the apartment where Hulda Wennersehn lived. Janice couldn't get in touch with him to tell him she couldn't make it. So he had gone to the parking lot where they had arranged to meet and had finally realized she wasn't going to be there. Assume he went to the apartment alone and that he went to Penny's place in the late afternoon and she let him in and he shoved the shears into her throat. He tracked some blood into the Wennersehn apartment. He cleaned it up, cleaned up his shoes and maybe pants legs, and burned the rags.

But he had expected Janice to be there. He had changed his plan. What could the original plan have been? Janice certainly would have an understandable motive for killing her husband's girl friend. Having her nearby at the time of the murder could establish opportunity.

So if he planned to frame Janice Holton for the murder of Penny, and if Janice couldn't show up to be the patsy, why would he go ahead and kill Penny anyway? Lorette Walker had found out from the cleaning woman that somebody had stretched out on Hulda Wennersehn's bed.

So he had some thinking to do. He could cancel out and try to set it up another time. The death of the nurse would, of course, bust up the little duet of Penny and Rick, the two who had the unshakable belief Sherman hadn't killed himself. Did Penny have some random piece of information that she had not yet pieced into the picture and that made haste imperative?

Or it could have been some kind of sick excitement that grew and grew inside the brain of the man stretched out on the bed, until at last he got up and walked to Penny's place and did it because he had been thinking of it too long not to do it, even though the original plan was no longer possible.

Of course, it was possible that he might have at last decided to just go talk to the nurse and see if she did have the missing bit of information that he suspected she might have. Then, while he was with her, she might have made the intuitive leap, and suddenly he had no choice but to kill her, suddenly and mercilessly.

But my speculations kept returning to what the original plan could have been. What good would it do to knock Janice Holton out or drug her and set her up for the murder when under interrogation she would explain why she was at the Wennersehn apartment and who she was with? I tried to figure out how he could have planned to leap that hurdle. Kill them both and set it up as murder and suicide? That would have been a complex and tricky and terribly dangerous procedure.

Suddenly I realized that he could have framed her very safely, very beautifully, if she were unable to remember how she came to be there, in fact could not remember the assignation with Pike or even being in the Wennersehn woman's apartment or in Penny's apartment.

I found myself pacing around the room with no memory of getting off the bed. Suppose Pike had some way of making certain Maureen didn't remember a thing. No memory of suicide attempts. Couldn't Janice have no memory of committing a murder? Suppose she found herself in Penny's apartment with the dead girl, with no memory of how she got there?

Penny had been going to tell me something Dr. Sherman said about memory and digital skills. Digital? Skill with numbers or with fingers? Manual skills, maybe.

Maybe that Dormed thing fouled up memory. Electrosleep. Portable unit, Biddy had told me.

I needed some fast expert opinions. I had no problem remembering the name of the neurologist in Miami. When your spine has been damaged by an angry man belting you with a chunk of two by four and your legs go numb, and somebody fixes what you were certain was a broken back and wasn't, you don't forget the name.

Dr. Steve Roberts. I got through to him in fifteen minutes. "Excuse me, Trav," he said. "This lady I live with has just handed me a frosty delicious glass. There. I have tested the drink and kissed the lady. What's on your mind? Back trouble?"

"No. Some information. Do you know anything about an electrosleep machine called a Dormed?"

"Yes, indeed. Nice little gadget. Very effective."

"If somebody used one a great deal, could it destroy their memory?"

"What? No. Absolutely not. Not enough current to destroy anything. If you keep hitting people with big charges, you don't destroy any particular process. You just turn them into a vegetable in all respects. Each series of shock treatments destroys brain cells. So do alcoholic spasms, if you have enough of them over a long enough period of time."

"How about convulsions? Like a woman might have if she had a kidney failure and lost a baby."

"Eclampsia, you mean? No, I doubt it. That sends the blood pressure up like a skyrocket, and before any brain damage could occur, you'd probably have a broken blood vessel in the brain. Where are you, anyway?"

"Fort Courtney."

"Practicing medicine without a license?"

"Practicing, maybe. But not medicine. Steve, can you think of any way you could make a person lose their memory?"

"*All* of it? Total amnesia?"

"No. Just of recent things."

"How long do you want this effect to last?"

"Permanently."

"Sometimes a good solid concussion will do it. Traumatic amnesia. Lots of people who recover after an accident lose a couple of hours or days out of their life and it seems to be gone forever. But there's no guarantee."

"Is there any chemical or medical way to do it?"

"Well . . . I wouldn't say that there's anything you could call a recognized procedure. I mean, there isn't much call for it, as I imagine you can understand."

"Is there a way?"

"Will you hold a minute. I think I can lay a hand on what I want."

I waited for at least two full minutes before he came back on the line. "Trav? I have to give you the layman's short course in how the brain works. You have about ten billion neurons in your head. These are tiny cells that transmit tiny electric charges. Each little neuron contains, among other things, about twenty million molecules of ribonucleic acid, called RNA for short. This RNA manufactures protein molecules—don't ask me how. Anyway, these protein molecules are related to the function we call memory. With me so far?"

"I think so."

"In certain experiments it has been shown that if you force laboratory animals to learn new skills, more RNA is produced in the brain, and thus more protein molecules are produced. Also, if you inject rats with magnesium pemoline, which doubles, at least, the RNA production, you have rats that learn a lot faster and remember longer. So they've tried reverse proof by injecting rats and mice with a chemical that interferes with the process by which the RNA produces the protein molecule. Teach a mouse to find its way through a maze, then inject it, and it forgets everything it just learned."

"What do they inject?"

"A substance called puromycin. At one university they've been treating goldfish with it, and they have some very stupid goldfish out there. Don't learn a thing and can't remember a thing."

"What would happen if you injected a person with puromycin?"

"I don't think anybody ever has. If it works the way it does on the lab animals, you'd wipe out the memory of what had recently happened, maybe forever. Personally, I'd rather be given magnesium pemoline. In fact, I don't know how I'm getting along without it. As to puromycin, I have no idea what the side effects would be."

"Could anybody buy it?"

"Any doctor could, or any authorized lab or research institute. What in the *world* have you gotten into?"

"I don't know yet."

"Will you tell me someday?"

"If it wouldn't bore you. Say, what about memory and digital skills?"

"What about it?"

"Well, make a comment."

"There seems to be a kind of additional memory function in the brain stem and in the actual motor nerves and muscles. We've discovered that a man can have a genuine amnesia, regardless of cause, and suppose he has been a jeweler all his life and you hand him a jeweler's loup. More often then not, without knowing why he does so, he will lift it to his eye, put it in place and hold it there, like a monocle. Give a seamstress a thimble, and she'll put it on the right finger. We had a surgeon here once with such bad aphasia he couldn't seem to make any connection to reality at all. But when we put a piece of surgical thread in his hand, he began to tie beautiful little surgical knots, one-handed, without even knowing what he was doing. Shall I go on?"

"No. That should do it."

"Don't turn your back on anybody holding a two by four."

"Never again." I thanked him and hung up.

An hour later I stood screened by the shrubbery on the grounds of a lake-shore house, empty and for sale, and saw the station wagon come out of the Pike driveway and turn toward me on the way to town. The two daughters of Helena, blond, dressed for the party, smiling, Biddy at the wheel and Maureen beside her.

I could reasonably assume that Tom Pike was already in the city, making certain of the arrangements, seeing that his guests would be taken care of. I moved through the screen of plantings, along the road shoulder, angled back along the property line to a point where I could look at the big house. Both cars were gone. Mosquitoes sang their little hunger note into my ears, and a bluejay flew to a pine limb directly over me and called me foul names and accused me of unspeakable practices.

I crossed the drive and the yard to the rear door and knocked loudly and waited. After the second try, with no answer, I tried to slip the lock, but there was too much overlap in the door framing, so I went along the back of the house and used a short sturdy pry bar on the latch of the first set of sliding glass doors. I had stopped en route at a shopping plaza and bought it, thinking of the sturdy construction of the steel cabinet I had seen in Maureen's bathroom. The metal latch tore easily and I slid the glass door and sliding screen open, glad that they had not yet adopted that most simple and effective device now being used more and more to secure sliding glass doors, one-inch round hardwood cut to proper length and laid in the track where the door slides.

I slid the foot-long pry bar back inside my slacks, the hook end over my belt, and went swiftly upstairs to Maureen's room. There was a party scent of perfume and bath soap in the still air, overlaying the constant undertone of medications. I knelt on the yarn rug in the bathroom and examined the lock on the metal cabinet. It was solid-looking, with such a complex shape of orifice for the key I could assume that trying to pick it would take too much time and patience. I bent the steel lip with the chisel-shaped end of the bar far enough so that I could work the curved nail-puller end into it. I held the cabinet with one hand and pulled slowly on the bar until suddenly the lock gave way and a flying bit of metal clinked against the tile wall.

There were all the usual bathroom nostrums and medications in the cabinet, things that could be harmful to children—iodine, aspirin, rubbing alcohol. There were syringes and injection needles laid out on a pad of surgical cotton. There was a box of disposable sterilized hypodermics. There was a little row of prescription medicines, pills in bottles and boxes, and there were only three small bottles of medication for injection, with a screw cap covering the rubber diaphragm through which the colorless solution was to be drawn into the hypo. Each had a prescription number, the same number. Two were full, one half empty. It seemed to be a very meager supply compared with enough needles for a nurse's station. The drugstore was Hamilton Apothecary, Grove Hills Shopping Center.

I knelt, pondering, automatically listening for any sound in the house. Biddy had said she had learned to give Maureen shots. So the prescription sedative could have been drawn off in whole or in part, and puromycin injected into the bottle. I took one of the two full bottles and the partially empty one. The twist caps on the full ones were still sealed. I realized that the placement of the three bottles bothered me. They were set out midway on the metal shelf, neither back against the rear, nor out at the edge. The other items on the other shelves were set back, taller items at the rear. So something could have been taken out, something that had stood behind the smaller bottles.

I got up and prowled and found a small flashlight on the nightstand in Biddy's room. I knelt again and shone the beam of light at a very flat angle against the metal shelf. There was a very, very faint coating of dust on the shelf, and I discovered that in the area behind where the three small bottles had stood there were four circular areas about the size of fifty-cent pieces where there was no dust. So four bottles or containers had rested there and had been removed very recently.

Deductive logic is self-defeating in that it is like the old-time taffy pull. Stretch it too far and too thin and it cools and sags and breaks. I had projected reasoning into an area where there were too many plausible alternatives.

Also I had the suspicion that all along I had been trying to make logical deductions on the basis of someone's actions and reactions who did not move in any reasoning predictable pattern.

If there had been something removed from the cabinet and if that substance was essential to keep Maureen Pearson Pike in her present childlike state, then either the necessity for keeping her in that condition had ended or she could not return to this house.

I reached my rented car in two minutes, no more. The sun was going down. A fat lady on hands and knees, grubbing in a flower bed, straightened up and stared at me from under the brim of a huge Mexican straw hat, her mouth a little round O as I went by at a full run, shoe soles whapping the suburban asphalt. I waved.

I made it into town in perhaps eight minutes, leaving a black spoor of rented rubber here and there. The new building was up on pillars, to provide parking room underneath. The earth around the building was still raw from construction efforts, the big sign listing prime contractor, architect, subcontractors, and future occupants still in place, portions of the sidewalk still fenced off, with temporary wooden walkways along the curbing. While still a half dozen blocks away I had seen, in the dusk, the lighted windows at the top floor. Perhaps forty cars were under the building, clustered in a casual herd over near the ramp and stairways that led up into the building. With no lights in the parking area, they looked like a placid herd of some kind of grazing creature, settling down for the night.

I started to park near them, then thought I might want to leave quickly, and latecomers might block me in. I swung around to the right, away from them, and parked, heading out, not far from the entrance I had used and off to the right of it. I got out and took my jacket off the seat and put it on. Revolver and pry bar were tucked away under the front seat, so I locked up.

Just as I took the first step toward the car cluster and the entrance up into the new building, I heard a faint cat sound, a thin yowl, then a thick, fat, heavy sound that ended the cat cry. It was a whomping thud, as if somebody had dropped a sack of wet sand onto the cat. There was a curious aftersound, a resonating, deep-toned *brong,* a vibration of the prestressed and reinforced structure overhead. I turned and went out that entrance driveway toward the sidewalk. The building was set back in that area, so that the roofing over the first part of the parking area was but one story high.

There were no pedestrians on the street. At the furthest corner cars were stacked waiting for the light to change. I went over to the temporary wooden walkway, roofed for pedestrian protection. I jumped and caught the wooden edge, pulled myself up onto the rough plywood roofing, and from there clambered up onto the permanent roof over that portion of the parking area underneath.

That roof portion was about fifty feet deep and a hundred and fifty wide. There was a long band of fading red across the western horizon, and the daylight had diminished everything to varying shades of gray. I could see from the construction thus far that doors opened out onto the roof area, and that it was designed to become some sort of patio, perhaps an outdoor dining area for a restaurant lease in the new structure.

Evidently large items of equipment had been derricked up onto that area and uncrated there and taken in through the double doors. The skeletal crates, pried and splintered, and various wrapping and packing materials were piled near the wall of the structure. That wall soared twelve stories straight up to the lighted windows of the top floor. I came upon the body of Maureen Pearson Pike just beyond the jumble of crates and packing materials.

She lay on her back about three feet from the side of the building and almost parallel to it. The upper part of her body was a little closer to the building than her legs were. She wore a gray-blue suit, a white blouse, one blue lizard pump. The other was nearby. I had seen the color of the suit when she and Biddy had gone driving by.

She was ugly, even though her face was undamaged. The impact had jellied her, inside the durable human hide. She was a long sack, roughly tubular, still enclosing all the burst meat and smashed bone, except where pink splinters came through the left sleeve of the suit near the elbow. Her mouth was wide open and unmoving. Her eyes were half open. She was flattened against the roof and bulged wrongly along the contours of her, so that the woman-shape was gone.

She had landed, as if with a purposeful neatness, with most of her on a crumpled sheet of heavy brown packing paper. It was that slightly waxy waterproofed paper they use to wrap pieces of heavy equipment when they are shipped in open crates, bolted down to heavy timber pallets. Where it was torn I could see that it was a sandwich of two layers of brown paper enclosing a black, tarry core.

I sat on my heels beside her. I touched the gloss of her hair, then closed her eyes. I smelled all those sharp familiar odors of sudden death. She was cooling meat, the spoiling process beginning. Still on my heels, I craned my neck and looked up. No row of heads up there, staring in sick fascination down the steep canyon drop to the disastrous impact.

I turned and looked at the building across the street. It was a much older building, an office building four stories high. All the windows were dark. I moved the edge of a crate that pinned the paper down. I gently moved her legs onto the paper. I brought a corner of it up and around her and tucked it under the flattened waist at the far side of her. I moved between her and the building and hesitated, then put my hands against the body and rolled it. That single piece was not big enough. I found another, bigger piece, big as a bed sheet, and swiftly straightened it out, put a corner under her and rolled her halfway up in it, then folded the top and bottom corners in, and rolled her up the rest of the way.

In the pile of crates I found some tangles of heavy hairy twine. I cut three pieces with my pocketknife and then I tied the long cylindrical bundle once around the middle and at points midway between the middle and each end.

I started to lose myself as I was doing the knots. I found myself making them too neat and making little throat-sounds of satisfaction at how neat and nice they were, and at what a splendid job I was doing. So I hauled myself back from that dark brink and made a quick search of the area and came upon a place a little better than I had hoped to find. It was a service hatch set into the side of the building, perhaps three feet square. Four big wing nuts held the metal plate in place. I took it off. The space was only about two feet deep behind it, ending at the grilled cover for some kind of big foam airfilters.

I went to her and looked up, looked at the windows across the street, and then picked her up. She was a stubborn, clumsy burden, improbably heavy. I had to stand it

214

on end, lock my arms around it, and carry it in a straining, spread-legged waddle, across sixty feet of roof to the open service hatch. The paper was cracklingly heavy, the body somberly resistant. I forced it into a sitting position, pushed it back-first into the space, then bent the legs at the knee and pushed them in. The body lay tilted against the grillwork.

Parcel. All tied and stowed. Girl in a plain brown wrapper. Suddenly I realized that though I knew from the weight distribution which end was head and which feet, I had lost track of back and front. So either I had forced her into a sitting position or she was . . .

It was a sick horror, a viscid something that wells into the brain and stops all thought and motion. I shuddered and slammed the metal plate back on and turned the wing nuts down solidly. Only when I straightened did I realize I was soaked. I had sweated through my shirt, jacket, and the waistband of my slacks.

I went swiftly across the roof, made certain I would not be observed, then dropped to the plywood roof of the walkway and swung down and dropped to the sidewalk. As I started in, a car horn gave a warning beep and I moved aside. More guests for the party. I took my time and let them go up in the elevator first.

18 *I STEPPED OUT* of the elevator into party time. Gold rug, deep and resilient. Air conditioning laboring against too much smoke and too much body heat. Jabble and roar of dozens of simultaneous conversations. Two men in red coats at the bar set up in the impressive reception room of Development Unlimited.

Waitresses edging and balancing their careful way through the crush with trays of cocktails, trays of cocktail food with toothpicks stuck in each exotic little chunk. Girl in a cloth of gold mini-something and a gold cowboy hat and a golden guitar, wandering about with a fixed smile she had learned to wear while singing.

As I had come up alone in the elevator I had stared at myself in the mirror in the elevator. My face looked grainy and did not seem to fit. I had prodded at it with my fingers to make it fit. And I wondered if one eye had always looked bigger and starier than the other, and I had just never noticed. My lightweight jacket was dark enough so that it was not too evident how I had sweated it out. But it had been nervous sweat. It had turned ice cold. Not only did I feel as if I smelled somewhat like a horse, I felt that the exercise boy should trot me back and forth in front of the stalls for a time and rub me down or I'd catch the grobbles.

The guests were the business and investment community, the successful men of Fort Courtney and their women. Professional men, growers, bankers, merchants, contractors, realtors, brokers. Forties and fifties and sixties. Booming voices that spoke of confidence, optimism, low handicaps, capital gains. Many of their women had brittle questing eyes, appraising the hair, dress, and manner of their friends and acquaintances, checking to see who had come with whom.

It was easy to pick out the office staff. They were younger, and they seemed tense with the effort to be sociable and agreeable. I picked up a drink at the bar as protective coloration and moved along into what was apparently the largest area of the office suite, the bullpen, soon to be filled with girls, files, desks, duplicators, and electronic accounting equipment.

I saw Biddy Pearson in a small group at the far side of the room, talking animatedly. I worked my way over toward her, circling other conversation groups. She wore a little turquoise suit with a small jacket and short skirt. The jacket and the skirt fastened down the left side from shoulder to hip with five big brass old-fashioned galoshes-clamps, three on the jacket and two on the skirt. Her stockings were an ornate weave of heavy white thread with a mesh big enough for the standard seining net for bait.

She spotted me and looked flatteringly pleased and beckoned me over, introduced me to Jack and Helen Something, Ward and Ellie Somethingelse, and I moved in such a way as to block her out of the group just enough so that it dispersed. I did not trust my voice. I was afraid it would make a quacking sound. But it came out with reasonable fidelity as I asked her, "How are things going?"

"Beautifully! Tom is *so* pleased. Don't you think the decorator did a fabulous job?"

"Very nice."

"And Maurie is being an absolute dear! She seems to understand how important this is, really. And she's really being quite gracious." She went to tiptoe and lifted her chin to look about for Maureen.

So you take the gamble as you find it, and you make it up as you go along. "She certainly looks very, very lovely. That's a good color on her."

"Oh! You saw her already."

"Yes. Down in the lobby."

She was still looking for her, so it was a slow take. She turned toward me. "What? Where?"

"Down in the lobby."

"When?"

"I don't know. I've been here just long enough to get a drink. Five minutes ago? She got off the elevator when I got on."

She clamped her fingers around my wrist. "Was she alone?"

"Yes."

"My God, Travis, why didn't you stop her and bring her back up here?"

"Look, Biddy. She looked fine. She told me to go right on up and join the party. She said she had to get something out of the car. She said she'd be right back. Was I

217

supposed to grab her and bring her back up here, kicking and screaming?"

"Oh, she's so *sly!* Oh *damn* her, anyway. Just when everything was going *so* well. Tom was dubious about bringing her. But she seemed so . . . kind of better organized. Excuse me. I'd better find Tom. I thought she was still with him." She made a wry mouth. "And he probably thinks she's with me. He'll be sick, absolutely sick."

I found windows and oriented myself and went to a wide corridor that led past small offices to the big offices at the end. People were roaming up and down the corridor, being given the tour by some of the Development Unlimited staff. I turned a corner and went into an office and looked out and down and estimated I was not more than fifteen feet too close to the street side. I moved back toward the corner of the corridor and realized it had to be a room with a closed door. Almost all the others were open for inspection.

A pretty little redheaded woman came trotting along and stopped and stared up at me. She wore green and a pint of diamonds and a wide martini smile. "Well, hello there, darling! Are you one of *his* darling new engineers? Christ, you're a towering beast, aren't you? I'm Joanie Mace way down here."

"Hello, Joanie Mace. I'm not an engineer. I'm a mysterious guest."

"With a lousy empty glass? Horrors! Wait right here, mysterious guest. Don't move. Don't breathe. I'm a handmaiden."

She trotted away. My side of the corridor was empty. I heard voices approaching. I opened the door and stepped into a small office, unlighted. As I closed the door I saw that it was stacked with cartons of office forms and supplies. I made my way to the windows and found that the center window was fixed glass but that the narrower ones on either side cranked inward. A sliding brace stopped them when they were open perhaps eighteen inches. They were five feet tall, and the sill was a foot from the floor. The one on the left was open. I leaned and looked down.

It was the right one. I closed it, then pulled my jacket sleeve down across the heel of my hand and pressed the turn latch until it clicked into the fully latched position. As I turned, my toe came down on something soft. I could tell by the feel of it that it was a small leather evening bag. I shoved it into the front of my shirt and tightened my belt another notch.

I opened the door a careful fraction of an inch. A chattering group was approaching. When they had passed, I took the chance and walked out, perhaps too exaggeratedly casual, but there was no one there to fault the performance. I leaned against the corridor wall. Mrs. Mace brought me my drink, scuttling, holding it high, proud of her accomplishment. It was an extraordinarily nasty martini. I gave extravagant thanks. She said I should come by Sunday and swim in her pool. She would round up a swinging group. We'd all drink gallons of black velvets. Delighted. Yes, indeed.

We drifted along behind a group and ended up in the big room. Biddy came quickly to me and drew me aside. She looked determined and angry.

"Trav, I haven't told Tom and I don't intend to. Sooner or later he's going to find out she's missing and that will be time enough. I'm just not going to let my sister spoil the best part of it for him. She's done enough spoiling already. Would you please do me a very special favor?"

"Sure."

"Go down and start checking every bar you can find, and there are quite a few within three or four blocks of here. If you find her and if she isn't in bad shape yet, bring her back, please. But if she's had it, stay with her and put her in the station wagon down below. The tag is——"

"I know the car."

"Thanks *so* much! Poor Trav. Always doing stupid favors for the dreary Pearson family. And look, dear, do *not* ever let Tom know that I knew she was missing. He'd kill me. He would think I should have told him at once. But, darn it all . . . and . . . thanks again."

I started the slow journey through the crush of guests. I had to pass a group standing in respectful attention, listening to Tom Pike. He stood, tall, vital, dark, handsome, a little bit slouched, a little bit rustic and cowlicky and subtly aw-shucks about everything, his voice deep, rich, resonant as he said, ". . . job-creating opportunities in urban core areas, that's the answer if we're going to continue to have a viable center-city economic base here in Fort Courtney. The companion piece to this fine building should be—if we all have the guts and the vision—an enclosed shopping mall taking up that short block on Princess Street. Urban renewal to help tear down the obsolete warehouses and get the city to vacate the street, and I don't see why we couldn't have . . ."

I was by him, and a pack of ladies whooping at something that had just about tickled them to death drowned out the rest of the visionary address to the potential investors.

I rode down with a silent couple in the elevator. She stared with prim mouth and lofty eyebrows at the ceiling of the small machine. With clamped jaw and moody brow he stared at the blue carpeting underfoot. As we walked down into the parking area she did not realize I was as close behind them as I was. In a thin, deadly, indifferent tone she said, "Sweetheart, why don't you let me drive home alone while you go right on back up there and stroke Gloria's vulgar little ass all you want. She may be missing the attention."

He did not reply. I walked to my car and unlocked it and got in and clenched the wheel so tightly my knuckles made crackling sounds. I shut my eyes so tightly I could see rockets and wheels of fire. Little improvements come along, because the luck can go either way, and when you play the longer odds you open up the chance of the good luck and the bad. Her reaction helped. I had not expected it. I had wanted her to tell him that McGee had seen Maureen leaving by a route other than the one he knew she had taken, and so that would target him in on me, bring him in close enough for me to see what he was. But it was better the way she was doing it.

And I had to find Stanger, and find him fast.

I didn't get to Stanger until nine fifteen. I told him that it might save a lot of time and a lot of questions later if it went down on tape on the very first go-round.

"You look funny," he said. "You look spooked."

"It's been one of those days, Al."

"What's this all about?"

"When the tape is running."

"All right, all right!"

So he left Nudenbarger on traffic cruise by himself and rode down to headquarters with me in my car. I said I'd like to do it in the car if possible. He came out with a battered old Uher with an adaptor for the cigarette lighter. I found a bright white drive-in on Route 30 and parked at the far edge with the rear against the fence. A listless girl made two long walks to take the order and bring out the two coffees and hook the tray onto the car. Stanger had checked the recorder. It had some hiss but not too much. The heads needed cleaning and demagnetizing.

He rewound and started it again on record and established his identity, the date and time, and said he was taking a voluntary statement from one Travis McGee of such and such a place, said statement having some bearing, as yet unknown, on the murder by stab wound of Penny Woertz, and that said victim had been acquainted with said McGee. He sighed and handed me the mike.

As soon as I got into it, he stiffened and he boggled at me. As I kept on he wanted to interrupt so badly he began making little lunges and jumps, so I didn't give him an opening. At one point he bent over, hands cupping his eyes, and I could hear him grinding his teeth. I finished. I turned the remote switch on the mike and said, "Want me to turn it back on for questions?"

"No. No. Not yet. Oh, good Jesus H. Jumpin' Sufferin' Christ on the rocks! Oh you lousy dumb bastard! Oh, why did I ever think you had one brain cell to rub up against another. You silly bastard, I have got to take you in and shut the iron door on you. For God's sake, it is going to take me half the night just to write up the charges. And you have the gall, the nerve, the lousy . . . impertinence to ask me to sneak down there and grab that dead broad out of that crazy hidey hole and make like I found her in a ditch, and keep anybody from coming up with the ID and keep her the hell on ice as a Jane Doe until God only knows how. . . . No! Dammit, McGee. No!" It was an anguished cry.

"Why don't you ask me some questions. Maybe it'll calm you down, Stanger. You've got all night to go collect her."

He nodded. I turned the mike on.

"Are you absolutely certain she was dead?"

"She fell a hundred and twenty feet onto concrete."

"So all right! Did you realize when you touched the outside and inside knob on that office door and messed with the window and picked up the pocketbook, you were removing evidence of a crime, if there was one?"

"He wouldn't leave anything useful. I moved the body too. Jumped, fell, or pushed, it would look just the same."

"But what the hell do you expect to accomplish?"

I turned off the microphone. "Al, you won't play it my way?"

"I can't! It's such a way-out——"

"Who can make a decision to *try* my way? Your chief?"

"Old Sam Teppler? He's going to keel over in a dead faint if I try to tell him, even."

"How about your state attorney for this judicial district. Gaffney?"

"Gaffner. Ben Gaffner."

"Is there any chance he'd buy it? There's all kinds of prosecutors. What kind is he?"

Al Stanger got out of the car and slammed the door. He walked slowly around the car, scuffing his heels on the asphalt, hitching at his trousers, scratching the back of his neck. He came and looked down at me across the hook-on tray.

"Gaffner is on his fourth term. He gets a hell of a lot of respect. But nobody gets very close to him. He likes to
222

nail them. He drives hard. His record keeps him in. He isn't fancy. He builds his cases like they used to build stone walls in the old days. All I can say is . . . maybe. You'd have to sell him the whole thing. All the way down the line. He's straight and he's tough, and he likes being just what he is. But I'd even hate to try to explain to him why you're not behind iron right now, McGee."

"Let's give it a try."

He went to a public phone booth on the corner line of the gas station across the highway. I could see him in the floodlighted booth, talking for a long time. I could not tell from his dispirited pace as he came back what the answer had been.

He got in beside me and pulled the door shut. "He's based fifty-five miles from here. In Lime County. He'll leave in about ten minutes, he said, and bring two of his people. They'll make good time. They'll plan on me opening up one of the circuit court hearing rooms in the courthouse and we'll meet them there."

"What did you say to him?"

"Told him I had a nut here that wanted me to help him hide the body of a murder victim."

"What did he say?"

"He asked me why I'd called him, and I told him because I thought maybe the nut had a pretty good idea. So he said he'd better come over and listen. I don't think he'll buy it."

"No harm in trying to sell it."

"Why don't I just lock you up nice?"

"Because at heart you're a dandy fellow."

I blinked the lights and the girl came and got the tray and her money. Stanger checked in and said he was going off shift a little early instead of staying on until midnight. He told them to have the dispatcher tell Lew Nudenbarger. We went down to the courthouse. He located the night man and had him unlock the small hearing room next to the offices of the circuit judge on the second floor, and told him to stay by the side door near the parking lot, as Mr. Gaffner would be coming along.

The countersunk fluorescence shone down on a worn

red rug, a mahogany veneer table with ten armchairs aligned around it. The air was close and still, and the room had no windows. Stanger fussed with the thermostat until something clicked and cool air began to circulate. We laid out the various items on the oiled top of the table. The two prescription vials, one partially used. The two-headed bug. The recorder, now with AC line cord plugged in. One blue lizard envelope purse that matched the blue lizard pumps wrapped up with the dead wife of Tom Pike. Holton's revolver. The pry bar, which could be matched to the forced entry marks on the sliding glass doors and the metal medicine chest.

We waited for Gaffner, with Stanger wearing a tired little smile.

19 BEN GAFFNER sat at the middle of the long table. He directed me to sit opposite him, Stanger at my left. His two men sat at his right and his left. The thin, pale one named Rico was his chief investigator. The round, red one named Lozier was the young attorney who assisted him throughout the circuit.

Gaffner was an orderly man. He arranged in useful order in front of him a yellow legal pad, four sharp yellow pencils, glass ashtray, cigarettes, lighter. Rico had brought along a recorder, a Sony 800. He plugged it in, threaded a new tape, tested it, put the mike on top of a book in the center of the table, tested it again, changed the pickup volume, and nodded at Gaffner.

Only then did Gaffner look directly at me. The tape reels turned at slow speed. He had a moon face and his small and delicate features were all clustered in the center of the moon. His hair was cropped close except for a wiry tuft of gray on the top near the front, like a handful of steel wool. His eyes were an odd shade of yellow, and he could hold them on you without shifting them or blinking them or showing any expression. It was effective.

"Your name?" he said finally. Uninflected. No accent, no clue to area of origin. Name, age, address, occupation, marital status, local address.

"It is my understanding that you are making a voluntary confession, Mr. McGee. I must warn you that——"

"I am aware of my rights regarding self-incrimination, remaining silent, right to counsel, and so forth, Mr. Gaffner. I waive them freely and voluntarily, with no threats, promises, or coercion on your part."

"Very well. You will tell me in your own words your actions in regard to the alleged crime which you——"

"We're not going to do it that way, Mr. Gaffner."

"We are going to do it my way."

"Then, you had a long drive for nothing. Al, lead me to that iron door of yours."

Gaffner kept those yellow eyes on me for a long ten count. "How do you suggest we do this, McGee?"

"I want to start over five years ago and tell you how and where I met Helena Pearson Trescott and her daughters. I won't waste your time with anything not pertinent to the case I hope you will be able to take to the grand jury. Some of the subsequent events will be guesswork."

"I am not interested in your conjectures."

"I am not interested in how much or how little interest you have in my conjectures. I am going to give them to you, right along with what facts I have. Without the conjectures the facts won't hang together. You'll just have to endure it, Mr. Gaffner. Maybe you could just tell yourself you might get some leads out of them."

After another long yellow unwinking stare he said, "Proceed, then. Try not to ramble. When I hold up my hand like this, please stop, because I will want to write a note on this pad. When I stop writing, continue, and try to continue where you left off. Is that clear?"

"Perfectly."

It took a long time. It took both sides of a five-inch reel of tape and half of another before we were done. He wrote many pages of notes, his writing swift, neat, and very small.

My chain of motive and logic went thus:

Dr. Stewart Sherman had indeed killed his wife, and in the course of his investigation the special investigator for Courtney County, Dave Broon, had come up with something that, if he reported it or turned it in, would have been enough to give a reasonable assurance of an indictment by the grand jury. A practicing physician would be far more useful to Dave Broon than a man indicted for murder. A man of Broon's shrewdness would probably lock it all up very carefully, perhaps by trading cooperation and silence for a written confession which could be tucked away.

Next consider Tom Pike's narrow escape when he was being investigated for unethical practices while working as a stockbroker. The intervention of Miss Hulda Wennersehn was almost too opportune. One might detect here the possibility of Dave Broon stepping in and doing Pike a great favor. It would be profitable to help Pike. Maybe he dug up information on the Wennersehn woman to use as leverage, or maybe he already had something and was waiting for a good chance to use it. This would give Broon a certain hold over Pike as well. Pike was becoming more and more successful, and possibly overextended.

Then we have Helena Pearson Trescott, before her first operation for cancer, telling her daughters the terms of her will and the surprising size of her estate. Maureen would certainly have told Tom the terms. Then we have the surgeon, Dr. Bill Dyckes, telling Tom Pike, but not the daughters, that Helena will not recover from the cancer of the bowel. Suddenly the expected baby is a potential source of loss compared to (under the terms of the will) the optimum solution. The ideal order would be for Helena to die first, then for Maureen to die without issue, and for Tom Pike to marry Bridget.

The family doctor is, by accident or plan, Dr. Sherman. One can assume that through a mutually profitable relationship Pike and Broon have become confidants. Trust could be guaranteed by putting various damaging pieces of information in a safe place, available only upon the death of either conspirator.

So pressure is put on Sherman to induce spontaneous abortion of the child Maureen Pike is carrying. There are drugs that can be given by injection that will dangerously inhibit kidney function. Do it, or face complete exposure and disgrace and perhaps a life term. It works almost too well, making Maureen dangerously ill.

Here there is an area of pure guesswork. Why was it so necessary to wipe out Maureen's memory of the immediate past? Did she suspect the shot Sherman gave her had killed the child? Or, more probably, when she appeared to be comatose, she could have heard too much of some quiet bedside conversation between Dr. Sherman and her husband. Nothing could make a woman keep her mouth shut about that. If memory could not be wiped out, she would have had to be killed, in spite of the money loss it would mean. Sherman had been doing animal experimentations on memory, on the retention of skills once learned, of retraining time when such skills were forgotten. As the doctor on the case, he could easily give Maureen a massive dose of puromycin. When it wiped memory clean of all events of the previous several days, one can assume Pike would soon realize how useful that effect could be. It could help him lay the groundwork for her death, which would have to come after Helena had died, and it would be a way of keeping Bridget there in the house, with the two of them, where she could fall in love with Tom Pike.

Once she is home from the hospital, Tom Pike, with Biddy's unwitting cooperation, keeps his wife on puromycin. Her day-by-day memory function is fragmented. Her learning skills are stunted. A side effect is a kind of regression to childhood, to sensual pleasure, to the naughtiness of running away. But this helps keep Biddy near. She cannot leave her sister. So while Helena still lives, he sets the stage for eventual successful suicide. There is no risk in feeding her the sleeping pills and wait-

227

ing a seemingly risky length of time before taking her in. She will have no memory of it. No harm in putting her in the hot tub, making the hesitation marks on her wrist, then one cut deep enough, and waiting, then breaking down the unlocked door. She will not remember. She will not know that it was he who fashioned the clumsily knotted noose instead of she.

But he was not aware of the way potential suicides stay usually with one method and never more than two. But here we have four.

The reason Dr. Sherman became ever more troublesome seems clear. He would slowly come to realize that there was a very small chance of their ever using the evidence of his wife's murder against him, because if indicted, he would certainly be expected to tell of the induced abortion performed at the request of Pike, with leverage by Broon, and tell of the drug that he had been supplying Pike to inject into Maureen, the drug that had caused the mental effects that baffled the neurologists and the psychiatrists. Meanwhile he had been induced to invest everything in Pike's ventures, even to cashing in his insurance policies and investing the proceeds.

Maybe Sherman began to talk about confession. Maybe he began to gouge money out of Pike in return for supplying the puromycin.

How was that murder done? A week before she died, Penny Woertz had a dream that reminded her of something. A trap door in Sherman's forehead, a little orange light like the one that winks on the face of the Dormed control. Count the flashes. Could she have remembered some casual comment that Sherman made about some trouble with the electrosleep device he had supplied for Maureen Pike and taught Biddy to operate?

A careful check might reveal that on the night the doctor died the daughters and Helena might have driven down to the Casey Key house. And it might reveal that Pike was out of town, in Orlando or Jacksonville. There he could have rented a car, gone home, gotten the Dormed and put it in its case and taken it down to Sherman's office to be tested. It was portable. The case was pale. The machine was heavy. A tall man had been seen leaving Sherman's office. Tall is relative. Pike was fairly tall. Six feet almost? Height is such a distinctive thing that a pair of shoes with extreme lift is a very efficient disguise. I have a pair of shoes with almost a four-inch lift. It takes my six four up to six eight. With them I wear a jacket a couple of inches longer than my normal forty-six extra long. People remember the size. They remember seeing a giant. They remember little else about him.

Simplest thing in the world to take it in for Sherman to check. "Maureen says it hurts her. Biddy and I have tried it. There are little sharp pains at first. Try it and see."

In moments the doctor is asleep, with the impulses set at maximum. Take the key out of the pocket. Unlock the drug safe. Roll the sleeve up. Tie the tubing around the arm. Inject the lethal shot of morphine. Untie the rubber tubing. Go and collect all the puromycin out of the backroom supplies. Wait a little while and then take the headpiece off, unplug the machine, repack it in its case, and leave.

Helen Boughmer promises trouble. Tell Broon to find a way to shut her mouth. Broon has no trouble.

Holton and Nurse Woertz begin to make a crusade of the whole matter. Nothing they can find out, probably. Broon discovers and reports to Pike that Holton and the nurse have become intimate. Then whisper the news to Janice because, disloyalty being contagious, she can be a good source of information about Holton's progress in his independent investigation. Make the casual contact with her. By being sympathetic, play upon her hurt and discontent. Keep it all on a platonic basis, but be as cautious and discreet as though it were a physical affair—because were Biddy to learn of it, some unpleasant new problems would arise.

Helena dies. Perhaps the new source of funds, a large lump sum from her estate, is becoming more and more imperative. Broon had gained a lot of leverage with the murder of Sherman and could become increasingly expensive to Tom Pike.

Enter McGee, a worrisome development to Tom Pike

when he learns that Helena has been writing to McGee. He does not know if Helena suspected anything. The story of tracing the *Likely Lady* seems implausible. Then he gets the little query from Penny Woertz. Did you tell the doctor you were having trouble with the Dormed? Did he check it for you?

Put Broon onto McGee. Then Broon reports that Holton has asked him to check McGee's room. Puzzling. Then, Broon reports, Holton and the nurse and McGee spent quite a bit of time together in 109 and then Holton left. The nurse stayed with McGee all night. But by then Pike has arranged how to take care of Penny Woertz. He has already arranged the Saturday date with Janice. He has temporarily transferred the Wennersehn woman to Jacksonville and has the key to her apartment, two doors from Miss Woertz.

At that point something made me aware of Stanger and I glanced at him and saw him glaring at me in anger and indignation.

"Sorry, Al. When he missed connections with Janice, I think he went to the apartment alone. Had he met her and had she followed him there in her car, I think that he would have spent a good part of the afternoon making love to her. After all, it wasn't going to be anything she could talk about later. Then, perhaps, when she napped, he would go over to Penny's place. She would let him in. He would kill her with whatever weapon came easiest to hand. Go back and perhaps pin down the sleeping woman and inject her with a massive shot of puromycin. Lead her in her dazed condition over to Penny's apartment. Shove her in and close the door. Drive away. She would not recall having any date, any assignation. She would be in the dead nurse's apartment, with the shears in the dead throat of the woman who was sleeping with her husband. Traumatic emotional amnesia. Not a terribly unusual thing.

"But he lay there for a long time thinking it over and maybe decided it was a risk he could accept. Blood spattered on his shoes and pants legs. He went back to the Wennersehn apartment and cleaned himself and the floor
230

and burned the rags in the fireplace. The maid swept the fireplace out on Monday."

"Who will verify that?" Gaffner asked.

"It better be Tom Pike. My source is not available. I completely forgot who told me."

"We can give you a long time to sit and think."

"I have a terrible memory."

Yellow stare. Small shrug. "Continue."

I told them that investigation would probably prove that Tom Pike landed in Jacksonville Sunday morning in plenty of time to direct-dial Rick Holton and whisper to him about the note, knowing that bullheaded Holton would track it down. And, having done so, because of the contents that Tom had conned out of Nudenbarger, might solve the McGee problem suddenly and dramatically, which would take Holton out of the play too.

When that didn't work, Pike had put Broon back to work on me. I mentioned that Broon could well own over forty rental houses in Southtown, and it might be interesting to find out how he could live so well and afford to buy real estate too.

"And that brings me up to the point where I burgled the Pike house and picked up this stuff. It's in detail on Al's tape, so I suggest you listen to that."

We all did. I was glad of the break. My throat felt raw.

One of the group was missing. When I had told of the letter and the check for twenty-five thousand forwarded to me by D. Wintin Hardahee, and how he had been cooperative at first and then had brushed me off completely, Gaffner had sent Mr. Lozier, who knew Hardahee, out to bring him in, with instructions not to tell him what it was all about.

Lozier came in alone and sat down quietly and listened to the balance of the tape I had made in the car.

Gaffner turned to Lozier and said, "Well?"

"Well, sir, that is just about the weirdest——"

"I was asking about Hardahee."

"Sir, I didn't tell him what it was about. He came willingly. And all of a sudden, halfway here, he started crying. I pulled over, and when he could talk, he said that he had promised Dave Broon he would cooperate and Broon had promised not to turn him in."

"For what?"

The young lawyer looked very uncomfortable. "Apparently, sir, Mr. Hardahee has been having . . . uh . . . a homosexual affair with his tennis partner, and Dave Broon bugged the cabin where they've been meeting for over a year."

"How was he asked to cooperate?"

"Broon wanted to know the contents of the letter Mrs. Trescot wrote to Mr. McGee. He convinced Broon he had never had a chance to read it. He told Broon about the check to Mr. McGee. Mr. Broon asked him to give Mr. McGee no advice or cooperation at all. Broon told him that he might hear from Mr. Pike about an investment opportunity, and when he did, it might be a good thing to go into it, substantially."

"Where is Hardahee?" Gaffner asked softly.

"He's sitting down in the car, sir."

"Well, Larry, suppose you go down and drive the poor sad silly son of a bitch home. Tell him we'll have a little talk someday soon. Tell him that in the absence of a complaint, there's no charge."

As Lozier left, Gaffner turned to Stanger. "Would it be asking entirely too much to have you go out and come back here with Broon, Lieutenant?"

"I swear to God, I have been hunting that man here and there and up and down the whole day long, and he is plain gone."

He shifted his unwinking stare to me. "And it is your thought, Mr. McGee, that Mr. Pike will suddenly crack under the strain and start bleating confessions at us all?"

"No, sir. I don't think he will ever confess to anything at all. I don't think he feels any guilt or remorse. But you see, if Maureen disappears, there is no proof of death. He can't bail out by marrying the younger sister. If he's in a tight spot, he'll have to make some kind of move." It astonished me a little to hear myself call him "sir." It is not a word I use often or loosely.

"Don't you think, Mr. McGee, that you are assuming

232

that a very intelligent man like Pike has committed some very violent and foolish acts?"

"Right now they seem violent and foolish because we all have a pretty good idea of the things he's done and why he's done them. But when things get more and more complex, Mr. Gaffner, it leaves more room for chance. For luck, good and bad. Where would we be with all this if I hadn't come into the picture? Not that I've been particularly bright about any part of this. I was something new added to the mix and I guess I've been a catalytic agent. His luck started to run the other way. The biggest piece of bad luck was when I decided not to park over by the other cars. When she hit the overhead, it was a hell of a sound. I didn't know what it was. I knew it was something right over my head. One hell of a smack to make the whole prestressed roof ring like a drum. Okay. No workmen around. Building empty except for the party on the top floor. So I had to find out what made that noise. Maybe I knew what it had to be. Maybe my subconscious fitting things together in a single flash of intuition. What if I hadn't found her?"

"He doesn't know you found the body."

"And so he's handling it according to plan. She ran off again. Big search. Worry. Then in the morning the workmen find it, and it fits with her recent history of suicide attempts and her condition. He's going through the motions now. He thinks he's home free. Violent, yes. Foolish, however, is another word. I think he's legally sane, but I think he's a classic sociopath. Do you know the pattern? Superficially bright, evidently quite emotional, lots of charm, an impression of complete honesty and integrity."

"I have done the necessary reading in that area, Mr. McGee," Gaffner said.

"Then you know their willingness to take risks, their confidence they can get away with anything. They're sly and they're cruel. They never admit guilt. They are damned hard to convict." He nodded agreement.

I told him about the couple who had worked for the Pikes. I told him of the golf club incident. Then I de-

233

scribed Tom Pike's bedroom, the strange sterility and neatness of it, how impersonal it seemed, without any imprint of personality.

Gaffner asked Stanger if he could add anything. "Not much on him," Al said, examining the sodden end of a dead cigar. "Florida born. Lived here and there around the center of the state, growing up. His folks worked the groves, owned little ones and lost them, took over some on lease, made out some years and crapped out other years. Don't know if there's any of them left or where they are now. Tom Pike went off to school up north someplace. Scholarship, I think. Came here a few years ago, just married, had money enough to build that house out there. I guess there must have been credit reports on him for the size loans he's got into and I guess if they turned up anything out of line, he wouldn't have got the loans. The people that don't like him, they *really* don't like him a damn bit, but they keep their mouths shut. The ones that do, they think he's the greatest thing ever walked on two legs."

After a silence Ben Gaffner said softly, "Ego. The inner conviction that everybody else in the world is soft and silly and gullible. Maybe we are, because we're weighted down with excess baggage the few Tom Pikes of this world don't have to bother with. Feelings. The capacity to feel human emotions, love, guilt, pity, anger, remorse, hate, despair. They can't feel such things but don't know they can't, so they think our insides are just like theirs, and they think the world is a con game and think we fake it all, just as they have learned to do."

I said, "You've done your reading, sir."

"What have we got right now? Let's say we could open Broon up and make him the key witness for the prosecution. If he confirms what you think he can confirm, McGee, then I'd take a chance on going for an indictment. But Pike is going to be able to get top talent to defend him. The jury is going to have to either believe Broon or believe Pike. Circumstantial case. Pike is likable and persuasive. And I'm saddled with a story to present that sounds too fantastic and I'm saddled with medical

234

experts who'll be contradicted by his medical experts. One long, long trial, a lot of the public monies spent on it, and I would say four to one against a conviction."

"About that," Stanger agreed unhappily.

"So what if there's no way to open Broon up? Or what if he's gone for good? Nothing to go on. I'd be a fool to go after an indictment."

"Gone for good?" Stanger asked. "Little cleanup job by Pike?"

"Only if Pike could be sure Broon wouldn't leave anything behind that might turn up in the wrong hands. Otherwise, on the run. Cash in the chips and leave for good, knowing that sooner or later Pike would want to get rid of the only link to all the rest of it."

"So where does that leave us, Mr. Gaffner?" Stanger asked.

"I think you and Rico better start moving. What time is it? Three fifteen. Best get a panel delivery. We'll have to make sure Pike isn't in that area anywhere. Get that body out of there at first light. Drive it back over to Lime City. Is that old phosphate pit on the Hurley ranch dry at the bottom?"

"Since he cut through, it runs off good."

"About eighty-foot drop down that north wall. Get hold of that big matron with the white hair."

"Mrs. Anderson."

"She can keep her mouth shut. I want the fancy clothes off that body, tagged and marked and initialed by both of you and put away in my safe, Rico, and I want her dressed in something cheap and worn out. Put her at the bottom of that drop, then, soon as you can, you get her found. You could tell Hessling to go check a report of kids messing around there last night. Then I can come in on it through normal channels and we'll process an autopsy request, and I'll make sure I have somebody come in to backstop Doc Rause and run a complete series on the brain tissue."

He turned toward me with the slow characteristic movement of his round head, moon face. "It isn't all that big a risk, in case we get nowhere. She kept wandering off

235

and had to be found. So she wandered off and hitched a ride maybe, and ended up dead in the bottom of a phosphate pit."

Stanger said, "Won't Pike make sure she's listed as missing, and won't she fit the description enough so that he might come over to make the identification?"

"We'd better make a positive on her. We can change our mind later on. Who do you think, Rico?"

The pale, mild investigator said, "That drifter girl that jumped bond on that soliciting charge four, five months back? If the prints matched, it could be a screwup in the filing system that we could catch later on."

"I like it," Gaffner said. Lozier had returned. He said Hardahee had pulled himself together. Gaffner said they would decide later on if they wanted an affidavit from Hardahee.

Then Gaffner swiveled his head slowly and nailed us each in turn with the yellow appraisal. "All of you listen carefully. We are engaged in foolishness. You do not have to be told to keep your mouths shut. I do not buy all of McGee's construction. I buy enough of it to continue the idiocy he started. We are all going to remember that our man won't get jumpy. He won't become superstitious and fearful. Psychos are notoriously pragmatic. If a body is gone, somebody took it. He'll wait to find out who and why, and while he is waiting he'll make the perfectly normal and understandable moves of the alarmed husband with a missing wife. Stanger, you and Rico better get going. And after Rico is loaded and gone, Stanger, your job is find Broon for me. Lozier, wait in the hall out there while I have a word with Mr. McGee."

The table had been cleared of gear. All that remained were the overflowing ashtrays. Gaffner looked as fresh and rested as when the session had begun.

He stood at attention and looked up into my face. "You're the bait, of course. When the woman is not found, Miss Pearson is going to feel more and more guilty. She is going to blame herself. And so she will confess to her brother-in-law that she knew Maureen was gone and didn't tell him. She will say that you saw Maureen leaving. Then you are the key, because you can supply the information about the body. No body, and the whole scheme is dead."

"So he has to talk to me."

"And he is still wondering what's in that letter Mrs. Trescott wrote you."

"And what he says to me, that's what you have to know. That's what you need so you can move. What if he decides to accept his losses, write this one off, go on from here? What if he can squeak through, assuming he is in a little financial bind?"

"As soon as the working day starts, Mr. McGee, I am going to make some confidential phone calls to some of the more important businessmen I know over here in Fort Courtney. I'll tell them it's just a little favor. I can say that as a matter of courtesy I was told that the Internal Revenue people are building up a case against Pike for submitting fraudulent tax returns, and it might be a good time to bail out, if they happen to be in any kind of joint venture with him. I think he might feel a lot of immediate pressure. You could provide the answers that would relieve it. I think we can hurry him along."

"So how do you want me to handle it?"

"I think the thing he would respond to best, the attitude he'd most quickly comprehend, would be your offer to sell him the body for a hundred thousand dollars. But I don't want to move, to set it up, until we have a good line on Broon. I'd like him in custody first. Additional pressure. So we'll get you back to your motel, and I want you to accept no calls and have your meals sent in until I instruct you further. Can you . . . ah . . . suppress your natural talent for unilateral action?"

"I bow to the more devious mind in this instance, Mr. Gaffner."

There was no trace of humor in him. "Thank you," he said.

20   *I SLEPT UNDISTURBED* until past noon. The door was chained, the DO-NOT-DISTURB sign hanging on the outside knob.

The first thing I remembered when I awoke was how, about an hour before first light, I had driven by the new building, with Gaffner beside me and Lozier following in the car they had arrived in.

I drove by knowing she was still up there, behind the metal plate of the service hatch, waiting out the first hours of forever, leaning against the interior grill, firmly wrapped, neatly tied.

Helena, I didn't do very well. I gave it a try, but it was moving too fast. Dear Tom sidled her into the little office past the boxes, perhaps kissed her on the forehead in gentle farewell, opened the window as wide as it would go, and told her to look down, darling, and see where the lovely restaurant will be. She would turn her shoulders through the opening and peer down. Then a quick boost of knee in the girdled rump, hand in the small of the back. Her hand released the purse to clutch at something, clutch only at the empty air of evening, then she would cat-squall down, slowly turning.

I showered, shaved. I felt sagging and listless. I had the feeling that it was all over. Odd feeling. No big savage heat to avenge the nurse, avenge the big blond childish delicious wife. Perhaps because nothing anyone could do to Pike would ever mean anything to him in the same sense that we would react to disaster.

He was a thing. Heart empty as a paper bag, eyes of clever glass.

As I was reaching for the phone, there was a determined knocking at my door. I called through it. Stanger. I let him in. He seemed strange. He drifted, in a floating way, as if happily drunk. But he wasn't. His smile was small and thoughtful.

He looked at his watch and sat down. "We've got a little time to spare."

"We have? That's nice."

"I did a better job of bugging Mr. Tom Pike than I did on you. Was it that wad of paper on the floor?"

"Lieutenant, I'm disappointed in you. Bugging people on your own team. Shame!"

"My only team is me. I had a lot of thoughts about you. One of them was you were smokescreening the fact maybe Tom Pike brought you in here for some reason or other. Was it something about that paper on the floor?"

I said it was and told him how it worked, then said, "So why didn't you let me know last night?"

"Wanted you to have all the window trimming there was. The more you could come up with, the better chance you had of selling Gaffner. You did good with that man."

"That was an expensive piece of equipment you planted on me, Al. City property?"

"Personal. It wasn't like planting it on a stranger. I knew I'd get it back. You might as well think it was Broon did it. But he didn't because the very last time anybody saw him at all was a little before noon, Monday. He went to the Courtney Bank and Trust and opened his deposit box, and it gave me the ugly feeling he was gone for good. So it was mighty comforting to hear I'm going to meet up with him."

"You keep looking at your watch."

"So I do. But there's still plenty of time. Don't you want to know how I bugged old Tom?"

"You're going to tell me anyway."

"Why, so I am! Who else can I tell? I went right to a fellow who happens to be the second oldest of those six brothers of Penny Woertz and who happens to work for Central Florida Bell, and I told him I was in need of a little illegal help, and first thing you know, we had a nice tap on both Pike's private unlisted lines. Nothing I can ever take to court, naturally."

"Naturally."

"Lord God, that man has had trouble this morning! Between keeping people busy hunting all over for his missing wife and trying to calm down the people who want to take their money out of his little syndicates and corporations, I bet you ol' Dave Broon had to try a lot of times before he got through. About ten of eleven when he did. Had to put in thirty-five cents for three minutes."

"So?"

"So thank God when Tom said they could meet at the usual place, Dave didn't want any part of it. Saves a lot of trouble. Dave Broon picked the place. Six miles southwest of town. I just got back from there, checking it over, getting something set up. Pretty good place to meet. Big piece of pastureland. Used to be the old Glover place. Pike and some people bought it up a while ago to turn it into something called ranchettes. Two-acre country estates. There's a gate with a cattle guard near the west side and a lot of open land and just one big old live oak shade tree smack in the middle, maybe a quarter mile from the nearest fence line."

"When do they meet?"

"Two thirty. But I left Nudenbarger staked out. We can swing around and go in the back way and cut across to where I left him. Less chance of running into either of them."

"You seem very contented, Mr. Stanger."

"Sure. Broon told him to bring a big piece of money. They haggled some. Pike said thirty thousand was absolute tops. Broon said it would have to be an installment. Broon told him not to get cute. It's sure empty out there. Bugs, buzzards, and meadowlarks. They'll meet by the tree and have a nice talk."

"And you bugged the tree."

His face sagged and his mouth turned down. "You take the pure joy out of things, McGee. I'm sorry I decided to bring you along for the fun."

240

"I'm sorry I spoiled your fun. I haven't had anything to eat yet. Is there time?"

"Fifteen minutes."

Stanger drove the city's sedan hard. He took a confusing route through the back country, along small dirt roads. At last he stopped and got out at a place that looked like any other. He extended the aerial of a walkie-talkie and said, "Lew? You read me?"

"I read you, Al. No action yet. Nothing. Hey, bring that bug dope out of the glove compartment."

"Okay. We'll be coming along now. Let me know if either one shows up before we get there."

He told me that he'd left Nudenbarger staked out with binoculars, a carbine, and the receiver-recorder end of the mike-transmitter unit he'd tied in the oak tree. He said we had a mile to go. He hadn't wanted to put the car on any directly connecting road for fear Broon or Tom Pike would drive a circuit around the whole ranch to see if everything was clear before driving in.

We had to crawl under one fence and climb over another. The air was hot and still, but there was a hint of coolness whenever the breeze stirred. Stanger seemed to be plodding along listlessly, but he covered ground faster than one would think.

We came out onto a dirt road, crossed it, leaped a watery ditch on the other side. I followed Stanger into a clump of small pines, thick ones, eight to ten feet tall. He motioned me down, and we crawled the last dozen feet to where Nudenbarger lay on his belly close to the fence, staring through the binoculars. He turned and looked with a certain distaste at me and said, "Nothing yet, Al. Maybe they called it off, huh?"

Stanger ignored him. He said to me, "Ringside. Like it?"

We were sheltered on three sides by the pines. We could look under the bottom strand of wire and see the big oak tree about five hundred yards away. Stanger pointed out the gate they'd drive through. "Five after two," he said. "Ought to get some action along about now."

And we did. A dusty beetle-green Ford two or three years old appeared in the distance, trailing a long plume of dust. The rain of yesterday had dried quickly and completely.

"Broon," Stanger said. The car slowed as it approached the open gate with the cattle guard steel rails paving the entrance, and then went on past, accelerating slightly. In a tone of approval Stanger said, "Took a look to see if Pike was early and now he'll swing around the place. About four miles to go all the way around it. He'll come right down this here dirt road behind us."

We waited. It stirred old instincts, old training. Terrain, cover and concealment, field of fire. The brown pine needles underneath me had a faded aromatic scent. Skirr of insects. Piercingly sweet call of meadowlark. Swamp-smell of the ditch water nearby. Sway and dip of the grasses in the breeze. The motor sound became audible, grew, and it went by behind us, shocks and springs chunking as it hit the potholes in the clay road base. Faded off. A drift of road dust filtered the sunlight for a few moments.

Long minutes later we saw, far across the flat pasture-land, distant glints as he drove along the opposite road, the one that paralleled the road behind us. He was behind the hedgerow of scrub pine and palmetto, chrome winking through the few open places.

When he returned to the gate, he slowed and turned in and drove across the open pastureland, through the grass that had grown to over a foot high since the stock had been moved. The car rolled and bounced and he made a swing, a half circle and parked perhaps fifty feet beyond the lonely live oak.

When he got out, Stanger reached and took the binoculars away from Lew Nudenbarger. "Not now, you damn fool! He'll be looking every direction, and you pick up the sun just right on a lens, he's gone."

"Sorry, Al."

We watched the man walk slowly over to stand in the

242

shade of the oak. Five hundred yards was too far for me to get much more than an impression of a smallish man with a trim and tidy way of moving, pale hair, brown face, white shirt, khaki trousers.

I thought I saw him raise a hand to his mouth, and was suddenly startled by a small, dry coughing sound that came from the monitor speaker of the receiver. It stood on a level place between Stanger and Nudenbarger, a few feet back from the small crest.

"Do the talking right there," Stanger pleaded in a low voice. "Right there. Don't, for God's sake, set in the car and talk. We want you right there, you slippery little scut."

Minutes passed. And then a red car appeared far away, pulling a high-speed dust tower. It braked and turned into the gate. It was the red Falcon wagon, and the last time I had seen it in motion, Helena's daughters had been in it.

It followed the same route through the grass that Broon had taken. It made a wider circle around the tree, in the opposite direction, and stopped on our side but not in the line of vision.

Stanger was looking through the glasses. He lowered them and hitched down and turned on the old Uher recorder, now functioning on battery pack and jacked into the receiver. He took another look through the glasses. "Dave got a gun in his hand," he said.

Broon's voice came over the speaker, resonating the diaphragm as he shouted across the sunlit space. "Whyn't you turn off the motor and get out?"

Pike was so far from the mike his answer was inaudible.

"Talk in the shade, brothers," Stanger pleaded. "Go talk in the shade of the nice big tree."

"I wanted you to see the gun right off, Tom," Broon called out to him. "So you wouldn't get cute until I told you something. If I don't make a phone call tonight to a certain party, an eight-page letter gets mailed special delivery to the state attorney. I spent half the night writing that letter. Now I'll toss this here gun in my car and we can talk things out."

We watched the distant scene and saw them both walk slowly into the shade of the big oak. "Real nice," Stanger whispered.

Broon's conversational voice over the speaker had a startling clarity and fidelity. His tone was mild. "I give you credit, Tom. You suckered me good. Never occurred to me there was something in that bottle different from what you were sticking into your wife. What the hell was it?"

"Mostly nitric acid. I estimated it would eat through the lead stopper in about twenty-four hours."

"What made you so sure I'd put it in my lock box when you told me to keep it safe?"

"I wasn't sure. If you hadn't, I was no worse off, was I?"

"You sure to God made me worse off. Turned everything in my box to a mess of dirty brown stinking mush. Papers and tapes and photos and one hell of a lot of good cash money. It even et a corner out of the box. That bank woman was real upset about the stink. Thing is, Pike, it ruined a lot of stuff that didn't have a damn thing to do with you and me."

"You forced me to do something, Dave."

"How do you figure?"

"You got too expensive. I couldn't afford you."

"With folks standing in line to hand you their savings?"

"But with you taking so big a cut, I couldn't show a return. Then the supply dries up. I had to cut down on your leverage."

"It didn't work. I've got a good memory. I got a lot of facts in that letter I wrote. They can be checked out. Pike, you just made it harder on yourself, because I got to collect all that money you burned up with that damned acid stunt, and we're starting with that thirty thousand you better damn well have brought along."

"Things are too tight. I didn't bring it."

"Then I'm going to pull the stopper, boy, and let you go right down the drain."

"I don't think so."

"Now, just what gives you reason to think I won't?"

"Because you're only half bright, David. But you're bright enough to understand the way things are now. And you're going to keep right on working for me. But your rates have gone down."

"The *hell* you say!"

"If you were bright, you wouldn't have left so suddenly. I knew from the way you acted that I'd destroyed the actual proof. You'd have made me believe you still had the edge. Now, letter or no letter, all you've got is your naked word against mine. Who will be believed, you or me? Think it over. With the Sherman tapes and the signed statement, you could destroy me, possibly. Now you're only a potential annoyance. I brought along thirty-five hundred dollars for you, to show good faith. You're bright enough to know I'm going to be a pretty good source of income for you. Nothing like before, of course. You'll accept it."

"You sure of that? You sure I'll settle for a little bit here and a little bit there?"

"As opposed to nothing at all, why not?"

"It won't pay for the risk."

"What risk?"

"Maybe I'm only half bright, like you say, but I'm bright enough to know you're not going to last. They're going to grab you, and when they do, you'll put me in it right up to the eyeballs."

"Grab me for what?"

"For killing folks. Maybe with Doc Sherman it was your only way out. But I think you liked doing it. You told me they'd grab Janice Holton for stabbing that nurse. But it went wrong somehow and you went ahead anyway, without any real good reason. Pretty soon you're going to set up that suicide deal on your wife and enjoy that too. Then you'll start thinking about somebody else. Maybe me. No, thanks. You've turned into a bug, Pike. I've seen them like you and seen what happens. Maybe it makes you feel so big you have to keep doing it."

"My poor wife threw herself out a twelfth-story window last evening, David."

"What! What the hell are you saying? There wasn't a thing in the paper about——"

"Believe me, she went out the window. I heard the sound of the impact and I know she didn't walk away. I thought the workmen would find the body, but it seems to be gone."

"What the hell do you mean—gone?"

"Today I learned from Biddy that her old friend, Mr. McGee, told her at the party that he saw Maureen sneaking out alone. Assume he knows the terms of the trust funds. So I think he'll get in touch with me to sell me a little information. Your next job is to get to him first, David, and see if you can encourage him to tell you all about it."

Broon did not respond. I found it hard to relate the voices that came over the little speaker to the two men standing under a distant tree across the sunny pastureland.

"You poor damn fool," Broon said.

"It's really quite imperative to get going on it," Tom Pike said, "because even if he hadn't interfered, it will take several months before they'll close out the trust and transfer the principal directly to Bridget."

"Somebody steals a body and you think it's some kind of an inconvenience! You damn fool!"

"Why get in an uproar, Broon? Body or no body, nobody can ever prove a thing."

"You don't even realize it's all over, do you? I'll tell you, there's only one way I can walk away from this one, partner."

Quite suddenly there was a grunt of effort, a gasp of surprise, over the speaker. The distant figures had merged abruptly, and as they spun around it looked, at that distance, like some grotesque dance. The taller figure went up and over and down, and we heard the thud of impact. Both of them were down and invisible. The grass concealed them. Dave Broon stood up, stared down for a moment. Stanger lowered the binoculars quickly. Broon made a slow turn, all the way around, eyes searching the horizon.

"Shouldn't we——"

"Shut up, Lew," Stanger said.

Broon trotted out of the shade and across the sunlit grass to his car. He opened the trunk. Stanger put the glasses on him as he came back.

"Coil of rope," he said. "Tie him up and tote him away, maybe."

"But if he drives off——" Nudenbarger started to say.

"If I can't punch that engine dead at this range with that there carbine, Lew, I'm not trying."

Broon squatted over Tom Pike for a little while, then straightened and took Pike under the armpits and dragged him about fifteen feet. He dropped him there and went quickly to the tree, jumped and caught a limb, quickly pulled himself up and out of sight in the leaves.

"Son of a gun!" Stanger said.

"Why is he climbing the tree?" Lew asked plaintively.

"He took the end of the rope up with him. What do you think?"

Nudenbarger looked baffled. I comprehended the shape and the sense of it. And soon it was confirmed when Tom Pike sat up in the grass quite slowly, slumping to the side in an unnatural way.

Then he rose slowly up from a sitting position.

"Oh, God!" cried Nudenbarger.

"Keep your damned voice down to a soft beller!" Al snapped.

Over the speaker came a strange sound, a gagging, rasping cry. Pike ran a few steps in one direction and was snubbed to a halt. He staggered back. He tried the other direction and did not get as far.

Stanger said, not taking his eyes from the glasses, "Got the fingers of both hands into that loop now, holding it off his throat."

"Broon!" the deep voice cried, cracked and ragged.

He seemed to run in place and then he moved up a little bit. Straight up. And a little bit more. His legs made running motions. He began turning. Then his shoes were above the highest blades of grass. Dave Broon dropped abruptly into view. Nudenbarger raised the carbine and Stanger slapped the barrel down.

Broon got into the red wagon and swung it in a quick turn and parked it close to where Pike hung.

He got out, backed off, looked at Pike, and then ran for his car.

"Now!" Al Stanger said. He snatched up the carbine and vaulted the fence with an agility that astonished me. By the time we were over the fence, he had a twenty-yard lead. As the green Ford began to roll, picking up speed, Stanger stopped, went down onto one knee, and fired four spaced, aimed shots. At the fourth one the back end of the car bloomed into a white-orange poof of gasoline, and as the car kept moving, Broon tumbled out the driver's door, somersaulting in the grass. He got up and started to run at an angle toward the far side of the pasture but stopped quickly when Stanger fired his fifth shot.

He turned, hands in the air, and began to walk slowly toward the tree. The car had stopped in tall grass, tinkling, frying, blackening. He walked more quickly. And then he began to run back toward the tree.

"Head him off, Lew. Grab him."

Lew had good style. He loped in that loose deceptive stride of a good NFL end getting down for the long bomb. Stanger and I headed for the tree. He jogged. I started to run by him and he blocked me with the barrel of the carbine extended.

Thus we all got to the red wagon at about the same time. Nudenbarger was taking no chances with Dave Broon. He had one meaty hand clamped on the nape of Broon's neck and had Broon's arm bent back up and pinned between Broon's shoulderblades by his other paw.

Broon was hopping up and down, grunting, struggling, yelling, "Cut him down! Al! Hey, Al! Cut him down!"

We looked up at Tom Pike. He turned slowly toward us. His clenched fists were on either side of his throat, fingers hooked around the strand of rope that crossed his throat. He looked like a man chinning himself, face blackening with total effort.

I saw that I could swing him over and up onto the roof of the station wagon and get the pressure off his throat immediately. As I moved toward him quickly, Stanger clanked the carbine barrel against the back of my skull. The impact was exquisitely precise. It darkened the day without turning the sun out completely. It loosened my knees enough to sag me to a squat, knuckles against the turf, but not enough to spill me all the way. I turned and stared up at Al, blinking away darkness and the tear-sting of skull pain.

"Don't go messing with the evidence, boy," he said.

"Don't *do* this to me, Al!" Broon begged. "Please, for God's sake, don't do it like this."

Nudenbarger, with Broon firmly in hand, was staring slack-mouthed at Tom Pike. "Jesus!" he said softly. "Oh, Jesus me!"

And Tom Pike continued the slow turn. He lifted his right leg slowly, the knee bending. Classic shoes, expensive slacks, navy socks of what looked like brushed Dacron. The leg dropped back.

"See him twitching any, Lew?" Stanger asked mildly.

"Well . . . that leg moved some."

"Just reflex action, Lew boy. Posthumous nervous twitch, like. Doesn't mean a thing."

Broon said, "You're killing me, Al. You know that."

"You're all confused. You killed Tom Pike, Davey."

"You're miserable, Al. You're a mean bastard, Al Stanger."

Slowly, slowly, Tom Pike turned back to face us. He had changed. The look of muscular tension had gone out of his fists and wrists. They were just slack hands, pinned there by the loop, fingers pressing into the flesh of the throat. His chin had dropped. His toes pointed downward. His face had become bloated and the eyes no longer looked at anything at all.

"See now how it was just the nerves twitching some?" Al asked gently.

"You were right, Al. He's dead for sure," Lew said.

I pushed myself up and fingered a new lump on the back of my head. "How long would you say he's been dead, McGee? All things considered."

"I'd say he must have been dead by the time Broon started to drive away, Al. All things considered."

"Guess we shouldn't touch a thing. Get a reconstruction by the lab people to match up with the eyewitness account." He handed me the carbine and went over and took handcuffs out of a back pocket. He snapped one around Broon's wrist, told Lew to bend him over a little, and snapped the other around Broon's opposite ankle. Lew let go and Stanger gave Broon a push. Broon sat in the grass, knees hiked up.

"Lew, you cut across and get the car and bring it around in here. Might as well stop and pick up our gear over there on the way. We'll be waiting right here."

With a last look at the body, Nudenbarger hurried off.

The body had stopped turning. Stanger stared into the distance, sighed, spat. "Sorry I had to rap you like that."

I looked into his small dusty brown eyes. "I guess it was the quickest way to stop me, Al."

"Feel all right?"

"Just a little bit sick to my stomach."

"Funny. So do I."

21   *I STAYED AROUND* and did what I could to help Bridget Pearson through the worst of it. In a conference about strategy, Ben Gaffner had accepted my suggestion that nothing would be gained by opening up the actual way in which Maureen had died.

It could bring down on us a lot of awkward questions from high places.

Better to make it an identification error over in Lime County and let the phosphate pit story stand.

He agreed that there was so little to go on that Dr. Sherman's death might as well remain on the books as suicide. But the Penny Woertz murder had to be taken out of the active file, and properly closed. That meant some acceptable explanation of motive. Dave Broon came in handy. He was smart enough to have started talking about strangling Tom Pike in a fit of anger and then, upon discovering he was dead, trying to string him up to make it look like suicide.

That gave Gaffner a choice—to play ball with Broon or to go for murder first. Murder first would need only the eyewitnesses to state that they had seen Pike trying to get free as Broon was slowly hauling him clear of the ground. Gaffner had Broon brought in for a private play-back of the tape of the conversation under the live oak. Broon then said it was his certain knowledge that Pike was having an affair with the nurse and had killed her out of jealousy. Gaffner, out of respect for the reputation of the deceased Miss Woertz, edited it down to Pike's pursuit of her, with the crime of passion occurring doubtless when his advances were repulsed. All this cooperation earned Broon the chance at a plea of guilty to murder second, with, whether the sentence was ten, fifteen, or twenty, a chance at parole in six.

Even though by funeral time—a ceremony for two, for Mr. and Mrs. Pike—the swarm of auditors and examiners were beginning to find that Tom Pike had been distributing newly invested capital to previous investors and calling it a distribution of capital gains, Fort Courtney was full of people who could not, and would never, believe that such a brilliant and warm and considerate and handsome and well-mannered man could have ever juggled a single account in any questionable manner, to say nothing of *stabbing* anyone.

No, it all had to be some kind of vicious and clever conspiracy, engineered by *Them. They* were the subtle, hidden enemy, hiring that Broon person, making some kind of intricate deal with him, and then probably taking over the wonderful properties Tom Pike had such great plans for at the time of his death.

So the funeral was well-attended. Biddy knew that all the allegations were so absurd as to be grotesque. And so did Janice Holton. Biddy was so certain, that I could not risk the slightest slur or shadow of doubt to color anything I said to her, or she would never have let me try to help her in any way. She kept going on tranquilizers and raw courage. I helped her close up the house. It would be sold once all estate and inheritance matters were straightened out, and the funds would go to the unfortunate who had invested in Development Unlimited. Fortunately, as there was no doubt of Maureen's having died first, the trust fund would go directly to Bridget. Because Maureen had signed certain papers in connection with her husband's enterprises, had he died first, it was possible the monies might have been diverted to the creditors of Development Unlimited.

She said she was going to drive on down to Casey Key and open up the old house and stay there for a time, quite alone. She said she would be all right. She would walk the beach, get a lot of painting done, sort herself out.

The morning I was packing to leave the Wahini Lodge, Lorette Walker stopped by and said she heard from Cathy I was checking out. I asked her to come on in. She leaned against the countertop and lit a cigarette and said, "Stayed you a long time, huh?"

"I couldn't tear myself away from this garden spot."

"Lot of things happened. Always like that wherever you go?"

"I'm happy to be able to say no."

"That's no good way to fold a shirt! Mess it all up for sure." She came over and took the shirt back out of the bag, spread it out on the bed, folded it quickly and deftly, and put it in the bag. "Best way," she said, backing off. "Sorry I couldn't do you much good on what you wanted me to find out."

"You did a lot of good. You'll never know how much."

"But nobody come hard-nosing around to try to make me say it twice."

"I told you I'd leave you out of it."

She said wistfully, "Could be better for me if you never did keep your word."

"How do you mean?"

"I told myself, back there when I wanted to trust you some, I said okay, gal, you just go ahead and he'll mess you up good. Be a good lesson. Stop you from ever going soft again for any whitey."

"That's why you did it?"

She put on a look of owlish innocence. "Well, then there was that chance of the airplane ride you mentioned. I figured on Paris. Anyway, here's the change from that two hundred. I spent eighty of your dollars on people that didn't have anything worth telling."

"So let's split what you've got left there."

She flared immediately. "So it means I got no right to tell myself I ever did a damn thing for you just for a favor? You buying me for this sixty dollar, you think?"

"Right off the slave block, woman. You did a favor, but I've got no right to do a favor, according to you. I know you didn't expect a dime, but by God you'll take that sixty dollars and you'll buy yourself a pretty suit, something tailored, maybe a good medium shade of blue, and you will wear that damned suit, and you will accept it as a gesture of friendship and trust."

"Well . . . I guess *you* don't need no lessons in coming on mean, mister. I . . . I guess I can take it like it's meant. And thank you very much. You're sure? The only thing I got a right to do with it is buy a winter suit?"

"That's how it has to be," I said, putting the sixty left over into my wallet.

She shrugged and smiled. "Well, then . . . got to get on back up to those rooms. We run pretty full last night."

I held my hand out. "You helped a lot. And a pleasure to get to know you, Mrs. Walker."

After a moment of wary hesitation she shook hands. "Same to you. Good-bye."

She opened the door and turned back, her hand on the knob, and looked at me and moistened her lips. "McGee, you have a nice safe trip back home, hear?" She bolted out and closed the door. My last glimpse and last impression of her was of the slender and vital brown of her quick legs. Another lady in a plain brown wrapper. No, that was not a good analogy, because there was nothing very plain about that sleek wrapper. It was special—flawless, matte finish and inordinately lovely.

I went back knowing that whatever had been wrong with me, any restlessness, irritability, mooniness, had come to an abrupt end. Seeing him hanging and turning so slowly had brought me back to the fullness of life, probably just because his was so evidently gone. I was full of offensive cheer, bounding health, party plans.

Three months later, on a windy gray afternoon in January, Bridget Pearson appeared. She apologized for showing up at Bahia Mar without any advance notice at all. She said it had been an impulse.

She came aboard *The Busted Flush* and sat in the lounge and took neat small sips of her drink and seemed to smile too quickly and too often. The weeks had gaunted her down and in some eerie way she had acquired that same slightly haggard elegance that Helena had evidenced at the time we sailed away in the *Likely Lady*. The long legs were the same, and the way she held her hands, and I knew that all of her was so much the same that it would be like an old love revisited.

She told me that she was restless, wondering what to do with herself, thinking maybe she might go on a trip of some sort. She said she kept coming up with strange little inconsistencies in her memories of Tom Pike. They bothered her. As if there had been something warped and strange that she had been too close to. Was everything the way she believed it had been? Could I help her understand?

Why, now, don't you trouble your purty little head about a thang, little sweetheart. Why, for goodness sake,
254

ol' Uncle Trav will take you on off a-cruisin' on this here comfortable and luxurious ol' crock houseboat, and he'll just talk kindly to you and comfort you and love you up good, and that'll put the real sunshine back in your purty little smile.

I thought of what it would do to her eyes and to the shape of her mouth if I ever told her how it had been for her mother and me aboard the *Likely Lady* in that long-ago Bahama summertime. I tried to sort out the intervals. I am X years older than this lovely young lady and I was X years younger than her lovely mother.

No, thanks. It was too late for me to take a lead role in a maritime version of *The Graduate*. And even had it been possible under my present circumstances, I did not want to astound myself with the unavoidably queasy excitements of an incestuous sort of relationship.

I let too many long moments pass. I could sense that she had thought it all over quite carefully and had come with the definite purpose of opening the door a little way, thinking that I would take over from there. The half-stated offer was withdrawn. We made a little polite talk. I told her I had not seen anything particularly inconsistent about Tom Pike. And that was the truth. She said she was going to meet some friends in Miami and she had better go. I told her I was sorry she couldn't stay longer. She turned when she was halfway along the dock and gave me a merry wave and went striding on, out of my life.

I went back below and freshened my drink and mixed some Plymouth with some fresh grapefruit juice for the lady.

She was sitting on the side of the big bed in the master stateroom, filing her nails. She wore a big fuzzy yellow towel wrapped and tucked around her. She lifted her head sharply to toss her dark hair back and looked at me with a twisted and cynical smile.

"A wealth of opportunity, McGee?"

"Or it never rains but it pours."

"Let me see. Finders keepers, losers weepers. How did she seem?"

"Gaunt. Haunted. At loose ends."

"Wanting comforting? How sweet! And did you tell the poor dear thing to come back some other day?"

"Any show of jealousy always comforts me," I said, and gave her her drink. She sipped it and smiled her thanks and reached and put it on the top of the nearby locker. I stretched out behind her and propped my head up on a pair of pillows.

"Sorry I was here?" she asked.

"Been the same thing. I would have had to go with my instinct. And it said no dice."

"She's very pretty."

"And rich. And talented."

"Hmmm!" she said. The file made little rasping sounds. I sipped my drink. "Mr. McGee, sir? Which really surprised you most? Her showing up or me showing up?"

"You. Definitely. Looked down from the sundeck and saw you standing there and nearly choked to death." I reached an idle finger and hooked it into the back of the wrapped and tucked towel. One gentle tug untucked it and it fell, pooling around her. She slowly straightened her long, slender, lovely back. She reached and picked up her drink and took half of it down, then replaced it.

"May I assume you are quite serious, Mr. McGee?"

"It is crummy weather out there, and you have an extraordinarily fine back, and you were pleasantly bitchy about Miss Pearson, so I am serious, my dear."

"Shall I bother to finish these last three fingernails?"

"Please do, Mrs. Holton."

"I shall try to finish them, Mr. McGee. I think it would be good for my character, what little I have left."

So I listened to the busy little buzz of the nail file and admired her, and sipped the drink, and thought about the way she had looked that day I had watched her spray-painting that old blue metal chaise.

And then I heard the wind-blown January rain move in from the sea and across the beaches and the boat basin and roar softly and steadily down on the weather decks of my houseboat.

Harold Coyle is "the Tom Clancy of ground warfare."
—W.E.B. Griffin

"Coyle is at his best when he's depicting soldiers facing death. . . . He knows soldiers and he understands the brotherhood-of-arms mystique that transcends national boundaries."
—*The New York Times Book Review*

Brigadier General Scott Dixon, sent by the Pentagon on a fact-finding mission to Colombia, has been communicating a message no one wants to hear. The U.S. military is slipping into a quagmire, leaving the men and women in the field to twist in the tropical wind—none more so than his old friend and comrade-in-arms Nancy Kozak. She broke a sacred rule in violating the chain of command. Now Dixon must decide whether to go by the book . . . or to follow his conscience.

Major General Charles B. Lane, division commander, 11th Air Assault, imagines himself an American Caesar, whose every word and whim are law. He arrived in Colombia determined to become known as the man who won the war on drugs for the United States. But even more important is the battle of public relations, where he covets victory at any cost.

"Coyle captures the stress, exhilaration and terror of combat."
—*Cincinnati Post*

"Coyle's examination of individuals caught in the complexities and cruelties of combat is first-rate."
—*Booklist*

Lieutenant Colonel Harold Cerro, Captain Kozak's battalion commander, is a man of proven leadership and valor under fire. He speaks with a voice that commands respect from every soldier who ever followed him into combat. But he is growing disillusioned with the Army—and with his division commander.

Jan Fields-Dixon, wife of Brigadier General Scott Dixon, is the senior correspondent for the World News Network (WNN) in Colombia. She knows that something is seriously wrong with the U.S. military's campaign, and when Captain Nancy Kozak is brought up on charges, Fields-Dixon sets off on a mission to uncover the truth. But it's a truth that may not exist. And it's a mission that could destroy her marriage.

"Coyle is good at conveying the confusion and freewheeling terror of modern combat. . . ."
—*Milwaukee Sentinel*

Books by Harold Coyle

Code of Honor
The Ten Thousand
Trial by Fire
Bright Star
Sword Point
Team Yankee

HAROLD COYLE

CODE OF HONOR

POCKET BOOKS

New York   London   Toronto   Sydney   Tokyo   Singapore

This book is a work of fiction. Names, characters, places and incidents
are products of the author's imagination or are used fictitiously. Any
resemblance to actual events or locales or persons, living or dead, is
entirely coincidental.

POCKET BOOKS, a division of Simon & Schuster Inc.
1230 Avenue of the Americas, New York, NY 10020

ISBN: 0-671-51029-0

First Pocket Books printing January 1995

10 9 8 7 6 5 4 3 2 1

POCKET and colophon are registered trademarks of
Simon & Schuster Inc.

Stepback art by Dru Blair

Printed in the U.S.A.

ACKNOWLEDGMENTS

In writing this book, I was ably assisted by a number of people from various walks of life who took time from their busy schedules to read the rough drafts and help me make this book a reality.

Lieutenant Jeff Givens, the executive officer of a 1st Infantry Division brigade, used much of his precious free time to plow through the manuscript and comment on it as well as pass it on to others in the Big Red One for their comments. Thanks, Jeff.

Captain Kristine K. Hayter, a JAG officer with the 1st Infantry Division, was kind enough to review the manuscript and comment on legal matters. Besides thanking her, I would like to apologize to her and just about every JAG officer in the United States Army for taking my liberties with the Manual for Courts Martial as well as the conduct of the investigation and court martial I have depicted. However, as Captain Hayter herself acknowledged, this is a novel and not a supplement to the Manual for Courts Martial.

Chet Burgess, my media expert, took time to go through the material I sent him despite the fact that he was knee deep in remodeling his new home and moving into it.

The New York City connection, Michael Korda and Paul McCarthy, as usual, tolerated my fits of passion and my incredibly creative spelling as they worked with me to make this a finished product. Good editors, I am told, are hard to find, which is why I am thankful that I have been blessed by two of the best.

A new addition to my circle of helpers is Melanie M. Martin, a dear friend who, from the start of this project to the very end, helped me in innumerable ways.

ACKNOWLEDGMENTS

In the course of writing this book, I lost a dear friend, a man who helped me on this book and others, for he knew no bounds when it came to a friend. Lieutenant Commander Gerry Carroll was a naval aviator, a veteran, a writer, and a man dedicated to his family, his friends, the United States Navy, and his nation. He died this past September, leaving a hole that no one will ever fill. Gerry, here's to you, kid.

Dedicated to Dr. C. H. Burgess, Ph.D.
Professor of English, V.M.I.

He was a scholar, and a ripe good one;
Exceeding wise, fair-spoken, and persuading;
Lofty and sour to them that lov'd him not,
But to those men that sought him, sweet as summer.
                    —*Henry VIII*, Act IV, Scene ii

CONTENTS

War is the unfolding of miscalculations.
—BARBARA TUCHMAN

It is better to die on your feet than to live on your knees.
—EMILIANO ZAPATA

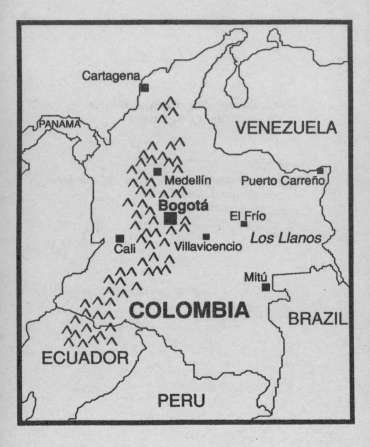

PART ONE

A
GATHERING
OF
DARKNESS

CHAPTER 1

September 21

LOOKING DOWN AT HER WATCH, CAPTAIN NANCY KOZAK decided that it would probably be a good idea to go over and check with her battalion commander. Though nothing had changed in the past thirty minutes, she was doing nothing where she was, and doing nothing was something that Nancy Kozak had never been able to do well.

Taking a deep breath, Kozak brushed from her face the stray wisp of hair that always managed to escape from the tight bun she put her hair into before an operation like this. Ready, Kozak set the butt of her rifle on the ground upright between her legs and grasped its forward grip with both hands. With a single heave, she pushed herself up and out of the dirt she had been lounging in. Her grunts and exertions caused none of the other eleven soldiers she had been waiting with to stir or follow suit. They were used to her need to be doing something, even if it was just trooping, checking things for the umpteenth time. With nothing more than a casual glance, if that, the men and women who made up Kozak's battle staff withdrew back into their own thoughts as they waited for the helicopters to arrive, provided, of course, they did arrive.

At the edge of the clump of trees she paused. From there she looked out toward the dirt runway, if the bare scraping of earth could be called a runway. To one side of it, closest to her, sat

3

the soldiers of Company A languishing in the oppressive late-morning sun. They were the assault company today, the first in. Followed by Company C in support, the unit she had been waiting with, the battalion had the mission of seizing and securing a suspected arms cache located in the Cauca River Valley some ninety-five kilometers from where they sat. Like most of their operations to date, it would be, as one of her sergeants put it, "a walk in the woods and a nice break from this hole."

For the briefest of moments she considered the wisdom of leaving the relative shade of the tree line just to go trotting out on a fool's errand. But then she shook her head and stepped off. She figured if she had put out this much effort already, she might as well follow through, and she headed directly for the first group of soldiers waiting at the edge of the runway.

As she approached, no one in the group she was headed for paid her much attention. It wasn't that the twelve people, mostly members of the command group for the first wave, were ignoring her. It was simply that after sitting in the hot Colombian sun for over an hour waiting to start an operation that was hopelessly behind schedule, all the energy and enthusiasm that they had been able to muster earlier in the day to psych themselves and their soldiers up for this operation had melted away. Even her battalion commander, Lieutenant Colonel Hal Cerro, merely looked up at her without speaking when she finally reached them. He was, she knew, like her, doing his utmost to contain the anger and frustration that he felt whenever he thought about the manner in which operations had been conducted in the last few months.

Stopping just in front of Cerro, Kozak mumbled something that Cerro didn't hear. He didn't bother to ask her to repeat it. Had it been good news, he knew Kozak's pace and tone of voice would have been far more animated. Her leisurely, almost sullen manner and subdued greeting told him all he needed to know; nothing had changed, everything was still proceeding as normal, late and getting later.

Looking up while she stood before him, the sun at her back, Cerro watched Kozak rearrange her gear and dust herself off as she looked down the line of waiting clusters of soldiers. She was, he thought, like everyone else in the 3rd Battalion, 511th Infantry Regiment, tired of waiting in the oppressive heat for the helicopters that were late and getting later by the minute. But rather than waste his time pondering what his operations officer was about to do, Cerro turned away and went back to thinking about the timetables and schedules Kozak's operations section had developed and published for the battalion's orders that were supposed to be driving this operation. Now, like so many other such efforts, those wonderful little schedules were worthless. Instead of being a well-synchronized effort, today's operation, like most of the operations the 11th Air Assault Division had conducted since arriving in Colombia, would have to be conducted on the fly. Not that either he or Kozak minded doing things that way. If the truth were known, both secretly preferred to operate on the run, for they were both part of that rare breed of soldier that not only thrived on chaos but could make that chaos work for them.

Looking down at Cerro, Kozak was about to ask if there had been a change in the estimated time of arrival for the aviation company that was supposed to be supporting them that day. Kozak stopped, however, when she realized that she had asked him that very same question not thirty minutes before. His answer now no doubt would be the same: "Brigade will call us as soon as they have any word." She looked down at her boots and shook her head before looking back at Cerro. "Sir, I'm going to take a walk down the line. Want to join me and kill some time?"

Though he knew that he should accept her invitation, at that moment Cerro had no drive whatsoever. After ensuring that everything that could be done in the way of planning and coordination had been done, he had finally managed to turn in just after midnight. Up three hours later, due more to the heat than nerves, Cerro had bounced about the battalion's base camp checking those things that a good battalion commander should. At dawn both he and Kozak had gone over the plan one more time with each of the company commanders and then from a distance watched the pre-combat inspections. In the process, Cerro, like Kozak, had skipped breakfast, believing, or more correctly hoping, that this operation would get off on time.

But it didn't. Like many others before, delays due to the overcommitment of the division's aviation assets in support of multiple operations left the 3rd of the 511th baking in the hot tropic sun along the flat dirt landing zone like lizards on a rock. After having been physically and mentally pumped up and then let down, Cerro had little energy or drive to spare for another inspection that would only serve to kill a few more minutes. Squinting as he looked up at Captain Nancy Kozak, Cerro shook his head. "If it's all the same to you, Nancy, I think I'll sit this one out."

Feeling much the same way he did, Kozak nodded. "Okay. No problem. I'm sure the XO back at the command post will give us a hoot as soon as he hears something."

Still squinting, Cerro didn't even nod his head. "Roger that." With that he let his head drop as if there were a lead weight tied to the brim of his helmet and allowed his mind to wander off in search of a thought or sleep, whichever came first.

With no need to say more, Kozak turned, held her rifle at her side by its charging handle, and began to walk down the line. That line consisted of groups of soldiers, numbering ten to twelve per group, spread every thirty meters parallel to the dirt runway. Like the command group, each of the small circle of soldiers represented a helicopter load, at times referred to as a slick. The distance between each group was based on the fact that each UH-60 utility helicopter with its blade unfolded measured about sixty-five feet, or approximately twenty meters. With ten meters added for separation between aircraft, the line of twelve groups that made up the first lift extended almost a quarter of a mile.

As Kozak approached each group, no one stood, though her appearance did cause a slight stir as the first soldier in each group to see Kozak would tap the senior man on the shoulder. If the sergeant or officer was too far away to reach, the soldier would throw a small rock to get his attention and let him know that the battalion S-3 was coming. Alerted, the senior soldier would prop himself up, look in the direction that Kozak was coming from, and prepare to greet her. Normally the greeting consisted of a glib comment such as "Mornin', Captain. Nice day for the beach," or "Doesn't brigade know that exposure to the sun too long causes skin cancer in lab rats?" While the officers' comments were for the most part less caustic, everyone who spoke found some means of conveying their displeasure. Though many of these comments were just this side of disrespectful, the quips and remarks Kozak heard that morning and on many other mornings were the only way her soldiers could legally let Kozak know that they were not at all happy with their predicament.

The fact that they were making them, however, often with a smile, was enough for Kozak. Had they simply sat there as she went by, glaring at her and saying nothing, then Kozak would have been concerned. For her part, Kozak would pause and return the comment with one of her own. To the sergeant who joked, Kozak shot back, "Well, Sergeant Wells, that's why they sent us out here instead of the lab rats. We wouldn't want to be guilty of being cruel to animals, would we?" This caused the soldiers in Wells's squad to crack up. One specialist toting a squad automatic weapon slapped the side of his weapon as he laughed out loud before he joined the exchange. "Yeah, Captain. We wouldn't want those animal rights activists coming down on us. Them folks from division is bad enough."

Not interested in any long-drawn-out conversations, especially when they involved any mention of the division or its bloated staff, Kozak would respond with a light laugh, make a comment or two, and move on to the next group. Because she was not the commander, Kozak could move about with greater freedom and less hassle. In Cerro's own words, she moved through the battalion area with the ease of a cat, while he could only do so with the grace of a bull. Being an astute commander, Cerro used this to his advantage, since he knew that the officers and NCOs would freely tell her things that they would hesitate to tell him. That, coupled with an incredible eye for detail and a knack for working with people, allowed her to see things that he couldn't. Since she had assumed the full responsibilities as the operations officer, after the major in that slot had been killed in a freak accident, Cerro had come to value Kozak's observations as much as his own.

Knowing this, Kozak tried hard not to miss anything. As she walked among the groups of waiting soldiers, her eyes would move from one soldier to the next, looking at his or her face, uniform, weapon, even boots. For often it was the condition of the soldiers' boots that betrayed how long they had been with the battalion. The newer the boot, the greener the soldier. This morning as she was parrying comments with her own and trying to gauge the condition of the battalion, the number of new boots Kozak saw served to remind her that the battalion was changing. It was no longer the well-trained and tight-knit group of professionals that had left Fort Campbell four months earlier. It was now a hodgepodge of tired veterans fast approaching burnout and new, partially trained soldiers fresh out of training centers in the States. A full 25 percent of the command now consisted of people who had joined them after they had arrived in country. With another eight months to go and the tempo and cost of operations increasing, Kozak was beginning to wonder how many of the soldiers she was looking at would make it to May, when they were due to pull out of Colombia.

Finished with Sergeant Wells's group, Kozak waved to Wells and slowly made her way to the next group without saying another word. Private Andrew Hayman watched her go by. New to the unit, Hayman found it difficult to relate the training and indoctrination he had received in his infantry training at Fort Benning to what was going on here. Nothing, from the manner in which the officers and sergeants conducted themselves to the way in which Staff Sergeant Wells ran the squad, bore any resemblance to Fort Benning. Everything, including the Army he was now serving in, was foreign. Of course, Hayman thought, with less than three days in a line unit under his belt, it wasn't surprising that things would be confusing. Still he was hoping that something, anything, that he had learned in basic and advanced infantry training would be of use. But so far this battalion seemed to do everything different. Looking over at the specialist with the squad automatic weapon who had spoken to the captain, Hayman longed for the day when he could face an upcoming operation with such casual disregard.

Kozak was deep in thought, her head slightly bowed, when she came up to the group that included Second Lieutenant Gerald T. Horan. A graduate of West Point and only recently assigned to the 3rd of the 511th, Horan jumped to his feet when he saw Kozak approaching and saluted. Surprised by Horan's sudden move, Kozak stopped in her tracks and looked up to see what the problem was. The image of a second lieutenant dressed in new camouflage that hadn't faded and boots that still betrayed a hint of polish beneath the thin covering of dust caught Kozak off guard. Not that there was anything wrong with Horan. It was just that Kozak hadn't been expecting such a display of military etiquette. As she looked Horan up and down, it finally dawned on Kozak how long it had been since a young officer in this battalion had behaved in such a manner. Were they, she wondered, getting too casual, too slack?

While Kozak stood there looking at Horan with a blank stare as if she were pondering what to do next, Horan's platoon sergeant jumped to his feet, glaring at his new officer and barely able to contain the muted obscenities that he was mumbling below his breath. While Horan was somewhat bewildered by Kozak's reaction, Sergeant First Class Timothy Banks knew exactly what was going on. Taking charge, as was his style, Banks gave a quick salute so as not to further embarrass his platoon leader and reported. "Good morning, ma'am. Second Platoon, Company A, at your service."

Shaken from her thoughts by Banks's response, Kozak looked away from Horan over to Banks and gave a rather casual hand salute in return. She began to say something to Banks, then paused, remembering that the Second Platoon, for the first time in well over a month, had a lieutenant as a platoon leader. Turning back to Horan, Kozak looked at the eager young officer. Again she did not speak. Rather she allowed her mind to stumble over a series of disjointed thoughts. The first that came to her was Kozak's regret that her battalion commander had agreed to accept Horan and another second lieutenant into the battalion while they were still deployed forward and involved in operations. Though she knew that eventually they would have to accept these officers as well as senior noncommissioned officers to replace losses that were beginning to accumulate, Kozak, like the other battalion operations officers in the 11th Air Assault, preferred to wait until their battalion had been pulled back to Eagle Base outside of Bogotá. There, as the division reserve and without the pressure of back to back operations, Kozak thought, the company commanders could spend the time necessary to properly integrate and indoctrinate the new people into the ranks properly. The idea that new soldiers, officer and enlisted, could be sent to them straight from the States and plugged into units without additional training or time to acclimate to the country, the climate, the unit, and the level of operations that they were conducting was in Kozak's mind worse than ludicrous. It was, as her brigade commander had once put it during a fit of anger, akin to being an accomplice to murder.

Still Kozak, like her brigade commander, was a soldier, and they had their orders. They would accept and integrate individual replacements into their ranks as quickly as they arrived in country in accordance with the division's policy. So young Horan, along with another lieutenant whose name Kozak couldn't remember at the moment, was out there along with the rest of the battalion waiting in the sun for helicopters that never seemed to arrive on time. This led Kozak to her next thought or, more correctly, observation. Horan was young, frighteningly young. As she stood there staring blankly at the nervous young platoon leader, Kozak couldn't help but think that Horan didn't look at that moment old enough to graduate from high school. The fact that Horan wasn't much older than the bulk of the platoon he was about to lead into combat didn't make Kozak feel any better.

Nor did it make the members of Horan's platoon feel too comfortable. To them, Banks was a known commodity. He had been their platoon sergeant back in Kentucky before the deployment. When their platoon leader came down with malaria six weeks prior, Banks had assumed command. To the soldiers of the platoon this was no big deal. They, the old-timers in the platoon, knew Banks and trusted him. They knew what he would do in a tight spot and had come to depend on his judgment. They knew that when he said do something, it was the right thing to do. In four months of operations they—Banks and the members of the platoon—had become a single entity. It came as no surprise to Kozak, therefore, that the assignment of Horan would be greeted with hostility. Only the direct intervention of the A Company commander had quieted their discontentment. Still, based on the looks on the faces of the old-timers, and even Sergeant Banks's, Kozak could tell that their company commander's efforts had not been 100 percent effective.

Shaking her head slightly, Kozak brought her hand up and with a casual flip swept from her face the stray wisp of hair that

10

had fallen out of place again. Looking in Horan's eyes, she noticed that he was staring at her, waiting for her to say or do something. Her presence and her failure to say anything up to now was, she realized, unnerving this young officer.

Still she said nothing as her mind wandered off again. Had she, Kozak wondered, been like this? Though only seven years separated her date of graduation from West Point and Horan's, the difference between the two seemed incredible. That she could stand there, the author of an order that was about to propel two rifle companies into battle, a battle in which she would function as the fire and air support coordinator, with no more on her mind than fleeting thoughts about the age of another officer, was to her unnerving. Had she, Kozak wondered, become too casual about all of this? Had war, and the agony and destruction that it visited on everyone and everything that it touched, become so much a part of her that she didn't even give what she was doing a second thought?

How terrible, Kozak suddenly realized, to be twenty-nine and so hardened to pain and suffering that your only measure of human worth was whether the person in front of you could stand up in combat or not. Perhaps, Kozak thought, that had been on the mind of her former boss, the operations officer she was filling in for. At about the same time that Horan's predecessor had been evacuated, the operations officer, a major with a bright career ahead of him, had gotten up from his desk one day and walked out of the battalion command post. Without a single word to anyone, he casually strolled over to the flight line and right into the rotating blades of a liaison helicopter that was preparing to take off. Had he, Kozak wondered as she stood there staring blankly at Horan, become so casual about death that even his own meant nothing?

Unable to contain himself, Horan finally took the initiative. "Captain Kozic, is there something that you need?"

Kozak blinked, looked at Horan, and finally spoke. "It's Kozak. Pronounced co-zack."

Though she hadn't meant to make it sound like a reprimand, her response stung Horan. "Oh, sorry, ma'am. I . . . well . . ."

Realizing that she had only shaken him further, Kozak forced a smile. "It's okay. Everyone screws it up the first few times."

Looking down at the ground between them, Horan sighed. "Well, I do apologize. It won't happen again."

My God, Kozak thought as the faint smile disappeared from her face, it had been a mistake to plug this lieutenant into the line so soon. Maybe, she thought, she could talk the battalion commander into leaving him behind. Maybe it wasn't too late. But as soon as that thought came to mind, she pushed it aside. It was too late. If Horan was pulled out of his platoon right now, it would be an embarrassment that he would never live down, with either his own men or the other officers in the battalion. No, she thought. As cruel and cold as it seemed, Horan was committed to this operation, ready or not. Besides, maybe she was being too cautious. Thousands of other officers, she thought, had had to face the same thing Horan was now facing, or worse, and had survived. Why should this young officer be treated any different? Without a pause Kozak's smile returned. "No, there's nothing I need. I'm just trooping the line one more time. Now if you excuse me, I need to be going."

Horan smiled and saluted. "Yes, of course, ma'am. By all means." He was in truth glad to be rid of Kozak, an officer who had a reputation and combat record that was the envy of every junior officer in the battalion.

Without acknowledging his salute, Kozak turned away and began to tread her way down the line again. She was halfway to the next group when she heard the faint sound of helicopter blades off in the distance beating the humid midmorning air. Instinctively Kozak stopped and turned to face the direction from which the sound was coming. Quickly slinging her rifle over her shoulder, she lifted both hands up to the brim of her helmet to shield her eyes from the sun as she searched for the source of the noise. When she finally caught sight of a small black dot on the horizon, she shifted her head first to the left then to the right as she prepared to count the number of other helicopters that were inbound. Only after watching for several seconds did she finally realize that there was only one inbound helicopter, and that one as it grew closer appeared to be only a light liaison aircraft.

Dropping her hands to her sides, Kozak was about to despair when the first happy thought of the morning popped into her mind. Maybe, she thought, Aaron was flying the inbound bird. The idea of seeing Captain Aaron J. Pierce, whom everyone called AJ, brought a smile to Kozak's face. For AJ was the first man that Nancy Kozak had allowed herself to become involved with. Though Kozak was by no means an advocate of celibacy, all of her affairs before AJ had been more or less purely physical. In her efforts to make it or break it as an infantry officer, Nancy Kozak had gone out of her way to avoid becoming involved in a relationship that could endanger her standing in the eyes of her superiors, peers, and even her subordinates. After all, she had reasoned, the image of a love-struck female fawning over her lover didn't quite fit the role model that infantry officers were expected to follow. So it was in the image of Iron Mike, the statue that stood in front of Building Four at Fort Benning, Georgia, the home of the infantry, that Kozak patterned her lifestyle.

It was only after she had met AJ that Kozak realized that living in the shadow of Iron Mike was perhaps overdoing things a bit much. Even Iron Mike, she thought, must have had someone that he went home to after a hard day of yelling "Follow me" and toting his rifle about. So when Kozak first gazed into AJ's pale blue eyes and found herself blushing, she decided it was time to reassess her position on the issue of love, men, and relationships.

Intently, Kozak watched and followed the approach of the inbound helicopter, just as everyone else scattered around the pickup zone did. While everyone, even the most hardened veteran in the battalion, could feel their pulse begin to quicken in anticipation, the reasons differed from one soldier to the next. For the old-timers, the increase in the heart rate and accompanying awareness had become as much a part of their pre-combat preparation as checking their weapons. When the time came for the final run into the LZ, each soldier who had been there knew they had to be ready for anything and everything, from jumping right into the middle of a firefight to a crash landing.

When it became obvious that there was only one helicopter coming in, the veterans of the two line companies waiting grunted or mumbled before turning their attention back to whatever they had been doing. The new men, including Horan, however, hadn't learned yet how to turn their emotions on and off with such ease. For them the sensations they felt as they watched the lone helicopter approach varied. For some it was akin to the sudden fear one feels when riding a roller coaster for the first time as it is slowly being cranked up the first long incline. Like the ride on a roller coaster, just beyond that incline, now clearly in sight, lay all sorts of unknown terrors that the rider had no control over. To others the thought of battle brought only images of a vague, unfathomable darkness.

Regardless of what they thought, the sudden realization that they were about to go over the top and there was nothing that they could do to stop it struck each new soldier to some degree. Every trooper in the battalion knew that, despite all their physical and mental preparation, only when they had reached the end of the ride would they know for sure that they could deal with it. Even the old soldiers, those who had been with the battalion since the beginning, wondered. No man or woman, after all, could be expected to be a hero every day.

Not everyone in the battalion, however, felt the strange grip of fear, excitement, and anticipation as they watched and waited. Of the soldiers waiting and watching, Kozak alone felt joy in her heart. Unable to restrain herself, she inched her way onto the runway in an effort to get a closer look.

Seeing Kozak wander out from the edge of the runway, the pilot of the helicopter assumed that she wanted him to land near her. With measured ease he slowed his aircraft and prepared to land near Kozak. Only when the helicopter finished its approach and slowed down just before landing in front of her did Kozak suddenly realize that AJ wasn't flying this aircraft. Always the cocky aviator, AJ never missed the chance to show off his skill and daring when he thought that Kozak might be watching by coming in a little too fast and far too low. Whoever was flying this helicopter, Kozak decided, was doing it by the book. Heaving a sigh of disappointment, Kozak watched as the pilot lightly touched down and allowed his single passenger enough time to dismount from the left door and walk away before he pulled up and away from the landing zone.

Crestfallen, Kozak was still watching the helicopter fly away when the passenger it had left behind called to her, ''Expecting someone else, Nancy?''

The familiar voice, which she had not heard in a long time, caught her off guard. Whipping her head around to face the owner of the voice, Kozak quickly brought herself to a position of attention when she caught a glimpse of the lone black star centered on the front of the helmet approaching her. Rendering the best hand salute she could manage, Kozak greeted Brigadier General Scott Dixon. "Yes, sir. But I'm sure he's busy."

As Dixon closed the distance between them, Kozak could see the sly smile shaded by Dixon's hand as he returned her salute. "Jan told me that you finally found a romantic interest that was worthy of your attention."

Kozak's eyes widened. "My God, does everyone know, sir? Excuse me, but did Jan, I mean Mrs. Dixon, report on my love life during a prime-time news show or something?"

Reaching up with his right arm, Dixon put his hand on Kozak's left shoulder and gave a slight shrug. "Jan, Captain, is a reporter, a female, and my wife. She told me that she came across you out here in never-never land, and brought me up to date on everything you were doing."

That comment caused Kozak's eyes to grow wider. "She told you everything?"

Understanding the meaning of Kozak's question, Dixon smiled. "Well, almost everything. At least everything that a broken down old tank general from the Pentagon would be interested in."

Taking a deep breath, Kozak tilted her head down but kept eye contact with Dixon. "Which brings up the next question, sir. Exactly what is a general officer assigned to the Army General Staff doing out here in the middle of nowhere?"

"The chief sent me down here to find out what you sky warriors were up to."

It was only with a great deal of effort that Kozak kept herself from replying that the only thing that they were up to was eye deep in bullshit, but she held her tongue. For although she had known Dixon and his wife for years, and theirs was a relationship that transcended the formal military boundaries, there had always been a fine line between maintaining a comfortable and relaxed professional relationship and being too familiar. After all, Dixon, Kozak reminded herself, was a general and the chief that he was so casually referring to was the Chief of Staff of the Army, General Paul M. Fulk. That he had sent Dixon didn't surprise Kozak. Of all the senior officers she had known, he always managed to stand head and shoulders above the rest when it came to calling the shots as he saw them and speaking his mind, damn the consequences. Such an attitude would have cost a lesser man his career long ago. But Dixon had in his own lifetime become something of a legend. It was said by those who knew him that he could do no wrong in the eyes of those who counted.

While the general and the captain stood in the middle of the dirt runway talking, the soldiers of Kozak's battalion looked on, wondering who the general was and more importantly why he was being so chatty and informal with Kozak. Of all the people watching, only their battalion commander, Hal Cerro, who was now making his way to where they stood, knew. Almost from the day Kozak had reported to her first unit at Fort Hood, Texas, an unusual friendship had sprung up between Dixon and Kozak as their careers and their lives became intertwined. Cerro knew all about this because he too was part of that relationship that merged professionalism and friendship. That Scott Dixon, who Cerro knew was assigned to the Pentagon, was standing here dressed for battle rather than sitting in an air-conditioned office overlooking the Potomac didn't surprise Cerro. Dixon was never one for staff work. He was a field soldier. That wasn't to say Dixon couldn't do what was necessary when he was serving on the staff. In fact he had a knack for it. But when the choice came down to going out and doing something in the field with a unit or sitting in an office moving papers about a desk, in Dixon's case the papers never stood a chance.

As he approached, both Dixon and Kozak turned to face Cerro. Smiling as he saluted, Cerro spoke first. "I heard that you were down here on some kind of fact-finding tour. What brings the newest general in the Army to our humble little corner of the earth, sir? General Staff need some fresh coffee and decided to send its junior general to find and secure Juan Valdez?"

"No, not quite, *Colonel* Cerro. Fact is, we need someone to empty the trash cans in the chief's office and he asked if I knew a lieutenant colonel who could handle the job."

16

Cerro said, "Oh, no, sir. I don't need to do time in the Pentagon. I've been a good boy. Ask my S-3. She'll tell you."

Kozak backed off, putting one hand up and waving it. "Sorry, sirs. I'd prefer to stay out of this one."

After an exchange of handshakes, Cerro got around to the same question that Kozak had asked Dixon minutes before, namely, What was he doing there?

Though there was still a hint of a smile, both Cerro and Kozak could tell that Dixon was getting serious now. "I thought that my last day in country would best be spent in the field with a unit on an operation. When I saw your unit was slated to hit a suspected weapons cache, I decided to join you."

Cerro, now slowly turning serious, shook his head. "Well, I'm sorry to disappoint you, sir, but if the reports from division intelligence are to be believed, this will be a real sleeper. The report, based on information provided by informers, *claims* that this is a Class B logistic site, small arms and sustenance only. All the Class A sites with the big stuff, heavy weapons and all, are up in Norte de Santander or Vichada. The rebel insurgents are active around here but not like to the north and east." After a slight pause, Cerro added, "Fact is, I think this is just going to be a drug bust."

Betraying no surprise, Dixon cocked his head to one side. "What makes you say that?"

Looking down at the ground for a moment, Cerro considered his answer. Though he suspected that Dixon already knew the truth, since the division commander's preference for drug-related targets was common knowledge, Cerro still hesitated. No one had ever offered him any proof, though the number of missions that the battalion had been given that had been labeled as FARC but instead turned out to be drug-related were too numerous to ignore. Looking back at Dixon, Cerro decided, What the hell! He had asked. Besides, Cerro knew of Dixon's knack for detecting BS in all its forms. It would do no good to attempt to bluff him.

"Well, to start with, the 'informers' usually turn out to be DEA agents. When these Rambos gone astray find something belonging to the cartel that they can't handle, they pass the word onto the local CIA. The CIA translates cartel into FARC and passes the information directly to the division G-2. Well briefed on their roles, the intelligence analysts in G-2 accept the CIA information as gospel and pass it on to division operations, who then task the brigades. This allows the division commander to tell the Colombians that he's going after the Farcees every chance he gets, while he's actually getting more druggies.''

As Cerro spoke, Dixon nodded. He already had found out much of this on his own and had pretty well figured out the rest. The "Farcees" Cerro spoke of was the popular name used by American forces when discussing the Revolutionary Armed Forces of Colombia. Officially known as the FARC, based on a shortening of the Spanish name, which stood for Fuerzas Armadas Revolucionarios de Colombia, the Farcees were the chief opponent of the 11th Air Assault Division. An aborted military coup nine months prior and the resulting purge of officers had left the Colombian military disorganized, dispirited, and incapable of dealing with both the drug cartel, which had never been under control, and a resurgent socialist movement aimed at ridding Colombia of a corrupt government, an oppressive military, and the drug cartel. Though the Colombian government tried to deal with its problems on its own, the President of Colombia finally was forced by circumstances to either accept defeat at the hands of the FARC or request American military intervention.

Through the use of strict controls and limitations, the Colombian President was able to convince the majority of his government that the Americans were the lesser of two evils. There was in his estimate little choice. As he told his confederates, in order to save their regime and their way of life they would have to risk alienating portions of their population and suffer the righteous and overbearing Americans for a while. So with great trepidation, the President requested that the United States dispatch a small expeditionary force to Colombia for a period of no more than one year to hold the line against the FARC while the Colombian government rebuilt its own military machine, starting from the top.

The United States, seeing an unparalleled opportunity to put a sizable military force that would have relative freedom of action into the heart of a nation noted for its illegal drug industry, decided the invitation was too good to pass up. Hence, while it was the avowed mission of the 11th Air Assault to protect the regime in power from the FARC while it put its own military house in order, the 11th Air Assault was under special orders to do as much damage as possible to the drug cartel while it was in country. With only one year to do it, the division commander, Major General Charles B. Lane, was determined to become known as the man who won the war on drugs for the United States.

While few people had a problem with going after the drug lords, it soon became obvious that the 11th Air Assault couldn't perform both its mission to suppress the FARC and tackle the druggies as well. That, of course, didn't keep Lane and his staff from attempting to do so. Thus started the vicious cycle of mixed priorities, overextension of divisional resources, and botched missions as the Colombian government put pressure on the American military to go after the FARC rebels, while the commanding general of the division and the DEA did everything they could to find and destroy the infrastructure of the drug industry. The problem here was that the industry they sought to destroy was far more resilient than anyone had suspected. While inroads had been made into the drug industry, the efforts by the 11th Air Assault against it were proving to be of little consequence, especially since the drug cartel had become, shortly after the coup and the resurgence of the FARC threat, the main supporter in Colombia of the ruling government. That Lane or anyone else in the military chain of command, not to mention the DEA or CIA, failed to appreciate this, was understandable.

That, however, only accounted for a small part of the problem facing the 11th Air Assault. Its biggest problem was internal. For it was becoming more and more obvious to the American media, as they freely roamed the battlefield and spoke to soldiers who were being worn thin by operations that never seemed to end, that they weren't accomplishing anything. That the mission of the 11th was not to win the war but just to keep the FARC from doing so until the Colombian Army was ready to resume its own burden had been lost to both the media and the general public as American men and women killed in the line of duty started coming home in body bags.

General Fulk, the Chief of Staff of the Army, decided that to allow the impression that the Army was wasting men and money in pursuit of a hopeless cause was not only inexcusable but detrimental to the American Army as a whole. Which was why Dixon found himself standing in the middle of a dirt runway on a hot September morning in Colombia. Fulk was tired of overoptimistic reports and muffled responses, coupled with statistics that showed that American casualties were on the rise. That was why he dispatched Scott Dixon down to Colombia to look at the situation for him. General Fulk's only instructions to Dixon were "Scotty, I don't want any goddamned Vietnams on our own watch. Go down there, find out what is going on, figure out what we need to do to fix it, and report back to me, ASAP."

There was silence for several seconds, silence while both Cerro and Kozak waited for Dixon to continue. Finally Dixon, looking over at the troops, spoke. "Well, regardless of where you're going, I'm going. After all, how would it look if I spent two months without ever getting my boots dirty." Turning back to Cerro, he added, "Provided you have room."

Cerro, relieved that the subject had been changed, turned to Kozak. "Well unfortunately every seat on my aircraft is taken. But I'm sure Captain Kozak can find an open seat with the second wave."

Dixon leaned over toward Kozak. As she was looking over a listing on the manifest, he whispered so that Cerro could hear, "Correction to that last transmission, Captain. First wave. Your boss's last message should have read first wave, not second."

Kozak grinned as she looked up at Cerro. Cerro rolled his eyes. "I stand corrected. First wave."

Nodding her head in acknowledgment, Kozak looked down the listing of helicopters and the number of troops, referred to as paks, assigned to each one in the first wave. Finding what she was looking for, Kozak called out her answer without thinking. "The fifth aircraft has two open slots."

"Perfect!" Dixon exclaimed. "More than enough room for a general officer and his ego."

While Cerro laughed, Kozak frowned when she saw that the

fifth aircraft was the same one Second Lieutenant Horan was on. Fearing that putting Dixon in the same load as Horan might unhinge the young officer further, she was about to recommend another aircraft when the sound of numerous inbound helicopters broke the morning stillness. In unison, Dixon, Cerro, and Kozak turned toward the sound. "Well, General, looks like show time. I'll take you over to where you need to go while Captain Kozak trots on over to the command group and notifies Brigade we're on the way."

Without another word, both Cerro and Dixon turned and began to walk away, leaving Kozak to look over to where Horan was standing, then at the approaching aircraft. This was going to be a simple raid, Kozak reasoned, a good first mission for him. There really wasn't any reason to make a big deal over where the general sat or whether or not Horan was ready to go on an operation. General Dixon was never one to make a big to-do about protocol. If he said riding with the Second Platoon was fine by him, he meant it. And if this indeed was a simple anti-cartel raid, then an easy operation would be perfect for Horan's initiation. Nodding, Kozak pushed her concerns about Horan's and Dixon's presence aside as she headed down the line of troops back to where the command group was beginning to stir. There were other things she needed to deal with that were critical to the success of this operation, and they had nothing to do with general officers or second lieutenants.

Kozak had just begun to turn her full attention to the operation that was about to begin when she suddenly turned around to face the incoming helicopters. Perhaps, she thought, AJ was flying one of them. The idea of seeing AJ, regardless of how briefly, was never far from Kozak's mind these days and always managed to soften a face that was becoming too old too fast from holding up a burden that had broken lesser people. Only the shouts of sergeants and officers rousing their men from their slumber broke Kozak's concentration, pulling her mind away from her forlorn hope and back to the task at hand. With a sigh, Kozak turned once more toward the waiting command group and began to make her way toward them. Still, every few feet she slowed and glanced over her shoulder, looking and hoping.

CHAPTER 2

September 21

THE SOLDIERS OF THE 3RD BATTALION, 511TH INFANTRY, weren't the only combat troops waiting to get on with it that morning. Nor were Nancy Kozak and the officers of that battalion the only leaders chafing at the unexpected delay in the operation.

Not far from the Cauca River, near a level patch of ground that broke up the steep slopes that rose from the riverbed, Hector Valendez looked at his watch, then scanned the skies. The Americans were late. According to his calculations, they should have been here a long time ago. Though recent experience showed that this was becoming more the norm rather than the exception, the uncomfortable delay was not welcome. There was too much at stake here, too much time and energy invested in this operation to have it compromised by simple ineptitude.

Turning his head this way and then that, Valendez debated what he should do while he waited. The idea of sitting there in the cramped confines of his covered observation bunker, which was nothing more than a small scooped-out hollow with heavy overhead cover in the side of the mountain, was not appealing. He could, he knew, leave its relative safety and concealment and walk among the waiting soldiers of the Revolutionary Armed Forces of Colombia one more time. As with Cerro and

22

Kozak, the unwelcome idleness weighed heavy on Valendez. He found the gap of time that existed between his final instructions and the commencement of a battle intolerable.

This feeling, Valendez knew, was not uncommon. He had first become aware of it as a problem for commanders when he had read Clausewitz's book *On War*. The passage in that book left little impression on Valendez at the time he had read it. Only later, as he himself became involved in military operations and rapidly moved up the chain of command within the FARC, did Valendez begin to appreciate what Clausewitz had been saying. Understanding of a problem, however, is only the beginning. Even now, though he knew that it was impossible to change anything, Valendez found himself fighting the urge to get up, go out, and do something. What that something was didn't matter.

But he didn't. Instead, he sat there looking out over a landscape that had in the past few days become as familiar to him as the garden of his former home in Bogotá that he had once tended with such care and love. In an effort to turn his mind away from the fears and apprehensions that were nagging him, Valendez carefully analyzed his own thoughts, an ability that made Valendez unique among the leadership of the FARC. He knew that all he was interested in doing was occupying his mind. A diversion, he decided, was what he needed. It didn't matter what it was. Just something to fill the time and keep his mind busy until the Yankees arrived. Behind him he noticed that the deputy company commander who shared the bunker with him was becoming impatient. "You are anxious, my friend?"

The young man nodded. "Yes, Jefe. I was just wondering whether the crew of the number-two machine gun finished clearing that brush in front of their position as you told them. Do you think there is time to go down there and see if it was done?"

Though that thought was at that moment rather seductive, Valendez knew that his tromping about would cause his men to become more nervous than they already were. And the last thing that Valendez wanted to do was rattle his soldiers. "No, my young friend. Little would be gained from going out now other than perhaps betraying our own positions, or maybe getting caught in the open. Best we stay here.'' Still, as he turned away from the nervous deputy commander, the urge to leave continued to be overpowering. He did not like the confinement of his observation post. Only the steel nerves that had led Valendez to this place kept him where he was.

That and of course American technology. After all, there was no telling when the helicopter gunships equipped with their all-seeing thermal sights would make their final sweep of the area before the troop-carrying helicopters came in. Of all the problems that Valendez faced, dealing with American technology was for him the most difficult. Though the FARC had sufficient funds with which to tap into the vast arsenals of the former Soviet Union, his force was and always would be a light force that had to rely on man-portable systems. That left them with few options other than ingenuity and cunning with which to counter the mobility, agility, and technology of the Yankees.

Not that this bothered Valendez. After all, he reasoned, the Yankees had often held the upper hand in weapons and technology and had more than once been embarrassed by a smaller force that had something that technology could not replace— determination. That and a blind belief in their cause were the primary tools that propelled not only Valendez's soldiers but Valendez himself. He was in fact becoming to many the personification of the movement.

From behind him he could feel the presence of someone else very close. Glancing over his shoulder, he noticed it was Rafael Dario, his radioman. Like the deputy company commander, he was becoming impatient. ''Jefe, I was wondering are we ready for this?''

Valendez liked Dario. A young man not much different in age than the deputy company commander, Dario had become more than a radioman. He was his traveling partner, orderly, bodyguard, and at times like this a friend. Dario in turn looked up to and admired Valendez, seeing in him more than a military commander. ''Well, Rafael, while it is true that the magnitude of what we are about to do dwarfs anything that the FARC has tried before, we can do it. After all, every man out there is a well-trained, hand-picked volunteer. For months now I have been telling those people in the central committee that it was time that we had the courage of our convictions. It is time for the FARC to come out of the shadows and start to apply pressure directly on the Yankees."

Valendez paused. To get to where they were now he had been forced to argue, sometimes quite strongly, to convince the rather conservative members of the FARC's ruling council that he was right. Finally after repeated efforts he had prevailed. No one in the end could seem to refute his arguments or his record of successes that belied his background and amateur status as a soldier.

For Valendez was by nature an intellectual, a man who had once been content to spend his days in the confined spaces of the classroom. At five feet, six inches, with dark hair and a pinched face that accentuated his lean, almost skeletal frame, Valendez looked like a schoolteacher. And for years that was exactly what he had done and had for the most part been content to do. Since joining the FARC, however, Valendez had found the experience of living in the jungles and mountains of Colombia among the people both enjoyable and liberating. Out here, free of the trappings of civilization, the restrictions of a man-made world, and a self-deluding society, Valendez found himself closer to the idealized world that his favorite philosopher, Karl Marx, had written so much about. He had quickly, with the drive of a zealot but the disciplined mind of an intellectual, found his place in the world.

Pushing through these idle thoughts one more time, Valendez again felt the need to suppress his nervousness. Finally resigning himself to the idleness resulting from the failure of the Yankees to adhere to their own schedule, Valendez moved over to the corner of the dugout and sat down on an empty ammo box. Folding his arms across his chest, he lowered his head and tried to close his eyes.

Following him, Dario asked if he would like some warm coffee. Without looking at him, Valendez shook his head. "No, not right now. If I drink anything else, my bladder will burst, and that," he said with a chuckle, "would be quite embarrassing in battle."

Turning his mind back to the pending battle, Valendez thought about doing what he had just told the deputy company commander he didn't want him to do. There was no point in going out into the open again. All had been set and ready since dawn. Nothing had changed. The soldiers of the provisional company that he had helped to train and the night before to emplace about the perimeter of the plateau jutting from the mountainside were ready. None had moved. He knew that. None needed to be reminded of their individual and collective tasks, for they had been well briefed and rehearsed in them by him and their company commander. All was set. All was ready. There was nothing useful that he could do but wait quietly and patiently for the Americans to come. For the moment they held the initiative, they set the time. But Valendez, the deputy military leader of the Revolutionary Armed Forces of Colombia, was determined to change all of that today.

One of the runners, new to this company, looked over to where Valendez sat. He was a farmer, or more correctly, the son of a farmer, who had left home and joined the FARC. Though he wanted to be a fighter like his brother, he had been assigned to this company as a runner. While he didn't much care for that duty, it did have certain advantages, including meeting men like Valendez. Screwing up his nerve, he began to speak in a faltering voice. "Jefe?"

Valendez looked over at the young man. He was still not very comfortable with the title El Jefe, which meant leader. Not that it wasn't deserved. At age thirty-seven Hector Valendez had become in a shockingly short time a very powerful figure within the FARC. It was just that he hadn't set out to become El Jefe. "Yes, my young friend. Is there something you need?"

"I have been told, Jefe, that you had been a professor at the university in Bogotá, and that when you left, instead of becoming an officer, you chose to be a common fighter, like I wanted to be. Why?"

"Yes, it is true. I was a professor of economics at the university, with a strong interest in military history, a hobby."

"That hobby," Dario said with a smirk, "has cost the government in Bogotá dearly these last few months."

Valendez looked up at his radioman and smiled. "Yes, well now that hobby has become my vocation. You see, though I had been successful and well liked at the university, I, like many thinking men such as you, became more and more disheartened by what I saw. In my case it was class after class of students, bright with the flame of social and economic reform while sitting in my classroom, who within a matter of years after graduating forgot those ideals. Instead they became a part of the system, which is corrupt, heartless, and socially depraved.''

A student of Karl Marx, a man he felt who was badly misunderstood, Valendez had chosen to combine the study of economics with history. In the classroom he had endeavored to lead his students, through the use of well-documented historical failures, to discover not only what had worked and what had succeeded in the combination of economics and society, but why. He had hoped since his early days as a student himself to be part of a peaceful revolution from within the system by enlightening and stirring the social conscience of the children of the privileged class themselves. But the students, when freed from the confines of the classroom, were mesmerized by the benefits and luxuries of power and money that their fathers commanded and defended. In their transformation he saw his dream of using education as the key to the salvation for the people of Colombia slowly wither and die. Discouraged, Valendez walked out of his classroom at the university on his thirty-fourth birthday and went into the jungle, where he offered his services to the Revolutionary Armed Forces of Colombia as a rifleman.

''My choice to become a soldier pitted against the establishment does not come from any deep desire to save our people or to change their fate. I have already tried that and failed. Instead, in the beginning all I wanted to do was to destroy those who had destroyed my dream. I left the university with an overwhelming belief that I had been betrayed. In my eyes I had been betrayed by a system that preached that there was a future for our people when there was none. We have all of us been betrayed by the realization that our dream of true social and economic change was merely a shimmering mirage, not a vision, held out by men who only want to line their pockets with money earned through our labors. And I felt betrayed by students I had hoped would become the agents of social and economic change but who instead used their education to reinforce the bands that bound an oppressive system together.''

Slapping his knee to add emphasis to his point he concluded his impromptu speech. "So it was the destruction of what was, and not an effort to work for what could be, that drove me to want to be a fighter."

Looking about the bunker, he saw that everyone was watching him, mesmerized by his explanation. Not wanting to leave things there, he looked down, bringing his hands together. When he spoke again his voice was calm, softer. "In the process of seeking to destroy, I was reminded that when destructive forces are given free rein, darkness enshrouds everything that it touches. From being a man of enlightenment working for true social reform for a system he believed in, I found myself becoming the foremost agent of the forces that threatened that system's very existence. Though I, in truth, do not really relish the notion of being known only for my powers to destroy, if that is what is necessary to bring the criminals who rule this country to justice, then so be it."

While the men gathered in the small bunker looked at him and each other, Valendez reflected upon his climb to power within the FARC. It had been his talents as a military strategist and trainer, together with his burning desire to lash out, at times with an abandon that was both blind and total, that had caught the attention of the FARC leaders. When they attempted to direct Valendez's fury, they found there was more to him than they had at first thought. Upon closer examination of this new and fanatical fighter, every leader that came in contact with Valendez found he commanded a useful wealth of military knowledge that he wielded like a weapon. Coupled with the disciplined and logical mind of a teacher of economics and the skills of a professional teacher, his hobby propelled Valendez into the inner circles of the FARC military command at a time when new problems and issues demanded new answers, answers that Valendez seemed to have.

He was quickly elevated to the position of squad leader, then deputy company commander, where his unique ability to combine the realities of his country and its people with his vast pool of military knowledge brought life to a military revolution that had for years been little more than an annoyance to the Colombian government. Though he was politically naive, none of the old-line leaders of the FARC could find fault with Valendez's methods or the results those methods yielded. He was, they thought, an important tool that with a little guidance could be very useful.

Somewhere during this almost meteoric climb the man was transformed. As praise and promotions were heaped upon him, Valendez came to the realization that he had never been mistaken about the revolution or his need to be part of it. The only error he had made had been a choice of means with which to pursue his goals. Now that he was on the right track, there was no stopping him. With the enthusiasm of a lost soul who had finally seen the light, Valendez redoubled his studies of military history while throwing himself into every task and assignment he was handed. So it came to pass that after much debate among those who made up the ruling council Valendez was recalled from the FARC's training base in Venezuela, where he had been serving as an instructor, back to Colombia, where he became the deputy and chief adviser to the FARC's military chief.

The debating did not stop with Valendez's appointment to such an important position. In fact that debate was only the beginning. For, once back in Colombia, Valendez moved the FARC's military campaign against the Colombian government forward with all the drive and energy that he could muster. Such drive, long absent in an organization that had grown old and set in its ways, caused concern among the more conservative members of the ruling council. Everything that Valendez did was aimed at one thing and one thing only: pulling down the Colombian government. He gave little thought these days to what would happen after that. "Those were issues," he told close associates, "best left to those with a knack for dealing with the trivialities of politics." While such statements might have been sincere, they did nothing to endear Valendez to many of the old-timers who wanted a country left after the revolution.

So it was, when Valendez pushed his boss into presenting to the central committee of the FARC his long-range plan for discrediting the Colombian government, that a major crisis erupted. Though the nominal head of the military arm of the FARC mouthed the words, few listening doubted that Valendez had been their author. "We have been presented a unique opportunity," the preamble of the paper stated, "with the involvement of American forces in Colombia. For us the conditions and the terms dictating their use could not be more favorable. First, the number of combat units and their support troops have an upper limit which the American President dare not exceed. Second, their commitment is also limited in duration and is not contingent on either the internal conditions or events in Colombia. Repeated assurances by the American President and a pledge by the American Congress to hold him to this deadline leaves us little fear of a protracted conflict with the Americans. Third, the Colombian military recovery is being hamstrung by relatively low-ranking officers who were not purged by the government after the aborted military coup and in secret are looking for an opportunity to exact revenge for the injustice of the government when it decimated the ranks of the Army's officers corps."

At home before a group, Valendez's mastery of oral presentation and his ability to draw his listeners into his way of thinking made him a powerful force to be dealt with. Even the hard-core members of the central committee were just so much clay in his hands as he molded their thoughts with the skill of an artisan. "This feeling, never far below the surface, is manifesting itself in many ways, in particular the reluctance of the officers of those units ready for field operations to use those forces against us, preferring to save their manpower for what they feel is the inevitable showdown with the government. Finally, the American media, as they invariably do, have followed American forces into Colombia and provide us with a source of propaganda which we could never muster ourselves. By drawing the American forces into heavy engagements that produce casualties which cannot be hidden by the American military high command, we will be given a spotlight into which we can present our case to the world and at the same time mobilize the anti-government sentiment that has been simmering below the surface of our country for years."

The plan, or more correctly the campaign, that Valendez presented to the council through his superior was hotly debated. While everyone had an opinion, no one had a good counter to the campaign. It seemed that the FARC, which had worked to overthrow the Colombian government for years, was finally being handed a set of circumstances and a plan designed to exploit those circumstances. In the end those with wise and cool heads recognized that they had become too accustomed to defeat, failure, and fear. It was time perhaps, they reasoned, to take big risks. And Valendez's plan was certainly a big risk. When the decision was made to give Valendez his way, the vote was unanimous, though for many different reasons. While there were those on the ruling council who felt that Valendez might be right, there were those who knew he was wrong or who simply feared him. The failure of such a high-risk and costly plan, they reasoned, would allow them the opportunity to do away with this upstart. They had without saying so told Valendez that it would be for him victory or death.

Slowly he shifted his weight as he sat on the ammo box and looked toward the small aperture of his dugout, listening for the telltale signs of American helicopters. Valendez could almost feel the cold invisible hand of the ruling council on his shoulder. This operation, though only the first of what he expected to be many, would make or break him and, he believed, the future of the revolution.

Sitting next to the open door, Dixon tried to occupy his mind by looking down at the landscape as it flew by him. Though he worked hard at studying the terrain, his mind was cluttered with self-recriminations and admonishments. It had been a mistake, he realized minutes after lifting off, to have come along with the lead element of Cerro's assault force. The idea that he was a general officer now, a rank that is surrounded by a mystique and aura that few understand but most are intimidated by, had not hit him until then. Even the platoon sergeant, who had seated himself next to Dixon so that one of his soldiers didn't wind up in the hot seat, couldn't ignore Dixon. General officers, after all, are the closest things to a god that most soldiers ever come to know, and gods, as we all know, are seldom friendly folk.

Often generals appear to move about without their feet touching the ground. The mere mention that a general officer might be in the area is often enough to send every officer and non-commissioned officer into a low hover. It is, after all, seldom a simple task to prepare for the divine visit. This feeling that general officers are demigods is not without foundation in reality. The fact of the matter is that generals, because of their position and their ability to make decisions that can only be overridden by bigger generals, have in their hands the power of life and death. Every soldier knows this. It is ultimately the generals who decide who will go where and when. It is the generals who give the orders to close with the enemy and decide when to pull back. While staff officers may draft the orders of battle and more junior officers lead their men and women into combat, the person who like a Roman emperor sits on the sidelines and gives the modern American gladiator the thumb up or the thumb down is without exception a general.

It wasn't that any of this was new to Dixon. He too had once gazed upon generals with that same spellbound look of awe that the young second lieutenant catty-corner from him now viewed Dixon. From the reaction that he had received, Dixon imagined that the soldiers of this rifle squad would have preferred having an alien from another world travel with them than a general. It wasn't that Dixon hadn't been warned. Even before he went to the special course for newly promoted general officers dubbed the charm school, Dixon had been watching, listening, and thinking about how generals acted and what sort of response those actions created. In a sort of naive way, Dixon had been able to convince himself that when his time came, if the gods in power smiled upon him and chose him to join their ranks, he wouldn't act any different as a general than he had as a captain, major, or lieutenant colonel. Before Jan Fields-Dixon and General Fulk had pinned the single star of brigadier general onto Dixon's shoulders, he had been able to believe that he could do so. And even after that landmark event, an occasion that had reminded Jan more of a religious ceremony than a civil procedure, Dixon had been able to continue to act as if the star he wore hadn't changed anything.

But that had been in the Pentagon, a place where one's value is measured by the number of stars one wore or in the case of mere mortals the number of stars one's boss wore. Until General Fulk had sent Dixon to Colombia in an effort to figure out what was going on down there, Dixon had not had the occasion to be with soldiers, real soldiers, as a general. Only after he had boarded the helicopter he now rode in and introduced himself to the squad he would be traveling with did it hit him that he was no longer one of them, a simple soldier. In the past he had always been able to move about and conduct himself in a manner that put those around him at ease and allowed his abilities and personality to transcend rank and position. The glaring sheen from his general's star, even the single black subdued star he wore on each collar of his battle dress uniform, however, now blinded the soldiers he was traveling with. They could not see Dixon as a man. They could not even see him as a fellow soldier. All they could see was a general, a person who had sent them there and in their minds had the power to take them away from this hell on earth. None of them could imagine that Dixon was as nervous as the rest of them as they drew near the landing zone. None of them even considered Dixon vulnerable to the same dangers and hazards that threatened their lives. He was, after all, a god.

A tap on his shoulder caused Dixon to look away from the lush green and red of the Colombian landscape. It was the crew chief. He was reaching over the heads of the soldiers across from Dixon and holding up two fingers. Over the whine of the engine Dixon could barely make out the words he repeated, "Two minutes, two minutes." They were two minutes from the landing zone. Nodding that he understood, Dixon looked down to check his personal gear, what little he had, without thinking that the crew chief, like the other soldiers on the helicopter, was so conscious of Dixon's presence that he made a special effort to tell Dixon first of their approach before informing the rifle squad Dixon was traveling with. They were, after all, just riflemen. Dixon was a general.

Even before Hector Valendez's radioman could say "They're here!" the whine and sudden rush of noise and wind created by a scout helicopter flying low and fast over Valendez's dugout told him battle was about to be joined. At first Valendez simply looked up, first at his radioman, then past him at the blinding daylight that streamed through the aperture of his dugout. For a second it seemed as if Valendez was frozen in place, unable to move. In truth he was briefly overcome by the significance of the moment. All the planning and preparation that he had put into this operation was about to be put to the test. Everything that he had worked for since joining the FARC, from the hardening of his own heart, body, and mind to the demanding training he had run his specially recruited companies through, was about to be tested. Everything, including the future of the revolution, was about to be risked in battle, one that would pit two dissimilar forces, each led by dynamic, thinking humans, against each other.

Standing up as best he could in the cramped confines of the dugout, Valendez moved over to the aperture. Without a word passing between them, the radioman stepped aside and allowed Valendez full use of the aperture. Valendez, after all, was the deputy military commander for all of the FARC. Though he lived with his soldiers, eating the same food at a common table in camp, sharing the hardships and burdens of long marches and demanding training, Valendez's position demanded respect and along with that a deference by subordinates that was never demanded but always shown.

From the narrow aperture Valendez could see two small scout helicopters buzzing about both the landing zone and the camouflaged arms-cache site like dragonflies searching a pond for prey. The scouts, themselves armed to the teeth, were in fact doing just that. They were looking for trouble, becoming bolder by the minute as nothing below them moved or showed any sign of responding to their presence. They had, Valendez knew, been sitting several kilometers away for some time watching for signs of his forces. Only when they were satisfied that there was no apparent danger did the scouts come charging in at treetop level in an effort to stir a reaction. Even this seemingly foolish move was not made without the presence of attack helicopters hovering off in the distance watching and waiting to intervene if necessary. Now, as Valendez watched, the scouts slowed down and began to circle areas where they feared the enemy might be hiding. With no outward show of fear or concern, Valendez watched as the helicopters flitted about from one place to another, turning this way then that as they made sure all was clear for the troop-carrying helicopters.

To his radioman, the deputy company commander, and the two runners that shared the dugout with Valendez, his calm demeanor was almost unnerving. They of course did not realize that he, like them, had his own fears. Unlike them, however, his were not of death, something that he had often wished for after he had thought himself a failure as a revolutionary at the university. Rather, his greatest fear was that his plan would not yield its desired results. He wanted to smash things, to destroy. After years of patiently trying to work within the system in order to reform it and seeing all of his efforts come to nought, he had resolved that he would spend the rest of his life if necessary trying to level that system. Destruction, complete and utter destruction, was his chosen tool now. And today his target, a mere stepping-stone to his goal, was the Yankees, the Yankees who belonged to the 3rd Battalion, 511th Infantry.

After the long and uneventful flight from the base camp to the LZ over the peaceful countryside, the sudden rush of events at the landing zone came on like a blur. Because he was sitting at the door, Dixon would be the first out on his side. To make sure that he didn't embarrass himself or slow things down by trying to exit the aircraft with his seat belt still on, Dixon undid his seat belt long before the wheels of the UH-60 helicopter even got near the ground. This response was not an imaginary fear. Dixon had, in the rush of events, tried to get up and out of a helicopter without undoing the seat belt a few times too many.

With that out of the way and prepared to spring up and out, he was still careful to hang on to the frame of the seat just in case the pilot made a sudden turn. Watching, Dixon saw the ground draw near as the helicopter coming in at a steep angle prepared to land. It was almost as if the ground itself was rising to greet them. As he braced himself for action, Dixon considered drawing his pistol, but then decided not to. That, he decided, would be a little too melodramatic even for him. All he waited for now was the thump of the wheels digging into the dirt to cue him and he would be gone.

The riflemen he was traveling with, however, weren't waiting for that. From behind him, Dixon heard the platoon sergeant yell, as much for Dixon's benefit as for his troopers, "EVERYONE OUT. NOW!"

Without so much as a pause, the platoon sergeant got Dixon moving and out the door with a nudge that was more of a shove before Dixon even had a chance to determine how far off the ground they still were. It was a good thing that he hadn't, for had he seen how high they were when the troops started exiting, Dixon probably would have stiffened up and really hurt himself after falling six feet from the helicopter to the ground.

Almost before he realized what was happening, it was all over. In a blur he went tumbling out of the helicopter, hit the ground, and instinctively allowed his body to collapse as he had learned a long time ago at airborne school. Though his intent was good, Dixon's form was terrible. Even before he stopped rolling, he knew that he had hurt and bruised at least a half a dozen spots on his body and would no doubt find more after he had time to think about it.

But there was no time to think about his personal injuries or anything else for that matter. The riflemen he had been traveling with, used to this kind of punishment, had already scampered past where Dixon still lay on the ground. Propping himself up on an elbow, he watched his traveling companions clear the landing zone and disappear into the waist-high brush and bushes that surrounded it to begin the process of deploying into a rough perimeter. Only the young lieutenant paused long enough to ask Dixon if he was all right, and even then he kept one eye on his platoon sergeant lest he lose track of the one man in his platoon who knew what he was doing.

Dixon, still too stunned to say anything, just waved the lieutenant on. By the time he had managed to get himself onto his feet and headed for the brush, the helicopters had already disappeared. The whine of their engines, now barely audible, had been replaced by the shouts and orders of officers and sergeants as they got their troops in hand and ready to move on. Off to his left, Dixon heard Cerro's clear and distinct voice driving on the company commander of the assault force. Officers and sergeants hearing Cerro didn't wait for their company commander to relay the order. They immediately redoubled their efforts and, trusting that their riflemen would follow, plunged forward into the brush and toward the arms cache.

As he watched, a silly thought popped into Valendez's head. As effortlessly as a cooling breeze it quickly replaced the nervous apprehension that he had felt earlier. While he stood there watching American troops sweep through the dummy arms cache a few hundred meters below them, the strange and silly vision pushed aside Valendez's conscious thoughts and removed him from that time and place. Rather than viewing the Yankee riflemen moving forward by short rushes and bounds from the lee of one covered spot to the next with concern or foreboding, Valendez's mind drifted back to his childhood.

For several moments Valendez felt the same giddy feeling that he would get when playing hide-and-seek with his brothers. It was, he remembered, such an exquisite feeling knowing that all your searching for the right spot, efforts at burrowing yourself into place just so, and supreme patience were about to pay off. He could tell as a child when he had his brothers dead to rights. He could tell by the look of concern that would creep upon his brothers' faces, a look that was poorly masked by a stern and falsely confident expression. When he saw that look, Valendez's own excitement would multiply. He would almost jump up and down with joy, knowing that regardless of what his brothers did he, Valendez, would win.

As important as the selection of the site and his patience had been, however, Valendez knew that timing was everything, both in the past when playing with his brothers and now as he prepared to kill Yankees. As a child he had learned that if he timed it right, he would be able to scare the devil out of his brothers, causing them such confusion and shock that he would be able to do anything he wanted for seconds, sometimes minutes, before his brothers would be able to recover sufficiently to react and make him pay for his trickery.

As he struggled to restore clear and conscious thinking, Valendez realized that what he and his soldiers were doing was nothing more than a grown-up game of hide-and-seek! They were playing now the same games that he and his brothers had played when they had been children. This action today, Valendez knew, would be no different. When he and his soldiers sprang their ambush, there would be a period where Valendez would be in control. How long that period would last Valendez did not know. He was prepared, as were his men, to wait until sundown before breaking and running, if they could last that long. But that, Valendez knew, was only one possibility. If the Yankees were well led, resolute, and able to quickly regain their balance and bring their overwhelming firepower to bear effectively, then Valendez and his men would need to break off the action sooner. For Valendez knew that, as terrible as the initial results of the ambush would be, psychologically as well as physically, the impact of fighting a hard battle that had been costly in lives would be greater if at the end of the fight the Yankees had few or no enemy bodies to drag before the cameras of the world and display like so many trophies. To bleed without having the opportunity to draw an equal or greater amount of blood was to a soldier a defeat of the worst kind.

Slowly the images of his childhood began to fade back into the recesses of his mind. Before they disappeared completely, Valendez the university professor wondered if the games he had learned as a child such as hide-and-seek had been nothing more than preparation for adulthood, or if what he, his soldiers, and the Yankees were doing at this very moment was simply an extension of childhood games. As interesting as this philosophical question was, Valendez realized that this was no time to deal with it. Leaning forward, he began to watch for the mystical cue he had used so well as a child, the subtle cue that would tell him it was time to initiate the firefight. That—and the need to start dealing with the next problem that he, the leader of his men, El Jefe, would need to address, which was deciding when they had done enough killing for the day— wiped the last vestiges of childhood memories from his mind.

The anger that Dixon felt over his treatment at the landing zone was finally beginning to subside when they stumbled upon the arms cache. While there had been a high level of tension as Cerro's lead company moved from the landing zone to where they were now, that tension seemed to redouble itself, almost becoming a real and tangible commodity that Dixon imagined he could touch as the squad he traveled with began to move in between the camouflaged huts and sheds. Hanging back ten to fifteen meters, Dixon conformed as best as he could to the movements of the rifleman to his front. As he did so, the fact that he didn't have a weapon worth mentioning other than his holstered pistol heightened Dixon's anxiety and nervousness. Not wanting to get in the way and wanting to create the smallest possible target, Dixon moved against a tree at the edge of the arms cache site and eased himself into a squatting position.

Effortlessly the riflemen of Cerro's battalion changed from the formation they had used during the approach march to the site of the arms cache into one that allowed them to begin the methodical process of clearing and securing it. From where he sat, Dixon could only see a relatively small number of people. But what he saw pleased him. Few commands were given. There was no need to. The soldiers were well trained and often anticipated the command before the squad leader or the platoon sergeant gave the order either by word or with a simple signal. Automatic riflemen eased into positions that afforded them the best field of vision and fire. Riflemen designated to lead off were up and moving forward without hesitation or confusion, headed for positions they had already selected that would allow them to cover the next group of soldiers to advance.

Here and there Dixon could tell who the leaders were by the manner in which they moved and acted. He could also tell which ones were new to all of this, like Second Lieutenant Horan, the young officer he had traveled with who had been so unnerved during the flight. Horan, Dixon concluded, was doing no better down here on the ground than he had in the helicopter. Though he was going through the motions no doubt just the way he had been taught at Fort Benning, Horan was always one or two steps behind his platoon sergeant, Sergeant First Class Banks, in thinking and acting. At least, Dixon thought as he watched Horan move up to Banks and hold a hushed conversation before issuing his next order, Horan had the common sense to use Banks's talents and experience.

Now that the lead or point elements had penetrated well into the site and the troopers who had been giving them cover from the tree line were moving forward to new positions to cover further advances, Dixon pulled himself up from his squatting position, using the tree he had been next to for support. In the process of doing so he imagined that he could distinctly hear several bones and joints crack and pop. This, Dixon realized, was no longer an easy game to play at. Activities and motions that had come to him so easily as a junior officer and those being displayed by the sky troops before his very eyes were neither easy nor came naturally anymore. The idea that he could not make the one hundred and seventy-two pounds that his five-foot, ten-inch frame supported perform like it used to often bothered Dixon, especially at times like this. Perhaps, he thought as he finally managed to straighten himself out, Jan, his wife, was right. Perhaps it was time that Dixon stopped playing cowboys and Indians and let what she called the younger lads do all the fun stuff while he did the thinking.

Ready, Dixon followed the last of the troopers into the site, looking closely at the huts and lean-tos for the first time. Ignoring the sound of helicopters heralding the arrival of the next wave of Cerro's battalion, Dixon began to wander through the site barely keeping track of the squad he had traveled with. Slowly Dixon began to realize that the huts and lean-tos were not very impressive up close. Nor were they well laid out or camouflaged. That last item, he thought, goes without saying, for if this site had been well laid out and camouflaged, no one would have found it. Only small, seemingly insignificant errors or omissions that Dixon himself had been able to discern in the aerial photos had allowed the division intelligence officer working with the CIA to pinpoint the arms cache so quickly and accurately. It was, he thought, almost as if the FARC had wanted the 11th Air Assault Division to find this cache and come here. It was—

Like being hit in the face by a ball bat, the sudden realization of what was happening struck Dixon. Like a bird of prey's, his eyes darted from one item to the next as he quickly sought confirmation of his worst fears. There were no trails, no beaten paths leading from one hut to the next or through the site that men carrying arms would have left. There were no signs around that soldiers, even highly disciplined soldiers, would have left behind as they worked, such as discarded scraps of paper, cigarette butts, bits and pieces of equipment. And even in the lean-tos, stacked high with boxes that should have held weapons and ammunition, Dixon saw that the boxes were old and weathered, stacked in a rather indifferent manner, and had no tarps or plastic coverings to protect them from the cruel jungle humidity and rains. This site, this supposed arms cache, was bait designed to draw them in.

Realization of course is one thing. Doing something with that knowledge, however, is entirely different. Having come along on this operation on a whim and merely as an observer, Dixon really didn't fit into the chain of command. To simply yell out, "AMBUSH," at the tops of his lungs might cause more problems and confusion than the ambush itself. With that thought, Dixon looked for an officer who was in the chain of command. Unfortunately the first one that his eyes fell on was Second Lieutenant Horan, a lad already overwhelmed by all of this. Rejecting that idea, Dixon next decided to find Cerro, Kozak, or the company commander. By going to them and working from the top down he could be sure that whatever Cerro's lead company did in the few seconds that it had left before the trap was sprung would be productive and orderly. At least that's what Dixon hoped as he turned and prepared to head for where he thought he would find the battalion command group.

For some reason Valendez had noticed the lone soldier wandering about the dummy arms cache behind the advancing line of Yankee infantrymen. This soldier, unarmed and unburdened by field pack or gear, struck Valendez as looking and acting different from the others. There was something special about him. His actions, his aloofness from the action, his detachment from the others all marked him as some kind of special observer. Though Valendez could not explain to himself why this special observer, whoever he was, wasn't traveling with the command group, a cluster of officers and radiomen he could clearly see gathering on the far side of a hut away from the lone soldier, Valendez suspected that this lone soldier was significant in some way. While keeping one wary eye on the command group as it milled about for a moment, with some officers talking on radios while others looked down at maps, Valendez studied every move the lone soldier made. He therefore was able to see the sudden reaction, the quick jerking of the lone soldier's head, and the rapidity with which he began to move toward the command group. Whoever this man was, he had, Valendez knew, figured out their game and was about to alert the others.

Taking a deep breath, Valendez began to give his orders as he continued to watch Scott Dixon. "Let us begin with the mortars now, if you would, please."

At once Valendez's radioman keyed the handset of his radio and called out, "Eagle, commence firing. Eagle, commence firing." With that the radioman released the push-to-talk button and waited. Over the earpiece of the handset, Eagle, the call sign for the leader of the mortar section, responded. "Eagle acknowledges. Firing now."

With that done, there was for the moment nothing that Valendez, the deputy company commander who stood next to him, or their radioman behind them could do but wait, watch, and pray.

The distinct thud of half a dozen mortar rounds being pushed out of their tubes broke the hushed stillness just as Dixon caught sight of Cerro talking on the radio. Both Cerro and Dixon, knowing the significance of the thuds, didn't try to determine where the noise came from. They knew that it would be a foolish waste of time. They therefore reacted appropriately by dropping to the ground and making themselves as small as was humanly possible. With few exceptions every soldier in or around the arms site did so, for they had been in Colombia long enough to have heard that terrible sound before. The only exceptions were the new troopers, the soldiers who had just joined the battalion and were, if they survived the stupidity of those who sent them into battle before they were ready and their own ignorance, about to become veterans.

CHAPTER 3

September 21

EVEN BEFORE THE FIRST MORTAR ROUND SLAMMED INTO THE midst of the soldiers of Alpha Company at the arms-cache site, Charlie Company, still going through the motions of forming up in preparation for movement to the arms site, was engulfed in a withering fire that swept the landing zone and the area around it. The surprise was complete and the effects for a unit that had sustained less than a dozen casualties in its first six months in Colombia were devastating. Before the commander and soldiers of Charlie Company really understood what was going on, half a dozen of their number were hit, including the company commander himself.

Nancy Kozak, who had been talking to him just before the firing had started, had turned away looking toward the arms cache when she had heard the mortars being fired. When she realized what was happening, Kozak had spun her head around to order Terry Kaplin, the Charlie Company commander, to get his unit on the move fast. But Kaplin wasn't there. Bewildered, she looked to her left, then to her right. Only when she heard the gurgling sound of Kaplin as he tried to spit up the blood that filled his mouth did Kozak look down at her feet. Then it all hit at once. The sound of automatic weapons firing, the zing and snip of bullets cutting through the air and vegetation around her, and the screams of wounded soldiers shocked and panicked at being hit mingling with the shouts of officers and sergeants to get down and open fire.

Without any further conscious thought other than being careful to avoid falling on Kaplin, Kozak threw herself flat on the ground. For a moment she lay there pushing her face down into the mud that smelled of stagnant water and rotting vegetation and tried to overcome her own shock and surprise and collect her thoughts. The sound of Kaplin lying next to her drew her full attention. Turning her head to face him while keeping it down, Kozak was appalled by the sight that greeted her less than two feet away. Kaplin, lying face up, was arching the small of his back up while clawing at the empty sky with wild and disjointed motions. His eyes were all but popping out of their sockets, fixed in an unblinking look of panic and fear as he spit blood from his gaping mouth. To see a fellow officer, a man who was little more than a year younger than she, reduced to such a state in a matter of seconds was as unnerving at that moment as the sudden hail of gunfire had been. For what seemed like an eternity Kozak lay there and looked at Kaplin, mesmerized by the sight before her eyes. In those seconds there was no feeling of fear, no conscious thought. Only horror, a horror that almost paralyzed her mind and body.

That feeling, however, only lasted a moment. As quickly as it had overwhelmed her it was gone, replaced by a flurry of action as she pushed her body along the ground closer to Kaplin and began to look for the wound that had felled him. This task, given that she could not raise her head up off the ground for more than a few inches, was difficult. The fact that Kaplin's face was intact and that he was spitting up blood ruled out a wound above the neck. That meant that he either had a chest wound, a stomach wound, or had been shot in the neck. Laying her rifle on the ground next to her, Kozak took one hand and began to feel Kaplin's abdomen and chest while she reached for Kaplin's throat with her other one.

As soon as her hand closed around Kaplin's neck, she knew she had found the wound. Ignoring the sticky warmth that coated her hand, Kozak felt for the actual site of penetration while feverishly working to free the compression bandage that hung on Kaplin's web belt with the hand she had been using to check his torso. The first small pouch she found and ripped open turned out to contain a compass, which fell out on the ground. Kozak ignored that and moved her hand further around the web belt until it came upon another small pouch that felt about the right size. Pulling the cover open, she found the plastic-encased bandage and pulled it out just as the fingertips on her other hand found the broken flesh on Kaplin's neck.

Working as fast as she could without fumbling, Kozak ripped the plastic pouch open with her teeth, pulled the bandage out with one hand, opened it up, and reached around with it until she had it over the wound her other hand had discovered. Quickly Kozak pulled the hand that had found the wound out of the way and pressed the bandage down over the wound. Using her bloodied but free hand, she slid it under Kaplin's neck. Once she had managed to reach all the way around the back of his neck, she put the hand over the top of the bandage and began to apply all the pressure on the wound that she could with both hands. Whether this would do any good was anyone's guess. It was all, however, that Kozak could do for Kaplin at the moment.

From behind her Kozak felt a slap on her thigh. Without letting up on the pressure she was applying to Kaplin's wound, she turned her head to see who it was. It was, to no surprise, Sergeant Andy Pender, the assistant operations sergeant who was serving as her radiotelephone operator that day. Pender, his body pressed flat against the ground and his face showing no sign of fright, was holding the hand mike of the radio out toward Kozak. "Captain, the old man's on the horn. He wants to know Charlie Company's status."

Kozak was perplexed. Forgetting for the briefest of moments that her hands were wrapped around the Charlie Company commander's neck in an effort to keep his life from oozing away, Kozak shouted back, "Hasn't anyone from Charlie reported in yet?"

In a matter-of-fact manner, one that appeared more suitable for a training exercise than close combat, Pender shook his head. "I haven't heard anyone other than the colonel on the radio since the shit hit the fan, ma'am."

Glancing back at Kaplin, whose eyes and expression showed no change, Kozak thought for a moment. Then she turned back to Pender. "I can't let go of this bandage right now. Get yourself around here so you can keep pressure on this wound while I check in with the colonel.''

Ignoring Cerro's frantic call over the radio, Pender clipped the radio's hand mike to his web gear and began to crawl over Kozak's legs and around Kaplin's head. As he was doing so, Kozak lifted her head slightly so that she could look around. Cerro, she knew, would want to know what their situation was when she finally was able to talk to him. That she couldn't do so at the moment caused her to curse. She had become so involved in dealing with Kaplin's wound that she had lost track of everything around her. It would take her several seconds, all the time that it took Pender to complete his maneuver, to figure out that Charlie Company for the moment was leaderless and pinned in place, unable to move and barely returning fire at assailants that up to now had been unseen.

The ringing in Scott Dixon's ears caused by the detonation of a mortar round that impacted less than twenty meters to his right was quickly replaced by a piercing scream. For a moment Dixon, stunned by the suddenness of the attack, simply lay there wondering if he was the one producing the horrible scream. Slowly, ever so slowly, he managed to regain control of his senses by slowing his breathing and simply letting himself relax, despite the impact of a second volley of mortar rounds. As each sense came back into play, Dixon was able to start piecing together the scene around him.

Even as he worked at that, the one thought that began to dominate his still rattled brain was that he was stupid. It had been wrong for him to come along on this operation, to place himself in the middle of a combat unit without prior notice, and to add to the burden of a commander, one he had always held in high regard and had a special relationship with. As heroic as the image of a general officer out front with the troops might seem in a cheap novel, Dixon knew the Army hadn't made him a general so that he could go running about like a rank second lieutenant absorbing shrapnel and bullets.

The screaming, which had subsided only for a moment, started up again with a vengeance. Taking care to make sure that he didn't lift his head off the ground more than a few inches, Dixon turned his head toward the screaming. A few meters away, ten, maybe fifteen, to Dixon's right, a soldier lay on the ground flailing his arms and legs madly as his head jerked from side to side, screaming with all the strength he had left and throwing off sprays of blood from numerous wounds as he did so. The motion of his head jerking from one side to the other gave the scream a strange warbling effect like the siren on a police car. The sight of a small pillar of smoke rising lazily up from the ground a few feet from where the wounded soldier lay told Dixon that whoever the poor bastard was he had taken almost the full blast of a mortar round. Odds were, Dixon knew, there was little that he or anyone else for that matter would be able to do for the wounded man other than put him out of his misery. And that simply was not the way the Americans did things normally.

That the body Dixon was watching belonged to Private Andrew Hayman, newly assigned to the 3rd Battalion, 511th Infantry, meant nothing to Dixon. Hayman was, as far as Dixon was concerned, just another image of war that would burn itself into his brain, where it would wait patiently with all the others he had collected over the years until the quiet hours of some night. Then like other images and sights, the vision of Hayman's death throes would come back in all its fury to rob Dixon of his rest and sanity.

Turning his head away from Hayman, Dixon forced himself to think about something else, like getting out of the open and under cover. At first he thought about heading to where he had last seen Cerro and his command group. To do so, however, would have forced him to move across open ground to a spot that was even more exposed than the one he was in. Besides, as he surveyed the route he would need to take, Dixon noticed clods of earth being kicked up by concentrated machine-gun fire stitching its way this way and that. No, he decided. First things first. Get out of the open and then take it from there.

Looking to his left, he spotted two soldiers crouching behind a slight rise of ground thirty meters to his front left. One of the soldiers had a radio whip antenna sticking up out of his rucksack, a sure sign that the other had to be an officer or at least a senior sergeant. Without another thought Dixon slowly began to push himself forward toward the antenna. Even if one of the pair he was headed toward wasn't an officer or sergeant, the cover offered by an otherwise insignificant dirt mound was a lot more inviting than his present position. As if to drive that point home, a stream of bullets cut their way across his path, throwing dirt up into his face and into his eyes, blinding him and causing Dixon to flatten himself on the ground.

While Brigadier General Scott Dixon was wiping the dirt from his eyes and preparing to restart his long and arduous trip across the thirty meters that separated him from the mound of dirt and the antenna, Second Lieutenant Gerald T. Horan finally began to look around. The only person he saw at first was his radioman next to him. Everyone else in his platoon it seemed had disappeared. Shaken by his first taste of combat, his current predicament further unnerved him. Were he and his radioman, Horan wondered, the only survivors of his platoon? Had the jarring mortar barrage and the ceaseless hail of small-arms fire killed everyone? Though commissioned and trained as an infantry officer, Horan suddenly found himself in a position that he realized he was not ready to deal with. Fortunately, he thought, he had his platoon sergeant. He'd be able to get a handle on this mess and give him, Horan, a chance to sort himself out.

As suddenly as that thought came to mind, Horan flashed back to his original thought: Is everyone else dead? As if to answer his question, the screams of Private Andrew Hayman caused Horan to look out across the open ground behind him. Immediately behind him he saw one soldier lying flat on the ground busily rubbing his eyes. Though exposed, this figure didn't appear to be in serious distress. Not far from him, Horan saw Hayman, still thrashing about madly, though not as much as he had been when Dixon had first set eyes on him. Even from where he lay, Horan could see that Hayman was severely wounded and needed assistance. For a second all thoughts of his platoon were pushed aside as Horan lifted his head higher off the ground and began to yell, "MEDIC," just as he had seen it done in dozens of war movies. Though he had no idea who the wounded man was, he was an American soldier who needed help.

Though many heard Horan's call for assistance, only one man responded. Noticing a head pop up from behind a mound of dirt, followed by yells that he didn't understand, the gunner behind a Russian-made PKM machine gun shifted the barrel slightly to his right, made a quick estimate of the range, tilted the barrel down slightly as he had been taught, then pulled the trigger.

While not every round fired by the FARC gunner found its mark, and the flak jacket and kevlar helmet that Second Lieutenant Horan wore deflected or absorbed most, enough found exposed portions of Horan's upper torso and head to do the job. Watching from where he lay, Horan's radioman found watching the death of his lieutenant both fascinating and horrifying. As he watched, the impact of bullets fired from very close range kept Horan's body propped up. It was almost as if they were working together, the first bullets holding the body in a vulnerable pose so that their brothers could catch up and do their job tearing into those portions of Horan's head, chest, and shoulders that were exposed above the mound of dirt. Only when the bullets stopped did Horan's lifeless corpse simply flop down into the pool of blood that was already beginning to form at the base of the dirt mound in front of the radioman's face.

For a second the radioman continued to stare wide-eyed at the shattered mass of bone and flesh that had once been a face. This sight, combined with the fear, the smell, and the strain of battle, was all at once overpowering, crippling, and numbing. In a single moment of spontaneous revulsion, the involuntary convulsion of the radioman's stomach muscles forced him to turn his own head to the side away from his shattered lieutenant and throw up with all his might. Though he had yet to be touched physically by the battle that continued to ebb and flow all around him, the radioman was as dead at that moment as his lieutenant. The fact was, though he didn't know it and wouldn't for years to come, that every bullet that had ripped into his lieutenant had in its own insidious way made its mark in his brain, a mark that time would never wash away.

From his bunker, Valendez darted his eyes from the scene before him to the sky above. Below him, on the small patch of level ground that jutted out of the mountainside where the dummy arms cache was located, all was going well. Actually, things were going better than well. As he watched in silence, Valendez could see individual American officers and sergeants scurrying about in an effort to organize a response to the devastating fire that rained down on them from an unseen ring of bunkers. Those responses, however, were being frustrated time and again as the Americans discovered that, rather than facing a single line of enemy positions, their tormentors were deployed in a series of well-placed positions that ringed the arms-cache site on three sides. Each FARC fighting position, the Americans were finding, was well placed, expertly camouflaged, and covered by at least two other positions. Any effort to isolate and deal with a single position would draw fire from two and sometimes three other bunkers to either flank or further back. It would take, Valendez knew, a well-coordinated force lavishly supported by fire support to crack the lines of bunkers his men occupied. And so far the Yankees had yet to recover from their initial beating and put together such an effort.

Satisfied with all that he saw before him, Valendez turned his attention for a moment in the direction of the landing zone. Off in the distance, further down the hill on another level patch of ground, he could see only faint signs that the ambush on the landing zone was still in progress. Like the commander of the company conducting the ambush, Valendez relied on radios for reports from the platoon leader at the landing zone. At that moment that platoon leader, like the two platoon leaders at the main site, reported all was going well. Report after report confirmed what Valendez himself could see, that return fire was sporadic and poorly directed, leaving their own firepower undiminished. Only the mortar platoon had ceased fire, and that was only because of the necessity of moving the mortar tubes to new locations, lest they become detected from the air and attacked by the Yankee gunships.

Thinking about those gunships caused Valendez to look up and search the sky again. Where, he wondered, were the vaunted American attack helicopters? Why hadn't they struck? Was the surprise so complete that the Yankees had been caught off guard and unprepared to react? How nice, Valendez thought, that would be. But this, he knew, was no time for such dreams and fantasies. They would come and attempt to extract revenge for the punishment that his men had rained down on the Yankee ground troops. But until they did, there was nothing he could do about it. The new trap was set, and all he could do was wait for the Americans to come rushing into it as their ground troops had done earlier. Still Valendez could not help but wonder and worry. Looking up, he whispered, "Where are you?"

Little more than two hundred meters away, down on the small level area that Valendez was watching between his incessant scans of the sky above, Lieutenant Colonel Harold Cerro was thinking the same thing. Though he and his command group had like everyone else been taken aback by the suddenness and severity of the FARC attack, the officers, sergeants, and the soldiers serving as radiotelephone operators with him recovered quicker than most and began to respond to Cerro's orders and their training. Under the dubious cover of the lee of one of the huts, some of the members of the battalion command group worked on the two wounded troopers they had pulled to safety. At the same time, Cerro and the fire support officer, a young captain named Peter J. Crippen, were attempting to get a handle on the situation so that they could bring in the attack helicopters, which were busily trawling about several kilometers away in search of targets that weren't there.

While Crippen, on the ground inches from Cerro, attempted to contact the commander of the attack helicopters loitering off somewhere north of them, Cerro's own radioman alternated his attempts to contact the commander of Alpha Company or Kozak, who was with Charlie Company back at the landing zone. Neither answered the radioman's call. Though Cerro understood that both were in tight if not tighter situations than his own at that moment, his inability to exercise anything resembling command and control infuriated him.

As bad as this was, the fact that he had been cautioned about going in with the lead element during such operations added to the anger that Cerro felt welling up in him. At least if he had taken his brigade commander's advice and used one of the helicopters he had been offered as a command and control bird, he would be able to get a picture for himself of what was going on, with or without reports from the elements in contact. Other battalion commanders in the division, flying just over the heads of their people on the ground, were doing so effectively. Except for an odd angry shot, the light weapons of the FARC had done little to discourage this practice. Only Cerro's determination to lead from the front, as his mentor Scott Dixon had always done, caused Cerro to reject the idea of commanding from above. Even if Cerro had known that less than fifty meters away his mentor was having similar thoughts and regrets, he would have still felt the anger that continued to well up inside of him. Both Kozak, at the landing zone, and Frank Spelvin, the Alpha Company commander, should have reported in already. They knew better. They damned sure knew how Cerro felt about reporting, and that to Cerro made all of this harder to tolerate.

Revelations as to the true nature of their situation at that moment were coming fast and furious. Already Kozak had a firm grasp of several important pieces of information. For one, they had not been subjected to the mortar fire that the main force with Cerro had been. This made it easier to look about and gather more information and assess the situation. Next, the volume of fire, the noise of battle, and the manner in which the troopers of Charlie Company were deployed led her to believe that they were faced by a FARC platoon, probably no more, deployed in a simple L-shaped ambush. Though this didn't make things easy, it could, she began to realize, be worse. On the debit side, the wounding of the company commander and the failure of the company executive officer to seize immediate control of the company left the three small platoons of Charlie Company on their own for several critical minutes. During those minutes only one platoon leader, Second Lieutenant Elie Tibbetts, was able to pull his platoon together and do something quite on his own that would set the pace for the rest of Charlie Company's fight.

That Tibbetts and the Third Platoon were able to do so was more an accident than good planning. Upon landing, Tibbetts had hustled his platoon out and away from the exposed landing zone, rapidly deploying them into a hasty defensive line. Though he had gone further than he should have, and he was about to correct this when the firing began, the effect of this misjudgment meant that a large portion of his platoon, including him, was outside of the kill zone. Free from the imminent danger, Tibbetts was able to take a moment to assess the situation. This was not his first firefight, since he was one of the "originals" who had been with the battalion before it deployed from Fort Campbell to Colombia. Though the volume of fire was greater and far more accurate than anything he had seen to date, the solution to the problem that he applied here was the same that had worked so well before.

With little more than a quick overview of the area from where he stood, Tibbetts ordered the one squad in contact to stay in place and keep up a good return fire. Correctly guessing that his one squad had found the extreme flank of the enemy positions, he would use that squad as a base of fire and a guide. With his other squads, now forming up to his left and right, he would pull further away from the ambush site before moving around and to the rear of where he thought the last enemy positions were. With luck, he could then take the enemy positions from the front, flank, and rear. If that succeeded, then it would be, he knew, a relatively easy matter of rolling up the entire enemy line by taking on one position after another using similar tactics.

While the squad leaders with him prepared their people for this, Tibbetts decided that he'd best inform his company commander of his plans and maneuvers lest the other platoons or attack helicopters mistake the movement of his men for the enemy. When Captain Kozak answered the radio instead of his own commander, Tibbetts didn't hesitate to render his report to her. He knew that Kozak had been traveling with Kaplin, and his own commander no doubt was listening in on his report.

When Tibbetts was finished, Kozak threw the radio hand mike back at Kaplin's radioman, who had given it to her when he had seen his own commander was wounded. It wasn't that Kozak was being disrespectful or anything. It was just that throwing the hand mike happened to be the quickest and most efficient, not to mention safest, method of returning it. Looking at her own radioman, Sergeant Andy Pender, Kozak considered Tibbetts's report before deciding that she had best get this situation in hand before doing anything else. Tibbetts's report and initiative were both encouraging and gave her something to work with. Ready, she began to issue her orders.

"Sergeant Pender, drag Captain Kaplin over there in that stand of trees. We'll collect the wounded there and set up a command post. When you're set, contact Colonel Cerro and let him know what's going on here."

Pender, unsure of what Kozak had in mind and wanting to make sure he got it right, shot back to her, "What exactly is going on here, ma'am?"

His question was not meant to be funny or critical. Only after Pender had asked did she realize that she hadn't taken the time to tell him. Quickly she blurted her plan. "Third Platoon is looking for the enemy's right flank. When they find it, they'll start rolling it up. I'm going to rally the rest of the company. If I can, I'm going to pull one of the other two platoons back and throw them around the right flank to reinforce Tibbetts while the platoon left in contact lays down a base of fire and pins the enemy in place."

Pender was about to comment that as far as he could see it was them and not the Farcees that were doing all the pinning down, but he didn't. Though Kozak enjoyed a little humor now and then, this was not one of those times. So Pender merely nodded that he understood and turned his full attention to dealing with Kaplin, his rifle, his radio, and keeping himself as close to the ground as the buttons on his uniform allowed him while Kozak turned away and began her search for whoever was in charge of the First and Second platoons.

Lieutenant Horan's radioman was still heaving when Dixon came up next to him. Dixon, not noticing what the radioman had been doing, suddenly found himself running his left hand through a vile pool of vomit. Jerking his hand back, Dixon cursed as he shook it. "Jesus! Damn you!"

Looking up at Dixon and noticing that the general was next to him, the radioman cleared his throat. "Sorry, General, I, I . . . The lieutenant, he's dead. All shot to shit."

For the first time, Dixon took the time to study the shocked, numbed expression that the radioman wore. Carefully lifting his head so that he could see over him, Dixon looked over to where Horan's corpse lay. The sight that greeted him explained without any need for words the radioman's reaction. Two feet beyond the radioman Horan's head was turned toward Dixon.

One couldn't call what Dixon saw a face, not anymore. Rather it was a beaten mass of pulp framed by the kevlar helmet that now served as a bowl that collected the blood, gray tissue, and bone that had once been Horan's head.

Without any further thought, Dixon allowed his head to drop down on the ground, where he let it lie for a moment while he sucked down several deep breaths in an effort to calm his own stomach. Watching, the radioman began to feel better about himself. If a general could be shaken by looking at a corpse, then he didn't need to worry about being embarrassed by tossing his lunch.

Blinking his eyes as if this would magically cancel out what he had just seen, Dixon turned his attention to his next concern. "Is your radio on the company or battalion radio net, trooper?"

"Company, sir."

"Give me the hand mike."

Fumbling about his web gear, the radioman pulled the hand mike free of the metal hook that it had been hanging from and handed it to Dixon.

"What're the call signs for your company commander and your platoon leader?"

"Alpha Six is the old man. The LT is, was, Alpha Two Six."

The use of such simple call signs, a violation of operational security, angered Dixon, but he let it pass. This was no time to bother about such trivial matters. Besides, since he had no call sign for himself within this unit, he would have to throw OpSec out the window himself as soon as he began transmitting. While the zing of bullets passing close overhead reminded Dixon of the need to keep low, he pressed the rubber-covered lever called the push-to-talk button on the side of the hand mike and began speaking. "Alpha Six, Alpha Six, this is Oscar Seven. Over."

At first, there was no response. Then a voice came back. "Unknown station, this is Alpha Six Romeo. Get off this net. Out."

Realizing that he had reached the Alpha Company commander's radioman who didn't recognize the ad hoc call sign Dixon was using to identify himself, Dixon decided to use the direct approach. Re-keying the mike, he tried again. "Alpha

Six Romeo, this is the general officer that was traveling with Alpha Two Six. Inform your Six that Alpha Two Six is dead and that the Alpha Two Six element is pinned under heavy fire. Over.''

Releasing the push-to-talk button, Dixon closed his eyes and tried to think. What, he wondered, would he do now? Before he came up with an answer, the speaker on the hand mike blurted, "Oscar Seven, this is Alpha Six Romeo. Alpha Six wants to know if you have contact with Alpha Two Six Alpha. Over.''

The platoon, Dixon realized, was out of touch with their commander. With this lieutenant dead and the company commander asking about Alpha Two Six Alpha, who should be the platoon sergeant, things had to be really bad. Keying the mike, Dixon responded without thinking. "Negative. I've no contact with any of the leaders of this element. I'll get the senior man up on the radio as soon as possible.''

Quickly the response came back. "This is Alpha Six Romeo. Alpha Six would appreciate that. Anything else? Over.''

"This is Oscar Seven. Negative. Out.''

Handing the hand mike back to the radioman, Dixon lifted his head in an effort to look about some. Off to his left he heard the familiar pop-pop-pop of several M-16s close at hand. Someone from this platoon, he decided, was over there and returning fire. That meant that he had to go over and find out who, if anyone, was in charge. Though the task of chasing platoon sergeants and squad leaders during firefights was definitely something that didn't fall within the job description of a general officer, Dixon justified his actions without much thinking about them by the seriousness of the situation. He began to back away from the dirt mound in order to crawl around the radioman. As he did so, he slapped the radioman on the bottom of his boots and yelled, "Okay, trooper, follow me.''

Without giving the radioman another thought, Dixon continued, following the mound of dirt as closely as possible while keeping his entire body pressed to the ground as best he could. This was no easy task, especially for a man in his late forties who had never counted low crawling as one of his specialties. He had and had always had a particular problem keeping his butt down, even when he was a somewhat spry young cadet at VMI. Still, for not having done anything like this for some time, Dixon was able to establish a rhythm of sorts. That, with the added motivation provided by an occasional burst of small-arms fire overhead, allowed him to make good time, reaching a point where he could finally see the line of troopers he had been following earlier. Confident that their platoon sergeant was among them, Dixon turned on his stomach slightly and began to crawl toward them, oblivious to the fact that the dirt mound that had protected him had long since disappeared.

It took Scott Dixon a few seconds to realize this. The fact was that he had become so oblivious to his surroundings, concentrating instead on maintaining as low a profile as possible while at the same time keeping an eye open for the platoon sergeant, he hadn't noticed that the mound that had been protecting him had diminished in height and thickness to the point where it ceased to exist. When belatedly he noticed that it had disappeared, he froze in place, carefully looking wide-eyed to his left and then his right to see if his error had drawn any unwanted attention to him. After several seconds that dragged on forever, Dixon let out a sigh of relief. Anxious to correct his oversight, Dixon prepared to move back behind the mound of dirt. Before doing so, however, he glanced back to make sure that the radioman wasn't in the way.

Only then, while he was lying flat on the ground totally exposed to enemy fire and sweating from every pore in his body, was Dixon startled by a second revelation: He was alone. There was no radioman behind him. At first he feared that the radioman had been hit and he hadn't noticed. Carefully Dixon twisted his head around further and looked back along his route. There was no sign of the radioman. Not until he saw a pair of boots, partially obscured by the dead lieutenant's boots, move, did Dixon realize what had happened to the radioman. He hadn't budged an inch. The bastard, Dixon realized, had simply lain where he had found him and had made no effort to follow. Though angry, Dixon did his best to suppress it. The last thing he wanted was to lose his temper, get excited, and draw attention to himself while he was in the open. With great care Dixon slowly began to reverse his direction. As hard as crawling forward had been, doing so backwards was slower, more awkward, and given Dixon's anger at being abandoned by the radioman, more nerve-racking. Still, propelled by his anger, an anger that had started the moment he had toppled unceremoniously out of the helicopter at the LZ and was now multiplied with every burst of small-arms fire that tore overhead or kicked up dirt nearby, Dixon made record time.

Dixon found the radioman in the same position he had left him. He was still lying next to the dead lieutenant with his head turned away. The only difference was that his eyes were closed. They were in fact being held shut so tightly that Dixon could see wrinkles in the corner of the man's eyes from the effort. For a moment it reminded him of a child who had seen something terrible and hoped by closing his eyes he could make it go away. That this was exactly what was going on inside the radioman's head didn't, however, occur to Dixon at that moment. Rather, Dixon's anger blinded him to any consideration other than the fact that he, a general officer, had given a soldier in combat an order and that the soldier, for whatever reason, had disobeyed him. It wasn't that Dixon was an unreasonable man. On the contrary, those who knew him and had worked with him knew him to be one of the most understanding human beings that had ever put a uniform on. But the fact was that Dixon was a human being, and as such he was as susceptible to all the frailties of human nature as the next man. At that moment anger and fear, and not compassion and understanding, were the emotions that were driving Brigadier General Scott Dixon. For not only had he given an order that had not been carried out promptly, he had in a very real sense been abandoned by this radioman, left alone to face the dangers of moving about in a firefight.

In the heat of the moment very little of this occurred to him. There was no time for rationality or compassion. Only later on, after the heat of passions and emotions flamed to a fever pitch by battle had cooled, would Dixon be able to understand and be reasonable. But with men dying all about and his own life in danger, reason was a scarce commodity. Dixon, already embarrassed at putting himself in an awkward situation that he knew had been a mistake from the beginning, could think of nothing else but doing something that would correct that error in judgment. His immediate response, getting the platoon sergeant of the unit he had been traveling with in contact with his company commander, was the only beneficial thing that he could think of. And a radioman, no matter how scared or shaken he was, was not going to stop him from doing so.

Reaching out, Dixon grabbed the radioman's shoulder and gave him a violent shake. This had the desired effect, causing the radioman's eyes to fly open. When he had eye-to-eye contact, Dixon lit into him. "I told you to follow me. I *ordered* you to follow me! Now get your shit together and do it. Understand?"

The radioman's eyes that had moments before been squeezed shut now grew to the size of saucers. His lips parted slightly, and he gave the appearance he was going to speak, but nothing came out. Instead the radioman closed both his mouth and eyes and ignored Dixon.

This reaction served only to multiply the anger that Dixon had already been building up, pushing rational thinking further and further from Dixon's mind and replacing it with blind fury. Letting go of the radioman's shoulder, Dixon took hold of his collar, gave it a twist, and jerked the soldier as close to his own face as he could. As before, this violent action caused the radioman's eyes to open wide. "Damn you, soldier. I gave you an order and you're going to comply. Do . . . you . . . understand?"

When the radioman finally answered, there was a slight quiver, almost a pleading quality to his voice. "I . . . I can't, General. Jesus, I can't deal with this shit."

As contorted with fear as the radioman's face was, Dixon's was just as twisted and disfigured with anger and rage. The real reason for having the radioman follow him no longer entered into Dixon's thinking. Dixon could have ripped the radio off of the man's back and taken it himself. But in the rage of passions that consumed Dixon's mind, the fact that a soldier in combat was steadfastly refusing his orders overrode all logic and reason. Twisting the soldier's collar tighter, to the point where he was beginning to choke the man, Dixon lowered his voice and hissed in the most menacing tone he could, "You're going to move your ass and follow me or you're going to die right here, right now." Dixon was about to add, Or I'll shoot you myself, but didn't, though that's exactly what he thought. Soldiers, after all, were fighting and dying around the two of them, and getting the radioman in contact with his platoon sergeant was to Dixon the only thing that he could do to stop it. And if that took radical and even illegal means to make it happen, then he was prepared in his current state of mind to follow through.

As dramatic as the confrontation between Dixon and the radioman was, another incident that would have far greater consequences was beginning to be played out. Cerro, between ducking every time a burst of small-arms fire struck near his command group and shouting orders and instructions to the soldiers around him, had managed to put together a reasonable picture in his mind of what was happening to his command. It was not at the moment a good one, but it at least gave him some hope. In addition, Pete Crippen had managed to raise the commander of the attack helicopter company supporting them and was waiting to hand off the radio hand mike to Cerro so that he could personally give them an update on the situation and issue them instructions.

When he was finished talking to Kozak, Cerro tossed the hand mike back to his own radioman and reached out toward the fire support officer for his. As he pulled the hand mike to him, Cerro muttered a curse, damning the division commander for insisting that attack helicopters in support of ground operations would operate on the artillery support net and not the battalion command net of the unit they were supporting. Had the helicopters been on the command net of the 3rd Battalion, 511th Infantry, Cerro and his fellow battalion commanders wouldn't have to waste valuable time telling the attack helicopter commanders what was happening on the ground. The attack helicopter commanders and pilots would already know simply by listening to the reports. Still there was no changing that, at least not now. Keying the hand mike, Cerro called the helicopters. "Bravo Five Two, this is Mike Seven Six. Over."

With the quick situation report that Crippen had given him, Captain Allen A. Bryson responded to Cerro's call with as much information as he had so that Cerro didn't have to play a thousand questions. "Seven Six, this is Five Two. I have four snakes coming in from the southwest. We can see two firefights in progress, one at the LZ and one at the arms site, but cannot identify who's who down there. Over.''

For a moment Cerro wondered how best to guide Bryson in without exposing his own positions. This was especially critical, since the enemy mortars in new locations were picking up their barrage where they had left off. Ready, he pressed the push to talk button on the hand mike. "This is Seven Six, the situation at the LZ is pretty much in hand. They are in close contact and rolling up the enemy bunker line now. We're still pinned, however, at the arms-cache site and cannot maneuver. I need you to locate and take out their mortars. From those platoons I've been able to contact and what I see here, none of my people are more than fifty meters from the outer edge of the arms site. The other people are in bunkers and beyond the fifty-meter mark. The greatest volume of the enemy fire appears to be coming from positions on the high ground north of the arms site. At this time, that's the best I can do for you. How copy? Over.''

Bryson, serving as the gunner for his own aircraft as well as the company commander and senior aviator on the scene, looked up from his sight and surveyed the unfolding battle before him. He did not like going in with such skimpy information concerning friendly dispositions and target data. This fear was a natural one given the amount of drilling that he and every attack helicopter pilot and gunner in the Army had been given concerning engagement criteria. After the First Persian Gulf War, with the numerous incidents of "fratricide," the modern term given to friendly fire, the need to have positive controls and clearly marked friendly front line traces had been driven home to them in the classroom and on the live fire range. This was not, Bryson realized, a classroom drill or a live fire exercise. This was the real thing with real men and women, American men and women, dying before his eyes. And unlike past engagements that he had been involved in since his arrival in Colombia, the enemy was standing fast, toe to toe with the Americans, giving apparently better than they were getting. Taking a deep breath, Bryson pressed his radio button. "Roger, Seven Six, I understand your people are in the open and all within fifty meters of the arms cache. I will split my flight, using two snakes to work over the area between the LZ and the arms site and the others concentrating on the forward slopes above the arms site. Over.''

Not knowing what else to say, Cerro looked at Crippen as he responded. ''Roger, that sounds good to me. I'm turning you back over to my Eight Nine. Work with him for further guidance. Over.'' Without waiting for a response, Cerro handed the radio hand mike over to Crippen. ''He's all yours. Just keep him in the game. Okay?''

Crippen, who had been watching and listening to Cerro, nodded. As an artillery man Crippen would have felt much more comfortable dealing with a tube artillery battery than with an understrength attack helicopter company. But given the fact that there was no way that the limited range of the field howitzers could reach every corner of the 11th Air Assault Division's area of responsibility, they had to make do with helicopter gunships in those areas where friendly guns couldn't reach. Besides, the only other alternative was relying on Colombian Army artillery units, something that no American ground commander in his right mind would do if he could avoid it. So as much as he disliked it, the helicopters were better than nothing, especially in situations like this.

Alerted to the presence of the incoming American attack helicopters, Valendez shifted his attention from the firefight on his immediate front to the horizon beyond. From the bunker apertures, built so as to give him a clear and unrestricted view of the river valley and skyline to the south, Valendez could barely make out the approaching attack helicopters. Though they were mere dots in his binoculars, their speed and the range of their weapons made them more than deadly, even now. Still the danger they presented didn't seem to bother Valendez. The truth was he was relieved to see them coming up the river valley. All was, Valendez suddenly realized, in order. Without betraying any of the excitement that he felt, Valendez began giving orders to his radioman, Rafael Dario. Dario in turn relayed them over the air as Valendez spoke. ''Contact Eagle. He will cease fire and shift his mortars to their next position immediately. Once there, he will notify me when they are ready and stand by for my order to fire again. Next notify Falcon. When they have all targets within range, he is to engage the enemy at will. All positions around the arms site are to begin reducing their volume of fire until Falcon has engaged.''

Having given his orders, Valendez went back to watching and waiting. He had no need to monitor Dario as he passed the orders to the various leaders scattered about the mountainside. Of all the men in his command that day, Dario was the one man he could depend upon no matter what. For Dario, a young man who had known nothing but poverty and deprivation, was more than a simple radioman. He was in fact a jack of all trades, serving as an aide, cook, driver, and personal bodyguard to Valendez, a man whom Dario saw as more than a military commander. He was in Dario's eyes the father that he had never had. For his part Valendez, a man who had never married, returned the affection and loyalty, taking Dario into his confidence and taking him by the hand as a father would a son. And like a son Dario followed Valendez, from the first day when Valendez as a deputy company commander met Dario, the raw recruit. When he had finished relaying all of the orders and had received acknowledgments from the recipients, Dario leaned forward and softly informed Valendez of that.

With a slight nod Valendez in turn acknowledged Dario's message. It was back to waiting, always waiting, Valendez thought. How well, he realized, the old German military philosopher knew war. Why, he wondered, had so few listened to what he had said? Indeed why?

Reaching a point where he felt that he could safely engage the Farcee positions without exposing his aircraft to their small-arms fire, Bryson ordered his pilot to slow down to a hover. His wingman, just to the right and rear of his aircraft, conformed to Bryson's actions. With little more than a quick glance over his shoulder to reassure himself that the other aircraft was ready, Bryson turned his attention to fighting his own aircraft. Putting his head down onto the sight that sat before him, he switched to the thermal viewer mode and began to look for targets. Identifying friendly ground troops, given that they were for the most part still exposed, was not difficult. Finding the mortars, however, was more of a challenge. Though he detected several hot spots out beyond the fifty-meter perimeter that the battalion commander had defined, Bryson passed them by in his search for something that looked like a mortar tube or a mortar firing position. Thus engaged, neither he nor his pilot noticed the telltale back blast and bloom of white smoke as a volley of Russian-made surface-to-air missiles leaped out of the jungle behind them and began to reach up for them. The only warning Bryson had that they were in trouble was the sudden scream of surprise from his pilot when he saw their wingman suddenly blow up. Bryson was so absorbed in opening his engagement that he didn't even have time for this before his own multimillion-dollar helicopter disappeared in a fireball that dwarfed everyone and everything below them.

Seldom in a war can a person, either during the war itself or even after it, point to a single incident and say with any degree of certainty that such and such a moment was a decisive moment, that after a particular incident the face of a war was changed forever. In modern history one such incident occurred on June 4, 1942, when Navy Lieutenant Clarence W. McClusky led his thirty-seven Dauntless dive bombers into a dive that wrecked three Japanese aircraft carriers off the Pacific island of Midway. Another moment, only slightly less dramatic but often ignored, took place near a small Vietnamese village named Ap Bac on January 2, 1963, when Lieutenant Colonel John Paul Vann, an American adviser with the South Vietnamese Army, watched helplessly as the Viet Cong for the first time stood their ground against overwhelming South Vietnamese ground forces and destroyed in quick succession three American helicopters and repelled a mounted attack by a Vietnamese mechanized infantry unit.

The destruction of the American attack helicopters above the dummy arms cache, both those searching for the mortars and those working over the area between the LZ and the arms site, by a section of Valendez's command code-named Falcon caused everyone on the ground to pause in whatever they were doing and look up. Although the angry explosions were ominous, they meant little to Nancy Kozak and her efforts to break the back of the enemy platoon engaging Charlie Company at the LZ. To Cerro, still pinned against the wall of a dummy arms shed, the loss of the attack helicopters meant that the firefight his command was engaged in would continue unchecked until the pinned remnants of Alpha Company finally were able to make a dent in the enemy bunker line or the enemy simply got tired of killing his men. For Dixon, still locked in his own personal struggle to motivate a soldier who had lost all ability to function, the destruction of the helicopters was another inconvenience, another incredible stroke of bad luck that like all the others that day was conspiring to rob him of his self-esteem.

Only Hector Valendez standing before the aperture of his observation bunker fully appreciated what he was seeing and what it meant. The shock waves created by the destruction of those four attack helicopters would not only continue to ripple their way across the valley where he had so carefully set up his ambush, they would sweep from the banks of the Rio Cauca at the bottom of the valley and reach eventually the banks of the Potomac River itself. And behind those shock waves Valendez felt, for the first time with a degree of confidence he had not felt before, the sound of victory for his cause would come. For he knew that even if he and every member of the FARC with him that day died, their achievements would change the face of the war against the Yankees and the reactionary Colombian government forever. From that day on, he, his men, and the FARC were fighting a new war, one in which they could not lose. For now they, and not the government in Bogotá or the commander of the 11th Air Assault Division, would choose the time and place of their battles. They had in their hands the most necessary commodity to victory that an army could have, initiative. And Hector Valendez was determined never to relinquish it.

CHAPTER 4

September 22

HAD HE BEEN A ROMAN GENERAL AT THE HEIGHT OF THE Empire, Major General Charles B. Lane would never have entered a meeting with less than six trumpeters to announce his presence. But he was not. Rather he had been doomed by fate to being an American general commanding at a time when pomp and circumstance, at least for the military, were viewed as both frivolous and too expensive. So Lane had to content himself with a crisp, sharp shout of attention as he walked into the briefing room for the 0700 daily update.

Still Lane refused to be totally denied what he considered to be his due. What little he could have and still be considered within bounds he took. This attitude resulted in making the headquarters of the 11th Air Assault Division a sort of show-piece within the Army when it came to proper procedures and military correctness. While everyone who had ever worn the uniform of the United States Army knew from day one that lack of order equaled failure and defeat, Lane's ideas and views bordered on compulsiveness. Everything in the division had a proper place, and every action and task had an estab-lished routine that was mandated and supported by reams and reams of policy statements, checklists, and standard operating procedures. Not that anyone expected anything less from a man who had from the beginning been referred to in the ranks and behind his back as Conan the Bureaucrat.

With the punctuality of a train pulling out of the station, the rituals surrounding the morning update briefing ran their course. As Lane made his way to his seat, his aide slipped into the room, heading straight for a small table where he set down his notebook and a metal coffee thermos. While Lane took his place between the assistant division commander for maneuver seated on his right and the chief of staff to his left, exchanging small talk with these two officers, his aide poured a cup of coffee for him.

Even this action was conducted with a ritualistic quality not unlike that of a Japanese tea ceremony. The thermos used to convey the general's coffee itself was part of the ceremony. It was covered with stickers that represented the division's shoulder patch and Lane's name and rank in large, neat black block letters running down the side. When the aide had filled the cup three-quarters full, he made his way to where Lane sat, holding the cup aloft as if it held sacred nectar for the gods. After handing his boss the cup over Lane's right shoulder, the aide disappeared, his role in the ceremony at an end. Without looking, Lane brought the cup up to his lips, took a sip, then brought the cup down until the arm holding it rested on the arm of the overstuffed leather chair that he sat in. Having thus partaken of the ceremonial coffee, Lane looked up at the assistant division intelligence officer, already standing at the front of the briefing room with pointer in hand, and nodded, letting him know that the briefing was now in session.

From the rear of the room came a click as a sergeant turned on the overhead projector. Every day when he heard this, Colonel Christopher Delhue, the division's chief of staff, watched the briefing officer. For as soon as the projector clicked on, the briefing officer sprang to life, whipping the long pointer he held in both hands horizontal to the floor across his body, bringing it to rest on the screen at the front of the briefing room within inches of where he wanted it. Without fail, this caused Delhue to smile, for it was as if the briefing officer was somehow connected to the overhead projector and switching on the projector served to activate both the projector and the briefer. The only thing that tempered Delhue's sense of humor was the realization that the briefing officer now presenting and the others that would follow spent more than an hour rehearsing this routine briefing every morning in an effort to achieve the level of perfection that Lane demanded of his staff.

As with all morning briefings, this one started with the same preamble. "Good morning, sir. Enemy activity in the past twenty-four hours has been moderate," or light or heavy, as the case may be. The intelligence officer would then point to various locations on the map of Colombia and in order of occurrence describe each contact or sighting made by a U.S. unit that involved an FARC squad or larger unit, starting with just after midnight of the previous day and ending at midnight of that same day. Though this left a seven-hour gap in reporting, no one felt that this was of any major significance. The division intelligence officer felt it was necessary to have such an early cutoff so that his analysts could sift through the information that was coming in and package it for the briefer in plenty of time for him to prepare himself adequately. Besides, the midnight-to-midnight reporting period fit nicely into Lane's way of thinking, with each reporting period equaling one twenty-four-hour day.

Though things did occur after midnight that were of importance, they were never allowed to interfere with the delicate routine that had become the standard. Once when an American infantry platoon on ambush patrol was engaged by a superior enemy force estimated to be at company strength after the midnight cutoff, the briefing officer on his own added this item to the morning briefing. Before the briefing officer finished, Lane turned to face Delhue. When he spoke, it made Delhue think of what it would be like to be a snake's prey as the snake looked into the eyes of its victim before consuming it. With measured ease and never bringing his voice above a quiet conversational tone, Lane in a mocking voice asked Delhue, "Is it too much to expect, *Colonel*, for the staff officers under your charge to follow established procedures?" Without waiting for a response, Lane rose to his feet, looked about the room, and announced, "When you people have your act together, have someone contact my aide." Finished, he turned and walked out of the room, leaving the gathered staff confused, embarrassed, and somewhat insulted that a senior officer

CODE OF HONOR

would behave in such a manner. Still, C. B. Lane got his way, as he always did, and broke the will of his subordinates, giving them the choice of conforming to his views or facing professional suicide.

So despite the fact that the battle between Hector Valendez's special action company and Cerro's battalion was the only operation of any significance during the reporting period being briefed, it waited for its chronological turn. When, after a detailed description of six questionable sightings and three minor squad-sized confrontations between units of the 11th Air Assault and elements suspected of being FARC, the officer giving the intelligence update turned to the fight at the arms cache, everyone in the room sat up and began to pay close attention. "At approximately 1145 hours, two companies of the 3rd Battalion, 511th Infantry, made contact with an FARC force here, estimated to be a reinforced company. The enemy were—"

Before the briefing officer could finish, Lane interrupted. "Who said that the enemy force was a reinforced company?"

Caught off guard by Lane's question, the briefing officer looked at Lane for a second before glancing over to the division G-2 intelligence officer. There was in his face a pleading request for salvation, or at least some guidance. Before the G-2 could respond, Lane asked his question again, a little more forcefully this time. "Who said that the enemy force was a reinforced company?"

Turning his face back to the division commander, the briefing officer began to field the question, groping about for the right answer as he did so. "Well, sir, the information concerning this particular incident was generated by the unit in contact and sent up the chain. To the best of my knowledge, there has been no effort made to re-evaluate this data."

"So," Lane pronounced as he stuck his right index finger in the air, "we have no independent confirmation concerning the size of the enemy unit."

Confused, the briefing officer looked at Lane for a moment before responding. "Well, yes, sir, that is, I suppose, correct. I don't know that there was—"

Again Lane cut off the briefing officer, this time by turning in his chair to face the division intelligence officer himself.

69

"Please correct me if I'm wrong, but didn't your office generate an assessment of enemy capabilities three weeks ago stating that the Colombians were incapable of conducting military operations above platoon level?"

Uncomfortable with the sudden attention of his superior, the G-2, who had been lounging in his seat, sat upright and shifted this way and that as he threw his hands out in front of him. "Well, yes, I believe we did make that assessment three weeks ago."

"Has anything," Lane continued, "developed or come to light, other than this farce the commander of the 3rd of the 511th calls a battle, to change that assessment?"

Though he had known, like all the other officers on the division staff, that mention of FARC units of company size was a no-no, the division G-2 had included the assessment of the forces that had engaged the 3rd of the 511th in his briefing. "How much trouble can I get into," he had asked in a rather cavalier fashion, "by telling the truth for once? Besides," he added, "the assessment is the 3rd Brigade's, not ours. If Lane doesn't like it, he can hammer *them*." Now with Lane glaring at him, the bravado the G-2 had displayed evaporated. Shaking his head more as a reaction than as the result of careful thought, the G-2 looked down at the floor like a puppy being scolded and muttered, "No, not that I have seen."

Casting his eyes across the assembled staff, Lane feigned a look of confusion. "Then I don't understand? How can one of our battalions get thumped so soundly by an enemy force the size of a platoon and then right here in my own headquarters have my own staff support the fantasies of an ill-informed and confused battalion commander?"

As Lane spoke, Delhue felt his stomach knot up. He already knew that Cerro had only two companies on hand, not his entire battalion as Lane was implying. Even worse, through his manner and pronouncement Lane was instructing his staff in so many words that any discussion of an enemy force in company strength or larger would not be tolerated. The reason for this, as he and every officer in the room knew, was that to admit that the enemy capability was improving rather than diminishing would be to cast doubt on the effectiveness of the division and in turn on the division commander. Lane himself had stated in the narrative of the monthly summary of operations sent to the Pentagon via SOUTHCOM less than a week ago that "the military balance in Colombia has tilted irreversibly in favor of U.S. and Colombian forces."

Had this been true, Lane's diversion of effort to deal with the drug cartel and his emphasis on those operations would have been appropriate. But since the FARC was not declining in power but on the contrary increasing its capability, Delhue knew that every trooper and weapon taken away from their efforts against the FARC was a dangerous weakening of their position. "We're failing to do what we were sent here to do," he told another officer. "Instead we're off playing cops and robbers while the Farcees are sharpening their knives and jockeying their people about for the big kill."

Delhue was pondering the consequences of what Lane was doing when Lane ended his visual sweep of the room by staring directly into Delhue's eyes. The sudden direct and piercing stare of Lane's narrowing eyes less than two feet from his own was as unnerving to Delhue as Lane meant it to be. When he saw that his gaze had achieved its desired effect, Lane smiled slightly but narrowed his eyes. "Chief, we need to get to the bottom of this. I want you to contact 3rd Brigade and have the battalion commander fly up here today to see me. Until then, make sure that all reports concerning this incident, including press releases issued by the public affairs officer, are screened to ensure that they conform with the reality of the situation. Understood?"

Caught off guard like everyone else, Delhue nodded and murmured, "Understood."

Satisfied that his point had been made and that nothing more needed to be said, Lane settled himself back into his large overstuffed leather chair, took a sip from his coffee, nodded to the briefing officer, still visibly shaken from being on the spot for so long, and smiled. "You may proceed, Major. We've wasted more than enough time on this incident."

Although she didn't need to be escorted to the restaurant or even to her table, Jan Fields-Dixon didn't object. It would have done no good, since every time she did so, the member of the hotel or restaurant staff escorting her, always a man, would offer profuse objections. Each man was quick to point out that it would be inappropriate for a woman of such beauty and importance to be allowed to go about in public unaccompanied. "There are many men," one maitre d' with a toothy smile had remarked to her when she objected, "who would take advantage of a woman in your situation." Knowing full well that she could count that particular maitre d' among them, along with scores of other Colombians and American businessmen in Bogotá, Jan had said nothing and followed, as was expected.

About the only class of males in Bogotá that seemed to leave Jan alone were those in U.S. Army uniforms. The fact was they gave her a wide berth, since most knew she was the senior correspondent for the World News Network in Colombia. Though Jan had never betrayed the confidence of a source, no one assigned to the military mission in Bogotá or the 11th Air Assault Division wanted to be the first. Equally intimidating, at least to the officers, was the fact that Jan was the wife of Brigadier General Scott Dixon. Conventional wisdom left little doubt that making a pass, or anything resembling a pass, would in short order be brought to the general's attention. "I would just as soon," one lieutenant colonel cautioned a major who had seemed interested in buying Jan a drink one night, "do a root canal on a hungry tiger. Odds of surviving that are considerably higher."

Still, Jan would not be ignored and she knew that. There were simply too many young men in and out of uniform who enjoyed the thrill of twisting a tiger's tail just for the hell of it. So when Jan was informed that Scott hadn't arrived yet, she decided to be seated at a table alone in the middle of Army officers and go into what Scott called her Mrs. Robinson mode. In a playful mood, despite having been stood up by Scott the previous evening, Jan had even dressed for the occasion on the off chance that Scott would be late, as he usually was. The time alone would allow her to have a little fun.

Wearing a short-sleeved white cotton dress with a full skirt that reached mid-calf, Jan stood out like a shining beacon in a sea of green uniforms. Simple gold jewelry sparkling in the radiant morning sun that streamed into the room drew her spectators' attention to all the right places. Her long lustrous brunette hair, pulled away from her face by a white hairband but left falling about her shoulders, nicely framed an oval face that was highlighted with a light application of makeup that accentuated her big brown eyes. Jan demanded second looks, and despite the decorum of the moment she got them.

Assured that she would draw the attention that she desired, Jan followed the maitre d'. Before taking her seat, Jan carefully gathered her skirt at the sides and brought it around to her front, pulling it tight across her rear as she did so. With a measured grace befitting her performance, she seated herself and allowed the maitre d' to push her chair in to the table. As she turned to thank him with a smile, she casually glanced around the room, knowing that somewhere in such a target-rich environment an adventurous heart was waiting for the right moment to come up and open a conversation with her on some pretext or other. Taking up her menu, Jan pretended to carefully study it, even though she already knew every entry on it by heart and knew what she would have. Selection of her meal was not her interest. Rather, this gave her the opportunity to look up from the menu every now and then and catch one of the officers at another table staring at her. When she did, Jan would divert her eyes while smiling before returning to her careful study of the menu.

She was still engrossed in looking the menu over when a voice from behind startled her. "You know, Jan, such antics are not in line with your public image."

Spinning her head about to see who belonged to the voice, she smiled when she recognized Colonel Chester Thomas, the military attaché assigned to the American embassy in Bogotá. Besides being one of the few military men who would talk to her, he was a genuinely friendly man, just a few months away from retirement. Thomas had not only been instrumental in helping Jan get her feet on the ground when she had arrived in Colombia, he had taken care to keep an eye on her, playing the role, as Jan liked to claim, of her surrogate father. Looking up at him, she smiled. "Is there nothing better for you to do, Chester, than prowl the local restaurants looking for people to scare?"

"Jan, you should know by now that I am very, very discriminating about whom I scare. You, for example, one of the most successful television correspondents in the world, with a list of credentials longer than my right arm, make a wonderful target of opportunity.''

Jan blushed. Though she was proud of her achievements, she took even greater pride in the fact that she, a woman, had achieved them in a still heavily male-dominated field.

''You realize, Chester, that if you don't go away, my public image, the one that my superiors in Washington have so carefully cultivated and are so concerned about, is going to be placed in jeopardy.'' This comment, which caused both of them to chuckle, was said only half in jest. At times it really bugged Jan that her credibility and appeal were tied by the producers of her news broadcasts to their network ratings. To protect her they often placed Jan in a bubble that she was not comfortable in. Hence she used every opportunity to be a little naughty in a rather harmless way. Though not an exhibitionist by any stretch of the imagination, Jan did enjoy being the center of attention as well as the object of admiring glances and mesmerized stares. While Scott found her behavior amusing, Jan, despite being the very portrait of sophistication and a role model for so many young female correspondents, found it nothing less than erotic.

''Would you care to join us, Chester?''

Making a great show of looking about, Thomas finally asked, ''Us?''

''Yes, Scotty and me. I'm expecting him any minute.''

The mention of Dixon's name caused the expression on Thomas's face to change. ''I think, Jan, it would be better if you two were alone.''

Noting the sudden change, she was about to ask why he had said that but decided not to. ''Well, I guess you're right. This is, after all, his last day in town and I'd like to spend some more time with him. He missed our dinner date last night.''

''Yes, I know.''

Seeing that Thomas now appeared to be anxious to go, Jan missed the tone of his last comment. Had she thought about it, she might have been a little better prepared for the unexpected, but she didn't. Making his apologies, Thomas turned and left Jan's table to go over and join another group of officers. Jan, finished with the menu and after placing her order sat back to enjoy her coffee and the show that she was putting on. While she sat there looking about with a carefully measured casualness, a sadness caused her brow to darken momentarily. The source of the unhappy thought was Scotty's absence the previous night. It was to have been, as far as she knew, his last night in Colombia before he departed for Washington and she remained behind searching for all the news that was fit to be reported. Since they often found that their separate careers took them in opposite directions, both Jan and Scott took great pains to make their times together meaningful and enjoyable. Last night was to have been a special night, just the two of them. Jan had arranged for a nice intimate dinner for two at a restaurant few Americans frequented, after which they would spend some time at a rather romantic establishment where they played old tango records, then . . .

Such thoughts caused Jan to forget about the leers and stares directed at her. In the bright sunlight amid the clatter of plates and silverware and light breakfast conversation. So involved had Jan become with her fantasies that she did not notice Scott when he approached her.

When she became aware of his presence and turned to greet him with a smile, her mood turned from pleasant surprise to stunned silence. The man standing in front of her was not the same man that she had said good-bye to the day before. Instead of smiling eyes and a warm smile that enhanced his usual confident and commanding expression, Jan was confronted by a man who looked like he had been dragged through a rat hole. While both his face and uniform were clean, Scotty had the look and demeanor of a man who had not slept all night and carried with him the burdens of the world to boot. Even more disturbing were the cuts and scratches, still red and swollen, that marked his face. Without having to be told, Jan realized that her husband had been involved in something serious.

Though concerned, Jan said nothing. Instead, as soon as she could recover her poise, she flashed the best smile she could muster, stood up, and reached out to embrace Scott, who for his part responded by stepping closer to her. Taking her in his arms, he gave her a stiff and somewhat perfunctory hug, breaking it off as soon as he could do so. Stepping back, he avoided her stare as he mumbled an apology for not being able to keep their date last night. With that he reached down, held Jan's chair, and motioned for her to sit. Sensing that he either wasn't in the mood to expand on why he missed last night's meeting or couldn't at the moment, Jan remained silent as she took the offered seat, watching Scott while he seated himself but doing so without staring.

For his part, Dixon dropped into his seat across from Jan with the grace of a sack of potatoes. Without looking over at Jan, he took the napkin, placed it on his lap, and immediately began to fiddle with the silverware. He was nervous, Jan thought. Very nervous and edgy. She had seen him like this before, too many times before. Normally this behavior came when something was troubling him, something that was to him very important and he had been unable to find a way of dealing with it, or it was one of those things that dwarfed him and threatened to overwhelm him. It wasn't that Scott Dixon was the strong silent type. On the contrary, Scotty could be very vocal and outspoken when he had something to say and the issues at hand needed to be addressed. He even had the reputation of being quite emotional in a violent sort of way.

What Scotty Dixon lacked, Jan had learned years before, was the ability to vocalize those thoughts and concerns that played upon his personal emotions and beliefs. Like most men of his age and position, he had been carefully trained by his parents, his society, and the Army to stuff his personal feelings and bear in silence those internal struggles and issues that had nothing to do with the performance of his assigned tasks and duties. In a way, Jan could understand the need for this. He had, after all, in his lifetime seen many things and participated in many actions that to a normal person would be unendurable. Scotty as a combat commander not only had to deal with such issues as death, fear, privation, physical discomfort and suffering, and the unknown, he was expected to inspire and lead others to not only endure these things but to willingly confront more of them. Men and women who allowed themselves to show their true feelings and allowed those feelings to dictate their actions could not do what the Army expected Scott Dixon and thousands of others like him to do. So men and women who considered themselves combat leaders, including Scott, were left on their own to learn how best to deal with their own human frailties in private while doing what needed to be done.

Knowing this, however, never made being with Scotty any easier for Jan. The only thing that she could do at times like this was to start a simple dialogue on a subject that was comfortable for the two of them and hope that Scotty would eventually respond to her and at least for the moment let the worries of the world go. Choice of topic at a time like this was critical, for Jan knew that being too frivolous would turn Scotty off. At the same time she wanted to ensure that she didn't accidentally stray into a subject that would only deepen Scotty's somber mood.

After taking a long sip from her coffee, Jan smiled. "I got the official word yesterday that we'll be working with some new equipment down here in Colombia, a new mobile transponder. It's the size of a small suitcase and has everything, including satellite dish and power supply, that a camera team needs to beam back a live report to Washington from practically anywhere in the world. The whiz-bang kids back at WNN headquarters call it a manpack satcamstay, which is short for man-portable satellite camera station. Of course, the first question I asked was whether this man-portable unit could be converted to a woman-portable unit."

The last part of her announcement caught Dixon's attention. Looking up at him, Jan saw a slight smile begin to creep across his face. She had his attention. Letting her last statement hang for a moment, Jan took another sip of her coffee. Scotty, not knowing whether she was serious or not, couldn't allow the comment to go past without finding out for sure. Finally he shrugged and asked, "And?"

Wanting to keep the conversation light for a moment, Jan set her cup down. "And what, my dear?"

"Is it or isn't it?"

"Is it or isn't it what, dear?"

Taking a deep breath, an exasperated expression lit across Dixon's face. Jan was doing it to him again, he thought. She liked to play these games, starting a conversation, getting his interest, and then dropping the matter before she finished. Sometimes he imagined that she did this just to piss him off, though he knew it was her own weird and twisted idea of fun. Playing along with her, Scott leaned forward. "Is your new man-portable camera unit—" Stopping in mid-sentence, he

77

suddenly realized how silly his question was. She had gotten him again. Jan enjoyed creating elaborate stories, capturing his interest, and then getting him to either lose his patience or make a fool of himself by asking silly follow-up questions. Though most of the time he didn't know why she did it other than to engage in her own perverted form of fun, Dixon knew what she was after this morning. With a shake of his head, Dixon looked at Jan and smiled. Yeah, he thought, he was not being very good company this morning, and Jan was doing the best she knew how to draw him out of his gloom. Finally he asked her, in an effort to avoid dwelling on his concerns and issues, how she was doing.

This caused Jan to raise an eyebrow. "Well, if you must know, I'm quite horny at the moment, thank you very much."

Ordinarily Dixon would have responded with a quip of his own. Though he tried hard to come up with an appropriate comeback that would equal Jan's off-color comment, he just didn't have it in him this morning. Instead he looked down at his cup of coffee. "Sorry about last night, Jan. I know how much it meant to you."

Dropping her playful smile, Jan reached across the table and touched the back of Scotty's left hand. As she did so, she noticed that it too bore several cuts and scratches. "The real question, trooper, is how are you?"

Lifting his cup midway to his mouth, Scotty brought his right elbow up onto the table and held the cup thus supported as he returned Jan's stare. "To tell you the truth, Jan, I don't know. I don't know what to tell you, even if I knew how to tell you. Fact is, right now I'm supposed to go back to Washington and in five days submit a report to General Fulk along with recommendations concerning our operations here in Colombia; and at this moment I don't know what I'm going to say."

"What about telling the truth?"

No sooner had she asked that question than she was sorry that she had, for Dixon's expression turned from concern to anger. When he responded, his words were short and sharp. "Whose truth, Jan? My truth? His Lord High Majesty Major General C. B. Lane's truth? Hal Cerro's truth? Private Andrew Hayman's truth? Whose truth do I report?"

Though Jan had no idea who Andrew Hayman was, she

realized that she had hit upon the raw nerve that Scotty had been trying to protect. And now that she had done so, she had to find some way of calming Scotty or changing the subject. Already his voice, louder with the sudden rush of emotions, had caused several of the diners sitting close to them to stop their own conversations and turn to look at her and Scotty. While she glanced around the room flashing a somewhat apologetic smile, Jan reached across the table and clasped Scotty's left hand between her own two. Looking over into his eyes, still showing red from lack of sleep, Jan tried to calm him. "I'm sorry, dear, if I've upset you. I didn't mean to meddle in your concerns."

Blinking his eyes, Scotty returned Jan's gaze and for the first time realized that he had lost it for a moment. Putting his cup of coffee down, which he had held suspended all this time, he took his right hand and put it over the top of Jan's two hands as they held his left hand. "I'm sorry, Jan, for snapping like that. It's just that . . ."

Jan tilted her head sideways and gave Scotty a sympathetic smile. "No need to apologize, dear. I understand." She didn't of course. She seldom did. But it helped to say so, she knew, when they both needed a quick out from an uncomfortable moment.

Accepting what Jan said at face value, Dixon saw this as a good out and used his right hand to pat their hands that were still joined together on the table. "Thanks, Jan. I appreciate that." Then with the awkward scene closed, he pulled both hands away and settled back into his chair. "Have you ordered yet?"

Taking her cue, Jan nodded her head. "Yes. I'm having the usual. One egg, toast, and fresh fruit."

With a quick glance at the menu, Dixon made a face. "That sounds good. I think I'll have the usual too, pancakes and sausage."

Though what he had just said wouldn't have made any sense to someone else, Jan understood him perfectly. Satisfied that the moment of crisis was over, Jan settled down and did the best she could to enjoy the rest of breakfast with her husband and make it equally enjoyable for him.

*　　*　　*

To the southwest, and almost two hundred air miles away, Captain Nancy Kozak was just sitting down to eat her breakfast. Finding a nice quiet spot not far from the dummy arms-cache site that they had hit the day before, Kozak dropped to the ground, crossed her legs, and took off her helmet. As she moved her head around in a slow circular motion, she realized that this was the first time she had had that damned thing off in almost twenty-four hours. The sensation that one experiences after taking such a burden off your head is one of wonderful light-headedness. For several moments it almost seems as if your head is floating. For a combat infantryman such feelings are as close to pleasure as one can get while in the field. At that moment Kozak was determined to enjoy her moment of pleasure regardless of anything else that was going on around her.

There was in fact a great deal going on. After having engaged in a bitter firefight throughout the afternoon the day before, the soldiers of Companies A and C of the 3rd Battalion, 511th Infantry, held their ground unsupported throughout the night in a tight perimeter. Only after dawn, when it became clear that the FARC units that had contested control of the area with the 3rd of the 511th so fiercely had slipped away under cover of darkness, did helicopters venture in to bring reinforcements in and evacuate the wounded out. Though this was accomplished quickly and efficiently, it was much too late as far as the soldiers of the 3rd of the 511th were concerned. They had, they felt, been left in the lurch, abandoned by everyone outside the small fire-swept circle of death.

While Nancy Kozak unsnapped her web belt and reached into her pants pocket for her Swiss Army knife, she looked about in an absentminded way. Off to her front several meters away a small squad of soldiers were carefully picking their way through the underbrush searching for enemy emplacements. Despite the fact that the battalion had been at this since dawn, not all the enemy bunkers had been located yet. Those that had been found showed beyond any doubt how badly misinformed the battalion had been about the enemy's strength and intentions.

On the hillside above the dummy arms cache Kozak could see markers used to tag each position uncovered arranged in a series of concentric rings layered one above the other. The

FARC commander had arranged his position like an amphitheater, using the arms cache as the stage. It was, she thought, no wonder that Company A wasn't able to effectively mount any type of effective drive from the arms site against their assailants from below. Every move was visible and every inch of ground was covered by more than one position. She and Company C had been lucky at the landing zone, where all they had faced was a single horseshoe ring of positions. Yet even those had been a bear to roll up, requiring nothing less than a full-scale platoon effort to crack each one. By the time they had finished their own fight and were able to reach Company A, the sun was already setting and the danger of fratricide was, in the battalion commander's mind, too great to warrant any further action that night.

In that, Nancy Kozak had concurred. What she couldn't abide, though, was the failure of brigade or division to commit additional attack helicopters in their support or even to send medevac birds in to dust off their wounded. Insistence that the battalion secure the high ground before any aircraft would be sent in by division aviation meant that the wounded spent a painfully long night on the field with only medics available to tend to their needs. Though the medics did more than could have been reasonably expected, their limited training and woefully inadequate aid bags could do nothing to help soldiers who had wounds that only skilled surgeons operating in well-equipped hospitals could have effectively dealt with. In the end several had died. Though most did so quietly, a few could not be quieted. One trooper, his bowels and intestines torn open and exposed by a mortar round, lingered on throughout the night. Only a single well-aimed bullet delivered at close range by a friend at the trooper's request brought him peace.

Like the other survivors of the night Kozak continued to do what was necessary in a rather mechanical manner. With the large blade of her Swiss Army knife she slit open the top of the brown plastic bag that contained her breakfast. Ignoring the detail of soldiers twenty meters away who were busy laying out their dead comrades in body bags, Kozak spilled the contents of her plastic bag on the ground before her. Sorting through it, she looked at each item, putting it either in her lap or throwing it over her shoulder into the undergrowth. Only after she had finished sorting out her breakfast in this manner did she begin to tear into the separate pouches of those items she had kept and eat whatever came out. There was no thought needed to accomplish this particular feat, for there was no enjoyment to be gained from what the Army passed off as food. It was a simple mechanical process, not unlike the one used by the soldiers filling the body bags. For them it was simply a matter of sorting too. After finding a body all they needed to do was drop it in the bag, mark the tag, and pull up the zipper. No thinking necessary. In fact the less thinking the better.

When she was halfway through her meal, Sergeant Andy Pender, her radioman, came trudging up next to her. Looking down at his captain while she ate, he waited for her to acknowledge his presence before speaking. When finally she looked up, he spoke, using the same slow, almost slurred speech that everyone seemed to be using that morning. "Colonel Cerro's looking for you, ma'am. Says that he will be catching the next helicopter out and needs to turn operations here over to you."

Kozak waited a moment to clear her throat before speaking. "Did he say where he's going?"

"Something about him having to go to division headquarters in Bogotá to see the CG."

When she let her head drop, it reminded Pender of a puppet collapsing after its strings had been cut. After a moment Kozak let out an audible sigh. "Well, Sergeant Pender, the Inquisition begins."

"Pardon me, ma'am?"

Looking back up at Pender as she reached for her helmet, Kozak just shook her head. "Nothing, Sergeant Pender. It was nothing. Now do me a favor and inform the colonel that I'll be with him in a minute."

"Okay. Will do."

Without saluting, Pender turned away and headed back to where he had left Cerro.

Entering the World News Network offices at a brisk pace, Jan headed straight for her office without pausing to enjoy the usual morning greetings. The only person she spoke to or acknowledged en route was her secretary, and even then it was just a quick "Have everyone in my office, right now" before she disappeared into it herself.

"Everyone," of course, didn't mean everyone who worked for WNN in Bogotá. The people Jan called for in her own verbal shorthand were the correspondents and heads of the sections working for her. Being a slow news morning, Jan's wish was easily and quickly accomplished.

When everyone was crowded into her small office, Jan got right to the matter at hand. "Something's gone down in the last twenty-four hours concerning U.S. forces. Anyone have any ideas what it was?"

For those who knew Jan, her announcement that something had happened delivered in such a positive manner was a signal that she had a lead on something but nothing solid to back it up with. What she was after at this moment was a pooling of rumors and observations from her staff in an effort to come up with a scheme for pursuing her lead. Though few knew where she got her information from, no one doubted that she was right. Her track record and careful methodical methods of developing a story made any doubt a noncontender. All they had to worry about was digging in the right places and finding the information that she and the other correspondents would need to support Jan's lead, whatever it was. And that, she knew, would be only a matter of time. For whatever had shaken Scotty, she told herself, couldn't be hidden from the prying eye of the news camera for very long.

From his desk Colonel Delhue watched through the open door of his office as the commander of the 3rd Battalion, 511th Infantry, left Lane's office and headed off toward the corridor. Even from where he sat Delhue could tell that Cerro had been through hell, both out in the field and in Lane's office. His hangdog look of exhaustion was now accentuated by a mix of shock and anger. Cerro, he knew, would stop and take advantage of a warm shower and change of clothes at the BOQ before fleeing back into the field and away from division headquarters. Bogotá under the best of circumstances was not a good place for a field soldier to hang around. It was, Delhue knew, even worse when Lane was angry at you.

The voice of the division commander coming over the intercom broke Delhue's train of thought. "Chief, could you come in here a minute?"

Reaching down, Delhue depressed the speaker button. "On the way, sir." But rather than jump up and bolt for the door, Delhue eased back in his seat for a moment. Damn, he thought, the bastard is going to can that poor battalion commander. Instead of trying to figure out what went wrong and learning from his experience, Conan is going to bury him and his battalion in a dung heap. After taking another moment to compose himself, Delhue stood up and strolled out of his office to the commanding general's office across the way.

Upon entering, he closed the door and remained standing, waiting for Lane's signal to take a seat. Lane, however, didn't give the signal. Instead he leaned back into his seat and looked at Delhue through partially closed eyes. "The 3rd of the 511th is due to rotate into Bogotá and assume the division reserve mission soon, isn't it?"

Looking down as if he were mentally checking notes attached to the front of his skull, Delhue thought a moment before responding. "Yes, sir. They are, in fact, overdue. The 3rd of the 511th should have been replaced by the 2nd of the 188th Infantry two weeks ago, but that move was delayed at the request of the 3rd Brigade commander."

"Well, as much as I hate to do it, we're going to have to bump the 3rd of the 511th back down the reserve rotation list again. Tell the G-3 to alert the next unit on that list to begin preparation for assumption of the division reserve mission."

Delhue waited for an explanation. When none was forthcoming, he asked, "Sir, why is the 3rd of the 511th being bumped? They have yet to be given a break from the field. We have even had to send their replacements forward to join them out there rather than wait for the unit to come back here. And if the initial reports from yesterday's actions are accurate, they need the time out of the line to pull themselves together."

Delhue's last comment caused Lane to bolt forward, slapping his hand on the desk. "The last thing they need, Colonel, is to be taken out of the field. If we pull them back now while they are shaken from yesterday's fiasco, they'll lose their cutting edge. No, they need to stay in the field at least for the foreseeable future and soldier on." Having vented his anger,

Lane eased back again. "It's like falling off a horse, Chief. If you don't get right back on you never will. You understand, I'm sure."

Of course Delhue understood. He understood that if the 3rd of the 511th came back to Bogotá, the home base of every news agency covering their little war in Colombia, word of the battalion's ambush by a reinforced FARC company would eventually leak its way into the news. It wasn't the officers Lane was concerned about. Most of them were still sufficiently concerned about their careers not to jeopardize them by saying something that might upset the division commander or Army high command. No, it would be a rifleman at first who would spill the beans. Somehow one of the enlisted men or women, perhaps even a sergeant, disgusted with what they considered pointless operations that wasted lives, would wind up in front of the camera telling the correspondent and the whole world about the dumb-ass mistake that had cost a friend his or her life. It had happened too many times before concerning other issues and operations the soldiers considered botched to expect something of this magnitude, regardless of precautions, to go unnoticed or commented on. No, Delhue knew, Lane couldn't take that chance.

Without any further comment, Delhue acknowledged Lane's order and left, headed to the G-3's office to personally relay the order. When he was alone, Lane reached out and hit his intercom. When his aide responded, he ordered him to put a call through to the deputy chief of staff for operations, a personal friend of his in the Pentagon. It was best, Lane knew, to start squelching Brigadier General Scott Dixon's story of the incident before he had a chance to tell anyone.

While Lane tended to the immediate task of preserving his career, Delhue slowly, almost ponderously, walked down to the division's G-3 operations section. He was dejected. He had been ever since the morning briefing and nothing that he had seen or heard that day had done anything to relieve him of his somber mood. That this required a visit to the operations section didn't lighten his dark mood.

He was, he knew, impaled on the horns of a dilemma, held in check by a code of honor that advocated loyalty to one's superior and devotion to duty above all else. But what was one to do, Delhue asked himself over and over again, when one's superior no longer abided by the same code that he himself so ruthlessly imposed upon his subordinates? And who, he wondered, would or could sit in judgment of such a man? After all, Delhue reasoned, nothing that Lane had said or done, either today or in the past, was technically wrong or inappropriate. As he had before, Delhue turned everything over in his mind two, three times, looking at every word, every order Lane issued in an effort to . . . To what? Delhue thought. What was he trying to do in his own mind? Build a case against his own commanding general? Collect information to present to someone in an effort to prove that Lane had acted and was acting inappropriately? To collect facts so that if the hammer fell, he would be able to cover his own ass? What exactly, Delhue thought, was he doing?

As he came to the end of the corridor where the G-3 operations section started, Delhue hung his head, looking at the floor tiles as he walked, shaking his head while he pondered these bothersome thoughts. Two enlisted members of the division staff headed in the opposite direction paid him no heed. They didn't even comment on Delhue's absentminded shaking of his head. Senior officers, everyone knew, were a rather strange breed of human being and it was best for an enlisted man to simply leave them alone. Passing into the offices where the G-3 and his officers worked, Delhue was stopped by the division operations sergeant. "Is there something I can help you with, Colonel?"

Looking up, Delhue stared at the sergeant major for a moment before answering. "No, Sergeant Major, no thank you. I need to see the G-3 on a matter."

Without any change in expression, the sergeant major shook his head. "I'm sorry, sir, but the G-3 is in a meeting right now with all of his staff officers. Professional development or something like that."

Glancing about for the first time, Delhue noticed that except for the Colombian Army major, a Major José Solis, who was assigned to the G-3 section as an adviser and liaison officer, all the officers were absent. Turning his head back to the sergeant major, he was about to ask exactly what "something like that" was but decided not to. Odds were the sergeant major didn't know. To ask him would only have borne that out and would have embarrassed him. Delhue, like the division G-4, agreed that the operations section was nothing more than a clone farm where Lane was raising a new generation of officers who saw Lane as the personification of the perfect general and slavishly patterned themselves after him. The idea of another generation of Lanes made Delhue shudder.

Deciding not to waste any more of his time, Delhue walked over to Solis, the Colombian officer. As Delhue approached his desk, Solis jumped up and flashed a broad smile on his face, causing Delhue to respond in kind. "How are you this afternoon, Major?"

When he spoke, there was only a hint of an accent. "We are doing quite well, Colonel. How may I help you?"

That Solis was not part of whatever kind of meeting the G-3 was holding didn't need to be explained. Lane had more than made it clear that he didn't like the Colombian Army officers, considering them lazy, incompetent, and untrustworthy. He therefore had as little to do with them as he could, and that attitude pervaded the division, especially those who felt the sun rose and set on C. B. Lane. "I have a message, Major, for the G-3. He is to revise his rotation plan for the division reserve battalion. The 3rd Battalion, 511th Infantry, will be bumped from the top of the list back down into the order someplace."

Solis nodded. "Yes, sir, I see. Is there anyplace on the list that the 3rd Battalion, 511th Infantry, should be moved to?"

That he hadn't considered that question surprised Delhue. He was letting his mind get too cluttered with trivial personal concerns and petty politics. He needed to forget about his misgivings and concentrate more on the business of running a division. That decided, he looked into Solis's eyes and thought for a moment. He had to give this officer an answer. Understanding Lane's intent, Delhue worked the issue over in his mind in an effort to come up with a good compromise. If left to Lane, the 3rd of the 511th would never be rotated into the reserve position just outside of Bogotá. That, however, would not do. Eventually the battalion would need to come in and be afforded the opportunity to stand down and rest. Even Lane, Delhue knew, would eventually have to agree to that. Knowing that six to eight weeks would be more than enough time for this issue to blow over and allow another one to creep in and dominate Lane's mind, Delhue told Solis to instruct the G-3 to arrange it so that the 3rd of the 511th would not assume the division reserve mission for at least six weeks. When Solis asked if there was any particular reason why this battalion was being held back from coming in, Delhue didn't provide an answer. He merely shook his head. "The G-3," he responded, "will know the reason."

With that, Delhue left. For a moment Solis stood there and watched the colonel as he slowly shuffled out of the office. There was something bothering him, Solis thought. There is more to this change in rotation than he is willing to tell. With that thought in mind, Solis sat down and pulled a notebook out of his right breast pocket. He would make a note of this. Perhaps, Solis thought, Hector Valendez would be able to use this information. Then, as he was writing the unit number down, it struck him like a thunderclap. This was the battalion that had been involved in the ambush the day before. Solis smiled. Yes, he thought, he must include this information in the daily update he fed his FARC contact.

CHAPTER 5

September 29

IN WASHINGTON, THE REACTION OF THE MEN WHO MADE UP the Army's senior staff was about what General Fulk had expected. He could tell by their reactions, subtle though they were, that they were not comfortable with what Dixon was saying about the situation in Colombia, especially Lieutenant General Richard Knol. Knol, the deputy chief of staff for operations, became particularly animated when Dixon spoke in terms that made the commander of the 11th Air Assault, one of Knol's fair-haired boys, appear incompetent or at best simply negligent. Dixon, of course, didn't use those words in his briefing. He didn't need to. All he needed to do was lay out the bare facts as he found them and let them speak for themselves. Perhaps, Fulk thought, that was what bothered Knol the most, the fact that what Dixon was saying was so self-damning that he or anyone else didn't need to add any embellishments to paint a clear and accurate picture of what Lane was doing to his division.

As Dixon approached the conclusion of his briefing, he paused for a moment and looked around the room. There before him, with few exceptions, was every senior officer on the Army staff and major Army command. What he had said up to this point he knew did not sit well with many of these men, men who took great pride in their personal integrity and ethics and those of their institution. To be told that one of their own had submitted reports that were misleading to the point of being false was painful to them. To realize in their heart that it was true was devastating. Dixon, who had been tagged to be one of them someday, understood this. That is why before he concluded his somber presentation he hesitated ever so slightly.

In those few moments of silence he could almost hear himself sweating. From around the room the gathered generals returned his stare, their personal feelings hidden behind masks of stone. Even the man who had sent him on the mission that he was now reporting on, General Fulk, gave Dixon no sign of encouragement, no warm, friendly nod of approval. He was on his own. For the conclusion, unlike the main body of the briefing which contained cold, hard facts, was mostly suppositions, his thoughts and views on what would happen if nothing changed. Suddenly the image of Ebenezer Scrooge standing before the Ghost of Christmas Future popped into Dixon's head. These officers, he realized, for all the confidence that comes with the attainment of high rank and their garnet-like veneer, were afraid of what he was about to show them. For he knew that no one, especially Americans, liked being told that they were going to lose.

Unable to postpone the moment any longer, Dixon looked down at his notes and began. "Based on the briefings I received from the commander and staff of the 11th Air Assault, discussions with commanders of troop units, both U.S. and Colombian, a thorough review of all pertinent records, reports, and studies, coupled with my personal observations, I have come to the following conclusions. First, the capabilities of the FARC's military arm have not been diminished by the presence of the 11th. On the contrary, the FARC has improved in all areas during the past six months despite the efforts of the 11th. This becomes all too clear when you consider the fact that when the 11th Air Assault first arrived in country, operations by FARC units in greater than squad strength were unheard of. Now there is no denying that they are not only capable of but willing to engage in company-level pitched battles with U.S. forces. This point stands in sharp contrast to the capability or apparent lack of improvement of the Colombian Army. Based on reports and studies from our military assistance teams in

Colombia submitted before the deployment of the 11th, I can find no appreciable change in the combat readiness of those units which I inspected. This is even more devastating when you add the fact that most of the units which I did see were supposed to be their showpieces.''

For the first time in the briefing, Fulk interrupted Dixon. He already knew the answer, since Dixon had pre-briefed the chief on everything the day before. Fulk, however, wanted to emphasize Dixon's next point, as well as give him some support, regardless of how minor it was. "You mentioned that the Colombian units you saw were supposed to be their best. Why do you think otherwise?"

"Well, sir, records show that we have been transferring huge amounts of weapons and equipment to the Colombians, more than enough as of last week to completely re-equip fifty to sixty percent of their Army. I could not find any evidence, however, that this equipment was being issued to those units considered to be their most reliable and best-trained. During my first visit to the brigade they have just outside of Bogotá, a unit they refer to as their Presidential Guard, I saw no new weapons or equipment. Vehicles, weapons, even the soldiers' web gear in that brigade were old and obviously well used. Before going to their next unit, one deployed in the most sensitive area of the country, I reviewed exactly what we had given them. Again I saw no sign of any new or modern equipment. When I asked the second brigade commander about this, he shrugged and smiled, telling me that the Presidential Guard Brigade had first priority on everything and his unit nothing.''

Leaning forward and folding his hands on the table before him, Fulk looked at Dixon. "Then where, Scotty, do you suppose all of this equipment is going?''

Relieved that Fulk had called him Scotty, a sure sign that he was on solid ground, at least with the chief, Dixon responded, looking at Fulk as he ignored everyone else in the room. "That, sir, brings me to my last point. Our efforts and those of the Colombian government have done nothing to relieve the tensions that existed before the military coup of 28 February. The ambassador and his staff made sure that I understood that the economic and political reforms that were introduced shortly after that coup have without exception failed to take hold. If anything, our operations and the efforts of the FARC have brought their reconstruction of the rural infrastructure to a standstill. Key crops such as coffee and cocoa have shown a steady decline since June of this year, one month after we arrived in force.''

Cocking his head back, Fulk looked into Dixon's eyes. ''Which means?''

''I believe, sir, that the Colombian Army is in fact rearming, but not in preparation to fight the FARC. Rather I believe that they are using the equipment we are sending them to outfit units that in a second coup attempt would be used against forces loyal to the government, provided, of course, there are any.''

''Scotty, you're asking me to believe that the Colombian government doesn't know what its own Army is doing. Do you expect us to accept that their own Army is arming itself to the teeth in preparation to get rid of them, and they can't see that?''

Taking a deep breath, Dixon prepared to throw out an answer that he knew would bring the briefing to a close. ''Why not, sir. For the past six months we have been accepting everything coming out of Colombia from our own people as gospel. I have no doubt that the Colombian government has the same capacity to believe whatever it chooses despite the facts.''

From out of the corner of his eye, Dixon saw Knol sit bolt upright in his seat. He didn't need to look over to where Knol sat to know that his last comment had the chief of operations on the edge of his seat, nostrils flaring and blood in his eyes. Turning his full attention back to Fulk, Dixon saw what he thought was a faint smile on the chief's face. Only slowly did Dixon realize that the chief had used him and his briefing to bring Knol down a peg or two in a high-profile Pentagon power game. Though he didn't like internal politics, especially in an institution such as the Army, where soldiers' lives and national security were at stake, Dixon knew that they were part of the landscape. The fact was it took some serious behind-the-door maneuvering by several senior officers who liked Dixon to get him his star, and Dixon knew it.

Pushing those bitter thoughts from his mind, Dixon turned his full attention back to the matter at hand. Fulk gave him the high sign to continue. ''In conclusion, sir, based on what I now know, I believe that there is nothing that we can do, now or in the next six months, to save the Colombian government.''

"Rather bleak outlook, isn't it?''

"It is, sir, more than bleak. I am assuming that the Colombian Army is simply waiting for us to leave before they decide to go into round two with their own government. And even that is assuming that the weight of FARC successes in the field and the failures of the Colombian government to deliver promised reforms don't beat the Colombian Army to the punch. In my opinion, sir, we'll be lucky if the current Colombian government holds up long enough for us to get out of there.''

He was about to pick up his briefing where he'd left off, but Knol interrupted. "General Fulk, pardon the intrusion here, but I've heard enough.'' Jabbing his index finger at Dixon while he faced Fulk, Knol's voice betrayed his anger. "Just who in the hell does he think he's talking to. I have seen nothing to support one allegation—''

Without saying a word, Fulk cut Knol short. A simple gesture of his head and a glance about the room so subtle that Dixon missed it told Knol that it was time to cease and desist. This also served as a warning to everyone present that another such outburst would not be tolerated. When he was satisfied that he had restored order, Fulk turned his attention back to Dixon. "Scotty, I would like to thank you for your report and observations. Now if you would excuse us, I have a few items I want to cover with these gentlemen before we all break for the day.'' With that Fulk turned away from Dixon, leaving him to slip quietly out the door and away from the firestorm that he suspected his briefing was about to generate. Pausing only long enough in the anteroom to stuff his notes and supporting documents into his briefcase, Dixon was about to flee out the door when Fulk's aide came up to him and touched him on the arm. "General Dixon, General Fulk would like to see you in his office as soon as he's finished here.''

Damn! he thought. Damn it, now what? Then, without having to think about it, Dixon realized that his involvement with the war in Colombia wasn't over. It was, he feared, if anything, just beginning.

To his surprise, Dixon didn't have long to wait. Fulk, his head down and muttering to himself, burst into the outer office where Dixon sat waiting and charged straight forward toward his door. His secretary, used to such entrances, shouted out as fast as she could while he stormed by, "General Fulk, a reminder that you're scheduled to meet with the Secretary of the Army and Sec Def in twenty minutes." The slamming of Fulk's door served nicely to punctuate the end of the secretary's announcement. Fulk's aide, unable to keep up with his boss, came trotting in a second later. As he came in, the secretary shot a knowing glance at him. The aide sighed. "Lions ten, Christians nothing." With that, the secretary shook her head once before going back to filling in the next day's schedule while the aide went over to his desk and began to sift through the pile of messages that had gathered in the center of it during his absence.

For the next minute or so the three of them, Dixon, the secretary, and the aide, sat in their own little corners, keeping to their own thoughts or busy work. To Dixon this lull was both a blessing and a time of apprehension. It was a blessing because for the first time since Fulk had given him the task of finding out what really was going on in Colombia he had nothing pressing to do. Dixon had hoped that the briefing he had just concluded and the written report on which it was based finished that project. But as he sat there watching the secretary and aide go about their separate jobs while waiting for him to leave so that they could gossip about what had happened at the briefing, he knew in his heart that that wasn't going to be.

"Martha, send General Dixon in." Fulk's sudden barking over the intercom that sat on the secretary's desk startled no one but Dixon. He looked at them for a second, then shook his head. They must be used to this sort of thing, he thought as he stood up, adjusted the coat of his uniform, and prepared to go in. Dying to see him go so that she could talk freely to the aide about what had gotten their boss in such a huff, the secretary smiled and pointed to Fulk's door. "The chief will see you now, General."

With the same dread that a schoolboy going to see the principal, Dixon walked into Fulk's office. The chief, his uniform jacket unbuttoned, sat behind his desk slouched down in his seat, surrounded by a haze of cigarette smoke, madly puffing away on a cigarette. This surprised Dixon, who had grown used to the anti-smoking campaigning of the Army. The surprise obviously showed in his face, for Fulk took the cigarette, held it at arm's length, and looked at it for a moment. "My wife will give me hell for starting again." He turned his gaze to Dixon as his took another puff. "She always knows. That woman has a nose like a blood hound." He chuckled. "Of course, whenever I start again, I always try sneaking into the house in an effort to get upstairs and change before she gets a good sniff of my uniform. You'd think after thirty-two years of marriage I'd finally get my act together, but no. There are just some things that never seem to change."

At a loss as to what to do and how to respond, Dixon simply stood there and nodded. Seeing that his efforts to put Dixon at ease were failing miserably, Fulk decided to drop the chase and get down to the matter at hand. Motioning to Dixon to take a seat, Fulk sat up, snubbed out the cigarette, and leaned across his desk, folding his hands and thrusting his head toward Dixon. "Scotty, in fifteen minutes I'm going to have to go into the Secretary of Defense's office and tell him that we are involved in another war that we cannot win." Fulk let that thought hang in the air for a second before he pushed himself back into his seat and looked up at the ceiling. "I don't like that. Not one bit." Looking back at Dixon, "And he isn't going to like that either, especially since he was the stupid son of a bitch who thought of sending combat forces to Colombia in the first place. The idea that a simple military show of force, that the image of American combat troops alone will solve the world's problems has been tried one time too many. And I'm the schmuck who's going to have to tell the administration that, in terms that even the Sec Def can understand."

As Fulk spoke, Dixon at once felt a sense of relief and one of sympathy. Relief that the chief himself was going to serve as the bearer of bad tidings to the Secretary of Defense, something that he had been afraid Fulk would require him to do. With that burden lifted, Dixon was free to feel a little sympathy for Fulk for having to do so.

"You know what the first thing the Secretary is going to do, Scotty?" Without waiting for an answer, Fulk continued. "He's going to say, 'Well, perhaps the Joint Chiefs of Staff were right. Perhaps we do need to send in Air Force ground attack units and use the Marines to deal with the Caribbean provinces.' I can see it all now. Jet jockeys with big watches and little penises zooming in at four hundred miles an hour dropping a couple of tons of ordnance on villages all over the place while the media have a heyday filming the jarheads splashing ashore like John Wayne in the *Sands of Iwo Jima.* Christ, in a month it will be a regular three-ring circus.''

While the chief vented his anger and frustration, Dixon simply sat watching him, nodding his head, and going over all the arguments in his mind that the Army had used to keep the other two services out of Colombia. The fact that this was in the beginning a low-intensity conflict, a simple guerrilla war and that the Army was trained to deal with it. The fact that only small well-trained, highly mobile combat units were needed to deal with the FARC threat. The fact that a single service with common techniques and a single clean chain of command would best serve our purposes, and finally the fact that we wanted to keep the lowest possible profile. All that had sounded good seven months ago when the intervention into Colombia was first being discussed. There had been, Scotty knew, nothing less than an in-house fight between the services in an effort to determine who got the lion's share of the mission and the funding. In the end it had been the Army's plan, submitted over Fulk's own signature, that had won out. Now Fulk was going to have to go in to the Secretary of Defense, the very man he had convinced seven months ago that the Army could do the job, and tell him that they were failing. Still, Dixon thought, this wasn't all bad. At least Fulk was taking a stand now, while he still had something to stand on. At least, he thought, this wouldn't be another Vietnam.

Then, just as that thought came to Dixon, Fulk shattered it. ''Scotty, I can't go into the Sec Def's office empty-handed. I've got to tell him something that will buy us some time so that we can sort this thing out on our own. That's where you come in.''

Those words, though he had been expecting them, hit Dixon like a sledgehammer. Tensing up in preparation to receive without flinching whatever the chief was about to throw his way, Dixon waited for the other shoe to fall. The wait was mercifully short.

When he spoke this time, Fulk's tone and voice were very deliberate and calculating. "I've come to the conclusion that Lane and the 11th Air Assault down in Colombia need closer supervision. Jerry Stratton can't do it from SOUTHCOM headquarters. Too far. What we need is someone on the ground representing Jerry and SOUTHCOM who can physically go out and personally verify reports and progress."

Fulk's obvious solution, as Dixon watched it unfold, both appalled and stunned him. Rather than seek a quick and direct means of resolving the problems as Dixon saw them, the chief was coming up with a solution that was at best a Band-Aid. Lane, Dixon thought, needed to be relieved and pressure from the State Department needed to be applied to the Colombian government in an effort for them to clean up their own house. Though Dixon thought that he might be jumping to conclusions, he feared that he wasn't. Pushing his own thoughts to the background, he continued to listen as Fulk outlined his solution.

"I'm going to have Jerry establish a forward command post for SOUTHCOM on Bogotá." Looking over at Dixon, Fulk pointed at him. "You're going to be in charge of it."

With that brief statement, Dixon's worst fears were realized.

"The mission of this command post, we'll call it SOUTH-COM Forward, will be assisting the 11th Air Assault in coordinating with and reporting to SOUTHCOM. You will serve as General Stratton's personal representative in Colombia and provide whatever assistance to the commander of the 11th Air Assault he deems necessary to facilitate the quick and accurate flow of reports and orders back and forth between SOUTH-COM and the 11th."

For a moment Dixon waited for additional instructions. But there were none. Rather than do something substantial about correcting the problems that Lane was creating, Fulk was putting a Band-Aid on the whole affair in the hope that it would stem the hemorrhage that Dixon was predicting. Though he didn't like it, none of it, he had spoken his mind and now he had his orders, though they were at this moment far from clear. For the first time since entering the chief's office, Dixon spoke. "Will this forward command post have any operational control over the 11th Air Assault?"

Dixon's question caused Fulk to think for a second. With a shrug and a slight shaking of his head Fulk responded. "No, I don't think so. At least not at this time."

The manner of Fulk's response confirmed Dixon's worse suspicion: Fulk was making this up on the spur of the moment and didn't have a clear idea in his own head what he really wanted. That meant that Dixon would be, as he just had been during the briefing, pretty much on his own. "When, sir, am I to have this headquarters established and functioning?"

Fulk waved his hand. "After you finish up with your written report, head down to SOUTHCOM and get with their chief of staff. Find out when he can put together a package using the staff and equipment he has on hand and get it down to Bogotá. When you have a good idea, let me know when you can be on the ground and running."

The sinking feeling that Dixon had begun to experience was slowly being replaced with one that was a mix of dark foreboding and acute depression. Nothing, it appeared right now, would be changed in Bogotá. Like a tenured professor who had long ago outlasted his usefulness, Lane would be maintained in place simply because there was no clean, graceful way of removing him without causing internal political problems. A compromise solution arrived at by the Army's highest counsel had been reached, and like most compromise solutions this one didn't really solve the problem.

Still General Fulk was the chief, Dixon's boss, and he had made his decisions and issued his orders. All Dixon had to do now, he knew, was to salute and carry on like a good soldier. That he would do so there was no doubt. In his briefing and in his written report Dixon had voiced his opinion and had made his recommendations. That the chief had opted not to listen to all of them was regrettable to Dixon, but there was nothing that he could do. To push the matter further just now would serve no useful purpose as far as Dixon was concerned.

Finished with him, Fulk dismissed Dixon, lit another cigarette, and leaned back in his chair as he pondered how best to deal with the Secretary of Defense.

Under different circumstances, the countryside which the troops of Company B, 3rd of the 511th Infantry, moved through would have been beautiful to behold. The lush green vegetation lining the sides of fertile valleys through which clear mountain streams ran down to empty into the Rio Cauca stood in stark contrast to the commanding mountains that made up the Colombian Sierra. But all of this natural beauty was lost to the men and women of Company B. They were not out there moving along at a snail's pace along narrow trails that wound their way up and down one hill after another for enjoyment. They were, as the orders that originated from Division stated, conducting a show of force, moving about the countryside in an effort to encourage the natives and intimidate the enemy.

Nancy Kozak, as well as most of the B Company troopers, doubted that they could encourage anyone, especially themselves. Nor did they believe that the Farcees would be very much impressed by the show they were trying to put on, not after giving the other two line companies in the battalion a sound beating and then slipping away in the dark. As one sergeant said loud enough for Kozak to hear, "We couldn't even awe the dullest donkey in these mountains right now if we wanted to."

Still the operation wasn't a total waste, at least not for Kozak, who marched along between the second and third rifle platoons in the column. The monotony of watching the same rucksack of the trooper in front of her as the file of soldiers snaked their way up one hill, and then down another didn't bother Nancy Kozak. Even the streams of sweat running down her face and soaking every stitch of clothing she wore didn't faze her. It was instead in its own way rather therapeutic. The one thing she was sure of was that it was a damned sight better being out here humping up and down the mountains than sitting back at the brigade base camp listening to the bickering and whining of the troops.

Word that the battalion had been taken out of the rotation for division reserve had come as a shock. Coming as it did, on the heels of the ambush at the arms cache, the men and women of the battalion, both officers and enlisted, couldn't help but draw the conclusion that they were being punished for their conduct during the ambush. The manner in which the troopers themselves reacted varied, depending on where they had been that day. The people who had actually been involved in the ambush

99

and resulting firefight were stunned, then angered. They knew what had happened. They knew that they had done everything that humanly could have been done given the situation they were thrown into. Fact was that most of them came out of it feeling rather proud of the way that they as individuals and units had behaved under appalling conditions. Their battalion commander himself, Lieutenant Colonel Cerro, had in fact congratulated them on their ability to maintain discipline and unit cohesion throughout the day despite appalling losses. Which is why when the word came down that they would remain in the field conducting combat operations instead of going to what the troopers in the 11th referred to as "The Big City," their sense of pride turned to one of bewilderment and anger. How they as individuals and squads could have done better was beyond them. Not even Cerro could explain with any degree of satisfaction why they were being forsaken.

Cerro himself was rocked back on his heels by the censure Lane had given him. Though he didn't go into specifics and limited his comments to one-liners like "That man's incredible" or "He has no earthly idea what's going on out here," Nancy Kozak knew that whatever had transpired between the two men had affected her battalion commander as nothing had before. "He was," she wrote in a private letter to her grandfather, "a man transformed, a knight of the realm suddenly exposed to the harshest deprivations of a system he had not only defended but believed in with his heart and soul. Though he continues to soldier, it is clear that this is out of habit now and not out of love for the profession and what it had once stood for. He is, in short, a broken man."

In the days that followed, and Kozak watched, nothing seemed to revive her sagging spirit as she watched a man she so admired tear himself up from within. In a firefight, the man gave the appearance of being fearless. He conducted himself in the same calm, almost remote manner during an engagement with the enemy as he did on training exercises. Some even commented that he actually appeared to slow down some during a fight, almost as if he were forcing himself to keep from being carried away by the chaos and confusion around him. Even his handling of personnel and administrative issues was almost faultless, a rarity for a combat leader with a background such as his. It had been Kozak's experience that most combat arms officers were either super troopers in the field and wanting in all other areas or they were whiz-bang staff officers who couldn't fight their way out of a paper bag. Cerro seemed to be both, which was why she so admired him and had fought so hard to be assigned to his battalion.

Had he only had to deal with the aftermath of the ambush, given a little time Cerro could have pulled the battalion back together and restored confidence to those shaken by the experience of that battle. But the mindless decision to keep them in the field indefinitely was too much for Cerro's skills as a leader, just as it was too much for the soldiers to understand. Complicating the issue was the fact that a rift within the battalion itself appeared as soon as everyone found out that they were not going to the rear for what they considered was a well-deserved rest. For those soldiers within the battalion who had not taken part in the fight at the dummy arms cache blamed those who had for the mass punishment that the division commander had brought down on them. In the charged environment that existed at the time word got out, there was nothing officers or NCOs could do to stop the fights, sometimes involving whole platoons, from breaking out. This ripped whatever was left of the delicate fabric called unit cohesion to shreds and left Cerro with a situation for which his training and experience had not prepared him.

The brigade commander, Colonel Henry R. Johnson, an individual who was outside of the division commander's circle of chosen favorites, did all he could do to lessen the impact of Lane's seemingly mindless decision. The division operations section, however, anticipating such a move, ensured that Johnson's brigade had more missions than it could handle with the units assigned to it. This move in effect forced Johnson to use the bulk of Cerro's battalion on a daily basis, leaving Cerro no time to sort out his internal problems.

For some people in the 3rd Battalion, 511th, this was fine by them. Kozak was one of those people. She saw what was happening and knew that eventually it would have severe and dire consequences. But, like Cerro, nothing in her training or experience equipped her to deal with the quagmire of internal resentment and self-recrimination that the battalion found itself in. Though she did have the people within her own staff section to deal with, Kozak was a staff officer, the acting operations officer for the battalion. Technically her job as the battalion S-3 had nothing to do with the maintenance of morale and discipline within the battalion. Those areas of responsibility belonged to the commanders and leaders of the battalion, called green tabbers because of the one-inch green felt cloth they wore under the unit crest on the tabs of their dress green uniforms. As a staff officer Kozak could concentrate on dealing only with the problems concerning the missions and tactical operations of the battalion. Though the morale of the battalion and its ability to function as a cohesive force did impact on its combat capability, she didn't need to deal with the factors that contributed or detracted from those delicate and pliable commodities. She didn't need to come up with solutions or become directly involved in efforts to revive them. She could and did put on mental blinders and kept her attention focused solely on doing her job, period.

It wasn't that Kozak didn't care about what was happening to the battalion. Like every officer who was worth a damn, she was very much concerned about the downward spiral of morale and effectiveness that showed no sign of ending. Nancy Kozak was too good an officer not to care. But caring and being able to do something about it were not the same thing. The problem of encouraging soldiers, shoring up flagging morale, and mending fractured cohesion required leaders who themselves were confident and together. While it is possible for someone to go through the mechanical process of producing operational plans or issuing orders without regard to physical or mental state, a leader who was shaken himself, whose face betrayed fear or who spoke with a voice that lacked conviction could do nothing to influence others. That in a nutshell was Kozak's problem and, to a lesser extent but only slightly, Cerro's too.

For they, like the soldiers who had been with them at the arms cache, had felt that the battalion had done well despite the odds. And because Cerro and Kozak were humans, just like their people they too felt the bite of Lane's seemingly arbitrary decision to deny them the rest that was not only well deserved but needed. Kozak in particular had been looking forward to spending time in The Big City with AJ, the aviation captain who had captured her heart as no other man had ever done before. To suffer the trauma of battle like the one that the battalion had been involved in, followed by word that the one thing that had been sustaining her for weeks, her dream leave with AJ in Bogotá, would be denied her was too much.

At a time when everyone around her was suffering the same sense of anger and frustration, there were few that Kozak could turn to for advice and comfort. She had considered confiding her feelings to the one intimate friend that she had at the base camp, another female captain by the name of Jessica Ann Cruthers, who was the assistant brigade intelligence officer, but quickly dismissed that idea. She had, or thought she still had, an image to maintain. To go to an officer on the brigade staff and cry on her shoulder, regardless of what their relationship was, would be in Kozak's eyes unprofessional. Though she suspected that Cruthers would as a woman understand, Kozak had since entering active duty carefully guarded her emotions and feelings, confiding in no one and dealing with her feelings alone as best she could. Now when she suddenly felt the needed to turn to someone, someone who could help her by lending her a sympathetic ear and easing her seemingly intolerable burden with a kind word and friendly smile, Kozak not only found that she had no one she could trust, she didn't even know how to.

There was, of course, AJ. Before the fight at the arms cache, Kozak and he would spend hours on the phone late at night when traffic over the military lines were almost nil. The two seemed to be able to talk about almost everything, from their day-to-day experiences in Colombia to memories of growing up and views on the world at large. Such conversations, free-flowing and uninhibited by rank, protocol, or the need to maintain a professional facade, had come to mean a lot to Kozak. After one such conversation that had gone on well into the early morning hours, Kozak suddenly realized how much she had given up in her pursuit of a military career. Like a blind person who had suddenly been given sight, she understood all the misgivings and concerns that her mother, even her own father, a former officer himself, had tried so hard to communicate to her. What she would do about AJ and how she would fit her newfound feelings and love into a promising career were questions still unanswered when they had gone into the arms cache.

Now, like everything else, her affair with AJ was on hold. For not only did she have to fight through the acute depression that hung over her like a gray winter day, she had to sort out how she felt about AJ, who was an aviator. Of all the surprises and shocks that had rocked the battalion during the firefight, the one that had hurt the most was the feeling that the aviators of the division, the people who made an air assault unit what it was, had abandoned them.

Not that it was the fault of the aviators in general or AJ in particular. They, like everyone else, up to the moment that the first surface-to-air-missile, or SAM, had been launched, had been working under the premise that the Farcees didn't have any shoulder-fired SAMs. As with the overly optimistic intelligence summaries that denied the FARC the capability of conducting company-level operations, no mention was ever made, officially or unofficially, about periodic reports of Russian- and French-made SAMs turning up here and there in Colombia. This failure to appreciate the potential danger led to the habit of not arming the helicopters of the division with anti-missile flares dropped by helicopters in their wake to lure away incoming heat-seeking missiles. On the day of the ambush, the flares of the aviation company supporting Kozak's battalion were safely locked away in their storage boxes at the division's main ammunition supply point. When word of the disaster of the arms cache reached the division, orders went out that no aircraft was to be permitted to enter into the battle zone until the FARC forces had broken contact and the area was secured or they had been armed with the flares. The operations officer of the aviation battalion took this order to mean all, to include medical evacuation birds. Thus, during the critical hours when the 3rd of the 511th's wounded needed evacuation and everyone still in the fight needed fire support from attack helicopters, the wings of the division sat idle, unable to respond while a frantic search of the division ammo dump was conducted to find the well-packed flares.

In her mind, the logical part at least, Kozak could understand that AJ had nothing to do with the decision not to arm the helicopters with the anti-missile flares. He had no say over the order preventing needed relief and support flights from reaching the 3rd of the 511th when they were needed the most. Kozak knew this. Yet, with the same irrational thought process that allows a woman who has been raped to blame a husband for not protecting her, even though he was physically unable to do anything to protect her, Kozak condemned AJ. She condemned him by virtue of the fact that he was an aviator and thus in a convoluted sort of way no better than the operations officer and whoever kept the choppers from coming to the rescue.

With her mind busy churning away at this and other personal concerns, Kozak missed hearing the first few pop-pop-pops of an M-16 firing at the head of the column that announced the initiation of a firefight. It was only when the rucksack that she had been staring at in front of her disappeared that she realized something was going on. Startled, she stopped and looked to the left and right before she understood what was happening. Then without another thought she threw herself to the side of the trail, just as everyone in front of her had.

From behind she felt a tap on her shoulder. Without needing to look back to see what it was, Kozak reached up with her right hand and let her radioman for today, Specialist Luis Haya, pass her the radio's hand mike. Set to the Bravo Company's command frequency, Kozak listened to the initial contact report from the platoon leader of the lead platoon to his commander. Like most young men involved in a sudden and unexpected fight, the platoon leader spoke just a little too fast and with a slightly higher pitch in his voice. "Bravo Six, Bravo Six, this is Bravo Two Six. My point element ran into a half a dozen armed people at a trail junction about one hundred meters up ahead. The other people didn't return fire. They just took off into the jungle headed northwest. Should I pursue? Over."

There was a pause. Kozak said nothing as she waited to hear the company commander's decisions. Though technically outranking him by virtue of her position, she had no intention of intervening in the manner in which the company commander ran his company unless of course he did something that was totally inappropriate. Like Cerro, she believed in allowing subordinates maximum leeway in exercising their prerogatives and authority. That she was present that day with Company B was only due to her personal desire to get away from the oppressive atmosphere that permeated the base camp and not from any wish to run the operation at hand.

In the few seconds that stretched between the platoon leader's request for guidance and the announcement of his decision, the commander of Company B had to juggle many considerations and options in an effort to come up with the best one. If he guessed right, he and his company would be successful, winning the day and another battle. On the other hand, if he made a bad choice, all he'd wind up doing was stuffing more body bags. In light of the recent past, the company commander opted on the side of caution. "Bravo Two Six, this is Bravo Six. Deploy your platoon and form a base of fire. I'll bring the First Platoon up on your right and move forward in pursuit. Third Platoon will follow and be prepared either to swing to your left or follow First. Do you understand? Over."

Without any hesitation, the Second Platoon leader responded, "I roger. We'll be set in a minute. Over." No sooner had that platoon leader stopped transmitting than another voice came over the radio. "Bravo Six, this is Bravo One Six, I roger your last transmission to Two Six. I am preparing to move my element around to the right as soon as you give the word. Over." Again, as soon as the last platoon leader let go of the hand mike, a fourth voice came up on the air. "Six, this is Three Six. I monitored your instructions to Two Six. I am closing up my people and standing by for further orders. Over."

Without waiting for any further response, the company commander came back. "Okay Bravo, let's do it. Out." As if on cue, the soldier in front of Kozak got up and began to move forward at the double with his rifle held close to his chest and ready. Taking the radio hand mike from her ear and thrusting it back without looking, Kozak yelled to her radioman, "Let's get moving, Haya, before we get run over." Once she felt Haya grab it away, she pushed herself up off the ground with the aid of the rifle, brought it up to the ready position, and took off after the platoon to her front. As she caught up, the first reassuring thought in days popped into her head. At least, she thought, the soldiers were still able to react well under pressure. Of course this was just one company, the one that hadn't been involved in the fight at the arms cache. Still it was something.

Up ahead, no more than two hundred meters from the trail junction where Hector Valendez and his small escort had stumbled into a group of American soldiers, Valendez ordered a halt. He had no sooner dropped down to one knee facing to the northwest when the squad leader of Valendez's small escort came up next to him and dropped to one knee next to him. The squad leader, a young man who had left an American-owned coffee plantation to fight for the land that had once been his father's, was winded, more from the excitement of running into the Americans and being fired on than from running.

While the squad leader waited for orders, Valendez looked over his shoulder, cocking his head to listen for a moment in the direction he and his small party had just fled from. In the distance he could hear the orders in English being shouted. When it became evident that the voices were growing no closer, a slight smile began to creep across his face. They were deploying first and preparing to come forward carefully. The Americans, he thought, had learned caution.

Turning to the squad leader, he studied him before he issued his orders. There was a hint of fear in the young man's eyes. Yet there was no panic. Though shaken, he was waiting patiently, as he had been trained, for his orders from the senior commander present. And no one in the entire FARC's military arm was more senior at this moment than Valendez. Without any flourishes or unnecessary embellishments, Valendez spoke. "You will hold here for five seconds after I leave with my party. At the count of five your men will open fire in the directions of the Americans for two to three seconds. Then, without delay, break and continue to move to the northwest as fast as you can for two to three hundred meters. Stop, turn, and fire your weapons again for several seconds. After that, change directions, moving to the southwest until you reach the river. Once you've done that, cross over, move upstream, and find someplace secure to hold up for the night near the river. In the morning move out and rejoin your unit as quickly as possible. Is that clear?"

There was no thought of questioning Valendez's orders. The squad leader knew where Valendez was headed and understood that he could best protect his commander now by drawing away the Americans so that he could continue to the secret meeting with the ruling council. Nor did he dread telling his men what they were about to do. Whatever apprehension the fighters of the FARC had felt about closing with the Americans in close combat had been eradicated by the fight that Valendez himself had planned and led. With a nod and a confident "Yes, it shall be," the squad leader stood up and turned away from Valendez, signaling his squad by hand to deploy in a firing line facing the direction from which they had just fled.

Finished with the squad leader, Valendez also stood, pointing to his assistant and radioman. With a quick wave of his right hand he signaled them to follow as he pivoted a quarter turn and ran north at a quick trot. After traveling for several seconds, the three came to a halt in a line several meters from the trail. The small party of rebels dropped down to one knee in unison and listened. To their rear they could hear the sound of a volley of gun fire. To their immediate front they heard or saw nothing. Satisfied that the Americans were still taking their time and deploying, Valendez signaled to his assistant. "Onto the trail and head north on the double." Though the radioman questioned the wisdom of getting back onto the trail so soon after running into an American force, he followed the assistant without hesitation, trusting the judgment of their esteemed leader.

When they were up and on the trail running north as fast as their loads permitted, Valendez hung back a little and turned around, running backwards as he did. His first instinct back there had been to turn and fight. He had found it necessary to use every ounce of restraint he had to keep from doing so. Not because the Americans they had encountered outnumbered them. Together with his radioman, assistant, and the escort, he had nine men versus the four Americans he thought had been a point element. With both sides equally surprised, his nine could have easily taken the four. But that, he knew, wouldn't have been prudent. For even if they had taken out all four and been able to get away before follow-on forces could come up, there was a good chance that his own people would have taken one or more casualties. That would have meant they would have had to stop and police up their wounded or leave them and face the possibility that they would betray under interrogation the identity of who had been traveling with them, where they had come from, and where they were going. The risking of such consequences wasn't worth the momentary thrill that participating in a stand-up firefight with the enemy would have brought him. So, like the good commander and tactician he was, Valendez looked, thought, decided, and acted appropriately.

Spinning back to face front, he picked up his pace in order to catch up with the rest. As he did so, he also decided that it would have been a shame if he had himself been struck down now when he almost had in his hands everything that he had been working for. At the meeting of the revolutionary council that he was headed for, he expected to be given carte blanche to step up the military pressure on both the American and Colombian forces as he saw fit and conditions warranted. The success of his six-hour battle with the Americans eight days before would be, he knew, more than enough to convince even the most skeptical member of the council that his ideas and plans were sound. Though he expected heated debates and some dissension, a feature of every meeting of the FARC's council, in his heart he knew that they would release control of the newly formed regular forces that he himself had organized and trained.

Though by most standards the twenty-seven companies of the FARC's regular forces were slight, when grouped with the special weapons platoons into nine provisional battalions, they would form a hard hitting force, one unlike anything that the FARC ever before possessed. Augmented with local rebel forces, the military arm of the FARC would then bring to an end the seeming pointless hit-and-run raids that stung but did no permanent damage and begin to concentrate on carving out permanent rebel enclaves. Such holdings, Valendez knew, no matter how trivial, would serve to discredit the government and force them to come to the FARC and fight them on their terms, in their time, just as he had done on a small scale to the Americans. That he and his forces, molded by his own hands, would ultimately be victorious was never in doubt in Valendez's mind.

Nor was there any doubt about how this would all end in the minds of the few Americans who took the time to carefully read the unmistakable signs of doom that were growing in number like a gathering storm as each day past. Rather than light at the end of the tunnel, all they saw was a gathering darkness. And it frightened them.

PART TWO

THE END
OF
INNOCENCE

CHAPTER 6

October 2

BEFORE THE FIRST SHOT WAS FIRED IN THE FARC'S NEW CAM-
paign, a different kind of battle had to be fought. It took place
at a remote site not far from Armenia, a city located in the
Cauca River Valley. The logic of choosing such a site baffled
Valendez, since the current leadership of the FARC could come
and go just about anywhere in Colombia without fear, but he
said nothing. Despite the fact that they were men of strength
and character, with few naive illusions left, they, the FARC's
chosen leaders, still needed on occasion to indulge their fantasies. One of the fantasies that many of them cherished as
fondly as his own manhood was the image of himself as a
struggling revolutionary hunted by the government and forced
to lead a secret and precarious existence. For each and every
one knew that one day, long after their victory had been won
and they were nothing but memories, the more heroic and
dangerous their lives seemed, the brighter those memories
would burn. So Valendez, despite the fact that his travel to this
meeting had almost cost him his own life, said nothing. He had
other issues that needed to be attended to and he had no intention of allowing trivial concerns to confuse or dilute his agenda.

This meeting, as all of them did, started with rivals on the
ruling council heaping praise and platitudes upon their most
bitter enemies on the council in an elaborate charade designed

to give everyone present the illusion that all was well between the leaders of the FARC. The object of most of the opening day's salutations and acclaim was Valendez, the hero of the moment. First came Simón Mortino, the chairman of the council and sharpest critic of what he called Valendez's mindless war of attrition. He opened the meeting by standing up and summarizing in the most glowing terms the political and propaganda benefits Valendez's ambush had already reaped. "We have shown," he crowed, "that we are men who are not afraid to stand up to the machines and firepower of the Yankees. We have given our people hope and pride. Hope that one day we will in fact prevail despite the odds, and pride that the courage to liberate ourselves from oppression is within our own hands. My good friend Hector Valendez, the man his enemies now call The Jaguar, has shown us the way, the way to victory."

Mortino's speech did not surprise Valendez. In fact, had he not spoken in such a manner, Valendez would have been concerned. Nor did the following speech, given by Mortino's archrival on the council, León Febres Cordero, contain any surprises or variations from the tired old line that he had been spouting for years. Cordero, a man who viewed political change from within the existing system as the only true way to meaningful success, and therefore an opponent of any form of armed insurrection, nevertheless could not allow his opponent on the council to reap all the fruit of Valendez's labors. No sooner had Mortino sat down than Cordero stood up and continued to heap praise in a backhanded sort of way on Valendez. "As you all know," he stated, "I am a man who has from the beginning advocated change from within, using the government's own laws to destroy it. But I am not a naive fool. I can, like many of you, appreciate the need to hurry things along with a little shove every now and then. Through the recent efforts of our deputy commander of the military arm, we have given the government in Bogotá and the Americans something to think about." Pausing, Cordero looked at Valendez and then at Mortino. "But I, as always, advise caution when wielding the bayonet. Pushing too hard too fast might cause our enemies to rally and our friends to shy away. We, the leaders of the revolution, must put our heads together and determine how best to use the victory that our heroic field commander, Hector Valendez, has given us.''

This last sentence, coming from Cordero himself, pleased Valendez for several reasons. The first and most obvious was an admission finally that the FARC's military arm had a viable role to play in bringing down the government in Bogotá. Like many of the pseudo intellectuals that had infiltrated the ranks of the FARC in recent years, Cordero had championed peaceful and legal means of effecting change to the exclusion of all others. To openly admit at a meeting of the full council that there was a place for military operations in his theory of revolution could only be viewed as a last gasp for a failed policy. Though he was tempted to smile as Cordero spoke those words, Valendez did not. Biding his time, he simply nodded in acknowledgment. Besides the moral victory of finally forcing Cordero to admit the need for armed confrontation, a more subtle and far-reaching victory for Valendez had been proclaimed by Cordero's simple statement. When Cordero referred to Valendez as ''our heroic field commander,'' and no one on the council bothered to remind him that Valendez was only the deputy, Valendez knew that from that moment on his voice and his opinions, when it came to military operations, would dominate. He had without any scheming or manipulation been given everything he needed to carry out his war against his enemies, both here in the council and out there in the forests, streets, mountains, and jungles of Colombia.

Even so, Valendez was rather circumspect about using his newly won power. For despite the praise and joy over the recent victories of the FARC's military arm over both the Yankees and the government forces in the field, there was still some opposition to the notion that it was time to accelerate the military campaign. Early on in the meeting, however, this opposition was easily swept aside. Valendez's success of the twenty-first of September assured that. Talk by the council members themselves that one day Colombians would look back to that date as being the military turning point of the people's war against an intolerably corrupt government gave the twenty-first of September more meaning than Valendez could ever have hoped for and silenced many naysayers.

Of course, the heady joy of an unexpected victory did nothing to end the unnerving practice of holding protracted debates and discussions on every issue and subject presented to the FARC's ruling council, no matter how trivial, before a decision could be made. This did not come as a complete surprise to Valendez. In fact he had counted on it. Still, as the council turned to the selection of which region this campaign would be waged in, he felt a pang of regret that men who considered themselves the leaders of the socialist movement in Colombia could allow their egos and personal agendas to interfere with the business at hand when, in Valendez's eyes at least, the issues at hand and their solutions were crystal clear and irrefutable. But there was no escaping the human and political elements that so complicated his efforts and those of his fighters. Thus resigned to his fate, Valendez leaned back in his seat, folded his hands on the table, and prepared to suffer in silence hour after hour of heroic speeches and discussions that contained more dogma and florid words than substance.

That resignation did not mean that he was abdicating decisions concerning the strategic direction of the upcoming campaign to the political buffoons who called themselves the council. Valendez's silence instead was a tactic, one which he used, like any combat tactic he employed, to achieve his desired objective. In the past it had been necessary to stand and shout toe-to-toe with opponents on many occasions. When his successes in the field followed one after the other, as he had predicted and promised, his need to scream, shout, and argue had diminished to the point where all he needed to do now was clear his throat to silence a speaker he was at odds with. Even his silence, as in this day's meeting, now made itself felt. As the discussions progressed and Valendez said nothing concerning the where and when of their next major move, more and more members of the council cast worried eyes in his direction, wondering and worrying what he was up to. None understood that he was letting them play themselves out with their own indecision and arguments. He was doing what most horse trainers did when breaking a new and undisciplined horse. He was letting the wild beast run itself down before applying a firm and guiding hand to it. As he did with the enemies he faced on the battlefield, he would let his opponents on the council exhaust themselves in pointless efforts before exerting his influence.

From his seat next to the nominal head of the FARC's military arm, Valendez watched the arguments go this way and that with the same deadpan stare that a sophisticated English gentleman watched a tennis game at Wimbledon. First there was the debate between those who wanted to go after the populated urban areas first in order to deny the government major nerve centers and provide bountiful recruiting grounds for the growing military arm, and those who favored a rural uprising. After much discussion it was pointed out that while seizing a city might be relatively easy, running and sustaining it and its population was beyond the FARC's means. The focus of the discussion then turned toward mountainous regions of the country where the FARC had been enjoying its unbroken string of successes in the past few months. Though this was tempting, the proximity of the capital and the heavy concentration of both American and government troops made this proposition risky at best.

It was at this point that Hector Valendez began to become personally involved. For while he listened patiently to the early part of the discussions and nodded when appropriate, he did so out of deference to the speaker and not in approval, since he had already decided not only when he would strike and where but how. Only when Mortino, the council chairman, was about to lose control of the meeting did Valendez decide that the time had come to speak. He announced his intent to do so by standing up and walking over to a map of Colombia displayed at the rear of the one-room country schoolhouse where the meeting was taking place. Without his saying a word, Valendez's simple action brought a hush to the room as everyone present watched and waited for him to speak. To heighten the dramatic effect he had achieved, Valendez stretched the pause for better than a minute. During that time, a time when all eyes and thoughts turned and focused on this former professor, he pretended to study the map. Only when he was ready did he turn to face the council.

"At a time like this it would be very easy to lose our focus, to become mesmerized by our own successes and power." Valendez lifted his hands up and open as if he were weighing pieces of fruit in each one. "Nine regular-force battalions and thirty-five local-force companies seems to us now like a powerful force. It is, in fact, the largest, best-equipped, and most thoroughly trained force we have ever had. But," Valendez continued as he dropped his hands to his sides, "we could throw it all away if we do not move forward with caution."

This last statement caused eyebrows all around the conference table to rise. To hear this from Hector Valendez, the man who was always advocating bigger and bolder military operations, was akin to hearing the devil renounce evil and sin. His had always been a shrill voice pleading for increased aggressiveness in all areas when most of the old-time members of the FARC were frightened by their own shadows. Now, when this voice spoke calmly of caution at a time when his bold and seemingly rash policies were bearing fruit, there was shock. Without having to raise his voice above that of a loud whisper, he had captured their undivided attention. Seeing this, Valendez put his hands on his hips and began to move about the room, just as he had done when he had been at the university.

"We have the tools, both military and political, to do much. But they are fragile tools, expensive ones that once broken we may not be able to replace. For each of the regular-force battalions is more than a collection of five hundred men. It is, like our own bodies, a complex organism composed of many specialized parts that when functioning together create something greater than the sum of the parts by themselves. For just as one cannot make a man by simply sewing together two arms, two legs, a head, a torso, eyes, hands, feet, a heart, and so on, so too is it impossible to gather up strangers in one place and call them a unit. Like the human body, the military unit needs the magical spark of life that animates it. For the human, the spark is what we call the miracle of life, given at birth by the mother. For the military unit, leadership, training, camaraderie, common purpose and respect, organization, and shared hardships all work in mysterious ways to make a collection of individuals an effective unit. Weapons and people are only tools. Spirit and determination, that's what makes a unit."

From his place at the head of the table Mortino interrupted. "Yes, yes, my friend, this is very interesting, but this is not the time or place for such discussions."

Raising his finger in the air, Valendez exclaimed, "On the contrary, Mr. Chairman. This is precisely the time to discuss this. You see, the same rules that apply to our units apply to those of the enemy. The same forces that hold our companies together hold theirs. If we understand this, if we bear this in mind as we plan our strategies, we can use this knowledge to diminish the effectiveness of his units while preserving ours, both physically and psychologically.''

Despite the fact that he had just been spoken down to as if he were a lowly college student in one of Valendez's classes, Mortino said nothing. This pleased Valendez, for Mortino's yielding to him only served to reinforce Valendez's stature in the eyes of the members of the ruling council. Though this was only a minor point, every such point gained reinforced Valendez's growing power.

''I do understand the logic behind each of the proposals presented here this morning concerning where and when to strike next. They all promise a quick gain, gains that can serve our purposes well. But each of them would, in my opinion, cost us too much militarily. The capture of a major city or province capital would secure us many headlines, but the government and the Yankees, with superior mobility, firepower, and manpower, would eventually return and throw us out. All we would have then would be a short-lived victory, a city in rubble, and a fresh defeat with no forces left to repeat such a stunt. To go into the mountains anywhere within two hundred miles of Bogotá as a start would be equally doomed. We would by our own hand be bringing into play a war of attrition in which we would be at a great disadvantage. Every bullet, every replacement weapon, every trained recruit would have to travel hundreds of miles through contested or enemy-controlled territory before it reached its intended destination. We could expect to lose a good percentage of everything, from men to supplies, before it reached the front. Besides, the enemy again would be able to employ its superiority in numbers and firepower. Until such time as the government forces are no longer loyal or become ineffective in the field, we cannot hope to go into the mountains, seize land, and hold it for long.''

''Where then,'' Mortino asked, ''do we use this marvelous weapon that you have so carefully crafted? Certainly not in the Amazon region. We have had virtual control over that region in the past without reaping the sort of benefits that we need to ensure a final and unchallenged victory.''

Valendez smiled as he shook his head and circled the table one more time before stopping his wanderings when he reached the map again. ''Yes, quite right. No, I was not thinking of the Amazon. That is where the government would like to see us go and linger about on the fringes as we have done in the past. There we would be isolating ourselves, out of sight and mind, at no cost to them.'' Using his hand to indicate the various regions that he spoke of, Valendez continued. ''Instead of along the coast or in the mountains or in the cities themselves, I believe we should concentrate our efforts, now and for the foreseeable future, in Los Llanos.'' With that, he slapped his hand, palm down, on the eastern region of Colombia, a vast area of flatlands and rivers, some 250,000 square kilometers that bordered Venezuela. It was, everyone in the room knew, an area which no one really controlled, a region that had hung in a strange limbo of near lawlessness for so long that a sort of peaceful coexistence between the guerrillas, government officials, narcotics growers, and ranchers who lived there had been long established and respected. It had no major cities and few towns worthy of the name. What roads existed were little more than trails. Rivers, instead, provided the only reliable surface travel year round.

''Here in the vast savannas we can let our revolution take root very quickly and with little interference from the government.'' As he pivoted about, Valendez's flashing eyes and excited yet deliberate tone spoke of a man possessed. ''The government in Bogotá will not be able to stop us, for they, and not we, will be at the end of a long and tedious supply line. Any efforts will spread them thin elsewhere in critical areas where our local forces will be able to fill the vacuum created by the absence of forces that they will have to send east to challenge us.''

For the first time since Valendez had started speaking, Cordero spoke. ''You seem sure that the government will come to us on our chosen ground when we are ready.''

Without hesitation, Valendez responded, making a fist as he did so. ''Yes! They will come to us as we want them. The government will have no choice. To allow us to hold land that is of some consequence, with easy access to the rest of the world and its all-seeing media, cannot be tolerated. With Los Llanos tamed by us, we will be able to protect the ranchers there and open new lands for farming and ranching to those peasants and Indians that the government has for years forgotten. We will be able to put into effect those reforms that we have discussed for so long but have never had the opportunity to try. And after as little as one season, when the crops of the land are harvested by the new landowners under our guidance and protection, in a land free of drug lords and corrupt governments, we, the FARC, will reap a harvest of popular support anywhere we choose in this country.''

"Provided," Mortino interjected, "the government does not destroy that which we have planted.''

When he spoke, Valendez did so with a gleam in his eye, a gleam that told of boundless confidence. "Yes, the Army will come. And perhaps the Americans too. But they will come slowly in bits and pieces, never large enough to do what needs to be done. We will meet them, each piece the fools in Bogotá offer us, as a raging grass fire driven by the winds meets all who stand in its way and consumes them." Lowering his head slightly, Valendez allowed a wicked smile to creep across his face. "Besides, when the government comes attacking us with their big guns and attack aircraft, the government troops will by their own hand be subjecting the very people that they have come to save to the cruelties of war. And as in so many other wars that the Americans have waged or supported, once their television cameras have captured for the American public the horrors of a government waging war on its own people, this war will become unpopular in the United States. In time this unpopularity will give way to protests that will eventually give the current administration in the United States a choice between staying in office or maintaining an unpopular war.''

"You speak with great confidence, a confidence, I fear, that I do not share. To challenge our own government, that is one thing. But to imagine that we can influence another country's, that is in my opinion quite arrogant, not to mention dangerous, thinking.''

Valendez met Mortino's comment with a shrug. He felt like telling Mortino that the reason that he could not share his confidence was summed up in a word he had just used, fear. Like so many of the other men at the table before him, Mortino had neither the stomach nor the nerve to risk all, even when there was no risk. Valendez, however, held his tongue. He had already flamed far too many sparks of anger that afternoon. Time now, he knew, to finish making his point and let others take up his case, as he knew they would. Yet he still could not resist the urge to take one more swipe at the timid men who called themselves leaders. "This will not be, my friends, the first time that members of this council have listened and doubted. Fortunately, every time the need to move forward has presented itself to this esteemed body of men, enough men of courage stood up and made their presence felt."

This insult and direct challenge to the manhood of some of the members of the council did not go unnoticed. Several of them became visibly upset or annoyed. And yet no one said anything. Again Valendez had thrown down a challenge that was not picked up by anyone. Though he knew he was playing a dangerous game, for the very men he was addressing would be in the beginning the heart of the new government once the one in Bogotá was gone, Valendez drove on. He was a soldier, not a politician. In time, he suspected, he would have to become one in order to survive. But for now survival meant little to him. Destroying his enemy was his only concern.

Besides, there was more to his confidence than sheer logic or bluff. His statement concerning the Army was based on solid intelligence that few in the room possessed. As far as he knew, only he and one other man knew how deeply involved the disenfranchised elements of the Army's officer corps were in the success of the FARC in the field. Those officers, though few in number at present, were so well placed that they would be able to influence without suspicion which units came east to challenge the FARC and how they came. When that day did come, and it would, Valendez had no doubt that the first units they would feed into his meat grinder would be those most loyal to the Bogotá government and least likely to support another coup. With little effort on their part, the sponsors of the next coup would be able to eliminate, at no cost to themselves, future opponents. Valendez did not understand how those men could be so disloyal to a government they were pledged to support, and what they hoped to gain from such treason. Yet he also believed that it was wrong to turn away gifts, regardless of bearer, on personal principles alone. War, after all, made strange bedfellows, and right now Valendez was prepared to crawl into bed with anyone who promised to give him what he and the revolution needed.

Having achieved the impact that he had desired, Valendez placed his right hand over his heart and lowered his head in a gesture of apology. "I have, my fellow patriots, been too long-winded. I hope that my case has merit and will be judged to be acceptable. That, of course, is for you to decide. And I am confident, as always, that whatever your decision, it will be the best." With that, Valendez returned to his seat to watch and listen as the others discussed his plan.

October 5

Once he had been sentenced to a term in purgatory, Scotty Dixon saw no sense in delaying his departure from Washington, D.C. The fact was, after his briefing to the Army staff concerning the situation in Colombia, the sooner he left the better he and everyone concerned would feel. That briefing had generated a blizzard of annoying questions concerning the conduct of operations and reporting procedures that was proving to be an embarrassment to the Army staff. Even the Secretary of Defense found himself in the awkward position of having to choose between his personal integrity and loyalty to the administration when the threat of a congressional investigation reared its ugly head. So no one was really upset when word was passed around the corridors of the Pentagon that Dixon, the bearer of the ugly truth, was going south, the term used when assigned to Colombia. It was hoped that with him out of sight the specter of defeat that he had fostered would fade. Though many believed that Lane's reports had been too good to be true, they likewise believed that Dixon's report was too pessimistic. "The truth," one general who had attended Dixon's briefing said, "no doubt lies somewhere in the middle." Not sure, as a result of the two extremes presented to them, where the truth was, many opted to trust the system. "All we need to do," conventional wisdom stated, "is to wait out the next six months, pull out the 11th on schedule, and we can all go back to business as usual."

Dixon, on the other hand, was faced with anything but business as usual. Rather than hide behind the conventional, he was now faced with the task of creating a job, not to mention a staff, out of nothing. This task included everything imaginable, from such simple considerations as where he would literally hang his hat once in Colombia, to where he and his tiny staff would get the phones and communications equipment that they would need to carry out their assigned tasks, whatever they turned out to be.

Such an assignment for a man of Dixon's talents and reputation was not impossible. He had found himself in similar circumstances before. During the First Persian Gulf War he and the tank battalion he was serving in as the operations officer found themselves thrown into an area of the world where the United States Army had never before trodden en masse, dangling precariously at the end of a long and vicarious line of communications. There they faced an enemy force that was numerically superior and fighting on its home soil. A few years later in Egypt when the United States found itself faced with a resurgent Russia bent on making its mark on the world scene, Dixon was given the command of a tank battalion at the last minute and ordered to lead it into battle. Following that, during a war with Mexico that was often referred to as "an unfortunate misunderstanding," he was charged with planning a mission that if it had failed would have put both him and his commander in the military prison at Fort Leavenworth, Kansas. And recently in Germany he had been cast into the eye of a storm that had set into motion political changes in Europe that were still being sorted out.

During his trip from what his wife, Jan, called Sodom on the Potomac to SOUTHCOM headquarters, Dixon pondered all of this and tried hard to find something from his past that he could use to guide him or at least provide solace. This effort, however, yielded nothing. The more he searched for some sort of parallel or a simple glimmer of hope, the more precarious and lonely his current situation seemed. There was nothing, no matter how far back he reached into the dark days gone by, that he could use to steel himself for the ordeal that lay ahead. The trials which he had passed through before bore no comparison to the one he now faced. Always in the past he had been in the company of friends or serving with soldiers who, though they were strangers, were skilled professionals. That he was leaving a hostile camp behind him and traveling into an even more hostile one depressed Scotty Dixon to a degree that he had never felt before.

Nothing at SOUTHCOM did anything to disperse his gathering gloom. If anything, it added new dimensions as he was bounced from one staff section to another, hat in hand, seeking the necessary personnel, coordination, and equipment that he and his staff would need in Colombia. The principal staff officers, brigadier generals themselves, inevitably fell back to the same position. "Sorry, Scotty, but we're already stretched to the max now with no prospect of getting any better anytime soon." Dixon, having reviewed the entire Colombian adventure from top to bottom, understood this, since the administration had opted to fight this dirty little war on the cheap, with no mobilization of reserves and no increase in the end strength of an already undermanned Army. This understanding didn't make Dixon's task any easier. In fact, it only served to heighten his anger and deepen his depression. After three days of walking into brick walls, Dixon threw up his hands and walked into the office of General Jerry Stratton, the SOUTHCOM commander-in-chief.

The meeting was brief and to the point. Though respectful, Dixon made sure that Stratton understood his frustrations. "We both have been in the Army long enough to know," Dixon stated, "that an order can be dodged only so long before someone gets bent out of shape, stops accepting excuses, and starts looking for results. Unless you know something that I don't, sir, this mission of mine isn't going to be canceled."

To his surprise, Stratton not only agreed with Dixon, he expressed a sincere and unabashed sympathy for Dixon's plight. "Scotty, I'm quite concerned about what is going on down there. Since your briefing I've done a lot of serious soul searching and have come to the same conclusion that you have; the 11th Air Assault is an accident waiting to happen. I've closed my eyes to what's been going on down there, hoping that we could make do with Lane, but as you have pointed out, that's not going to work anymore. Of course, knowing that Lane is not up to the job and as a result something bad is going to happen is one thing. Accurately predicting what that bad thing is going to be, let alone when it's going to happen, makes doing something about it difficult. Though I don't agree with the chief that sending you and a tiny staff down there to play 'I Spy' will solve our problems, I have my orders just like you. With that matter settled in my mind, I've come to the conclusion that you can be very valuable to me up here, and despite the grief that Lane and his staff are going to give you, you may, when push comes to shove, quickly find yourself in the position of being their savior.''

"Or," Dixon quickly added, "their scapegoat."

Stratton took a deep breath as he looked down at the blotter on his desk. "Yes, that too."

Though he still had another two weeks before he would be able to leave for Colombia, and his mission was still far from clear, let alone satisfactory, those weeks went fast. The doors of SOUTHCOM were slowly pried open to Dixon, allowing him to scavenge among the meager resources available to that staff in search of the men and material needed to build his own staff. In those weeks, during long conversations with Stratton, Dixon began to appreciate that Stratton was coming to view Dixon's forlorn hope mission in a new light. Dixon's newly created SOUTHCOM Forward, as his tiny staff was officially designated, was being designed to be a bridge across the gaping abyss that both he and Stratton found themselves peering into. Failing that, Stratton hoped in private that Dixon and his people would be able to provide him with a safety valve to stave off disaster.

October 15

Had Scotty Dixon and his wife, Jan Fields-Dixon, compared notes, they would have been hard put to tell who had to deal with more stonewalls and frustrations. Like Scotty, Jan was finding herself dealing with a situation that bore no resemblance to anything that she had faced in the past as she tried to put together a story that she knew was out there somewhere, but for now was simply beyond her grasp. The differences between the problems each faced were like night and day. While the issues and people that Dixon found himself up against were rather straightforward and upfront, the roadblocks that were faced by Jan were very circumspect and subtle. In fact, had she not known intuitively that the line of bull she was being fed by the public affairs officers at the embassy and the 11th Air Assault was just that, bull, she would have shrugged off her hunch as just another dry hole and left the issue alone.

But she knew that all was not well. There was something going wrong, seriously wrong, in Colombia. She had seen it in the eyes of her own husband the day he left in September. Though he was, as always, careful to keep his thoughts and feelings to himself, Jan had spent too many nights easing her husband back from the brink of recurring nightmares to know that what he had seen during his visit to Colombia had shaken his very soul. In itself Scotty's behavior could have been ignored. But when it was linked by Jan the next day to a sudden change in policy regarding the announcement of U.S. casualties, her suspicions grew. Rather than give information concerning losses and injuries on a daily basis, as had been the practice to date, it was announced from the Pentagon that only weekly totals would be provided, totals that did not separate battle and non-battle losses. One of the more astute correspondents observed dryly that this was what happened in Vietnam when the high personnel losses became an embarrassment. "Much better," he said, "for the public-affairs officer to have to waffle an answer during a press briefing only once a week than seven times." Finally, and most telling to the media gathered in Colombia, the policy imposing restrictions on the travel of correspondents and the pooling of them to cover military operations was revived and immediately enforced by both the U.S. military and the Colombian government.

Suspecting something and being able to build a story, however, were two different things. And Jan knew it. Being confined by a very stringent code of ethics that she followed, and insisted that everyone who worked in the Bogotá bureau conform to, didn't make it easy for her or her staff. Still she had no intention of compromising her professional integrity and would not tolerate anyone around her who did. "Nothing," she told her people, "leaves this office unless we can verify it using reliable sources and facts." Unfortunately, their efforts so far to discover what exactly Scotty had seen which had resulted in the gathering cloak of secrecy that was now obscuring military operations in Colombia had yielded nothing of substance. The weekly press briefing given by a member of the American embassy staff concerning military operations provided little information. Though facts and figures concerning those operations conducted the previous week were shown in large multicolored graphs and charts, the nature of those operations, let alone their locations and results, was withheld due to what the military labeled operational security.

Jan Fields-Dixon would not be denied. There was something going on, and she knew it. Travel restrictions, non-informative briefings and press releases, and military commanders who made themselves unavailable for comment be damned. She was going to get to the bottom of this story no matter what. And those veterans of the press corps in Bogotá who knew Jan knew what that meant. So it was with a certain amount of humor that her fellow correspondents looked upon Major General C. B. Lane and expressed their sympathy for him. Eddie Bauer of CNN summed it up best when he said, "Unless he mends his ways and starts giving Jan a little something of substance, the Farcees are going to be the least of Lane's troubles."

Bauer, of course, was like every other American in Bogotá. Used to the small-scale operations that had become the accepted pattern of life for the 11th Air Assault since their arrival, they, like the American public, had come to view the activities of the FARC as little more than dangerous entertainment. That view was about to change forever.

CHAPTER 7

October 20

WATCHING THE ANCIENT C-130 TRANSPORT PLANE ROLL TO A
stop, Major General C. B. Lane felt a twinge of apprehension.
He was not accustomed to such a feeling. Though he had felt
it before, usually when he was faced with a situation which he
did not completely control, he had always managed to find
some way of attacking the cause of his apprehension head-on
and crushing it. Which was why he was here at the military
airport waiting on this particular C-130. He would, as soon as
Brigadier General Scott Dixon stepped off it, roll over him like
a steamroller, leaving no doubt in Dixon's mind that he, *Major
General* C. B. Lane, and nobody else was calling the shots
down here, the Chief of Staff of the Army be damned.

Lane liked being in control; he needed to be in control.
Where and how this obsession with dominating everything and
everyone that came into his life originated was buried deep
inside of Lane's psyche. Only the physical manifestations of
that need mattered anymore to those around him and, to an
extent no one appreciated, to Lane himself. With the rank of
lieutenant general assured and that of full general within his
grasp, he really didn't care anymore, if he ever had, what
drove him. The why no longer was an issue. Only the how, the
process that had gotten him this far, mattered. After all, he
rationalized, it had gotten him this far. There was no reason,

none at all, to imagine that it wouldn't get him the rest of the way. So control and domination, always the strong suit in Lane's limited repertoire of skills, became so prevalent that any others that he might have possessed at a younger age were pushed aside and lost.

But the current situation was not his to dominate, at least not for the moment. Things had changed and were still changing fast. In the beginning the opportunity that the deployment of his division to Colombia had been was to him a gift. Added to this gift, as a benefit, were restrictions imposed by the Colombians governing every aspect of American military operations in Colombia. These restrictions included the number of troops, the duration of their commitment, the rules of engagement under which they would operate, where they would operate, and even the manner in which they were controlled. The 11th Air Assault was so tightly regulated by the terms of the agreement that governed their use that many in the military, including Lane himself at first, felt they were unworkable. But the administration had made its decision, and General Fulk, despite his better judgment, had saluted the President and issued the necessary orders.

Especially galling to the Army had been the decision made by the State Department to place the operational control of the 11th Air Assault Division in the hands of the Colombian Ministry of Defense. In part this was a sop given by the Colombian President to his senior officers. After the military coup the previous spring and the brutal purges that followed, the government had to give something back to the military, if only their pride. Seizing any opportunity offered to them, the generals that had survived the coup and the purges insisted that only those U.S. officers and control headquarters that were absolutely essential would be allowed to enter and operate in Colombia. They did not want American generals coming into their country, taking over everything and telling them how to do things, a habit, most noted, that was as American as McDonald's. It wasn't that they didn't like the Americans or that the American generals were evil. It was just that their manhood would not tolerate having a foreigner, especially a Yankee, sitting in their capital, telling them how to defend it. Such a practice, the generals had told their President, would only serve as grist for the FARC's propaganda machine. Besides, there was the need to make sure that when the time came for the military to re-exert its influence over the conduct of internal politics there would be no interference from anyone, foreign or domestic.

For Lane this arrangement was ideal. In theory he received the orders that governed his tactical operations from the Colombian Minister of Defense. The Minister of Defense, however, was a former lawyer who was chosen for his personal loyalty to the President of Colombia and not his military knowledge. In the past the Minister of Defense had always been an Army general. The coup by the Army, however, had made that practice seem unsafe to the new President. So he had chosen from his ranks of loyal supporters a man he could trust to assume that post.

Though he had picked as wisely as he could have, the new Minister of Defense, José de Contrilla, was not up to the task. He had no experience with military tactics of any kind, let alone those used by an air assault division. Seeing an opportunity, Lane used Contrilla's shortcomings to his advantage. At their first meeting, before the 11th Air Assault even began deploying, Lane suggested that it would be to the advantage of all concerned if Contrilla, rather than trouble himself with the grimy details of day-to-day operations, simply assigned areas of responsibility and general guidelines to the 11th Air Assault. His staff and subordinate commanders, Lane assured Contrilla, would handle the planning and execution of their operations. Pleased to be relieved of such a burden and left free to deal with the final decimation of officers of questionable loyalty from his own Army, Contrilla readily agreed.

For four months that arrangement had suited Lane just fine. He was, as a result of the State Department's efforts, the senior American military officer in Colombia, commanding the only major American military headquarters. He controlled his own operations and his staff, chosen as much for personal loyalty to him as for their skills. He also controlled the flow of information concerning those operations not only to the Pentagon but also to the media. Such an opportunity, Lane knew, came only once in a lifetime. So he, with the help of his staff, was determined to make the most of it while it lasted. During the first few months, when the war in Colombia was new, popular, and going all his way, Lane and his staff made even the simplest search-and-destroy mission appear to be a heroic epic planned and controlled by Lane's hand-picked staff. The media, as a result, became an unwitting partner in Lane's campaign of self-promotion.

But somewhere, unnoticed at first, things started to go wrong. Without any fanfare, with no true warning, a new element, one that no one had planned on, began to enter into Lane's carefully orchestrated march to promotion. In a way, the success of the American forces in the first few months was responsible for the change. As long as it was just an all-Colombian affair, the leadership of the FARC had seen no need for any changes in its tried and true methods. They had in fact become as much a part of the political landscape of Colombia as the government itself. And like the government, the FARC was always there but never quite fully in control. The presence of the 11th Air Assault Division, viewed by most Colombians as nothing less than an invasion from the north, brought forth a hue and a cry from many. It was, many Colombians shouted during riots in Bogotá, a surrender of the nation's manhood. The same type of rebellion that rocked the capital shook the ruling council of the FARC. Those members of the FARC who had been restrained by the old guard broke free of their former leaders and in a matter of days joined in fanning the flames of discontent. "How can any man," one popular FARC slogan that began to appear just as the 11th Air Assault began to arrive read, "who considers himself a man freely submit to a government that must be propped up with Yankee bayonets." The wave of enthusiasm that swept away the FARC's old line brought forth new faces, methods, and ideas. Foremost among them was the former university professor Hector Valendez.

Unfortunately, the G-2 intelligence section of the 11th Air Assault and the CIA in Colombia never suspected that the increasing change in fortunes of the FARC in the field paralleled the ascendancy of Valendez through the ranks of the FARC's military arm. Though they were able to note changes, both the G-2 and the CIA credited those changes to other people or circumstances. Valendez, never rising above the position of deputy to the military chief, remained hidden from the view of the American intelligence network.

But his efforts didn't. Slowly, almost unperceived, things began to change. There were no sweeping announcements, no single striking event that heralded the altering of the tactical and strategic balance. The presence of platoon-sized FARC units where only squads had operated before was easily dismissed at first as nothing more than exaggerated reports made by hysterical or nervous commanders in the field. This "error," like so many others, was easily remedied. For example, in the case of reports of platoon-sized units, the division G-2 adopted the practice at division headquarters of halving the number of enemy forces that American troop units reported contacting and doubling the number of dead FARC soldiers every contact yielded. Thus a thirty-man FARC platoon that had suffered six casualties in a firefight with an 11th Air Assault unit became a reinforced squad that was all but wiped out by the time the report was briefed to Lane. This good news, of course, was duly passed on to both the Pentagon and the media. "The troopers of the 11th," Lane would tell reporters, "can put another notch in the stocks of their rifles," meaning that another FARC combat unit had disappeared.

Of course when it became evident that FARC units were not only failing to disappear but were in fact multiplying, the gears of the 11th Air Assault Division's reporting system had to be thrown in reverse. By the time the division had been in country for three months, both the G-2 and the G-3 found themselves working to downplay rather than magnify the level of operations that the division was involved in. Soon it became the policy of the division's public-affairs officer to discount any contacts that involved less than a company of American soldiers or a battalion of the Colombian Army. And even when reported, the size and nature of the units involved were not given, "in the interest of operational security." To further tighten up the flow of information, reporters and correspondents found the free rides to units in the field becoming harder and harder to get. Only when they had the permission of the public-affairs officer were selected members of the media, members who were still considered pro-Lane, allowed forward to brigade or battalions in the field. Jan Fields-Dixon, of course, was not one of them.

Still, had everything continued to run at the pace that it had been going, Lane could have survived the Colombian experience not only unscathed but with his career enhanced. September, however, put an end to that. First came Scott Dixon, sent by the Chief of Staff of the Army on a fact-finding tour. There'd been little time to prepare for him when Dixon came waltzing into Lane's private theater of operations. Then at the tail end of Dixon's visit the 3rd Battalion, 511th Infantry, stumbled into a massive ambush and got its nose bloodied in the single costliest operation to date. On the heels of this disaster, and partially as a result of it and his unsuccessful efforts to cover it up, the media turned on Lane and his division. These elements, all of which Lane had thought he controlled, became unglued at the same time and left him with a handful of problems. That they could be dealt with effectively was never in doubt. In a meeting of his key staff officers Lane pointed out quite proudly that "the media can be muzzled, Dixon can be stonewalled, and the tempo of our operations can be regulated so that we can ride out the next few months without a care." Lane's chief of staff, Colonel Delhue, sitting opposite him, was about to add, Well, that only leaves the FARC to deal with, but did not. Lane had a vision, and no one, no matter what his rank or position, was going to be allowed to obscure it with facts.

Even before the C-130's foot ramps were in place, Lane saw the figure that he knew to be Scott Dixon come bounding down from within the aircraft. Not wanting to wait until Dixon had his feet, so to speak, firmly planted before confronting him, Lane had decided to meet him here in person on the very first day. Another meeting of the two was inevitable, he knew, and Lane had decided to make it at a time and place of his choosing. What better way, he thought, to throw Dixon off than to hit him in person right between the eyes as he was stepping off the bloody airplane.

The image of Major General C. B. Lane taking long and measured strides had greeted the tiny staff of SOUTHCOM Forward before they had finished filing off the plane. At the rear of the C-130, Scott Dixon and Lieutenant Colonel Jeffrey K. Worsham were talking when Lane and his aide-de-camp came out of the building where they had been waiting. Worsham, who was serving as the chief of staff of Dixon's small staff, saw the two of them coming over Dixon's shoulder and motioned in their direction. "Looks like the welcome wagon is acomin', sir."

Twisting his head about in the direction Worsham was pointing, Dixon drew in a deep breath when he saw who it was. "Well, he sure as hell isn't wasting any time coming out to mark his territory."

When Dixon had recruited his small staff of officers and NCOs, he made sure that they understood that the reception and cooperation that they could expect would be at best strained. So his comment to Worsham came as no surprise. With one eyebrow cocked, Worsham volunteered, "Would you like me to stand fast or make myself scarce?"

Without looking back at his chief of staff, Dixon responded with a dry halfhearted order. "Best you check on the unloading of the gear and equipment. If we lose it here at the 11th Air Assault's airhead, we'll never see it again." Then, turning to him, Dixon added, "And, Jeff, if you see me fold my arms and start tapping my right foot, do us both a favor and come over and rescue me."

"From Lane?"

"No, from myself. You see, the Army takes a dim view of generals striking other generals in public."

Giving Dixon a wry smile as he saluted, Worsham added before he turned to leave, "Well, sir, I wouldn't worry too much about that. In Major General Lane's case, I'm sure if you plead temporary insanity, you'll get no argument from the judge and little more than a verbal reprimand."

Putting on a stern face, Dixon returned Worsham's salute. In the past he would have been upset if a subordinate had spoken of a general like that to him. But after having met and spent the better part of a week trying to work with Lane, Dixon didn't feel the slightest urge to correct Worsham or defend Lane. Of all the general officers he had ever met or known of in his career, Lane was in Dixon's eyes without doubt the least worthy of the respect and honors that his rank accorded him. With Worsham disposed of, Dixon spun about to face the man who would be for him the real enemy.

As Lane closed the distance between them, Dixon studied the person. He always thought of Lane as a person, since he didn't consider him fit to bear the title general or even that of man. In stature, Lane was exceedingly unspectacular. Of medium build, he stood at six foot one and appeared to be in good physical trim. His starched BDU uniform, spit-shined boots, blocked BDU hat with the two large stars centered in the front, and a well-polished general officer's belt and holster tagged this person as an officer who was more at home in an office than in the field. None of this in itself set Lane apart from any other officer who believed that exaggerated uniform standards were the mark of a good soldier. Not even the dark sunglasses, the kind that hide the wearer's eyes, marked Lane as anything other than a simple martinet.

What gave Lane his distinct personality traits, the ones that automatically set people he met to disliking him, were his carriage and stride. He walked with an exaggerated casualness, the type that is not casual at all but that requires much practice, not too unlike the one that Douglas MacArthur had used. This casual stride and carriage were meant to show that he, C. B. Lane, was confident and in control, that he didn't need to worry about trivial worldly concerns because the world around him was his to command. The only detraction from his almost carefree image was Lane's habit of slowly sweeping his head from side to side, looking at all around him. He did this, Dixon imagined, not to survey and take in information but rather to detect dangers and threats in much the same way that a search radar automatically scans the horizon for the enemy. For Dixon knew that Lane viewed him as nothing less than a direct and immediate danger to his career. Which was why Lane was there that afternoon to greet Dixon and his staff. It made sense to Lane and it made sense to Dixon, since both men, from their earliest years in the Army, had been taught that when dealing with an enemy victory can best be achieved by seizing the initiative and striking when your foe is off balance.

When Lane was within six feet of him, Dixon brought himself to a rigid position of attention and rendered a sharp hand salute. "Good afternoon, sir. I hadn't expected to see you so soon. It was my understanding that I had an initial office call with you tomorrow morning."

Returning his salute, Lane closed the gap between him and Dixon. "Well, yes, that's true. But, you see, we have a major operation scheduled for the morning that my aide neglected to consider when he was making up my schedule. A two-battalion sweep south of Medellín. Since I'll be tied up keeping an eye on that, and I didn't want to wait for several days before talking to you, I thought I'd pop on out here and get this over with now so that we both understand each other from the start.''

Since he couldn't see Lane's eyes because of the dark glasses, Dixon watched his mouth. Though Lane wore a smile, Dixon imagined it was like the one the wolf had when he was speaking to Little Red Riding-Hood.

When he dropped his salute and stopped in front of Dixon, Lane planted his feet shoulder width apart and grasped the front of his leather general officer's belt with his hands on either side of the shiny brass buckle. Seeing that Lane had no intention of offering him his hand, Dixon likewise spread his feet apart. But instead of putting his hands in front of him, he placed them in the small of his back, sticking them palms out under his own leather belt.

Puffing out his chest and rocking forward on his heels slightly, Lane exaggerated his commanding height. "Let me get right to the point, General Dixon. The Colombian Minister of Defense is not at all thrilled with the idea of SOUTHCOM establishing a headquarters here in his country. He feels that this is a clear violation of the status of forces agreement that his government and ours agreed to months before.''

This statement threw Dixon, and the smile on Lane's face told Dixon that his expression had betrayed his surprise. To get around the status of forces agreement, the Colombian government had been told that Dixon and his staff, who would be housed in the American embassy's compound, were nothing more than an augmentation of the ambassador's staff. The real purpose of Dixon's small staff, their role as the forward element of SOUTHCOM, had been classified secret, no foreign dissemination. Since only a handful of senior officers and members of the embassy staff knew of Dixon's real mission, the only conclusion that Dixon could come to was that someone violated the U.S.-only restriction on revealing the nature of his headquarters and told someone in the Colombian government. Not having any use for this person, Dixon naturally jumped to the conclusion that if Lane hadn't himself been the perpetrator of this security violation, he at least was involved in making it so. Yet with no proof of any type, Dixon could say nothing. Instead he took a deep breath. "Well, sir, I guess the first order of business for me and my people is to put the Colombians' mind at ease and let them know that we are not coming down here to expand our presence or role."

The smile on Lane's face grew larger for a moment when Dixon said this. Then, feigning concern, Lane looked down at his boots and shook his head. "Well, Dixon, I'm afraid that's going to be quite a chore." Looking back up at Dixon, Lane began to give a little lecture to the new kid on the block. "These Colombians, General Dixon, are quite suspicious of us. They're proud people who really don't want us here at all and see everything we do as a potential threat to their sovereignty. It's taken me quite a while to convince them that we're not here for any other reason but to help them hold the line against those socialist guerrillas that are threatening them and their people. I hope that your presence doesn't interfere with the ability of my division to work in harmony with the Colombians. It would be too bad if it did."

What Lane was telling Dixon, or at least alluding to, rocked Dixon even more than his initial announcement. If he was taking Lane's meaning right, Dixon saw him, C. B. Lane, hard at work making Dixon and his headquarters the scapegoat for any and all failure in joint U.S.-Colombian operations from this point on. The fact that Lane's overbearing attitude and his barely veiled contempt for the abilities of the Colombian military had already doomed any hope for effective and meaningful combined operations would be lost to most. One Colombian general staff officer had confided in Dixon during his last visit that most Colombian officers would rather link arms with the FARC than join Lane's American forces in the field. Of course Dixon didn't know that some Colombian officers were already doing that. All he knew at that moment was that he now had two major foes to contend with before he even got started. Besides Lane and his loyal staff, who no doubt would only grudgingly cooperate with his own staff, Dixon now had a hostile host nation to deal with, which meant a possible international incident to boot.

Recovering his poise, Dixon looked into the dark lenses of

Lane's glasses. "Well, sir, I'm sure that we'll be able to muddle through this problem somehow."

Lane smiled. "Yes, General, I'm sure you will. Just as I'm sure you and your people will remember that you are here to serve the commander-in-chief of SOUTHCOM as nothing more than a sort of clearinghouse of information needed by my divisional staff and his staff."

Carefully picking his words and watching his tone, Dixon slowly responded. "I can assure you, sir, neither I nor my staff have any intention of doing anything that would interfere with the conduct of your operations. We're here to ensure that the information needed by both you and General Stratton gets to all the right places."

Taking his right hand away from his belt, Lane raised it chest level and jabbed his index finger at Dixon. "Good! And make sure you don't forget that, General."

With all his strength, Dixon pressed his jaws together, almost as if he were locking his mouth down for fear of saying something he would regret. The only action he could safely bring himself to take at that moment was to bring his arms up and fold them slowly, across his chest.

Seeing that Dixon had no intention of responding to his intentional provocation, Lane put his right hand back on his belt, looping the thumb behind it. He was preparing to continue to lecture Dixon when a lieutenant colonel quickly came up behind Dixon and tapped him on the shoulder. In a whisper that he was sure Lane could hear, Worsham spoke to Dixon. "Excuse me, sir. Hate to bother you with this trivial matter but . . ." Not having thought of an excuse that seemed reasonable enough to interfere in the conversation between Lane and Dixon, Worsham stopped in mid-sentence.

Lane, looking into Dixon's eyes and seeing the anger, knew that he had done what he had set out to do. He had served him notice that he, Major General C. B. Lane, was the only bull in this pen that mattered and he had no intention of letting go of anything to anyone. Seeing no need to stay any longer, he used the interruption to make his exit. "Well, I see you have housekeeping matters to tend to. I have an air assault division to run. If you need anything, have your chief of staff contact my chief of staff, and I'm sure we can do something to help."

Still struggling to keep his tongue in check, Dixon was barely able to utter the words "Yes, sir" as he saluted Lane. With that, Lane smiled and walked away, proud of the way he had put Dixon in his place.

When he was out of sight, Dixon relaxed his stance, though Worsham could see that he was still shaking from his anger. Finally, though he kept watching the door behind which Lane had disappeared, Dixon spoke. "Jeff, this is going to be a *looong* seven months."

Looking at the same door, Worsham thought about Dixon's comment. "We have met the enemy and he is him?"

Cranking his head around toward his chief of staff, Dixon let a smile light across his face. "Yeah, something like that. Now let's get this show on the road."

With that, both men turned and began to walk toward the C-130, now disgorging its cargo. Standing at a respectful distance, far enough to be out of the way yet in a position where both his staff NCOs and the Air Force ground crewmen could see them, Dixon and Worsham watched. Worsham informed Dixon that their senior sergeant had already left with the officer serving as the headquarters commandant to check on the quarters they had arranged for before arriving, leaving the senior operations sergeant in charge of the off-loading of the C-130. At the moment, with all of their communications equipment bundled up on huge pallets, there wasn't much he or anyone else could do. It was at that moment that Worsham remembered what he really needed to tell Dixon. "Oh, by the way, sir, I checked with the ground crew. There's a phone over in the air-ops shed that you can use to call to any commercial line here in Bogotá."

In all the haste and associated stress of preparing his staff, Scott Dixon had neglected to call Jan and tell her that he was coming. Though he had meant to many times he had just never made the time. When finally he thought of doing so and had the time, a funny idea began to rattle about his head. Why not just pop in unannounced after he had arrived in Bogotá. That, he thought, would really make Jan's day. Pleased that he had come up with such an idea and had stuck to it, Dixon smiled as he began thinking to himself that this time it was going to be his turn to surprise his wife with a sudden and unexpected entrance.

* * *

In the town of Puerto Carreño, located on the eastern fringe of the region known as Los Llanos that jutted into the western border of Venezuela, Colonel Marco Agustin of the Colombian Army was waiting for a different kind of surprise. The town, a small provincial affair with a population of a little over five thousand wedged into the far eastern corner of Colombia, was about to become the subject of an experiment in terror in which the soldiers of the commander's garrison were to be the test subjects.

That something was about to happen in his area of responsibility had only slowly become evident to Colonel Agustin. The commander of the region that encompassed most of the province of Vichada and the brigade that garrisoned it, Agustin had recently been made aware of subtle changes in the habits of the people of the region. It began after the first week of October, when his senior sergeants and junior officers began to comment that the local people were starting to act strangely. They were, most of his other sergeants and officers agreed, becoming less friendly, more reluctant to engage in conversation, or even trade with them. Concerned about this, Agustin traveled to the outlying police stations and outposts in his area of responsibility. At each stop he heard the same thing from all of his subordinates. By the time he finished his tour, he knew. Something was about to happen, and soon.

Knowing that something was going to happen and being able to predict with any kind of accuracy exactly what was going to happen, let alone where and when, was a different matter. Agustin's intelligence officer, a young and dedicated major, the son of a wealthy hotel owner in Cartagena, was alerted to his commander's concerns. His efforts to gather information, however, yielded nothing positive. After several days of trying his usual methods, the major reported back that all of his otherwise reliable sources seemed to have disappeared. "No one," he told Agustin, "even my contacts with the drug cartel, can be found. It is as if they had been gobbled up by the earth itself."

With nothing but negative intelligence, which often can be as valuable as solid information, Agustin flew up to the headquarters of the division responsible for the region in which

HAROLD COYLE

Puerto Carreño was located. That trip, however, was for Agustin wasted. Though the division commander and his staff listened intently to everything that Agustin reported, and they all agreed that the signs indicated that something was astir in Agustin's region, there was nothing, he was told, that they could do for him until he had something tangible to report, or actual contact. "We cannot," the division commander told him, "target and attack shadows generated by a man's fears and suspicions." Besides, as the division chief of staff pointed out over lunch, all indications were that the FARC's new efforts were being concentrated in the Cauca River Valley. "Ever since the eighth of October, the enemy has become very, very active between Cali and Medellín. Both the Ministry of Defense and the Americans have been shuffling forces into that region in the hope of drawing the FARC into a major fight."

That the date of the increased activities to the west coincided with the change in attitude of the people in his region Agustin considered for a moment before he answered. When he did, he was careful in his choice of words. "What, my friend, if the real threat was here in our own backyard and all the noise along the Cauca was nothing but a diversion?"

A frown swept across the division chief of staff's face. Leaning back in his seat, he looked at Agustin and thought for a moment before answering. Reaching out, he took his drink, swirled the glass, and took a long sip. The thought of an offensive in their region had never dawned upon him. Still, right now it was nothing more than that, a thought, a formless and unfounded fear. Ready, he reached over, slammed the glass down on the table, and spoke. "*If* that is the case, *if* our area and not the western mountains is to be the scene of the next battle, then we must in the beginning make do with what we have. We will hold until the government in Bogotá can decide where the real danger is and shift their attention and whatever forces they can afford to us here in the east."

The chief's answer did little to mollify Agustin. "And if we cannot hold on?"

This last comment brought a smile to the chief's face. "We are talking about the FARC here. They have been around so long, like our own politicians, that their methods have become institutionalized and somewhat ossified. Though things could become a little rough for a few days, there is nothing out there that we cannot handle on our own until help arrives.''

The efforts of the division chief of staff to calm Agustin's apprehensions failed miserably. If anything, the attitude of the division's commander and his staff only served to heighten his own suspicions. If, as Agustin feared, the FARC's operations in the western mountains were a diversion, then the FARC had already won the first half of the opening battle. Everyone, it seemed, accepted the obvious, and there was nothing that he could do to change that.

Thus, when he returned to Puerto Carreño, Agustin threw himself into a frenzy of preparation. He began by increasing the readiness of his command, especially the small garrisons in the outlying areas. These, he felt, would be the first to feel the pressure of a new enemy drive, a drive he expected would open with small probes against weak points and numerous ambushes through the region. To meet this threat he encouraged all of his subordinate commanders to increase the number of patrols and their own ambushes along likely routes of infiltration out of Venezuela and along the few roads and many rivers of Vichada. To augment the efforts of those units already deployed, Agustin stripped Puerto Carreño of most of its garrison. This allowed him to establish new company-sized outposts at key points along major transportation arteries. Like the others, the commanders of these new garrisons were instructed to keep alert and not to disperse their command.

Agustin's drive, however, was not shared by many of his subordinates. They, like the chief of staff, felt that there was little need to worry too much over the prospect of battle with the FARC. One company commander even told him that he was reluctant to do anything out of the ordinary for fear of spooking his own men. ''Even if they come at us in the dead of night,'' he told Agustin, ''we will be able to hold them and still have a reasonably peaceful breakfast.''

Ignorance, of course, is often the basis of confidence. Agustin thought of this as he stood in the open doorway of his office and looked out across the enclosed square that served as a parade ground for the last two companies in Puerto Carreño that were co-located with his own headquarters. One of those companies, broken down into platoons, had been deployed to small blocking positions and strongpoints around the town of Puerto Carreño. The other company, serving as a reaction force not only for Puerto Carreño and the immediate area but for Agustin's entire region, was scattered about the parade ground in small squad-sized groups. The men of the company, cleaning their weapons and sorting through their gear, were preparing for another evening of patrols, ambushes, and waiting, just as they had been doing every night for the past week. In the growing shadows of late afternoon, here and there the sergeants and officers of the company moved about singly or in pairs checking on their men's progress. None of them, Agustin thought, were moving with any real sense of purpose. They, like everyone else, were infected by the status quo. When, Agustin thought, the FARC come, heads will roll. They will start here, he knew in his heart, and continue to roll until they topple every self-serving politician in Bogotá.

Mired in these grim thoughts of the future, Agustin stood in the doorway and watched his men slowly go about their daily chores. Neither he nor his men heard the deep yet distant thud of a dozen 120-millimeter mortars firing the opening volley of Hector Valendez's offensive to seize Los Llanos. In the span of a second, perhaps two, the entire scene before Agustin's eyes was transformed. Everything—men, equipment, trucks, buildings, even the ground itself—was torn apart and heaved into the air by blinding explosions that were magnified by the strong outer walls of the courtyard. Never having been exposed to such an attack, no one, not even Agustin himself, had any idea what to do. While some of the soldiers instinctively threw themselves flat onto the ground, others dropped what they were doing and attempted to run for safety.

There was, however, no safe haven for the company. As if to underscore this point, a volley of small-arms fire, partially drowned out by the second volley of mortar rounds impacting on the parade ground, announced the commencement of the ground attack. Even before he knew exactly what was happening, Agustin somehow understood that there was no way that he would be able to rally his forces there in the compound and beat off an attack. Picking himself up off the floor of his headquarters building, Agustin turned away from the unfolding horror that the parade ground had become and turned to head out the rear door of the building just as the FARC assault teams forced their way into the open gate of the compound. Shouting as he ran through the building for his staff to follow, Agustin made it to a side entrance seldom used by anyone that had once been a sally port meant for just such an occasion. Prying the heavy metal door open with the help of a sergeant who had followed closely behind him, Agustin shouted to the few members of his staff who had managed to make it this far to head out of town to the westernmost platoon strongpoint. There he would rally his forces, assess the situation, and do what needed to be done.

Just as Colonel Agustin had already found out, there was absolutely no subtlety about the manner in which Hector Valendez threw the FARC's military arm into its new task. Across the entire length and breadth of Los Llanos, from Villavicencio in the west to Puerto Carreño in the east, dozens of small police detachments and military garrisons located in the villages like the one Agustin had commanded were eradicated in a single night. Striking an hour before sunset, six of Valendez's main-force battalions, many of them operating as whole units for the first time, swept all before them. The government forces, dispersed into small garrisons with few of them company strength or greater, withered under the combined impact of the FARC's total surprise, their unexpected firepower, and the boldness of their daytime attacks. In those cases where stunned survivors of this initial onslaught managed to escape death or capture, few would manage to make it through the night, for the night belonged to the FARC's local-force companies supporting Valendez's main-force battalions. Together with the task of policing up the battlefield after the main-force battalions had done their duty, the local-force companies established control of their own home regions and prepared to provide security for the political, governmental, and administrative branches of the FARC as they moved in behind the combat forces. Thus in the span of a few days the FARC was able to make the transition from being a clandestine guerrilla organization of little note to being a sovereign power in its own right and a serious contender for control of Colombia.

* * *

It was just like Scott Dixon, Jan thought as she rushed through the last few stories that she needed to review. Damn him! To show up just like that and expect her to fall all over in a rush to hop into bed with him was, was . . . Nervy, that's what it was, pure and simple. That man, she thought as she tossed a finished piece into her out box and reached over to her in box for another, had got more nerve than he knew what to do with. And his weak, wimpy excuse of, "Well, you do this to me all the time." That to Jan was even more contemptible. What made him suppose, she fumed, that just because she had the habit of popping in and out without notice he could do that to her at a time like this. As she told her assistant editor, a young woman by the name of Genny Conners, after Dixon had gone storming off that afternoon, she couldn't help it if her job suddenly snatched her up and then just as suddenly dropped her back home on a moment's notice. She didn't do it for fun. At least most of the time she didn't.

From the doorway, Genny called out, "Well?"

Looking up from a draft story that she had been staring at for a few minutes and yet had no idea what it was about, Jan shot back, "Well what?"

"Well, Jan, are you going to go meet him tonight?"

"What do you think? My God, with all the increased activity in the western mountains, the shifting of more and more of the 11th Air Assault's combat battalions into the Cauca River Valley, and reports of threats against Medellín itself to deal with, the last thing I need to do is go running about Bogotá chasing an arrogant, inconsiderate fool who thinks playing 'Guess Who?' is romantic."

Genny smirked. "Oh, come on, Jan. You've got to admit it was sort of funny. I mean the look on your face and everything."

"Funny? You think being made a fool of in front of everyone on the staff is funny?"

"Oh, not everyone was here. Remember, Frank and Eddie were out making arrangements for your piece on the Ministry of Defense."

Jan glared at Genny. "Very funny. Am I the only one here interested in doing her job?"

"Okay, boss lady. Without looking, tell me what the piece

in your hands, the one you've been studying so intently for the last five minutes, is about.''

Jan cocked her head to the side and looked up. "It's about . . . it's the one Carol did on the, ah.''

"I thought so. Your mind is so befuddled by that man you keep referring to as the last of the Neanderthals that you have no idea what you're doing, do you?''

Narrowing her eyes, Jan gave Genny a dirty look before looking down at the pages of copy she held. As her friend had guessed, Jan had no idea what the piece was about. The story she had supposedly been working so hard on was one done by Terry Freeman, not Carol. Genny was right. Her mind was on Scotty, and there was no getting around it. Dropping the paper on the desktop, Jan leaned back in her seat and looked up at Genny, her expression softening to one of complete puzzlement. "You know the most infuriating thing about this, Genny, is the fact that Scott knows I'll be there. The bastard knows.''

With a sly smile, Genny folded her arms. "Well, you know the old cliché.''

Jan shook her head and waved her hand at Genny, "Yes, yes. You're right. You're absolutely right. Can't live with them, can't live without them. But damn,'' Jan mused, "I'd sure like to try someday.''

Dropping her hands to her side, Genny cocked her head. "Honey, I've tried it. Believe me, I've *really* tried. If I found a way of doing that, I'd copyright it and make a couple of million on the secret.''

Folding her hands in front of her on the desk, Jan surveyed the folders and files and draft stories that hung out of her boxes and cluttered her desk. "I don't imagine I'm going to make it through this mess tonight. So I might as well throw in the towel.'' Standing up, she shuffled a few more papers about the desk, then gave up completely. Looking at her watch, then over to her friend, Jan sighed. "Well, I guess I'd better go get ready for Hagar the Horrible.''

"Jan, be nice. That man loves you.''

She thought about that for a moment. Then with an impish grin on her face and a gleam in her eye, Jan looked up at Genny. "Yeah, I know.''

CHAPTER 8

Evening, October 20

WHILE HE SAT AT THE TABLE PLAYING WITH HIS DRINK AND waiting for Jan, Scott Dixon thought about his love for her and their life together. How terrible, he thought, that they had so little time together. It seemed, as he looked about the dining room, that most of their lives in the past year had been spent in dining rooms not unlike this one, here and in Washington, D.C. There always seemed to be a reason, he knew, why they couldn't spend more time together at home like a normal couple did. What with Jan being a world-renowned reporter, in demand to cover every major hot spot in the world, and him a newly promoted general officer with the promise of more stars to come if, of course, he measured up and punched all the right tickets. Still, excuses now didn't make up for all the lost time that they individually and collectively let slip away.

For a while, when his name had come out on the list for promotion to brigadier, Dixon had considered turning in his retirement papers and taking a job with a consulting firm in the Washington area or going back to finish his degree and look for a job teaching history in college. Though Jan would still be up to her eyeballs with the World News Network, at least one of them would have his feet on the ground and be there, when the opportunities made themselves available, for the other. He would even be able to bring his sons home from their military boarding school in Virginia for the first time in years and give them a real home. Both boys would soon be in college, and there was little time for him to create the father and son bond that he had for so long been postponing due to "the needs of the Army."

But when decision time came, when he had to pick between fading into the background or pressing on higher and higher up the career ladder, Dixon found he couldn't do it. He couldn't leave the Army and start his life again as second fiddle to Jan. He wondered how much of that was nothing more than male pride and how much the need, his need, to keep pitting himself against the system and taking on new and more interesting challenges. It wasn't that every job in the Army was a challenge. Far from it. Many of his past duty positions, like the one he had just left at the Pentagon, were nothing more than staff positions in which he did the stubby pencil work for a more senior officer who made all the decisions. The only challenge Dixon found in those jobs, he had once told Jan, was keeping his sanity, biting his tongue at the appropriate times, and preventing his mind from turning into mush. The Army, of course, considered each and every duty position critical to the overall mission of the Army, and Dixon's superiors had always taken great pains to ensure that they frequently expressed to Dixon how important his contributions were to the success of the unit, the section, the Army, etc., etc., etc. Like everything else, Dixon reasoned, you had to take the good with the bad. And in the Army that often meant enduring no-mind jobs as you marked time and waited for a good, meaningful assignment to come your way.

So Dixon stayed and took the promotion. Jan was, he knew, a little disappointed. For she too had hoped that one of them would hang up their spurs and become the continuity in the relationship. Jan, however, had faced the same dilemma more often than Dixon did. It seemed that every time a new assignment in her news agency was offered her, she would ponder whether this was the time to call it quits or stick it out for another year, maybe two. For she was very much like Dixon, a person who loved challenges and had made a living by meeting them head-on and when necessary defying conventional wisdom and practice to do a job that she believed in. She, like he, lived for the thrill of being there out front, doing something that meant so much to her and gave her life meaning and purpose. Alive, Jan had once told Dixon when she was defining how she felt when she was hard at work on a tough assignment. "I feel alive." And so the two of them made the necessary accommodations in each of their own lives as they learned to live together while spending so much time apart.

Lost in his private reflections, Dixon didn't notice Jan's grand entrance. Nor did he bat an eye as she approached the table slowly, doing her best to give him something to think about. He didn't need anything more to think about, Jan realized as she watched him stare in her direction without seeing her. With a sigh she realized that his mind, as usual, was lost in space. Though the body was here, the look on his face told her that the thoughts were out there somewhere far from this room, maybe even this country. Perhaps, she feared, the momentary playfulness that had been such an embarrassment to her that afternoon was gone, beaten out of him by a hard afternoon dealing with C. B. Lane and the staff of the 11th Air Assault. Trying to do anything with those morons, Jan knew, was enough to depress a hyena. With this in mind, Jan decided to soften her desire for revenge somewhat as she came up next to Scott.

It took Dixon a moment to realize that someone was standing next to him. It was a scent, her scent, that finally jogged him out of the depths of his own mind. Turning slightly and looking up, a halfhearted smile lit across his face. "Hello, Jan. I'm so glad you were able to make it." Almost as an afterthought he stood up, took her hands in his, leaned over, and gave her a light peck on the cheek. Stepping back a bit, he looked at her, head to toe, before he spoke again. Her brown hair, normally worn down about her shoulders or held back with a barrette or bow, was pulled up and held in place on her head with decorative combs. She wore a black cocktail dress with a scooped neckline that went from her barely covered shoulders and dropped to where her breasts began to rise. A simple rhinestone necklace was all she wore to decorate her soft exposed skin. Sheer black lace sleeves encased her arms, their delicate elegance standing out in contrast to the simple dress that curved about her figure and stopped two inches above her knees and left her smooth, shapely legs exposed for all to see and enjoy. Scott gazed into her eyes. It was those eyes that made Jan who she was. For those large brown eyes could both penetrate to the very soul of a person and in the same instant speak louder than any words he had ever heard. At that moment he saw a warm, gentle, and loving look in those eyes. Without a word having been said, he knew that he had been forgiven. Leaning forward again, he gave her a kiss, this time on the lips, and moved his hands up her lace-covered arms to her shoulders. Any lingering thoughts Jan had of exacting revenge for the crummy way that he had come into her office that afternoon and made a fool of her disappeared in the warmth of that moment.

Pleased that she had been able to shake him out of his deep meditative state without having to play any mind games, which she was in no mood to engage in, Jan returned Scott's warm kiss for a moment and then pulled away and looked at him. He was wearing his Class A's tonight, his green uniform with all the badges. She flashed a shy smile. With her cheeks now highlighted by a redness that told all who were crass enough to stare that her passions were rising, Jan leaned into his embrace slightly and brought her hands up and rested them palms down on his chest. When she spoke, it was a warm, quiet breathy tone meant to arouse rather than chide. "Scotty, please. Not here and now, at least not until we've eaten. I'm starved."

The mood was broken, but the passions remained. Dixon smiled and shook his head. "I've never seen a woman who could eat so much and keep her shape like you do."

Placing her hands lightly on her hips, Jan smiled. "This figure ain't what it used to be, Scotty. Not by a long shot."

Pulling her back to him, he gave her another light peck on the lips and then eased back. "Woman, to this broke dick tanker, that body of yours is heaven."

With a flourish, he stepped back. Using exaggerated motions, he pulled out her chair and bowed at the waist, motioning her to be seated. "Madam, your table is ready."

The evening, despite Dixon's clumsy and aborted attempt at humor that afternoon, was turning out to be a pleasant one. Their conversation was light and engaging as they discussed everything and anything that had nothing to do with Colombia, the Army, or the World News Network. It was, Jan realized, as if they both had by unspoken mutual consent agreed that this night would be theirs and theirs alone and nothing, not job or country, was going to change that.

Finished with the main course, Jan and Scott were busy weighing the pros and cons of whether it would be more enjoyable to sit there together and enjoy a cup of coffee and dessert or if they should just chuck romance to the wind and run upstairs to the room he had taken for the night when Jan saw Scotty sit upright in his seat. A concerned look that quickly turned to one of despair flashed across his face as he looked at someone in the distance behind her. Sitting up, Jan turned, asking as she did what was wrong. Dixon growled, "Well, it didn't take long for them to find me."

Across the room Jan could see the headwaiter, his eyes fixed on their table, headed toward them. He moved like a man with a mission, and the expression on his face told her that it wasn't a social call he was about to pay them. Turning around to face Scotty, Jan reached out with her right hand and grabbed Scott's. "I suppose you told whoever your number-two man is where you could be reached?"

Sheepishly he looked down. "Of course I did. Jan, I'm a general officer. I can't go running about in the middle of a war zone disappearing like a kid playing hooky."

Shaking her head, Jan squeezed his hand. "Damn you and your dedication."

Just then the headwaiter arrived at their table, placing himself at the corner of the table opposite from where Jan and Dixon sat. Facing Dixon, he bowed slightly and apologized for having to interrupt their meal. When Dixon nodded and said that he understood, the headwaiter smiled and then turned to Jan. "Señorita Fields, there is a call waiting for you in the lobby from a Señorita Conners. She says it is very, very important and you must talk to her immediately."

For a moment Jan didn't think. She thanked the headwaiter and turned to Scott, wondering what Genny found so damned important to call here about. She was pondering this question when she saw her husband looking at her with an incredulous stare. "It would seem," he said dryly, "that I'm not the only one at this table suffering from a severe case of dedication to duty."

Jan winced a little. "Sorry, Scotty, but you do understand how it is. I am, after all, the bureau chief here in Colombia."

Reaching up with his right hand and sandwiching the hand she had laid upon his left hand, he smiled and nodded. "No need to apologize. You never promised me a rose garden, et cetera, et cetera. Now best you go tend to business and I'll settle up with the waiter."

For a moment she held his gaze and allowed herself to feel the warmth of his two hands clasping hers. Then without another word she pulled it away, stood up, and followed the headwaiter to where her phone call was waiting.

The FARC's progression from guerrilla force to political power, or any other concerns other than simple survival, was the furthest thing from Colonel Agustin's mind that night. Like many other officers commanding tiny garrisons throughout eastern Colombia in similar circumstances at that moment, he assumed that his command alone had been the target of a brief yet determined raid. In the beginning he was confident that, as bad as things seemed then, the situation would stabilize and with a little help from division he would be able to re-establish control. Only after being turned away from two of his own platoon strongpoints by enemy gunfire did it begin to dawn on him that what had happened at the garrison's compound was something more than a raid. It wasn't until he reached the third and final platoon strongpoint east of Puerto Carreño that Agustin and his small band of survivors found sanctuary.

The relief he and the men who had come out of Puerto Carreño with him felt was short-lived when the terrible truth of the whole situation became apparent. Upon entering the strongpoint shortly after midnight, Agustin was greeted by the commander of the company that had been manning the strongpoints around Puerto Carreño. "Thank God, Colonel Agustin," the young captain shouted when he ran up to meet his brigade commander and embraced him. "You have made it. I knew that it was only a question of time before you would lead a relief effort and save us from annihilation."

Shaken by his experiences of the day and the physical exertion of moving about in the dark cross-country in an effort to avoid FARC patrols, Agustin didn't respond to the captain's greeting at first. Only after he was led to the command bunker of the strongpoint and handed a canteen of water, which he all but drained with a single swig, did he speak. "Relief effort? I am leading no relief effort, Captain. What you saw follow me into this post were the only ones who made it out of Puerto Carreño alive." Seeing the expression of joy on the captain's face turn to shock, Agustin hurriedly continued. "What is the status of your command?"

It was a minute, maybe more, before the captain was able to shake himself out of the sudden panic that swept over him when his brigade commander announced that there was no relief force coming. Finally in halting sentences he rendered his report to Agustin. "Not long after we heard the sound of explosions coming from the direction of the compound, the platoon commander of my First Platoon, holding the strong-point on the west side of town, made one frantic call over the radio. He reported that his unit was under attack. When I tried to contact him to find out more information, I got no response. Two hours later, after nightfall, the platoon commander of my Third Platoon, charged with manning the northern strongpoint, informed me that his positions were under heavy mortar fire. He told me that the bunkers his men were manning, built to withstand only small-arms fire and light mortars, were collaps-ing under the weight of the enemy attack. From here we could see the flashes on the horizon and hear the explosions of the attack he was reporting."

The young captain paused, sat down on the ground in front of Agustin, and let his head droop between his shoulders before he continued. In the dim light of the cramped bunker, Agustin could see that the captain's shoulders were shaking. When he spoke again, he was barely able to choke back the sobs that stuck in his throat. "The enemy shelled the Third Platoon's positions on and off for an hour. After each attack the platoon commander would report, adding the names of more of his platoon to the list of dead and wounded. Finally, after one particularly long mortar attack, the platoon's senior sergeant radioed me and informed me that his lieutenant was dead, along with better than half of the men in his platoon, and that enemy assault parties had penetrated the perimeter of their strongpoint. Only the command bunker and two others were still resisting at that time. He asked for instructions. By the time I responded, the Third Platoon went off the air. That was an hour or two ago."

"And here," Agustin asked, "what has happened here?"

Looking up at his colonel, the captain was about to speak when a sergeant came into the small bunker. Ignoring the presence of the colonel, the sergeant dropped to his knees behind his despondent company commander. "Excuse me, Commander. But is it true? Has the garrison of Puerto Carreño been wiped out just like the other platoons?"

At first the captain did nothing. He simply sat there before Agustin. For several minutes the silence in the bunker was as oppressive as the hot, humid air. Finally the captain looked at the sergeant with tearful eyes. He tried to answer him, but no words came out. None, however, were necessary. The look on his face and his inability to answer him told the sergeant all that he needed to know. "What are we going to do, then? Sit here, like the Third Platoon, and wait for them to come and kill us?"

Again the captain did not answer. This time he turned his mournful face toward Agustin and stared at him. He was, Agustin knew, looking to him for the answer to the sergeant's question. It was only natural that he do so, for Agustin was the senior officer present and he alone would make the final choice as to what they would do. But, he wondered, sitting there in the cramped confines of a bunker filled with frightened men, what choices did they have, realistically? Since this had been a platoon strongpoint, the only communications that it had were two short-range radios and a single land line, now useless, that had connected the strongpoint with Agustin's headquarters in Puerto Carreño. There was no news from the outside world, nothing other than what the company commander had already reported, none of which was encouraging.

Given this pittance of information, Agustin forced himself to think in a logical manner. The enemy, it seemed, had struck the compound in town first, destroying it with both mortar fire and ground attack. That meant that they had been able to infiltrate sizable forces past the platoon points. Now, with the company in the compound eliminated, the enemy could move about as they pleased. After achieving this freedom of action, they had begun the methodical elimination of the platoon strongpoints. Starting in the west, then moving to the north, the enemy were toppling them like dominoes. The fact that the Third Platoon, alerted and ready, wasn't able to resist the enemy attacks left little prospect that this position would be able to do much better.

With as firm a grasp of what the enemy was doing as he could hope for, Agustin turned his attention to what he and his diminished command would do. There were, he realized, only three options to choose from. First, he and the tiny garrison of this strongpoint could stand and fight in place. This would, of course, be a last stand. And like most last stands it would be an empty gesture, one that would do no one outside of Puerto Carreño any good and would simply hand the FARC another victory.

If that was true, the next logical thing would be to surrender. Such a thought, however bad the situation was, was quickly cast aside. Agustin had little doubt that if he offered himself up to surrender, he would not live to see the next dawn. His reputation as a fierce and uncompromising anti-guerrilla fighter was well known. There were too many incidents of brutalities visited by men under his command in his past to be ignored by the enemy. Besides, Agustin reasoned, there was still too much pride and too much fight left in him and many of his soldiers. While it was true that everyone was at the moment despondent because of what appeared to be their impending doom, positive leadership and the hope of survival could motivate them to carry on. But carry on and do what?

That question led Agustin to the last and in his mind only reasonable choice they had. Ready, he looked at the captain and the sergeant. "There is nothing to be gained by staying here and dying. We will therefore abandon this post and make our way west, where I expect we will be able eventually to link up with either relief forces sent to save us or other garrisons still holding."

Though he was thankful that his commander had given them a solution to their dilemma, the captain was not instantly carried away with enthusiasm. His first response instead was one of skepticism. "But the enemy, they are to the west of us and no doubt coming our way."

"Yes," Agustin snapped, "they are. That is why we are

going to go east, away from the enemy, before attempting to make our way back to the west and safety.''

"Into Venezuela?''

"Yes, Captain, into Venezuela. That is where the FARC have operated from for so long and, I'm sure, where the forces that attacked us came from. We will do what they have been doing for years, only in reverse. Once in Venezuela, we will move south along the border and re-enter Colombia.''

Still unconvinced of the feasibility of his commander's plan, the captain continued to pelt him with questions. "Won't the Venezuela border patrols be alerted and on guard due to the attacks against us here today?''

Losing his patience, but still determined to show his shaken subordinate that his plan was a reasonable one, Agustin leaned over and lowered his voice before responding. "Look, Captain, we know most of the FARC's old infiltration routes in and out of Venezuela, right?'' The captain nodded. "Yes, and tonight we will use one of them to slip past them and the Venezuelans, just as they have done so many times before. Now do you have any more questions?''

Looking over at his sergeant, then back at Agustin, the captain shook his head. "No, sir. No questions.''

"Good! For there is much to do, and not much time. Sergeant, pass the word that we will be breaking out of here in the next thirty minutes. Have your men load up as quickly as possible as much food and ammunition as they can reasonably carry. No personal gear or effects. No heavy weapons either. Machine guns and rifles only. We must travel fast and that means traveling light.'' When the sergeant left, without turning to verify Agustin's orders to him with his own company commander, Agustin turned his attention to the captain. "Now I need you to pull out your map of the area between here and the border that shows all the FARC's infiltration routes and bring it to me. We must be quick, for I doubt if they will leave us alone for much longer.''

Just as he'd expected, the two men, given a reasonable mission and orders that made sense, responded as they were trained. Though Agustin himself was starting to have doubts about their chances of even getting out of the strongpoint without being torn apart by the FARC, he knew in his heart that he had to try. He was, after all, a soldier, and it was his duty to fight as long as he could. Though the thought of fleeing this battlefield now began to bother him, he reasoned that this was only the beginning of a new and more deadly war. And if that was true, if the FARC was now as strong as he feared, there would be many more battlefields on which he could avenge his honor and this defeat. How many more, or where they would be, he had no idea. Only one man that night knew with any degree of certainty. And Hector Valendez was not about to tell anyone, at least not for the moment.

In the quiet hours after midnight, when Captain Nancy Kozak found that she could not sleep, she took up the habit of wandering about the brigade base camp, going from one unit's operations center to the next. In each of them she would stay awhile, sharing information with the officer and sergeants on duty while sipping coffee and, when the mood took them, digressing into swapping war stories and news from back home. The men and women who made up the night shifts in command posts, Kozak had found, were a breed apart. Freed from the stringent protocol that the presence of senior officers dictated, the people who ran the war and maintained the vigilance for their units from dusk to dawn were a more easygoing, sociable lot. This was especially true for the night crew manning the 3rd Brigade's tactical command post, where Nancy Kozak's closest friend in the entire brigade, Captain Jessica Ann Cruthers, ran the S-2 shop from seven in the evening until seven the next morning.

Cruthers, nicknamed Jack because of her initials, was only a few months older than Kozak and in many respects her opposite. Four inches shorter than Kozak, Cruthers was petite. Even her fingers, thin without being bony, were small. She wore her mousy blond hair short and cropped close to her head, unlike Kozak, who despite the misery kept as much of her flowing auburn hair as possible. This was a source of much amusement for Cruthers, who never missed an opportunity to hassle Kozak. Every time she came into the brigade tactical operations center and removed her helmet, Kozak would automatically reach up with her right hand and begin to vigorously scratch her head, causing the hair piled high and held down by legions of bobby pins to start to unravel. As soon as Kozak uttered a word of complaint, Cruthers would start on her from wherever she happened to be standing. "Girl," she'd call, "when are you going to realize that no living mammal worth mentioning is going to give you a second look. Get with the program and lose those long stringy locks."

Proud of her hair, Kozak would often shoot Cruthers a glance of feigned anger. "My hair is not stringy. It happens to have quite a bit of body. I just need to wash it and comb it out some."

"Some!" Cruthers would exclaim. "You have more knots and snags in that mop of yours than a four-quart pot of spaghetti. It would take a whole platoon of parachute riggers a week to sort them out. Why do you insist in keeping all of that hair? Trying to provide a home for orphaned bugs?"

Looking about before answering, Kozak would give Cruthers a shy glance. "Jack, you know damned well why I keep my hair this long."

Like the rest of the ritual, repeated time and time again, regardless of the time of day or night or the presence of others in the operations center, Cruthers would let out a decidedly unfeminine laugh. "Nancy, who are you kidding? What, with those two bars on one collar, the crossed rifles on the other, and those baggy-ass BDUs you wear, do you really think any man around here is going to give you another thought?"

Sometimes this would anger Kozak. Sometimes she would give a sly smile. With a twinkle in her eye, she would remind Cruthers, "Ah, got you there, girl. AJ likes my hair."

The mention of Captain Aaron J. Pierce would cause Cruthers to put her hands on her hips and laugh louder. "Ha! AJ Honey, let me tell you something. AJ's an aviator, and like all male aviators, the hair he's interested in isn't on your head."

If Cruthers hadn't managed to anger Kozak up to this point, her making fun of AJ in this manner would push her over the edge. Usually all Kozak needed to do was simply flash a look that told Cruthers that she had gone too far. When she saw that look, Cruthers would quickly change the subject and not mention hair or AJ for the rest of the day. Yet inevitably the next night, when Kozak came into the brigade operations center, removed her helmet with her left hand, and began to claw away at her itchy scalp with her right hand, Cruthers would start the whole routine again.

That was how Cruthers knew that something was wrong when Kozak came into the operations center this evening and plopped down in a chair next to her. Seated half on and half off the metal folding chair, Kozak held her rifle between her knees so tightly that her knuckles began to turn white. She said nothing, did nothing as she stared vacantly at the Intel map on the wall across from her that a sergeant was working on. Even from the side, Cruthers could tell that Kozak's brown eyes were puffy and red. Though everyone in the brigade had blood-shot eyes, especially those who worked the graveyard shift, Cruthers could see that her friend had been crying.

After Kozak sat there for several moments without comment or even removing her helmet, Cruthers decided that whatever it was that was bothering her friend couldn't wait. She had something, Cruthers guessed, that she wanted to talk about, but either didn't know how to start or, for whatever reason, was embarrassed about. Setting aside the list of moving target indicator grid coordinates that she had been calling off to the sergeant who was plotting them on the Intel map, Cruthers looked over at Kozak and studied her for a second. Between the look in her eyes, the despondency that she was displaying, and her failure to initiate what other members of the brigade staff referred to as the Jack and Nancy comedy show, Cruthers knew she had a real problem on her hands. Moving her head around so that it was in Kozak's line of sight, Cruthers looked her in the eye. "You okay?"

Without breaking her expressionless stare, Kozak nodded. "Yeah, I'm fine."

Laying her right hand on Kozak's shoulder, Cruthers shook her head. "Sure, like you expect me to believe that. I know you better and you know that I do. Feel like talking?"

Looking up into Cruthers's eyes, then around the room, and finally back to her friend, Kozak tried to answer, but the word "yes" got caught in her throat as she fought back a sob. Moving her hand across Kozak's back and giving her a slight reassuring pat between the shoulder blades, Cruthers called over to the sergeant at the map board that she was going to take a break. Having watched what had been going on without

160

making it look too obvious, the sergeant nodded and turned back to the map where he continued to work cleaning up stray marks here and there. Neither he nor any of the other officers or NCOs of the night shift paid the two female captains any heed as they left the brightly lit operations center and wandered into the still night air.

Though there was no breeze to push the sullen night air about, the two women at least were able to escape the stuffiness of the blacked-out command post. Though no brigade base camp had yet been attacked by guerrillas, the brigade commander wasn't taking any chances. Unlike other senior commanders, he took heed of what had happened to 3rd of the 511th. Since the twenty-first of September he had been taking every prudent precaution he could think of to ensure that he and his command weren't surprised like that again. Still, many unwarlike conveniences dotted the brigade area. One of them was a crude wooden picnic table banged together by some soldiers after setting up the brigade base camp months ago. Sitting under a drooping camouflage net that needed tightening, the picnic table was used by members of the brigade when eating lunch or taking smoke breaks away from their posts. It was for them the nearest thing to a sanctuary where they could for a moment forget about their duties, their responsibilities, and most of all the war.

Blinded by their emergence from the bright lights of the operations center into the deep darkness of the night, the two women slowly half walked, half shuffled about in the moonless darkness, searching for the table where they had shared a lunch many times before. Cruthers found it quite by accident when she hit her shin against the weathered board of the bench. After she let out a short damn, they seated themselves on the bench, facing away from the table, side by side. Though there were others somewhere out there, pulling their tour of guard duty or manning operations centers, the darkness and the camouflage net made Cruthers and Kozak feel very much alone. As they settled down, Cruthers wrapped her right arm across Kozak's back while her friend placed her rifle off to one side. Without a word, Kozak slumped and began to cry. Placing her left hand on Kozak's left shoulder and squeezing her tightly, Cruthers tried as best she could to comfort Kozak as she sat there, her face buried in her hands, and began sobbing.

As Kozak let herself go, Cruthers tried to imagine what exactly had finally brought this on. She and just about everyone else outside of Kozak's battalion had seen it coming, not only in Kozak but in just about everyone associated with that battalion. Harold Cerro, the battalion commander, best reflected in appearance and conduct what was happening. He was fast becoming a psychological basket case. The once proud and cocky infantry officer had as a result of the grind of war and the aftermath of the twenty-first of September become sullen and withdrawn. His gaunt face, need to avert his gaze when addressing people, and halting conversation when he did made everyone on the brigade staff uncomfortable. Even his physical stature was changing. Daily his sagging shoulders seemed to sink closer and closer to the ground under the weight of untold worries and concerns that he kept locked in his mind. "It's only a matter of time," Cruthers had heard her boss tell the brigade operations officer, "before Cerro goes off the deep end. Let's just hope he doesn't take too many of his people with him."

Cerro, of course, wasn't Cruthers's concern. Hers was a more personal stake. Right now in her arms the one person that she really cared for was sitting there falling apart. What to do to help right now was foremost in her mind. Of course, being the intelligence officer she was, Cruthers immediately reverted to her training. It was, after all, only natural. With eleven years of service behind her, Cruthers's way of thinking and reacting had become instinctively military. To really be able to help Nancy, she knew she had to find out what it was that was bothering her the most. So as she tried hard to comfort Kozak and wait until her crying jag had run its course, Cruthers began to assess the situation and determine what evil forces were arrayed in Kozak's mind against her sanity.

Was it the cold and mindless manner in which the division had dealt with 3rd Battalion, 511th Infantry, after the twenty-first of September? This, of course, was a very real possibility. Her own battalion commander, after all, was demonstrating his inability to deal with that event. Was it the trauma of war? Had Kozak allowed all the nightmares of past battles to gang up on her and steal her ability to cope? That possibility sounded reasonable, especially given her recent bout of nocturnal wanderings. Perhaps there was bad news from home, a sickness, a divorce in the family, or other such problem. Such a thing, combined with the stress and strain of the recent month, would be, Cruthers reasoned, enough to cause a Marine to cry. Or maybe, she thought as she began to exhaust her list of possibilities, it was that silly bastard that she had been pining for during the last few months, the aviator with straight teeth and no brain. Though Cruthers hoped that this wasn't the case, the more she thought about it the more she began to suspect that some way, somehow, AJ the throttle jockey was the root cause of Kozak's current state. It wouldn't be the first time, Cruthers sighed, that she had had to sit by and watch as an intelligent, capable female officer impaled herself on the love of a man who had no idea what the word love meant.

Noticing that Kozak was beginning to wind down some, Cruthers leaned over and moved her face close to Kozak's. Softly, calmly, she spoke. "Feel like talking or would you rather just sit awhile?"

With nothing to blow her nose into, Kozak sniffed back the liquid that was threatening to gush down the front of her face. Sitting upright, she used the index finger on her right hand to wipe away the drop of mucus that had managed to escape. Wiping her hand on the pants leg of her BDUs, Kozak turned, faced Cruthers, but then froze as the thought of her mother popped into her head. For the briefest of moments Kozak imagined what her mother would say if she had caught her wiping snot on her own clothes. Strange, Kozak thought before dismissing that idea. Here I am, a full-grown woman, a combat infantry officer, and I'm still paranoid about my mother. But then, she reasoned, right now she was a little paranoid about everything, including the future. When the vision of her mother's disapproving face was gone, Kozak began to talk in a mournful, shaky voice that warned Cruthers that more tears were only a breath away. "It's AJ, Jack. We . . . I had a fight with him."

Drawing in a deep breath herself, Cruthers didn't try to disguise the look of disgust that flashed for an instant across her face. She knew it! Damned if she hadn't guessed right. That weasel, with his oversized watch and an ego to match, had either picked a fight with Nancy or had dumped her now, at a time when she needed his love and understanding the most. Pulling Kozak closer to her and comforting her for a moment, Cruthers looked over Kozak's shoulder, her face contorted with anger. Damn him! Damn them all. Nothing, she had decided a long time ago, could fuck up a good woman and her career faster than a fickle lover boy whose maturity hadn't managed to keep pace with his chronological age. Though she had tried to warn Kozak many times that this was neither the time nor place to be getting involved in a romance, Kozak had ignored her friend and had allowed herself to drift into an affair that now, from all outward signs, was coming to an end. This was not the time, Cruthers knew, to tell her, "I told you so." No, not the time at all. Later maybe. But tonight the best she could hope for was to find some way of calming her down, getting her mind off the shit-for-brains boy scout that had gotten her into this state, and give her friend something positive to look forward to. It was, she knew, a tall order, but one that she had to try to fill.

Pulling back out of their embrace, Cruthers looked into Kozak's eyes. Taking Kozak's hands, still moist with her tears, into her own, Cruthers tried to sound as empathetic as possible. "You ready to talk about this yet, or do you just want to sit here quietly for a while and settle down?"

Without any further prompting, Kozak let it all come gushing out. "Oh, Jack, I don't know what to do, who to turn to, or even what to think anymore. I'm even beginning to question whether I can think straight anymore."

"Nancy, in case you haven't noticed, you and your unit have been through a rough month."

"I know. I know that. I keep telling myself, 'Girl, you've seen worse.' But then I look around and I realize that I haven't. In the past there was always someone there to prop me up when I needed it or give me a kick in the butt when I deserved it. Colonel Cerro and I go back to the Mexican incident when he was a captain on division staff and I was a fresh lieutenant, and he has been sort of an inspiration to me. When I needed an ideal infantry officer, one that I could model myself after, he stepped into my life and gave me that."

Taken aback by this oration on her battalion commander, and not the person she had previously indicated as being the guilty bastard, Cruthers gave Kozak a questioning look. Realizing that her friend wasn't making heads or tails out of where she was going with this conversation, Kozak tried again. "After the twenty-first of September, when the colonel started getting, well, funny, I began to feel a little lost myself. I mean, after all, here's the one person that I had held up as being the personification of the infantry combat leader going to hell in a handbasket right before my eyes. I was beginning to feel . . ."

Noticing her hesitation, Cruthers shook Kozak's hands and moved her head closer to Kozak's. "Feeling what? You can tell me. Please, what were you feeling?"

With her eyes wide open and her face drooping in the saddest expression that Cruthers could ever imagine, Kozak reminded her at that moment of a little girl. "Jack, I felt lost. Lost and vulnerable. There wasn't anyone in the battalion that I could turn to and talk to this about. Everyone, from the XO on down, was either feeling sorry for themselves or angry as hell, sometimes both."

"Well, why in God's name didn't you come to me? Nancy, I would have listened."

Kozak looked into her friend's eyes and thought for a moment before responding. No, she thought, it wouldn't do to tell her the truth. She just wouldn't understand. While Jack was a good friend and they were close, Cruthers wasn't a combat arms officer. She hadn't been there! She hadn't seen what Kozak and Cerro had seen, felt what they had felt, or suffered inside as they did for every failure, real and imagined, that combat arms officers suffer after losing people entrusted into their care. Kozak had needed another officer, another combat veteran who had been there in battle and knew what she felt without her having to say anything. Cruthers, for all her friendship and good intentions, could never fill that role. So, shaking her head and averting her eyes, she lied. "I don't know, Jack. I guess . . . I guess I just wasn't thinking straight."

"But you told AJ."

Looking back at Cruthers rather sheepishly, Kozak nodded. "Yes, I went to AJ."

"And he didn't understand. He didn't understand what you

told him and he didn't understand the pain and suffering you were feeling, did he?''

Kozak took a couple of deep breaths, looked down at their hands clasped and resting on her thigh, and simply nodded her head.

Releasing Kozak's hands, Cruthers half turned, leaned forward, and embraced Kozak again. "Nancy, Nancy, Nancy. How many times do I have to tell you. AJ's a fool. The only thing he's capable of understanding is that damned machine of his. He's like most men. They have little idea what makes women work and even less inclination to find out. Comprehension of anything that doesn't run on electricity or liquid fuel is beyond them.''

Though Kozak felt that Cruthers, now as always, was being a bit too negative about men and the way they acted, she said nothing. Breaking their embrace, she pulled away from her friend slightly. "It's not only that, Jack. I think I could have dealt with his lack of compassion. He is, after all, an aviator and he doesn't appreciate what it's like to lead soldiers into battle. What really got me . . . Well, what I mean to say, the thing that I found the hardest to deal with was me and my own thoughts.''

Oh, God, Cruthers thought. Here she goes blaming herself and making excuses for that moron. When's she ever going to learn?

Not noticing the incredulous look in her friend's face, Kozak went on without pause. "Although I knew that he wasn't involved in this operation, I couldn't get it out of my mind that he didn't, that he couldn't, do anything to help me. All afternoon as we inched our way through the enemy positions, cracking one bunker at a time, losing people all the way, I kept looking up at the sky, hoping that he would come in like the cavalry and save us. When finally we were able to contact the brigade aviation officer and call for med evacs and resupply and he informed us that division aviation was not able to fly any missions in until they had found their decoy flares and mounted them on the helicopters, I felt betrayed. I felt like the man I loved, even though he was a hundred miles away and unable to change anything, had deserted me. Even after we got back. Even after I had been able to push those silly thoughts out of my head, when I saw him for the first time last week, the same ugly feelings of betrayal and abandonment came back."

"Did you tell him, Nancy, how you felt? Did you explain any of this to him?"

She shook her head. "I tried. I really tried. But all he could talk about was how much of a bummer it was that the battalion had been taken out of the reserve force rotation and how he had been looking forward to spending time with me in Bogotá. Imagine that, Jack. Here I am on the edge, with no one to turn to, and all he can think about is how terrible it is that he didn't get to shack up with me. To hell with me. To hell with my problems. I . . . I just . . . I just couldn't . . ."

As Kozak began to get choked up, her voice trailing off into a sob, Cruthers, now half hanging off the bench while she faced Kozak, put both hands on Kozak's shoulders and smiled. "Honey, believe me, I understand. I really understand." She ignored Kozak's comment about having no one to turn to and instead sat back on the bench, pulled Kozak's head down on her shoulder. Then slowly she began to run her fingers along the side of Kozak's face and neck, telling her as she did so that everything would be all right, everything would be fine.

The two women sat there like that for a minute, maybe two, with Cruthers's right arm around Kozak's back and the hand on that arm gently playing about on the side of Kozak's face and neck. It felt good to Kozak to feel another person's warm body close to hers. To have a shoulder to lean on and to have a sympathetic ear to talk to. Unburdened, at least for the moment, of her dark thoughts and pain, she was for the first time in a month beginning to feel at ease, at peace with herself. God, she thought, this feels so, so . . .

Slowly, almost unperceived at first, Kozak began to feel uncomfortable. Despite the warmth of Cruthers's embrace, or, more correctly, because of the warmth, Nancy Kozak began to realize that sitting here, with Cruthers like this wasn't . . .

Wasn't what? Kozak wondered. Right, or appropriate, or normal? What was it that was bothering her? she wondered. Was it that she didn't want anyone to see her like this in the dark with Cruthers, a woman that everyone more or less knew was lesbian? Or was her uneasiness due to the fact that she had allowed herself to give way to her foolish emotions and cry like a silly girl in the presence of another officer? Or was there something else? Perhaps, Nancy thought as she felt Cruthers's fingers gently stroking the back of her neck, she was beginning to enjoy this too much. Perhaps, she was . . .

Like a thunderclap, Kozak jumped up, brushing Cruthers's left hand from her and moving out of her embrace. The suddenness of Kozak's reaction startled both women. Spinning around wide-eyed, Kozak stared down at Cruthers still sitting on the bench. She in turn stared up at Kozak. Kozak opened her mouth to speak, but no words came out. Only air, as she began to pant, passed her lips. Disgusted, frightened, and very much shaken, Kozak turned and began to rush off into the night when she heard Cruthers call out. "Nancy! Your rifle."

Stopping in place, Kozak clenched both of her fists and shut her eyes. In her rush to get away she had run off without taking her rifle. Pivoting about, she opened her eyes and saw Cruthers standing there in front of the bench holding Kozak's rifle out. Though she knew she had to go get it, she hesitated. What do I say? she thought. What can I say?

Slowly, hesitantly, Kozak inched forward. With great reluctance she reached up and grasped the offered rifle. For a moment Cruthers held on to it, looking into Kozak's eyes as she did so. Neither woman said anything, neither woman moved. They just looked at each other, one frightened and badly shaken, one surprised and embarrassed.

Kozak tried to pull her rifle away from Cruthers, but she held on. As their eyes met, Cruthers began to speak. "Nancy, I . . ."

It was at that moment when a voice from the direction of the operations center called out to Cruthers, "Hey, Captain. Hot stuff coming in from division. You better get here quick."

Glancing back, she saw her sergeant at the entrance of the operations center. "I'll be there in a moment."

"Better hurry, Captain. The ops people have already sent for the old man. The Farcees have lit up the entire eastern part of the country and are hammering every military airfield in and around Bogotá."

"I said I'll be there in a minute." The sharpness of her response was enough for the sergeant. He had done his duty. He had passed on the word, given her a warning, and that, he figured, was all an officer deserved. Satisfied, he disappeared back into the operations center. When he was gone, Cruthers looked at Kozak, a sheepish, apologetic look replacing that of surprise in her eyes. "Nancy, I'm sorry. Believe me, I'm terribly sorry. I thought . . ."

She didn't finish. Letting go of Kozak's rifle, she turned and hurried off, disappearing into the brigade operations center. Behind her she left Nancy Kozak still standing in front of the bench, staring straight ahead into the darkness, alone, more alone and lost than she had ever felt in her life.

CHAPTER 9

October 21

A FORMER BOSS OF SCOTT DIXON'S HAD ONCE TOLD HIM THAT it was far more advantageous to add to those whom you can count on as friends than to multiply one's own enemies. Though not always successful, since people such as C. B. Lane seemed to make it a hobby of alienating those who did not share their views, Dixon worked hard to be cooperative, open, and friendly, or at least to avoid intentionally pissing someone off when the more open approach failed. In Colombia this policy was to prove its worth in spades.

Colonel Chester A. Thomas, whom everyone called Cat or the Cat because of his initials, had been serving in Colombia as the military attaché for close to three years when Dixon arrived there to begin his fact-finding tour for the Chief of Staff of the Army. Thomas, a man who was fast approaching the end of his career in the Army, had found himself on the outside when C. B. Lane and his staff arrived in Colombia. During a meeting not unlike the one that took place between Lane and Dixon, Lane had informed Thomas that his thoughts, ideas, advice, and presence were not welcome in his division. "We have a job to do," he told Thomas, "and we don't need a limp-wristed colonel from the embassy poking around here." Though appalled by this mindless rebuff, Thomas said nothing. Instead he decided right then and there that if that's the way

Lane felt, fine. He'd get his wish. With less than a year to retirement, Thomas decided to do something he had never done in his twenty-seven years in the Army; he'd start taking it easy. Though he would do his job and serve the ambassador as his adviser on military affairs, Thomas had no intention of beating himself up trying to force his views and observations on Colombian affairs on Lane or his staff.

That changed, however, when Dixon had first arrived in country. Dixon, like Thomas, was rebuffed and stonewalled by Lane despite his credentials. Even the staff of the 11th Air Assault Division ignored and stonewalled him when they thought they could. That was why Dixon found Thomas to be an invaluable source of information, a guide through the Byzantine labyrinth of Colombian politics, and a key to unlocking countless doors for him throughout the country. Any difference in rank was quickly put aside as Dixon and Thomas worked side by side whenever possible to fulfill General Fulk's mandate to find out what was really happening in Colombia. "General," Thomas had told Dixon when he was departing in late September, "you're ever down these parts again, you know you have a place to rest your head and a sympathetic ear you can chew on."

So it was no surprise that when Thomas found out that Dixon was coming to Bogotá as the head of SOUTHCOM Forward, he went out of his way to do everything he could to make sure that the embassy and its staff were ready and willing to accommodate them. He even badgered the ambassador until the ambassador put in writing an agreement that placed Thomas on Dixon's staff as adviser and liaison officer for the ambassador. Thomas, despite having been given such a backwater assignment, was still in every respect a good soldier who simply wanted to do his duty. By aligning himself with Dixon, he had the chance to be productive and make a meaningful contribution.

It was the Cat's efforts and preparations that allowed Dixon's staff to be operational and ready to deal with the crisis that was enveloping the eastern part of the country one day after stepping off the aircraft. Even more vital than the physical accommodations and the rapidity with which Dixon's communications became operational were the sources of information, both formal and informal, that Thomas was able to share with Dixon's intelligence and operations staffs. For while Lane and his division staff openly scorned and ignored the wealth of information that Thomas used to augment the normal U.S. intelligence sources, Dixon's young and energetic intelligence officer, Major Herman M. Hagstrom, reveled in the wealth of information offered by Thomas like a child let loose in a toy store.

Hagstrom was, as one staff officer at SOUTHCOM stated mildly, a real piece of work. When Hagstrom was introduced to Dixon as a candidate for his staff, Dixon all but rejected him out of hand. Dixon told Jeff Worsham, his chief of staff, that Hagstrom looked too much like a cartoon character rather than a G-2 intelligence officer. At five feet eleven and one hundred and forty pounds, Hagstrom had the physique of a stick person drawn by a four-year-old. His head, topped by a tuft of hair that looked too small to cover it, was almost egg-shaped. Even his glasses, the black plastic-framed type issued by the Army that everyone referred to as "no fuck" glasses, added to Hagstrom's image as a certified card-carrying nerd. While Worsham agreed that Hagstrom was far from being a picture-perfect model of an officer, he countered that Hagstrom had a unique talent. "When it comes to pulling diverse bits and pieces of information together with seemingly meaningless information and producing an accurate estimate," Worsham told Dixon, "no one does it better." Still leery, Dixon had done some checking of his own. What he found out more than supported Worsham's claim, for when no one else in SOUTHCOM could make sense of something, Hagstrom got it. "The kid," said the deputy chief of staff for intelligence at SOUTHCOM, "treats a challenge like that as a game. Behind those godawful glasses is a brain that's as close to a Cray computer as a human being can get."

Now as he sat in the early-morning briefing and staff brainstorming session listening to Hagstrom go through his paces, Dixon was pleased he had been able to overcome his dislike for the man based solely on appearance. Hours before the CIA's chief analyst was even ready to sit down and start sifting through the mishmash of information on his desk, piecing together the scant information that his sources had made available to him, Hagstrom, drawing off the same sources, which were supplemented by Thomas's connections, had a full estimate of the situation prepared and on Dixon's desk.

That estimate and his briefing did not paint a very bright picture. "Were I to make a historical comparison of the magnitude and scope of this offensive," Hagstrom stated at the beginning of his briefing, "I would have to use the Tet offensive of January 1968. The main difference, however, between the VC in 1968 and the FARC yesterday is that, to the best of my knowledge at this hour, the FARC has succeeded in destroying every target they hit and secured all the objectives that they have attacked. As of oh six hundred hours this morning, it's the FARC ten, Government forces zip." While hedging slightly by stating that bad news in situations like this is often exaggerated and has a tendency to overwhelm any good news that may be coming in, he warned Dixon and the rest of the staff not to hold their breath.

Continuing his briefing, Hagstrom turned his attention to the western part of the country for a moment. "The recent operations being conducted by the FARC in the western mountains along the Cauca River now appear to have been nothing but a deception whose aim was to draw the government forces and our own 11th Air Assault away from the true area of operations." Using a map that covered all of Colombia and large tracts of neighboring nations, he then began to explain the flow of FARC operations, as best he could, based on the fragmented reports, observations, and downright assumptions in the eastern zone. For each major incident he gave the location, the time it started and ended, if known, the government forces involved, the size and nature of the FARC units involved, and the nature of the attack, such as a mortar barrage only, or sapper teams, or ground assault accompanied by mortars. The area in which these operations took place, now being referred to as the Eastern Zone of Operations, was quite extensive. It measured some 230 miles east to west and anywhere from one hundred to one hundred and fifty miles in width, north to south. The defining terrain feature in the north was the Rio Meta, which ran northeast from the eastern mountains near Bogotá to the Venezuelan border. To the south, another river which, like the Meta, originated in the eastern mountains, ran more or less to the northeast also. A tributary of this river, the Rio Ariari, created the western boundary of the zone while the Venezuelan border itself, the eastern. In all, some 54,000 square miles.

In his efforts to piece together some type of coherent picture in his mind, it wasn't until Hagstrom was midway through his briefing that Dixon stopped him and asked him to clarify a point. Putting up his hand, Dixon called out, "Woo, Herman. Hold up there, lad. For the past ten minutes you've been talking about local and regular forces. Where did that difference come from?"

Surprised, Hagstrom looked at Dixon for a moment and blinked his eyes as if he were changing programs in his mind before he answered. "Oh, well, I was going to get to that later in the briefing, sir. But I guess now's as good a time as any, if you would like."

Dixon nodded. "Yes, Herman, I would like."

Shuffling through the stack of note cards that he was using for his briefing, Herman looked for those concerning the enemy's order of battle. When he found them, he looked at the first one for a moment, cleared his throat, blinked his eyes, and began to speak without looking up at Dixon. "Well, sir, as soon as I knew I was coming down here with you, I started going over all the reports that I could get my hands on. You know, after-action reports, spot reports, Intel updates, the works. As I was going through them trying to create my own order of battle for the FARC, I noticed that the nature of some of the enemy units was beginning to change. It wasn't until last night, when I was able to go through Colonel Thomas's files, that I was able to confirm my theory.

"Starting back in late June, stray reports of FARC units, all wearing the same pattern of camouflage uniform and armed with the same type and caliber of weapon, began to crop up. By mid-July the reports of these well-equipped and uniformed units started to increase, coinciding with reports of platoon-sized forces used in quick raids against well-defended Colombian outposts, or in large ambushes. It was the reports from August, however, with the sightings of company-sized enemy forces, supported by mortars in most cases, which convinced me that we were dealing with well-equipped regular forces that were different from the ragtag part-time warriors that had been the mainstay of the FARC up to then. For lack of better terms, I adopted the same terms used in Vietnam to differentiate VC forces. In my opinion, the FARC now has two distinct categories of forces in the field. Local forces, as before, are made up of people from a community who support the FARC but on a part-time basis only and seldom if ever leave their home region. The new forces, which I have been calling main-force units, are mobile shock troops. Well armed, the main-force units are trained to fight as platoons, companies, and maybe, if these reports are to be believed, battalions anywhere in Colombia.'' Finished, he looked up at Dixon and waited for the general to say something.

There was a pause as Dixon weighed the information that he had just been given. How in the hell, he thought, could he and everyone else who had studied the same reports have missed something as obvious as the information that Herman had just briefed? Still thinking as he spoke, Dixon asked Hagstrom why he hadn't mentioned this to him before.

An embarrassed smile flickered briefly on Hagstrom's face as he looked down at the floor and shuffled his right foot. ''Well, sir, to tell you the truth, it wasn't until early this morning, at about zero two-thirty, that it hit me. I mean, I had been writing all the information down as I saw it, but it never all came together for me until just a few hours ago. When the idea sort of fell on me, I went back, looked at my notes again, and blam, there it was, clear as a bell. The enemy the government forces are trying to deal with today is not the same one that they have been trained to fight. This is, in my estimate, day one of a new war.''

Slumping in the seat next to Dixon, Worsham let out a low but audible ''Oh, shit! Katy bar the door.''

Without even bothering to glance over at Worsham, Dixon mumbled, ''Jeff, I concur.'' Twisting halfway about in his seat, Dixon scanned his entire staff, speaking as he did so. ''Ladies and gentlemen, based on what the G-2 has just stated, I want all of you to begin to adjust your reports and estimates accordingly. Though there may be an outside chance that he's wrong, I don't think so. And,'' Dixon added as an afterthought, ''if he is, at least we'll be erring on the safe side.''

Looking back at Hagstrom, Dixon asked if he could hold the

rest of his briefing for a moment, indicating that he wanted the operations officer, Major Don Saventinni, to give the staff a quick and dirty overview of how the Colombian military was reacting to the FARC's offensive. Saventinni, at six foot two, one hundred and eighty-five pounds, and a close-cropped ranger haircut, was everything imagewise, that Hagstrom wasn't. An infantryman, Saventinni's uniform was covered with every badge and special skill patch imaginable. From Pathfinder to scuba, he wore them proudly on a chest that filled his BDU shirt and covered chest muscles that gave the appearance of being as hard as marble. With the swagger of a man confident in his ability to take on all comers, day or night, Saventinni moved to the front of the room, dropped his pre-positioned overlay into place on the map, and startled everyone in the room by shouting, "GOOD MORNING, SIR!" with a sharpness that damned near split Dixon's eardrums.

Feeling good about his staff and how things were going, despite the disasters that were befalling their Colombian allies outside, Dixon turned to Worsham. "Jeff, if that trooper is on steroids, cut him to half rations. I think he's a little overdone."

The general's comment caused Saventinni to break out in a grin that ran from ear to ear. Turning his broad shoulders sideways so that Dixon could see the ranger tab on his left sleeve, Saventinni smiled. "No steroids necessary, General. It's airborne ranger, through and through."

Looking up at the ceiling, Dixon shook his head and mumbled so that all could hear, "Lord, save us from the infantry." When the laughter died down, Dixon nodded at Saventinni. "Okay, Don. What do you have?"

Pointing to the blue symbols that represented the 11th Air Assault Division's brigades and separate battalions, Saventinni explained that, as of six that morning, the division was continuing to conduct operations against enemy forces that Hagstrom had during his briefing tagged as nothing more than diversions. When asked if the 11th had shown any indication that they might be holding back and preparing to redirect their attention against the new threat in the east, Saventinni shook his head. "I spoke to their operations people just before this briefing started, sir. At this time there are no plans to suspend, delay, or cancel any operations in progress or planned for the next twenty-four hours. The division hasn't even issued a be prepared warning to the brigades to do so. It is, at this time, business as usual." There was in Saventinni's voice a note of disgust when he made that last statement.

Looking over to Thomas seated to his right, Dixon asked if the Colombians had asked for any assistance from the 11th yet. Thomas shook his head. "No, sir, not that I know of. And even if they need the 11th's help, which I think they do, it will be a long time before they ask."

"Why? Pride? The Colombian generals aren't foolish enough to let simple pride interfere with military necessity, are they?"

"Yes, sir, they are. You have to remember the new reformed military has to prove its value and manhood. We are, after all, dealing with Latinos, proud men who often value their machismo more than their own lives."

Dixon thought about Thomas's comments, then looked at the symbols that represented the 11th and the blue circles and boxes marked on the clear overlay that indicated unit zones of operations and assembly areas, and said nothing. After a minute he nodded. "Okay, while we're talking about them, what about the Colombians?"

Though he stated from the start that it was still too early to tell, what reports had been received told of, as Saventinni put it, "nothing but gloom and doom." Just as Hagstrom had done for the enemy forces, Saventinni briefed Dixon and the staff on what the Colombian Army had done in the past twenty-four hours and what they were planning to do over the next twenty-four. While explaining the former was no easy matter, given the dearth of confirmed information, projecting what the Colombians would do was even harder. "About the only operation going on, in or outside the Eastern Zone of Operations where the enemy hit, was the dispatch of one battalion of the Presidential Brigade out of Bogotá, early this morning by truck to reinforce the garrison of Villavicencio. A second battalion of that brigade is scheduled to leave within the hour."

"Villavicencio?" Dixon cut in. "Why Villavicencio?"

"It is," Thomas explained, "the main source of food for Bogotá. Its population of 200,000 makes it the only major city of any value in the Eastern Zone."

Dixon nodded and looked over to Hagstrom. "Okay, but except for an attack against the military airfield there, I don't recall you mentioning any real danger posed against that city. Or did I miss something?"

"No, sir," Hagstrom responded. "You didn't miss anything."

Next Dixon looked at Saventinni. "Why reinforce a garrison that's not in danger, using your only reliable reserve force in the capital? And why trucks? Why not airlift?"

"The last part of the question is easy, sir," Saventinni stated. "As the G-2 briefed, sapper teams and mortar attacks pretty well nailed all of the military airfields in and around Bogotá. It's estimated at this time that upwards of two-thirds of the Colombian Army's rotary-winged aircraft and fifty percent of the Air Force's fixed-wing transports have been destroyed or rendered nonoperational. Those aircraft that are still available are being held back to rush forces around to deal with a real emergency."

With an askew expression on his face, Dixon looked at Saventinni. "Real emergency? Do they expect things to get worse or are they simply waiting for the situation to stabilize in the east before they rush in reinforcements?"

While Saventinni shrugged and shook his head, Thomas chimed in. "A coup. You said so yourself, General, in your report to the Chief of Staff of the Army. Up until today the Colombian government has considered their own Army the greatest threat to its existence. We can't expect them, the Colombian administration, to be able to change gears overnight and recognize the fact that we are fighting a new war. After all," Thomas added by way of example as he pointed to the blue symbols representing the 11th Air Assault Division's positions in the western mountains, "even an elite professional organization such as the 11th hasn't adjusted to the new realities of the war in the east."

Though he didn't respond to Hagstrom's reply right away, Dixon shook his head. Then after looking at the entire map one more time, Dixon stood up. Everyone who had been seated jumped to their feet. "Good job, people. Though I will need to go over the rest of this briefing with you sometime before noon, I really need to get on the horn with General Stratton and give him a quick and dirty rundown on what we know. While I'm doing that, Jeff, how about seeing how fast this motley crew can turn their work here into a coherent report we can zap up to SOUTHCOM.''

Reaching over and rifling through a stack of blue folders, Worsham pulled one out and handed it to Dixon. ''Ready for your review and comments, sir.''

Taking the folder, Dixon opened it, glanced through the report, drafted and ready for faxing, minus the blank section where Dixon would add his own comments. Closing the folder, Dixon cocked his head and gave Worsham a slight smile. Doing his best Humphrey Bogart, Dixon patted Worsham on the shoulder. ''Frenchy, this could be the beginning of a beautiful friendship.'' Without further comment, Dixon tucked the folder under his arm and began to leave the room, Worsham calling the staff to attention as he did so. Returning their salute, Dixon had reached the door when he stopped, turned, and faced the staff, who had already began to congratulate themselves.

Caught off guard by this sudden about-face, everyone in the room froze in place and looked at Dixon, half expecting to be chewed out for some infraction that they might have just committed inadvertently. But they relaxed when as Dixon spoke they realized that he had suddenly remembered something. Pointing first to Hagstrom, then to Saventinni, Dixon gave them some additional guidance. ''You two work together. Herman, if what you say is true, that the FARC achieved near total success yesterday, I expect them to conduct follow-up operations today or open up a new series of operations somewhere else. So far those people have been doing everything right. No reason to assume that they'll start dicking things up now. Saventinni, I want you to keep close tabs on the relief force motoring to Villavicencio. Troops in open trucks are just too inviting a target.''

''An ambush, sir?'' Hagstrom asked.

''Why not? The VC did it all the time. Threaten an important target with what seems to be a major attack, cause the South Vietnamese Army to react, and blow away the relief force as it comes trundling up the road, fat, dumb, and happy. If you follow your own logic, whoever is pushing those people's buttons for the FARC did some reading on—'' Suddenly it struck him. He himself had started it by using the Vietnam analogy in his report to the Chief of Staff of the Army. The ambush of the 3rd of the 511th, he had stated in his report, was nothing more than the January 1963 battle at Ap Bac revised. Hagstrom's reference to Tet and the division of enemy forces into local forces and main-force units had in turn grown out of Dixon's own observations. The North Vietnamese initial strategy for securing the Central Highlands of Vietnam in 1965 had followed the same script that he had just described. The government's holding back of key elements of the military as anti-coup insurance mirrored the Republic of Vietnam's paranoia. And given the FARC's extensive use of a deception plan to draw attention far away from the main area of battle, just as the NVA had done at Khe Sahn just before Tet '68, the parallels were simply too close, Dixon reasoned as he stood there, not to be a coincidence. It all made sense. Wide-eyed at this sudden revelation, Dixon forgot about Hagstrom and Saventinni and turned his attention to Colonel Thomas. "Chester, you familiar with the story of Mobile Group 100?''

"Yes, sir. The ambush of a French battalion-sized task force in June 1954 somewhere in the mountains near Pleiku, I believe.'' Then Thomas, cued to the danger by Dixon, began to stare back at him. "I'll be goddamned!''

"Right!'' Bounding over to the map through a parting sea of staff officers, Dixon jabbed his finger on the map right on the road that lay between Bogotá and Villavicencio. Thomas, who had followed Dixon to the map, looked at where Dixon's finger was and nodded in agreement. Satisfied, Dixon turned to his staff. "Gentlemen, the next major fight is going to be there, somewhere along that road.'' Dixon glanced back at Thomas. "Cat, I recommend that you scoot on over to the Colombian Ministry of Defense and explain all of this to them. Maybe they can do something in time to save that battalion.''

"Excuse me, sirs.'' Both Dixon and Thomas turned to where Worsham stood. "Aren't we going a little overboard by making that kind of assumption? I mean, the FARC aren't the most mobile people in the world. They can't be everywhere at the same time. And their ability to pick up and move about, especially the type of units that Herman is referring to as main-force units, is rather limited. How could they know that a government battalion would be dispatched from Bogotá to Villavicencio?"

"Because, Major Saventinni," Thomas responded, "during the coup attempt last spring, when the garrison in Villavicencio appeared to be wavering between staying loyal to the government and going over to the rebels, as soon as the capital was secured, a battalion of the Presidential Guard Brigade was dispatched by road to stiffen the resolve of the local commanders. That this happened was no secret. If the FARC military people are half as good as the general gives them credit for, they would have made note of this reaction and taken it into account when they were planning this offensive. Even if you toss that theory aside, the fact that Villavicencio is the gateway into the Eastern Zone and the foodstuffs that come from that area are critical to the survival of Bogotá, one of the standing contingencies is to do exactly what the Colombians are doing now—rush reinforcements to Villavicencio when danger threatens it. There is more than enough evidence available to us that proves that the FARC intelligence network has made its way into the Ministry of Defense. Any plans dealing with operations of the magnitude that we are seeing in the Eastern Zone would never be adopted by any commander worth his salt until he had war-gamed every angle, particularly the reaction of the other people."

"Like I said, Jeff," Dixon added, "whoever is driving the train for the other people is good. This is not the time to assume that there's a flaw in his thinking or that he's going to start screwing up." Finished, Dixon pointed his finger at Thomas. "Cat, get going."

Without needing to hear any more, Thomas headed for the door. "On the way, sir."

Looking over at Worsham, Dixon pointed. "Jeff, first find out when that helicopter we're supposed to have available to us will be ready. Next, have someone get on the line and get a handle on the Colombian Army officer who's been assigned to us as liaison. If you can't find him before the helicopter's ready, have one of our people who's fluent in Spanish standing by."

"You planning, sir, to head up the road and try to stop the battalion that's out there?"

"I don't know," Dixon responded. "But I would like to make sure that at least the man in charge of that unit knows what he might be headed into if the Cat can't get his own people to understand and explain it to him."

Though Worsham knew that what Dixon was proposing was well outside of the charter of this tiny headquarters, he could see nothing wrong with what they were about to do. While well-defined and prescribed tasks and responsibilities were nice, war, as he and every officer above the rank of captain knew, often demanded the adoption of expedient measures and solutions that often fell well outside previous plans and orders. "It was the side," a battalion commander that Worsham had once served under had said, "that recognized this need for flexibility and did it best that often won."

Time, circumstances, and luck were not riding with the 1st Battalion of the Presidential Guard Brigade. With three companies of infantry, reinforced with a battery of six 105mm howitzers and a platoon of armored cars, the 1st Battalion had left the capital just before dawn. The trip from Bogotá to Villavicencio, a straight-line distance of seventy-five kilometers or forty-five miles, should have taken no more than four hours, tops. But delays along the route of march caused by local traffic, narrow village streets, and an occasional breakdown made the trip take much, much longer. Although some of the delays were intentional, they were so well conceived and merged so nicely with naturally occurring problems that the obstructions thrown in the 1st Battalion's path by the FARC were never seen for what they were.

These delays did more than simply slow the speed of the column. When the battalion rolled out of Bogotá, it had done so in the manner prescribed by the Colombian Army's regulations governing road marches. The armored car platoon led out, followed by the lead infantry company five hundred meters behind. After them the artillery battery, also at a distance of five hundred meters. Another infantry company, the battalion logistics trains, and the final infantry company all followed in that order at intervals of five hundred meters between company march units. In addition to the distance between companies, there was a distance of fifty meters between each vehicle within the company march units of the battalion. Though this made the length of the entire battalion march column quite long, a little over seven kilometers or four and a half miles in length, these intervals, if maintained, would make it extremely difficult to ambush more than a small portion of the convoy. But those distances, because of the delays, anxious commanders who always pushed on every chance they got, and drivers who were awakened at midnight and on the road for hours, were not maintained. Every time the front of the column slowed or stopped, the following vehicles closed up, reducing or eliminating the intervals. By midmorning, the column had been reduced into a single march unit with less than twenty meters, and in some places ten, between vehicles. Though still large, a little over two kilometers, a reinforced battalion under ideal conditions could ambush most, if not all, of this compressed column. That, of course, was exactly what Valendez had counted on.

Ten kilometers west of Villavicencio the road from Bogotá leaves the valley floor that it had followed most of the way. It goes up over a small mountain, going through a series of twists, turns, and loops before descending on the other side into Villavicencio. Though this was when everyone should have been at their highest state of alert, just the opposite was true. The disturbed night's sleep, the pandemonium of preparing to move out and lining up in the dark, their departure before dawn, and the boring and tortuously slow march had eroded the vigilance of the most dedicated officers and soldiers of the battalion. With the end of the journey literally on the other side of the mountain, the only thought that ran through the minds of the officers and the drivers of the 1st Battalion was to get on with it and get the march over with as soon as possible. With the reduction in speed made necessary due to the steep incline, practically every factor that makes for an ideal ambush was present by the time the column was halfway up the mountain.

As the armored cars at the head of the column finished going around one particularly large loop on the western side of the mountain, a series of explosions to the left, above the roadway, ripped away a large outcropping of rocks. By the time the debris from this rock slide reached the road, it had gained enough momentum and additional material to sweep away into the gully below the first two armored cars, one of which belonged to the platoon leader. Caught totally off guard, the surviving armored car crews, exhausted by the long and difficult march begun before dawn and lulled into a state of inattention, failed to react at all. This, of course, made it easy for the FARC anti-tank gunners on the hillside above to dispatch the only armored fighting vehicles in the column. Having made short work of the escort element, those gunners were free to turn their attention to other vehicles of the column, now brought to a dead halt by the destroyed armored cars and the rock slide further up the road.

The rest of the FARC regular battalion, reinforced by two local-force companies, didn't wait for the anti-tank gunners to finish their initial task. Though each company, fighting from well-prepared emplacements above the roadway, opened fire at slightly different times, based upon when the echo of the initiating blast reached them, the time gaps made no difference for the 1st Battalion. Automatic weapons, light and medium mortars, and machine guns of every caliber ripped through the column, toppling row after row of soldiers sitting in the open rear of the trucks like tenpins. Especially hard hit in the opening minutes were any jeeps or vehicles that had antennas, a sure sign that an officer was riding in them. Though not all officers fell in the opening volley, far too many did to make a rapid recovery possible.

Besides the effects of the bullets, anti-tank rockets, and mortar shells, trucks crashing into each other or rolling over off the road into the gully to the right added to the 1st Battalion's casualties and the chaos. During this confusion the attackers experienced little or no return fire. That which was directed against them was poorly aimed and had no real effect. So the withering fire controlled by FARC platoon and company commanders continued to rain down on the stricken column, becoming more focused as squads and whole platoons began to concentrate their attention on a single vehicle or a cluster of government troops when they appeared to be rallying.

Within minutes the battle degenerated into a long string of separate little fights as the surviving officers, generally young lieutenants who had been riding in the trucks and not jeeps, and senior sergeants began to exert control over the panic-stricken soldiers. Here and there, despite brutal fire from above, small islands of resistance began to form. Though there was no way to form these isolated groups into a single coherent defense, the battle at least began to become a two-way fight. Ten minutes into the fight, a lull seemed to settle as there a was a noticeable slackening of fire.

At first the government troops took this decrease in their assailants' volume of fire as a sign that the FARC forces were breaking off the attack. Those officers, sergeants, and soldiers who stuck their heads up prematurely to see what was happening often paid for their curiosity with a bullet through the head or chest. Within each knot of soldiers, one or two casualties inflicted in this manner were more than enough to convince the others that the enemy was still in place and very dangerous. Pulling back behind whatever cover they could, the government soldiers prepared to wait for the situation to develop a little more or for someone to tell them what to do.

They didn't have long to wait. Already the FARC fighters, rehearsed by their leaders in what to do, were preparing to finish the fight quickly and decisively. While sporadic fire held the government troops in place, FARC company commanders, basing their plans on reports from their platoon commanders and their own observations, prepared for the next phase of the ambush. Once the pockets of government troops were accurately plotted, mortar fire was shifted onto them. With a steady rain of mortar rounds pinning the government troops, preventing them from moving or returning fire, FARC commanders shifted their forces. Machine guns were moved from positions that no longer could bring effective fire onto the enemy below to ones that could, while assault parties assembled under cover and prepared to infiltrate down onto the road under the cover of the redirected mortar and machine-gun fire, to physically root out survivors.

Since the situation facing each FARC company commander was different, the resumption of the fight was disjointed. First here and then there the crash of mortars and the chatter of long machine-gun bursts announced the renewal of the attack. Though the officers and sergeants on the road had used the lull as best they could to organize the pitifully few men they had under their control, there were not enough men, heavy weapons, or good positions to fight from. Spread out in a thin line, hiding under or behind their own trucks, the defending government troops were easy prey.

Slowly, methodically the pockets of resistance began to disappear. While the mortars, machine guns, and FARC fighters left in place hammered the government troops, the platoons chosen for the assault infiltrated down onto the road at those places where there appeared to be no government soldiers left alive. Occasionally they would stumble upon one or two men trying to hide or huddled under or behind a truck. Sometimes the frightened soldiers would offer to surrender, sometimes they would resist. Either way, all such individuals were dispatched with a quick volley of fire as the assault teams swept by and began to work their way toward the flanks of the pockets of organized resistance.

When set, the leader of the assault team would make a decision. If he thought he could eliminate the enemy in a single rush, he would radio his commander and have the mortars lift their fire. As soon as the last round impacted, the assault team would be up and charging forward. Hit by fire from above and a sudden attack from the flank, the small pockets quickly crumbled. Again, as before, the government troops had but two choices, try to surrender or keep fighting. Sometimes both reactions would occur at the same instant as one soldier jumped up and raised his hands while his companion next to him continued to fire away at the oncoming foe. As before, the FARC fighters responded the same way to both, killing everyone before them. If, on the other hand, the pocket he was closing on appeared to be too big or too well organized, the leader of the assault team would deploy his men and pour fire into the flanks of the enemy, slowly working his men forward, with the weight of fire from the flanks chewing away at the defenders, one by one, as the fire from above kept the other government troops pinned and unable to react. Only when he was sure that the enemy was about to break or his losses would be small would the leader allow the final assault to go forward. In this manner the pockets went under, one by one, until finally silence returned all along the road.

It took no more than an hour to finish the elimination of all organized resistance. No sooner had the last echoes of fighting ended, to be replaced by the moans and pleas for help from the wounded that littered the two-kilometer stretch of road where the 1st Battalion had died, than the third and most brutal phase of the operation began. Teams of FARC fighters flocked down to the road and went to work. Some picked their way through the wreckage of the 1st Battalion searching for weapons and equipment that would be of use to them later. Others went from vehicle to vehicle checking them out, identifying those that could be used to haul away the weapons and equipment being collected and stacked neatly along the side of the road. Medical teams and stretcher parties tended to their own wounded, bringing them to a hasty aid station where they could be given elementary first aid and then in selected vehicles loaded up and driven off along seldom used trails to hospitals awaiting their arrival.

Amid all this activity, four-man teams methodically combed the road in front of each company, checking each government soldier that they came across. Pausing only for a moment, the members of these teams would place the muzzle of their rifles against the head of each government soldier and squeeze off two quick rounds, regardless of whether he was already dead or still clinging to life. By this means Valendez hoped to send a message, a brutally cold message, one which he expected would not only be understood by the relief force that would come but by all those who heard of it. It was, Valendez explained to his field commanders, their way of announcing to the government that this was now a full-scale war, a war which the FARC intended to fight to the finish.

While the field commanders understood this explanation and accepted it with few reservations, few imagined the true reason behind it. Only Valendez, ever mindful of the complexities of war, knew that the introduction of such a level of brutality would bring into play a new level of terror and fear. He expected the government soldiers to repay in kind this terror by overreacting and dropping all pretenses of humanity during this next deadly phase of the war. "Within a week," he told a confidant that night, "Americans will be treated to the images of government artillery pounding every village in their path and heaps of dead civilians stacked high by the indiscriminate use of attack aircraft, artillery, and sophisticated helicopter gunships. In this way we will turn the benevolent government in Bogotá fighting to preserve the freedom of their people into murderers bent on destroying the very people they are supposed to be protecting in order to save their own skins. Slowly we will isolate this government from its own Army, from its own people, from its own allies. In the end, without American support, this corrupt government will die by its own hand.''

PART THREE

BY
IRON
AND
BLOOD

CHAPTER 10

November 10

JAN CHATTERED WITH A CHEERFULNESS THAT REMINDED Willie Freeman, the senior WNN soundman in Bogotá, of a girl on a school trip. "You know what I really enjoy about doing work in the field?" she blurted out as they drove from pothole to pothole on the poorly maintained national road on the fringe of the region called Los Llanos. "Trotting from one troubled spot on the face of the earth to another can be exciting. I don't think I'll ever tire of the adventure of going someplace I've never been before or seeing the world as it really is." Knowing that all she would get from Willie was a grunt or a perfunctory uh-huh, she turned to JT Evens, her cameraman. "Don't you just love being able to experience the cultural, ethnic, and social diversity of a new land and its people?" Then without waiting for his answer, for her question roused JT from a fitful sleep, she continued. "It's like a fringe benefit. Not even the stress and strain of constantly being on the move, having to rush off from one place to another, often on short notice, to cover a breaking story bothers me."

JT responded with a cynical look. This didn't seem to bother Jan as she continued. "In fact, I think I rather enjoy the challenge. You know, every situation different, having to be handled in its own unique way. And even when there are similarities between stories, especially ones that involve armed

191

conflict, the background of the war, the history of the people, the principal players involved, and the settings are always different. No, no pat formula or single set of rules applies out here, huh?''

Finally stopping her nervous chatter long enough for JT to respond, the only answer he gave as he shoved his baseball hat further back on his head was a rather halfhearted "Yeah, right, Jan. You sure are right there.''

JT's apathetic response took some of the wind out of Jan's enthusiastic commentary. Looking over to Willie, she saw that he was busy trying to pretend that he was too absorbed with driving to respond. Without a receptive audience, Jan turned and looked out the window of the van, continuing her thoughts in private. Her professional dedication was coupled with a true love of her job. Together with the recognition that her unique ability to bring the many diverse aspects of a story into play, giving her pieces meaning and impact, Jan was a gem in the eyes of her network and those who heard her stories. Though she had tried different jobs within the World News Network, from being an anchor on one of its prime-time programs to doing shows of her own, she always came back to the work she did best and the assignments that she so loved. As one of the owners of World News Network half jokingly told an associate, "When the going gets tough, we send in Jan.''

As it was for those who actively pursued a career in the real world, not every aspect of her job was enjoyable. There was in most stories some element of tragedy, suffering, and, as in the case of all wars, death. Though these by-products of the events that made up the news seldom touched her or the crews she worked with, Jan in all of her years as a dedicated, hard-nosed correspondent had never been able to come up with an effective means to shield herself psychologically from the pain and trauma of her stories. It was this element of her makeup and her profession that allowed her to see beyond the coldness and remoteness that her husband often dropped like a shield between them. Often she wondered how Scotty found the strength to go on when she, a mere spectator of this horror, was often troubled by it in her dreams. Though they never spoke of it, this shared experience served as a bond that made their love for each other and their relationship so much more valuable to each of them.

Even before the Land-Rover carrying her and her camera crew reached the village of El Frío, which reportedly had just been wrested away from the FARC, the signs that this would be another one of those occasions when any joy of being a correspondent would be submerged by the sheer pathos of the situation began to manifest themselves. First there was the lingering pillar of black smoke in the distance. Like a marker it stood in stark contrast to the pale blue sky, serving for all to see that another objective in the government's slow, bloody counteroffensive had been achieved. The smoke also allowed Jan an opportunity to steel herself for what she was about to see. Like a ship's crew preparing for a storm at sea, Jan Fields-Dixon started to stuff her emotions away into the deepest recesses of her consciousness where her willpower, like bands of steel, would keep her true feelings in check.

The sight of the smoke and Jan's withdrawal served to end the casual conversation that Jan had been sharing with JT Evens from Athens, Georgia, and Big Willie Freeman from East St. Louis, Illinois. It was said in Jan's office in Bogotá that a more diverse crew couldn't have been picked if someone had wanted to. JT Evens was every bit the southern cracker, in speech, dress, and manner. He took great pride in being called the last of the good ol' boys. Big Willie was so named because there were two Williams in Jan's office; and Freeman, who towered over the other by better than a head and a half, was a city kid. He was a fighter, a man who had fought, literally, his way out of the ghetto. Even in high school, where his peers regularly beat him up because he chose to study and his high grades set him apart from the other black youths in his class, Willie Freeman had to face adversity on a daily basis. Whereas Evens was laid back and easygoing, everything about Freeman, from the manner in which he carried and expressed himself, to the way he went about his job as a soundman told all who saw him that he was not to be trifled with. And then there was Jan, a self-actualized woman who made her way through life with charm and grace when she could, bluster and blunder when it was necessary, and sheer determination and courage when it was demanded of her. Though not always popular, Jan Fields-

Dixon was admired by all who saw her for what she was, a free and independent person, beholden to no human yet a part of the whole, as much a piece of the society that had bred her as any other man or woman, great or small.

Slowly the familiar signs of battle began to unfold as the WNN crew drove on in silence. First they came across a battery of howitzers. Jan watched the Colombian soldiers going about their chores. Near each of the six guns set up on the side of the road in the open was a stack of empty shell casings. This meant that the government forces had found it necessary to use their heavy artillery to overcome the FARC's resistance. Since artillery was rather indiscriminate and men under fire have a tendency to use it too lavishly, Jan thought, odds were that civilian losses were high.

No sooner had she finished that thought than they saw the first of the refugees, led by several soldiers, headed west and away from the place that they had once called home. Their gaunt, vacant expressions told Jan that they had felt the sting of the big guns just as much as the FARC fighters had. Within minutes, this was amply confirmed when another knot of refugees, walking a little slower than the others, came into sight as the van got closer to the village. In this group were the freshly wounded, the crippled, the very old, and the very young. Watching from his window, JT mentioned that none of the soldiers leading them away seemed to be interested in helping the stricken villagers. Willie, driving the van, responded in the same cold, dry manner he always used when he was trying to control his anger. "What do you expect, cracker? You think they give a damn? You think they care what happens to those people? They're the ones who screwed up those people in the first place. The only thing those soldiers care about is the fact that it's the villagers and not them bleeding all over the road."

Though Jan wanted to say something, if for no other reason than to keep the two men from opening a fight with each other, she couldn't think of anything. Willie was right. Besides, the sight of a small child, not more than two, crying as she bent over a lifeless form on the side of the road, was enough to silence everyone in the van. It was, Jan knew, an ageless image. She had seen old photos of such scenes from World

War II, Korea, Vietnam, and countless other wars. She herself had been witness to such images of tragedy, made more painful by the fact that when she saw them in person they were not images. Rather they were real people, flesh and blood like her, that she could reach out and touch. In the beginning Jan had done that. She had tried to help the people she saw stricken through no fault of their own by a war they did not want and did not understand.

But when you touch someone, they often touch back. In trying to relieve pain, you often absorb more than you can handle yourself. When Jan realized that she was losing her ability to deal effectively with such incidents, she withdrew within herself, not out of callousness but out of the need for self-preservation. When you had no effective means of helping, Jan learned, it is far more cruel to pretend, both to the people you are trying to help and yourself. Hence the need to steel herself beforehand so that she could look upon such things with dry eyes and walk away when she had done what she had come there for. Yet even her best efforts would never be enough to erase the sight of the child and the fallen adult now receding in the rearview mirror of the van. Like so many others, Jan would carry that one with her forever.

From behind her, JT let out a mumbled curse. "Bastards. Look at that. All these trucks sitting around and they couldn't even shake a few loose to help their own kind. Bastards. Soldiers killing soldiers, that's one thing. This . . . this is too much."

Shaken from her thoughts, Jan looked around just as Willie started to slow the van. On either side of the road a number of military trucks sat in open fields attended by their waiting drivers and a few stray soldiers. Jan, who had grown used to seeing precision in all things military because of her life with Dixon, always sat up and took note when she saw a sloppy military unit. In this case the trucks that JT had alerted her to were not in any type of order or line. Rather they were scattered about, some parked together in clusters, others sitting quite alone and unattended. Even the drivers, wearing every variation of their uniform imaginable, added to the chaotic scene. Again it was JT who spoke. "Boy, I hope the grunts in this unit look better than these old boys."

Jan, still looking about, finally responded. "Don't hold your breath back there, JT. You've been pounding this beat long enough to know better than that."

"Yeah, I do. Thing is, Miss Jan, if the Farcees can be pushed around by a sorry lot like this, then what's the big deal about the Farcees. Seems to me either they're not what they're cracked up to be or someone back in Bogotá is pulling the wool over our eyes, trying to make the Farcees look meaner than they are."

Turning around, Jan smiled at JT. "That, friends and neighbors, is why we brought you and your trusty camera along. It's time to play truth or consequences with these good ol' boys now, ain't it?"

JT smiled. He knew Jan was making fun of him and his manner of speaking. But he didn't mind. They all needed a little humor, even if it was at each other's expense, to keep themselves from going crazy in this sick and twisted world. After all, at that moment they were at the less than tender mercy of an Army that had just brutally pounded one of its own villages, people and all, and all they had was each other. So JT smiled and nodded. "That's right, Miss Jan. Now all we need to do is convince that city boy sitting next to you to take his foot off the brake and drive this thing."

Unmoved by the levity that Jan and JT were sharing, Willie responded in his deep dry voice. "I'm afraid those soldiers with the machine gun behind the roadblock up ahead have a different idea."

Turning to look ahead, Jan saw the checkpoint that Willie was stopping for. Though the weapons they held were menacing in themselves, the manner in which the soldiers held them and their rather lackadaisical stances made the whole scene before them nonthreatening. Popping his head up from behind so that it was even with Willie's and Jan's, JT grunted. "Um, sleep safely tonight, Bogotá, your Army is on guard."

Ignoring JT's comment, Jan continued to watch the soldiers at the roadblock. "Okay, Willie, show time."

Bringing the van to a slow and easy stop off to one side of the road, Jan and Willie opened their doors and began to approach the roadblock, careful to make sure that they didn't do anything that might be interpreted as hostile. When they were several feet away, the two Americans stopped. Without any need to be prompted, Willie called out in Spanish, slowly reaching into the pocket of his equipment vest in search of the government papers authorizing them to be in the forward zone. "We are a news team, with permission from your government, here to report on your great victory today."

When the two soldiers heard this, they looked at each other and began to laugh. This caught Jan off guard, since Willie was not known for his humor. Glancing over at him, Jan asked what he had said. When he'd repeated word for word his greeting, Jan cocked her head, then looked back at the soldiers. Since Willie's Spanish was impeccable, there was something wrong here that she didn't quite understand. In Jan's mind the attitude of the soldiers, both here and back down the road, was not that of men who had just finished a hard and costly fight. That thought triggered another as she turned first to one side, then to the other. Not seeing what she was searching for, Jan looked over to Willie. "Have you seen any wounded soldiers or ambulances headed back up the road?"

Understanding what she was getting at, Willie shook his head. "None, Jan. The only blood I saw was on those civilians we passed."

Further speculation was cut short when an officer came around the end of the roadblock nearest Jan and walked up to her. With a broad smile, he introduced himself. With two quick steps to the side, Willie was next to Jan and translating. "He says he's Captain Emmanual Elmoro, commander of the company that took the village of El Frío early this morning."

Smiling, Jan offered her hand to the Army captain while she introduced herself and Willie translated. With chivalry more appropriate to the ballroom than a recently contested field of battle, the captain made a slight bow and raised Jan's hand up to his lips. While he was engaged in this little ritual, she studied him. He was clean-shaven, his uniform was neat and almost spotless, and even his hands were free of dirt and mud. "How long ago, Captain, did you finally secure the village?"

Looking up, though still holding her hand, Elmoro smiled. "Not more than an hour ago, señorita."

Lowering her eyes, Jan glanced over to Willie, who nodded. Looking back at the captain, she flashed a shy smile to hide her surprise. Firmly, yet without showing any undue haste, Jan pulled her hand away from the captain's. "Willie, tell the dear captain who we are and see if you can negotiate our way into the village."

The idea of having an international news team cover the exploits of his company seemed to excite the young captain. His smile broadened as he quickly responded, reaching out to grasp Jan's arm with one hand and sweeping the other in a wide motion of welcome. Willie had no trouble keeping up with the captain as he announced his intentions. "Oh, señorita, it would be my pleasure. Come, let me personally escort you and your crew."

While Jan was being led away past the soldiers at the roadblock, Willie rushed back to the van where JT was already hefting his camera over one shoulder and his battery pack over the other. "Guess Jan charmed her way past the roadblock, huh?"

Willie, busy pulling his own equipment out, didn't look over when he responded. "The boss lady smells a rat. According to the captain we were greeted by, his boys just blew into town an hour ago and he looks like he just stepped out of the shower, not a firefight."

Pausing for a moment, JT let his face fall into a reflective stare. "So you two don't think there's been much of a fight here, huh?"

"JT, I'm not sure what the boss lady's thinking. All I know is that she wants both of us to be on our toes. Watch for her cues and shoot anything that you think she might want."

Jan, never sure how a story would go, and always looking for the less than obvious, often asked questions that seemed innocent enough at the moment. It was often her commentary, shot afterwards, combined with video and the sound bites caught by an attentive crew that gave what should have been a mundane story power and impact. Seldom did her crew understand exactly what she was looking for or what she was after, since Jan herself was always looking, searching, thinking as they went. That was why anyone working with her had to be able to shoot what she told them to, shoot what she really wanted, and shoot what they themselves saw and felt was important. Though there were occasions when Jan, the cameraman, and the soundman were not in sync, more often than not their efforts were rewarded. Today would be a case in point.

Within minutes Jan's party, led by the fast-talking captain, was in the village. The damage was considerable. What few motor vehicles had been in the village before the attack began littered the streets, shattered and burning. The oily black smoke from burning tires and rubber mixed in with the acrid smoke of homes and shops that were reduced to rubble. Though not every structure was totally demolished, none that she saw escaped damage. Busy explaining how the other two companies of the battalion he belonged to surrounded the village during the night while his command prepared to make the final assault, it was several minutes before the captain noticed Jan's preoccupation with the amount of damage. Waving his finger about in a random fashion at the devastation, the captain explained. "We started the shelling shortly after midnight in the hope of catching the rebels while they were sleeping."

JT, filming as he went, held the camera steady while he leaned over and whispered in the ear Willie had not covered with the headphones, "Yeah, not to mention the local populace."

Willie ignored JT's remarks. Following several paces behind, he repeated in English the captain's remarks so that Jan and his mike would pick his words up. Though she was thinking the same thing JT was, Jan simply nodded as she continued to walk alongside the Colombian captain. "So," Jan responded, "most of this was done by your artillery before the attack began?"

When he heard Willie's translation of the question, the captain nodded his head and smiled. "Yes, our artillery and your helicopters. They both did a marvelous job of preparing the target for our attack."

When Willie had finished repeating the captain's last comments, Jan shot a look back at him. His face, impassive, was fixed on her, waiting for her response. "Did he say *our* helicopters, Willie?"

He nodded. "Yes, ma'am. He said ours."

"Ask him if he means American, I mean United States Army helicopters."

Even before the captain finished responding to this inquiry, the gleam in his eye, his head nodding, and his immediate response of "Sí," made Jan feel a little sick. As Willie spoke, that feeling deepened into one of depression. "Yes, AH-64 Apaches, a flight of four. They flew in support of our attack, using rockets and 30mm cannon to hammer likely pockets of resistance just as our assault began this morning. Very effective, they were very, *very* effective."

Busy keeping her expression in check, Jan didn't notice that they had reached the town square. It was a rather small affair, yet well defined, as most squares and marketplaces were in these small villages. Though there were soldiers here and there, mostly sitting about in the shade in small groups chatting, smoking, and waiting, it was the civilians that caught Jan's eye. On any other day, the center of this village would have been filled with the people of the village and the smells of fresh produce, meats, and coffee for sale. Today, however, the only villagers in the square were either dead, lined up to one side in two long rows, or languishing in an open-air aid station in front of the local church. Too wounded to join the migration west, they were being tended by two civilians in bloodstained shirts and a priest and a pair of nuns. Stopping, Jan looked around and took in a deep breath before she proceeded. This, of course, was a mistake. For the air she drew into her lungs hung heavy with the stench of death, that weird mixture of stale blood, loose bowels, charred flesh, and human sweat. Finding herself horribly close to gagging, Jan froze, her eyes bulging and her checks turning red, then white as the color ran out of her face. "Control," she mumbled to herself under her breath. "Get control of yourself, girl."

Seeing that she was experiencing a moment of distress, both JT and Willie stopped recording. Watching her, they waited, ready to dash forward to help if necessary. Closing her eyes, for the briefest of moments, she managed to regain her balance. When she was ready, Jan opened her eyes, looked at JT and Willie, nodded to them, and picked up her questioning of the captain as if nothing had happened. "Losses seem to have been quite high, Captain?"

Canting his head to the side and looking down for a second, he nodded. "Well, yes, of course. These type of operations are seldom undertaken without cost. As you can see, this poor village paid a heavy price."

Not wanting to linger there in the presence of so much pain, suffering, and death, Jan ignored the captain's efforts to dehumanize the suffering around them by talking about the village as if it were an inanimate thing and quickly cut to the point. "What price did your company pay?"

This brought a smile to the captain's face. Puffing out his chest, he beamed as he answered. "We, my company and the rest of the battalion, were very fortunate today. We suffered no casualties. The combined weight of the artillery and helicopter attacks smashed all resistance before we entered the village."

Incredulously, Jan asked what exactly that resistance had been.

Raising his right hand to them as a sign he wanted them to follow, the captain led Jan and her crew to a part of the square where six corpses lay stretched out under the baking sun. Three of the bodies belonged to men who had to be well over sixty. Two were mere boys. Only one, a rather heavy-set man, looked like he was of the proper age to be bearing arms in an active guerrilla unit. At their feet, neatly laid out, were a shotgun, two ancient bolt action rifles, and a pistol of questionable value. "These men," the captain claimed as he pointed to the bodies, "are FARC. They kept this village terrorized and the villagers praying for deliverance."

Though she didn't mean for her actions to be as obvious as they were, Jan looked at the six bodies before her, then turned abruptly to where the civilian dead lay, then back at the captain. Her expression betrayed her thoughts, for any traces of smile that were left on the captain's face faded. In its place there was a sneer. When he spoke, there was bitterness in his voice. Even Willie, who up to now had managed to remain aloof from all before him, found it difficult to maintain his poise. Though Willie's translation was spoken without the anger that he heard in the captain's voice, Jan understood it. "How dare you come into our country and pass judgment on what we do to defend ourselves against our enemies. This is our war. These people, all of them, the civilians over there and the enemy at our feet, are all Colombians. Just as my soldiers are Colombians. If those people had been loyal, they would have left long ago or died resisting the enemy. But they chose to stay, and for their decision they alone are accountable. I am accountable to my commander and responsible for the soldiers in my command. When we leave here tomorrow, I will never see this village again. Its death means nothing to me. But the soldiers who follow me out of here will be with me tomorrow, the next day, and for a long time. For Colombia, and for my own sake, I dare not risk their lives foolishly. Today I had artillery and helicopters, your helicopters, to help me protect them. So I used them, just as your own Yankee officers taught us to do. This, señorita,'' the captain exclaimed, sweeping his arm about the square, "is not a Colombian invention. This is the Yankee way of war. Even the guns and the shells which we used are American, made by your countrymen, given to us by your government, to be used in the manner in which your officers trained us. So do not cast those accusing eyes on me as if you were innocent. In this war that word has no meaning.''

Too angry to continue, the captain took a deep breath, turned, and stalked off, leaving Jan, JT, and Willie standing speechless in the middle of the square. It took Jan a minute to collect her thoughts and decide that it was time to leave. There was, she reasoned, nothing more to be gained by staying there. They had in every sense worn out their welcome. So without further ado the three Americans left as quickly as they could.

It wasn't until they had put a mile or more behind them that anyone in the van spoke. Finally JT broke the silence. "Any idea what you're going to do with this stuff, Jan?''

Though she had heard him, Jan didn't respond immediately. This one, she knew, would be a hard story to put together. It could go any of several ways, and at that moment she was just too wound up and overwhelmed by what they had just witnessed to make a sound call. That, she decided, would best be left until after they were back in Bogotá. Perhaps, she thought, it would come to her during the long ride back. It always did. Finally Jan answered, without turning to face JT, in a manner that betrayed her uncertainty. "I have no idea what we're going to do with this one. None whatsoever.''

For the longest time everyone in the van left it at that. Then as if to signal that she wanted to drop the subject, Jan turned her head to JT and gave him a small smile. "JT, would you reach into the ice chest and pull out something for me to drink?''

Her request told both JT and Willie that the subject of the piece they had just shot was closed for the moment. Without another thought, JT returned Jan's smile. ''Sure thing. Your usual?''

Jan smiled. ''Yes, that would be fine, thank you.''

Steadying himself as Willie rounded a sharp turn, JT reached over, popped the lid of their cooler, and began to fish for Jan's drink.

As the van slowed to take the turn, a FARC gunner hefted the butt plate of his 7.62mm American-made M-60 machine gun onto his shoulder. Pulling the weapon back until it was snug, he sighted down the barrel as his thumb clicked the safety off. When the front-sight picture was resting dead center on the windshield of the van, he let his right index finger slowly ease itself around the trigger of the weapon. Slowly he let his breath out, then began to draw one final breath in, which he would hold before shooting.

From behind, a voice, as firm as it was low, intervened. ''No, this van is nothing. Leave it pass.''

For one final second the gunner looked down his sight into the front window of the van. Then, as carefully as he had placed it there, he removed his finger from the trigger. Letting his breath out, the gunner eased the butt of the machine gun off his shoulder and laid it gently on the ground, all the while watching his intended target finish the turn and continue its journey west to Bogotá. Though it would have been an easy mark, the gunner knew his squad leader was right. This van meant nothing. It was the Colombian Army battalion in El Frío that his local-force company, working with two regular FARC battalions, was after. Far better, he knew, to wait until darkness when everyone was set. There would be, he knew, more than enough targets fleeing their planned attack in a few hours to satisfy even his wildest dreams of revenge for the murder of his village.

And in the morning, when that lust was satisfied, he would go up the road to find his family. As so many other soldiers in his battalion had already done in other villages, he would find those of his family who were still alive. He would join their mourning, help bury their dead, and then go back to the task of cleansing his country of the corruption that had allowed such atrocities to visit them. The war for this machine gunner had become very real and very personal today, and it would never end until he was satisfied that the dead in his family were properly avenged or he himself had joined them.

Colonel Delhue didn't notice Major José Solis standing in the open door of his office until Solis softly rapped on the door. Slowly, almost absentmindedly, Delhue rotated his chair a quarter turn away from the window he had been staring out of, until he was facing the Colombian Army liaison officer. Throughout this process he made no effort to sit up or alter his deadpan expression. Only his feet moved, making the short side steps necessary to propel the chair. When he was set, facing the new direction, Delhue raised one eyebrow slightly as he looked at Solis.

For a moment Solis looked over at the division chief of staff. Even as he sat there slouched down and almost swallowed up by his overstuffed executive's chair, Delhue's tall bearlike frame presented a commanding presence. Only his face, its puffy skin dragged down about his eyes and mouth by months of stress, concerns, and unrelenting verbal and professional abuse, detracted from the image of the powerful man that Delhue's physical stature spoke of. From the moment he had set eyes on this man, Solis knew that he was a soldier, a man who would not tolerate fools or compromise either his own personal honor or that of his nation's. How fortunate for Hector Valendez, Solis thought as he suppressed a smile, that it was General Lane and not Colonel Delhue who commanded the 11th Air Assault Division. For he knew in his heart that had Delhue been running the division, the FARC would not be comfortably poised on the brink of their most ambitious effort with little to fear. Only one man in Bogotá that morning was seen as a threat by the FARC, and Hector Valendez had ordered Solis to find out all that he could about that man.

Without any introductions or pleasantries, Delhue raised his right hand from his chair's armrest and motioned toward a seat next to his desk. "Please, Major, have a seat."

While the Colombian major crossed the room and settled

into the offered seat, Delhue sighed. Here, he thought, was another wasted soldier. A man, a native of this country and a professional soldier whose entire military career had been spent pursuing the Farcees and other guerrillas through the same jungles and over the same mountains that our people were operating in, and no one, by intent, was using his knowledge or experience. How many good soldiers, Delhue mused, had our self-righteous arrogance cost us? Seeing that Solis was settled and ready, Delhue threw his body forward with a noticeable effort, stopping it by bringing his arms up and to rest on the desktop. "What, Major Solis, can I do for you today?"

"I would like to thank you for taking the time, Colonel Delhue, to talk to me like this. I mean with no previous appointment."

Solis's comment almost made Delhue laugh. It was general knowledge that Lane's manner of doing business left little for Delhue to do throughout the day. Lane's G-3, a lieutenant colonel almost as arrogant and egotistical as Lane himself, was the real center of power on the division staff. From his first day with the division, Lane had made sure that Delhue understood this and did nothing to hinder this arrangement. Though he had at first tried to do his duties, by mid-July the pain of daily confrontations and public reprimands had taken too much of a toll on Delhue's pride. So, like others in the 11th who were not favored by Lane, Delhue did what he could to avoid the division commander and busied himself doing those things that Lane and his chosen few had no interest in yet needed to be done. Since Lane's background and passion was plans and operations, Delhue worked closely with the division's support command, helping them deal with the monumental task of keeping an air assault division running.

Shaking his head, Delhue did smile, but it was a friendly, disarming smile. "Major, you are always welcome."

The colonel's comment struck home, for Solis knew that Colonel Delhue, like him, was an outcast. Though he understood Army politics and personality cults that often displaced professionalism, the practice still annoyed and angered him. He, unlike so many of his brother officers, had joined the Colombian Army to serve and protect his nation, not as a steppingstone to power and wealth. It was this dedication to his personal convictions and his unflinching dedication to high moral standards that made his decision to support the FARC an easy one.

Pushing aside his personal thoughts, Solis went right to the heart of the matter. "My superiors, Colonel Delhue, are somewhat perplexed by Brigadier General Scott Dixon and his staff. You see, we are not sure what role they now play in your chain of command. When General Lane first told the Minister of Defense of General Dixon and his mission, we were very suspicious and quite alarmed."

Delhue fought the urge to smile, since no one was more alarmed and suspicious about the introduction of Scotty Dixon and SOUTHCOM Forward than Lane himself. It had been a grim day when Lane's aide handed him the message signed by General Stratton announcing that Dixon was coming south for the express purpose of establishing a headquarters to monitor and report on American and government military operations in Colombia. Violent was too mild a word to describe Lane's reaction. Delhue, however, had no trouble finding words to define the manner in which Lane attempted to deal with this threat to his private domain. To Delhue, the orders that Lane issued to his staff, both specific and implied, crossed over the line between questionable conduct and downright unethical and unprofessional behavior. That Lane was capable of such behavior was a given. As one battalion commander stated to Delhue in private, "Within five minutes after meeting the man, you get the urge to take one hand and cover your wallet while using the other to protect your balls."

Personal behavior is one thing. Unethical behavior in an individual is excusable. What was not, in Delhue's mind, was Lane's demand that his subordinates conform to his moral standards or lack of them. To force another officer, especially a subordinate officer, to choose between compromising his own ethics or ruining his career was to Delhue worse than murder. Dignity and pride were in Delhue's mind the only things that a man can take to his grave. A man without dignity and pride, on the other hand, had nothing. In his view of the world, such a person was the lowest form of life imaginable, one step below an animal, since animals, unlike humans, have no choice.

When the distant look descended over Delhue's eyes like a transparent screen and the colonel withdrew into silence, Solis realized that he had hit a nerve. Unsure how to react, Solis settled back to wait for the answer that the chief of staff was obviously framing in his troubled mind. In the silence that followed, Solis began to appreciate how Hector Valendez could so easily discount the American division. Though their soldiers were, man for man, superior in training and firepower to any that Valendez could muster, the inability of their leaders to overcome their pettiness doomed their efforts. It was, Solis thought, as if the gods of war, after creating the magnificent fighting machine that the 11th Air Assault was, decided it was too perfect and therefore dangerous. So to even the playing field of war they gave the 11th leaders hamstrung with character flaws that would prevent them from leading in a manner that befit the courage and skills of their soldiers. Both Valendez and Solis realized that so long as these flawed leaders were left to their own devices, the 11th Air Assault would never become a serious threat to the FARC and their operations. And until Brigadier General Scott Dixon and his small staff came into being, this prophecy was unfolding as Valendez had foreseen.

But there was something disturbing happening that no one, including Valendez himself, understood or could explain. Despite the fact that the tempo of American operations was slowing down, those that were being conducted were bringing more pressure on the FARC. The old ratio of one operation against the FARC versus three against the drug cartel had been reversed within a matter of weeks. It was, Solis knew, a result of Dixon and his staff. How they were achieving this was not exactly clear, either to Solis or Valendez. It was, therefore, his task to find out how this new informal system worked so that the FARC could either short circuit it or if necessary destroy it.

Only after he noticed that Major Solis was still in his office and staring at him intently did Delhue realize that he had let his thoughts wander too far afield. Shaking his head as if that would clear it, he looked over to the major and smiled. "You'll have to excuse me, Major. I seem to have deserted you there for a moment."

Solis flashed a quick smile. "Please, sir. There is no need for you to apologize. It is I who should apologize for bothering you with such a minor question that should be so obvious.''

This comment caused the smile to disappear from Delhue's face. He grunted. ''Nothing, I'm afraid, is obvious or simple in this division, especially the relationship between SOUTH-COM Forward and us.'' While he had meant to say General Lane instead of us, Delhue's own code of ethics prevented him from being so openly disloyal to his superior, regardless of how poorly that man repaid such dedication. ''When they arrived, their sole purpose was what we told your Minister of Defense. They were to have been nothing more than a link between this headquarters and the commander-in-chief of SOUTHCOM, General Stratton. In a nutshell, Dixon and his people were to be nothing more than a glorified message center. The FARC's offensive in Los Llanos, however, changed that. During the first few days, the superlative manner in which Dixon's small staff tracked and predicted its progress, scope, and intent made people at SOUTHCOM and the Department of the Army sit up and take notice. It didn't take long for General Stratton at SOUTHCOM to begin disregarding our intelligence summaries and basing his decisions and directives to us on General Dixon's reports and recommendations. An aside that is not too obvious was the realization that our staff was out of touch with the reality of the situation down here, which in Stratton's mind meant that he needed to give us orders that were, to say the least, very specific and could not be ignored.''

Shifting in his seat, as if he found Delhue's explanation uncomfortable, Solis thought for a moment, then responded to Delhue's revelation. ''Do you mean to say, Colonel, that your General Stratton would take the word of a junior officer with so little time in Colombia over that of a more senior commander who had been here for months?''

''If you and your Minister of Defense knew Scotty Dixon, you would understand.''

''But, Colonel, we do not. That, I imagine, is why we cannot understand what is happening in the American command system. Perhaps if you could tell me a little about General Dixon, that would help.''

''Brigadier General Scott Dixon is one of the unique individuals that come along once in a lifetime. For him and those associated with him, the normal rules do not apply. Though to the best of my knowledge he is not an ambitious man who set out to do so, it would be a great surprise to just about anyone in the Army if he didn't eventually become the Chief of Staff of the Army."

If, Solis wondered while Delhue spoke, Dixon was not an ambitious man, how could he attain the high rank he had already achieved? Solis spoke what he was thinking. "I do not understand, Colonel, how this can be. Officers in my Army, regrettably, simply do not make it to the rank of general just by being good soldiers. What, sir, is this officer's secret?"

"No secret, Major. Luck, pure and simple. Luck has put him into some incredible situations where he was able to demonstrate his natural talents as a soldier and unique leadership skills. I can think of a dozen other officers with as much time as Dixon has in the Army who are smarter, have more formal schooling, are better leaders, and present a sharper image than General Dixon but haven't to date achieved one tenth of what he has. If there is a key to Dixon's success, it's his ability to keep his head in unusual circumstances, use all the people he has to the best of their abilities without abusing them or wasting them, and to persevere."

"You seem to admire him."

Delhue grunted. "Any soldier worth his salt has to admire Scotty Dixon and his achievements."

"Why then," Solis fired back without thinking, "does General Lane hate him so and scheme to discredit him?"

The bluntness of the question rocked Delhue back in his seat. That there was an open rift between Lane and Dixon was no secret. Anyone with eyes and ears could see it and its manifestations. But to openly speak of it, that was an entirely different matter. For several seconds Delhue looked at Solis and considered ignoring his question. Then in an instant he dropped all pretenses. Taking a deep breath, Delhue let go. "Because, Major, Lane resents Dixon. Dixon is everything that he isn't. Dixon has every chance to become what he wants. And the most disturbing thing in General Lane's mind is that while he has worked, probably from the time he was a second lieutenant to now, to reach the top, fortune and chance have catapulted Dixon into the limelight and high regard that Lane so craves. To General Lane, Dixon does not deserve what he has achieved." Delhue paused, thought about what he was about to say, then decided to go ahead. "General Lane has made it his mission in life to punish General Dixon."

"Punish him for what?"

"For being the man that *he* isn't."

Though he had known that these American officers had clay feet, like many of the senior officers in his own Army, Delhue's blunt and unabashed condemnation of General Lane in the harshest terms struck Solis with a force that he wasn't prepared for. After a minute Solis looked up at Delhue and mumbled half to himself, "Then all of this, it is a personal matter after all, isn't it?"

Nodding, Delhue dropped his head down and looked at the blotter on his desk. "I'm afraid so, Major. As much as I hate to admit it, we are making major decisions based on personal feelings and not military necessity."

"But the shifting of your 3rd Brigade from the west to support our operations in the Eastern Zone, that was a sound and logical decision."

Looking up, Delhue shook his head. "The only reason that brigade went east was because General Dixon pointed out to General Stratton that the counteroffensive by your Army would very soon run out of steam without our support. It is his opinion that unless we keep the pressure on the FARC in the Eastern Zone, the Farcees will keep on rolling west, straight into Bogotá. The order to move the reinforced brigade east originated with General Stratton, not Lane."

The realization that Valendez was right, as he had always proven to be, startled Solis, though it shouldn't have. Hector Valendez was always right, just like this General Dixon who so worried him. In an instant everything that had been confused was clear. The contest now was no longer one between government and rebels. It wasn't even a struggle between the opposing forces. It was all a series of bouts between individuals. It was Hector Valendez against General Scott Dixon. Everyone, Solis realized, was merely a pawn in this fight. The question now, one that Valendez would need to ponder, was how he would play the pawn that General Lane had become.

Thanking Delhue for his time and insight, Solis got up and left the office, turning this last thought over and over in his mind. Finally confident that Hector Valendez would find a way, Solis smiled. Victory, he suddenly saw, was theirs for the taking. All the pieces were there, all the cards were neatly stacked up. All that remained to be done was to tug at the right card and everything would come tumbling down. "Yes," Solis whispered, "victory *is* ours."

CHAPTER 11

November 12

THOUGH SCOTT DIXON WAS NEVER FAR FROM HIS MIND, THERE was much that C. B. Lane had to do to shore up his sagging reputation. For while it was true that Stratton was listening to Dixon, Lane was still the senior commander on the ground. The 11th Air Assault was his. In the end, when all was said and done, it would be the achievements of the division that would be remembered by promotion boards and not the staff work of an ad hoc headquarters. All Lane had to do was to make sure that his name, and his name alone, was associated with those achievements. "Let that little shit whisper all he wants in Stratton's ear," he told his aide one day. "It's my name that goes on the orders that start the battles, and after this is all over it will be my name that will go down as the man who fought and won the war in Colombia."

Saying this and making it so were two entirely different matters. On the surface it seemed simple. All Lane needed to do was to act the role, to ensure that the people in his command and the media saw him as a fighting general. That role, however, was not one that he wore well. From start to finish, Lane was as tied to his headquarters as a sailor lashed to the mast to weather a storm. In World War I the French referred to such commanders as château generals because of their practice of never leaving their elegant palaces and châteaus well in the rear of artillery range. In the calm, cool, clean atmosphere of their confiscated estates, the château generals of World War I and their staffs worked in comfort and almost splendid isolation. Though no one ever thought of doing so, the comparison between Lane and his World War I counterparts would have been striking.

C. B. Lane, a man who had built his reputation upon his administrative prowess and not his war-fighting abilities, knew he would be out of his element in the field. Like the French generals of the past, he had difficulty absorbing, sorting, and using the information that assailed a front-line commander like a machine gun. Lane's mind just couldn't deal with more than one or two things at a time. That was why he built around him a large staff manned by people who wouldn't rush him and would cater to his needs. In the quiet, well-appointed headquarters of the 11th Air Assault Division, hand-picked staff officers kept him from being overwhelmed with data, sorting it out and feeding it to him in digestible packages as he needed it. Safe in the cool quietness of his well-lit office, C. B. Lane worked on one problem or issue at a time in the same patient and orderly manner that a farmer plows each of his fields in its turn. Though he personally did not accomplish much, what he did produce was masterpieces. In the past, such well-crafted masterpieces delivered at the right time to an appreciative superior were enough to mark Lane for promotion. Now with events turning on him faster than he could comprehend, he realized that he needed to change his style, and neither he nor his division was ready for that.

As they walked toward Lane's command-and-control helicopter that morning, his young aide noticed his general did so with a deliberateness and stiffness that reminded him of a man approaching the electric chair. His demeanor and his expression, so unlike those that he used at staff briefings and command visits, betrayed Lane's apprehensions. While some would interpret his behavior as advance signs of cowardliness, his aide knew better. "While the general," he had been told by the G-3, "was afraid of no man, embarrassment was a different matter. The old man is deathly afraid that he's going to find himself in a situation which he has no control over, and that he's going to make a dumb move. Our job," the G-3 summed up for the aide, "is to make sure that he doesn't get himself into a bind like that." When the aide asked how exactly they were supposed to do that, the G-3 shrugged and patted the aide's shoulder. "Good question." With that, the G-3 had turned and walked away.

With all the formalities of a dress parade the crew chief of the UH-60 helicopter that Lane would ride in today greeted him and handed him his aviator's helmet. The aide, scurrying about the helicopter and entering from the other side, quickly took his place in front of the massive radio panel that controlled all the radios as well as the intercoms in the rear of the helicopter. As he settled himself in, placing the general's map where both could see it and use it, and began to check to make sure that all the radios were set properly, the aide was still wondering how he was going to keep his boss from messing all over himself.

The situation they were flying into, briefed at the 0700 hours morning briefing, had all the makings of a real circus. Even the manner in which the 11th Air Assault had become involved was in itself somewhat of a farce. It all began two days prior when a Colombian Army battalion seized a town named El Frío on the Meta River. This effort was part of the northern arm of a government counteroffensive aimed at rolling back the spectacular gains made by the FARC. Unfortunately, the battalion that had taken El Frío was unsupported, leaving it vulnerable to attack, which the FARC promptly did. Pounced upon by an FARC force estimated to be two battalions plus, the Colombian battalion was quickly isolated and mauled. Though they had managed to hang on throughout the eleventh of November, the last remnants of the Colombian battalion had been overrun just before dawn on the twelfth.

Because the purpose of the relief effort to save the Colombian battalion that was to be mounted by two battalions of the 11th Air Assault's 3rd Brigade was no longer valid, the mission was canceled immediately by the 3rd Brigade commander. Lane was not informed of this decision until his 0700 hours briefing. Not waiting for the G-3 operations briefer to finish describing the situation, Lane stood up, walked to the front of the room, and began to speak. As this was the first time that Lane had ever done this in all their months in Colombia, no one knew what to do or what to expect. In silence they watched as he took a fighting stance, feet apart and hands on hips, before speaking. When he began to speak, he had their attention. "There isn't a damned thing we can do to save those poor bastards in El Frío. I'm sure they did as well as they could," he said in his finest fighting-general voice. "But just because that battle's over doesn't mean the whole game has to be given up." Several staff officers turned and looked quizzically at each other, each wondering where their commander was headed. Lane, either ignoring this or not seeing it, continued. "We can still go in there and extract a pound of flesh from the Farcees before they have a chance to break up their battalions and melt away into the bush."

While his staff gazed at him bewildered, wondering what he was driving at, Lane took inspiration from his own speech. Looking to his aide at the back of the room, he bellowed, "Jimmy, get me Henry R. Tell him I have a new mission for his brigade." The assembled staff officers followed Lane as he moved to the rear of the room with a slow deliberateness that spoke of confidence and power. Except for Lane's footfalls, the only sounds being generated in the room were those made by the aide as he placed the call to Colonel Henry R. Johnson, commander of the 3rd Brigade. When Henry R. came on the line, the aide responded to him with a solemn voice. "Colonel Johnson, please hold for General Lane." By that time, Lane was there waiting for his aide to hand him the phone.

Grabbing the phone as he seated himself where his aide normally sat, Lane settled down and began speaking. "Henry, I know that relief mission of yours is a bust. Seems like the Colombians in El Frío just couldn't hack it."

This comment caused Major Solis, seated off to one side, to draw in a deep breath and glare at Lane. No one except Delhue noticed Solis's reaction. When, after the briefest of seconds, Solis saw Delhue staring at him, he knew that his face had betrayed him and quickly dropped it into a deadpan stare as he turned back to where Lane was berating the 3rd Brigade commander.

"You know, H," Lane said with the expression of a father admonishing an errant son, "I'm rather disappointed that you scrubbed the whole thing. Christ, we got the bastards out in the

HAROLD COYLE

open. Now's the time to hit them, when we know where the little bastards are.''

For a moment there was silence as Lane listened. Slowly the watching staff could see Lane's facial muscles tighten up. He was becoming angry. They had all seen that look before and they knew what was coming. When he spoke this time, any hint of warmth or understanding, real or faked, was gone. Lane was angry and he wanted the commander of the 3rd Brigade to know it. "Listen, Colonel, you just listen. I have no intention of coming down there and showing you how to run your brigade. But if I have to, I will." The air in the room was heavy with tension. Once Lane got himself worked up like this, anything could happen, and what usually happened wasn't good. Today would be no different.

"We have been given a hell of an opportunity to smash two Farcee battalions, and I'll be damned if an unimaginative brigade commander is going to blow it." By now Lane's face was red. As he spoke, he was jabbing his free hand forward, index finger extended, as if trying to poke the brigade commander on the other end of the line in the chest. "I expect a maximum effort on this. The G-2 people here feel that those people are going to pull in their horns and run back east as fast as they can. If you drop one battalion well east of El Frío into a blocking position and another to the south to keep them from slipping away that way, with the Meta River to the north, we'll have them in a box. If you pull your 3rd Battalion out of whatever it's doing, drop them west of town, and have them sweep east, we'll have the Farcees between a rock and a hard place. That should be simple enough for even you to understand."

From his seat at the front of the room, Delhue hung his head and shook it. How embarrassing, he thought, it had to be for Henry R. to be spoken to in such a manner. H.R. was an exceptional commander, a natural when it came to leadership. He had proven his mettle in every assignment and had won his current position on merit, demonstrated ability in peace and war, and plain hard work. Now, in what would ordinarily be one of the high points of any soldier's career, to have to suffer such undeserved abuse was, to Delhue, unconscionable. That he and every other officer in that room should sit there in

216

silence and allow Lane to berate Colonel Henry R. was just as onerous. To Delhue, the idea that Lane believed that he, by virtue of his rank and position, could do as he pleased, unchecked, and treat people in such a manner was indicative of a system gone wrong. But what, he wondered, could he do? What options did he have available? As bad as it was to turn a blind eye to such goings-on, any alternative went against everything that he and every other officer in that room had been taught. Lane was by virtue of his commission and rank their superior ranking officer. And they, every man and woman in the room, by virtue of their oath of commission, was obligated to obey his orders so long as they were legal and moral. Nothing, after all, said that you had to like your superior, only obey him.

By the time Delhue looked back up, Lane was finishing his rather one-sided conversation with the 3rd Brigade commander and preparing to hang up. As bad as the previous part of his tirade had been, the last portion bothered Delhue even more. "You will, " Lane told the brigade commander, "make whatever coordination and reconnaissance you need to do in the next two hours and get this operation moving. This is an air assault division. Speed and mobility are what we're about. Now get to it and start earning your pay for a change."

Delhue was not the only person in the room that winced at Lane's last comment. It had been, several officers felt, totally uncalled for. That it was not unusual for their commanding general to degrade people in such a manner did not justify it. Finished, Lane handed the telephone back to his aide and smiled. "Gentlemen, if all goes well, by nightfall we will have two enemy battalions in our hip pocket and another streamer to hang on the division flag."

While Lane stood there before his assembled staff, Delhue turned away and looked into the faces of the young captains and majors beaming glowing smiles at their division commander. That Lane and his abusive manner were beyond help was a given. He would, Delhue knew, continue to ride down his subordinates until the day he left the Army. What bothered Delhue the most at the moment was the idea that there, in a room full of admiring and still impressionable young officers, a new crop of officers was being trained to carry on that perversion of leadership on officers who were yet to come forth. How sad it was, Delhue realized as Lane walked out and his entourage of loyal staff officers followed him out of the room. How sad it was for their nation and his Army.

Of course, not everyone was disappointed with the results of Lane's actions. Major Solis knew without having to be told that the hasty operation directed by Lane would be welcome news to Hector Valendez. For the trap that Lane expected to set would snare nothing. It would be the FARC rather than the Americans who would end the day with another victory. For Hector Valendez had never had any intention of turning and running back east into the hinterlands of Los Llanos. Westward, now and until final victory, had become the watchword for the FARC. The days of cautious hit-and-run operations, a sudden strike here or there followed by rapid dispersion, were over. It would be the battalion landed west of El Frío that would become the hunted, not the hunter.

Glancing down at his watch, Solis quickly calculated the time he had. Though he would have preferred to use his usual secure means of passing his information back to Valendez, that was far too slow. He therefore decided to use his emergency backup system for direct and rapid contact. Though it was risky, and there was little danger that Lane's master stroke would yield anything, the potential damage that prepared regular-force battalions could inflict on an unwary American infantry battalion was, Solis felt, well worth any chances he took.

Doing his best to mask his haste or eagerness, Solis walked out of the Ministry of Defense building and onto the busy street. After he cleared the final checkpoint, he headed toward the post office, where he would use a public phone to send his flash traffic. Freed from the prying eyes of the Ministry building, Solis could relax and smile. Two, he thought, could use speed and mobility. Besides, as one senior Colombian officer once pointed out to him after listening to a briefing given by the staff of the 11th Air Assault Division, the ability to go forward rapidly often does nothing but get you into trouble that much faster.

* * *

Within minutes, warning orders implementing Major General C. B. Lane's inspiration were en route to the units that would be involved. For the two battalions that had been slated as part of the relief operation, adjusting themselves to their new tasks was relatively simple. The companies that made up the 1st Battalion of the 417th Infantry and the 1st Battalion of the 513th Infantry were ready to go in minutes. All pre-combat checks in preparation for their previous mission had been made. All supplies, from combat rations to ammunition, were still on hand, distributed, and in the hands of the troopers of both battalions. All the staffs of those two battalions needed at that moment were line of departure time, the location where they were headed, and a mission statement that told them what was expected of them once they got there.

In the 3rd Battalion, 511th Infantry, things wouldn't be so easy. Not only would its ultimate mission be more difficult, for they had been designated as the sweep battalion in this shoestring operation, but their companies were scattered about the brigade area executing diverse missions. Company A, still under the command of their former executive officer, First Lieutenant Barbara O'Fallen, was the most available and was assigned the mission of providing security to the brigade base camp and serving as the brigade reserve. Company B, under First Lieutenant Dan Krammer, was one day out on a three-day sweep of the area around the brigade base camp. Though they were only fifteen kilometers northeast of the brigade command post when Lane was issuing his orders to the brigade commander, it would take them three hours by foot to make it back. Company C, the only line company still under the command of its original commanding officer, Captain Frank Walters, was at that moment en route back into the brigade base camp, having completed a four-day dismounted sweep to the southeast. Though they were closer than Company B, four days of patrolling during the day, ambush duty at night, and incessant marching in the late fall rains and heat had taken their toll. The time needed to pull them in and turn them around for their new mission would be equal to or greater than that for Company B.

The senior leadership of the 3rd of the 511th was just as scattered. Still anxious to escape facing the problems that the September 21 ambush had visited upon his battalion, Lieutenant Colonel Harold Cerro continued to seek refuge by going out into the field with one of his units every chance he could. Today he was with Company B, the one company that carried the least amount of animosity as a result of their perceived plight.

Major Edward J. Bond, the new battalion executive officer, was with the brigade supply officer and the 3rd of the 511th's own S-4 supply officer, paying a visit to the division support command where he hoped to learn something about the mechanics involved in keeping an infantry battalion deployed in Colombia supplied and maintained. Only Captain Nancy Kozak was at the battalion command post when the initial warning order came in over the land line from brigade alerting her that they had a mission.

That message, relayed by the brigade operations officer himself, was short and deceptively simple: "3rd of the 511th will, on order, conduct an air assault into a land zone or zones, to be designated, west of the town of El Frío. 3rd of the 511th, in cooperation with 1st of the 417th and 1st of the 513th, which will be taking up blocking positions to the east and south of El Frío respectively, will conduct offensive operations to find, fix, and destroy two FARC regular-force battalions currently operating in and around El Frío." When Kozak asked the brigade S-3 when they could expect to receive the brigade operations order, there was a pause. When the brigade ops officer finally did speak, he told Kozak in a very guarded manner, "Nancy, don't expect much more than what I just gave you." With that, he terminated the conversation and left Kozak the task of pulling the scattered elements of the battalion back into the brigade base camp while preparing an order based on the sparsest of information and guidance.

Flown back to the brigade base camp in the brigade commander's own aircraft, Cerro was greeted with Kozak's estimate of the situation. In it she listed three variations or options of how she thought the battalion would execute its assigned mission. Of the three, Cerro picked the one that Kozak herself favored and had spent the most time developing. It wasn't that she had driven her commander toward it. On the contrary, after having worked with Cerro for so long, she intuitively knew how he preferred to operate and what he would have done himself if he had been left to his own devices. Good operations officers are supposed to do that, and no one who saw Kozak at work would deny that she was good.

The plan, like all plans that Cerro and Kozak developed, was simple. After landing five kilometers west of El Frío, the battalion would move forward with two companies abreast, with A under First Lieutenant O'Fallen on the right, and C, commanded by Captain Walters, on the left. B Company, led by First Lieutenant Krammer, would follow A. Krammer's job would be to react to the situation as it was developed by either one or both of the lead companies. Following far enough behind so that his company didn't get involved right off the bat in any firefight A Company might stumble into, Krammer would, on order, move forward to reinforce or attack through A, swing left to reinforce or attack through C, or go right and extend the battalion's frontage or outflank any opposition A or C ran into. This formation, two up and one back, gave Cerro sufficient flexibility to meet just about any contingency while providing the widest possible frontage they dared present.

This last item was of great importance, for the enemy situation in and around El Frío, even after the attached cavalry troop finished its recon of the area, was ambiguous as hell. Though Cerro had wanted to go with one company forward and two back, his mission required him to cover as wide an area as was prudent. "Your battalion," Henry R. told him during his briefing, "will be the beaters. Your task is to drive the Farcees out of hiding and into the waiting guns of the 1st of the 417th and the 1st of the 513th. Failing that, if the enemy chooses to turn on you and fight, you must become the hammer while the other two battalions provide you with an anvil upon which to smash him."

While all of this sounded good at the orders briefing in the safety of the brigade base camp, Cerro knew in his heart that his battalion, if called upon to play hammer, would be a very fragile one at best. The battalion, he pointed out to Henry R., was not ready and could not be ready for at least twenty-four hours for this type of operation. Even A Company, assigned to base security, was not well rested, given their need to keep 50 percent of their strength up and alert all night securing the base perimeter or lying in ambush. The other two companies were worse off, having been involved in operations at the time of the alert. "At best," Cerro pointed out, "I'll have twenty, maybe thirty minutes together with my staff and all my company commanders before we have to load up on the slicks and move out. Add to that the fact that I'll never even have the opportunity to talk face-to-face with the commanders of the other two battalions involved and you have, sir, the makings of a potential disaster."

Though Henry R. listened patiently and attentively, and the excuses that Cerro was giving were all valid, he knew that the real reason Cerro was uncomfortable with the idea of this operation was confidence. For both men knew in their hearts that after the September 21 ambush both Cerro and the soldiers under his command had lost confidence in themselves and each other. No one spoke of this openly, no one said so in so many words. They didn't need to. A trained eye could see it in the faces of the leaders and soldiers of the battalion and in the manner in which they carried themselves and performed their assigned duties. The battalion had been broken in spirit. Henry R. tried to protect Cerro and his battalion while at the same time giving his battalion small, easy missions in the hope that these would help collectively to restore their confidence. But this did not happen. As the days and weeks slipped by, Henry R. realized that what had happened during the ambush and immediately after had left a mark on Cerro and most of his officers that was beyond his ability to erase. "They are," he told Colonel Delhue in a confidential conversation one night, "nothing but a shadow of their former selves. I dread the day when I'll have to put them into another hard fight."

That day, Henry R. knew, had come when Lane had issued him his marching orders that morning. At first he tried to work out a plan in which the 3rd of the 511th would go in as one of the blocking forces. This option, however, was quickly shot down by his own operations officer. "The blocking forces, sir, must be in place first, both to the east and south. Since the 1st of the 417th and the 1st of the 513th are on hand and ready, they have to be the blocking forces. Besides," he added, "since the Farcees will be pulling back to the east, or maybe even to the south, it will be the blocking forces and not the sweep battalion that will bear the brunt of this fight. The sweep battalion's only task is to hurry them up and clean up any stragglers.''

Seeing the logic, Henry R. let the order of deployment and tasks to the battalions stand. Still, he wasn't ready to give up. As much as he hated to do so, he went back to division shortly before noon and asked that the division reserve battalion be released to his control for this operation. ''The 3rd of the 511th,'' he explained to the division G-3, ''is still scattered all over hell's half acre. It will be hours before they'll be in place, and even then they will not be in any shape for a really tough stand-up fight.''

The G-3 didn't even take Henry R.'s request seriously. ''You know General Lane's feelings on the use of the division reserve, sir,'' he responded in a rather uninterested voice. ''The only way we can get the old man to release it is in an emergency. Since my morning sitrep shows your brigade having three battalions available and the operation calls for only three battalions, I don't see how I can justify adding another to your troop list.'' Then with a sarcastic tone in his voice the G-3 added, ''You can always call General Lane yourself, sir, and take the matter up with him.'' The G-3, of course, knew that Henry R. wouldn't do that, especially after the verbal beating he had taken that morning. Having tried his best, he faced the inevitable and told Cerro as best he could that he and his battalion were going.

Cerro and his staff had never assumed otherwise. Almost to a man, everyone who had been involved in the September 21 incident went about their duties in preparation for this mission with a rather fatalistic attitude. When Nancy Kozak, in the midst of writing the brief operations order that they would use to launch the battalion into the attack directed by Lane, turned to her operations sergeant and said, ''Well, this is it,'' he knew what she meant.

It was no secret, once word got out, that this mission was *it*, the test. There would be no chance for Cerro to escape his problems, which included a crippling lack of confidence in himself and the battalion. Today his skill as a battalion commander and his ability to coordinate the activities of all three line companies at once and lead soldiers in battle would be tested for the first time since September 21. His operations officer, Nancy Kozak, wouldn't be able to use her staff work and activities to busy her mind so that it wouldn't be free to dwell on the personal issues and concerns that had been eating away at her self-confidence like ravenous parasites. Though the methods of escaping coming to terms with their personal issues had been different, as different as the two people themselves, the results were the same. Issues that needed to be dealt with were ignored. Personal problems, frailties, and wounds that could have a serious impact on their performance, and hence that of the battalion, had not been tended to. Only the absence of a crisis had kept the 3rd of the 511th, and the soldiers and officers in it, from self-destructing. All that had eyes saw this, from the brigade commander on down the line. And now that afternoon, as commanders and staff officers rushed about preparing for the arrival of the helicopters, everyone realized that just such a crisis was at hand. The day of reckoning was here.

CHAPTER 12

November 12

IT WAS LATE AFTERNOON BEFORE THE FIRST LIFT, CARRYING A and C Company of the 3rd Battalion, approached the two landing zones west of El Frío. B Company, following the first two waves, was due to follow A Company fifteen minutes after that company had landed and departed the landing zone. Hal Cerro, as was his custom, was going in with the first wave. Since First Lieutenant Barbara O'Fallen was the most junior of the company commanders and Captain Frank Walters of C Company the most senior, Cerro opted to move initially with O'Fallen's unit. Kozak, having learned from the September 21 incident, would remain airborne during the initial phase of the operation. There, together with the battalion fire support officer, Captain Peter Crippen, the battalion intel officer, First Lieutenant Marion A. Dietz, and Sergeant Andy Pender of her own section, she would provide a communications link with brigade, the other two battalions involved in the operation, and the two batteries of 105mm artillery supporting the operation. If and when attack helicopters were committed to the fight, she would coordinate their activities also. By this arrangement Cerro on the ground was left free to concentrate on maneuvering the battalion while Kozak, quite literally above and away from the fight below, could call on and control whatever support was called for by the situation.

225

Kozak's UH-60, with extra man-portable radios lashed into vacant seats and their antennas hanging out open doors, was not alone in the skies above El Frío. Zipping about over one unit on the ground or another, like an impatient dragonfly skimming from lily pad to lily pad, Major General C. B. Lane's command-and-control helicopter fluttered about. He was there to make sure that his operation went down the way he had envisioned it. "Sometimes, Jim," he told his aide, "you got to sit on these people if you want results."

Traveling about the same circuit but at a discreet distance was Colonel Henry R. Johnson's command-and-control aircraft. He, like Lane, was moving from one place to another, landing every so often to talk with battalion commanders on the ground while waiting for Cerro's battalion to appear. Worried over the total lack of reaction from the Farcees, Henry R. spent the balance of the afternoon glancing at his watch, watching to the south for the appearance of the 3rd of the 511th, and casting every now and then a wary eye toward Lane's helicopter.

The two senior commanders and Kozak were joined on occasion by other people flying about. They were either waiting for something to happen, like the two senior commanders, or going about their duties oblivious to them. One of the aircraft waiting was a liaison helicopter from the division's attack helicopter battalion. It made its appearance just as the first of the two blocking forces went in. Cerro's request that the attack helicopters work over his landing zones before his unit went in was denied. "It would," he had been informed, "serve no purpose other than to give away our intentions." Though he argued that the Farcees would know what was afoot by the time his unit arrived, Henry R. ended the discussion by blandly stating, "That's a call from Division, Hal." So with nothing to do, the helicopter simply loitered about lazily, waiting for the enemy to show themselves so that it could bring to bear the devastating firepower that the attack helicopters of the battalion could deliver.

Another helicopter carrying correspondents drawn from the media pool to cover the operation also joined the traffic aloft. Like a frog jumping from one small American-controlled pond to another, this helicopter would spring up out of the bush and quickly touch down whenever a group of American soldiers were seen gathering below. Added to these and an occasional stray helicopter darting in and out of the area to deliver supplies and equipment to the 417th, 513th, and the artillery batteries already in place were other aircraft with no apparent task at hand, which only contributed to the cluttered air space. From Kozak's helicopter, Sergeant Pender watched all of this activity. Never known to hold his thoughts, he commented over the intercom to no one in particular, "Looks like the New Jersey Turnpike on a Labor Day weekend."

Kozak, though she heard him, ignored his comment. For no sooner had he finished his halfhearted attempt at humor than she saw two groups of dots coming in fast and low from the south. At first they looked like a swarm of insects, insignificant and distant. Those dots, she knew, were companies A and C. A quick glance at her watch told her there wasn't much time before sunset, three, maybe four hours at best. She, like everyone else in the brigade, knew that if the Farcees couldn't be brought to bay before that, then the thin line of troops that the two blocking battalions had out on the ground would never be able to keep the enemy contained. "In the darkness," the brigade commander had stressed to Cerro, "the other people would go through the 417th and the 513th like water through a sieve."

Against this deadline the soldiers of the 511th had rushed their preparations as best they could. Though nothing major was overlooked, no one felt completely comfortable. From beginning to end this was, Kozak knew, a thrown-together affair. Still, as she watched the distant dots to the south grow rapidly in size and slowly start to take the shape of transport helicopters, it was an event that would not be postponed or canceled. Rock Six, the radio call sign for the division commander, had a personal interest in this affair, and nothing short of divine intervention or a cataclysmic disaster could stop it. Ordering the pilot of her own helicopter to move off to the west, away from the battalions' approach to their landing zones, Kozak watched as the first of the helicopters carrying A Company slowed, flared out, and began to land. They were committed.

* * *

Below in that helicopter First Lieutenant O'Fallen unsnapped her seat belt, pulled herself up into the open door, and prepared to exit the aircraft as soon as she felt the wheels hit dirt. Looking back over her shoulder, she was about to yell something to the soldiers behind her when her entire body was suddenly thrown back against another soldier waiting to exit. The noise of the helicopter masked the sound of gunfire coming from the ground. Only when she flopped back onto the floor and her head flipped back, revealing lifeless eyes that were rolling back up into her head, did the troopers with her realize that she had been shot. Three days before her twenty-fifth birthday, Barbara O'Fallen, the only child of a Wisconsin couple, died, ending her parents' dream of grandchildren and a normal happy life.

Like a string of firecrackers, gunfire erupted from two adjoining sides of the landing zone, raking the incoming helicopters that hung for a moment like suspended clay pigeons in a shooting gallery. In this sudden and unexpected hail of gunfire, the courage and skill of each helicopter pilot was laid bare. Some, with nerves that never failed them, continued to bore on, altering neither their speed nor rate of descent. Others, anxious to get out of the grueling cross fire as quickly as possible, practically did a nose dive, jerking up on their controls at the last second and thumping their aircraft onto the ground with a jarring thud. A few flinched, jerking to one side or the other so as to avoid the streams of tracers they saw racing toward them head-on. One pilot, totally unnerved by the experience, pulled up and away from the maelstrom below. That only one minor collision occurred was nothing short of a miracle. Even more miraculous was the fact that most of the soldiers survived that collision.

This fact, however, even if known, would have brought no comfort to Hal Cerro as his own helicopter came in at the tail end of A Company's wave. A disaster, he thought. He had another fucking disaster in the making, and his battalion wasn't even on the ground yet. Intently he watched, blocking as best he could all emotions and feelings as he took in as much as he could before landing. So intense had his concentration been that it was a moment or two before he noticed that not only was he not getting closer to the ground but it seemed as if he was moving away from it. Dumfounded, he looked away from the spreading firefight below and over to the pilot. Without an aircraft crewman's helmet on, Cerro had to yell to get the pilot's attention. "What in the hell are you doing? Land! Take this thing down, *now!*"

Cocking his head back, the pilot tried to tell Cerro something, but he didn't hear. Instead, Cerro leaped up and at the pilot, bumping their Kevlar helmets as he did so. Contorting his body around the pilot's high-backed seat so that his face was almost in the pilot's, Cerro yelled at him, spitting as he did so. "You take this piece of shit down there now or I'll blow your fucking brains out all over the inside of your pretty fucking helicopter."

The young aviator glanced from the firefight below, over to Cerro's face, twisted beyond recognition in anger, and then at his instrument panel. Without another word, he shoved his control stick down and over to the side, throwing Cerro off balance but bringing the helicopter around and back into the landing zone. Pulling himself away from the pilot, Cerro looked out the door, saw the ground rushing up, and prepared to jump as soon as it was close enough. This would be it. In his heart he knew it. And although the idea had never really formed itself into a clear, coherent thought in his mind, Lieutenant Colonel Hal Cerro had no intention of surviving this fight.

From their perch well above the landing zone, Kozak saw it all. Though she didn't know of the distress that her battalion commander was in, or of the death of First Lieutenant O'Fallen, the severity of the situation was immediately and brutally obvious. Keying the intercom that linked her, the fire support officer, the intel officer, and Pender, she called for immediate suppressive fires from the supporting artillery batteries. Crippen, the fire support officer, shot back without thinking, "They won't fire them until the helicopters have cleared. We have to wait."

Kozak, animated by what she was seeing and her own feeling of being unable to help A Company through direct action, shot back without turning her face away from the scene below. "Call them, damn it, and get them ready. Shoot as soon as you can." No sooner had she finished that order than a call from the brigade commander came in over the radio asking for an update. Turning her head toward Pender, she keyed the intercom. "Tell Henry R. that Company A is catching hell in their LZ. We're calling for fires now. Status of C Company is unknown." With that she turned back to look out the open door of the helicopter in an effort to sort out the chaos on the ground. The thought that she and her aircraft might be in danger never crossed her mind. And even if it had, she wouldn't have done anything different. As much as she didn't like the idea of being up there, away from the fight itself, she knew she was where she belonged and had no intention of leaving, regardless of the risk, real or imagined.

From the north bank of the Meta River, Hector Valendez paced back and forth in front of a concealed 14.5mm anti-aircraft machine gun. Every few steps, he would stop, cock his head to one side, and listen as best he could to the sounds of battle. At the end of his little circuit, he would again stop and look down at his radio operator, Rafael Dario. Without having to be asked, Dario would look up and inform his commander that there still was no word that the local-force platoons covering the landing zones were withdrawing. With a huff, the only sign that he showed that he was getting angry, Valendez would turn around and start his circuit again. The plan, he knew, was unraveling, and there was nothing, nothing at all, that he could do from where he stood to pull it back together.

It had been a simple plan. It had to be. There was just not enough time for anything more ambitious. With the little time he had been given to prepare, Valendez had broken his three local-force companies down into platoon-sized elements and scattered them about, with each one covering any large open area that could accommodate an air assault force. His two main-force battalions, in the meantime, had been withdrawn to the southwest, where they would remain hidden. During the day, the scattered local-force units were to have developed the situation. At night, if and when the American units pulled into defensive perimeters, Valendez intended to throw one or both of his regular battalions at the most vulnerable of the three American battalions.

That, at any rate, had been the plan that he had briefed. He had made it clear to the commanders of each of the local-force companies that their units were to harass the Americans but avoid decisive engagements. He had carefully picked his words so that there would be no mistaking his intent. "Units," he had instructed each of the local-force company commanders, "that make contact at landing zones will take the Americans under fire for no more than five minutes at the most. After that you will break contact before the Americans bring the full weight of their awesome firepower to bear. If you tarry too long, if you try to take advantage of an advantage that you have achieved, no matter how great, you and your men will pay for your delay with your lives. So don't wait. Fire, confuse them, draw some blood, then break it off."

Someone, Valendez realized, had not listened. Instead, as he reached the anti-aircraft machine gun again, the sounds of small-arms fire, now mixed in with artillery fire, continued to drift across the river to him. Stomping his foot, he cursed. He cursed at whoever it was that had chosen to disobey him. He cursed at the Americans flying so arrogantly above the town of El Frío in their helicopters. Finally he cursed at the pair of 14.5mm anti-aircraft guns he had deployed north of the river. Though his choice had been a good one when he had made it, they were unable now under present conditions to do anything of value. Though the gunners continued to track any aircraft that appeared to be headed their way, they didn't fire. To do so, unless the aircraft drifted out over the river itself, would be useless. So, like Valendez, who stood there and mumbled beneath his breath, the anti-aircraft machine gunners watched and waited for things to work themselves out.

It was the fighters of the Number 2 Platoon, 27th Local Defense Company, recruited from the town of El Frío and its surrounding area, that had added the unexpected friction to Valendez's plan. Local men, every one, they had no intention of giving ground when they had the enemy to their front. They were tired of watching. They were tired of waiting. They had watched three days before as the Colombian battalion moved forward and brought devastation down on their families and homes. Their discipline had held. And the next day, when they supported the attack of the two main-force battalions against

231

the government troops, they had held themselves in check, providing a base of fire while the better-trained regular-force fighters closed with and broke the back of the enemy's forces. Even after walking through the streets asking stunned survivors about the fate of their loved ones, the men of the 27th Company refrained from killing the government soldiers who had gone over to the FARC at the last moment rather than die.

But now with their blood lust unquenched, with revenge burning in the mind of every man in Number 2 Platoon, neither the orders from their own platoon leader, himself the father of three who had once been a shopkeeper in El Frío, nor Valendez's plan could keep them from meting out the vengeance that they so much needed to purge from their souls. To a man, without a word having to be spoken, the fighters of Number 2 Platoon had resolved to stand where they were and bring the bastard Yankees to their knees. It wasn't that any of them were fanatics. It wasn't that they had a death wish. On the contrary, they were all simple men, each and every one. They were men who had answered Valendez's call to arms and had come forth to defend their homes. Now, however, many of those homes and the families that they had tried to defend had been wiped away by the army of a corrupt government that ruled from a strange, distant capital. All that mattered now to these men was that they extract what they believed was justice, simple, brutal, biblical justice. So, against Valendez's wishes and plans, Number 2 Platoon stood its ground, pouring volley after volley of fire into the confused and shattered ranks of A Company, 3rd Battalion of the 511th Infantry, as fast as they could.

Out on the fireswept clearing, the soldiers of A Company, now under the command of the only surviving officer in the company, Second Lieutenant Tyler Wiezman, were flooded with images of the September 21 debacle. For the second time in as many months they found themselves in a desperate situation, pinned by heavy enemy fire and taking casualties at a prodigious rate. The memory of the previous encounter, the brutal heat, the devastating small-arms fire, and the ever-present specter of death all about them had a numbing effect. Even the best efforts of the sergeants and Lieutenant Wiezman couldn't shake the sixty-odd men and women who were still alive and unwounded from their inactivity. Singly and in small groups of two and three, the sky troopers of A Company hugged the ground with all their might and prayed for darkness or deliverance.

Only two things kept those soldiers from breaking and running, despite the tremendous volume of automatic weapons fire that was being thrown at them. The first was immediate and effective artillery fire, called for and directed by Nancy Kozak and Peter Crippen from above. Heeding Kozak's order, Crippen brought down volley after volley of 105mm howitzer fire as soon as the last helicopter had dropped the troopers of A Company off and cleared the landing zone. Firing ICM, or improved conventional ammunitions, at first, Kozak quickly realized that the Farcees were well dug in, and she requested that the supporting batteries switch to high-explosive rounds with delayed action fuses. This, she reasoned, would allow the artillery rounds to burrow into the ground first before detonating and hopefully dig the enemy out like a gardener rips into the earth to pull out a bothersome weed by its roots. Once that was having an effect, Kozak worked with Crippen to adjust the artillery batteries' pattern of fire so that all the rounds impacted evenly along those enemy positions that they could identify from the air.

The other factor that saved A Company, for the moment, was Hal Cerro's conduct. Once on the ground and in the thick of the firefight, Cerro gave up all pretense of caution and moved about the kill zone in a rather cavalier manner. While he didn't totally throw caution to the winds by walking about as if nothing was happening, neither did he take any extraordinary measures to conceal himself or take cover. With the calmness of a man who looked forward to his own imminent death, Cerro moved about from one group of soldiers to the next, encouraging them to fire and directing that fire against the nearest or most dangerous positions. Some of his troopers, wrapped up in the depths of their own fear, were startled to see Cerro crouched next to them looking about the field as if he were searching for wild game and not the enemy. When the flash of an enemy weapon firing revealed a Farcee position, Cerro would point to it and tell the soldier he was next to, "There, trooper. The enemy is over there. Start putting some fire on him for a change." Looking up at Cerro, most reacted partly out of habit and partly out of shame. Only after he had succeeded in getting the soldiers he was with up and returning fire would Cerro leave. Afterwards, when the survivors were able to compare their impressions of the battle, the one thing that all would agree on was the manner in which Cerro conducted himself. "He was," one sergeant commented for the record, "going about as if he were on the rifle range giving us a block of instruction on small-arms marksmanship. All the time he was with me, he wore a strange sort of half smile on his face. You know, the kind that an officer gets when he sees a training exercise going well. I've never seen anything like it. If it wasn't for him, I think we'd all still be there, dead or eating dirt."

What most of his people did not appreciate was that the smile Cerro was wearing was not because he was satisfied with what was going on. Cerro, unbeknownst to them, was oblivious to what was happening around him. He, like the soldiers he was directing and encouraging, was merely reacting, doing what came naturally to him because of training and practice. The smile that the sergeant would speak of was there because he knew that any second now an enemy bullet would bring his moral pain and suffering to an end. He would in the twinkling of an eye be relieved of all his worldly concerns and problems. In the back of his mind, over and over again as he moved about the landing zone, the ancient Japanese saying swirled about: "Duty is heavy. Death lighter than a feather."

Above the drama being played out between the Number 2 Platoon of the 27th Local Defense Company and A Company, Nancy Kozak was working at full speed. On one hand she was keeping the artillery coming in where it was needed, coordinating it with rocket and gun runs being made by attack helicopters. On the other hand she was trying to get Frank Walters, who had managed to overcome the enemy resistance at his landing zone, to move over to A Company's landing zone. Crippen sat next to her, radio handset pressed to one ear and air crewman's helmet pulled down on the other. Sergeant Pender, across from Kozak, bounced back and forth from the battalion radio net to the brigade command net, relaying situation and spot reports to Colonel Henry R. as they became available and requesting additional attack helicopter support from the brigade operations officer every time Kozak told him to do so.

In the midst of this confusion and activity, neither Walters nor Kozak realized that the Number 3 Platoon of the 27th Company had broken contact, not because of pressure put on them by C Company but because it had been planned that way. They had been ordered to. Nor did anyone realize, American or rebel, that in the course of this withdrawal away from the Americans, the platoon leader of Number 3 Platoon did as he had been trained to do. Based on his assessment of the situation as he perceived it, on his own initiative he altered the direction of his retreat. The ongoing firefight at A Company's landing zone, clearly audible after his breaking contact with C Company, drew him in that direction. By moving that way, he was unknowingly applying the old military axiom that advised commanders to march to the sound of the guns. Though his sole motivation was to go to the aid of his fellow platoon leader, the effect would be the same. The FARC fighters of Number 2 platoon, and not the troopers of A Company, would receive reinforcements first.

The idea of reinforcing the battle in progress was also on the mind of Henry R. Within minutes it was obvious that the plan that he had based his operation on was no longer valid. Rather than being the hammer, the 3rd of the 511th, for whatever reason, had now become the anvil. Without hesitation, Henry R. contacted the commander of the 1st of the 417th in the east and ordered him to conduct a movement to contact toward the 3rd of the 511th's current positions. The 1st of the 513th, in the south, would be prepared to support either the 417th or, on order, to reinforce the 3rd of the 511th once they had stabilized their situation.

After the commander of the 417th acknowledged the order, Henry R. contacted Kozak. Sergeant Pender, answering at first, tugged on Kozak's pant leg and yelled, without bothering to key the intercom, "Captain, Henry R. on the horn. Needs to talk to you now." Kozak, who was busy consulting with Crippen concerning the use of white phosphorus and smoke rounds to cover the withdrawal of A Company, told Crippen to hold his thought and switched radios. As Kozak gave Henry R. a quick update, explaining that C Company would be moving out in the next minute or two to relieve A Company, Henry R. listened, then explained to her what he was in the process of doing.

It was at this moment that the situation was exacerbated by the appearance of the battalion executive officer, Major Edward Bond. Frank Walters and his company had been delayed by the enemy from responding immediately to Kozak's order to rush over and relieve A Company. This and the need to re-form his company into attack formation headed south rather than east took Walters several minutes. Walters was about to move out when Major Bond's voice came over the battalion command net. Having been informed that no one could contact Cerro and that A Company was in dire straits, Bond assumed control of the fight from Kozak. Next he directed that the flight carrying B Company land in C Company's landing zone, not A Company's as originally planned. His intention was to form both C and B companies up before moving out. Over the radio, before he landed, he told Walters, "We can't go off half cocked into the middle of a firefight. Hold Charlie Company until Bravo arrives." Reluctantly Walters acknowledged the order and signaled his platoon leaders to spread their units back out while they waited for the arrival of his new commander.

In his aircraft, with the door open and the rush of air coming in at him, Bond was beside himself with excitement. Originally he had come along on this operation for no other purpose than to observe and learn. He was fresh from the Command and General Staff College at Fort Leavenworth and an abbreviated Spanish language course in Monterey, California, and this assignment was not only his first troop assignment in over seven years, it was his very first time in combat. Even the low morale and sullen mood he found in the 3rd of the 511th did little to diminish the thrill of finally being in an infantry unit in an active theater of operations. This thrill, as was normal for most Americans approaching their first battle, was tempered ever so slightly by a host of concerns and apprehensions.

Whatever concerns he had about his own abilities were washed away by the sudden rush of adrenaline when he heard, as the aircraft drew near the landing zone, that the battalion operations officer was unable to contact the battalion commander and was running the operation. Though Captain Kozak's response that she was too busy to give him an update had irritated Bond, for he had perceived it as a rebuff by a subordinate, he let it drop for now. There would be plenty of time later to discuss the chain of command with young Captain Kozak.

Having finished her discussion with Henry R. and Crippen, who was now busy coordinating the shifting of fires to cover the withdrawal of A Company, Kozak called Walters and asked if he was moving yet. Walters, a little confused, responded that he wasn't. This both surprised and upset Kozak. Mashing down on the radio transmit button, Kozak yelled into the boom mike hanging in front of her mouth. "Charlie Six, this is Sky Rider Three, why in the hell aren't you moving? Over."

Before Walters could answer, Bond cut in. "Sky Rider Three, this is Sky Rider Five, I ordered him to stand fast until Bravo Six and his element landed and linked up with them. If you had been monitoring this net like you should have, you'd know what in the hell was going on. Over."

From where he sat, Sergeant Pender could see Kozak's face turn red with anger. Only with the greatest of effort did she keep herself from shouting back at the new major. Not that he gave her much of a chance to respond. Before she could compose herself, Bond was back on the air. "Sky Rider Three, this is Sky Rider Five. Until we find out what happened to Sky Rider Six, I am assuming command of this battalion. Do you acknowledge? Over."

Taking a deep breath, Kozak looked straight ahead with a deadpan stare, depressed the transmit button, and acknowledged with a perfunctory "Roger."

Satisfied in his mind that all was in hand, Bond looked out the open door of his helicopter as it made the final run into the landing zone. Despite the fact that he was more anxious to get out and on the ground than anyone in B Company, by the time he undid his seat belt and pulled himself up and out of the nylon seat, he was alone in the cargo bay of the aircraft. All of the troopers he had been traveling with were a long time gone and already scattered in the prone position on the landing zone. Though this startled him a bit, he recovered his composure, made a mental note that he would have to be faster than this in the future, and climbed out of the aircraft.

Once on the ground, he paused for a moment and looked about as the last of the aircraft in his lift pulled pitch and flew off. Satisfied that all was in order, he scanned the landing zone, half expecting the C company commander to run up and report to him. After several seconds of searching the surrounding brush and tree line, he saw two soldiers, whom he took to be Walters and his company command group. Remembering that this was war and not a peacetime maneuver, Bond shook his head at his own foolishness, made another mental note, and began to walk over to where he had seen the two troopers.

Out beyond the tree line, from a small covered spider hole, a fighter left by the commander of the Number 3 Platoon to delay the advance saw the lone American standing out in the middle of the open field before him. He watched him for a moment, wondering why this man was behaving like he was. Only when the enemy soldier, wearing what looked like a new crisp, clean uniform, stepped out with deliberate, unhurried pace, did the fighter conclude that this man was an officer. Though he had been told to wait until the enemy column had started to move before firing, the FARC fighter decided that the impudence of this Yankee officer needed to be punished. With great care he raised his rifle, took careful aim, and fired.

From where he sat waiting with Dan Krammer of B Company, Frank Walters watched Major Edward Bond start to walk toward them like he was strolling across the Plain at West Point on a Sunday afternoon. Walters no sooner shook his head in disbelief than a burst from somewhere out beyond the perimeter of the landing zone cut loose. Without having to look, Walters knew that it was from an AK-74, a Russian-made assault rifle. He also knew what the target was. When he saw Bond spin about like a top, he didn't rush out or get excited. Instead he stuck his right hand over his right shoulder. Seeing Walters's hand, his radiotelephone operator slapped the hand mike of the radio on the battalion net into it without having to be told. While he continued to watch where he had seen Bond go down, Walters keyed the hand mike. "Sky Rider Three, this is Charlie Six. Sky Rider Five is down. I say again, Sky Rider Five is down. You have the helm again. Any change in orders? Over."

From somewhere above him Kozak's voice came down and through the radio. It answered his question in a matter-of-fact manner. "Charlie Six, you will assume command of both your element and Bravo. Move out as quickly as possible and link up with Alpha as soon as you can. Those people are in deep trouble and need your help now. Over."

Looking over at Dan Krammer, commander of B Company, Walters called out, "You hear that, Dan?"

Krammer nodded and waved. "Okay by me. Let's get moving."

Turning to the platoon leader of his lead platoon, Walters waved his free hand over his head and then brought it down, pointing in the direction of A Company's landing zone. Without a word, the young lieutenant stood up, waved his right hand over his head, and stepped off headed south toward the sound of the guns. Satisfied, Walters called Kozak. "Sky Rider Three, this is Charlie Six. Bravo Six acknowledges your last. We're moving now. Over."

Finished, he handed the hand mike back to his radiotelephone operator and prepared to follow the lead platoon. Before he did, he took one last glance back to where he had seen Bond go down. A medic from a B Company platoon was out there in the knee-high grass tending to Bond. As his company moved by him, Walters shouted out, asking the medic if the major was alive. The medic, looking up at Walters for a moment, smiled. "He took one in the left lung and two in the shoulder. This here officer's lucky. He's earned himself the combat infantryman's badge, the right to wear the 11th Air Assault patch on his right sleeve, a Purple Heart, access to all them VA benefits, and a free trip home, all with less than sixty seconds of combat time. Now ain't that some lucky shit."

Walters grinned back at the medic, waved, and turned to march off with his company. If that was luck, he decided, he didn't want any part of it.

Above all this confusion, listening over the radio to the orders and counterorders of the 3rd Brigade, the 3rd of the

511th, and other units involved, C. B. Lane hung in the sky like an impatient vulture. Things were not going as he had envisioned them. Someone, he realized, had screwed up. Though he couldn't tell for sure yet who that someone was, he swore to himself that as soon as he knew, he'd nail the son of a bitch to the front door of division headquarters as an example. With no one else but his aide to talk to, Lane turned to him and threw his hands out in disgust. "Listen to that garbage. In all my years in uniform, I've never heard such amateurish behavior."

The aide, Captain James William Adderly III, looked at Lane, as was his habit, and nodded without thought. Only his eyes, if Lane had cared to look, would have betrayed Adderly's true thoughts. Responsible for operating the sophisticated radio system found in all true command-and-control aircraft, Adderly heard everything that Lane did. In the course of the battle so far that afternoon, he had heard or seen nothing really wrong, not like Lane was trying to make out. All battles, he knew from his own experiences in the Persian Gulf as a second lieutenant and every training exercise he had ever been on, took on a life of their own and seldom evolved in the manner that commanders on either side had envisioned. Having been a platoon leader, a company commander, an assistant brigade operations officer, and a watch officer in the 11th Air Assault Division's operations center, Adderly had enough of a background to judge what was happening on the ground and between the various commanders of the 3rd Brigade. In his opinion, an opinion he didn't share with Lane, everything was going about as well as could be expected.

Looking over at Lane, Adderly shook his head. The idea that this man was not the great warrior that he made himself out to be had been slow to sink in. From a distance and in small doses, as he had viewed the man when he had been assigned to the division operations section, Adderly had been fooled, like so many before him. Lane, as he would breeze into and out of briefings, training inspections, and short visits to the field, talked the talk, as the saying went. It was only when he had been assigned as Lane's aide-de-camp that Adderly found out that Lane couldn't walk the walk. "The man," he wrote his wife, the only person whom he could confide in and pour his heart out to, "is a paper soldier. In a pinch, I fear he could cost us lives. Were I not at odds with my obligation to adhere to the stringent code of honor that depends on unflinching loyalty and adherence to orders that binds the officer corps into such a tight-knit professional group, I would have spoken to someone about what I saw a long time ago. But I fear, my love, that I, like many around me, am morally bankrupt and a coward hiding behind the words Duty, Honor, Country."

Across from Adderly, Lane was beside himself. Peering through the windows of the closed doors of his aircraft, Lane tried to pick out which cluster of men on the ground were A Company, 3rd of the 511th. Every now and then, when he caught a glimpse of something he thought he understood, he'd say something, more to himself than to Adderly. On one pass, just as Frank Walters was finally getting his and Dan Krammer's company moving to where A Company was pinned, Lane mumbled, "Too slow, too slow. Everyone is moving too damned slow down there." Then to the pilot he yelled out, "Take it around again, lower this time."

As he had done for the past twenty minutes, the command pilot of Lane's aircraft banked to the right, swinging wide and away from the 3rd of the 511th's fight for a moment. Leveling out just this side of the river, the pilot headed east for a minute or two, then brought his aircraft around to the right until he had completed a 180-degree turn. Slowing, he dropped some and began another low, slow pass over the 3rd of the 511th, watching as he did so for the other aircraft that hovered over the area or darted this way and that in all directions. If he had any concern about enemy anti-aircraft fire, he didn't show it.

Of course, had he been aware of the pair of gunners smoothly tracking his helicopter with their 14.5mm machine guns every time he made an eastbound pass along the south side of the river, Lane's pilot would have been a little more attentive about what was going on down there. But since no one had been fired on all day, and he was there to serve Lane's needs come hell or high water, the command pilot concentrated on his flying and left all the thinking and ground watching to Lane. He was, after all, the division commander.

Had anyone bothered to ask the soldiers of A Company how long they had been out there in the middle of the landing zone under fire, none could have answered. It was without exception an eternity for each and every one of them. Only Cerro, still up and wandering about, seemed unfazed by their terrible predicament. It wasn't until he came across Second Lieutenant Tyler Wiezman, now wounded for the second time that day but still in command, that he begin to consider their overall situation. "Colonel," Wiezman yelled as Cerro approached, "we've got smoke and willie pete coming in to cover our withdrawal."

To Cerro, a man who had not considered the possibilities of surviving the day, the idea of leaving the landing zone was a revelation that he had to pause and think about. "Where are you going to go, Tyler?"

Struck by Cerro's question, Wiezman looked at his commander and wondered if he had heard right. Blinking, he shook his head and pointed toward the northeast corner of the landing zone. "Over there, away from the enemy and closer to C Company."

Squatting between Wiezman and his radioman, Cerro studied the area that the young officer had pointed to, then looked back down at Wiezman. "Yeah, that's probably a good idea. When are you going to move?"

Suddenly it dawned upon young Wiezman that his commander was out of it. Somehow, in all of the confusion, Lieutenant Colonel Cerro had lost track of the situation. Although he still appeared to be functioning after a fashion, Wiezman decided to take matters in his own hands. Over on the edge of the landing zone, where the enemy positions were, he saw that the smoke and white phosphorus were finally having the desired effect. Though tongues of small-arms fire still lashed out of the billowing white smoke, it was wild and very much diminished. Struggling to stand up, Wiezman looked up and down the ragged line of riflemen that represented A Company. From where he stood he could clearly tell which of the prone figures were still fighting and which were dead, dying, or severely wounded. What he couldn't tell in the confusion of the moment was which of his sergeants were still with him. Deciding to wait until they were under some sort of cover to sort that out and reorganize, he shouted, first to his left, and then to his right while he pointed, "Everyone up and to the rear over there. Re-form in the tree line. Everyone up and to the rear. Re-form in the tree line.''

Slowly, in ones and twos, the survivors got to their feet and began to drift back in the direction that Wiezman was motioning them toward. Most, mindful of their stricken comrades, attempted to help those who couldn't respond. Grabbing the nearest wounded trooper, they dragged or threw him over their shoulder as best they could. Though there was no guarantee that all of the wounded were being policed up, Wiezman was grateful that there was still enough discipline left in the soldiers of his company to think about someone other than themselves.

Wiezman's actions and the response of the survivors of his company finally began to bring Cerro out of his despondency. Standing next to Wiezman, he noticed for the first time that his radioman wasn't with him. Somewhere, without realizing it, he had lost him to enemy fire. Knowing that this was no time to go around and look for him, he turned to Wiezman. "Lieutenant, I've lost my radioman. I need to borrow one of yours. Can you manage things without a company radio net for a while?"

Looking at Cerro, Wiezman tried to hide the anger he felt. "Sir, there isn't enough of a company left to make a radio net worthwhile." Seeing the surprised look in Cerro's eyes, Wiezman realized that he had come on too strong. Not that he cared, it was true. A Company was now down to little more than two platoons. Still . . . Reaching behind him, he grabbed the first radioman his hand fell on. "Smitty, put your radio on the battalion command net and go with the colonel. Now."

Smitty looked at Wiezman. "But, sir, it's already on the battalion push."

"Okay, then just go now."

When Smitty moved over next to Cerro, Cerro nodded. "Great! I appreciate the loan. We're going to double-time over to the tree line and set up a battalion CP just inside the tree line, where the north and east side of the field come to a point. I'll get a hold of Frank Walters and we'll meet you there."

With a nod, Wiezman acknowledged and Cerro turned to head off for the spot he'd designated. Glad to be rid of his commander, Wiezman got back to matters at hand. With a quick scan he checked out the area where the company had been pinned. Satisfied that everyone that was able to was up and headed back to the rear, he turned his back on the enemy positions and followed his radioman. As he limped along, he kept shouting to the ragged line ahead of him, "Come on, get a move on. Keep it going over there. We don't have all day. Keep it moving."

It wasn't until Hal Cerro and Smitty, running now ahead of the rest of the people clearing off the landing zone, reached the cover of the tree line and bounded in, without looking, that they realized that they were in trouble. Suddenly, without so much as a warning, a lone fighter of Number 3 Platoon, 27th Local Defense Company, jumped up off the ground right in front of Cerro and Smitty. Leveling his AK-74, he let fly, hitting Smitty in the stomach with a long burst that sent him sprawling backwards. Seeing that the first American was finished, the FARC fighter turned and prepared to fire on Cerro, now less than three feet away from him and closing fast.

CHAPTER 13

November 12

THE SHIFTING OF A COMPANY FROM THE OPEN TOWARD THE northeast corner of the landing zone caught just about everyone off guard. Involved in dealing with other concerns at that moment, no one besides Wiezman's soldiers and the fighters in Number 3 Platoon took notice of the vicious little firefight that had broken out at point-blank range at the edge of the tree line. Even the platoon commander of Number 3 Platoon, who had been waiting for the fleeing Americans to close, was taken aback when one of his people opened fire without waiting for his order.

He didn't know, of course, that the young fighter, a tenant farmer from birth, had seen that he had no real choice. Cerro and his radioman were only a second away from stepping on him. In the split second before he fired at the radioman, the fighter knew he was violating his platoon commander's order to wait until he gave the command. But there was no way he could comply with such an order. Like much of what had happened to him in the last forty-eight hours, the rebel fighter was reacting to the situation as best he could. That his action had initiated the engagement and cost the Number 3 Platoon its surprise was not his immediate concern. He hadn't made an error. It hadn't been a mistake, at least from his standpoint. For him it had been necessary, a simple matter of life and death.

245

But that individual's decision and action gave the troopers of A Company several vital seconds in which to drop to the ground and spray the tree line they now faced with a wild but very intimidating volley of fire.

Hovering to the north of A Company's landing zone, Kozak was busy looking for the lead element of Frank Walters's combined command when the fight between A Company and Number 3 Platoon broke out. Caught up in her thoughts and concerned that Walters was taking too long, she was wondering if it would do any good to call to hurry him along when Pender, looking out the other side of the aircraft, called across to her. "Captain, A Company's stepped in some shit. There's another enemy unit down there taking them under fire."

Shifting herself in the nylon seat, Kozak looked out the right door of the helicopter. From where she was she could make out a ragged line of soldiers fifty meters or so short of the northeast corner of the A Company landing zone, shooting in the direction of that corner. At first she looked around the helicopter, then at the horizon, wondering if they had become disoriented and were south of the A Company LZ and not north, as she had assumed. That such a thing in the heat of battle could occur was not unheard of. But the river, the village, and the lingering smoke from fire caused by the barrage of smoke and white phosphorus rounds against A Company's first assailants told her that they were where they should have been.

That didn't make any difference, however, at that moment. Something new and unexpected had been added to the tactical equation and was at that moment threatening to finish the destruction of A Company. Once she was satisfied that she was seeing the true situation, Kozak blurted out a rare expression of surprise. "Damn! Where did they come from?" Then, without hesitation, she pointed to Crippen. In a voice that betrayed no excitement, no confusion, Kozak began to issue instructions to her battle staff. "Have one battery repeat the fire mission of smoke and white phosphorus and the other stand by for an immediate suppression of the new enemy positions. But tell them not to fire until I give the word. We don't have a good handle on the location of B and C companies." Without waiting for an acknowledgment, Kozak turned to Pender. "Contact Walters. Tell him what's going on and that we're preparing to

246

fire artillery on the northeast corner of the landing zone. We need a solid fix on his lead element now. If necessary, have him pop smoke." Finished with Pender, she looked over to Lieutenant Dietz. "Marion, get on the radio with the attack helo liaison. Find out if they have anyone on station and ready to go in." Though he was the intel officer, Dietz didn't hesitate. He did what needed to be done. With a nod that Kozak didn't see, since she was already looking back out the open door, he keyed the mike attached to the radio set on the attack helo liaison frequency and began to call.

With everyone in the cargo bay of the helicopter busy relaying information or requesting it, Kozak keyed the intercom to the pilot and pointed in the direction of the firefight. "George, get me over there fast." Then, with nothing further to do until Crippen, Walters, and the pilot responded to her flurry of orders, Kozak turned and leaned out the door as far as she could, trying hard to catch a glimpse of what was happening on the ground and wondering what she would do when she got there.

To the southeast, the brigade commander was on the ground talking to the commander of the 1st Battalion, 417th Infantry. Out of the loop for only several minutes, he would miss the crisis that was building as C. B. Lane's helicopter, now finishing its eastward run over the 3rd of the 511th's fight, prepared to make its turn. Adderly, Lane's aide-de-camp, saw the new firefight at the same moment that Pender did. Pointing, he keyed the intercom. "General, looks like there's a new firefight erupting over in the 3rd of the 511th's area."

Lane, who had been busying himself studying his map, looked up and in the wrong direction at first. Realizing his error, he leaned over to look where Adderly was pointing. Too late to see what his aide was talking about, Lane called out to his pilot, "Take this thing around fast. I want to see what Jim is talking about."

Jerking his collective over hard, the pilot threw both Lane and Adderly off balance as he began a banking turn that took them over the Meta River and its north bank.

*　　*　　*

On the north bank of the river, Hector Valendez, now standing next to one of the two 14.5mm anti-aircraft guns, heard the chatter of rifle and machine-gun fire to the southwest. The momentary silence that had followed the barrage of smoke and white phosphorus rounds on the Number 2 Platoon's position had been a good sign. Finally, he thought, they were disengaging. His plan was salvageable. That illusion, however, was shattered with the renewal of firing and the sudden and violent maneuvering of the helicopters over the area occupied by the 27th Company. Standing there listening to the last glimmer of hope for his hastily laid battle plans fade, Valendez became angry. Angry at the local-force commanders for ignoring his orders. Angry at being faced with his first military failure. Angry at his inability to reach out and do anything about it. But most of all, as he stood there and listened, he realized his greatest anger was aimed at the American helicopters, machines that gave their commanders the mobility to flit about from one crisis to the next, reacting and adjusting their plans with the greatest of ease while he stood there rooted to the ground like a tree.

Hector Valendez was barely managing to hold back his anger, clutching his fists until his knuckles turned white as he did so, when the shadow of a helicopter passing overhead fell upon him. He looked up and saw the underbelly of the aircraft only yards away, and he lost whatever control he had held on to up to that moment. Turning to the gunner of the anti-aircraft gun, Valendez thrust his arm skyward and yelled, "SHOOT THE BASTARD, DAMN IT! SHOOT! KILL HIM. KILL THEM ALL."

Hearing the order to fire, the anti-aircraft gunner ignored Valendez's red, contorted face and his wild gesturing. Continuing his smooth and steady tracking of the helicopter overhead, the gunner leaned into his sight, made a minor adjustment, and squeezed the trigger until his weapon began to buck, spewing out a stream of ball and tracer rounds at C. B. Lane's helicopter.

Everyone on Lane's helicopter noticed the sudden series of small jerks and muffled thuds but didn't pay any heed to them until the co-pilot saw a stream of tracers go racing up past his windshield. With understanding came a moment of panic. "Jesus Christ, we're under fire."

The pilot, only a second behind in his partner's discovery, stiffened in his seat, then began to twist his head to the left, to the right, then to the left again. He thought for a split second about jerking his aircraft further into its turn, but then decided against that. Unless he knew for sure where he was taking fire from, that wouldn't be a smart move. For all he knew, he could be maneuvering himself and his crew into the enemy fire and not away from it. Still frantically scanning the cockeyed horizon while he held his aircraft in its tight bank, he yelled over the intercom. "Where? Where are we taking fire—"

The crew chief's shout drowned out the pilot's harried question. "Christ! We're hit! We're being hit! Jesus H. Christ!"

The pilot, knowing this, jerked his head around to admonish his crew chief and tell him to stick his head out the damned window and see where the fire was coming from, but he cut himself short when he saw the crew chief jumping out of his seat, shifting his body wildly from one side to the other in an effort to avoid the shower of sparks and fragments that were filling the rear of the aircraft. The enemy had their range. Without hesitation, the pilot began to jerk the stick in the direction opposite to the sharp bank he was already executing, but not before he felt a sharp rap at the base of his spine as a round struck the bottom of his armored seat. Without realizing it, he shut his eyes and began to mutter repeatedly, "Hail Mary, full of grace. Hail Mary, full of grace."

The aircraft was just beginning to respond to the pilot's radical maneuver when he felt his joy stick go slack. At the same instant the earphones in his crewman's helmet came alive with the shrill voice of the co-pilot and the buzz of the malfunction warning alarms. Excited, he started to yell over and over, "We're losing it! We're losing it!"

Popping his eyes open, he looked down at the bank of warning lights, now a crazy quilt of orange flashes. In his worst nightmare, during his most demanding simulation, he had never beheld such a sight. Again he closed his eyes and whispered a silent prayer as he leaned as far to his left as he could with the joy stick.

Behind him, C. B. Lane sat frozen. Even the warm stream

of urine running down his pant legs failed to shake him from the paralysis that locked his mind and body in place. Across from him his aide, Captain Jim Adderly, was caught up in the confusion of the moment. Like the crew chief, he was turning this way and that, trying hard to take everything in while looking for some way of helping, for he too had been witness to the accuracy and effectiveness of the enemy anti-aircraft fire. Unlike the crew chief, he knew without having to think that jumping up and dancing from one side to the other would do no good. Unable to predict the pattern of the impacting rounds, a shift to the right could be the kiss of death rather than salvation. Only the pilot and co-pilot had any armor protection from ground fire. Everyone else, including the general, had to rely on luck and the skill of the pilot.

It was then, in a sudden flicker of thought, that Adderly turned to Lane. Ceasing his rapid but measured scanning of the aircraft's interior, Adderly looked straight at Lane. When his eyes focused on his superior, he was taken aback. Across from him the man he had so looked up to, the man who had made a reputation as a severe and harsh master, brutal and uncompromising to anyone he felt was a lesser man, sat riveted in his seat, ashen-faced with unblinking eyes that bulged like an excited blowfish's. In an instant he took it all in, even the spreading darkness running down the general's leg. "Oh, God," Adderly shouted as he realized that Lane had been hit.

In a flash he unhooked his seat belt and pushed himself up from where he sat. The wild gyrations of the pilot didn't make this easy, causing Adderly to lurch forward. Losing his footing, Adderly had to alter his effort from one of trying to reach Lane to that of trying to keep from smashing into his wounded commander. Throwing his hands up and out to either side of Lane's head, Adderly barely managed to grab the side of the seat and stop himself from colliding with him. Hanging on to the sides of the seat, Adderly steadied himself, took a deep breath, then froze as his nostrils filled with the pungent odor of loose bowels and urine. Without thinking, he glanced down at Lane's crotch just as Lane, shaken out of his coma by Adderly's advance, looked up at his aide's face as it contorted itself in disgust.

Embarrassment quickly followed by anger were the first conscious feelings that Lane had as he stared into Adderly's eyes. "What the fuck are you looking at, Captain?"

Shaken as he had never been shaken before, Adderly pushed himself away from Lane's face, now screwed up in rage and turning beet red. "I—I thought—"

"For Christ's sake, don't think, Captain. Do something!"

"I thought you were hit. I was trying to see if I could—"

"I'm not hit. But I will be if you don't do something."

Recovering his mental balance, yet now totally thrown by this experience, Adderly shot back without thinking. "What? What in the hell do you want me to do, sir?"

It was the snide slur that Adderly used when he pronounced the word "sir" that hit Lane the hardest. As much as Adderly's discovery of his momentary panic bothered him, Adderly's outburst and sneering rocked him more. Here was a subordinate, a mere captain, talking to him, a major general, like he was a rank second lieutenant. Without thinking, Lane lashed out at him. "Call for artillery fire, you asshole. Get on the radio and get some suppressive fires on the enemy triple-A positions."

In the heat of the moment, Adderly let his own anger get the better of him. He knew he didn't have any idea where the enemy fire was coming from. And he damn sure knew that Lane didn't either. With a sharpness that he didn't intend, Adderly shot back to Lane, "Okay, General, where do you want me to put this fire?"

Though the question was a sound one, Adderly's response stoked Lane's growing anger. Intending to take Adderly to task, Lane glanced out the right side of the aircraft just in time to catch a glimpse of 14.5mm tracer rounds from the last volley of anti-aircraft fire arching back and down to earth toward the village of El Frío. At that moment, as if a snapshot had been made in his mind, Lane took an association between the anti-aircraft fire and the village of El Frío.

Without hesitation, he thrust his arm in the direction of El Frío. "There, the enemy anti-aircraft fire is coming from that village. I want every gun in range to blow that dump off the face of the earth."

Looking over toward the village, then back at Lane, Adderly realized that his boss was regaining his equilibrium. Still the stern look on his face and the tough words couldn't hide the smell of piss and shit that filled the rear of the command-and-control aircraft. Though he still wore the stars, Adderly knew that from that moment on he would never be able to look at Lane as he had before.

Watching and waiting for his aide to respond, Lane could see the disdain well up in Adderly's eyes. He knew what it was about. He knew what Adderly was thinking. Though he couldn't do anything to change that, Lane was bound and determined to make sure that the pissant little captain across from him did what he was told. Leaning forward, Lane thrust his face at Adderly. "Mister, I gave you a goddamned order. Now you do what I told you or you turn over your bars. Is that clear?"

For the longest of seconds Adderly paused and returned Lane's stare.

Above the chaos and confusion that A Company's firefight had degenerated into, Kozak and her tiny battle staff were racing to get the artillery fire that Wiezman and his shattered command so desperately needed. When Crippen was finished and he had a response from the fire support center controlling the two 105mm howitzer batteries, he tapped Kozak on her shoulder and shouted, "Okay, Nancy, we got both batteries up and ready to fire nonstop, danger close."

Kozak was still half hanging out the open door watching the flashes of small-arms fire stabbing out from the tree line and the return fire from the ragged circle that A Company had formed in the open. Though greatly diminished, fire was now coming from the southern and western edge of the landing zone again, indicating that the enemy who had originally initiated the ambush had shaken off the effects of the last volleys of artillery. For a moment she wondered if this was what the Little Big Horn looked like at its climax. After shaking off the shudder which that thought sent down her spine, she lifted her left hand over her right shoulder, gave Crippen a thumbs-up, and yelled, "Send it, now!" without bothering to take her eyes off the drama being played out below.

Though she didn't see it, and Crippen didn't bother to look up at her, he returned Kozak's thumbs up, keyed his radio hand mike, and ordered the batteries to fire at will. The response he was given to his last message, however, was not what he expected. Instead of saying "On the way," the radiotelephone operator at the fire support center gave Crippen a "Wait. Out."

Pulling the hand mike away from his ear for a moment, Crippen looked at it as if he didn't believe what he had just heard. Tucking it back up under the rim of his helmet, he keyed the hand mike and shot back. "Wait. Out? What in the hell do you mean. Wait. Out? We got a whole bunch of people down there on the ground with their ass in a wringer that are going to die unless you shoot now! Do you copy? Over."

There was no hesitation when the voice on the hand mike responded. "Roger, Sky Rider Nine, I understand your situation. We have a priority mission that we have to fire before we shoot yours. How copy? Over."

Crippen flushed. Though technically a member of the artillery battalion that was providing the fire support, he, like most fire support officers, trained with, lived with, and identified more with the infantry battalion to which he was assigned. Providing them the best fire support was his assigned duty. Taking care of the men and women of the 3rd of the 511th, people who had become his family since deploying to Colombia, was his passion. With all his might, Crippen mashed the push-to-talk button on his hand mike and shot back, "PRIORITY? PRIORITY? What in the hell is more important than saving an entire company from getting wiped out?"

Bothered that he was being badgered like this, the radio operator's voice at the fire direction center was noticeably sharp when he replied, "Eagle Six has a mission that overrides yours. Do you copy? Over."

Crippen didn't know which angered him the most, the detached and unmistakably arrogant tone of the radio operator sitting some distance away in the safety of the artillery fire direction center or the division commander whose radio call sign was Eagle Six. Not that it mattered, for Crippen shot back, raising his voice noticeably as he dropped all efforts to hide his anger, "What in the hell could Eagle Six have that is more important than saving the lives of his own men?" Then, before the radio operator could respond, Crippen managed to seize control of his anger. "Listen, trooper, before you say another word, put Red Sky Six or Red Sky Three on. I want to talk to them.''

Looking about him, the radio operator saw the artillery battalion commander who used the call sign Red Sky Six sitting in front of the situation board being briefed by the duty officer. He paused for a moment, considering if he should bother his battalion commander or not, then decided to. Maybe the battalion commander would be able to get Captain Crippen, who was obviously quite hyper at the moment, to calm down or at least back off some. ''Colonel Day, Captain Crippen needs to talk to you, sir. He's pissed off about the CG's fire mission.''

There was a pause as Day, the artillery battalion commander, hesitated. He knew when the duty officer told him of the two missions that it wouldn't be long before the infantry battalion in contact would come up on the net and bitch about losing their fire support. For a moment Day even considered ignoring the call. He was a battalion commander, after all, and was under no real obligation to respond to Crippen's request. Ignoring Crippen by falling back on the prerogative of his rank, however, was a poor answer to his dilemma, and Day knew it. A subordinate was in a bind and wanted an answer, needed an answer, a real answer, right now. Twisting in his seat, Day picked up the radiotelephone hand mike that was attached to the remote set sitting on the duty officer's table, turned the volume on the speaker up, and keyed the push to talk button. ''Sky Rider Nine, this is Red Sky Six. Send your traffic. Over.''

Crippen, though somewhat calmed down when he heard Day, jumped right in, his voice betraying the pressure, stress, and excitement he felt as Kozak's helicopter continued to orbit about the desperate struggle that continued below them unabated. ''This is Sky Rider Nine. We need fires and we need them now. The Farcees have one whole company stuck in the open between two forces and are chewing them up. Without those fires a lot of good soldiers are going to die.''

Day felt his stomach begin to knot up. He knew that. He had known that when he had heard Crippen's initial call for fires come in not more than a minute or two before, followed immediately by Lane's order, relayed by his aide, to concentrate all fires on El Frío. Yet he had said nothing. Even when the duty officer looked over at him with a questioning look on his face that asked him what to do without having to speak, Day had done nothing. In the back of his mind he had hoped that he wouldn't need to do anything. That perhaps they could fire the mission on the village, satisfy the division commander, and then return to supporting the 3rd of the 511th. That was what he had hoped, for he, like every other battalion commander in the division, feared Lane. They feared the repercussions of crossing him. They feared having him drop in out of nowhere and degrade them in their own command post, in the presence of their own soldiers and staff. They feared having him and his staff turn on their commands and ride them into the ground, just as they had done to the 3rd of the 511th and other battalions that had in Lane's opinion screwed up. And secretly, hidden way back behind these other fears, there lurked another, the fear that Lane, whose star was still on the ascendant in the Army, would one day sit in judgment of their professional career.

None of this, of course, had anything to do with duty. Not really. It was all personal feelings, all perceptions and fears. Still, people cannot escape those fears and feelings. They can stuff them, deny them, even mask them, but they are always there waiting to crop up when circumstances permit. Even in a situation as clear-cut as this one, all of Day's thoughts and decisions were being tainted by such personal fears and apprehensions, for the circumstances laid bare every aspect of his soul, good and bad. Only a man with blind dedication to duty and moral courage can overcome, in a situation like the one Day found himself in at that moment, his own shortfalls, real and imagined.

Crippen was still waiting for a response from Day when Kozak, noticing that they weren't receiving the fires she had requested, turned to face Crippen. "Pete, what's taking so damned long? Are we going to get the fires or not?"

Embarrassed by the perceived ineptitude of his own parent artillery battalion and confused by what was going on between Lane and Day, Crippen moved the radio hand mike away from his mouth as he shrugged. "Don't know for sure. I think they're debating who gets priority of fires."

Not knowing about Lane's priority mission or who "they" were, Kozak's eyes flew open as her face dropped in surprise. "Trying to decide? Why in the hell do they need to decide anything? We're the only people in contact, aren't we?"

The last part of her comment was directed at Pender. Listening to the conversation, Pender shouted out, "That's right, Captain. Except for some anti-aircraft fire directed at a helicopter over there, north of the river, we're the only people being shot at."

Though Pender was pointing out his door, to the north, Kozak ignored him after he had confirmed her suspicions. Moving in from the door, she leaned closer to Crippen. "Here, give me that hand mike."

Peter Crippen could see the anger in her eyes. He had no doubt that if she got on the artillery fire support net and started talking to Day, she would say something that everyone would regret. Though he himself was angry and ready to dump on Day for what he believed was indecision and moral cowardice, Crippen knew that in these circumstances it was better if he handled the artillery battalion commander. Raising his hand to wave her off, he was about to tell her that he could deal with it when he heard Day's response. Looking down at the floor of the helicopter, Crippen shoved the index finger of his left hand into his exposed ear and squeezed the receiver end of the radio hand mike tight against his right ear.

Without asking, Kozak and everyone else in the cargo bay of the helicopter knew that Crippen was listening to someone on the radio. Silently they waited. Finally Crippen pulled his finger out of his ear and with his free hand gave Kozak a thumbs-up. After acknowledging the call he had been listening to so intently, he looked up at Kozak and smiled. "Okay. We're in business. Colonel Day says you got both batteries as long as you need them."

Still not understanding everything that had gone on between Crippen and the fire direction center, or Lane's priority mission, Kozak was unimpressed with Crippen's minor victory. With hardly a change in expression, she shot back at him, "Good, now get those fucking guns shooting, *now*." With that, she slid over to the open door again, pausing only long enough to grab the door gunner's arm and shout to him. "Shoot, damn it. Use that gun and draw some fire."

The door gunner, a young kid not more than twenty, looked at Kozak. What did she mean, draw fire? he thought. Did she mean she wanted him to shoot at the enemy so that they would shoot at them? That was crazy, crazy. But as he watched the female captain continue to slide over to the open door, stopping only when the loose seat belt about her waist snapped taut, he realized that everybody was getting a little crazy, everyone in this helicopter. The pilots were whipping the bird about like mad, flying lower and faster than he had ever seen them do. The officers and sergeants on the radios were chattering a mile a minute, cursing and screaming at each other and other officers and sergeants over the radio. And the enemy, they seemed to be everywhere down there, chewing up those poor bastards on the ground. It was crazy. But maybe it all made sense? Maybe these officers knew what they were doing?

What the hell, the door gunner thought. Everyone else was going nuts. He might as well join in. Leaning into his gun, he scanned the landscape flashing below him looking for targets. When he saw movement in the bush along the tree line, he braced his arms, squeezed the trigger, and let loose a long burst from his gun.

Just inside the edge of the tree line in the northeast corner Harold Cerro opened his eyes. It took him a moment to realize that he was lying on his back. It took him even longer to realize that he had been shot. But when he finally did, the spasms of pain that swept though his body were horrific. Where he had been hit, how bad it was, how long he had been there, and many other questions were all mysteries to Cerro that would have to wait until the waves of pain that assaulted his brain subsided.

At first Cerro did nothing, did not even think. He simply lay there looking up at trees, waiting. Only after the passing of the dark underside of a helicopter clipping treetops and spraying machine-gun fire out of both sides as it flashed overhead, did Cerro begin to wonder what was going on. Slowly, painfully slowly, he asked himself what it was he was waiting for. When that thought finally managed to take root, he began to listen and look about. He was not alone. From every direction came the crack, chatter, and pop of small-arms fire, rifle and light machine guns. There were many different caliber weapons being fired, some of which Cerro didn't recognize offhand. While this bothered him, the idea that the reports of weapons that were strange to his ears were drowning out the familiar pop-pop-pop of the American-made rifles began to bother him. He was closer, he figured, to the enemy than to his own people. But how far? And why?

Slowly he rolled his head to one side, then the other. Though there was pain, it wasn't as bad as he had feared. To his right there was nothing, at least nothing that he could see, since there was a thick tree root less than a foot from his head that blocked his view. When he twisted his head around in the opposite direction, his eyes fell upon the soles of a pair of shoes two feet from his face. He knew right away that whoever wore those shoes wasn't an American. The soles lacked the intricate stamped pattern common to combat boots. Intrigued, Cerro thought for a moment, then with an effort lifted his head up off the ground and peered over the toes of the shoes.

Surprisingly, he was able to keep his head up and look about. Though it was painful, the pain now had receded to a numb throbbing that stayed in the background, sufficient to remind him that he had been shot but not enough to stop him from continuing his slow investigation of the area around him. The man or, more correctly, Cerro thought, boy he was looking at was definitely a Farcee. Letting his head drop back down to the ground, Cerro thought about this for a moment. Images of the last few seconds before he lost consciousness began to tumble about in his mind. During this, he remembered that he had run into the woods accompanied by a radioman. Hoisting his head up again, he turned to the right and looked over the tree root.

He was there, lying face down, unmoving. Both arms were tucked in tight to his sides and his hands were hidden under his body, as if he had been clutching something close to his chest. His wound, Cerro figured. He was clutching his wound. What he was doing, however, soon became academic for the moment as the earth beneath Cerro heaved up and quivered. The shattering blast of artillery impacting near at hand startled Cerro for a moment, but then he relaxed when he concluded that it was a good fifty or more meters away. Again he let his head drop back to the ground. He was safe, he thought. There was no danger for now. Though surrounded by the chatter of enemy small-arms fire, none of the rebel fighters seemed to be interested in him or the other bodies on either side. And the artillery was far enough away that he didn't need to worry about it.

That thought, however, triggered a new chain of thoughts. Cerro's mind, still racked with an occasional spasm of pain, was far from being fully functional. So each idea had to queue up behind another and wait to be dealt with in its turn. In this way Cerro was able to piece together as clear a picture of his plight as was possible. He and his radioman had made it to the tree line in the northeast corner of the landing zone. They had run into a Farcee fighter. The Farcee had shot the radioman. Cerro had shot the Farcee, but not before the Farcee had turned his gun on him. And now he was still there in the middle of the Farcee position, wounded, listening to the firefight. It was these last two thoughts that stuck in Cerro's mind. If he was in the middle of their position, he thought, and the artillery wasn't hitting here, it was missing the enemy.

Without any need to consider his situation, Cerro lifted his head again and looked over to the radioman. The radio on his back, little more than an arm's reach away, looked like it had survived the ordeal unscathed. For the first time since regaining his consciousness, Cerro began to move. And although his efforts were rewarded with pain, Cerro had a purpose in life now, a quest. Focusing all of his attention on the radio, Cerro began to inch his way toward it.

Straining against her seat belt, Nancy Kozak was for the moment helpless to do anything more than she was doing. It was now up to the artillery fire and Frank Walters to save A Company. That, however, would take five minutes, maybe more, according to Walters. In the meantime, A Company continued to lie out in the open with nowhere to hide, suffering punishing fire from two directions.

Kozak was about to key the intercom to ask Sergeant Pender if the attack helicopters were finished rearming yet when a familiar yet unexpected voice came up on the battalion net.

"Sky Rider Three, this is Sky Rider Six. Adjust Fire. Over."

The shock of hearing Cerro's voice, the first time she had heard him since A Company went in, caused Kozak to bolt upright in her seat. Jamming the push-to-talk button on the long cord that connected her air crewman's helmet to the radio, Kozak responded. "Sky Rider Six, this is Sky Rider Three. Where are you? What's your status? Over."

Ignoring her question, Cerro started to give her directions. "This is Six. Your fire mission is missing the enemy's main body. From the gun-target line, drop five zero, left five zero, and fire for effect. How copy? Over."

Puzzled, Kozak looked down over to the tree line and thought for a moment about where that correction would put the strike of the rounds. When she had a mental picture in her mind, she rekeyed the push-to-talk button. "Six, this is Three. We are already firing danger close. If we bring it in closer, A Company might be hit."

There was no pause as Cerro responded. "They're already being hit. Your fires are missing the enemy main body. They are right on the edge of the tree line, in the open and exposed. Either make that correction or stop firing. The artillery isn't hitting a damned thing, and the Farcees aren't bothered by it. That's an order, Captain."

Though she paused, concerned about what Cerro was telling her to do, Kozak dropped it and turned to Crippen. "Pete, have the battery that's firing on the northeast corner of the tree line adjust fire. From the gun target line, drop five zero, left five zero."

Without hesitation, Crippen looked at his map, then out the door of the helicopter, then up at Kozak. "No way. You'll hit A Company."

Kozak, not wanting to argue, leaned closer to Crippen. "I know what the hell I'm doing. Make the correction and fire for effect, now."

Things, Crippen knew, were desperate. But he wondered if they were that desperate. Maybe they were, he thought. He wasn't on the battalion radio net, so he wasn't sure what was going on down there. With little more than a shrug, he turned his attention to calling in the adjustment of the fires and prayed that Kozak knew what she was doing.

*   *   *

When Lane saw the impacts of artillery over in the 3rd of the 511th's area and not on El Frío, he threw a fit. The full force of that rage, of course, was directed at Adderly, the person who had made the call for fire. "What in the hell is going on, Captain? Didn't I tell you to have the artillery take out that town?"

From where he sat, Adderly looked at Lane. At that moment he wasn't sure what he felt. Was it anger? Was it loathing? Was it disgust? Odds were it was a combination of all of them and more. Regardless of what was driving him, Adderly felt like taking his helmet off and throwing it at Lane, telling him to call his own stupid and pointless fire mission in. For even though he, like everyone else in the command-and-control bird had been shaken by being hit by ground fire, Adderly knew that the 3rd of the 511th was in deep trouble and they needed the fire support.

Still Adderly held his temper and he held his tongue. Though he was a little afraid to unclench his teeth, he managed to respond to Lane's outburst with a controlled and very tempered answer. "The mission was called in, sir, as you directed." He thought about adding on that perhaps there was a more important mission that needed to be fired, but didn't. Hell, Adderly thought, that's got to be obvious, even to Lane.

That, of course, was an assumption, just as Lane assumed that the fire had come from a town no longer occupied by the enemy. Adderly's assumption that the tracers he had seen had been arching up instead of streaking away reinforced this collective assumption, and without anyone from the helicopter's crew able to confirm or verify, even had they been asked, Adderly deferred to both Lane's judgment and orders. So circumstances continued to run their own misguided course.

Lane, shaken by what was his first near-death experience, was too excited to leave things stand as they were. He had given an order and it was going to be carried out. "Get me the artillery fire direction center."

Knowing what Lane was about to do, Adderly said nothing. It wouldn't make any difference if he did. In the past Lane had taken great joy in berating battalion commanders over the radio, and this, he figured, was going to be just another one of those whipping sessions. When he had switched Lane over to the fire direction radio net, Adderly keyed the intercom between him and Lane. "Your radio is set, sir. The call sign for the artillery is Red Sky."

The only response Lane gave Adderly was a glare before he mashed the push-to-talk button. "Red Sky Six, this is Eagle Six. Over."

During the pause that followed Lane's call, Adderly looked away from his boss and tried to imagine the scene in the fire direction center. There would be a silence for the briefest of moments while the radiotelephone operator sat upright in his seat, turned to find his battalion commander, and then in a sonorous monotone announced that the division commander wanted to speak to him. With a slow yet deliberate pace, the battalion commander would walk over to the radio like a condemned man walking the last mile. How many of them, Adderly wondered, were tempted to have the radiotelephone operator make an excuse for them, to tell Lane that they weren't there or were unavailable? Probably all of them, he thought. Yet they always answered. They had to. Postponing the event would only make things worse. Besides, Lane's lack of professionalism and compassion in his dealings with subordinates didn't mean that they could in turn ignore protocol and etiquette. So they always answered, just as Lieutenant Colonel Day did. Still Adderly noted that he didn't, or wouldn't, use Lane's call sign. Instead Day simply keyed the radio and announced, "This is Red Sky Six. Over."

When Lane spoke, he dropped all call signs, all radiotelephone procedures. "Did you or did you not receive the fire mission I sent you?"

"This is Red Sky, affirmative. Over."

"Then why in the hell did you choose to ignore it?"

For a second, a very brief second, Day pondered his answer. He even considered not answering at all such a patently absurd question. Christ, he thought as he stood in his own fire direction center, didn't that man know what was going on?

The pause was too long for Lane. He jumped back on the radio. "I asked you a question. Either answer me or put the next man in your chain of command on the radio."

Tilting his head back, Day took a deep breath and responded.

"This is Red Sky Six. We acknowledged your mission and will fire it as soon as we complete the missions going in to support Sky Rider. Over."

"To hell with Sky Rider. They have nothing to do with my fire mission. I am giving you an order, Colonel, and I expect you to carry it out. Do you understand?"

Day was now becoming angry. Little by little he was losing his ability to contain himself. "This is Red Sky. I say again, we *will* fire your mission as soon as we complete those fire missions in progress. Sky Rider is in serious trouble. I must complete those missions before I can—"

"Mister, you ain't going to be able to finish anything. You put your next in command on—"

Without another word, Day leaned over, turned the radio off, and walked away, leaving his staff where they stood or sat stunned into silence.

Confusion was fast becoming total. Though the artillery fire and corrections requested were coming in, Crippen yelled to Kozak that he had lost contact with the fire direction center. Switching over to the batteries' internal net, he prepared to make any additional corrections that might be called for. Pender added to Kozak's concerns, announcing that the attack helicopters were still several minutes out and that he had been unable to raise either the brigade commander or his operations officer. They were, he told her, in some kind of meeting somewhere in the 417th's area.

Turning her back to her battle staff, Kozak looked down at the ground, grasping the intercom-radio transmit button in her right hand. With her left hand balled up in a tight fist, she absentmindedly pounded her left thigh again and again. Though it hurt, and eventually would leave a deep dark bruise, she didn't notice it. She was, like everyone else in the cargo bay of her helicopter, in a high state of excitement.

Below her she could see the soldiers of A Company. At that moment that was all that mattered to her, all that mattered to anyone in the helicopter. Though she was doing all that she could, Kozak felt the urge to undo her seat belt and leap out onto the ground just meters below them and rush forth into a fight that was just as chaotic and confusing as the one she and her staff were waging on the radio nets.

In the midst of this, Second Lieutenant Wiezman finally came up on the battalion radio net. "Sky Rider Three, this is Alpha One Six. The enemy in the northeastern corner has broken contact. Request you shift fires to cover our rear. Over."

Though she was glad to hear that, Kozak delayed responding to Wiezman's request at first. "Alpha, this is Sky Rider. Are you in contact with or near Sky Rider Six? Over."

"Negative, Sky Rider. He took off with one of my radiomen before we were hit the second time. Over."

"Where did he go? Can you reach him? Over."

"He went over to the northeast corner of the woods, where I was taking the company. I think he's down. Over."

Wiezman's last transmission sent a shiver down Kozak's spine. "Dear God in heaven."

Crippen, hearing her yell, reached out and tapped her on the shoulder. "What happened? What's wrong?"

Turning to face him, she yelled, "Have the battery firing on the northeast corner cease fire immediately."

"What about the other mission, should we keep—"

"Yes, Pete, yes, keep firing it. Just lift fires on the northeast corner. Now."

She was about to rekey the radio when a strange voice came in over the net. "Sky Rider Six, this is Eagle Six. What in the hell are you doing down there?"

Kozak didn't make the connection. She had no idea who this Eagle Six was and had no intention of finding out. Cramming the push-to-talk button down as hard as she could with her right thumb, she shouted at the radio boom mike hanging in front of her lips, "Unknown station, this is Sky Rider Three. Get off this net. *Now!*"

There was no pause. As soon as Kozak let up on the push-to-talk button, Lane jumped back on. "This is General Lane. Who the hell am I talking to?"

Just as she was about to respond, Crippen yelled from behind her. "That's the last volley going in on the northeast corner now."

Keying her radio, Kozak yelled out over the net to Wiezman. "Alpha Six, go, go, go. That's the last of the artillery fire to your front. Move out now."

"Sky Rider Three, we're—"

Wiezman's transmission, made over a lower-powered man-portable radio, was drowned out by Lane's transmission, which was made using powerful helicopter-mounted radios. "Listen, soldier, I don't know who in the hell you are, but I want to speak to your battalion commander right now."

Enraged by these senseless interruptions by someone whose call sign or voice she didn't recognize, Kozak shot back without pausing to think, "I don't give a shit who in the hell you are. Get off my net and stay the hell off it. Out."

Raising her left hand level with her shoulder, Kozak brought it down onto her thigh with all the force she could muster, screaming out the door, "GO! GO! GO!" as she watched A Company's ragged line of riflemen rise off the ground and cover the short distance between them and the northeast corner of the woods.

Alone in his thoughts, Lane considered having his pilot take them over to where the 3rd of the 511th was and ripping Sky Rider Three a new asshole right then and there. But he couldn't do that. The dampness in his crotch and the smell of loose bowels told him that he wouldn't be able to leave his helicopter even if he could safely land over there. He was pondering what to do when Adderly broke the silence. "General, the pilot says we've taken too much damage to hang around here. We need to leave now or we won't be able to make it back to Bogotá."

He was about to object, but decided that it would be pointless. There wasn't anything to be gained by staying here and watching this screwed-up operation any longer. No, he thought, someone's going to pay for trashing my plan, and they're going to pay big. Lane keyed his intercom button. "Fine, let's go back. And while we're headed back, contact Division. I want Colonel Webb to meet me at the airport the moment we touch down."

Adderly looked into Lane's eyes. In those eyes he saw anger and rage. There was no need for him to ask or even to wonder why Lieutenant Colonel Frederick Webb, the division's staff judge advocate, was being summoned. Lane, Adderly knew, was going to have a public hanging. Some poor schmuck, he thought, was going to get screwed, blued, and tattooed simply because they did their job and Lane was an asshole. Though he didn't like it, Adderly knew that this was the way things were, and that there wasn't a damned thing he could do about it. All he could do was the same thing everyone who hated Lane did, put in your time, do what you had to do, and endure. After acknowledging Lane's order and telling the pilot to head on back, Adderly turned away from him and watched the battle west of El Frío as it faded in the distance. Yeah, he thought, someone is going to hang.

CHAPTER 14

November 15

IT WAS FITTING THAT THE DAY WAS HEAVILY OVERCAST WITH an occasional spasm of drizzle when the advance elements of the 3rd Battalion, 511th Infantry, assembled on the military airfield outside Bogotá. Any anticipated joy or relief in having finally been rotated to that city as the divisional reserve had been crushed by the weight of the circumstances that put them there. For most, it was exhaustion and the delayed stress of battle just beginning to assert itself. It was a strange sensation, one that was as much mental as it was physical. Others, too many, in the words of one first sergeant, were finally allowing themselves to mourn the loss of a close friend or a well-loved sergeant or officer.

Foremost among this last category was Lieutenant Colonel Harold Cerro, killed by an artillery barrage that he had called in on top of himself. As Jan Fields-Dixon went from company to company, soldier to soldier, within the battalion, she found that the feelings over the circumstances surrounding the death of Cerro varied. Company A, which benefited directly from his sacrifice, was especially torn up. Second Lieutenant Wiezman, who had thought that Cerro had lost it during the chaotic rush from the landing zone, had harbored a great deal of anger at the time Cerro had taken one of his radiomen away from him. Though he told no one of this, the remorse and guilt he felt at

267

having doubted such a man and defiled his name, if only in his mind, troubled Wiezman greatly, leaving him withdrawn, sullen, and badly shaken. The sergeants in A Company were less troubled by such considerations, though they still mourned Cerro in a practical sort of way. "If there had been any other way of it," one sergeant told Jan, "I would be really upset. But we were at the end of our rope. He made all the difference, Ms. Fields. Out in the LZ walking around in the middle of the firefight, getting people to hang in there and return fire, in the end he did what he had to do. As hard as it may be for some people to understand, he had no choice. Not really. He picked dying so the rest of us could live. It ain't fair. And it ain't right. But hell, lady, what is anymore?"

That wasn't necessarily the view taken by others within the battalion. Many felt that Cerro was forced to take such a radical step because of A Company's ineptness. Few spoke about it, at least not publicly. One trooper in C Company, who had landed north of A Company at the same time, felt very keenly about this, however, and didn't care who he told about it. When Jan shoved a mike in the young soldier's face, he just started to talk, becoming more and more angry as he did so. "We landed in a hot LZ, just like them, and didn't have half the problems they had. Neither did we leave the colonel in such a bind that he got himself killed. I'm not calling those people over there in A Company a bunch of losers. Hell, I'm even friendly with a couple of guys there. But they got the colonel killed because they screwed up. And that pisses me off, big time."

Regardless of their opinion, all were united in the collective heartfelt feeling of personal loss. Though there would be another battalion commander, the men and women in the battalion knew there would never be another Harold Cerro. His passing more than anything marked the loss of innocence. For if he, a soldier of his drive and reputation, could be killed, then all of them could. Even the youngest troopers in the ranks now realized that they were all mortal, and unless things changed, few if any would come out of this war alive.

Against this somber background, Major General C. B. Lane delivered what many felt was the coup de grâce to what little confidence and self-respect the soldiers in the battalion had when it was announced that Captain Nancy Kozak would be charged with disobedience of a direct order, conduct unbecoming an officer, and disrespect to a superior officer.

Even the manner in which she had been notified of the charges infuriated the soldiers of the battalion. Few had little doubt that the occasion had been intentionally staged that way, for the Judge Advocate General, or JAG, officer arrived at the airfield just as Kozak was assembling the battalion. Refusing to be delayed from the execution of his duties, the JAG officer walked up to Kozak, standing in front of the survivors of the 3rd of the 511th, and presented himself with little fanfare, no warning, and a voice that even troopers in the rear rank could hear. "Captain Nancy Kozak, by order of the commanding general of the 11th Air Assault Division, it is my duty to inform you of the following charges that have been brought against you." Taking great care, the JAG officer then read them one by one as Kozak stood before him ashen-faced and too stunned to react.

Only a growing murmur from the ranks of combat veterans behind broke the reading of the charges. From the rear of the battalion, the command sergeant major was shaken from his shock when he heard the voices of the soldiers become louder and their cries of astonishment begin to slowly turn into sharp comments of rage sprinkled with muted threats. Though his soldiers' response mirrored his sentiments, he kept his feelings and reactions in check. He had heard of such humiliations being played out in the '70s and '80s but never, in his wildest dreams, did he expect to be a witness to such a spectacle. Responding in the same professional manner that Cerro had taught the officers and noncommissioned officers to react when faced with a crisis, the command sergeant major called out in the best parade-ground voice he could manage, "Silence in the ranks. Silence in the ranks. First sergeants, get control of your people and keep them quiet."

Watching this spectacle from one side, Jan Fields-Dixon neither understood what was going on nor how exactly to deal with it. Only JT had the presence of mind to keep the tape running, catching as best he could the battalion's response to this spectacle and Kozak's reactions. They were, JT thought as he watched through the eye of the camera, surprisingly subdued. Kozak's only comment to the JAG officer when he finished was a question. "Am I under arrest?"

Showing no sign that what he had just done had any effect on him, the JAG officer shook his head. "No, you are not under arrest. You will continue with your assigned duties until further notice. Do you have any questions at this time concerning the charges being preferred against you?"

Whether she meant it as an insult, or whether she reacted in an effort to keep from saying something she would later regret, Kozak turned away from the JAG officer and faced the battalion, still being held in check by threats from the senior noncommissioned officers. Slowly she scanned the battalion from left to the right, taking deep breaths as she struggled to contain the anger and tears that welled up inside of her. Finally, when she was ready, she held her head up and, looking into the vacant sky above the heads of her soldiers, she shouted her last order. "Company commanders, take charge of your units." As they saluted, she stepped off to her right and marched briskly away. Only her training and discipline kept her from fleeing the scene of the single greatest humiliation she had ever experienced or imagined.

Later, off camera, the battalion command sergeant major summed it up best when he told Jan Fields-Dixon that Lane's decision to prosecute Kozak was "the dumbest thing that he could have done. Hell, he might as well put a gun to every trooper's head in this outfit now and pull the trigger, 'cause no matter how this comes out, he's lost himself a battalion." In the process of talking to the leaders and soldiers of the 3rd of the 511th, Jan began to see what the command sergeant major meant.

While there was a great difference between how the soldiers felt about the death of their battalion commander and the circumstances that led up to it, to a man they knew that what Lane was trying to do to Kozak was wrong. That he was doing it, and that no one seemed to be stopping it, shattered what little morale and stability the troopers individually and collectively had managed to hang on to up to that point. So strongly did they feel about what Lane was doing to Kozak and them, few had any qualms about expressing their opinions before Jan's camera. "It makes no sense," Captain Frank Walters told Jan.

"He was wrong. Dead wrong. His treatment of this battalion after the big ambush in September was wrong, his handling of the artillery over El Frío was wrong, and his decision to bring charges against Nancy was wrong. That he doesn't realize it and that no one above him is doing anything to stop this insanity is, is . . ." Unable to find the right word to express himself, Walters stopped. He looked down at the ground, shook his head once, shrugged, then turned and walked away from Jan and her camera crew without another word.

And that was the way it stood that morning as helicopter after helicopter brought the soldiers of the 3rd of the 511th in from the field, shattered in spirit and body.

Sitting alone in her darkened office that night, Jan didn't quite know how she was going to approach Scotty on the matter of Nancy Kozak. In all the years she had been with Scotty, first as a lover, then as his wife, Jan had always made sure that neither one took advantage of the other. How easy, Jan knew, it would have been on numerous occasions to dig for or pry information from Scotty. What an advantage she would have had, being married to a living legend who knew just about everyone worth knowing in the Army and who was privy to information few had access to. The cost, though, to her pride as well as their relationship, would have been far too heavy. Both of these, not to mention her career, meant a great deal to Jan. When asked by a young female just entering the field of television news which was more important to her, Jan looked at the bright young face set in an expression that showed how deadly earnest she was and smiled. "Please don't ever ask me to answer that question, for I really don't think I could, not honestly." Tonight, however, as she looked at the phone and waited, Jan began to fear that she was going to have to answer that question soon. How much better, she thought, this would be if Scotty were here in Colombia instead of in Washington going ten rounds with the bureaucrats, which was how he described his frequent trips north.

When the phone finally did ring, it startled her. Jolted from her deep, troublesome thoughts, Jan shot forward and reached for the phone. Though she had no doubt that it was Scotty returning her call, she answered it as she answered all calls, in the office or at home. "Jan Fields speaking. How may I help you?"

When Scott spoke, his voice betrayed his exhaustion. "Sorry, Jan, about calling so late. I was called back by the chief for another round of discussions with the Secretary of Defense. People are starting to get really worried up here about what's going on down there." It was not only the way he sounded, harried and worried that caught her off guard. He was often worried as of late. It was the fact that he had blurted out, without any prodding on her part, who he had met with and their concerns that really took Jan aback. Things had to be bad if he was getting that careless, Jan thought. In the next instant, as Scott continued to recount some of the people he had briefed that day, Jan began to wonder if this was a good time to approach Scotty. Turning this thought over in her head while Scott continued to rattle on, Jan didn't hear much until he was about finished. "I just got into the hotel and saw the message light on the phone flashing. The front desk screwed up the message, naturally, and it took my tired old brain a few minutes to make sense of it. But I'm sure you didn't have me call back just so that you could listen to the pre-senility rantings and ravings of a broken-down old tanker. What do you have for me, babe?"

Jan hated it when he called her babe, hated it with a passion. Ignoring it, since she saw no point in putting him on the defensive before it was necessary, Jan prepared to respond, but paused. She was still unsure how to broach the subject. Though she could be as devious as the best of her co-workers in twisting and turning a conversation until she eased gently into the heart of the matter at hand, Jan didn't feel up to such manipulations. Nor was this a matter that she felt comfortable playing with. Instead, she opted to launch into it with all the grace of a cavalry charge. "You've heard about Nancy Kozak."

Not sure what she was talking about, Scott waited before feeling his way into the discussion. "You mean about what happened to her battalion outside of El Frío? Yes, Jeff Worsham has been keeping me well posted on operations down there. "

"That's not exactly what I'm talking about, although the issue at hand is a direct result of that fight."

Now Jan could hear an audible drawing in of breath before Scott answered. With a voice that was more authoritarian than conversational, he began to inch his way forward into a position. "Jan, I have been informed that there may be charges brought against Captain—"

"No, Scotty, there's no maybe about it. They have been dropped on her today. In fact, she no sooner stepped off the helicopter, bringing the survivors of her battalion in from the field, than wham, she gets informed by the division staff judge advocate himself, in front of her entire command, that she's under investigation for a laundry list of stupid charges."

"Jan," Scott cut in, "disobeying a direct order from a superior ranking officer in battle is not a stupid charge. The Army takes obedience and chain of command rather seriously, especially in the middle of a fight."

Scott's tone and what she perceived as his efforts to lecture her angered Jan. It was a natural reaction, for Jan hated it when a man, any man, got on his high horse and spoke to her like that. Forgetting in her moment of blind anger that Scott was her husband, and not some nondescript information officer who was giving her a bad time, Jan shot back. "I talked to those soldiers in Nancy's battalion, and what she did was right. The company on the landing zone, A Company, I think, was pinned down and badly cut up, facing annihilation. If she hadn't hung tough and told Lane where to get off, how many of those soldiers would still be alive today? Can you tell me that, mister?"

"Can you tell me, Ms. Fields, with any degree of certainty, that what Lane was trying to do was wrong? Have you spoken to Lane? Have you spoken to the brigade commander? Were you there?"

"I didn't have to be there. I don't have to be shown every day that Major General C. B. Lane is a moron who doesn't know his ass from a hole in the ground."

"Jan, Jan, wait a minute, just hold on here. Listen to what you're saying. You've already passed judgment on Lane when it's not him on trial. It's going to be Captain Nancy Kozak and her actions in relation to Lane over El Frío, and not Lane's personality or his past record that will be brought to question.

273

Kozak's actions, and only her actions, will be judged in a court of law."

"So you have no intention of doing anything, do you?"

Half angry, half frustrated, Scott tried pleading with her. "Jan, what do you expect from me? I have no authority in this matter. I'm not in the chain of command. Anything that I do would be inappropriate and unethical. You know that."

Though she heard the tone of his voice, Jan didn't back off. She was angry and to a large extent disappointed. "Scott Dixon, don't talk to me about ethics. What you and Big Al Malin did in Mexico was unethical as hell and you know it. Besides, speaking of Mexico, how can you stand to turn your back on Nancy Kozak? She saved my life while—" She was about to say "while you sat on your ass" but managed to check herself.

During that pause Scott jumped in. "Jan, please stop before you say something you and I will both regret. And for God's sake, listen to what you're saying."

"And what's that supposed to mean, Dixon?"

"Jan Fields, you're acting like a woman."

Though rather oafish, Scott's last comment had its desired effect as Jan took a moment to think about what she was saying. After giving her that moment, Scott continued. "You've lost your objectivity in this whole affair. I've forgotten nothing, not a damned thing about what Nancy Kozak did for you in Mexico. But she did exactly what she was ordered to do. She did her duty, just like any other officer in her place would have done. That you are grateful to her for it is natural. That you have become great friends, because you are both independent and professional women, is also natural. But you can't deal with Kozak as you would anyone else. Nancy Kozak is an officer in the Army, bound and obligated to a system that requires strict and unquestionable loyalty."

"Even," Jan jumped in, "if that loyalty is to a man more responsible for the death of his own soldiers than the enemy?"

Jan's refusal to give ground on this issue and her last comment finally broke Scott's restraint. With a roar he thundered back, "*YES*, damn it. Even to Major General, By-God C. B. Lane. So long as Kozak wears the uniform and draws the pay,

274

she lives and dies by the rules she willingly and freely obligated herself to, just like Hal Cerro."

It wasn't Scott's tone or his argument that finally checked Jan's fury. It was the simple mention of Cerro's name that caused her to halt. Though there was no appreciable break in the conversation, when Jan came back her tone had changed from that of an angry lioness to one of quiet and concern. "Did you . . . were you able to talk to . . ."

Sensing the change in his wife, Scott didn't wait for her to continue. Like her, when he spoke again, his voice was subdued, almost hushed. "Yes, I spoke to Kay today." He was about to say more but couldn't think of anything appropriate to say.

Kay, the wife of Hal Cerro and mother of his three children, had also become a close friend of the Dixons. Hal had, while in Germany, served as the operations officer on Scott's brigade staff and, even earlier still, as the training officer for Scott when he had been the division operations officer before and during the American incursion into Mexico. In truth it had been Cerro and not Nancy Kozak who had led the raid that had saved Jan, along with other hostages being held by a group of mercenaries that were employed by a Mexican criminal. "I suppose this sounds dumb, but how is she doing?"

"I don't think it's really hit home yet. These things never really seem to hit the wives until the funeral. I don't know what it is, whether it's the twenty-one-gun salute, or the playing of Taps, or when the officer in charge hands the widow the folded flag that breaks wives. Whatever it is, that's when Kay will need you the most."

"I know."

"You do intend to be there as a friend, don't you?"

"Yes, Scott, I will be there. But you don't intend to be here for Nancy, do you?"

There was an audible sigh before Scott answered. "Jan, please. If I did anything, even hinted at being interested in this matter, I'd be in the wrong, and it just might make things worse for Nancy."

"How much worse can they be? My God, her career is in jeopardy. Do you realize how much her career means to her?"

"Jan, I know how much her career means to her. But I've

got to be honest with you. Her career is over. Regardless of how favorable the decision is, her future as an Army officer was sealed the instant the division staff judge advocate issued those charges against her. Even if she is totally exonerated and Lane is proven to be the ass that he is, the stigma of this affair will follow her about as long as she wears the uniform.''

"Then you've already tried and sentenced her, haven't you?''

Sensing the renewal of Jan's anger, Scott decided that he wasn't up for another round with his wife. "Look, Jan. It's late. I'm tired and frustrated and I think you are too. Could we please drop this now before one of us says something that we'll regret as soon as we hang up?''

Though she was reluctant to end this argument here, Jan knew that Scott was right. If either one of them went on much more, something would be said and both of them would suffer. No, she thought, this was something best done face-to-face, after he returned to Colombia and had been given some time to think things over. For now Jan decided that she had made her position clear and hoped that it would be sufficient to motivate her husband into some kind of action. With a hint of reconciliation in her voice, Jan agreed. "Yes, Scott, we're both tired. It's been a rough five or six days down here, and I don't think things are going to get much better. If half of the reports filtering out of the bush are true, the FARC have no intention of letting up their pressure on the Bogotá government or its army.''

"They smell blood, Jan, and they're going for the throat.''

Picking up Scott's meaning, Jan perked up. "You think the Farcees are preparing for the kill?''

"Jan, don't you dare quote me or come out in any of your stories stating that an unnamed high-ranking official said this or that, but—'' Scott paused and drew a deep breath—"if the government of Colombia doesn't do something in the near future, and I mean near, nothing these pencil-necked geeks in Washington or the noble troopers of the 11th Air Assault do will make a difference.''

"That bad, huh?''

He was about to say that it was worse than that, but didn't. In his frustration, he had already said too much to Jan, his wife and bureau chief for World News Network. Instead he changed topics without warning. "Listen, Jan. I think I'm going to order some room service, turn on some mindless TV program, and veg out for a while."

"I understand. I'd do the same, but I'm not impressed with Colombian sitcoms. Do you think they'll get better after the revolution?"

"I doubt it. The Farcees don't strike me as having much of a sense of humor."

"No, I didn't think so. Well, honey, take care of yourself, for me, and hurry back."

"Oh, you don't need to worry about that. As soon as the chief says 'That'll be all, General Dixon,' I'm outta here."

"Okay, that's good. Love you."

"Love you too, Jan. Night."

Reaching out, Jan rested the receiver back on the phone's cradle slowly. Holding her hand on it for a moment, she stared at it. He had no intention, she thought, of doing anything to help Nancy. As far as he was concerned, she was on her own. Though that didn't set well with Jan, in a twisted sort of way she understood why Scotty took the stance he was taking.

Letting go of the receiver, Jan threw herself back into her seat and folded her arms. "Well, *mister* General Dixon," she said to herself out loud, "that's all well and good for you. But I can't stand by and watch that bastard take Nancy down like this. It's not right, it's not fair, and it's not going to stand, not so long as I can do something about this whole stinking mess." Without knowing exactly what she was going to do or how she was going to help Nancy Kozak, Jan was determined that Nancy wasn't going to face the lions alone. Not as long as she had something to say about it.

On the other end of the phone line, Dixon sat propped up against the headboard of his hotel room bed and stared blankly at the opposite wall for a moment. Though Jan's call had bothered him, the reaction of the Army Chief of Staff upon hearing the particulars of El Frío and the charges against Kozak shook him even more. "Scotty," he said, "Lane's beginning to really worry me."

Dixon had felt like asking incredulously, "Beginning?" but held himself in check.

"Everything you said about the situation down there," General Fulk continued, "has been right on the money or too damned close for me. What's more, from what we're seeing now, I don't think Lane can handle it. The El Frío affair, if everything I'm being told about what led up to it is true, is only a case in point."

Watching the chief as he took deep puffs of the cigarette he nervously handled as he paced to and fro in front of his desk, Dixon felt like asking what he intended to do about Lane. That, however, would have been inappropriate. Besides, after this buildup, he suspected Fulk was going to tell him anyway. Though he wasn't disappointed in this regard, Fulk's comments that followed served only to deepen the gloom Dixon felt over the news of Cerro's death.

"Scotty, Lane isn't doing well at all, not at all. But he hasn't really screwed up yet, not enough to justify his relief. Hell, if every commander got relieved for making a bad tactical call, no one would be left to command."

Unable to hold back, Dixon finally chimed in. "Major General Lane, sir, is making a habit of making bad tactical calls."

Rather than being angry, Fulk paused in front of Dixon and nodded in agreement. "Yes, true, true. But we still can't relieve him."

"What does that man have to do, sir, to convince you he's unfit for command?"

Fulk took a deep drag on his cigarette, squinting his eyes as he did so. "That, General Dixon, is my concern. Yours, I'm afraid, is to go back down there and do what you've been doing and be ready to pick up the pieces if this thing becomes unglued."

Dixon had been ready to counter with "*when* it becomes unglued" but again held himself in check. Instead he gave Fulk a firm "Yes, sir," and left, knowing that he had pushed Fulk as far as he dared at that moment and knowing that in the end what had to be done now would eventually be done.

What bothered Dixon at that moment and now as he sat on his bed staring at the wall was that more good men and women would die before that day came. In the meantime he was stuck in a moral and ethical dilemma unlike any he had ever faced before. For while the Chief of Staff of the Army could shrug off the Lane-Kozak affair with no more than a wave of a hand, Dixon could not. Just as he could not forget his duties and obligations as a soldier, Scott Dixon could not forget those he called friends.

PART FOUR

A
QUESTION
OF
DUTY

CHAPTER 15

November 16

AFTER SPENDING THE BETTER PART OF TWO HOURS TRACKING down the person he was supposed to defend, Captain Samuel Ulrich was beginning to think that she either didn't want to be defended or didn't exist. Arriving at the battalion headquarters of the 3rd of the 511th shortly after nine in the morning, Ulrich was directed to the battalion adjutant by a sullen soldier on guard. Entering the adjutant's crowded office, he introduced himself to the harried female first lieutenant who bordered on just this side of being chunky. When asked if he could see Captain Nancy Kozak, the lieutenant informed Ulrich in a rather offhand manner and without looking up from the paper she was holding in front of her that Captain Kozak was taking the newly arrived battalion commander on a tour of the battalion area. Though she had a sweet, round face, the female lieutenant conducted herself as if Ulrich were nothing more than a nuisance that she wanted to shed as quickly as possible. After reluctantly taking the time to give him some rudimentary directions on where in the battalion area the captain might be, the lieutenant went back to shuffling papers from one side of her desk to the next, leaving Ulrich to begin his chase.

As crowded as the battalion headquarters was, with squads of soldiers busily generating paperwork for the companies or responding to paperwork dumped upon them from higher headquarters, the barracks area was deserted. Alone, Ulrich blundered his way through one set of cinder-block barracks buildings to another. Were it not for the neatly packed and rolled gear of soldiers, Ulrich would have sworn no one had been in those buildings in days. It wasn't until he was roaming about in the fourth barracks building that he was challenged by a nasty little first sergeant.

Coming up quietly behind Ulrich, the first sergeant made his presence known only when he was two feet away from Ulrich. "*YOU!* Is there something I can help you with?" The ferocity of the first sergeant's words was matched only by the suddenness with which they were delivered. After jumping what seemed like a foot, Ulrich spun around and found himself looking at the top of a neatly blocked camouflage cap. Glancing down, he saw heavy jowls set in a stern and defiant posture, just like the rest of the first sergeant's squat but muscular body. Looking Ulrich up and down as if he were inspecting him, the first sergeant noted that the intruder he had accosted was an officer, causing him to add a "sir," reluctantly.

Recovering his composure, Ulrich unconsciously tugged at the bottom of his camouflage shirt and took a deep breath. Though he was quite pissed at the first sergeant for what he had just done to him, not to mention the disdain that he showed for his rank, spitting out the delayed sir as if the word had left a nasty taste in his mouth, he knew the first sergeant had achieved his desired effect. Ulrich was off balance for the moment and on the defensive. "I was, I am looking for Captain Nancy Kozak. Your adjutant said that I would find Captain Kozak somewhere around here. Have you seen her, First Sergeant?" Squaring back his shoulders, the stocky first sergeant put his hands on his hips and barked out his answer as if it were an order being given on the drill field. "You missed them by ten, maybe five minutes, *sir*."

Ulrich waited for several seconds for the first sergeant to continue before he realized that this little obnoxious man had no intention of surrendering any additional information unless he was forced to. Finally Ulrich, becoming annoyed at the first sergeant's attitude, not to mention his tone, tried again. "Well, you wouldn't happen to know where exactly they went to, would you?"

Folding his arms across his chest and squeezing them together, the first sergeant cocked his head slightly, almost as if he was pondering whether or not he should give such valuable information to this stranger. Finally, just as Ulrich began to part his lips to ask once more, the first sergeant spoke. "The captain is taking the colonel on an inspection of the perimeter, *sir*."

Again, as before, there was a pause as the first sergeant waited for Ulrich to ask what perimeter he was talking about. For a fleeting moment Ulrich considered not asking and playing the first sergeant's waiting game. But he didn't have time for that. More correctly, Captain Nancy Kozak didn't have a lot of time. The charges filed against her had received the personal attention of the division staff judge advocate. The appointment of an Article 32 officer, responsible for conducting a preliminary investigation into the incident, had been accomplished the same day as the incident, and the officer selected for this task left no doubt in anyone's mind that the outcome of those proceedings would be the one most desired by C. B. Lane, the man initiating the charges.

As fast as the prosecution had worked, the defense, which was what Ulrich was responsible for, had lagged behind. Part of this delay was to be expected. The 3rd Battalion, 511th Infantry, had remained in place west of El Frío after the fighting around the landing zones had died down. It wasn't until late the following day, after sweeping the area to ensure that the region was secure, not to mention tending to the collection of its dead and accounting for all personnel and equipment, that Kozak's battalion was relieved.

Speaking of the 3rd of the 511th as Kozak's battalion was not an idle thought. The discovery of the battalion commander's body at twilight on the evening of the twelfth of November, and the wounding and evacuation of the battalion executive officer earlier that day left Kozak as the senior ranking officer within the battalion. Only two other captains were still with the battalion, and both of them, Frank Walters of C Company and Dale Pulaski, the battalion S-4, were considered too junior to take over the shattered battalion. So, despite the charges leveled against her, the brigade commander kept Nancy Kozak with the battalion and persuaded the division chief of staff not to attempt a change of command until the battalion was out of the field and in Bogotá.

Though he was already tired of doing so, Sam Ulrich continued to pry information out of the rude and taciturn first sergeant, who in turn yielded every kernel of information with great reluctance. "You'll have to excuse me, First Sergeant, but I'm not familiar with this area. Where exactly is this perimeter you're talking about?"

For the first time, Ulrich detected the traces of a grin. The bastard, he thought, was mocking him. Looking down at his boots, then back up at Ulrich's face, the first sergeant broke out into a broad grin. "Well, *sir*, that doesn't surprise me. *The* perimeter is a network of defensive bunkers and fighting positions that surround the division's main support area and helicopter park here at the airfield. The reserve battalion has certain responsibilities along that perimeter. Captain Kozak, who assigned the companies to their sectors of responsibility, is walking the new battalion commander around *the* perimeter in preparation for his assumption of command, *sir*."

"Well, yes, of course. Now if you would be so kind, *Sergeant*, as to tell me where exactly your battalion's area of responsibility is, I'll be on my way."

Noting that Ulrich was starting to become visibly upset, the first sergeant changed his approach, but only marginally. "Well, it would be my pleasure, *sir*."

For the next forty-five minutes Sam Ulrich went from one post to the next along the wire entanglements and barriers that surrounded the sprawling military installation. Colonel Christopher Delhue, the division chief of staff, often referred to the main support area as the heart of the division, since practically everything, from men to material, used by the 11th Air Assault arrived and was distributed from here. It was in itself the size of a small Midwestern town, complete with its own streets neatly laid out and a police force, an MP platoon, to be exact, to patrol them. On any other day Ulrich would have enjoyed this time away from the madhouse that the 11th Air Assault's division headquarters had become. The chance to get out, around real soldiers and the equipment that made this division the fearsome weapon that it was, served to renew Ulrich's conviction that what he was doing made a difference. Unfortunately, the need to get his case together quickly, coupled with the piss-poor attitude of the soldiers of Kozak's battalion, wasn't letting Ulrich enjoy this outing. The fact was, he was about to reach the end of his patience when he finally caught sight of two people that he assumed were Kozak and her new commanding officer.

Relieved, Ulrich picked up his pace, being careful to make sure that he didn't run, since that would be undignified. He managed to reach the pair just as they finished inspecting a pair of bunkers guarding an entrance into the aircraft park. Deep in conversation, neither Kozak nor the lieutenant colonel noticed Ulrich's approach until he called out, "Captain Kozak?"

Turning, both Kozak and the lieutenant colonel looked over at Ulrich as he slowed his pace. Saluting as he neared the two infantry officers, Ulrich stopped and faced the colonel. "Sorry to disturb you, sir, but I'm Captain Samuel Ulrich from the staff judge advocate's office. I need to speak to Captain Kozak."

The look on the colonel's face told Ulrich that he was not happy with this interruption, nor the reminder that Kozak was up on charges. Without returning Ulrich's salute or even acknowledging his presence, except for a cold, sharp once-over, the colonel looked at his watch, then over to Kozak. "I have seen enough for now, Captain. Your dispositions appear to be impeccable and the soldiers are some of the best I've seen. Tend to this officer's business and meet me in my office at sixteen hundred hours. I want to go over our contingency operations as soon as possible."

When Kozak raised her right arm to salute the colonel, she did so slowly and without a word. She held her salute for several seconds, watching her colonel as he returned her salute, turned, and walked away. Only when he was out of earshot did she slowly let her right arm fall to her side, whispering, "Bloody pissant," under her breath loud enough that Ulrich heard.

Taken aback by her obvious disrespect, Ulrich's eyes widened as he looked at the colonel, then back at Kozak. "Excuse me, Captain Kozak."

Turning toward him, Kozak showed no sign of repentance for what she had just said. Instead she launched into a tirade.

"He's a jerk, an idiot. What in the hell does he know about fighting positions, let alone what soldiers are supposed to look like? He hasn't seen a real combat infantryman in six years, maybe seven. Christ, I'd like to have five minutes alone with the moron who pulled him out of the Pentagon and sent him down here to take command of this battalion."

Pausing only long enough to catch her breath and bring her temper under control, Kozak eyed Ulrich before she spoke again. "I suppose you wouldn't understand what I'm talking about, would you?"

Barely able to hold back the anger that had been building up inside of him as a result of the frustrating morning he had spent going from one angry and rude soldier to the next, Ulrich kept at Kozak, though now there was a pronounced edge in his voice. "Listen, I don't pretend to know what's going on here, but I do know that every soldier in this battalion I've come into contact with so far has a chip on his or her shoulder the size of the state of Montana. I know that you've taken your sweet time about tending to the charges that have been preferred against you, ignoring my calls and refusing to furnish me or anyone else with a statement concerning the incidents at El Frío." Preparing for his summary as if he were in a courtroom, Ulrich raised his right hand and pointed his index finger up toward the pale blue sky. "And I know that if you and the people in this battalion don't start giving me and my office some cooperation, you'll have to find some other dumb bastard who is willing to put up with your deplorable attitude and high-handed arrogance."

"What," Kozak countered nonchalantly, "do you expect?"

Taken aback by her question, Ulrich shook his head. "Excuse me?"

"I asked you, Captain, what do you expect?"

"I'm sorry, Captain Kozak, I don't understand."

This caused Kozak to smirk. "I wouldn't expect you to."

Though his anger at her manner continued to push him closer to the breaking point, he kept his temper in check. "I'm sorry, but I simply don't understand what you're talking about, just like I don't understand why you've been avoiding me."

Kozak squared off in front of Ulrich with her feet placed shoulder-width apart and her hands on her hips. "It's easy, Captain Ulrich. You're from Division. Nothing good comes from Division. Not to this battalion, not to anyone who is out here on the line."

"If, Captain Kozak, you feel that way about me, why didn't you ask for another defense council from outside the division?"

Folding her arms across her chest, she threw her head back. "Who? I don't know any JAG officers, at least none worth mentioning."

Her attitude and this last comment in particular were insufferable to Ulrich. Still he persisted in as even and unemotional tone of voice as he could manage. "You could have asked for a civilian attorney, you know."

"Listen, Captain, both you and I know how everyone in uniform feels about civilian attorneys. Only the guiltiest bastard would turn to a blood-sucking shyster lawyer. If I were to go into that courtroom with a civilian pleading my case, that would be my third strike."

"What are your first two?"

"First, and most obvious, is the fact that the commanding general himself is involved in this case. That in itself, is—"

"Is what, Captain Kozak?" Ulrich shouted as he cut her off. "Enough to make this wimpy JAG officer quake in his boots and piss all over himself? Listen, I don't care who is involved in this case or who preferred the charges, my duty is to defend you, and I intend to do that, in spite of yourself. Is that clear?"

Now it was Kozak's turn to be rocked back on her heels. Even as he spoke, the bitterness in her eyes began to fade away. During the tense and uncomfortable pause that followed his outburst, Ulrich noticed for the first time how tired she looked. It was more than the dark circles under her eyes and the droops on either side of her mouth. It was her eyes, sad, lusterless eyes that he finally took the time to look at, that spoke of her exhaustion and weariness. When she did break the silence, she tried to speak with an even, unemotional tone but couldn't. Her exhaustion, made more pronounced by a faint note of personal grief, came through. "They're starting to call themselves the Orphan Battalion. To a man, they feel that they and every officer that has stood up for them have been betrayed, berated, or screwed. It's no wonder that you, sporting that nice new shiny uniform, all clean and crisp, and sporting the wreath and quills of the JAG corps on your collar, got the treatment that you did. No one in the battalion area, I'm sure, took the time to find out if you were a good guy or a bad guy. All they saw was an outsider. And right now," Kozak continued as she looked over in the direction in which her new battalion commander had disappeared, "anyone who's an outsider is a bad guy."

"And you? What do you think?"

Ulrich's direct and simple question caused Kozak to look back and study the JAG officer standing in front of her. Though she knew he had to be in his mid-twenties, he looked older in a mature sort of way. His sandy blond hair, too long for regulation by better than half an inch and cut in a box cut instead of being tapered like the infantrymen of her battalion preferred, lay against the side of his head in soft, easy waves. The most striking feature, six-foot-one-inch slim frame notwithstanding, was his china blue eyes. Rather than being piercing, as that color is in some people, Ulrich's eyes were gentle, comforting. As she looked into them, they seemed to draw her into them. For a moment Kozak forgot what she had been talking about as she stared at him and searched for words that would describe the eyes that were staring back at her.

This silence made Ulrich feel uncomfortable. Averting his eyes, he reached over and began to fumble with the thin briefcase he had been carrying. Finding the paper he was looking for, he pulled it out and offered it to her. "I have been appointed to represent you. Do you have any objections to that, Captain Kozak?"

Realizing the embarrassment that she had caused Ulrich, and somewhat startled by her own indiscretion, Kozak looked away from the JAG officer as she answered quickly, "No, not at all. You're as good as anyone else, I suppose." Then, thinking about what she had just said, Kozak looked back up at Ulrich and added quickly, "I didn't mean that to come out the way it did."

Ulrich, still flustered by the momentary confusion and not paying attention, looked up at Kozak. "Excuse me, Captain Kozak?"

Not understanding that he was as off balance as she, Kozak blushed and began to explain away her comment as quickly as the words came to her. "Well, what I mean is that we, I mean I, really don't know any lawyers, not personally, like I said before. There isn't anyone I'd rather have . . ." Catching herself, Kozak paused, a pause that only served to accentuate her last few words. When Ulrich's eyes registered his surprise at that comment, Kozak became totally flustered, something that was truly rare.

In an effort to save her from further embarrassment, Ulrich tried to make a joke. "Well, don't worry. I know exactly how you feel, Captain Kozak. Until two minutes ago I didn't know any female infantry captains, not personally."

Without thinking, Kozak stuck her right hand out. "It's Nancy, Captain Ulrich."

Taking the hand offered to him as a sign of her efforts to make amends, he grasped it firmly and smiled. "Sam. Just plain old Sam."

Though reprieved from her own awkwardness, Kozak still wanted to make sure that what she was trying to say was understood. "What I meant, Sam, was that I had no intention of looking for a lawyer other than the one appointed to me. To have made a big fuss over the lawyer, especially a civilian lawyer, will leave a bad taste in some of the jury's mouths."

"Wait a minute, Nancy. Who said anything about a jury? There's always the possibility of lesser charges, plea bargaining, and—"

The easiness that had crept into their conversation suddenly evaporated as Kozak pulled her hand away from Ulrich. "There will be no plea bargaining, no acceptance of lesser charges. I want a general court-martial, with jury."

The transformation that swept over Nancy Kozak amazed and bewildered Ulrich. Her eyes, eyes that had a moment before been wide and on the verge of smiling, were narrowing down to mere slits as furrow after furrow cut deep into her brow. Even her nose perceptibly changed shape, crunching up to conform to the wild and uncontrollable contortions of her face. For a moment he was almost afraid to speak, unsure of what her response would be. Finally recovering his nerve, he began cautiously. "You know, of course, this may never come to a court-martial. You may be offered an Article 15, or even a simple reprimand."

"No. I want a general court-martial." There was no hesitation, no give. Kozak's response was as firm and uncompromising as the stance she took, clenched fists on her hips and jaw jutting. "That bastard is going to atone for what he did to Harold Cerro and this battalion. His ineptness and callousness are going to be laid bare for all to see."

Though he suspected that he knew who she was talking about, Ulrich wanted to be sure. "Nancy, exactly who is it you're after?"

"Lane."

"The division commander?"

"Is there another Lane in this division that anyone gives a damn about?"

Ulrich looked down at the ground between his feet as he shook his head and folded his arms across his chest. "No, not that I'm aware of." Looking up, he saw that Kozak was still standing before him defiant and angry. "Look," he started, "as your defense counsel, provided you still want me, I have to make sure that you understand that it is you and not General Lane that is up on charges."

Shaking her head as she followed suit and folded her arms, Kozak straightened up slightly. "That, sir, is where you are wrong. It was his ineptitude that bled this battalion white. It was his stupidity that put us asshole deep into the shit four days ago. And it was his blind arrogance that damned near cost us an entire company. Imagine trying to take all the fire support away from a unit in contact, just because someone shot at him and caused him to mess his pants."

Ulrich's jaw dropped. "You know about that?"

This caused Kozak to laugh. "Hell, Sam, everyone in the division knows about Crap in his Breeches Lane. Lane's own pilot was griping to everyone over on the flight line this morning that he still hasn't been able to get the smell out of his aircraft."

Like everyone else involved in this case, Ulrich had been told officially to keep to the facts at hand and make sure that nothing, absolutely nothing, concerning the commanding general was mentioned unless it pertained directly to the matter at hand. Unofficially he had been told to do whatever he could to downplay Lane's role and performance. Nancy Kozak, in the first five minutes of his initial interview, had made it painfully clear that she had every intention of doing just the opposite, leaving Ulrich with a real dilemma. Regaining his balance, Ulrich decided to push the fact that they needed to be discreet about what was said before and after this case came to trial, if it made it that far. "Nancy, please. I know that you are upset and anxious to find a target for your anger and frustration. It's only natural in a case like this to seek to excuse one's actions by making someone else the scapegoat. The fact is—"

"The fact is," Kozak shouted before Ulrich could finish, "that Lane was out of line. While he had every right to be where he was, playing Cowboy Bob or John Wayne, or whatever the hell he was trying to do, he screwed up when he started interfering with a military operation that was reaching a critical juncture. He jumped the chain of command and threatened to unhinge the whole operation. If it weren't for the fortitude of Lieutenant Colonel Chris Day, the battalion commander of the artillery unit supporting us, we would have lost our fire support just when we needed it the most. And since we're looking into this whole sordid mess, why is it just me who has been brought up on charges and not Colonel Day, who also refused a direct order from Lane?"

The issue of Colonel Day's role in this case had been discussed, but briefly. Like many other things, though, that discussion had been short, inconclusive, and summarily dismissed by Colonel Webb, the division staff judge advocate. "The only matter, gentlemen, we need to concern ourselves with at this time," he had told Mark Moretti, the prosecuting attorney, and Ulrich, "is the case of the United States versus Captain N. Kozak, period. Anything else, any other issues, will be dealt with in their time and by other means." Ulrich, of course, knew that Webb's comment meant that Kozak, and Kozak alone, would be charged, regardless of what was fair or appropriate. He had come out to the military airfield with the full intention of making sure that his client understood the official and unofficial rules of engagement for this case.

But any thought of doing so was, to say the least, history. Everything about Nancy Kozak, from her piercing stare, to the uncompromising and defiant stance she was holding, told Ulrich that she would not be denied. "You understand, Nancy, that if we go to a court-martial, your career is shot."

"Sam, my career ended the moment I keyed the radio net to tell Old Crap in his Breeches where he could go. You know as well as I do that in today's Army even the hint of any adverse action, whether it makes its way into your records or not, is the kiss of death. Besides, C. B. Lane must be made to atone."

As she spoke, Ulrich could feel his heart sink lower and lower. By the time she finished this last pronouncement, accentuated by a thrust of her right index finger down toward the ground, Ulrich felt as if his heart had struck rock bottom. It wasn't justice she was interested in, he thought. This woman was seeking vengeance. For a moment he considered shoving his papers into his briefcase, thanking Kozak for her time, and heading straight back to division headquarters to tell Colonel Webb that his client was crazy and needed a shrink instead of a lawyer. Then it struck him. Like so many others in the 11th Air Assault, he had seen and been subjected to, directly and indirectly, C. B. Lane's tyranny and arrogance. He had personally watched Lane on numerous occasions belittle field grade officers and senior sergeants whose only crime had been being too close to him when he lost his temper or, even worse, when he felt like demonstrating his power over other people. Such antics from a junior officer would have been to Ulrich intolerable. Coming from a general officer, a man who was the closest thing to a god on earth, they were beyond contempt. Suddenly, like a lightbulb being turned on in his mind, Ulrich saw what he could do, what he had to do. For here in the person of Captain Nancy Kozak and the defense he was charged to deliver on her behalf he was being offered the perfect opportunity to make Lane pay for all those little crimes against human decency that he had committed for as long as Ulrich could remember against the officers and soldiers of the division.

To Kozak's surprise, Ulrich flashed a smile. "Okay, you got yourself a lawyer. But from here on in you play the game by my rules. If anyone, and that includes your closest friend, gets wind of your Avenging Angel routine, we're both screwed. Is that clear?"

Now it was Kozak's turn to be thrown off guard. Up to that very moment she had thought him to be nothing more than a useless division staff toady. His last comment, however, set her to thinking. Maybe, she thought, there's a man hiding somewhere in those clean, well-pressed fatigues. If there was, and Kozak hoped there was, perhaps she could do what she had set out to do, consequences be damned.

Standing there facing each other, the two officers began anew to consider what it was each would need to do in the coming weeks to achieve what was required of them by fate, duty, and design. In their thoughts, neither was troubled by issues of professional ethics or morality. Such concerns, much ballyhooed in the pristine environs of the Command and General Staff College at Fort Leavenworth or the Army War College in Carlisle, had long since become meaningless to the officers and troops in Colombia. Not that anyone who cared to look seriously into the matter could have blamed the two young captains. How could they, after all, be expected to live up to high professional and moral standards when in the middle of a war the very people who should have been enforcing those standards were themselves incapable of living by them.

So the two of them, joined together by circumstances, made their way past the men and women of the division support command busily going about the task of keeping the heart of the division pumping and working hard to survive one more day in a hell not of their making. None of the young troops, each tied up in his own struggle, bothered the two captains as they passed by, headed toward a fight that they knew would be more vicious and brutal than anything the FARC could ever hope to wage.

From across the busy Bogotá street, Major José Solis could see the man he had been instructed to meet. Nervously he glanced first to his right, then to his left. He hoped that to anyone watching him he was checking the stream of cars and trucks that whizzed by him. While this was true and very necessary, given the way people in Bogotá drove, the traffic before him was at this moment the least of his worries. It was the National Police, or Terrorist Police, a branch of the National Police that specialized in anti-terror operations. They, and not the steady stream of vehicles, were foremost on his mind at that moment.

He had tried to convince himself that there was no need to

worry or be so cautious. After all, worrying about being picked up by the police at this point made no sense, for he knew that if he had been followed by counterintelligence people, any precautions he took now would be pointless. Other officers, after all, had been arrested for less than simply being in proximity to a FARC officer. No one, Solis knew, was above suspicion anymore, not since the aborted coup of last spring.

Still his training as well as his natural instincts caused him to look back. It was foolish, he thought, to go tromping about in broad daylight in the middle of the capital, meeting rebels like this. Even wearing the clothing of a day laborer, clothes that did not fit his stature and carriage at all, did nothing to ease his discomfort. Since leaving his apartment, Solis had felt like every eye was on him. This is mad, he kept telling himself, foolish and mad.

Yet despite his better judgment, he stepped out into the street and began to cross, headed for the sidewalk cafe, walking as a condemned man marches to his death. Almost as if to confirm this image that clouded his mind, the sudden screeching of a truck's brakes behind him just after he reached the middle of the street caused his heart to skip a beat. Without looking, he could see in his mind's eye hordes of national policemen pouring out of an unmarked car, racing up behind as they prepared to wrestle him down onto the pavement like a common criminal. Freezing where he stood in the middle of the street, Solis cringed before reluctantly looking over his shoulder. Only after he had located the source of the noise, an old truck overburdened with produce, did he relax as best he could. Recovering, he felt himself flush as he pulled himself together and, hurried on by the honking of impatient drivers angered at his unexplained delay in clearing the road, continued across the street. Once on the sidewalk, Solis moved quickly over to the cafe and slipped into the chair across from the man he had been told to meet.

The man, amused by Solis's antics, grinned. "It is fortunate that you have not attempted to make a living by being a member of the Terrorist Police, for I fear that your family would starve to death."

Solis's cheeks flushed with anger. "Not everyone, Señor Valendez, takes the dangers about them as you do."

Hector Valendez's grin broadened. "My friend, I do not take anything lightly. If I did, do you think our movement could have gone as far as it has?"

Though Solis in theory worked for Valendez, he would not let this man make light of his concerns. Nor did he like anyone telling him that he was part of the insurgency sponsored and controlled by the FARC. He was a Colombian soldier, an officer sworn to defend his country against its enemies. It just so happened that at this moment the greatest enemy, in his eyes and those of many of his fellow officers, was the government itself. His choice to provide the FARC with information at the direction of a very senior officer on the general staff was, he had been told, a political necessity, nothing more. Solis held no love for the man across from him. He didn't understand his ideology or the cause for which he was fighting. To Solis, Hector Valendez and all members of the FARC were tools, instruments to be used to achieve his goals and those of the Colombian Army. In an effort to ensure that Valendez understood that he was a man and not a mere pawn, Solis stared into Valendez's eyes with a firm and defiant gaze. "There are those who feel your movement would do better if you exercised a little more caution."

Rather than wipe the smile from his face or cause him to reconsider his comment, Valendez's smile only grew larger. "And if I listened to those people, men who huddle in the corner like frightened old women in the night, we would still be out there hidden away high in the mountains gathering moss, no nearer to pulling down this corrupt and inept government than we were last spring." Suddenly he dropped his smile. Leaning forward, Valendez took his fist and softly yet firmly brought it to rest on the table before Solis. "No, this is not the time to give in to groundless fears and apparitions. We must stand up like men and go forward. And we must do it now, while we have the upper hand and the government itself is still reeling from the blows it has received both from us and from within." Having made it clear that he was serious, Valendez sat upright, throwing his left hand out with a flippant gesture as he continued his argument. "Why, even the vaunted American Army is beginning to tear at itself from within. The trial of a mere captain, as you have pointed out, has the entire officer corps of the division in an uproar and has captured the attention of the American media.''

Whether Valendez's comments were meant to be a slur on the timidity he had just shown when crossing the street or not, Solis took it as such. Feeling the need to defend his actions and honor, he leaned forward and faced Valendez almost nose to nose. ''It would not be wise, my friend, to make too much of the affair between the general of the American division and the female captain he has brought charges against. She, like any other soldier, is only a small piece of the whole, and to judge the workings of the machine by studying just one piece would be a terrible mistake.''

Sensing Solis's mood, Valendez chose to defuse the confrontation. Leaning back into his seat, he signaled the waiter. Without having to be told, the waiter brought two beers over. Watching the performance, Solis suddenly realized that he had in part been right about being watched. The only thing that he had gotten wrong was the who. Rather than members of the Terrorist Police, the people watching him had been FARC. Glancing around, he wondered how many of the men lounging around in this small nondescript cafe, busily chatting with one another or lazily reading the daily paper, were armed and on guard.

''You are correct,'' Valendez countered, ''to a point. While it would be foolish to consider the events at El Frío that brought the American general and the captain into conflict as cataclysmic in themselves, the incident is symptomatic of a rot in spirit and morale that is infecting everyone charged with defending this government. And if this one tiny piece of the American division does manage to destroy herself, it will not mean an end to the division's effectiveness. But if we help matters along, perhaps we can cause other little pieces to malfunction. How long, Major, can that fine watch of yours continue to work if half the little wheels and gears one by one stop working?''

The openness with which he spoke of the American division and even the casualness with which he used his title convinced Solis that this cafe was a safe haven, if only temporarily. Relaxing, Solis took a sip of his beer, eyeing Valendez as he did so. Following the bottle down with his eyes as he set it on the table, Solis spoke without looking up. "You obviously have something in mind, my friend. Some way of sprinkling grains of sand into the workings of the American division."

Slowly the smile returned to Valendez's face. The confrontation was over. Major Solis was now in the frame of mind necessary to discuss the matter for which he had been summoned. "While the initial phases of the battles around El Frío yielded the results we had hoped for, the final operations, those we had not planned, the ones involving the Americans, did not live up to my expectations. The Yankees were simply too strong, too well supported, too quick, and our own local forces too unpredictable." Reaching out with his right hand, Valendez took his beer, sipping it as he reflected on what he was about to say. Only when he was ready did he continue. "Still, what happened there on the twelfth cannot be considered a total defeat. On the contrary, after looking at the fallout from that affair, there is much we can use to our advantage."

Solis nodded his head in agreement. "Yes, all of that is very true. There was much dissatisfaction over how the operation was carried out and what happened. There are still howls of recrimination echoing through the halls on our side of the Ministry of Defense as one general blames the other for the massacre of the infantry battalion during the initial fight. The report filed by the American correspondent, the woman who is now making the court-martial of the female captain such an issue, has done nothing to calm the anger of the general or the government. Everyone, from the President on down"—Solis started to make wild gestures as he twisted his face in a mock look of confusion—"is running around like a frightened chicken, squawking. In front of the entire general staff, the Minister of Defense stood up and shouted in the face of the chief of staff, 'Who is responsible for all of this? Who? Is anyone in charge of anything anymore?' " For a moment he joined Valendez, who was already chuckling. Then, on a more serious note, he continued. "Not even the Americans came away from the fight satisfied." Then as an afterthought Solis corrected himself. "Especially the Americans. Even though their 3rd Brigade was left in control of the battlefield and they annihilated two local-force platoons, the American media have made El Frío look like a thoroughly bungled affair. I saw this morning on the news channel that the Americans monitor in their headquarters a congressman complaining that their Army was using sledgehammers to kill ants.''

"Ah, yes," Valendez cut in, "the American media." His smile broadened again. "It was this powerful tool of democracy that gave me the idea which I want to discuss with you."

"I had hoped, Señor Valendez, that there was a reason, other than making me nervous and treating me to a beer, that you called me here."

Delighted that Solis was now comfortable enough to make light of his own fears, Valendez lifted his beer toward him for a toast. After the two men clinked their bottles together and took a long, hard pull at them, Valendez launched right into the matter at hand. "In terms of combat power, resources available, control of land and population, the position of the FARC is very, very shaky compared to the government, its military, and the Americans. That is a fact. But it is a fact that means very little these days. We have achieved, through operations that have been anything but militarily decisive, psychological and moral ascendancy over our enemies."

Though he did his best to maintain his impassive air as he listened, the frankness and accuracy with which Valendez summed up the FARC's military effort impressed Solis. He found himself intrigued by the man whom the Colombian Army's intelligence bureau referred to as nothing more than "a gifted amateur." "It is true," Solis interjected. "We, the Colombian Army, have failed to bring our full might to bear at any point. The loss of a few battalions and companies," Solis said as he waved his hand as if he were shooing a fly, "can be made good. But the loss of our reputation and confidence in our ability to deal with you," emphasizing the last point by pointing his index finger at Valendez, "that is an entirely different matter. As you have said, what you have gained, my friend, in these small battles far exceeds your investment of manpower or blood."

"Yes," Valendez agreed after hearing Solis out. "Now we have a new problem."

Before he could continue, Solis sat back in his seat, took his beer, and pointed the long neck of the bottle at Valendez. "Exploiting your success and maintaining the pressure."

"Exactly, Major Solis. Exactly. Unfortunately, we do not have the military strength to do so. Though I have tried hard to maintain a reserve, the tempo of our operations and the vast area over which we have been stretching ourselves in an effort to create the illusion that we are more powerful than we are have worn my main-force battalions thin. Now, when a couple of fresh battalions could make a real difference, I do not have them. While we do have local forces that have yet to be committed, the incident outside of El Frío proves that they, the local force units, are a poor substitute for well-trained and -led regulars. Besides, in concentrating our efforts in preparing the nine battalions of regular forces, I have through necessity been forced to postpone providing the local forces with battalion-level staffs and training. Now," Valendez concluded with a frown on his face, "when I need such battalions, I do not have them."

"So what is your solution to this problem, señor? You obviously have something in mind, otherwise you would have not risked your neck in a casual visit to the capital."

Valendez smiled. "You make too much of the risks you or I take. The fact is, I am safer here in the capital than I am out there in Los Llanos. Many members of the central committee, you know, think that I am too modest, that I should not shy away from the publicity that they themselves crave so much. But in their efforts to inflate their egos they forget that they are only setting themselves up as targets. You can, no doubt, close your eyes and see the face of each of the principal members of the central committee, thanks to the interviews they so freely granted to our friends the media. I, on the other hand, have been able to retain my anonymity, and thus I am free to come and go pretty much as I please." Looking around the cafe and then out into the crowded street, Valendez shook his head. "I can do what no other member of the central committee can. I can hide in plain sight."

While all of this was to Solis very interesting, it did nothing to explain why he had been summoned. His look of impatience, he realized, must have shown through, for Valendez quickly went back to the matter at hand with very little fanfare. "In lieu of reserve battalions, which we do not have, I intend to use the media and well-aimed and directed terrorism to keep up the pressure while the regular battalions rest and refit.''

"That is dangerous. If you commence such acts of violence you will lose the support of those in the military who hate the government as much as you do and have to date worked more or less in concert with you.''

"Does that," Valendez asked pointedly, "include you?"

Without any hesitation or effort to hide his convictions, Solis nodded. "Yes! Most definitely. For I am still a soldier dedicated to the defense of my people.''

This answer seemed to satisfy Valendez, for he smiled. "And so I suspected, which is why you, my friend, will be so important to us during this next phase of our little war. You see, I intend to sever the shield arm that has been defending the government.''

"I am sorry, señor, but your analogy escapes me.''

"The Americans. They have been protecting this government from us, from your Army, from its own people ever since the spring coup. Using the Americans like a shield, the government has hidden, free to continue the purge of the Army and delay the social and economic reforms so necessary to the people. By concentrating our attacks against the Americans now, when their own media are laying them bare to criticism, perhaps we can make this war too uncomfortable for them. Perhaps we can encourage their people and Congress to do what we ourselves cannot do—get them to leave.''

Relieved that Valendez was not creating a moral dilemma for him by striking at his own Army, Solis saw the plan's merit. "It is well known," he stated, "that American staying power is quite fragile. We discuss that among ourselves in private frequently. If you can through your efforts make this war politically uncomfortable and costly to the American politicians who put their troops here, then you are correct, they will leave.''

"Besides," Valendez added, "such attacks would serve as a warning to the Army.''

Though he thought he knew the answer, Solis looked over at Valendez. "Oh? And how?''

Realizing that he had in his enthusiasm threatened the Army that Solis was so dedicated to, Valendez quickly explained.

"We are going to do that which we have refrained from to date. We are going to embarrass the Americans right here in Bogotá where all the eyes of Colombia and the world can see. We are going to kill so many senior American officers and soldiers in the streets of this city that they themselves will be begging their government to pull them out. And in the process, as each American officer goes down in a hail of gunfire, every senior Colombian officer will have to ask himself, Am I next? We, of course, will make it clear in a quiet, gentlemanly way that such a thing will not happen, provided . . ."

"Provided what?"

"Provided the Army, your Army, steps aside and leaves us a clear path to the presidential palace once the Yankees are gone."

In the silence that followed, Solis thought about Valendez's comments and about the feelings that he and many of his fellow officers shared concerning their role in the current struggle. He knew that there already was a great deal of sabotage from within the Army itself aimed at doing exactly what Valendez was proposing. He knew that the units being deployed to fight the FARC in Los Llanos were not the best and those that were being committed to that fight were being fed into it in a piece-meal manner. Even the dispatch of one of the battalions of the Presidential Guard brigade and its subsequent massacre had been a setup, an effort to weaken those forces that were un-shakably loyal to the government. No, Solis thought, what Valendez was plotting was no mere dream. It was as cold and ruthless as it would be effective. In fact it was the very ruth-lessness of their acts to date and what Valendez was proposing that made everything he did so effective. It left those who survived with the thought planted firmly in their mind that they were fighting a heartless killing machine that had no remorse, that held to no constraints. Satisfied, in his own mind, that he understood what Valendez intended to do and that he could with a clear conscience support it, Solis peered into the rebel's waiting eyes. "Your strategy has merit. What, señor, do you require from me?"

CHAPTER 16

November 19

OF ALL THE CONCERNS AND UNRESOLVED ISSUES THAT SCOTT Dixon brought back from his extended visit to the Pentagon and SOUTHCOM headquarters, the one that he had the least desire to deal with was Jan's anger. She was, he knew, upset with him because he had done nothing to help Nancy Kozak and had, as he had told her in so many words, no intention of helping.

It wasn't the fact that she said anything, for Jan never said a word about Kozak and the trial from the moment she picked him up at the gate of the military airfield, through supper, and into the evening. On the contrary, it was precisely her avoidance of the subject that cued Scott to the severity of her anger. Scotty knew, from dealing with other lesser matters in the past, that the longer she held back the worse it would be. "It was," he told a friend once, half in jest and half in earnest, "like watching a uranium atom becoming excited, pinging about madly in its own little orbit until, POW, it reached critical mass."

"Well," his friend asked, smirking, "what does a well-trained professional soldier like you do when faced with that kind of peril?"

"I do," he responded as he continued to grin, cocking one

eyebrow, "what the pioneers did when faced by a savage attack; I circle my wagons and keep my eyes open."

"For a chance to attack?"

"Attack? Don't be foolish. I wouldn't last a minute. Don't forget, this woman is a trained correspondent. Her specialty is dismembering notable public figures, particularly men, before the all-seeing eye of the TV camera. No, when faced with Jan's fury, your only chance of surviving with your dignity and sanity is to turn into the wind and weather the storm. Then, when she has spent her anger, you seek an honorable surrender at the earliest opportunity under the best conditions possible."

This caused his friend to break out in a broad smile. "So you don't say anything. You just sort of let her run her course, tire herself out, and then apologize."

"That, good buddy, is about the size of it."

The "storm" struck home that night in the hotel room they were sharing, just after they had turned in on what normally was neutral ground. Scott, finished first in the bathroom, moved about the room like a cat. As Jan rose from her chair, he slipped around her and hopped into bed, leaning back on two pillows to do some reading while he waited for her to reappear. Unlike most nights, when she insisted in keeping up her conversation with him from the bathroom, despite the fact that he couldn't hear her over the noise of running water and he was trying to concentrate on the book he was reading, Jan said nothing. This Scott took as a bad sign, a sort of calm before the storm.

With this thought running through his head, he was unable to concentrate on the book he held propped up on this chest. Instead he watched her move about the room from one place to another, picking her outfit for the next morning. She's very much like me, he thought, down to her habit of laying everything out the night before, allowing her to lie in bed until the last possible moment, snuggled up to her pillow or me, when I'm here. Even her habit of going against the odds, standing on principles that few in her line of work could understand or appreciate, becoming the champion of causes that others shy away from, is no different than my habit of accepting what others consider preposterous missions with nothing more than a hand salute, a well-trained poker face, and a hearty "Can do, sir." Watching her move about in front of him clad in a white linen dressing gown that only came down to her mid-thighs, flipping her head to the side every so often to shake her long brunette hair from her face, Scott wondered if she did it all as much for the excitement that such challenges presented as for the high ideals that were often used to justify such fights.

Finished, Jan turned to Scott, flashed her famous smile, and cocked her head in a very charming manner. "Ready for bed, or would you like to read for a while longer, dear?"

Dropping his chin on his chest, he looked up at her over the reading glasses that he needed so badly but seldom used in public. "Well, I don't know. Why? Do you have something else in mind?"

"Well," she said, averting her eyes slightly, "we could talk, couldn't we?"

Like a soldier hearing the blare of the enemy's bugle sounding the charge, Scott winced slightly and prepared for the attack that was about to be delivered. Closing his book, he laid it on the night table and slowly removed his glasses, setting them on top of the book before turning to face Jan, arms folded across his chest. "My failure to do anything to help Nancy," he stated without fanfare or prelude, "has been bugging you since this whole thing hit the street, hasn't it?"

Seeing that he had opted to take a defiant and combative stance right off the bat, Jan dropped all pretense and drove right to the heart of the matter. "I'm sorry, Scott. I simply cannot understand how you can so casually turn away from a person who has been a friend, not just a good little loyal minion, all these years. Like I told you the other night, what she did in Mexico, in my opinion, ranks somewhere above and beyond the call of duty."

Jan's last comment angered Scott. With all the effort he could muster, he clenched his teeth lest he yell or say something that he would immediately regret. From the foot of the bed, Jan watched him, satisfied in part that she had struck a nerve while at the same time a little afraid that she had just pushed the wrong button too soon in this discussion. It would be terrible, she realized, to let this degenerate into an angry shouting match before she had made her point. Slow down, she told herself. Make your case. There's too much at stake here to lose it all in a fit of rage. In an effort to retrieve the situation, Jan dropped the accusatory tone in her voice and instead switched to one that was more conciliatory. "Scottie, dear, I understand that there are things that regulations and custom prevent you from doing. I'm not asking you to do anything that's illegal."

Though he was tempted to come back and accuse her of not understanding diddly about military law or regulations, her change in approach kept him in check. Though he too tried to change the tone of his voice to one that was more conciliatory, it came out instead as if he were delivering a lecture to a confused student. "Jan, darling, I'm afraid that you don't quite understand my position. Even the mere appearance of my trying to use my rank or influence in this matter would go against just about every principle—"

"Principle?" Jan shot back as she hastily brought her hands up to her hips and leaned forward at the waist toward Scott, chin jutting and eyes ablaze with passion. "You can lie there in your bed and talk to me about principle? Are they the same principles that his highness Major General C. B. Lane has been using to run this division? The ones that permit him and his staff to generate erroneous reports and information designed to further their own personal careers? Are they the same principles that allow young men and women to be sent out day after day on poorly planned and ill-advised missions, to die in this shithole of a country for political reasons that our own government can't explain? And why, sir, do you feel so obligated to live by some holy principles that no one else understands or even cares about?"

When Scott responded, there was no anger in his voice. "For the same reason, Jan, that you feel obligated to stand by Nancy even when common sense and your duty as a correspondent dictate that you step back and hide behind your camera."

Having expected a violent reaction, Jan pulled her head back, as if Scott's words had hit her square in the face. The manner in which he had delivered his last comment and the need for her to think drew the vehemence from her tone and argument. Standing upright, she gave Scott a quizzical look that slowly softened to one that bordered on being embarrassment. Since she had learned of Hal Cerro's death, she had become so drawn into fixing the blame on C. B. Lane that she lost her objectivity. She was out to prove a point, using her reports, and didn't give a damn anymore about balance, objectivity, or relevance. Now that she appeared to be more rational and receptive, Scott began to make his case. Pulling the sheet back, he swung his legs out of bed and pulled himself up till he sat at the edge of the bed. Thus seated, he covered his lap with the sheet and turned to face Jan, still standing at the foot of the bed.

"If there was something, anything, that I could do that was within my power to help Nancy Kozak, that was both legal and within bounds, I would."

"Couldn't you," Jan shot back, "at least come forward as a character witness?"

"Even if Nancy or her attorney asked, which they haven't, my vouching for her past character would do nothing to change the facts of this case. By her own admission, she did tell Lane over an open radio net where to get off while he was exercising his command prerogatives. She was wrong."

"But so was he. He had no right to interfere with Nancy's conduct of the battle. She was in the middle of an engagement, a fight in which a good part of her battalion was in danger of being wiped out. Lane was going to take away her artillery support."

"And," Scott interrupted, "he was well within his bounds to do so. Those guns belong to him, just like every soldier, weapon, and piece of equipment in that division. He is not only the division commander, he is the senior U.S. commander in country, charged by the President of the United States in executing policy. He had every right to divert those guns to a new target."

"But it was wrong, Scott. The official statement from his pilot indicates that Lane's aircraft was out of danger when he had his aide call for the artillery. He didn't need those guns anymore. Kozak did."

Caught off guard by what she had just said, Scott hesitated for a moment. "How, Jan, do you know so much about this case, including what the pilot's statement said? They haven't even convened the Article 32 investigation yet."

Throwing her head back, she thought about his question before giving him an answer that was somewhat aloof and snooty. "I have my sources."

Raising his right index finger, Scott shook it at her. "For your sake and your source's sake, you'd best be careful. You can get your pompous little behind thrown out of this country if you're not careful. Don't forget, the President of this country has declared himself and his nation at war, and both he and Lane have the right to invoke any part of the martial law restrictions they deem fit. Interfering with an official investigation would be more than enough justification for Lane to get rid of you."

He was right. Jan knew it. Moving over to a chair facing the bed, she plopped down and let her arms fall to her sides. Scott could see a hint of moisture in the corner of both her eyes. "He killed Hal, Scotty. As sure as I sit here, he killed him. And he's out to ruin Kozak simply because she called him a name while she was doing her duty. That, by anyone's measure, is not right."

Lowering his head, Scott pondered Jan's comments. Yes, he thought, Lane was responsible for ordering the operation that had resulted in Cerro's death. And yes, his insistence on bringing Kozak up on charges for ill-chosen words spoken in a burst of passion was, in Dixon's mind, inappropriate. To do so, however, was well within his right and, some could argue, his duty. War, whether it was a small one-division sideshow being waged in a remote corner of a minor third world country or on the plains of northern Europe, demanded disciplined and professional armies. Breaches of the discipline that held units together were dangerous and left unchecked could lead to future breaches of that delicate and necessary commodity. While it was not unusual for subordinates deeply involved in a fight to become frustrated and lash back at superiors they felt were interfering too much or were out of touch with the situation as they saw it, such incidents were nonetheless wrong and contrary to the maintenance of discipline. Equally common, Scott knew, was the practice of making an example of one soldier, officer or enlisted, who had erred, regardless of the circumstances which prompted them to do so.

Scott looked at Jan and stared at her for the longest moment.

He was familiar with every aspect of the fight at El Frío. His chief of staff, Jeff Worsham, while Dixon was in Washington, had looked into the matter, assuming correctly that he would want to know. As much as he wanted to find fault with what Lane had done during the battle and immediately after, all his actions were, as best he could determine, well within regulations and policy. Yet, he wondered, how could he explain this to Jan? How could he make her understand that on any given day he would do the same. The fact was, as he thought about this, that the image of the radioman, back on the twenty-first of September, flashed across his mind. He had on that day come within a hair's breadth of bringing that trooper up on charges. That he didn't do so didn't make him a better man. In fact, by failing to do so, Scott realized that he had allowed a serious transgression of his secret discipline to go unpunished. Voltaire said it best when he claimed that an admiral had to be put to death every now and then to encourage the others.

That witty saying, however, wouldn't do him much good at the moment. Dropping his head, he sighed. How, he wondered, could he explain that to her? How could he explain it to anyone who hadn't lived with this kind of thing their entire adult life? You couldn't, Scott thought. You simply couldn't put such ideas into words that could be understood by someone who had been hurt by war. Sitting there, he couldn't even explain it to himself. Like many others before him, he had long ago given up any hope of applying rationality to a human pursuit that defied rational explanation. War, as William T. Sherman told a Union Nashville matron who was hosting a dinner in his honor, was hell. It was that simple, period. The real sadness in this whole affair, Scott realized, was that no matter what anyone did, the cost of all this insanity was lives, lives of good people. On the twelfth it had cost Hal Cerro his life, and in the next week or so, unless she was damned lucky, it would cost Nancy Kozak her career.

He looked back at Jan, who continued to sit in her chair staring at him. "I'm sorry, Jan, but Hal Cerro died in the line of duty. If I had been given the same information that Lane had that morning, I would have done the same. Lane seized a fleeting opportunity to destroy two FARC battalions using the units available and the mobility of his division. To have allowed that opportunity to pass without doing anything would have been negligence on his part. It just so happened that one of those units was Hal's. On another day it would have been someone else's. And if that had been the case, the death of that battalion commander would have gone unnoticed by you, and because you had no association with the individual involved, the entire American public would not have noticed.''

Though she doubted that Scotty would let Hal's death pass in such a casual manner, Jan let that point slip by. Instead she continued to hammer at the incident that resulted in Kozak's pending trial. ''That still does not make right what Lane's doing now. Besides, I doubt that you would choose to crucify a subordinate just because he or she got a little excited and let words pass between you. I've heard more than enough stories bantered about concerning your indiscretions with higher ranking-officers when you got yourself excited.''

Scott leaned back some as he dropped his arms down to his lap and shook his head. ''Just because I did it and got away with it doesn't make such behavior right or even justifiable. The only reason I didn't get drawn and quartered was because the officer involved chose to ignore the incident or handle it in a different manner. In that regard, I was lucky. Nancy Kozak wasn't. And don't be so quick, Jan, to pass judgment.''

Slowly she shook her head as she spoke through the tears that she fought to hold back. ''Scott, he hurt me. He hurt me by hurting people who mean something to me. I can't let that go by simply by saying that it was nothing more than the luck of the draw. If it had been some other poor bastard instead of Hal, would that have made it any more right? Less painful for me, yes. Right, no. And now he's going after Nancy.''

She paused, wiping away a stray tear that had escaped her efforts to keep it in check and ran down her cheek. In her mind the issues at hand, avenging Hal Cerro's death and saving her friend Nancy Kozak, were flip-flopping about and merging together. For the first time, Jan began to fear that she wasn't making any sense. Finished, she caught her breath and continued. ''I know I don't understand everything the military did. I never have pretended to do so. And I know that at times I let my emotions get the best of me, causing me to react before I think. But I, Scott Dixon, am able to live with that and with myself. There's nothing I can do to help poor Hal. He's gone in all but memory. Though I wish there was something that I could do to help some other poor devil from going through what he did and sharing his fate, that is as important right now as doing something for Nancy. She is still here and very much in need of help and, more importantly right now, a friend.''

Scott listened, watching Jan's face as she spoke. While he could mask his fears and emotions behind an impenetrable poker face, Jan's face, especially her eyes, spoke legions. What he saw now in that face and those eyes was blind determination. She was, he knew, hell-bent on doing something, consequences be damned. Though he had never in his heart disagreed with that assessment, his stubborn adherence to the code of honor and the regulations that were so much a part of his life and his personality held him in check like twin anchors holding a ship. But Jan was not bound by those principles. She, unlike he, could do something. But what, he wondered, could she accomplish on her own? "And what, Jan, do you propose to do? What in God's name can you accomplish by giving this story more attention than it deserves?''

The anger that she felt helped her draw back her tears. From one of forlorn sorrow, her face slowly transformed itself into a mask of angry resolve. "I intend to make sure that the American public sees Lane for what he is. I'm going to give him the type of coverage that he should have had months ago, before his ineptitude and his campaign of personal gratification cost lives. I intend to be there, camera in tow, ready to catch him each and every time he trips or stumbles.'' Fired up by her resolve, Jan jutted her chin and drove her index finger into the arm of the chair she was seated in. "I can't bring back Hal, but maybe I can save Nancy and others from paying for Lane's climb to the stars with their blood.''

From the bed, Scott studied her. Her poise and tone left no doubt that she was determined. Perhaps she was right. Perhaps Scott thought, she could even accomplish something. Though the odds were against her, since many a reporter had set out on just such a crusade, perhaps Jan, with her camera, charm, reputation, and incredible luck, could do what he himself was unable to do.

Then it struck him. At first he felt ashamed that he even

considered the idea. But he did. He was, after all, a human being possessing all the emotions and drives that everyone else had. That included anger, disgust, and the need to seek retribution or revenge on those who deserved to be punished. Though he himself couldn't be the agent of that retribution, because of his obligation to his office and position, perhaps he could help someone like Jan who was both willing and eager to bring Lane down, if only a peg or two. Even a simple humiliation in public would satisfy Scott's lust for revenge, for he was wise enough to hope for little more.

Putting aside any last-minute qualms or doubts, Scott locked eyes with Jan. "What you're proposing isn't going to be easy. If you have any hope of doing what you claim you want to do, you're going to need help, and a lot of it."

There was a brief moment before Jan realized what Scott was saying. When finally she did, her eyes opened wide, for in all the years that they had known each other, as lovers and husband and wife, he had never, even as a joke, hinted at giving her information or assistance that would be harmful to the Army or anyone connected with the Army. That he was willing to violate this self-imposed code of ethics, a code she thought no one else in the Army bothered to live by, was nothing less than a shock. Lowering her head slightly, but keeping eye-to-eye contact with her husband, Jan carefully picked her words as she spoke. "Are you proposing to help me bring Lane down?"

It was Scott who broke the eye-to-eye contact, but only for a second. When he looked back at her, his face was relaxed, as if he had made a great decision and it had brought him physical as well as mental relief. "Just now, Jan, it dawned upon me that when all the old soldiers said that there were no rules in war, they meant just that, there are no rules. To do what is right for you or me as an individual does not always mean doing what is deemed proper by others living by their code. Lane, because he has chosen to violate the paper-thin code of honor that he as an officer is obliged to live by and enforce, has left me no choice. I either turn my back, as I have done for so long, and let him continue to drag his division down, or I do what I can to put an end to it." He paused, dropping his eyes to his lap. "I don't like doing this. Not one bit. But"—shaking his head, he continued—"there's no other way." He looked up and repeated in deadly earnest, "There's simply no other way."

"Then you really intend to help me?"

Reaching behind him, he grabbed a handful of sheets on her side of the bed and lifted them. "Jan, I have no real idea what I or anyone else in the Army can do to help. But that doesn't mean I can't try. Come on over and let's discuss this together. After all," he said with a slight smile, "some things that must remain in the dark are best discussed in the dark."

Without another word, Jan rose from her seat, switched off the light, and slipped quietly into bed next to Scott. There in the darkness the two of them discussed in hushed voices how best to achieve their mutual goal.

Downstairs in the lobby bar of the same hotel the object of their concern, young Captain Kozak, was sitting across from Sam Ulrich discussing the exact same thing. More correctly, Ulrich was telling Nancy what he intended to do in her defense. "We have to remember," he repeated at measured intervals, "that the charges in isolation are quite justified. While even I can understand how someone like yourself can do what you did in the heat of battle, this fight will not be waged in the same pressure-filled, kill-or-be-killed environment that the incident took place."

While he was well meaning and quite serious about what he was doing, Kozak all but laughed every time he used his colorful terms to refer to the battlefield, especially when he came out with "kill-or-be-killed environment." Only the severity of the charges against her and her burning desire, made sharper with each day of reflection, kept her focused and listening. He might be somewhat of a wuss, she thought, but he seems to know what he's talking about. But even more important to Kozak, he appeared to be as determined, for some reason, to thump Lane as she was.

"Throughout the trial, Nancy, we have to work hard to re-create the image of that battlefield in the minds of the jury. When we finish, they need to understand everything that was going on, not only between you and Lane, but between the enemy on the ground and the forces you were commanding."

"In other words, you need to make Lane look like a bungling fool tactically."

Kozak's interjection caused Ulrich to visibly recoil. He thought about what she had said, shook his head, then corrected her. "No, we don't. In fact, the last thing we want to do is give the appearance that we are trying to make the commanding general look bad."

"We," Kozak cut in, "don't have to do much to make him look bad. He does a great job of that on his own."

Drawing in a deep breath, Ulrich leaned forward and threw out his open hands. "Nancy, damn it, we've been over this again and again. You, and not Lane, are on trial. If we vary from our course—"

"Your course, Sam. Don't forget this grand plan is yours."

"It's yours too. I am your defense counsel. I'm not doing this just for shits and grins, you know."

"That's right, you are my defense attorney, and as such, you're . . ."

Across the room, in a group of strangers, a familiar face flashed into Kozak's view, causing her to seize up in midsentence. For the first time since early September she looked upon the face of Captain Aaron J. Pierce, a man she had once thought she was in love with. That she still had deep, unchecked emotions for this man became painfully obvious as her eyes locked on him and every thought in her head faded into obscurity.

Noticing the sudden midstride change in Kozak, Ulrich looked at her eyes. Seeing that she was staring at something or someone intently, he turned his head in an effort to see what she was staring at. Noticing a group of aviators of the division, he assumed that one of them was the object of Kozak's attention. Facing back to her, he quipped, "Old boyfriend?"

She ignored his comment. In fact for several seconds she ignored everyone and everything about her as she focused on sorting out her feelings toward AJ. In the process of doing so, memories both good and bad flashed through her mind. She knew she hadn't been fair to AJ when she had, without fully explaining herself to him, broken off their relationship in the emotionally charged aftermath of the September ambush. Nor had she answered his calls or responded to his messages, leaving him wondering what he had done wrong.

He had, she knew, done nothing wrong, not really. The root cause of their breakup, Kozak knew, was her own inability to deal with the crisis that the ambush and Lane's actions afterwards had plunged the battalion into. That, and the unreasonable blame she leveled against AJ simply because he was an aviator and the aviators had on the day of the ambush failed to support her battalion as she thought they should have, led to their estrangement.

But how, Kozak thought as she watched him and his friends as they began to move toward the bar, do I explain all of that to him? And at that moment she suddenly thought, Do I want to bother doing so?

As if her thoughts drew his attention to her, AJ turned and looked right into Kozak's eyes. His reaction, like hers, was one of surprise and momentary confusion. Stopping in midstride, AJ caused a minor pile-up in the center of the lobby as two of his friends behind him bumped into him. "Hey, hot shot!" one of them kidded him. "How 'bout using your brake lights next time?"

Mumbling a muddled apology, AJ broke away from the knot of aviators and made his way over to Kozak, who slowly began to stand as he approached. Pausing several feet away from her, he stopped, looked her in the face, and slowly began to speak. "Nancy, I heard your unit was in Bogotá. I was meaning to—"

Embarrassed, Kozak spoke, her words coming out in a hesitant, faltering manner. "I was too. I mean, I was going to contact you as soon as I took care of some things. I've been quite busy these past few days."

Without thinking, and looking for something to say, AJ blurted out, "Yeah, I've heard. Do you think you can beat the charges Lane's brought against you?"

Kozak was upset that AJ had broken the magic of the moment by reminding her of her problems. She was searching for some way of steering the conversation away from that subject and back onto the one that she really wanted to talk about, which was their relationship, when Ulrich stood up and cut in. "Well, her chances will improve immeasurably if she listens to me."

Annoyed by the interruption, AJ turned and looked at Ulrich. With a sneer that betrayed the contempt he felt for JAG officers, AJ commented dryly, "You must be her lawyer."

Miffed that he had all but said "scum-sucking lawyer," Ulrich put his hands on his hips. "Yeah, I'm her lawyer."

In horror, Kozak watched the two men as they squared off against each other. "God!" she called out in a sudden burst of anger, shouting out the first thing that popped into her head. "Why do men always feel this compelling need to hack away at each other before they shake hands?"

Stung by her comment, AJ turned and faced Kozak. "Oh, I'm sorry, Nancy, for bothering you. I just thought I'd come over and say hi." He looked down at the floor, thinking for a moment, as if he was trying to find a word to smooth things out. He was still doing so when one of his buddies called out, "Hey, AJ, you coming?"

Turning to where his friends were waiting, he looked over at them, then faced Kozak again. "Well, I see that you're real busy, and my friends are waiting. So I'll just leave you two here alone. It was nice seeing you again, Nancy, and good luck."

Without waiting for a response, AJ turned and walked away, leaving Kozak glaring at Ulrich and for the moment caught between two burning desires. The first was to burst out and call for AJ, which was something that her pride wouldn't allow her to do. The second, equally compelling desire that she suppressed was to turn and rip out Ulrich's heart for screwing up the one chance she had of making amends with AJ. That she didn't do so would for days amaze her and, as the trial began, cause her grief.

CHAPTER 17

November 21

HAD THEY NOT BEEN SO WRAPPED UP IN THEIR OWN CON-
cerns, the sudden shifts in Major José Solis's attitude would
have been obvious to the dullest member of Lane's oversized
division staff. That, however, would have required both parties, Solis as well as the American officers, to change their
habits. Nothing, however, could shake the division staff of the
11th Air Assault from its myopic view of the world. Not even
the steady stream of grim news from the east seemed to deter
the division staff of the 11th Air Assault from its precious
routine as it labored ponderously forward. Like a great, mesmerized bull elephant, the officers of the division staff continued to stumble about with no apparent goal, no purpose in life
other than to keep themselves fed and busy.

Not even Colonel Christopher Delhue, normally the only
person on the 11th's staff who, in Scott Dixon's words, bothered to pull his head above the daily mire, did so anymore. He,
like everyone else on the division staff, was beginning to miss
what was happening in the real world outside the walls that
housed them, and certainly didn't notice the change in a person
few bothered with during the best of times, Major José Solis.
If Delhue or anyone else had bothered to do so, they would
have seen a new man, one who was possessed, a person with
a mission in life and anxious to get on with it.

Today, less than two weeks before a scheduled commander's conference, was no different. As the captains, majors, and lieutenant colonels from the various staff sections in the division headquarters ran about, much to the amusement of their sergeants, who were content to stand aside and watch the spectacle of officers running around in smaller and smaller circles, Solis moved about the floors of the Colombian Ministry of Defense building occupied by the division staff. Unnoticed, except by an occasional harried staff officer in a rush to get by him in a crowded corridor, Solis moved slowly, thoughtfully, from one room to the next, up the stairwells and through the corridors. While he allowed his American counterparts to charge forward, eyes fixed straight ahead, Solis took his time, looking at everything and everyone he met during the course of his solitary journeys. During frequent halts he would make a note or two in the little green notebook he kept in his left breast pocket, closest to his heart. Had an unbiased observer been present to compare Solis's comings and goings with those of the American officers, they would have without doubt claimed that Solis and not the Americans was nonproductive.

To have understood the truth, however, would have required closer observation and a mind uncluttered by the trivial pursuits that Lane's headquarters passed off as staff work. José Solis, being as unintrusive as possible, was refamiliarizing himself with the building, learning all he could about this part of it. Though he had been through every room before and knew what staff occupied what section of the American wing of the building, he was looking at that same structure now through different eyes. Now, as he walked into a room looking about and taking in what he saw, he did not concern himself with desks or the people who occupied them. Instead, as his eyes danced about the room, he saw entrances and windows, supports and pillars, any opening or obstruction that would dissipate or block an explosion. He also looked for and noted as he glanced about where boxes and containers were kept, making careful note of their size, shape, and composition as well as how often, if at all, they were used. Such observations, he knew, would be important when it came time to smuggle the large quantities of explosives that he envisioned.

In his endeavors, Solis was not alone. After thinking about

the task given to him by Hector Valendez, Solis had rushed back to the revolutionary with his idea. "Though they have been in the same place since they arrived here months ago," he told Valendez, "the Yankees insist upon being able to pack up and move out at a moment's notice." Leaning over the table of their cafe rendezvous, Solis's eyes danced with delight as he explained to the puzzled FARC military man. "To accommodate this, they keep hundreds of boxes and special containers stacked up along walls and in corners in practically every room in the building. They even have blocked off stairways, partially for security reasons, using containers used to ship computers, copying machines, and other such devices."

Understanding immediately what Solis was driving at and infected by his excitement, Valendez immediately dedicated his best men to the mission. To handle the explosives, two of his best demolition experts, one of whom was famous throughout South America for his creative use of explosives, were put in charge of a sapper platoon and smuggled into Bogotá with all the high-grade explosives they could lay their hands on. To assist these men, Valendez had, through his former associates at the university, assembled a team of engineers and architects, including men who had worked on the Ministry of Defense building from its inception through its completion. Armed with his notes and observations gathered during his daily wanderings, Solis met each night with Valendez's team of experts. He would give each in turn the information that they had requested or that Solis felt they could use. Finished with that, the team members would give Solis a new list of information requirements and questions that he would need to answer the next day. In this way the FARC team by now knew more about the internal organization and layout of the 11th Division's headquarter than the headquarters' commandant himself. They, of course, had to, for each man involved knew without having to be told that they would only have one chance to strike at the heart of the Yankees' headquarters. For once they had made the effort and experienced success or failure, the shock value and potential for a cheap, decisive strike would never be available to them again.

Reaching the end of his tour for that day, Solis found himself standing outside the door of the main division conference room.

A military policeman standing at parade rest was posted outside the door. Not remembering seeing any briefings or special meetings scheduled for that day, Solis stopped and looked at the MP. "Excuse me, but who is using this room today?"

The MPs, like most troopers in the 11th, were normally not impressed with the Colombian Army officers and tried hard to pretend that they didn't exist, but Solis delivered his inquiry in such a manner that the MP could not ignore him. Though he didn't come to attention, he responded quickly, "The division staff judge advocate is using the room to conduct an Article 32 investigation."

Though he noted that the Yankee didn't add the customary "sir" that his rank demanded, Solis made no comment. Instead he looked at the MP and then the door. Forever curious about how and why the American military did what it did, Solis moved past the MP and began to enter the room. The MP, caught off guard, wasn't sure what to do. He had been posted at the door to ensure that no one accidentally entered the room in the middle of the proceedings. His first inclination, as it was with everyone in the division headquarters, was to challenge the Colombian. But then he caught himself. This investigation, to the best of his knowledge, wasn't a classified or a closed session. If it had been, he would have been told and been given an access roster listing all those who were authorized to attend. Unable to justify keeping Solis out based on his skimpy instructions, the MP allowed Solis to pass through the door. Closing it behind him, the MP shrugged his shoulders. Oh, well, he thought, shuffling his feet and looking up and down the hall for a moment, maybe no one will notice. Resuming his relaxed stance, he shifted himself slightly to the right. This allowed him to get a better view into the office across the way. Fixing his gaze straight ahead, the MP hoped that the five-foot-three brassy blond female sergeant with a bosom so ample that even her loose camouflage uniform couldn't hide it would return to her desk, which faced out into the hall where he stood.

Inside the conference room, Solis hesitated at the door before taking a seat. Though he had acted with authority and confidence in front of the MP, he wasn't sure if the Yankees wanted an outsider here watching what must be for them an embarrassing affair. Such a proceeding, he knew, in the Colombian Army would have been conducted in secret, far from the prying eyes of uninvolved outsiders. After looking about the room and noticing that no one, except for a lone sergeant standing at the back of the room, took note of him, Solis quickly and quietly moved over to the first open seat he saw near the rear of the room, sat down, and began to watch.

The tables at the front of the room were arranged in a horse-shoe with the open end pointed at the rear of the room, where Solis sat in one of several rows of chairs set up for spectators. Seated at the head table in the center was a major whom Solis recognized as belonging to the division's operations section, and a captain of the division's staff judge advocate corps, which they referred to as JAG. The major appeared to be running the investigation while the JAG officer sat there in silence, scribbling an occasional note on a pad set before him. Though Solis couldn't remember the JAG officer's name, he knew the major, having dealt with him on several occasions. He was, Solis knew, a dedicated if somewhat dull-witted man. He did exactly what he was told to do to the best of his ability. No brilliance there, he thought, and no backbone. Familiar with the charges brought against the female infantry captain seated at the table that made up the left side of the horseshoe, Solis understood why the major at the head table had been selected to conduct this preliminary investigation. He would do as he was told and, as he did with everything else, deliver the results his commander desired without question, without protest.

The female captain, a woman allegedly with a reputation and combat record that put every officer on the division staff to shame, sat quietly next to another JAG officer. The two of them, sitting as if they were uninterested in the proceedings taking place before them, said nothing either to each other or to other people involved in the investigation. Even when the major conducting the investigation turned to them and asked if they had any questions for the current witness seated in the center of the horseshoe after the prosecuting attorney finished, the female captain's attorney merely glanced up from his notes, shook his head, and murmured, "No, sir, not at this time." It was as if, Solis thought, after watching witness after witness come up, be questioned by the prosecution, and then be dismissed by the defense without a counterquestion being leveled at him, the female captain and her attorney had given up. Perhaps, he thought, they had. Or maybe, he thought, this was a sham trial, a mere formality that had to be acted out in order to satisfy the judicial niceties that the Americans seemed to be so fond of.

That this proceeding was of interest was obvious based on the people he saw in the audience. Almost directly in front of Solis sat the division commander, Major General C. B. Lane. He was positioned, Solis noticed, so that the investigation officer had to look at him. There is, Solis thought, no subtlety in the intimidation that the Yankee division commander was using this day. Even a blind man, Solis thought, would be able to see that this whole affair was set up to deliver only one result. The charges against the female captain would be found proper and a court-martial would be convened. Unless he had missed something earlier, that was the only way that he could see this.

Glancing over to his left, Solis looked toward the female television correspondent, Jan Fields, who was seated in the rear of the room, like him. How, he wondered, would she report this affair? Her mounting criticism against the manner in which the commander of the 11th Division was conducting operations was becoming a bother, an irritant, and an embarrassment to everyone in this headquarters. Even more than the female infantry captain under investigation, Jan Fields was a puzzle to him. How, he wondered, could she, the wife of an Army general, be allowed to openly stalk and criticize a senior Army field commander? That she had been allowed to remain in Colombia, especially in light of the bitter tone that her reports had taken after the disasters at El Frío, was a wonderment not only to Solis but to every officer in the Colombian Army, not to mention the FARC. "Were it not so amusing to watch her make that jackass general who struts about like a peacock squirm so," one Colombian colonel told Solis in confidence, "we would have arranged a fatal accident for her." That the Americans hadn't done so, and probably never would, only lowered Solis's opinion of them a bit further.

He was lost in this last thought when something that was said by the witness then being questioned caught Solis's attention. Turning his head away from the female reporter, he looked up and saw Captain James Adderly, Lane's aide-de-camp, sitting in the witness chair. The prosecuting attorney, seated at his table, was reading off a list of questions. "Then the enemy anti-aircraft fire from the village was effective?"

Looking over at the attorney, Adderly nodded. "Yes, that's right. We were taking effective fire."

"From the village?" the investigating officer added.

There was a pause as Adderly looked down at the floor, lost in thought. When he finally did look up and answer, he spoke in a hushed, almost hesitant manner. "Yes, I believe that's correct."

In the rear of the room, Solis shook his head. No, he thought. No, that's not correct at all. Based on all the reports he had seen, both Colombian and unofficial FARC accounts Hector Valendez had shown him, there were no FARC fighters in El Frío. And the only anti-aircraft guns on the field had been north of the river, well away from the village. Valendez himself had confirmed this. At one of their meetings he recounted how in a moment of utter frustration he'd ordered a pair of guns he was standing by to fire on the helicopter he thought was a command-and-control aircraft. Either the general's aide did not know for sure what had happened, or . . .

Like a brilliant flash of lightning streaking across his mind, Solis twisted his head over to where Jan Fields sat, then back at Adderly. If, Solis thought, Adderly was lying and this whole investigation was a sham being conducted under the watchful eye of the division commander, revelation of the truth to the American public would be an embarrassment that could create a furor that could not be ignored. Though he did not know how it would be done, Solis was confident that Hector Valendez, once convinced of the value of such a propaganda stunt, would find a way.

Not needing to hear more, Solis got out of his seat and moved quickly to the door, attracting no more than a casual glance from Nancy Kozak as she sat there trying hard to ignore what was going on around her.

* * *

Nancy Kozak wasn't ignoring everything. Her time, she knew, to speak out would come. But not here, not in this kangaroo court. All this was, she thought, was a rubber stamp, a ticket punched by Lane's legal staff as they went about carrying out his desires. When her eyes swept away from the departing Colombian officer, they fell on Lane sitting in the front row, watching intently as his personal aide answered the prosecuting attorney's questions. Instinctively her eyes narrowed as her face screwed itself up in a tight expression of determination. As God is my witness, she swore to herself, you're going to pay for Hal Cerro's murder. You're going to pay.

Ulrich was too busy paying attention to his friend and counterpart, Captain Mark Moretti, the prosecuting attorney, to notice what Kozak was doing. Moretti, Ulrich knew, was enjoying this, for he realized from the beginning that Ulrich was not going to make much of a contest here during the Article 32 proceedings. Ulrich had as much told him that, not to mention the whole world, when he informed Lieutenant Colonel Webb that there would be no witness for the defense today. "Are you sure?" Webb probed.

"Sir," Ulrich responded, trying hard to hide the anguish he felt over Kozak's decision, "the witness and I have discussed this matter in great detail. *She* knows of no one at this time who can materially assist her in her defense." The manner in which Ulrich stressed *she* every time he mentioned the word left little doubt in Webb's mind that Ulrich was against such a course of action. But, other than asking, he did nothing to change anything. The sooner this case was disposed of with a favorable verdict, the happier Webb would be.

A favorable verdict, of course, meant one that suited Lane.

As Sam Ulrich had predicted, given Nancy Kozak's desire to air her case during a general court-martial, the Article 32 investigation was turning out to be little more than a formality. Everything was going quickly, with the prosecution presenting its witnesses and the defense none. Even when the few witnesses called forth did step up to the stand, they to a man deferred to the written statements already in the hands of the major appointed to conduct the Article 32. No doubt, Ulrich thought as Lane stepped up to the witness chair, Lane will do the same.

The unannounced appearance of Major General C. B. Lane, as well as his agreement, or rather insistence, that he be questioned by the investigating officer, did little to shake his or Kozak's resolve or stance, although he wished she would have allowed him to start what he called his preparation of the battlefield. In the confines of the clean, well-lit conference room being used for the proceedings, each of the witnesses called by the major serving as the investigating officer recounted his version of the incident, delivering each word with well-practiced precision and no apparent malice or emotion. This is all too clean, too neat, too comfortable, Ulrich thought. We're going to have to work real hard to make the members of the jury feel what Kozak felt. For now, however, Sam Ulrich had to content himself with watching Mark Moretti do his thing with Lane.

Standing up after Lane had taken his oath, Moretti walked to a spot six paces before Lane. Holding a manila folder up in his right hand, he began to question Lane. "Sir, I have here in my hand a copy of the statement concerning the incident in question that you prepared immediately after that affair. Is there in this statement anything you wish to change or add at this time?"

Dropping his voice so that it sounded more commanding, more manly, Lane shook his head as he responded. "No, there's nothing that I need to add that isn't already part of the record. As far as I'm concerned, that statement and those of the other witnesses you've had up here today pretty well speak for themselves."

Though he wasn't sure if Lane's last comment was a warning or a summary designed to bring these proceedings to a close, the major conducting the investigation had no doubt in his mind what Lane was saying. With a nervous twitch in his eye, he looked at Moretti. "Captain, if you would please continue with your questions, if you have any?"

For a moment Moretti looked into Lane's eyes. Even from where he was seated, Ulrich could notice them as they narrowed slightly. That action reminded him of a cat narrowing her eyes as she focuses on her prey before pouncing. Moretti, no doubt, saw Lane's action in the same light, for he turned his gaze away from Lane and faced the major. "No, sir, I have no further questions at this time."

Nodding as Moretti turned to make for his seat, the major looked over to Ulrich. "Does the defense have any questions for the witness at this time?" To everyone's surprise and discomfort, Ulrich stood up as if he were going to walk out before Lane and ask him something. He was tempted, very tempted, to have a crack at Lane then and there. But then, just as he was about to go forth, he held back. Looking over to the major conducting the investigation, Ulrich allowed him to quiver a few seconds longer before he finally announced, "No, sir. Not at this time." Taking his seat, he allowed his division commander, against his better judgment, to leave the witness chair unmolested by cross-examination.

Shaken by Ulrich's last action, the investigating officer looked first at Ulrich, and then over to where Lane had taken his seat. "Does either the attorney for the defense or the prosecution have any further witnesses they wish to call on?"

Moretti and Ulrich, both men unsettled somewhat by the manner in which this whole affair had been handled to date, merely shook their heads. Not waiting for anyone to change their minds or giving anyone time to spring a surprise on him, the major began to bring the session to a close. "Let the record show that both attorneys indicated that neither had any further witnesses to call on. I therefore declare these proceedings at an end and thank everyone for their cooperation." With the closing of his notebook, the major ended the hearing.

Kozak, in a hurry to escape the accusing eyes of Lane's division staff, left as soon as people began to get up and leave the room. Ulrich, knowing that she was uncomfortable with what was going on, let her go without comment. There was, after all, he thought, no need to discuss anything further. He had played his hand the way she wanted it. Unless something dramatic happened between now and then, Kozak would get her court-martial just as she had wanted. Maybe, he wondered as he took his time and gathered up his notes and papers, Nancy was hoping that the stories her friend the TV news correspondent was running on Lane and his performance would do her some good. Though he didn't see how they could, and

Kozak had never mentioned anything about Jan Fields's efforts, Ulrich began to wonder if somehow those two weren't up to something.

Ulrich was still pondering this when he walked out of the room into the crowded corridor. It was there in the corridor that the real shock of the day came. Just outside the door Lane stood talking to the investigation officer who stood with his back against the wall. When Lane saw Ulrich emerge, he promptly turned away from the major and faced him, flashing a smile that unnerved Ulrich. Reaching out, Lane placed his right hand on Ulrich's shoulder and gave it a firm, almost playful squeeze. "You did a fine job in there, Sam. As much as this incident is regrettable, I am glad to see that we"—he paused as he looked at the investigating officer, then back at Sam—"are all working together to get this affair out of the way so we can get back to some serious war fighting. It will do us no good to squander our time or the reputation of this fine division in a protracted and possibly bitter courtroom slugfest." Then, as his grasp tightened on Ulrich's shoulder, Lane leaned forward and stared into Sam's eyes, dropping any hint of a smile and replacing it with what could only be described as a menacing glare. "You understand that, don't you, *Captain*?"

The tone of Lane's voice and the manner in which he emphasized the word *captain,* coupled with the painful digging of his fingers into his shoulder, left no doubt in Ulrich's mind that this was not a question. Rather, Sam realized, it was a warning. Lane was serving him notice, more directly and bluntly than he had imagined even Lane, for all the gall and arrogance that he had displayed in the past, would dare. The impact of what was happening in full view of the officers who had taken part in the just convened investigation stunned Sam. After all, Sam thought, here he was, the man appointed to defend another officer, to the best of his ability, being told by the most senior officer in the country that he was expected to do his part, just as the hand-picked investigation major was doing, to find Kozak guilty and ensure that the trial was conducted with as little fanfare or theatrics as possible.

Stunned by what he took to be Lane's meaning, reinforced by his close physical presence and Lane's grasping hand on his shoulder, Sam was speechless for several seconds. After several long, almost intolerable seconds, the smile returned to Lane's face as he let Sam go. Finished with Sam and the major he turned and without another word walked away. Sam, for his part, was so thoroughly shaken that he didn't even bother looking back at the investigation officer before he too turned and walked away, or more correctly, fled. That he should have stayed a little longer and questioned the investigation officer about whether he too had understood Lane's meaning as Sam did didn't occur to Sam until he reached his office, an office that he shared with two other JAG officers assigned to the division as defending attorneys.

In a daze, he wandered about the empty office for a moment, pondering what to do. Both of the officers with whom he shared the office and the duty of defending personnel in the division were gone at the moment. One, the most senior of the three, was working another case. Detached by Major Oberson, the Regional Defense Counsel and their superior, to the brigade operating to the southwest in the mountains, he had been gone for several days and would not be back for another week, maybe two. He was assisting in an investigation concerning an alleged case of willful negligence by a mechanic that had led to the crash of a helicopter. The investigating officer needed, according to Oberson, to take his time in putting his case in order, since there was the chance that the mechanic might be brought up on charges of murder. Though both Sam and his office mate seriously doubted that such charges could be supported, the other defense attorney left for the field without a protest. "Any chance to get away from the flagpole, Sam," he had said with glee, "is too damned good to pass up." The second JAG officer who worked out of the office, also senior to Sam and by all rights a better choice to defend Kozak's case, was back in the States. He was on leave, a leave, Sam suddenly realized, that was granted the day after the incident involving Lane and Kozak had occurred, and before Kozak's attorney had been appointed.

Stopping in midstride, Sam shook his head, looked up blankly at the ceiling, and uttered a mournful "Oh my God!" as it dawned upon him that not only Kozak but he had been set up by Lane. At a time when he was in the greatest need of his colleagues, when their collective wisdom, advice, and support were needed the most, he had been systematically stripped of them. He, like Kozak, had been isolated and left on his own.

Still recovering from this latest shock, Sam refused to believe that a senior Army officer, a general commanding a division in battle, could stoop to such blatantly unethical behavior. Looking down at the floor, he twisted his head first to his right and then to his left, mumbling to himself, "No, no," each time his head turned. It was as if he were arguing with an invisible opponent.

When a voice from behind interrupted his disturbing internal debate, the surprise caused him to jump literally off the floor. Spinning about as quickly as his feet hit the floor and he regained his balance, he turned to see his friend and fellow JAG officer Captain Mark Moretti leaning against the frame of the doorway, arms folded across his chest, with a smirk on his face. "Can't do any better in court, so you decided to come back here and argue against yourself?"

His fright turning to embarrassment, then anger, Sam managed to calm himself before he responded. "Mark, I've got to talk to someone about this case, another JAG officer."

Moretti threw his arms up. "Woo, buddy, I'm the prosecution, the enemy. Don't think it would be too swift an idea for you to talk to me about anything concerning Miss Nancy Kozak or this affair. You've got enough problems already."

Undeterred by his friend's attempt at keeping him from discussing the case, Ulrich shot back, "You ain't kidding there, partner. Fact is, I think we all have a problem."

"Who," Moretti asked, "do you mean by 'we'?"

"Anyone involved in the Kozak case. I think that there are some serious breaches of ethics, not to mention the illegal use of command influence, going on here."

Though he kept his arms folded, the smile disappeared from Moretti's face as he arched one eyebrow up. "Oh? And by whom?"

"The division commander, for starters. Colonel Webb and Major Oberson too, I think, might be involved."

Looking behind him into the corridor, Moretti finally left his position in the doorway, careful to close the door as he came into the office. Pulling out a chair from behind Ulrich's absent officer mate's desk, he spun the armless chair around, straddled the seat, and sat down, resting his arms on the chair's backrest. "Okay, you've got my attention. What brought you to this conclusion?"

Walking over to his own desk, Sam pulled his chair out and plopped down before he spoke. When he told Moretti of the confrontation he and the investigation officer had just had with Lane, Moretti could tell that Sam was both shaken and concerned. "My God," Sam exclaimed when he finished, "if that isn't abuse of rank and command influence to throw a case under investigation, then I don't know what is."

"Is that," Moretti responded in a rather casual tone, "what you think? Do you really believe that Lane's interest in ending this case is an effort to sway either you or me from doing our duty?" Then, he chuckled. "Sam, you're overreacting to this command influence thing. Best you forget about looking for something that you can't control and start concentrating on Miss Nancy Kozak's defense."

Not catching the significance at first of Moretti's inclusion of "or me" in his statement, Sam looked his friend squarely in the eyes. "Listen, I've been around long enough to know when someone is playing their macho-bullshit games of intimidation and browbeating with me. Lane wants me to roll over like a good boy and watch the judge and jury hang Kozak out to dry for what amounts to nothing more than a moment of indiscretion in the heat of battle."

"You said the investigation officer was there. How did he view Lane's comments? What did he think?"

There was a pause before Sam responded sheepishly that he had not asked the investigation officer about the incident. "I was too stunned," he explained, "to think straight. I mean, my God, I never in all my years expected to have a major general come up to me and all but order me to screw a client by not doing my duty."

To Sam's surprise, Moretti smiled. "Hey, buddy, don't feel like the Lone Ranger."

"What do you mean?"

"I mean," Moretti said as he stood, "that you're not the only person involved in this mess to feel the strongarm tactics of Conan the Bureaucrat. At least he was nice to you."

"You mean Lane's approached you?"

"Summoned is more like it. Before I even knew who the hell Captain Nancy Kozak was, let alone what she had done to offend his imperial personage, Lane had me in his office. He explained to me in no uncertain terms that my career in this man's Army depended upon my ability to bring Miss Captain Nancy to justice. 'We need,' he said as he spread his arms out before him like a TV evangelist preaching to the gathered masses, 'to make an example of that officer. We need to ensure that this flagrant violation of orders, breaches of discipline, and unwarranted disrespect for rank be punished quickly and severely, if for no other reason than to serve as an example to other officers in this division.' Hell, standing there in his presence, unaware of what exactly he was talking to me about, damned near scared the daylights out of me. I thought we had another My Lai massacre on our hands."

With his alarm growing by the moment, Sam cut short Moretti's description of Lane's rantings and ravings. "What," he all but shouted, "did Webb say when you told him about this?"

Pausing, Moretti looked at Sam as if he were an idiot. "What do you mean, told Webb? There was no need to tell Webb anything. He was sitting there the whole time Lane was giving me my marching orders, listening to all of this. Webb, I guess, had already received his fire-and-brimstone speech." Then cocking his head to the side, Moretti chuckled. "The only surprise, I guess, is that Lane waited as long as he did before he collared you."

With a feeling like a great ball of bile was rising slowly from the pit of his stomach, Sam felt himself become sick. It must have shown in his face, for Moretti stopped smiling. "What, are you surprised by all of this?"

"Shocked," Sam responded as he fought down the growing sense of nausea that was slowly spreading throughout his body.

"Jesus, you are naive, aren't you? I mean, what in the hell do you expect? A captain, a runny-nose little runt of a captain told Lane off, told him in front of God and country, over a radio set on a battalion command net, to go fuck himself."

Angered by his friend's attitude, Sam forgot his nausea and fired back. "Mark, she did so in the heat of battle! My God, a company was in the middle of being decimated and Lane was taking away their only hope of survival just to save his own precious lily-white ass.''

Indignant that Sam would talk to him in that manner, Moretti pressed the chair forward and jabbed his index finger on the desk before him. "Major General C. B. Lane was the senior tactical commander present. He was well within his rights to divert whatever assets he deemed necessary to deal with a new and unexpected threat to his entire command. In his judgment, at that moment the safety of the entire brigade, and not just a lone infantry company, was in jeopardy.''

"Do you, Mark, for one moment, believe that Lane was thinking about the security of his brigade, let alone one company, when he ordered the artillery to fire on that village?''

"It doesn't make any difference what I believe. Nor does it really make any difference what the tactical situation was. The facts are that your client challenged a valid order issued by a duly appointed superior officer, in the face of the enemy, and conducted herself, when challenged by that superior officer, in a manner that was prejudicial to the maintenance of discipline and morale of the units and personnel present.'' Finished, Moretti stood up and shoved the chair he had been sitting on back against the desk. Turning, he started to storm out of the office but stopped. Spinning around, he glared at Sam. "My advice to you is that you forget about improprieties on Lane's part, a man who is not on trial, and start worrying about putting a case together for your client, or Miss Nancy Kozak is going to be in Leavenworth well in advance of her year group and long after they've all finished with their staff college course.''

Though he didn't appreciate Moretti's attempt at humor or his advice to him, Sam said nothing as he watched Moretti leave. Though he hated to admit it, what Moretti said was right. Though Lane and everyone else who allowed him to get away with what he was doing might be wrong, such concerns were at the moment academic. There was no chance of getting Kozak to change her mind and appeal for a trial somewhere else. She was bound and determined to have it out right here and as soon as possible. With his hands tied, all Sam could do now was to save her from herself and C. B. Lane, a goal, Sam began to think, that was beyond his grasp.

So deep in thought was Sam over the gloomy prospects of Kozak's chances that he hardly noticed Major José Solis as he stuck his head through the open door. Remembering that he had, in his excitement to discuss his plan with Hector Valendez, forgotten to finish his inspection of this floor, Solis had all but run back to do so. Mumbling a brief apology to Sam, Solis looked around the room quickly, noted the windows and a stack of three computer shipping crates in the corner, and then disappeared without another word.

CHAPTER 18

November 24

FINISHING THE LAST BIT OF PAPERWORK HE INTENDED TO DEAL with before taking a break for lunch, Scotty Dixon closed the manila folder before him. Picking up the neat, clean file, he gave it a backhanded toss into his out box, murmuring to himself, "Take that!" With a shove at the edge of his desk, he pushed himself away from it, stood up, and prepared to leave when Jeff Worsham stuck his head through the open doorway.

"Jeff, just the man I wanted to see. I'm done with the morning dump of drivel and trivia and ready to flee this place for a quiet lunch with my bride."

Worsham managed a smile. He was glad to see his boss, who had been brooding since his return from Washington, in such an obvious good mood. Never the friendliest man, Dixon's view of the situation in Colombia over the past week had made him grumpier than usual. "It's as if," said Major Herman M. Hagstrom, Dixon's intelligence officer, in a private moment with Worsham, "General Dixon, after running around screaming that the sky was falling, suddenly realized it was true." Worsham, who agreed with Dixon's glum assessment of the situation in Colombia, nevertheless had attempted to do all in his power to keep Dixon's morale up. Which was why as he entered Dixon's office he was upset. Sensing his chief of staff's mood, Dixon stopped what he was doing. "Why so down in the mouth, trooper?"

"Well, sir, it's about your luncheon date with your wife."

There was no need to say more. Like a puppet that had just had its strings cut, Dixon's shoulders slumped down. "Don't tell me, Madam Media called and had to cancel."

Worsham nodded. "Yes, sir, she did. Not more than five minutes ago."

Cocking his head to the side, Dixon sighed. "Jeff, war may be hell, but being married to the media is a bitch. Thank God we never decided to have children. Jan would never be able to keep a due date, and the poor kid would spend half its life penned up in her belly waiting to be born." Though meant to be funny, his tone betrayed both his disappointment and irritation. Looking back at his desk, then over to Worsham, Dixon mused, "Oh, well, Jeff, me boy, looks like I've got enough time to finish going through all that crap the staff keeps piling on my desk before Colonel Agustin arrives."

"Well, sir, that's the other thing I need to tell you. Colonel Agustin is already here. He has been for ten minutes."

Surprised, Dixon looked at Worsham. "Here already? Was the office call he asked for set for—"

"Yes, sir, it was scheduled later this afternoon. But he showed up here and asked if he could wait."

"Why in the hell," Dixon demanded with a decided note of anger in his voice, "didn't you tell me he was here? Colonel Agustin is the new commander of the Presidential Brigade, an important assignment in their Army. Whose brilliant idea was it to let him . . ."

Worsham threw his hands up and diverted his face as if he were trying to protect himself from Dixon's verbal blast. "I told him I would announce him to you, sir, twice. But he declined both times, insisting, no, demanding, that he wait."

Understanding Worsham's gestures and puzzled by Agustin's insistence that he not be disturbed, Dixon calmed down. "Please, Jeff, do me a favor and show him in."

Without another word, Worsham left. When he reappeared, a tall, well-turned-out Colombian officer followed him into the room. Stepping aside, Worsham motioned to Agustin with his right hand. "General Dixon, Colonel Marco Agustin, commanding officer of the Presidential Brigade."

Walking over to the colonel, Dixon smiled and offered his right hand. Rather than take his hand, Agustin saluted stiffly. Caught short by his action, Dixon stopped and returned the salute. Only then did Agustin drop his hand and reach out for Dixon's. When they finally did shake hands, the Colombian gave two quick shakes that were as formal as his salute and then pulled his hand away. "It is, sir, a pleasure to meet a soldier with your reputation and background." Even his words were delivered with a rigidity that gave no hint of emotion or even sincerity. It was, Dixon thought, as if someone were holding a knife in this man's back and dictating his every word and action. That, of course, didn't mean that he had to respond in the same cold manner. Nodding in acknowledgment of Agustin's compliment, he smiled. "Your reputation is quite legendary itself. The leadership you displayed during the withdrawal of the garrison at Puerto Carreño and your trek through enemy-held territory is in itself quite extraordinary."

If Dixon had meant mention of his retreat from Puerto Carreño as a compliment, it had failed, and he quickly realized it when Agustin's face went flush with anger and not embarrassment. Agustin, realizing that his reaction had shown through his frigid exterior, quickly tried to change the subject. "General Dixon, I am in your debt for allowing me to interrupt your busy schedule on such short notice."

Sensing that Agustin wanted to get down to business, Dixon motioned to Worsham, who quietly withdrew, closing the door behind him as he left the room. "Please, Colonel, sit down." Moving over to the overstuffed chairs that his sergeant major had managed to liberate from the embassy staff, Dixon sat, crossed his legs, and then leaned over on his left arm which was perched on the chair's arm. Agustin followed, seated himself, but did not relax, not at first. "I assume, Colonel, that this is more than a social call."

With those words, Agustin allowed his rigid frame to slump over, letting his back ease itself into the chair, his knees coming apart, and his arms going limp. It seemed to take a long time and a great deal of effort to arrest his change from his exaggerated formality to near total collapse. When he looked up, the face Dixon saw was not the same one Agustin had worn during the introductions. Dixon could now see the haggard face of a man who was both exhausted and worried. There was much more to this meeting, he realized at that moment, than a simple social office call. Only when the Colombian colonel appeared to have finally come to rest, did Dixon speak. "Though I have just met you, Colonel, it is obvious that you are troubled and that you are hesitant to speak. If for whatever reason you wish to leave without going any further, please do so. I will forget this entire incident, and we can both go about our duties as if this meeting never took place."

There was no immediate response. Instead, Agustin looked into Dixon's eyes and studied them for a moment. Whether he was looking into them in the hope that he could see past the exterior and get a measure of the man before him or whether Agustin was merely searching in his own weary mind for the right words with which to answer him, Dixon could not tell. Though the suspense was beginning to irk him, Dixon chose not to rush the colonel. He would, Dixon knew, either tell him all in his own time or get up in another moment and leave.

"Have you ever, General Dixon, committed treason?"

Totally taken aback by the question, Dixon let his jaw drop. "Excuse me, Colonel?"

Agustin narrowed his eyes and spoke slowly, more distinctly as he repeated his question. "Have you ever committed treason?"

Dixon thought about that. In Mexico, both he and then Major General Al Malin had exceeded their authority in launching a raid that freed several hostages including his wife, Jan. And in Germany during the Ukrainian nuclear weapons crisis he had helped Malin lay out an operation that gave the illusion of being treasonous. But the outright committing of treason, the act of aiding or assisting in the compromise of his nation's security, no, he hadn't. With his face frozen in a well-controlled stare, Dixon shook his head. "No, I have never done so."

Averting his eyes, Agustin sighed. "It is not, señor, an easy thing to do. I have until recently never even imagined that I could bring myself to do so. But circumstances, well, as they teach in your command and general staff school at Fort Leavenworth, extreme situations sometimes call for extreme measures.''

Though he was anxious to get to the heart of the matter, Dixon realized that he dare not rush the colonel. Instead he simply nodded. ''Yes, that is very true. Sometimes we are presented with situations that are beyond the scope of our training and past experience.''

''I have, General Dixon, dedicated my life to the military with the understanding that by doing so I would be serving the people of my country. I have always in the past trusted my superiors and performed my duties without question and demanded that those under me do likewise, for I believed in the Army, my Army.'' As he spoke, he began to become animated as the anger inside of him began to build. ''I was always taught, from my cadet days on, to do what is right and have trust in your superiors. Yet now,'' he said, throwing out his arms to emphasize his point, ''now I find out that it is impossible to do both. What I believe is right no longer appears to be in concert with what my superiors are doing.''

Pausing to catch his breath, Agustin looked down at the floor, spoke without looking up. ''How could I be so blind? How could I be so naive? I have been a fool, a fool for a very long time. And yet now when I realize it, I do not know what to do about it.'' Looking up at Dixon, he said, ''I am like a junior lieutenant lost in the jungle with no map and no one to guide me. I am, señor, worse than useless. I have become a traitor.''

Unable to restrain himself, despite his realization that Agustin seemed to be pushing himself to the verge of a mental collapse, Dixon began to prod him. ''I realize, Colonel Agustin, that there is something troubling you. That I have gathered. But what, sir, causes you to discount your loyalty to your government? And why discuss this issue with me?''

''Because, General, I am not the only traitor to my nation. You see, I can no longer willingly follow my superiors, because they have taken it upon themselves to deal with the enemy. While your division was roaming the mountains to the west and my garrison was being wiped out in the east, those officers who had sent us out there were busy preparing for another coup. And even worse, since the disasters of the past two months have made it clear that the FARC is a force to be reckoned with, regardless of who controlled the seat of government here in Bogotá, the General Staff of the Colombian Army has been holding preliminary discussions with the FARC's central committee. They are, as we speak and our soldiers fight, seeking to strike a deal with them.''

Though he had been told by both Colonel Chester Thomas, the military attaché, and his own intelligence officer, that there existed a strong possibility that the Colombian Army might be considering another coup, to have it confirmed by one of their own officers, the commander of a key unit that would play a major role in just such an effort, was a bit shocking and unsettling. It took Dixon a moment to recover his balance. When he did, he wasn't quite sure where to start. Stalling for time, so that he could sort out the implications that Agustin's pronouncement gave rise to, Dixon changed the course of the conversation for the moment. "Why, Colonel, have you chosen me, a foreigner whom you have never met before, to discuss this matter with?''

There was a hint of resignation in Agustin's voice when he answered. "To start with, señor, there is really not much to discuss. I fear that what will happen will happen regardless of what you or I do. You see, my superiors have taken care to correct all those deficiencies that the last coup revealed. Even if my President were to be told today that another coup was coming, any efforts he made to round up the ringleaders or to rally units he might believe are loyal to him, would fail. One by one the units that the General Staff felt uncomfortable with have been scattered to the far reaches of our country or fed into the FARC's meat grinder. Underequipped and sent in piecemeal, the officers and men who would have stood by the President have been eliminated. As your own report submitted months ago suggested, the modern equipment that your government has given us has not gone to the units most likely to be used against the rebels. It has gone without exception to those units which the General Staff deemed loyal to them and not to the government.''

The mention of his report, a highly classified project that was not meant for distribution outside the U.S. Army, troubled Dixon. Though who and why someone had released it to the

Colombians troubled Dixon, he didn't pursue the matter. That he knew was academic at the moment. What was important was ascertaining, if at all possible, whether this Colombian colonel sitting before him was reliable and how true his story of gloom and doom was. Agustin, for his part, was watching Dixon during the uneasy silence, and answered as best he could the unspoken question, the one that Dixon was trying to find words for. "It is difficult, I am sure, for a soldier from your Army to believe the word of an officer who appears to be betraying his nation."

Not quite sure how to react, Dixon simply sat and stared at the Colombian colonel. In his silence, he confirmed what Agustin had just stated. Well, Agustin thought, it is his privilege to believe what he will. It is my duty to do what I must. Leaning forward, he rested his elbows on his knees and clasped his hands together. When he spoke, the whining softness of his voice was gone. In its place there was a firm, almost accusatory tone. "There are many ways a man can betray his country, General Dixon. Some men do it out of a misplaced sense of loyalty. Others, more vile creatures, do so for personal gain. Regardless of why they do it, the results are the same. Solemn oaths and pledges are forgotten as the traitor begins to create his own standards of conduct, ethics, and morality so that he can justify his actions. In the process, those under him suffer, sometimes physically but always in their hearts, as they watch their ideals and principles being surrendered one by one by those they are pledged to follow and obey. That death, Señor General, the death of the spirit and the heart, is the more painful of the two." Sitting up, Agustin puffed out his chest. "I know, for my heart has bled itself white. I am, like you, still a soldier." Then, he let himself go limp and shook his head. "But I am no longer a man. This war and the politicians, both in and out of uniform, rebel and loyal, have killed my pride and my faith."

Of this last part, Dixon heard little. The first thought that popped into his head was that Agustin was talking about him. Then without any conscious effort he asked himself if he was talking about Lane. Or was he talking about both him and Lane? It was this last thought, the idea that he could no longer tell the difference between himself and a man whom he de-

341

spised, that finally shook Dixon to the point that all displays of outward control were lost. Without a word, he jumped to his feet and turned away from Agustin. He stormed across the room several feet, then checked himself.

By the time he turned, Agustin was on his feet, standing erect and watching him. "Perhaps, General Dixon, this was a mistake. I apologize for disturbing you." The colonel's voice was anxious and worried. Dixon tried to say something to calm him, to keep him from leaving, but no words came. Like a fish stung into senselessness by a man-of-war, Dixon stood in the center of his office and watched Agustin pivot about and flee as quickly as he could.

With Agustin gone, Dixon was left on his own, left to sort out and account for his sins, both real and imagined.

En route to the cafe where she and Willie Freeman were scheduled to meet with someone alleged to be a member of the FARC, all Jan could think about was her missed luncheon appointment with Scott. It was becoming harder, she realized, to put her career and work before her relationship with him. It should be getting easier, she thought. By now their need to demonstrate their love and devotion to each other should be less, not more. Instead it was becoming demanding, more demanding than anything that she had ever known before. Is there always, she wondered, the need to reaffirm one's love and devotion over the years? Is there a break-even point where both parties settle into a comfortable routine? Or would there always be the need to recommit herself emotionally and phys- ically to a person whom she was already legally and morally bound to? Looking out the window of the taxi as it bumped and ground its way through the busy, narrow streets, Jan pondered these questions, all but forgetting their meeting.

Big Willie, however, hadn't. Sitting next to her, he inter- rupted Jan's train of random thoughts again and again. "How do we know, Jan, that we can trust these people? For all we know, this could be a setup by the Colombian government. You know they're anxious to get rid of anyone who doesn't toe the party line. The way you've been hammering away at them isn't exactly winning you friends in this town."

When she bothered to answer, those answers were quick and short. "It's not a setup. Trust me."

Jan's confidence, however, didn't put Willie off. "I trust you. No need to worry about that. I just don't trust the people who set this whole thing up. I mean, if they are real rebels, what happens if they try to grab you, you know, for propaganda reasons? Or they could be setting you up for a hit. I can see it all now, 'Famous Yankee newswoman and trusting sidekick killed in bold broad-daylight terrorist attack in the heart of the Colombian capital. More on this story and others at eleven.' "

Turning to face him, there was anger in Jan's eyes. His nagging and persistent interruptions were getting to her. "If you're so worried, stay in the taxi while I handle this."

Willie shook his head. "No way, Jan. Someone needs to save you from yourself."

"Oh, and you're elected? You got the duty today, I suppose?"

Quite literally he did, but he could not say so. When Jan had been approached that morning by a woman claiming to be connected with the FARC, to arrange the meeting they were headed for, both Willie Freeman, Jan's soundman, and JT Evens, the cameraman, agreed between themselves that one of them had to go with her. Since Willie knew Spanish, and his size and bearing were more imposing than JT's, both men decided that Willie was the natural choice. Neither Willie nor JT, of course, told Jan how they came to their decision. That, however, was not necessary, since both men, as Genny Conners liked to say, were always tripping over themselves in an effort to outmacho the other and save "poor little Jan" from the imaginary big bad wolf.

As reassuring as this attitude could be, there were times, like now, that it grated on her nerves. She was about to turn and snap at Willie when the taxi slowed, then pulled over to the curb. In Spanish the driver announced that they had arrived. Glancing out the window, then back at Willie, Jan decided to postpone her talk with her self-appointed guardian. Without a word, she was out of the cab, leaving Willie to pay. Might as well let him be of some use, she thought.

Used to meeting people under such circumstances, Jan stood

there on the sidewalk waiting until someone approached or
showed an interest in her. That did not take long. From behind
a man came up and took her arm. "This way please, Ms.
Fields." Though his grasp was light, it was firm enough to
direct her to a table where a man somewhat short in stature sat
watching their approach. With dark hair and a pinched face that
accentuated his lean, almost skeletal frame, the man reminded
Jan of a professor, not a revolutionary. When he stood and
extended his hand across the table by way of greeting, Jan
could see that she was an inch, maybe two inches, taller than
he. "Señorita Fields, I am so glad that you were able to come
on such short notice."

Taking the hand offered, Jan allowed him to take hers and
shake it. South American men, she knew, didn't take kindly to
having a woman challenging them, even symbolically, as many
people did in the United States when shaking hands. No need,
she thought, to get this guy bent out of shape unless she needed
to. With a smile, the tone of her voice was both light and
cheery. "It is, señor, a pleasure."

Standing, the Colombian eyed as much of Jan as he could
see of her. "Your beauty, señorita, is surpassed only by your
reputation." The words, Jan thought, were spoken with the
same obvious glee in his voice that a child uses when describing a bowl of chocolate ice cream covered with chocolate spills
and chocolate syrup. Though she often was accused by Scott of
being overly sensitive to such things, Jan could tell from the
way this man was looking at her and talking that he saw woman
first, correspondent second.

Easing into the chair being held by the man who had escorted her to the table, Jan folded her legs and began. "Your
kind invitation, señor, was too good to pass up." Jan made a
slight nod of her head toward Willie, who had finally come up
and joined them at the table. "Though some of my staff feel
that accepting your invitation is neither prudent nor wise, I
believe that if you meant to do me or anyone on my staff harm,
you could have done so without going through all of the trouble
of arranging a meeting such as this."

Hector Valendez smiled. They had been right. Everyone
who spoke of this woman said that she was as straightforward
and as blunt as she was beautiful. There would be no room, he

realized, for dancing in the shadows with this one. Directness and openness, these were what she respected and insisted upon. Well, he thought as he nodded, then let us drop the chase and get on with this. "We have no intention of bringing any harm to you or your staff. Though I do not mean to denigrate your status, there are many, many targets that better deserve our attentions and efforts. And besides, we are revolutionaries, not murderers. Though the government makes no distinction between its own people and those who are fighting against its corrupt rule, we have no such problem." Leaning forward, Valendez's eyes narrowed as his voice softened to a hiss. "We know who our enemies are and how to deal with them."

Jan realized that the Colombian's statements were meant to both reassure her and to threaten her. By agreeing to this meeting and coming this far, she knew that she had already made a pact with the devil, a pact that he would insist be fulfilled.

From her silence and expression, Valendez knew that Jan Fields had taken his meaning. Easing back into his seat, he let his face go calm, and raised his right hand to signal a waiter who had been hovering nearby. "Would you care for something, señorita?"

Jan nodded. "Coffee, please." Though she was dying for an ice-cold Diet Coke, she knew it would be impolite and in bad form to order one. Keep the natives happy, she thought, as long as you can. After the order had been placed and the waiter disappeared, Jan decided to regain the initiative if possible. "You went through a great deal of effort and have placed yourself in some risk asking us here. There is a reason, I trust, for doing so."

"There has been recently a great deal being made by the Colombian military and your own about how our operations are placing innocent civilians at risk. Stories, such as the one recently published in the government-controlled press, about us using small children to carry messages and explosives through their lines, are patent lies, poor attempts to make us, and not them, appear to be the evil ones."

With as little expression as possible, Jan agreed with a slight nod, knowing that this Colombian and his masters were as guilty of lying to the media as was the government he spoke and fought against. Though the abuses were not as widespread as the government claimed, this rebel group, like all those before it, used civilians when it suited them. Even as they spoke, though she didn't realize it, a group of women employed by the Colombian Ministry of Defense to clean their building nightly were being trained in the fine art of smuggling, emplacing, and setting explosives.

Ignoring Jan's less than enthusiastic endorsement of his denial, Hector Valendez continued. "Another fine example of the government and the American military trying desperately to smear my cause with innocent blood is being played out here in the capital by your own senior military commander. In a court of law he has lied. He fabricated a fantasy, and you supported him."

Thrown and confused by this last comment, Jan cocked her head. "What fantasy are you talking about? If you are talking about the case against Captain Kozak, I was there during the proceedings. Nothing that came out then, to the best of my knowledge, was a lie. What exactly did General Lane say that was incorrect?"

He had hit a chord. Though Jan tried to keep her expression in check, he could tell by a slight flutter of her eyes and the pace with which she now spoke that he had been right. "Your general," he continued, "during that hearing claimed that he was fired on from the village of El Frío, a village which had already been brutalized by government forces. No one, however, was defending El Frío at that time. In fact it was all but deserted. After the government force raped it, an event that you so courageously recorded and publicized, the FARC retook the town but did not reoccupy it. There was, as you know, little left to occupy. The few survivors who were left among dead, having suffered enough, were left alone by our fighters."

"Then why," Jan injected, "the second battle? Why did the FARC choose to fight for a worthless objective? And where were the guns that fired on General Lane's helicopter? He was fired on, you know. That part of the story is too well documented."

Though he wanted to smile now that he had Jan snarled in his trap, Valendez forced a frown. "No land, no village in my country is worthless, Ms. Fields. Though El Frío may not measure up to your ideas of an ideal community, it is for my countrymen a home.''

Not sure if the indignation was feigned or real, Jan apologized. She did not want to lose this lead, a lead that could be important to Nancy Kozak's defense. "I did not mean to imply that El Frío was useless. I just don't understand why three battles in as many days were fought over it.''

Propping his elbow on the table, Valendez raised three fingers. "The first was waged by the government against its own people. It punished El Frío in the manner that it did in order to discourage its own people in other villages from joining us and fighting for their own rights and freedom." He dropped a finger. "We, the FARC, went back into El Frío for revenge. It would have been wrong to allow the government to commit such a crime and go unpunished. Though it was their soldiers and not the corrupt politicians who ordered the attack who paid, the message we left was clear.''

That, of course, was a lie. The FARC counterattack, ordered and directed by Valendez himself, had been well planned and prepared for. El Frío had been the bait that the government had readily taken, just as Jan Fields was now taking the bait that he was dangling before her. Letting the scowl on his face grow, Valendez dropped his third finger. "The final battle, initiated by your Army, only had one purpose in mind, to kill Colombians. And as your General Lane admitted during an interview with another news correspondent after the operation, he didn't much care whether the people they killed were civilian or military.''

The Colombian's accusation angered Jan. Most of the Army officers she had come to know, over the years, would never do such a thing. In all the operations her own husband, Scott, had been involved in, he had been scrupulous in avoiding any unnecessary suffering or harm to the civilian populace. But then she realized that Scotty hadn't been in charge of this operation. In fact, since he had arrived in Colombia, he had been uneasy and at times upset over the manner in which Lane was doing things. Maybe this, she mused, was why he had been so willing to offer her advice the other night, advice that could only be damaging to a fellow officer. Like his self-imposed silence on discussing any current military matters with her, he had never spoken badly of a senior officer in her presence. Perhaps, Jan thought, there is some truth to what this Colombian was saying. Like many of the reporters covering this war, she had read up on Vietnam, especially after her own husband began to openly draw that parallel. In that war, cases of killing civilians in order to inflate body counts, while exaggerated, were too numerous to ignore or deny. Had, Jan wondered, the American Army here in Colombia reverted to that brutal practice? Pushing that thought aside for the moment, she restated her third question. "If the guns that fired on General Lane's helicopter were not in the village, then where were they?"

"North of the river, a good three kilometers away from the village. In the pre-trial proceedings held the other day, the pilot of General Lane's helicopter stated that they were flying at three thousand feet, just north of the river, when they were fired upon. From the village, it is impossible to see an object, even one as large as a helicopter, flying at that height while moving along the north bank of the Meta River."

"How do you know this for sure?"

Valendez leaned back in his chair, throwing out his chest in a show of pride. "Because, Ms. Fields, I was there. I was beside the guns and I gave the order for them to fire on General Lane's helicopter."

This announcement was enough to even solicit a response from Willie, a man known for his ability to remain unflappable under the most harrowing circumstances. Jan and Willie looked at each other for a moment, then at the Colombian. "Can you prove this? I mean the part about the guns being north of the river and not in the village?"

"I am willing, Ms. Fields, to have your team escorted to the site of the battle, both where the guns were and in the village, where your general claimed that they were. You will be free to roam about as you please, interviewing the gun crews, the villagers, and anyone you like. I will even arrange for a helicopter to fly at the same altitude and on the same course that Lane's pilot claims to have flown when they were taken under fire. You and your camera will be able to see clearly that no one in El Frío could have fired on your general while his aircraft was flying over the river as his pilot testified."

It was only then that Jan realized that she had no idea who this man was. It was clear from the manner in which he was now talking that he was no lackey, no mere messenger boy. "Can I interview you on tape?"

Valendez shook his head. "No, I am afraid not. You see, I am a modest man, and in reality what I have to say would add little to this that isn't best answered by the people who actually did the shooting and the villagers who saw it all."

Jan looked over at Willie again. He gave her a blank stare in return. Facing back to Valendez, Jan asked how soon he needed her answer. "Tonight, Ms. Fields. I will need to know by then so that I can make sure the arrangements are taken care of and you can be back in time for the upcoming trial."

The fact that the Colombian seemed to know a great deal about Nancy Kozak's trial didn't strike Jan as strange. Nor was she bothered by the possibility that this could, as Willie pointed out, turn out to be nothing more than a propaganda event staged for her benefit by the rebels. What was important, as she and Willie stood up and prepared to leave, was that she was going to be able to do something, perhaps something really big, to help Nancy Kozak. That, and only that, at this moment was her chief concern. All others, including her personal safety, were forgotten.

When the two North Americans had gone, the waiter who had served Valendez and Jan their coffee came over and sat next to Valendez. "I will be glad," he stated, "when we are finished here and can go back to the jungles and mountains. I will never again, Commander, complain about carrying your radio."

Rafael Dario's comment made Valendez laugh. "You never complained before. In fact, the only time you are a nuisance to me is when you get this crazy idea in your young head that carrying a gun and pulling a trigger is more important than what you do for me."

"Important, perhaps, in your eyes. But I have never given up the hope that you will someday show mercy on my humble soul and let me once, just once, stand up and fight for my country like a man."

"We all must do our duties, my friend, regardless of how mundane or unglamorous."

Looking around at the street, Dario grunted. "Well, I do hope that our duties will soon take us away from this city. It is without doubt the filthiest and unfriendliest place I have ever seen on earth."

"But it is the heart, my young friend. It is the heart of this country and of our enemy. And one well-aimed stroke delivered here, held true to its mark, is worth a dozen great victories out there. No, we still have much to do here, and if we are patient we might be able to bring all of our efforts together soon."

"But how soon?"

Valendez ignored his radioman's impatience. Instead he too looked around, sipping his coffee as he did so. Slowly returning his cup to the saucer, Valendez smiled. "Soon. Very, very soon, my young friend."

CHAPTER 19

November 28

THE MORNING HAD PROGRESSED AS ANTICIPATED. ONE BY ONE the witnesses for the prosecution were called forward by Captain Mark Moretti. Each in turn recounted his version of the incidents surrounding the insubordination and disrespect that Captain Nancy Kozak had allegedly committed against Major General C. B. Lane on November 12 over El Frío. Prompted by Moretti's questions, the witnesses without exception repeated their stories almost word for word as they had recorded them on their written statements some two weeks prior. Everything, Lane thought as he watched from the front row of seats provided for the spectators, was going well. He liked things that not only went well but did so in a neat, orderly, and predictable manner, like a train running on schedule.

First came the crewmen of Lane's helicopter, in ascending order of rank, starting with the door gunner. As he had during the Article 32 investigation hearing, Mark Moretti started his questioning by holding up each of the witnesses' statements and asking, "To the best of your knowledge, is this statement of yours a true and accurate description of the events of November twelfth?"

Without hesitation, each man in turn nodded, responding with a firm and unflinching "Yes, sir, that statement is correct."

"Would you please, for the benefit of the jury," Moretti would continue, "summarize what you saw and heard that day, while operating over El Frío?" Each man did, of course, respond to Moretti's request, using the same firm and steady voice that they had used when answering Moretti's first question. Jan Fields-Dixon, seated in the rear of the temporary courtroom between JT Evens and Big Willie, groaned every time Moretti started his routine. "You know, he could have saved the government a fortune if he had recorded his witnesses' statements at the Article 32 and simply replayed them here."

"Yeah," JT responded. "But then your friend General Lane and mine wouldn't have had another chance to tromp Captain Kozak's face into the mud again."

Mention of Lane's name caused Jan to glance over to where he sat like a fat cat watching mice at play in his snare. "You're probably right. Though I don't understand it, he's no doubt enjoying this."

"Not for long," Willie intoned in his deep, solemn voice. When Ulrich would wipe the smirk off Lane's face, however, remained a good question. When Jan had approached him with the videotape that Hector Valendez had been so instrumental in orchestrating, Sam Ulrich had initially rejected it out of hand. "I can't use that! That's the enemy you were dealing with."

But Jan would not be denied. "What in the hell do you think Lane is, Santa Claus? He's out to get Nancy Kozak, and since you're the attorney for the defense, that makes him the enemy."

Reluctantly he accepted the film pledging that he would use it during his cross-examination of Lane's helicopter crew. "If I can show that they were so badly confused that they couldn't tell where the enemy fire was coming from," he told Jan as he began to see the possibilities the video offered, "then perhaps I can start setting the stage for when I call Nancy's people to tell how difficult things really were that day. And even if the judge throws it out on some pretext or another, at least the jury will have seen some of it, and a shadow of a doubt concerning the prosecution's statements will start to muck up his case."

Jan, of course, had little confidence in Ulrich. "He reminds me," she told Willie after her meeting with him, "too much of an office boy I had when I was covering the war in Egypt years ago. Nice kid, but a little short on common sense and decidedly lacking in the backbone area." This, and a chronic cynicism that had settled down over everyone who was trying to do something to save a deteriorating situation in Colombia, left Jan, Willie, and JT worried as they watched the morning's proceedings go on like a dress parade. Even the defense seemed to be on line with the program. When offered the opportunity to cross-examine the witnesses called forth by Mark Moretti, Sam Ulrich cross-examined them in a subdued, almost hesitant manner. One by one Mark Moretti walked them through their stories, just as the investigating officer had during the Article 32. And one by one Sam followed the prosecution, asking no brilliant questions, making no startling revelations, only asking each witness to clarify a point or rephrase a comment he had made before. One, two, three, the witnesses came and the witnesses left, like batters facing an ace pitcher.

Sitting next to Sam, Nancy Kozak watched with a face that was as set and expressionless as a young art student's first sculpture. No words were passed between her and her attorney while he waited for his opportunity to cross-examine the current witness, no sidewise glances, either from him or Kozak, were cast while he was doing so. It was, one spectator noted, as if the two were strangers sharing a bus ride, each absorbed in his or her own thoughts and not interested in the person seated next to them.

Jan, however, more than made up for Nancy's lack of emotions as her squirming increased as the morning and Sam Ulrich's uninspired performance wore on. Though she knew that Kozak's attorney had an ace in the hole, an ace that only she, her crew, and Nancy Kozak knew of, she was becoming angry at the young JAG officer. "He can do better than that," she would comment to no one in particular. Or she would whisper to Willie, "He needs to be a little more aggressive, more probing." While Willie ignored her, Jan was beginning to wonder if, rather than to shock the jury, Ulrich's strategy was to lull them to sleep or bore them to the point that they gave in and demanded the trial be brought to a close. Hoping for a short recess, Jan, despite her pledge to remain in the background, told JT, "I swear I'm going to give Sam Ulrich a swift kick if he doesn't start acting like a defense attorney soon."

It wasn't until he got to First Lieutenant Clarence G. Kelly, C. B. Lane's pilot, that Sam started to come alive. Starting as he did with all those who had gone before, Sam approached the witness, statement in hand, and asked questions that were meant to emphasize certain points at issue, points which until now seemed totally unrelated. "Lieutenant Kelly," Sam said in a rather casual manner, "you stated that at the time you began receiving fire from the ground you were over the river."

Quick to point out the JAG officer's error, Kelly cut in. "North of the river, sir. We had drifted over the north bank of the Meta River."

Looking down at the sheet of paper, Sam pretended to look for the passage that Kelly was talking about, then exclaimed, even though he had not found it. "Oh, yes, so you did." Looking at Kelly, Sam's face dropped into a pronounced inquisitive stare. "Are you sure, Lieutenant?"

Bothered by being brought to task for such a trivial matter, Kelly's answer was sharp, almost to the point of being rude. "Yes, Captain, I am positive. As the aircraft commander, I am responsible for keeping track of where we are at all times."

Sam thought about that for a moment, shaking his head before he continued. "Why, Lieutenant, were you there?"

"We were executing a sharp, steep bank in order to turn around quickly."

"And this bank, it was to the left?"

Again displaying the same impatience as he had before, Kelly responded quickly and pointedly, "No, to the right, just as I wrote in my statement and stated for Captain Moretti."

"And while you were making this bank, where were you looking?"

"To the right, naturally."

"I'm sorry, I'm not an aviator. You'll have to explain that to me," Sam blurted as he reached out behind him and tossed the pilot's statement onto the table where Kozak sat. Only Kozak, who leaned back slightly as the statement came flying toward her, and Jan caught the significance of Sam's gesture. He had symbolically thrown down the red flag.

"In such a steep bank, I have to use the ground as a reference to make sure that I don't bank too far."

"Why not use your instruments? Aren't your instruments more accurate than your eyesight and judgment?"

"Sir, I am an experienced pilot. Though I do use my instruments, I have more than enough experience to make such an elementary banking turn I was executing when we were taken under fire."

Sam noted the hint of arrogance that was slipping into the pilot's voice. "Back to the point. You said you were looking to the right, correct?"

"Yes, sir, that is correct."

"What, Lieutenant, did you see?"

Kelly paused for a moment, in part because he needed to search his memory in order to recall the images of that day and time, and in part because he was confused. This, he thought, had nothing to do with the incident. Nor had anyone made such a fuss over these details before. It was, he knew, not part of the prepared script that his superior and Captain Moretti had drilled him on. Still it was a simple, harmless question, and he prepared to answer it as best he could, making sure that he didn't surrender any more information than he needed to, just as Captain Moretti had instructed him. "I saw the river, which was just at the bottom of my view. In the center was the area where the village should have been. And above that the southern horizon. Here and there along that horizon, there were several helicopters, a couple of scouts and several UH-60s."

"You said, Lieutenant, where the village should have been. Didn't you see the village?"

"I saw the church steeple. It was a great terrain reference point, the only really reliable one, as a matter of fact, other than the river, that we had."

"And," Sam continued as he turned away to face Kozak, "what happened while you were making your turn and watching this church steeple?"

"We were taken under fire."

"How did you become aware of this?"

"That we were under fire?"

Sam glanced over his shoulder and nodded. "Yes, that you were under fire."

"Well, sir, the whole aircraft suddenly started to jerk and buck, as if someone was underneath it rapping it with a hammer."

One member of the jury and a couple of spectators who had not yet been lulled into a near state of inattention realized the significance of Kelly's last statement. One of them, an aviator, shot upright in his seat, his eyes opening wide. This sudden reaction acted as a cue, alerting those around and behind him, that something had just happened. What it was they didn't know. But there had been a change, and now they were attentive to what was happening in the front of the room.

"What, Lieutenant Kelly, was your first reaction?"

"To look around, first at my instruments, then to the warning lights on the control panel, and finally about the cabin."

Turning to face Kelly again, Sam eased himself back so that he rested half sitting on the table. Folding his arms, he narrowed his eyes. "Before you turned away, away from a village that was obscured by so much vegetation that only its church steeple was visible, what did you see?"

As before, he paused. Cocking his head, Kelly looked down as if he were scanning the inside of his mind in an effort to review the images of that scene he had stored there. When he was ready, he looked up at Sam, his confusion now obvious. "Just the church steeple, the far horizon, and the other helicopters. That's all."

"You didn't see any tracers?"

"No, sir, I didn't see any tracers."

"None, none at all? You saw no indication of ground fire directed at you before your aircraft was hit?"

"No, sir. As I said, the first clue I had that we were under fire was when we started getting hit, from underneath."

Over where the jury sat, an aviation captain who was one of the jury bolted upright as he kept his eyes fixed on Kelly and muttered an abrupt exclamation. In the silence of the conference room, his soft "Oh, shit!" caught off guard those who were still unaware that something significant had happened. Even Moretti, who had been listening intently, took several seconds to catch on to the fact that the pilot of Lane's aircraft had just stated in so many words that the fire they had received could not possibly have come from the village. Slowly, as that revelation began to sink in, Moretti's mouth dropped as he shook his head.

In the rear, Jan, watching intently, broke into a broad smile and turned to smack JT on the shoulder with a clenched fist. "Yes!" she whispered. JT recoiled from the unexpected blow, and Willie looked over at her in surprise. "Yes! He did it. The wimp did it. He's going to do it."

While a wave of hushed conversations and murmurs broke out throughout the conference room, Sam turned to face the spectators. Spinning his briefcase around on the table, he opened it, reached in with his right hand for the videocassette that sat in the center of the case, laid his fingers on it, and paused. Looking down at the cassette, he thought for a moment. Then, pulling his hand away as if he had just been burned, Sam slammed the briefcase shut and pivoted about to face the judge. "Your Honor, I have no further questions for this witness."

Lieutenant Colonel Edward Cole, serving as the judge in this case, was, like everyone else in the room, caught completely off guard. This, Cole thought, was not expected. Not expected at all. As he considered what Sam had just done, Cole looked over at Lane. Lane, visibly shaken by the last few minutes, locked eyes with Cole. There would be hell to pay, Cole knew.

In the rear, Jan's exuberance suddenly turned into a stunned silence. Not caring who heard her, she exclaimed out loud, "What in the hell is he doing?"

Willie, glancing about him, leaned over and whispered to her to calm down, that she was drawing attention to them.

Jan, however, would not be put off by Willie. "The idiot had him by the throat. He had his knife right there, ready to drive it home, and he flinched! The little rat bastard flinched!"

As forcefully as he could, Willie told Jan to keep quiet. Looking past her at JT, Willie nodded his head. Together, each man grabbed an arm. Standing up, they all but lifted her out of her seat and escorted her out of the room while Cole slammed down his gavel, calling for the audience to be quiet. Giving in to Willie and JT's efforts, Jan allowed herself to be led away, though she continued to protest.

Once in the hall, JT and Willie let her go. Jan, spinning around to face her camera team, threw her hands up in the air.

"Doesn't he realize that we're going to run the full video tonight on the prime-time news program? He's going to lose the shock value of our efforts."

Glancing about in order to see who was watching them, Willie in a calm but firm voice tried to settle Jan. "He knows what he's doing. He's in charge of this case, Jan, not you. Maybe he's going to show it later."

Growing angry at Willie's attempts to mollify her, Jan pulled away from him as soon as they were in the corridor. Turning to face him, she hissed as she spoke. "He doesn't know his ass from a hole in the ground. He's as limp-wristed as the rat bastards on this division staff. By delaying his defense, he's giving Lane a chance to recover and work him and Cole over."

In a calm, slow voice Willie spoke. "What happens in there, Jan, is out of our hands. We did what we could and now, well, it's up to Ulrich. We've got to trust him." Jan's angry glance told Willie that she didn't like that part. "Besides, Jan," Willie continued, "we've got enough to worry about."

"Yeah," JT added. "Like getting hung out to dry by the Colombian government as soon as that video hits the evening news."

Though she hated to admit it, Jan knew they were right. What would happen to Nancy was, and probably had always been, beyond her control. And they were probably also right about the reaction that the FARC El Frío tape would create as soon as it was aired. Jan was already on the outs with most officials, both American and Colombian, for the harshness of her criticism since September, and the El Frío tape would in all probability be her swan song in Bogotá.

Without a word, Jan dropped her head, turned, and began to head out of the building. There would be hell to pay that night, and she needed to get ready for it.

Back in the courtroom, Mark Moretti had already called the next witness, Captain James William Adderly III, Lane's aide-de-camp. Cole, on the verge of calling a recess, remembered that Adderly was up next. Reasoning that there could be no harm in letting Lane's aide testify, Cole leaned back in his seat and allowed the proceedings to continue.

Adderly approached the stand with a tight, expressionless

face. There was nothing unusual about that. Most everyone who worked around Lane for a long period of time wore that look, one that showed no feeling or emotion. If you looked close enough, you could see that the bearer was holding on to his or her feelings and thoughts tightly, as if afraid to let go. In many ways that was exactly how Adderly felt that morning, especially after the revelation that Lieutenant Kelly had just made. Taking the oath, he reminded himself over and over that he would have to be careful about not only what he said but how he said it.

Confident that he was on firm ground with Adderly, Moretti cut the preliminaries and got right to the heart of the matter. "Captain Adderly, could you tell the court what you saw and heard that day over El Frío?"

He didn't respond at first. Rather, he looked beyond Moretti, as if his gaze was fixed on a distant object at the rear of the room. Everyone assumed that he was reviewing in his mind the events of the day and trying to form them into a coherent answer. If it had been as simple as that, Adderly would have responded instantly. But it wasn't. For the image that came to Adderly's mind first and sharpest was that of a frightened old man, panicked and unable to control himself, let alone a division. Even as he sat there in the cool quiet of the courtroom, Adderly imagined that he could smell the pungent odor of Lane's loose bowels. He could see, as clearly as if it were happening then, the growing darkness about Lane's crotch and pants leg as urine and shit flowed as freely from Lane's body as the fear his face betrayed.

Jerking his head to the right, he looked over to where Kozak sat. Like him, she wore a mask that hid all emotions. All signs that she had any feelings one way or another over what was transpiring in that room at that moment were safely hidden behind her expressionless face. Still, as bland as she tried to make it, Adderly could see a strong, determined look. Everything about her face, the manner in which she held her head, the set of her jaw, the steady stare she gave him in return, spoke of pride. It wasn't the flashy assumed pride that Lane and his staff wore on their sleeves like a badge. Rather Adderly saw that Kozak's pride was born from her skills and achievements as a soldier.

That, Adderly suddenly realized, was the difference. With a slight cocking of the head, he looked over to Lane, who was becoming annoyed over his delay. Kozak, he thought, was a soldier. Despite the fact that she was a female and had never made any pretenses to the contrary, she was something that Lane wasn't and could never be. And Lane hated her just as he hated anyone who was smarter than he was. And just as he degraded, belittled, and crushed anyone who showed any sign of success or intelligence that he could not lay claim to, Lane was determined to crush Kozak. For months, from his desk outside of Lane's office, Adderly realized that he had watched a parade of good men and women, soldiers each and every one, go in and be brutalized by a man who didn't deserve to wear the title. And now today he was going to participate at the direction of his boss in the destruction of another good trooper, all to satisfy some unfathomable personal need of Major General C. B. Lane.

"Captain Adderly," Moretti finally asked, "is there a problem?"

Adderly wanted to say yes there was, but he didn't. Instead he shook his head. "No, sorry. I was just making sure I understood what was going on here."

The perplexed look on Moretti's face didn't bother Adderly as he began to speak. "We were, as I stated in my affidavit, operating near El Frío."

After waiting several seconds for Adderly to continue, Moretti realized that Adderly had no intention of doing so. Not understanding what was going on, Moretti began to prod Adderly. "What, Captain, were you doing there."

"We were observing operations of the 3rd Brigade."

Again after waiting for an expansion on that theme, or any other for that matter, Moretti realized that Adderly wasn't coming forward with one. Deciding to lead Adderly through his questioning piece by piece if necessary, Moretti began again. "What occurred that day, at El Frío, Captain Adderly?"

In a manner that was as cold and detached as he could manage, Adderly responded, "The 3rd Brigade conducted an air assault operation in the vicinity of El Frío."

Cocking his head to one side, Moretti looked at Adderly with a puzzled expression on his face. What in the hell, Moretti wondered, was going on here? He felt like asking Adderly why he was being such an ass, but he managed to maintain his composure. Whatever the reason, Moretti figured, I have no patience right now to deal with this man. Determined to get him off the stand as quickly as possible, Moretti continued, deciding to be as direct and exact with his questions as possible. Moretti's tactic, and Adderly's short, precise responses resulted in a quick, almost comical series of exchanges. "What happened when the commanding general's helicopter was taken under fire."

"The pilot took evasive actions."

"What did the commanding general do."

"He had me call for a fire mission against the village of El Frío."

"Did the artillery respond to this call for fire?"

"Yes."

"I mean, did they fire the mission requested."

"No."

"Why not."

"They were firing another mission."

"What other mission."

"One in support of the 3rd Battalion, 511th Infantry."

"Why didn't they respond immediately to the commanding general's request."

"I don't know."

"Could you venture a guess."

"No."

By now it was obvious to everyone that Adderly, for whatever reason, had no intention of volunteering information other than that which he had to by the rules of the court. And those answers given were, to Moretti's growing frustration, not coming out the way he wanted them. Still he was determined to finish up what he had started, even if it were only for appearance sake. "When the artillery unit in question refused to fire the commanding general's fire mission, what did the commanding general do?"

"He called the artillery unit."

"And?"

"And what?"

Moretti drew in a deep breath as he held his growing anger

in check. "And what happened when the commanding general called the artillery unit?"

"I believe they told him that they were firing another mission."

Unable to hold back, Moretti turned to Cole. "Your Honor, permission to consult with the witness in private?"

Before Cole could respond, Ulrich jumped to his feet. "Your Honor, I object. This would not be in the best interest of my client." Though he had no idea what Adderly was up to, it was obvious that he was not cooperating with the prosecution. Though that didn't necessarily mean that he would cooperate with the defense, Ulrich was ready to grab at any opportunity that presented itself.

Without thinking, also rattled by Adderly's performance, Cole shouted out, "Objection sustained."

Stymied, Moretti called out while Ulrich was bending over to speak to Kozak as he took his seat, "Your Honor, I would like to call for a recess until tomorrow."

Caught off guard, Ulrich turned and stood up again, prepared to ask that he be allowed to cross-examine Adderly before the recess, but he was too slow. Seeing an opportunity to bring this distressing and confusing session to a close, Cole slammed down his gavel. "This court is in recess until zero nine hundred hours tomorrow morning."

Pushing their way past a group of Colombian cleaning women who had been waiting patiently to go into the conference room to prepare it for the big meeting of all the primary commanders and staff officers the next morning, Adderly followed Lane to his office. He ignored his boss's mutterings as he kept turning over and over in his mind what he had overheard between Kelly and the defense attorney as he waited to go in and testify himself. He had been there. He had experienced the same sensations that Kelly described as the helicopter had been hit, the hammering sensation on the bottom of the aircraft. And he had seen the tracers. He had looked out the door toward the village and seen the tracers. He knew that. Adderly had no doubts about that. Even now in his mind's eye he could see the tracers.

When he stopped, as if he had smacked into an invisible

wall, a major who had been following Adderly ran into him. Jarred out of his deep thoughts by the commotion behind him, Lane looked at his aide and the major for a brief moment before he growled, "Captain, quit screwing around. We've got a lot to do between now and tomorrow."

Dazed more by his sudden revelation than by the collision, Adderly apologized to the major and then stumbled a few steps behind Lane, making no effort to catch up. He had lied. That thought, swimming about in his head, couldn't be casually pushed aside. He had lied in his statement concerning the incident over El Frío. At the Article 32 investigation he had reconfirmed that lie. And now, because of it, the career of a fellow officer was on the line. But what, he wondered, should he do now? If he went back, if he tried to change his statement to read that the tracers he saw were falling toward and not rising from the village, what would they do to him? He had made a sworn statement, a statement that had already been introduced in an official investigation as evidence and which he had reaffirmed under oath during the Article 32 investigation. Would changing his statement, he wondered, constitute the admission of perjury?

Reaching Lane's office, Adderly drifted in as Lane bellowed out to the sergeant who served as secretary, "Get me Colonel Cole on the phone. No." Lane paused, thrusting his index finger out at the sergeant. "Have Cole see me in my office immediately." Without waiting for an acknowledgment, Lane stormed into his office, slamming the door as he went.

Easing over to his desk across from the sergeant, Adderly plopped down into his seat and stared at the wall over the sergeant's head absentmindedly for several minutes. The sergeant, while dialing Cole's number, looked over at him. Though he was dying to ask what had happened, he knew better than to ask. After working in this office as long as he had, the sergeant knew that it was best to keep his head down and mind his own business, especially when the head bull was on a rampage.

Adderly was still staring at the wall, his expression as blank as the wall itself, when Cole came into the office. Without bothering to stop, Cole went to Lane's door, knocked once, and then entered after Lane screamed a stream of indistinguishable curses through the closed door by way of acknowledgment. Shaken out of his deep and troubled thoughts, and unable to sort out how his sudden revelation concerning the incident at El Frío would affect him, let alone what to do about it, Adderly leaned forward and over the desk and opened a large planning calendar. Picking up a mechanical pencil, he clicked it a few times to draw the lead point out and prepared to write in the time when the court would reconvene. It was then that he noticed that the commander's conference, the one that everyone had been preparing for, was scheduled to start the next morning at nine.

"Damn," Adderly moaned when he realized the court-martial now conflicted with the division commander's conference. With Kozak's trial going awry, Lane would insist upon being there the whole time. Yet he needed to be at the commander's conference. Every primary staff officer, his deputy, and all special staff officers on the division staff, not to mention brigade commanders and key members of their staffs, were scheduled to be there. Arrangements and preparations for this all-day round of briefings and discussions had been in the works for almost a month. It was a cinch that Lane wouldn't be able to skip it just for a court-martial. He would have to be told of the scheduling conflict so that the trial could be delayed.

Yet Adderly, listening to Lane as he paced back and forth across his office, yelling and screaming at Cole, knew Lane would become even more unglued when he was told of this. When he got himself going, Adderly knew, and pinging off the walls, he came down on any target, even an innocent bystander, to vent his wrath upon. Looking up at the sergeant, Adderly considered for a moment having him tell Lane of the problem. That, however, would be cowardliness of the first order, something that Adderly despised in an officer. No, he thought, I'll have to do it myself.

But not right now. Even though it would be the perfect time, with both Cole and Lane together, the last thing Adderly wanted to do was to stick his head into the center of the hellfire and damnation Lane was raining down on the shaken staff judge advocate. He'd wait, he figured, till later in the day, hoping to find a time when he could pop the bad news on his boss. Maybe after Lane'd reviewed the G-3's pre-brief on the commander's conference he'd be in a better frame of mind. That at least was what Adderly hoped. Pushing the calendar away, and all thoughts of the trial aside, Adderly turned his attention to the in box holding all the actions and messages that had found their way onto his desk en route to Lane's office. After wading into the heap of files and papers sitting in front of him, he began to forget the conflict entirely.

Major José Solis felt no trepidation today as he approached the cafe for his daily meeting with members of the special team that Hector Valendez had assembled for the operation against the headquarters of the 11th Air Assault. He hoped that Valendez himself would be there, for he had some reservations concerning the timing of the attack. Though there was little that anyone could do, since so many of the explosives had already been emplaced and their timers set, Solis hoped that the least he could do was to get Valendez to agree to have the charges that were placed in the main conference room changed so that their detonation would coincide with the opening of the division commander's conference.

Crossing the street with care, for the late-afternoon traffic was quite heavy, Solis walked into the cafe. Spying Valendez seated with two leaders of the special team, he headed over toward them. As he did so, he caught the eye of Rafael Dario, who stood attentively near the entrance of the building. With a motion of his hand, held as if he were drinking from a cup, Solis let Dario know that he wanted coffee. A young and serious man, Dario nodded before he disappeared into the building, and half a dozen other FARC men, scattered about the busy cafe for security, went back to whatever they were doing before Solis had entered.

Standing up to greet Solis, Valendez reached across the table and offered his hand. "We have, Major, come to the end of our little project." As they shook hands, Solis noticed that Valendez wore a broad and unabashed smile on his face. He was pleased, Solis thought. Satisfied and pleased with how things had turned out. Not that Solis wasn't. On the contrary, he too was quite content with the way things had gone so far. Accepting Valendez's warm hand and shaking it once vigorously, Solis took his seat across from the rebel leader.

Dropping his friendly smile after exchanging greetings with the other two men, Solis launched right into the business he felt compelled to discuss with Valendez. "As you know, I am not completely satisfied with the time selected for the attack. I still feel that nine o'clock, and not nine ten, would be more appropriate."

Picking up his cup of coffee, Valendez nodded, the smile still on his face. "Yes, I know that you are not happy with ten minutes past the hour. Neither were these gentlemen," he added, pointing his cup at the two leaders of his special team. "Too difficult to set the timepiece, this one complains. It adds another opportunity for error, the other said. But"—he paused as he took a sip—"I added the extra ten minutes just to avoid any errors. Few meetings, even those of our vaunted central committee, start on time. I want to make sure that we have a margin built into our plan to cover any and every contingency imaginable."

Solis shook his head in disagreement. "These people are not Colombians. Especially not that jackass who calls himself a division commander. He insists that every meeting start on time and holds his staff to that requirement. In all the months that I have had to endure working with them, they have yet to start any later than the time announced."

Waiting for Dario to finish serving Solis, Valendez nodded, still smiling. "Yes, yes, I know that one's habits and history. But I also know about human nature. And if there is one thing that I have learned, both as an educator and as a military leader, it is that there is a first time for everything. Mistakes and miscalculations often crop up at the most inconvenient times. So we plan as best we can to ensure that such errors, which are out of our control, do not hinder our efforts."

"So," Solis sighed, putting his cup of coffee down, "you have no intention of making the change."

"No. We will go as planned."

"Well, then it is settled. We go forth as planned."

"What?" Valendez exclaimed. "You are not going to protest our plan to fire on the Yankee supply and support center at the military airfield with some of our captured artillery?"

Now it was Solis's turn to smile. "No, not at all. Though I am still, as a professional soldier, appalled that you would so

366

casually throw away four good 105mm howitzers, I understand the overall propaganda value of such an attack. I think that doing so will be a nice touch. Executed in conjunction with the attack on the headquarters, the artillery attack will magnify the shock of the other. Such a strike by conventional artillery will show that the raid on the Ministry of Defense is not simply an isolated terrorist attack. Since the government is responsible for the defense of the capital, the attack by large-caliber artillery will demonstrate how ineffective our security measures are. The retribution from the Yankees, I expect, will be most violent."

"Ha!" Valendez shouted as he looked at one and then the other of the special team leaders. "See, I told you we would make a revolutionary out of this young man, didn't I?"

The four men laughed, sipped their coffee, and chatted for several minutes. In the course of the casual, almost idle talk, Solis mentioned the trial, and how the lawyer for the defense had failed to show the video that Valendez had arranged to be made. Shrugging, Valendez showed that he was not overly concerned. "As I said before, we cannot plan for everything. Besides, the video will be seen. The lady correspondent, who thinks like me, made arrangements to run a modified version of it on the news show her network runs. There will be howls, I am sure, from our dear General Lane once he gets wind of that."

Solis chuckled. "He is already howling. All the planning and preparations that he personally put into rigging the trial of the female captain were beginning to come unglued today just before the attorney for the prosecution asked for a recess. Rumors are that he spent the rest of the day calling in each and every person involved in those proceedings in an effort to ensure that there would be no more mistakes."

"Isn't that," one of the other men asked, "according to their system, illegal?"

"Yes," Solis responded. "Quite. But General Lane, the senior commander here in Colombia, has been doing what he pleases for so long that he now believes that he can do anything. And his staff, isolated here, as it were, from the rest of their Army, is for the most part hand-picked and intensely loyal to him. Those who are not are kept in line by those who are through peer pressure, inertia, or simple despondency. One officer whom I heard the other day complaining passed off his failure to do anything about Lane's abuses simply by saying that dealing with such things was not in his job description." Solis paused, took a sip of coffee, and then chuckled again. "Have you thought, Señor Valendez, that we might be making a mistake in killing off General Lane and his staff? After all, they are already a known commodity. You have for months been taking advantage of their ineptitude. They, every one of them, will be replaced quickly. We have no guarantee that their replacements will repeat their errors."

"Major," Valendez chided Solis, "remember who our target really is. I am not interested in killing Yankees. We have, after all, proven that we can do so quite effectively for months. The corpses we add to that pile tomorrow will be just that, additional corpses. Our target, Major, for tomorrow is the psyche of the Colombian staff and the collective will of the American politicians. If we wanted a quick, cheap propaganda victory, we could have struck at the American embassy, just as the Viet Cong did in 1968 during their Tet offensive. But we would have lost the impact on the Colombian Army's general staff that our attack tomorrow will have. Think of it, Major. Every day after tomorrow the senior officers of your general staff will walk into a building partially destroyed by us, knowing that we can at any time destroy the rest of it along with them. Their lives, and not some foreigners', will be in jeopardy, and the ruins of the building, not to mention the smell of burnt wood and flesh, will be there in their faces to remind them of it. In the end," Valendez claimed with all the confidence of a man who saw the future, "they will come to their senses and see that their future lies in a coalition with us and not defending the government that has since the spring so ruthlessly decimated its ranks."

Lifting his cup in a salute, Solis smiled. "I hope, for all of us and our people, you are right. If not . . ."

Valendez threw out his right hand and shrugged. "And if I am mistaken, we will meet here again, or somewhere else, and come up with a new plan next week." Then without any further ado, he stood up and looked at the faces of the three men he had been sharing coffee with. "In the meantime, I have work to do, as we all do. Tonight I return to the field.'' Looking at his watch, he thought for a moment, then looked up again. ''Tomorrow night at this time four regular-force battalions, supported by two dozen howitzers provided to us compliments of the Army, will open their attack on Villavicencio. Just in case the Colombian Army doesn't understand the message we will be delivering at nine-ten tomorrow morning, the fall of Villavicencio will suffice.''

Reaching down, he took his coffee cup and raised it over his head. ''Gentlemen, to the New Violence.''

In response, the two special team leaders stood up, raised their cups, and shouted as loudly as they dared, ''To the revolution.''

Solis, witnessing this ritual for the first time, didn't quite know what to do. Then, when he saw all eyes in the cafe were fixed on him after Valendez and his captains had finished their toast, he rose slowly. With a determined look in his eyes, he lifted his cup just as Valendez had done. When he spoke, his words were firm and sure. ''Gentlemen, to Colombia.''

Though they were spoken with a hushed dignity, every man in the cafe heard them. One by one they rose, lifting their cups above their heads. Valendez, seeing this, smiled broadly as he puffed out his chest, before he, and every man present, repeated Solis's toast. ''To Colombia!''

Led by a Marine guard to the overcrowded offices where Scotty's small staff worked, Jan skipped the usual lighthearted conversation that she often shared with Marines of the embassy staff. Though by training they were quite formal and dedicated, most of the tall young Marines who escorted her through the building were eager to talk to a celebrity who was both a female and good-looking, once of course they were out of earshot of the commander of their relief. ''Woe be it,'' Scott explained to her one night, ''to the poor jarhead who lets down his guard while on duty. A Marine,'' he told her, ''has no friends when he's on guard.'' Jan, always anxious to disprove Scott's pet theories, didn't need to try very hard to prove him wrong. One young Marine told her one night as they wandered through the corridors how much of a treat it was to talk to a real American girl who wasn't connected with the government or the military. "We get," he told her, "mighty lonely for real female company, even if it's just for a short chat." Flattered at what she took to be a compliment, Jan had made it a point to be friendly from that point on with all the Marines.

Tonight, however, the disappointments of the day, plus her pending expulsion from Colombia, were just too heavy a burden for her to shove aside. As she walked behind the Marine, her shoulders were slumped forward and her eyes were glued to the floor in front of her. To those few people still working at that hour who saw them go by, Jan and her Marine escort looked like a guard taking a prisoner to her execution. Though no one said so to her, Jan would have been inclined to agree.

Reaching the area occupied by SOUTHCOM Forward, the Marine took her through the maze of offices, now almost vacant except for the skeleton crew that pulled night duty. Reaching Scott's office, the Marine was about to enter when Scott's aide-de-camp, First Lieutenant Wally Frazier, came popping out. Bumping into each other, both men took a step back. Though each mumbled an apology, Jan could tell that the Marine's was forced and rather short, almost as if he had to cut himself off before he added "idiot."

Frazier, noticing Jan behind the Marine, called out to her. "The general's still in, ma'am. Just go inside and take a seat."

He was about to go past them headed down the hall when the Marine objected. "Sir, we cannot leave a civilian who lacks a security clearance unescorted in this section of the building."

With a look of distress on his face from some kind of physical discomfort, Frazier stopped and looked at the Marine. "Look, Private, I'll take responsibility for Ms. Fields. You can go."

With a wary look in his eyes, the Marine saluted and walked away. When he was out of sight, Frazier turned to Jan. "Ma'am, the general's on the phone with General Stratton at SOUTHCOM. I gotta go real bad and can't stay here with you. So please, go in and take a seat in my office. He shouldn't be too much longer."

Without waiting for her to even say hello, Frazier turned and fled down the hall toward the latrine. Left alone, Jan shook her head and walked into the office where Frazier and a sergeant usually sat outside Scott's tiny office. Noticing that the door to his office was ajar, she walked over to it and peered in.

With the exception of a small desk lamp, all the lights in the office were out. Sitting sideways to his desk, with his back to the door and his feet propped up over an open desk drawer, Scott held the phone with his right hand while his left hung listlessly over the arm of his chair. Though she knew that she shouldn't, Jan leaned against the door frame and listened.

In a voice that betrayed an exhaustion that was accentuated by frustration, Scott responded to his commander on the other end of the secure telephone. "No, sir, I don't like it any more than you do. But I am still convinced that everything out there in Los Llanos has been nothing more than a preliminary operation. The Farcees are getting ready to dump the big one on us and when they do I think the Colombian Army is going to buckle regardless of what we do."

There was a pause as Scott listened to Stratton. In the course of that part of the conversation, Scott lifted his left hand up to his forehead. With his thumb and pinkie he rubbed his temples. He's tired, Jan thought. Worried and tired. Suddenly all her troubles were by comparison trivial. Though they could be far-reaching for her and Nancy Kozak, none of her failures today, she thought, would result in anyone's death.

Clearing his throat, Scott responded again. "Yes, sir, I know that neither the CIA, DIA, nor any other intelligence agency has come across any hint that the Colombian Army is now dealing directly with the FARC or preparing for another coup. But neither can they deny it." A pause. "Yes, sir, I know General Fulk isn't thrilled with the idea of revising and preparing to implement our contingency plans for a hasty withdrawal. But neither was Churchill in May of 1940 when Gort told him the battle on the continent was lost and it was time to leave."

Making a mental note to ask Scott who Gort was, Jan shuffled her feet and folded her arms across her chest while Scott listened to Stratton speak. "The revised contingency plans my staff submitted to you three weeks ago remain fundamentally unchanged. All we need to do is to present them to Lane's staff." Taking his hand away from his temple, Scotty twisted the phone receiver so that the receiver end stayed over his ear but the lower half was away from his mouth. Covering his mouth with his hand, he coughed, then lowered the phone back to his mouth. "No, sir, I don't think that it will be necessary to issue those plans from your end, though I would appreciate it if you would give General Lane a call and let him know what we're up to. He's not going to like having to listen to me or anyone else on my staff, but he will."

Dropping his left hand down on the desktop, he began to slowly drum it with his fingers. "Tomorrow, sir, I've been invited to the 11th's commander's conference at zero nine hundred. I'll take my planning staff with me, and when Lane starts talking about future operations, we'll brief those contingency plans to him."

Tired of drumming the desktop with his fingers, Scott lifted his left hand up to the top of his head and ran his fingers through his thinning hair while he listened. "No, sir. There will be no Saigons, not here. Whatever happens, I will do my best to make sure that the American government isn't seen escaping from the rooftop of its own embassy by the skin of its teeth."

This last statement hit Jan like a hammer. Though there had been a great deal of loose talk about this being another Vietnam, to hear Scott talk about the final evacuation of Saigon in 1975 like that to his superior was frightening. Suddenly the severity of the whole situation came crashing down upon her, and for the first time in a long time Jan felt herself shudder with fear.

She was still pondering the dark images that Scott's conversation was conjuring up in her mind when she heard him mention her name. "I haven't spoken to Jan all day, sir. I was informed by a member of the embassy staff that the Colombian government had asked that she be out of the country by tomorrow. Not that I can't blame them. I saw her televised report on the El Frío incident, and it was, well, quite a piece of propaganda. But other than seeing it on the evening news like everyone else. I know nothing." Suddenly he dropped his hand and chuckled. "Yes, sir, she certainly does know how to keep a secret. I'm afraid that once again I'm literally the last to know."

As quickly as the sudden laughter in his voice came, it was

gone. Now he was deadly earnest again. "Other than rumors, I have no proof that there have been irregularities in the manner in which the Kozak affair has been handled. I do not have a JAG officer on my staff and haven't been able to spare anyone to keep an eye on those proceedings."

Slowly he craned his neck back and stared up at the dark ceiling. "As much as I hate to, sir, I have to agree with you. For me or any member of my staff to go over there and poke our nose into that trial at this time could be counterproductive. It's going to be hard enough to get Lane and his people to sit down and listen to my people without my sticking my nose into an affair that he is so personally involved in, regardless of how wrong it is." There was a sigh, then a pause as he held his breath for a second. "I will keep my ears open, and if anything solid does come my way I'll give your inspector general a call. Till then I do agree with you, we have to keep our eye on the ball."

Lifting his legs, Scott reached out, shoved in the desk drawer that his legs had been resting on, and then let his feet fall to the floor. "Thank you, sir. I appreciate your confidence. I only wish I could give you better news, but I'm afraid we've not yet seen the worst. Good night, sir."

Leaning forward, Scott eased the receiver into the cradle of the desktop unit. But rather than letting it go, he stopped, frozen in midmovement, with his hand still holding the phone as he stared at it. Figuring that he was finished and that he could use a little cheer and a hug, Jan pushed her concerns aside and softly knocked on the partially opened door.

Without looking up, Scott grunted, "Yes?"

"Hey, sailor, looking for a good time?"

Caught off guard by Jan's favorite little ditty, Scott spun his head around to where she stood. "How long have you been here?"

"Oh, I just got here."

Noticing the wicked smile on her face, Scott let go of the phone, eased back into his seat, and twisted it around. "Ah-huh, sure."

Pushing the door open just wide enough for her to enter, Jan reached in, turned on the overhead lights, and entered the office. "Are you practicing to be a mushroom or do you miss being in the Pentagon?"

"No one, Jan, in their right mind, misses working in that puzzle palace. Now back to the question. How much, my dear, did you hear?"

"Not much, just the end. And who, dear, is Gort?"

Scott rolled his eyes, realizing that she had heard more than just the end. Knowing, however, that there was no point in saying anything about that now and making a note to find out where his aide had been while Jan had been eavesdropping, he answered her question. "Lord Gort was the commander of the British Expeditionary Force in France and Belgium in 1940 when the Germans invaded the Low Countries. When he realized that his army was in danger and that there was no way they were going to be able to stop the Germans, he began positioning his forces so that they could be evacuated from the continent despite his government's insistence that they stand and fight a battle that was already lost. When, belatedly, Churchill realized that Gort was right and ordered the evacuation, units of the BEF were in the proper positions. Had Gort not done so, the miracle at Dunkirk would never have taken place."

"Are we," Jan asked hesitantly, "preparing to stage a miracle at Cartagena?"

With his eyes closed, Scott nodded. "Something like that."

"How soon?"

Standing, Scott stretched out his full length and yawned. "God, Jan, I wish I knew. I really wish I knew."

Jan moved next to him, wrapping her arms around his waist when she was close enough, and laid her head on his chest, and sighed. "Well, if it does come to that, do me a favor?"

Dropping his arms down to her sides, he encircled her with them and gave her a gentle squeeze. "Name it."

She returned his squeeze. "Don't be a bloody hero. You're getting too old for that kind of thing."

"What kind of thing?"

She pushed away from him so that she could look him in the eyes, and her face clouded. "Scott Dixon, you know what I'm talking about. You and your motto, 'First in, last out,' that's what."

"Oh, and that from a woman who spends her day tromping

about in the jungle with armed revolutionaries shooting stories about evil generals who eat their own dead.''

Letting her face go blank, Jan looked down for a moment, then she looked back into Scott's eyes. "How much do you know about that?''

He smiled. There was, he realized, no point in being upset over something that had been done. Besides, by now he had become used to her unpredictability. "I know everything that's worth knowing. The only thing I don't know is when you have to leave.''

Laying her head back against his chest, she squeezed his midsection tight. "Tomorrow morning at eight-thirty.''

At first he said nothing as they held each other close. Finally he kissed the top of her head. "I'll run you down to the airport, if you don't mind.''

Slowly rocking back and forth, Jan responded with a quiet, almost mournful tone. "No, I don't mind.'' Then she added as an afterthought, "But won't you be late for your nine o'clock meeting with Lane?''

"Nah. I should make it in plenty of time. And even if I'm a few minutes late, no one will notice. And if they do,'' he said as he pulled away and looked down at her with a big grin, "fuck 'em! I'm a general. Who's going to yell at me?''

Jan was going to say his highness Emperor Lane, but didn't. She didn't want the mention of his name to ruin this moment. Instead she smiled. "Have you eaten yet?''

Scott lifted his arm up behind her back and, sticking his head over her shoulder, looked at it. This caused Jan to laugh. "Since when does knowing the time have anything to do with whether or not you've eaten?''

Dropping his arm, he looked at her with a serious expression. "Jan, you just don't understand, do you? It's an Army thing.''

"Yeah, right. Well, I'm hungry and I don't need to look at a watch to know that. How about we go back to the hotel, get a bite to eat, and then go up to our room.''

"I got a better idea. Let's go back to the hotel, go to our room, and have room service. I got a feeling it's going to be a long time before I have the pleasure of eating dinner in the buff with a lovely woman.''

Jan's face went into a scowl. "Well, Mr. God Almighty General Dixon Himself, unless you're planning a trip to Washington, D.C., in the near future, let's hope that's the case. Otherwise, Colombian revolutionaries and maverick division commanders are going to be the least of your concerns."

Without another word, Scott reached out and snapped off the overhead light, leaned over, and began to kiss Jan passionately. They were just getting into it when the outer door of the office flew open and Lieutenant Frazier came bursting into the office and looked around. Not seeing anyone in the outer office and the lights in Scott's office off, he went barging in there. In doing so, he managed to smack Jan's tilted head with the door and scrape Scott's forearm with the edge of the door, thus bringing their romantic interlude to an abrupt and painful end that only a young lieutenant could manage to engineer.

PART FIVE

OLD
SOLDIERS
NEVER
DIE

CHAPTER 20

November 29

WHEN HE WALKED INTO THE ROOM THAT WOULD SERVE AS court that morning, Sam Ulrich had no more delusions, no doubt about what today would be like. He knew he had screwed up. The moment that Cole had slammed down his gavel yesterday, he knew he had lost his only chance to derail Lane's drive to crucify Captain Nancy Kozak. What he would do today was still very much in question, especially since the person he had been charged to defend had managed to avoid him, his calls, and every effort by his office to contact her. Not that he could blame her. Nancy Kozak did not appear to be the type of person who tolerated weakness and indecisiveness well, especially in a man.

Swinging his briefcase up onto the table that had been set up for the defense, Sam looked around the room. Behind him at the prosecution's table Mark Moretti sat alone, pretending to be busy. Sam could tell by the look on his face that he too had been keelhauled by Lane yesterday, either in person or through the good offices of their superior, Lieutenant Colonel Cole. Cole, already seated at the table set up for the judge, sat staring at the door at the rear of the room, glancing down at his watch every few seconds, then back at the door. He, like everyone else, was waiting to see if Lane would show up today or attend the division commander's conference.

Sam had heard that morning about the lively debate throughout the previous evening, accompanied by a good deal of betting, on where Lane would show up. Smart money, he had been told, was on the trial. Though Sam doubted that even Lane would forsake his duties in such a manner, he knew in his heart that Lane would be there. Lane had by now clearly demonstrated to anyone who cared to see that his interest in this affair was more than one would expect from a commander interested in punishing a violation of the Uniform Code of Military Justice. No, Lane had been wronged, in front of God and country, and he was determined to inflict his vengeance on the wrongdoer.

Besides that, Sam had never had the kind of luck that would have had it otherwise. As a kid, he had never managed to get away with anything. If he had broken something at home, his mom had always found it no matter how well he had covered up the evidence. If he had been involved in trouble at school or had failed a test, his mom was always waiting for him, ready to question him concerning the offense as soon as he got home. Maybe this was the reason he had never been able to stand up effectively to a strong-willed woman.

Sitting down, Sam reached into his briefcase, pulled out a file, and set it down before him. Perhaps there was something Freudian about all of this. Maybe his acceptance of the plan hatched by Nancy Kozak and Jan Fields was nothing more than buckling under, as he had done with his mother when she confronted him as a child. They had approached him concerning the video. When told of its existence and content, Sam had refused to even discuss the matter. "How can we possibly show this in a military court?" he had shrieked. "Jesus, Nancy, those people are the enemy!" But Jan Fields, an older woman, and one even more determined and practiced in the fine art of persuasion, took over and, against his better judgment, persuaded him to use it. That he hadn't used the video, Sam was convinced, was as much a fault of the system as it was a personal failing. For he, like so many other people involved in this sordid affair, found it impossible to violate the code of honor that had been pounded into him since the day he had accepted his commission. The film was to him first and foremost enemy propaganda. To have used it would have been aiding the enemy. Of course, not using it aided Lane's efforts to punish Kozak. Stuck between these extremes, Ulrich had chosen the easiest, safest way out, thus allowing an important piece of his strategy to defend Kozak to fall and shatter on the floor, like his mother's crystal vase.

He was pondering this analogy as he fiddled with the file when the door at the rear of the room opened. Like everyone else in the room, he turned to see if it was Lane. When Nancy Kozak, and not "The Man" himself, came through the door, all but Sam turned back to whatever they had been doing. Anxious to talk to her outside, in the hall away from prying eyes and curious ears, Sam jumped up and began to head toward her.

When they met midway in the aisle left open in the space opened to spectators, Nancy Kozak avoided his eyes and all but shoved him out of the way. Embarrassed, Sam looked about and noticed that several people, including Cole and Mark Moretti, were watching. Taking a deep breath, he regained his composure and returned to his table where Nancy Kozak was already seated with her arms folded across her chest and her stare fixed straight ahead. "Nancy, I tried to contact you last—"

Turning to face him, her eyes were reduced to narrow slits, like a cat's that was about to pounce on its prey. "That's Captain Kozak to you, Mister Ulrich."

The contempt in her voice was as sharp as it was loud. He lowered his voice. "Listen, for better or for worse, I'm still your defense attorney and I have a job to do. Now I tried to get hold of you last night so I could explain why—"

"Save your breath, mister, because in five minutes you're going to be out of a job."

Stunned, Sam blinked and pulled away. "Do you mean you want to postpone this, or ask for a change in location for the trial?"

Leaning forward to close the space between them, Nancy continued to stare at him with the hard, cold look in her eyes that told him that she was offering no quarter this morning. "Listen, you spineless excuse of a soldier. You threw away my best chance of a win yesterday. Not yours, not anyone else's.

Mine. You had your chance. Now I'm taking over my own defense.''

Blinking, Sam shook his head. "You can't do that. You're not a school-trained attorney.''

"But I am an officer in the United States Army, schooled in military law, and entitled to defend myself. If you don't have the—'' She was about to say balls, but for the first time she pulled her punches. "If you can't stand up to Lane and this mockery of a court of law, then I will.''

Looking about in an effort to see who had heard or was listening, Sam raised his hand and tried to calm Kozak down. This effort, especially his absentminded "Shush,'' infuriated her. She lifted her finger and pointed it at his nose, just like his mother had done to him. "Don't you shush me, mister. I listened to you. I trusted you. Even Jan Fields trusted you, despite her misgivings.''

Taken aback by this last part, Sam wondered why Jan Fields had felt uneasy about trusting him. Though he would have liked to know, Nancy didn't give him a chance to ask. Instead she continued to lecture. "Now Jan's gone, thrown out of the country in disgrace, and I'm sitting here with a noose around my neck waiting for you and the rest of this vigilante gang to kick the chair out from under me. Well, if I'm going to go, it will be by my own hand, just like Hal Cerro.''

The seriousness of her commitment, as evidenced by her reference to her former battalion commander, escaped Sam for the moment as he continued his efforts to dissuade her. In a calm, steady voice, he spoke slowly so that Nancy heard every word and there was no chance that she wouldn't understand. "Nancy, if you go up there and try to defend yourself, they will tear you apart limb by limb. This trial, already a shambles, will become a massacre.''

Straightening up, she took a deep breath. "Good!''

Again unable to comprehend Nancy's frame of mind, Sam shook his head and looked at her in surprise. "Good? What in the hell do you mean good? Don't you understand? They are going to nail you to the wall.''

"They may, mister, but not before I get my licks in. Yes, there's going to be blood on this floor today, but not all of it is going to be mine.''

Turning away from her, Sam looked down at the file in front of him, his mind going a mile a minute. Somehow, between now and when Cole reopened the trial, he had to come up with something, some way of stalling. Looking down at his watch, he saw that it was eight fifty-nine. Convinced that talking to Kozak was useless, he was about to stand up and go forward to have a word with Cole when the door of the room opened. As before, everyone turned to see who entered. When Captain Adderly, Lane's aide, came through the door, a sudden and perceptible tension swept over the room. Then, when he did not announce Lane but instead walked to the front of the room alone and took his seat, there was a moment of confusion, followed by a collective sigh of relief.

Sam, on the other hand, couldn't relax. He needed time to organize his thoughts. He needed to come up with some way of saving Nancy Kozak from herself, not to mention what little dignity and self-respect for himself that he could still muster. Most of all, he needed a break.

Looking down at his watch, Colonel Cole asked the MP standing near his table to call the court to order at precisely nine o'clock. Seeing what could be an opportunity to question Adderly without Lane present, Sam Ulrich decided to seize it. Jumping up before the bailiff finished, he called out, "Your Honor, I would like to call Captain James Adderly back in order that I may cross-examine him."

Hoping that they were finished with Adderly, Moretti looked up to Cole with a pleading look on his face. Cole, however, said or did nothing, at least in response to Moretti. Instead he nodded his approval. Over at the table where Kozak and Ulrich were, Kozak glared up at her attorney. "I told you I was going to—"

Now Sam leaned over and whispered, "Listen, you'll be given more than enough opportunities today to slit your own throat. At least let me get a crack at Adderly. After that you can do as you damned well please." Without waiting for a response, Sam stood erect and called over to Adderly. "The defense calls on Captain James Adderly to take the stand."

Standing bolt upright, Adderly marched up to the witness chair. He held his head rigid, looking neither left nor right, as if he were on parade. Though neither Moretti nor Sam had any idea how Adderly would go, Sam was willing to play his hunch that Adderly had finally reached the breaking point and was about to tell the truth.

In the conference room where the gaggle of officers from the division had gathered, they were pondering the same question that the people in the courtroom were agonizing over: Where would Lane fly his standard today? Near the front of the room the assistant division commander for logistics, Brigadier General Ken Overten, was speaking with the division G-4 and the commander of the division's support command. Together they formed one of many little knots of officers scattered about the room that were discussing that issue. Overten had no sooner stated that even Lane would not let something like Kozak's court-martial keep him from a conference as critical as this, given the changing situation they faced, when Lane entered the room alone and unannounced. A major from the division operations staff posted at the door to cover just such a contingency called out, "Gentlemen, the division commander."

Stopping in midsentence or where they were, everyone in the room came to attention. Lane, a bit edgy that morning, didn't give the order "At ease" right away. Rather, he made his way to the front of the room, going by the little groups without paying them or any of the senior officers in the room any attention. His mind was preoccupied with other matters. Only after reaching the front of the conference room, well decorated with the crests and the flags of the division and various subordinate commands, did Lane stop, turn, and order the gathered commanders and staff officers to take their seats. In silence the participants made their way to their places, took their seats, and prepared for the opening of the conference. A few already seated took note that it was three minutes past nine, making this the first time in division history that a meeting Lane had called and attended was starting late. Not that this fact brought them any satisfaction. On the contrary, it was ominous. "Only death, or an act of God," Lane often stated, would serve to excuse a late start. Since neither was in evidence, that meant that Major General C. B. Lane, scornfully known as Conan the Bureaucrat, was going to have to eat his own words. And when Lane was made to look bad, even if by his own hand, everyone suffered.

But as he stood there in front of the assembled leadership and key staff members of the division, Lane shuffled his feet for a moment, looking down at the floor as if he were lost in thought. In the quietness of the room, silence broken by an occasional nervous cough, everyone watched and waited. Finally, as if he suddenly woke up to the realization of where he was, Lane looked up and scanned the room. Placing his hands on his hips, he threw his head back. Looking about the room for Colonel Delhue, it took Lane a second to realize that he wasn't there. Delhue was, Lane suddenly remembered, at a meeting called at the last minute that morning by someone in the office of the Colombian Army chief. Major Solis, informing them of this meeting, suggested that he and Colonel Delhue represent the division. Glad to be rid of Delhue, who always managed to irritate him during conferences like this with his questions, Lane had agreed and sent the two of them packing. Looking down at his watch, Lane noted the time and began to speak. "We, ah, need to get on with this, I'm sure."

The total lack of emotion or anger, accentuated by the absentminded manner in which Lane's words came out, threw everyone in the room. The old man, Overten thought, does not have his stuff together today. Though he had seen Lane rattled before, on occasion in private when something unexpected suddenly happened to him, he had never seen his boss so unstrung in the presence of subordinate officers. He knew that Lane, like many of the senior officers in the Army, had perfected his ability to portray his presentation as the man in charge to the point where he could kick into action without thinking. Leaning over, Overten whispered to the commander of the division support command, "Well, at least he knows where he belongs."

As disrespectful as that comment was, it was appropriate, and the commander of the support command nodded. Lane, in the past month rattled by the changing situation and the growing role of Dixon's SOUTHCOM Forward, had been making a lot of bad calls, almost on a daily basis. Now, before the commander of every major subordinate command and key staff officers from throughout the division, Lane made another one.

"I am sorry for the delay in opening this conference, but, ah, there is a conflict between this meeting and another affair that demands my immediate attention. Though I expect to be back for the open discussions this afternoon with the brigade commanders, I am afraid that the ADC for maneuver will have to hold the fort during this morning's round of briefings." Then, without another word, Lane briskly walked to the rear of the room, not looking back and totally unaware that no one, in the stunned silence that followed, had bothered to call the room to attention to mark his departure. Only after a moment or two passed did the commander of the division support command lean over to Overten and announce in a rather matter-of-fact manner, "Well, sir, you owe me five bucks."

Down on the street level, Scott Dixon's sedan pulled up in front of the entrance used by the staff of the 11th Air Assault. Glancing down at his watch before getting out, he noted that it was now seven past the hour. Though he had been rather casual about being late last night while he had been talking to Jan, Scott was rushed and anxious. Already on Lane's shit list just by being in Colombia, coming in late for his commander's conference wasn't going to make the plans that he and his staff were about to force-feed him any more palatable. Hurrying up the steps to the building, he was about to go through the door when he heard Jeff Worsham call out to him, "General Dixon, sir."

Stopping, he looked around to see where Worsham was. "Over here, sir, behind you."

Turning his head, he saw Worsham come trotting from under a tree across the street toward him. Behind him, Dixon could see the other officers, Major Don Saventinni and Major Herman Hagstrom, sitting under a tree in a small plaza across the way. Coming about completely, Dixon slowly began to descend the steps, headed for Worsham. Confused as much as he was surprised, Dixon raised his hand in a gesture to stop Worsham. "No, you wait over there," he called out. "Let me come to you. Maybe, just maybe, by the time I reach you, I'll have figured out why you and Tweedledum and Tweedledee are over there lounging about in the shade and not in there mixing it up with the lions."

Stopping at the curb, Worsham went limp, letting his shoulders drop forward and his head hang down a bit. The general was mad. Though he often joked with his staff, and usually used humor to make a bad situation a little more tolerable, Worsham could tell by Dixon's voice that this was not one of those times. While Dixon was waiting for a car to pass, Worsham started talking. "Sir, I can explain."

Dixon shook his head. "God, I hope so."

"There was a screw-up on the access roster. The division G-2 security officer put a new access roster into effect today because of the commander's conference. Added security, the guard at the door said."

Without another word, Dixon knew what had happened. "Wait, let me guess. We're not on it."

"Well, sir. You are, but we," Worsham said as he pointed over his shoulder at Saventinni and Hagstrom, now on their feet, "aren't."

Dixon slowly twisted his head around. Looking up at the wing of the Ministry of Defense that housed the headquarters of the 11th Air Assault Division, he muttered a silent curse. Facing Worsham again, he raised his right hand. "You and your trusty companions stay there. I'll go in there and get this thing squared away. This should only take a minute."

"Captain Adderly," Ulrich started, "you were an assistant operations officer in an infantry battalion, weren't you?"

"Yes, back at Campbell."

"And you served as an infantry company commander during the Second Gulf War?"

Adderly nodded. "Yes. I was with an airborne unit in that one."

"I submit," Ulrich called out as he turned to Cole, "Your Honor, that his experience, as well as his formal military education at Fort Benning and Fort Leavenworth, makes Captain Adderly a competent judge of infantry company and battalion combat operations. I therefore intend to question him, using his expertise, to establish the situation as it existed on the ground that day as well as the responses of Captain Kozak, both to the situation and General Lane's actions."

Moretti stood up. "Objection."

Cole didn't bother looking over at him. "Overruled. Captain Ulrich, proceed."

In contrast to the short, blunt responses that he had given the day before, Adderly spoke quickly yet clearly in response to Ulrich's questions. With great detail he described the situation as he saw it, taking great pains to emphasize that they, he and Lane, were only catching glimpses of the fight. When he got to the part where Lane started to call for the artillery mission against the village, Ulrich raised his hand. "If you please, Captain Adderly, allow me to sum up, for my sake and the jury's, the situation as it stood at this moment. And please correct me if I'm wrong. The lead companies of the 3rd of the 511th are dropped into two hot LZs and are pinned."

"That—" Adderly nodded—"is correct."

"The commander of one of those companies, a First Lieutenant Barbara O'Fallen, is killed in the first few minutes of that fight and the battalion commander accompanying O'Fallen's company loses touch with the rest of his company."

"Yes, that is correct. I was able to gather that by listening to their battalion command net."

"So Captain Kozak then assumed command."

"As soon as she was convinced that her commander was not in a position to command or control the fight, yes, she assumed tactical control of the fight."

Ulrich shook his head. "Then from the rear, the battalion executive officer, a new man to the unit and this theater of operations, comes in, disrupts the flow of operations as he assumes command without first consulting with Kozak, and then promptly gets himself wounded."

"Again, correct."

"Was it wise in your opinion, Captain Adderly, for the new major to come into a situation that he was unfamiliar with, one which was being controlled by a competent officer already, and start changing things without consulting with the officer in charge?"

Adderly smirked. "Well, while it was totally within his prerogative as the next officer in the chain of succession, no, it was a dumb move on his part. His insistence on exercising that prerogative cost the unit valuable time and created unnecessary confusion."

Nodding, Ulrich turned away, looked at the jury. "I don't think there is any officer, at least not one who had been in combat, who would dispute that." Turning, he stared at Adderly intently for a moment. Then slowly he continued. "Using that same measure, that same subjective call, how do you, as a veteran combat commander and a subject-matter expert in infantry operations, judge General Lane's efforts to deny Captain Kozak use of the artillery at a critical point in time, when he had no idea what her battalion's situation was and he and his aircraft were out of danger from the enemy?"

Adderly was about to answer Ulrich's question when the door of the temporary courtroom swung open and Lane entered the room. There was silence pause as every eye in the room turned to look first at Lane then back at Adderly.

Adderly, standing up, was about to call out "Attention" when the detonation of dozens of explosives scattered throughout the American wing merged into one earsplitting roar. Though everyone, surprised by the sudden rocking of the building and the flicking of the lights caused by the explosions, braced themselves as best they could, Lane pulled back against the wall and crouched. His expression as he did so caught Adderly's eye. It was, Adderly thought, the same wide-eyed fear that he had seen when their helicopter had been fired on over El Frío.

Heedless of the commotion breaking out about him, Adderly stood there and watched as Lane's head, tucked down in his shoulders, turned this way, then that, looking up at the ceiling as if he were waiting for it to fall on him. The bastard, Adderly thought, had no more idea where the enemy fire had come from than anyone else in the helicopter had. He had, like Adderly himself, assumed that it was coming from the village, a place that all the intelligence reports up till then had indicated was occupied and heavily defended. The tape made by the Colombian rebels was right on the money.

Turning his head, Adderly caught sight of Nancy Kozak standing at the front of the room. Around her the officers and noncommissioned officers of her battalion, brought into the court today in anticipation of their use by the defense, rallied around her. Alternately they turned to her for guidance while scanning about the room, watching for either an escape route or danger. Though Kozak herself was unsure of what to do, Adderly could see her eyes darting about, checking out every exit and all of the actions of the others in the room. She was thinking, preparing to give orders to those around her, and jump one way or the other as soon as she figured out which way was the best. No, he thought, she didn't deserve to be screwed over by—

Turning back to face Lane, Adderly shook his head. Though he didn't know what had happened and, like everyone else at that moment, wondered if this could be their last, Adderly knew for sure what he would do as soon as he got the chance. Consequences be damned.

Jeff Worsham would later describe the scene on the street that he and the rest of the SOUTHCOM Forward staff had witnessed like a scene from the movies. "One moment we were all standing there watching General Dixon reaching for the door of the building, the next, chaos. A low rumble from deep inside the building, then bang, every window and pane of glass is blown out along with body parts, paper, scraps of furniture, and huge yellow flames. Before we realize what's happening, the whole one wing of the building comes tumbling down around General Dixon, just like a house of cards. When we saw that, we all took off, to a man, at a dead run to where we last saw the general, each of us praying that we'd find him in one piece and alive but knowing in our hearts that he was . . . Well, not alive.''

CHAPTER 21

November 29

EXCEPT FOR THE SHUFFLING OF CHAIRS OR A HUSHED APOLOGY when someone accidentally bumped into another person as the staff of SOUTHCOM Forward made their way into the semi-circle about the wall where the maps of Colombia were displayed, there was silence. It was, Colonel Christopher Delhue thought as he sat near the front next to Colonel Chester A. Thomas, like sitting in a funeral parlor waiting for the bereaved family to enter. Not knowing what to say or how to act, no one did or said anything unless they had to. He was about to turn and make a comment to Thomas when someone in the rear of the room that served the SOUTHCOM staff as a combination operations center and briefing room shouted a crisp, sharp "Attention."

Coming to their feet like everyone else, Delhue and Thomas looked toward the center of the gathered SOUTHCOM Forward staff officers as they parted to make room for the assistant commanding general of the 11th Air Assault Division. Slowly, dragging his left foot slightly, he made his way forward. Looking at his face, Thomas could tell that Scott Dixon was still suffering from shock and the loss of blood. At least, he thought, Dixon had the good sense to keep the medics from shooting him up with all sorts of painkillers. The last thing they needed, he knew, was a commander with a foggy brain. Though he had no doubt that Dixon was in pain, as evidenced by the slight wince he made every time he put some weight on his left leg, Thomas knew that Dixon was an old warhorse, like him, and could handle a little discomfort.

Taking his place in a seat between Delhue and Thomas, Dixon eased himself down into the chair. After pausing to catch his breath, he spun the gray steel office chair about and looked into the faces of the staff officers before him. Being careful not to lean back into the seat lest he put pressure on the freshly stitched wound that ran almost the length of his back, Dixon managed a smile. "Why so glum?"

There was a heavy silence until Jeff Worsham, looking to either side of him, finally spoke. "We were . . . well, concerned, sir."

Dixon chuckled. "Jeeze," he responded, rolling his eyes and doing his best to smile, "I thought by now you guys would have figured out that I'm a tanker, an old one at that. There isn't a damned thing the Farcees have that can penetrate this hide."

Picking up on the fact that Dixon was trying the best he could to shake his staff out of the shock they felt over the string of disasters that had befallen the 11th Division and the sudden change in their mission, Thomas chimed in. "Ah, General Dixon, they were under the impression that your skull was the only impenetrable part of your anatomy." While this comment caused everyone in the room to break into spontaneous laughter, Christopher Delhue looked about. No one, he thought, would have dared make such a comment in the presence of C. B. Lane, let alone about him. This staff, he realized, from Dixon on down, was an entirely different creature.

Gathered about, sitting in a chair or on the floor, standing, or leaning against a wall or piece of office furniture, there was no rhyme or reason to them. Sergeants, both those on and off duty, were mixed in with the officers. Each and every man and woman, eyes riveted to Dixon, had broken out into a broad and uninhibited smile or laugh after Thomas's comment. They were younger, fewer in number, and lower in rank than the division staff they had just been ordered to replace. But Delhue suddenly realized that they were more than ready for the challenge. If Dixon, battered and knocked about as badly as he was, could generate this kind of response with just a few well-chosen words, then the people gathered in this room could do just about anything.

Raising his hand to signal an end to the chatter and laughter, Dixon hung his head in thought for a moment. When he raised it, the smile was gone. So was the mask of pain that he had worn when he first came in. His expression was now one of deep resolve. When he spoke, his words were clear and firm. "Each of us in his own way feels a great sense of shock and grief over the loss of so many of our comrades and fellow soldiers. It is right and proper that we should mourn their deaths and honor their memory as best we can. But," Dixon stated, accentuating this with a sweep of the room, taking the time to look into the eyes of every officer he could while he did so, "we are at war. Those people over in the Colombian Ministry of Defense fell while performing their duties. It has now been left to us, by order of the commanding general, Southern Command, to fall into the ranks left vacant by today's attack and continue to press forward. As cruel and as cold as this may sound, the senior officers and the staff of the 11th Air Assault Division killed this morning are beyond feeling, beyond help. Behind them they have left over fifteen thousand men and women scattered about this country who are no doubt as badly shaken by today's events as you are. We, each and every one of us, must show them that we are in control and have confidence not only in them but in our own abilities to carry on with the division's assigned duties." Waiting a moment for his words to take root, Dixon added, "Is that clear?"

While everyone else was nodding, Herman Hagstrom slowly raised his hand. Dixon could always depend on Herman to ask the question that everyone else was thinking about but afraid to ask. Looking directly at Hagstrom, Dixon nodded. "Yes, Herman?"

"Then, sir, it is official. General Lane has been relieved and you have assumed command of the 11th?"

Looking over to Thomas and then Delhue, who in turn looked at Dixon, Scott took a deep breath. The official order announcing that SOUTHCOM Forward would assume all duties and responsibilities of the now decimated 11th Air Assault Division staff had not been specific on that point. Only after a round of phone conversations between General Jerry Stratton, the SOUTHCOM commander-in-chief, and Dixon, Delhue, and Lane was the matter clarified, to a degree. Leaning over, Thomas whispered in Dixon's ear. "Best you get this over with now, General."

Nodding that he agreed, Scott squirmed in his seat, making himself as comfortable as possible before speaking. When he did, he picked his words carefully, in order not to open his superior, General Stratton, to later criticism. "Major General C. B. Lane has not been relieved of command. And my title, pending approval by the Chief of Staff of the Army, is assistant division commander for maneuver. As the ADCM, I am the second in command of the division, responsible for operations and command of the division in the absence of the division commander. General Lane has been ordered to report to the commander-in-chief, SOUTHCOM, immediately. At this time I am not privy to the reason why he has been so ordered or how long he will be absent." Delhue, leaning back in his seat, glanced over to Thomas, who in turn faced Delhue. That, they both knew, was not true. It was Stratton's intent to take Lane out of the picture and give Dixon as much time as possible to pull the division back together as best he could. Though neither man, professional to the core, liked the way this matter was being handled, the two colonels had agreed in a private conversation that, given the current situation, this was the best solution. To leave Lane, already badly shaken by the day's events, in Colombia would be tantamount to exposing the division to total disaster.

Turning back to the front, the two colonels continued to listen in silence as Dixon went on. "While we will integrate those members of the 11th Division's staff that were not on duty at the time, none of the principals or even their deputies escaped death or serious injuries. We, this staff, will therefore assume those duties."

Dixon lifted his right hand and pointed his thumb at Delhue. "Colonel Delhue will, of course, continue to serve as the chief of staff. Listen to him and listen to him good. He knows the division and will serve as the chief engineer and unifying element throughout this transition. Jeff Worsham, our old chief, is now the division operations officer. Everyone else falls into their appropriate staff position. Herman the Horrible is now the division intel officer, God help us.'' There was a slight interruption as a muted chuckle rippled through the gathered staff and Hagstrom blushed. ''Mary Anderson is the division G-4, Pete Northrup the division G-1, and everyone else per the assignments listed on the sheet Jeff posted earlier this afternoon. One appointment that I just managed to confirm before this meeting started was Colonel Thomas's.'' Turning to face the military attaché, Dixon smiled. ''Chester here has agreed to pull his retirement papers and accept the position as the assistant division commander for logistics. Given his knowledge of this country, the people, and his contacts, I didn't have too much trouble convincing General Stratton he was the right man for the job.'' While some of the gathered staff officers simply nodded their approval, others clapped, causing Thomas, a man who had always been well liked by Dixon's staff, to blush, as Hagstrom had.

''A liaison officer from the Colombian Army,'' Dixon continued, ''will be provided by Colonel Marco Agustin.''

''Is there any reason,'' Delhue asked, ''why we can't simply use Major José Solis? He's already familiar with the division.''

''While that would be a good move, we have a problem here in the embassy that you didn't have over at the ministry. The CIA insists on clearing everyone, and their procedures take a long, long, time. Colonel Agustin's man is almost finished with that. To start that nut roll again, with everything else going on, wouldn't be a good idea.''

Though he would have liked to keep José Solis, Delhue was unable to find a good reason for challenging Dixon's decision. Letting that issue pass, he decided to get on with the evening briefing. ''Sir, we have a great deal to cover. Are you ready to start?''

Carefully shifting in his seat, Dixon nodded.

Signing Worsham with a wave of his hand, Delhue turned to Dixon. ''I thought we'd start with a quick overview on the status of the division and where we stand concerning today's events before we launch into the full evening briefing, sir.''

Dixon nodded. ''Proceed.''

Moving into the center of the semicircle, Jeff Worsham opened his notebook, found where the notes he needed started, looked up at Dixon, and began. "I spoke to the commander, headquarters and headquarters company, just before you arrived, sir. Recovery operations at the Ministry of Defense are being delayed due to the discovery of unexploded devices scattered throughout the American wing. While he couldn't say if the devices were intentionally set to go off at a later time or they had simply failed to function properly, they are slowing the search and the rescue teams."

"Have there been any more wounded and injured found?"

"No, sir," Worsham responded in a solemn voice. "No change since the last report I gave you."

Closing his eyes, Dixon nodded for him to continue.

"Thanks to the efforts of the division signal battalion, we now have data as well as voice contact with all major subordinate commands as well as backup. This has allowed us to transmit the warning orders for the redeployment of the division with full graphics."

"How long ago did those orders go out?" Dixon asked.

Glancing up at the clock on the side wall, Worsham made a quick calculation in his head. "Two hours and thirty-five minutes ago. All commands acknowledged receipt."

Satisfied with the answer, Dixon motioned to Worsham to proceed.

"Though we are still short computers, each staff section does have access to at least one tactical computer and is able to access their appropriate computer network. Division support command operations out at the military airfield have returned to normal. Colonel Thomas and Major Anderson were out there a short while ago and talked to all the officers in charge of all the principal organizations and sections out there. Mary will cover what they saw and were told, in detail, during her portion of the briefing."

Dixon now leaned over toward Thomas. "What exactly were the Farcees aiming at?"

Thomas threw out his right hand and shrugged. "Nothing, sir, in particular. It was a nuisance raid. If their aim hadn't been so good, I would have said they were firing at random. But they hit too much for beginners' luck."

From his perch on the edge of a desk, Herman Hagstrom chimed in. "Amazing what they can do with guns they don't

one looked at him for a moment. For weeks he had been
warning anyone who would listen to him that the artillery
pieces being lost by government forces would turn up, sooner
or later and be used against them. The CIA chief at the embassy and the G-2 of the 11th Air Assault had both come on
line and stated that the FARC lacked both the training and the
know-how to use the guns, if indeed they still had them.

Ignoring Hagstrom's snide remark, Thomas took up where
Worsham had left off. "Though they did manage to score a
direct hit on a C-17 that was unloading and damage two other
Air Force planes, most of our helicopters were in revetments
and escaped damage. The fuel dump took a few hits and they
had a devil of a time controlling those fires, but that was about
it. By the time they turned their attention to the support command headquarters, everyone was pretty much under cover and
a pair of attack helicopters were in the air sniffing out the
locations of the guns."

"Seems a waste," Delhue mused, "of four good howitzers."

"Not really, sir," Hagstrom added. "The shots the news
cameras got of the fuel depot blazing away, added to the devastation of the American wing of the Ministry of Defense, were
quite impressive. If they were only after a propaganda coup,
then they achieved what they were after, in spades."

While Dixon shook his head, Thomas continued. "Herman's
right. The people back home are already being told that the
American military hasn't suffered this kind of setback since
Tet, 1968."

Not wanting to dwell on an analogy that he himself had been
instrumental in starting, Dixon pointed to Worsham. "Continue, if you please."

Jeff Worsham was about to open his mouth to go on when
the door at the rear of the room swung open, banging against
the wall behind it, and a hurried, surprised "Attention" followed. Everyone except Dixon, who took his time, jumped to
their feet. Like the parting of the Red Sea, the officers and
sergeants standing or seated between the door and the front of
the room separated, making way for C. B. Lane.

Reaching the front edge of the semicircle, Lane faced Dixon.

There was anger in his eyes, an anger and contempt that distorted his face. Looking first at Delhue, then at Thomas, Lane scanned the faces of the newly designated division staff. Finished, he looked at Dixon, square in the eye. "I want a word with you, mister, in private."

Though he felt awkward and quite uncomfortable, Dixon didn't show it. Focusing on the pain that shot through his leg and up his spine, rather than on his feelings, Dixon managed to return Lane's cold, angry stare without flinching. Only when he turned to Delhue, instructing him to continue, did he take his eyes off him.

Delhue's manner and matter-of-fact response to Dixon infuriated Lane. But he held himself in check. He was saving himself for his showdown with Dixon. Delhue, he thought, could be dealt with later.

Moving toward his private office, Dixon made no effort to keep from brushing Lane's sleeve as he passed him in the crowded semicircle. Breathing deeply and quickly, like a teakettle about to boil over, Lane followed him, slamming the door closed once he was in Dixon's office.

From the door of the main office, Captain James Adderly watched the two generals disappear into the smaller office. When the door was closed, he looked over to the front of the room and managed to catch Delhue's eye. "Colonel Delhue, could I have a word with you in private?"

Not knowing what Adderly wanted, but sure that he wasn't going to like it, since Lane often left his aide to pass on messages that he didn't want to convey, Delhue turned to Thomas, excused himself, and walked to the rear of the room to where Adderly stood. When he spoke, there was no mistaking the contempt he felt for Adderly. "Yes, *C*aptain?"

"Sir, I need to talk to you about . . ." He paused.

"I'm in the middle of a meeting, *Captain*. Now if you don't mind."

"Sir, it's about the incident over El Frío."

Delhue's ears perked up. "What about that incident?"

Committed, Adderly blurted his words. "I lied, sir. I lied about the whole incident, on my statement and at the Article 32 investigation. And General Lane knew I lied."

* * *

Alone with Lane in his office, Dixon hadn't even managed to get himself turned around and leaning up against the front edge of his desk before Lane started hammering away at him. With his index finger held up and inches away from Dixon's head, he went to it.

"Did you issue a warning order to my brigades alerting them to a redeployment that will pull them out of the western mountains and the eastern plain, away from the battle?"

Dixon nodded. "Yes, sir, I did. The 2nd Brigade will be flown north by the Air Force from Cali to Cartagena within forty-eight hours. The 3rd Brigade will move, starting tomorrow, to a new base of operations just north of here. And 1st Brigade—''

"I know what the order said. I want to know what gave you the idea that you could just go around on your own and issue such an order?"

"It is," Dixon corrected him, "just a warning order. General Stratton and I discussed—"

Without waiting for him to finish, Lane cut Dixon off again. "We'll get to him in a minute. As if that wasn't bad enough, just before I walked out the door, I got informed that you have instructed Lieutenant Colonel Cole to postpone indefinitely Kozak's court-martial. Then, to make matters worse, you go and return her to duty, as if nothing had happened. Do you realize how foolish that makes me look?"

Dixon was speechless, appalled that Lane would bring up the Kozak matter at all, let alone discuss it in the manner he did. My God, Dixon thought, you've just lost, for all practical purposes, every senior commander in your division and most of your staff. And the biggest concern you have is how you look. This is the Caine Mutiny in living color, strawberry ice cream and all.

Lane didn't wait for Dixon to recover his balance before he continued his tirade. "I don't know what in the hell you think you're trying to pull here, but whatever it is, you and that motley crew out there are going to pay."

Finally Lane had gone too far. Folding his arms across his chest slowly, so as not to pull at the tape holding the bandage on his back, Scott stared at Lane with cold, emotionless eyes. Seeing that he was not succeeding at riling Dixon up, Lane continued. "I don't know what Stratton told you, but make no doubt about it, I am still the division commander, and you and your staff work for me, not him."

"Neither I nor my staff believe otherwise." That, of course, was only half true. Scott had already made it clear to both Delhue and Thomas that as soon as the plane carrying Lane lifted off that evening, he was to be kept out of the loop. Any orders from Lane, given verbally or in writing while he was out of country, were to be acknowledged but not acted upon, by order of General Stratton. Though Dixon didn't much care for playing that kind of game, and fully realizing that it could blow up in his and Stratton's face, he also realized that if they were to have any hope of holding things together, Lane had to be out of the way. "We'll pay the piper, Scotty," Stratton had told him, "when the bill comes due. Until then I want you to sort out that mess down there and minimize our losses. Hopefully, by the time I run out of excuses for keeping Lane up here, the people in Washington will realize the wisdom of our efforts."

"And if they don't?" Dixon asked.

"Then, Scotty, we'll both be out on our butts, selling insurance or real estate."

Realizing that Dixon was deep in thought and not paying attention to him, Lane stopped his monologue. "You haven't heard a word I said, have you? Who the hell do you think you are, mister?"

Shaking his head as if he had just woken up, Dixon let a slight smile crease his lips. "Oh, I've heard every word you said, sir. Something about your still being in command."

Had he been a violent man, Lane would have punched Dixon in the face right then and there. Instead he just glared at him. As he pushed himself away from the desk, a spasm of pain raced up Dixon's leg, easing his smile for a minute. Looking down as he carefully rubbed his upper thigh, Dixon mused, "Second Purple Heart, you know. Or is it my third?" He looked up at Lane. "Hard to keep track of those things after a while, isn't it?"

The slur on Lane's combat record, which was nonexistent until he had arrived in Colombia with the 11th Air Assault, was too much for him. Clenching his left hand, Lane raised the index finger of his right hand up again and pointed it at Dixon's nose.

For a moment the anger in Lane's face left no doubt in Dixon's mind that the two men were about to come to blows. But then, just as suddenly as he had leaped toward Dixon, Lane pulled away and pivoted. Facing the door, he allowed his head to drop down between his shoulders, his arms going limp to his side. With Lane standing there like that for several moments, Dixon was unsure what to do. The only motion Dixon could see was the heaving of Lane's shoulders as he took in deep breaths in an effort to calm himself.

Finally cocking his head over his right shoulder, Lane spoke. When he did, Dixon was for the first time that night taken aback. For the bitterness and anger in Lane's voice were gone. Instead it betrayed a hint of sorrow and reflectiveness. His words were no less compelling. "You know, General Dixon, I was about to curse your medals and ribbons like I have cursed those of so many other officers who, due to the luck of their assignments, were given the chance at a young age to test themselves in battle. I never had that opportunity. I never was, as they say, in the right place at the right time." He dropped his head and shook it, his voice dropping to an almost inaudible mumble. "God knows, I tried. I tried. But . . ." When his voice trailed off, the two men, Lane still with his back to Dixon, stood there, alone in the heavy silence of the room, lost in their own thoughts.

Standing there looking at Lane, Dixon began to wonder if he had been too hard on him. Perhaps this man was after all just a simple soul like so many others he had come across in the Army, doing the best he could. Perhaps had he himself not been afforded the opportunities, through incredible luck for him and all too often misfortune for others, he would be standing there across the room in Lane's shoes. Perhaps. But then like a mist rising from the recesses of his mind, the memory of Hal Cerro served to remind Dixon of what Lane had done to Hal. This, of course, led to what he was trying to do to Nancy Kozak, a person who was more than a good soldier and a friend to Dixon. She had in many ways become a sister, a peer, if not in rank then in achievements and spirit. Realizing that if left unchecked by someone, Lane would be free to do her damage,

Dixon began to draw himself together, stomping out any thoughts of mercy or sympathy in his mind like a man beating out a grass fire. No, Dixon thought. Might-have-beens are not part of my job description. I must, he reminded himself, stay the course and follow through now while the bastard is vulnerable. He would, as Stonewall Jackson always implored his men to do when things were tough, "give the enemy the bayonet."

Dixon had renewed his resolve just as Lane was drawing in a final deep breath. Turning to face Dixon, Lane looked at him. Any doubt or confusion that had been there in Lane's face a moment before was gone. In its place was a steady resolve. "I did my time, serving in one hole after another, going from one thankless assignment to the next, just like every other officer. I may not have been as bright as some, nor did I ever possess the brave, dashing figure that so many expect of a combat arms officer. Like you and everyone else I did the best I could with those skills and talents I have. And do you know what, General Dixon? I succeeded. I made my way to the top, and I am not about to let a bunch of frightened politicians or desk generals in Washington pull the rug out from under me now. I'm leaving here within the hour, headed for Washington. By the time I get back, you and your goddamned medals won't be worth the scrap iron they're made from."

For the second time tonight Lane's words elicited a response from Dixon. Not believing what he had heard, he gaped slightly before he caught himself. Was Lane, Dixon wondered, intending to go over Stratton's head? Not even Lane, noted throughout the Army for his arrogance and disregard for protocol, was that foolish. Or was he? Though tempted to ask the obvious, Dixon didn't. If he's willing to slit his own throat, I'm willing to let him.

Still not satisfied that he had made an impression, Lane was about to launch into a new round of threats when there was a knock on the door. Before Dixon could respond, the door opened and Jeff Worsham stuck his head around the corner. "Sorry to disturb you, sir, but I think you need to come out here for a minute."

Lane turned toward Worsham and snapped, "You're interrupting us, Colonel."

He's gone too far, Scott thought. Raising his hand as Worsham started to back away, Dixon called out. "Hold on. What do you have, Jeff?"

Worsham cast a sideways glance at Lane before facing Dixon. "We've just got several reports in that the Farcees have launched a major attack on Villavicencio, artillery and all. There's even a rumor that the garrison commander has capitulated."

Knowing a saving throw when he saw it, Dixon nodded. "I'll be right out." Noticing that Worsham left the door open, he turned back to Lane. "Is there something else we need to cover before you leave, General?"

Unable to think of anything appropriate, Lane took one more hard look at Dixon, then turned and walked out, leaving the door to Dixon's office wide open. While he had wished that they could have avoided that scene completely, Scott was glad it was over. Moving around to the back of his desk, he pulled the center drawer out and started rummaging about in search of a bottle of aspirin.

With his head down, absorbed in his search, he didn't see or hear Delhue enter through the open door. Only when he heard the door close did he look up. "Yes?"

"General, we need to talk."

"About?"

"General Lane. I just had an interesting talk with Captain Adderly, his aide. I think it's time we sat down and placed a conference call to General Stratton and his inspector general."

"What about the reports concerning Villavicencio?"

"Sir, Villavicencio can wait."

There was something in Delhue's tone that told him that as bad as things might be down south for the Colombian Army, they were at this moment far worse for his own little piece of the American Army. Easing himself into his seat, Dixon called out to his aide. Lieutenant Frazier opened the door and stuck his head into the room. "Wally, would you be so kind as to pass the word to the rest of the staff that the evening briefing will reconvene in thirty minutes. And when you're finished doing that, put a call through to General Stratton. I need to speak to him."

When Frazier was gone, Dixon leaned forward and folded his hands in front of him on the desk. "Lane?"

Delhue nodded. "Yes, sir, it's about General Lane."

"Well now, Chris, now's as good a time as any, I guess, to compare notes. Shoot."

Some seventy miles to the south of Bogotá, what should have been a joyous and exciting moment for Hector Valendez was turning out to be something of a letdown. Sitting in the front seat of an open jeep at the head of a column of trucks filled with his fighters, Valendez rode through the streets of Villavicencio. Though he was without a doubt the most realistic man who belonged to the FARC's central committee, he was still disappointed at the lack of enthusiasm the populace of Villavicencio showed as his convoy wound its way to the city center. There were no cheering crowds, no reception committee. Only a smattering of pedestrians going about their daily business moved about the streets, paying little heed to him or anyone else. Despite the strong sense of realism that kept him on track, Valendez was genuinely upset that somehow someone had cheated him of his storybook entry and triumphant march. Folding his arms across his chest, he tried hard not to let his disappointment show as they reached the city's main plaza.

Pulling out from the narrow streets into the open plaza, Valendez was stunned by the sight that greeted him. On one side of the plaza, he saw the garrison commander, a Colombian Army colonel, waiting in front of the town hall with his staff. Across from him, separated by an open space of no more than ten meters was the commander of the lead FARC regular-force battalion, Commander Julio Nariño, and his staff. Milling about a short distance behind their respective commanders were armed soldiers and rebels, eyeing each other like rival packs of dogs waiting for the word to pitch into each other.

Since he had been under the impression that the Colombian Army garrison had surrendered, Valendez was both shocked and momentarily excited. "Stop, stop the jeep," he yelled as he pulled his crossed arms apart and fumbled some while grabbing for the rifle on his lap. Hearing the squeal of the jeep's brakes, Nariño turned and saw his superior, whom he had always called El Jefe. Not understanding why he was reacting in such a manner, Nariño turned away from the Colombian Army colonel and calmly walked over to where Valendez's jeep finally came to a halt. Only when Valendez shouted, "What in God's name is going on here?" did Nariño finally realize that his commander didn't understand the situation.

Seeing the troops in the trucks that had followed Valendez into the plaza begin to spill out onto the street, weapons at the ready, Nariño raised his hands, palms down and signaled them to lower their guns. "Jefe, please call off your men before someone gets hurt."

Confusion replaced Valendez's excitement. Throwing his legs out of the jeep, he eased himself out of it and slowly laid his rifle on his seat. "I assume, my friend, that you can explain this?" he asked as he waved his right arm about the plaza filled with armed men from both sides.

"I was, Jefe, hoping that you could help."

Valendez's eyes grew large. "Oh? I come into the center of a town, one in which its garrison is supposed to have been subdued. But instead of a vanquished foe and a triumphant command, I find one of my battalion commanders all but chatting and drinking coffee with the enemy, who, by the way, is still armed. And when I ask him to explain, my veteran field commander, a man known throughout all of Colombia for his skill as a fighter, asks *me* to help him explain what's going on. How interesting."

The expression on Nariño's face showed his frustration. "Fighting is easy. Politics and diplomacy aren't."

"I sent you in here to attack the place," Valendez countered. "How is it you managed to convert yourself into a diplomat?"

"As ordered, we followed the initial barrage in as closely as possible. But no sooner had my lead element penetrated the first row of buildings than the firing stopped. When I came forward to find out why, I found myself face to face with a group of Colombian officers standing in the street with a white flag of truce. They led me here, with my troops following, where I met the commander of the brigade responsible for this city and region."

"And?" There was a distinctive hint of impatience in Valendez's question.

"It seems, Jefe, that Colonel Guillén Montes wants to declare his command neutral in the fight between us and the Bogotá government."

Valendez turned his head sideways and gave his lieutenant a look that left little doubt that he thought him crazy. The battalion commander, however, maintained his gaze without flinching. Looking over Nariño's shoulder at the Colombian army colonel, Valendez thought about the situation for a moment, then let the expression of doubt leave his face. Reaching out, he placed his hand on Nariño's shoulder, spun him about, and came up next to him. Pulling Nariño as close to him as possible, Valendez spoke to him in hushed tones. "This, my friend, is a test."

Now it was Nariño's turn to stare incredulously at his commander. Seeing the doubt in his eyes, Valendez explained. "Whether our friend the colonel over there knows it or not, he is testing us. We both know that the Colombian Army is only waiting for a chance to try its hand again at bringing down the same government we are trying to throw out. Maybe, just maybe, this is the Colombian Army's way of telling us that they are willing to let us do it for them."

Nariño's face showed his disbelief. "Do you think they will stand aside and let us march on Bogotá?"

"Why not? Even a blind man can see the writing on the wall. They know they are losing this war despite the American presence. They have watched week by week while our strength and skills grow and theirs diminish. Slowly their officer corps is being reduced day after day from the attrition they suffer fighting a losing war. In the meantime the government they are supposed to be defending continues to purge their ranks one by one of officers they don't trust. They are surrounded, with us to their front and their own President in the rear. Don't you think that they would want to do something before we kill all the soldiers that they depend upon for their own power?"

"If this is true, if they are willing to treat with their enemy and betray the government they are pledged to defend, then how can we trust them? Won't they, as soon as *we* finish pulling down the government, turn on us?"

Pulling away, Valendez smiled. "Yes they will, my friend. In time, I agree, they will. But for now," he said with a glance over to the Colombian Army colonel, who stood with legs shoulder-width apart and hands behind his back impatiently rocking back and forth on his heels, "we must see what we can do to turn them and this situation to our advantage. If we handle this right, then perhaps other garrisons may be encouraged, either on their own or on order from the general staff of the Colombian Army itself, to follow suit. With their shield lowered, and the Americans preoccupied with sorting out the mess we made of their command structure, we will be free to cut directly into the malignancy that has been slowly killing our country for years."

Nariño shook his head. "This, Jefe, is quite risky."

"War, my friend, is a risk. It always has been and always will be. And victory has more often than not gone to the side that has been willing to take the biggest risks." Valendez smiled. "Come, let us speak with the colonel and see if we can't come to some sort of understanding. We both claim, after all, to be fighting for the people of Colombia. Perhaps it is time that we sit down and see if we can work with each other, for a while."

Though uncomfortable with the whole idea of dealing with government forces while they were still capable of resisting, Nariño nodded. When Valendez dropped his arm and turned away to walk over to where the Colombian officers waited, Nariño followed, just as he and every FARC fighter had for many hard and bitter months.

Several hours later, just before midnight, a different convoy, an American convoy, wound its way through the dark and deserted streets of Bogotá. When the lead vehicle reached the gate of the American embassy, the Marine guards, arrayed in full battle gear and protected by newly reinforced sandbag bunkers, challenged it. Ordering the driver to turn out the humvee's headlights and stop, Captain Nancy Kozak dismounted from her vehicle and approached the barrier set up in the middle of the gate. The corporal of the guard, a six-foot-plus Marine, came out from behind the sandbags and met her.

When he was close enough, Kozak called out. "I'm Captain

Kozak, the operations officer for the 3rd Battalion, 511th Parachute Infantry. I've got Company B with me. We're here by order of Brigadier General Dixon to augment the embassy security force.''

Upon hearing Kozak's voice, the Marine felt like telling her ''No thanks, lady,'' but kept his tongue in check. They had been told before going out for their tour of duty to expect a company from the Army units out at the airfield. This, in light of the events earlier that day, had brought jeers from the assembled rifle squad. ''How in the hell are they going to protect the embassy,'' one lance corporal moaned, ''when they can't even protect their own division headquarters?'' Though privately he agreed with his men, the captain commanding the security detachment at the embassy squelched all such talk and set about preparing for their arrival.

Now as the corporal stood facing Kozak waiting for his gunny to come up and verify her identity, he laughed to himself. The skipper, a Marine through and through, wasn't going to much like working side by side with a female infantry captain, especially one, he figured, that might outrank him, if only by date of rank. Life, he mused to himself, was about to get interesting around here.

CHAPTER 22

December 6

WHEN THE END CAME, IT CAME WITH THE RAPIDITY OF A house of cards tumbling down, with the fall of Villavicencio, without a fight, being the card that started the collapse. But it was not only the rapidity that rattled all the parties involved in the struggle. Everything about it was unexpected. "Even Herman," Scott Dixon commented one night in private to Colonel Chris Delhue, "in his wildest fantasy could never have dreamed this one up." Delhue's only comment, as he gazed at the map showing the disposition of both the FARC units and the government units reported to have "gone neutral," was to correct Dixon's choice of words, substituting nightmare for fantasy.

For the Colombian government, the nightmare began the first day of December. On that date, during a meeting between the American ambassador and the Colombian President to discuss the possibility of additional military commitments by the United States, the President was handed a note by an aide. From where he sat, the American ambassador watched as the blood drained from the Colombian's face. When he asked what the problem was, the Colombian President stood up, excused himself, and walked out of the room. Only after he returned to his own embassy did the ambassador find out that the Colombian Minister of Defense had committed suicide in his own office. Neither Dixon nor Thomas believed that the Minister of Defense had died by his own hand, especially since the minister's successor by default was the chief of staff of the Colombian armed forces. That this man was related to Colonel Guillén Montes, the man who had started this current crisis by stepping aside and opening Villavicencio to occupation by the FARC, escaped no one's attention. "If you had any doubts," Dixon warned the ambassador, "about the seriousness of this whole affair, I hope this latest move by our dear friends has changed your mind."

Unfortunately, from Dixon's standpoint, it didn't. Obligated by the foreign policy dictated from Washington, D.C., the ambassador continued to work with the Colombian government as they tried to stem the collapse that gained momentum as garrison after garrison followed Colonel Montes's example. By the simple act of tying a red strip of cloth about their left arm, the soldiers of the Colombian Army went from supporting the government in Bogotá to a state of armed neutrality.

This deteriorating state of affairs placed Scott in an awkward position. On the one hand, everyone in the military chain of command concurred with his analysis and decisions, encouraging him to expedite his shifting of forces from their widely scattered outposts to locations that would facilitate their extraction from Colombia. On the other, the ambassador, still hoping to salvage the unsalvageable, had Dixon review the military situation and come up with a list of military recommendations that he could forward to both the American and Colombian presidents.

As November gave way to December, Dixon began to feel more and more like Lord Gort, the commander of the British Expeditionary Force in Belgium in 1940. While he did as the ambassador directed, dedicating several officers to the development of plans he knew would never see the light of day, the bulk of his energy and that of his small ad hoc staff was bent toward salvaging all they could while they could. Though this contradiction led to confusion, not to mention frustration on the part of Dixon's staff, Chris Delhue managed to keep the staff's attention focused, leaving Dixon free to deal with the ambassador, General Stratton, and the Army staff back in Washington. Only once during this time of confusion did Lane's name come up. As he was explaining on the phone to the ambassador that the 11th's redeployment was nothing more than an effort to prepare for future operations, which was the truth, Dixon was informed that Stratton was on another line asking why it was taking so long to shift units north. Covering the receiver's mouthpiece, Dixon turned to Delhue. "Where's Lane when you need him?"

Lane, of course, was in Washington, pending an official inquiry into his conduct of the Kozak trial. So was Jan, stranded and unable to return to what she called the "cockpit of the war," because the Colombian government, branding her El Frío videotape leftist propaganda and Jan an undesirable, refused to grant her a visa. Jan being the type of woman she was, however, wasn't idle. Using her time, her proximity to the seats of power, and her connections, she worked tirelessly to complete the undoing of Major General C. B. Lane that she had started in Colombia.

These machinations, though resented by some in the military, served her purpose well, ensuring that the Army could neither ignore nor postpone the investigation of charges that Lane had used his influence as a commander in a manner that was both unethical and in violation of regulations. Not that General Fulk, Chief of Staff of the Army, cared to do otherwise. In a private conversation with General Stratton, Fulk mused. "You know, Jerry," he said the day after the President of the United States ordered Lane relieved of his command and Dixon named as interim commander of the 11th Air Assault Division, "last night was the first night in months that I was able to turn out the lights in the office and go home to a sound sleep."

Stratton, equally pleased to have Dixon's status and position secured in such a manner, agreed. Only Dixon at that moment would have taken issue with this momentary euphoria. For while one problem was solved, a whole new crop awaited Dixon's attention.

Capitalizing on his success of November 29, and anxious to test his theory, Hector Valendez pushed his victorious regular-force battalions north in the direction of Bogotá. The Colombian Army promptly sent a small brigade, taken from the

411

command charged to defend Bogotá, south to meet this threat. Officially it was the capitulation of this brigade to Valendez, without even making any pretense at a show of resistance, that caused the Colombian Minister of Defense to commit suicide. Rumors, of course, circulated that the minister had been assassinated by a military aide. These rumors could neither be proved nor disproved, since the incident took place in his office and the people finding the dead man were all members of the Colombian general staff.

Failure of the Colombian Army to stem the northward march of the FARC led the Colombian government to appeal to the American Army for assistance. "If you can but buy us a little time, a few days," the Colombian President pleaded with the American ambassador, "we will be able to muster troops still loyal to me and deal with this threat in our own way." Accepting the call, the ambassador put pressure on Scott to provide the Colombian President the time he needed. Though neither he nor anyone else who understood the true political and military situation believed that such an effort would do anything other than lengthen casualty lists already too long for a cause that was hopeless, Dixon complied. On the second of December a battalion of the 3rd Brigade, redeploying from the east, was dropped astride the main road leading from Villavicencio to Bogotá.

Not wholly unexpectedly, Valendez and his battalion commanders simply bypassed the roadblock that the American infantry battalion established. Leaving local-force companies, reinforced with two heavy mortar batteries, to deal with the American roadblock, the main-force units continued their march north. Even steady day-and-night patrols of attack helicopters and armed aeroscouts throughout the area made little difference. "It's like turning on the light in a room full of cockroaches," one disgruntled attack helicopter pilot complained to Dixon after returning from a mission. "You may get one or two if you're quick, but that's all. The rest disappear like magic into the woodwork and hide until after we leave."

The woodwork that the pilot was talking about was the villages, homes, farms, and towns that lined Valendez's path to the capital. While Dixon had been told by the Colombian President that the stringent rules of engagement that had so re-

412

stricted American operations in the past had been suspended, Scott knew better than to turn his division's firepower loose in the densely populated areas where the FARC sought shelter. When the ambassador took him to task on this issue, telling him that he had no choice, Dixon stood his ground. "You seem to forget," he pointed out to the ambassador, "what happened when we did that in Saigon and Hué in 1968. In the process of winning the battle, we leveled the country we were supposed to be saving and lost a war, not to mention our pride and self-respect." When Dixon's chain of command backed this stand all the way back to the President, the battalion dropped across the FARC's advance, chewed up after proving to be nothing more than a speed bump, was withdrawn. Though no one knew it at the time, this effort was to be the last one conducted by the United States with the aim of supporting the Colombian government. From that point on, everything the 11th Air Assault did had but one purpose: "to cut our losses," Dixon told his staff, "and salvage what little pride we can still carry out with us."

The last night in Bogotá started as all the others had with an unrealistic, artificial silence settling over the sprawling city. Within the compound of the American embassy, the combined Army and Marine security force went about their tasks of buttoning down and preparing for another long night's vigilance. In the operations center of the security force, located to one side of the main lobby of the embassy, Captain Nancy Kozak received the reports from the outposts scattered about the perimeter of the embassy compound. Absorbed in this effort, neither she nor the skeleton staff that worked for her noticed Scott Dixon when he came up behind her.

Taking a break from his own efforts, and not wanting to interfere with hers, Scott stood a short distance away from the cluster of tables, chairs, map boards, and desks as he watched. Like any well-drilled team, they went about their tasks with a minimum of effort. Scott enjoyed watching good people working together. It gave him a sense of accomplishment and pride. This was especially true when he had in some way had a hand in molding and training the people involved, and felt the pride of knowing that he was part of something bigger than himself and that their combined efforts made a difference.

As quickly as these thoughts raced through his mind, a sadness clouded them. How terrible, he thought, that all of our efforts, all of our sacrifices in the past months, will come to nought. Rather than being portrayed in the light that they deserved, the people and their efforts would be pushed aside like all failed ventures and forgotten as quickly as possible. "Until someone has the courage to tell the truth of what really happened down here," Chris Delhue mused in a moment of deep reflection, "we'll be viewed as losers." As heavy as that burden seemed to Dixon, the people that he felt for the most at that moment were the families who had lost sons and daughters, husbands and wives in Colombia. Jan said it best one night after getting over Cerro's loss. "To lose a loved one is hard, the hardest thing I can imagine. But to lose them for no good reason, that's cruel, bitter and cruel."

Lost in his own melancholy thoughts, Scott wasn't paying attention when Kozak, finished with her duties for now, stood up and walked over next to him. "Is there something, sir, that I can do for you?"

Shaking his head as if to clear away his dark thoughts, Dixon managed a slight smile. "No, nothing right now. Just thought I'd take a break from pondering the imponderables and wander about. I've been penned up in that little cubbyhole of mine too long and need to get some exercise."

Reaching up and stretching her arms above her head, Nancy looked back at her people as they went about their duties. "That, sir, sounds like a great idea. Care to join me while I walk the perimeter?"

After telling his aide, Wally Frazier, to head back up to the office and inform Colonel Delhue that he was going to take a short walk about the grounds of the embassy, Dixon looked back at Kozak. "Sounds like a winner. Lead off, Captain."

Walking out onto the steps of the embassy, the two officers stopped and stared at the night sky of Bogotá. They stood there for several minutes in silence, each lost in their own thoughts. Finally Nancy mused almost to herself after watching the lights of the city wink on one at a time, "It's strange. Out there just beyond the wall and barbed wire people are going about life as if nothing out of the ordinary was going on."

Scott sighed. "For them nothing is. Political upheaval and violence are as much a part of the social fabric of this country as the birth and death of its citizens. Those people out there, the ones turning on all those lights, they really don't much care who is in charge. Their lives, they realize, will change very little. Only the name of their President and maybe the ruling party will change. Within a month after we're gone, it will be as if we were never here."

Raising her eyebrows, Kozak looked at Dixon. "You certainly are in a cheery mood tonight, sir. What's the matter, did your dog die upstairs or is Jan in the middle of running one of her notorious crusader rabbit series on TV?"

Standing in front of the embassy out of earshot of the Marine guards at the door, Scott said nothing. Instead he just hung his head, looked over at Kozak, and started to walk. For the longest time neither said anything, each retreating into their own private thoughts. Though they were both thankful to have someone there next to them, each was thankful that the other made no demands on them or cluttered this peaceful moment with idle conversation. Only when they came to the rear of the main building did Dixon finally come to a halt and say something. Even then he was in no rush. Rather he stood motionless in the shadows with Kozak watching truck drivers and assistant truck drivers go about checking their vehicles. When he finally did speak, he spoke in soft, almost hushed, tones. "Are they ready?"

"They" referred to the trucks gathered in the embassy compound for the purpose of whisking away any Americans, including the security force, that still remained in Bogotá. With scattered reports of FARC units probing the suburbs, both Dixon and Kozak knew that such an evacuation could come at any time. Kozak, responsible for developing and implementing the evacuation plan, nodded. "If we decide to go by land, we can be on the road and out of here in less than thirty minutes."

"I'm not comfortable, you know, with the idea of splitting the column."

"Both Captain Trainor and I agree that doing so is best," Kozak countered. "He'll take his Marines and lead off, taking the ambassador and what's left of his staff out along the most direct route out of town. I'll stay here until he's reached the outskirts of the town. If he gets stopped before that, I can either come to their rescue with B Company or hold the embassy open as a safe haven for them to return to."

"You," Dixon said looking over to her, "will of course be here until the very last."

"Of course, General. I was, after all, trained by a rather hard-core tanker who always insisted on doing the same. I believe he was quite insistent about ensuring that all his officers understood what his 'first in, last out' motto meant." This caused Dixon to chuckle. She did likewise before turning serious. "There's no way I can persuade you to leave now and go north where the rest of your staff is, is there?"

"So long as the ambassador stays, I stay."

"What," Kozak asked, "does he hope to accomplish from here? It's all over, isn't it?"

"Like me, Nancy, he's a hard case. And like me he knows it isn't over until the fat lady sings. Though I don't believe in miracles, not anymore, he still does. And so long as the President of Colombia remains in Bogotá, he stays and, ditto, so do I."

Folding her arms across her chest, Kozak shook her head. "You know your presence is only making my job harder."

He smiled. "Well, as you know, I've always been interested in providing all my subordinates with challenges commensurate with their abilities."

Though she heard his words, her mind was already drifting off to a new thought. Without looking away from the trucks, Kozak asked Dixon with no preamble, "Do you think Hal Cerro knew what he was doing?"

When he had been told of the circumstances surrounding Cerro's death, Scott had asked himself the same question. More pointedly, he wondered if Cerro had in any way engineered the situation that resulted in his death. After several days of deep reflection, Dixon had finally come to the conclusion that he hadn't. Cerro was simply too good a soldier for such foolishness. And at that he had let the matter rest, until now. Looking over at the Bogotá skyline, then over at the trucks again, he watched the young soldiers as they went about their duties. Finally he spoke. "Hal Cerro was a soldier, first, last, and always. He did what he did that day outside of El Frío, because he saw no other choice."

Kozak thought about Dixon's answer for a moment, then mused half to herself, "If I have to go, that's the way I want to go. In battle, at the head of troops, just as the battle turns to our favor."

When she spoke those words, there was, Dixon thought, a clear note of wistfulness that shone through. He studied her face for a moment. In the glow of the lights from the temporary motor pool, he could see the dreamlike quality in her eyes, as if she were lost deep in a daydream that pleased her. Had she, he wondered, become so jaded by her experiences in this war, especially the death of a man she so admired and a court-martial that was so trivial in nature that she was . . .

Without any need to continue, Dixon moved around Kozak until he faced her. "Listen, Captain Kozak. I know these past few months have been hell on you. Though they've been tough on everyone, believe me, I know that you and, before his death, Hal Cerro were put through hell. There is nothing I or anyone else can do to make good the wrongs that have been done against you. Even if C. B. Lane is brought to justice, we'll never see Hal Cerro again. He's dead. And wishful thinking or your death will not make that fact any more palatable."

Rather than being upset or repentant, Kozak looked up into Dixon's eyes. For a moment, she saw the same fire that he had seen in hers on other such occasions. No wonder she admired this man so much. Both he and Hal Cerro had been tempered by the same fire, the fire of war.

"Do you, sir, remember the story of General Garnnett of the Confederate Army?"

"The one who commanded the Stonewall Brigade at the First Battle of Kernstown and was killed later at Gettysburg?"

"Yes, sir, the same. Do you remember how he felt being charged by Stonewall Jackson for disobeying an order but never having a chance to clear his name and how he went into Pickett's charge mounted, the only mounted officer in the entire attack?"

"Look, Nancy, I better than anyone else know what's going on in your mind. I know that you are just as anxious to attach some value to Hal Cerro's death in order to make it worthwhile as well as clear your own honor. But I have learned that when a soldier dies, he doesn't ascend to a higher plane or become something more than he was before. He's just dead.''

"Are you trying to tell me that Colonel Cerro died for nothing? That he gave his life up for no good reason?''

"No. Like I said before, he made a conscious choice when he was faced with a whole host of bad ones. In reality he probably didn't even have a choice between living and dying. He probably just picked the agent of his death. You, on the other hand, have a choice. And so long as you do, I hope that you pick life, for this world would be a damned sight less exciting without you.''

"The court-martial, regardless of what happens, is the death knell of my career.''

"Then,'' Dixon shouted, throwing out his arms, "start another. Jesus, woman! You're still young, not much over thirty. You have done nothing wrong and you have no sins, either real or imagined, to atone for. To throw away your life just because you think you can't be a soldier anymore doesn't make sense. Not one bit.''

Though she wanted to find some way of countering his argument, she couldn't. He was right, at least as far as what she had been thinking. The idea of finding an honorable and noble end had more and more crept into her tired mind. And despite what the general said, Nancy Kozak in her heart knew that Cerro had done exactly that, sought and found himself a death befitting the warrior leader that he was in thought, word, and deed.

They were still standing there, Kozak going over in her mind what Dixon had just said, and Dixon looking at her while he waited for a response, when Wally Frazier found them. In his usual style he blundered forward without regard for what was going on. "General Dixon, sir. Colonel Delhue needs to see you right away.''

For a moment Scott neither moved nor spoke. Instead he continued to look into Kozak's eyes. He hadn't, he realized, made an impression. Not in the least. With a sigh he looked away to his aide, who stood off to one side shifting his weight from one foot to the next, like a little boy that needed to go to the bathroom but wanted to finish what he was doing first. "What seems to be the problem, Wally?"

"Sir, the Colombian President, as well as his entire cabinet, has resigned. They up and pulled out of the capital an hour ago headed for some other country."

"And we're just finding out?"

"The ambassador is just as pissed, sir. The only way he found out about this was when Colonel Marco Agustin, commander of Bogotá's garrison, sent one of his staff officers here a few minutes ago with a personal message from his colonel."

"Did Agustin's message say where he and his command stood?"

"Sir, Colonel Delhue told me to tell you that the staff officer carrying the message was wearing a red band on his left arm."

Looking over to the trucks, Dixon thought for a moment before he turned back to Kozak. "Okay, Nancy, the time has come to get your people and Bill Trainor's Marines mounted up and ready to roll."

"Then we're going by land?"

"Yes. The ambassador's been stricken with the same phobia everyone in Washington has about leaving the capital in a helicopter off the roof of the embassy like the people in Saigon did in '75. Seems everyone is under the insane impression that it's more dignified to leave in a limousine."

Kozak shook her head and said nothing.

"As soon as I can pry the ambassador away from that beautiful mahogany desk of his, we'll get this circus on the road."

Turning, Kozak began to walk away with a rapid pace, calling over her shoulder as she went, "We'll be ready."

Watching her go, Dixon wondered who else out there in the darkness would be.

Realizing that there was now nothing he could do to stop the first convoy of trucks and jeeps that had suddenly spilled out of the American embassy onto the dark streets of Bogotá, Julio Nariño contacted his company commanders and made sure that they understood that he would not tolerate another oversight such as that. Though he doubted that he would have another opportunity such as the one that had just passed, he ordered a roadblock thrown across the route used by the fleeing Yankees.

Though his men were tired and grumbled about the foolishness of closing the door after the horses had escaped, the platoon commander charged with this mission kept them at the task. "This," he told his men, "will soon be over. And when it is, and you have returned to your fields and shops, you will look back to this night and all the others we've shared with great fondness and longing." Though none of his men believed a word he said, they continued to work, hauling whatever material was handy over to their makeshift barricade.

Impatiently Scott Dixon sat in his humvee listening to the steady grinding of the engine as the convoy snaked its way through the deserted streets. Never a good follower, Scott hated being stuck in the middle of the column with nothing more to do than keep track of where they were on the small city map that had been issued to every vehicle, and to enjoy the ride as best he could.

Further up in the line of march was Nancy Kozak's vehicle. Though she was in charge of the overall movement, she found herself, like Dixon, with little to do. Lieutenant Dan Krammer, the commander of Company B, was in charge of the actual movement. All Kozak had to do was monitor the silent radio net and hope that their luck, like that of the Marine convoy before them, held.

Just as the lead vehicles turned a corner up ahead, the radio speaker mounted to her front and connected to the radio next to her that was set on the convoy frequency came to life. The call she heard coming in was from the lead platoon leader. That broadcast, however, wasn't finished when outside her humvee the rip of automatic rifle fire drew her attention away and cut the transmission short. Instinctively she reached behind her to grab her rifle. Fighting the urge to jump out of the humvee, Kozak stayed put and waited for the initial reports to come in. She knew Dan Krammer would report as soon as he had something to report. So she sat there clinging to the stock of her rifle with one hand while grabbing the radio hand mike with her other, fighting the urge to call Krammer and ask for a report. "He'll send me one," she kept repeating to herself, "as soon as he has one to give. He'll send it."

As if in answer, the radio came to life again. "Skyrider

420

Three, this is Bravo Six. We have a roadblock up ahead, covered by fire. I'm dismounting my First Platoon and going forward with them to check it out. Will advise you as soon as I know the score. Over.''

Anxious to get in touch with Krammer before he dismounted and was away from his radio, Kozak keyed the radio hand mike and spoke into it. "Bravo, this is Three. Is there a bypass? Over?'' The silence, however, told her that she had missed him. Seeing no point in trying again, since his response would have been immediate if he had heard her, Kozak let the radio hand mike drop and looked down at the street map on her lap. In a flash she could tell that the Farcees had chosen their site well. Any bypass at this point would take the convoy through the narrow and twisting streets of a slum district. Besides, she realized as the sound of M-16 rifle fire began to drift back to her, by now Krammer was heavily involved in a standup fight and chances were they weren't going to be able to break it off too easily. Deciding the best thing to do right now was to bring up the engineers and prepare to bull through, Kozak turned to her driver, yelled to him that she was going up to see what was going on, and disappeared into the darkness.

Further back in the column, Dixon heard the same report and, like Kozak, looked to see if a bypass was possible. He too, however, soon dismissed that idea for the same reason that Kozak had. Unlike Kozak, there was even less that he could do. To start with, though he was the division commander, he was so far out of the chain of command that any efforts on his part to influence the situation at this moment would be counterproductive. Besides, his wounds, though healing nicely, limited the amount of running and ducking he could do. If he, like Kozak, ran forward, he would present a large, slow moving target. As much as he hated doing nothing, that for the moment was the only logical course of action open to him. Reaching over to his side, he unsnapped his holster and pulled his nine-millimeter pistol out. Jerking back on the upper slide, he let it go when it reached the stop on it. Sliding forward, it chambered a round. Throwing the door open, he remembered his speech given to Kozak less than two hours before and wondered what he would do if things didn't work out this time.

HAROLD COYLE

Forgetting all the bull he had given her about there being no honor in death and that she needed to forget silly notions of such things, Scotty Dixon made up his mind then and there that he would not allow himself to become a war trophy.

When she reached the corner, Kozak lowered herself as far as she could before peeking around it. The vehicles of the lead platoon, Krammer's First Platoon, were stopped in the middle of the street, where they had been when the firing had started. On either side of the street she could see soldiers of the First Platoon crouching low in doorways or behind the corners of buildings. Emerging from behind their cover only briefly, they would fire a three-round burst and then duck back before their efforts brought down a hostile response. The Farcees, she thought, were no doubt doing much the same thing. If that was true, that meant that they were involved in a stalemate, something that Kozak knew they would eventually lose once the Farcees started funneling reinforcements into the fight.

Looking about a minute, she noted where Krammer was across the street. Bracing herself like a runner ready to do the hundred-meter dash, Kozak leaped up, sprinted across the street, and made a wild dive for cover as her movements began to draw fire, allowing herself to roll on the pavement in order to avoid breaking anything. Dan Krammer started rendering his report before she had time to recover. "We have one man down, wounded I think, and can't do anything from here. They have us pinned, big time."

Gathering herself up, Kozak threw herself against the wall that Krammer and two other troopers from his company were sharing and thought for a minute. So far, she thought, it seemed as if they had gotten off lightly. If the Farcees had meant to ambush her column, then someone on the other side had blown it. But if all that the people up ahead were supposed to do was hold them until reinforcements arrived, then they were in deep trouble.

Finally, without looking over at him, she began to speak. "Dan, this is no good. We can't stay here for very long. If these people are already here in place and set up like this, you can bet that they have friends nearby."

"Yeah," Krammer shouted as he leaned around the corner,

squeezed off three quick rounds, and then pulled his head back. "And you can bet every one of their smiling little faces is headed this way."

"Dan, you stay here and keep those people occupied. I've already got the engineers coming up, just around the corner, waiting to clear the barriers. I'm going to head on back, gather up the Second Platoon, and make an end run to the left. I'll take a radioman with me and contact you as soon as we're in place. Once the firing has stopped and the engineers have cleared the road, don't wait for me to give you the word. Start pushing the trucks through. I'll have the Third Platoon move forward while we're maneuvering around the roadblock to the head of the column. Once everyone is on the move, Dan, hop in your vehicle and get the convoy and the First Platoon out of this city. The Second Platoon and I will bring up the rear as soon as everyone is clear. "

With no more words or orders necessary, Krammer looked over to Kozak. "Will do. We'll be ready and waiting here. Good luck."

As before, she prepared herself for her return across the street by balancing herself on all fours. When Krammer and the troopers with him were ready to spring around the corner and cover her move, he yelled, "Now," and Kozak was off.

By the time she reached the portion of the convoy where his humvee sat, Scott Dixon had managed to pull himself out of the passenger seat. Standing next to the vehicle, holding the door for support, he saw Kozak running down the line of trucks to his front, gathering up the soldiers who had already dismounted and stood ready to fight or flee. Making his way up to where she stood giving instructions to the platoon leader with her, Dixon heard the last of her instructions. Only after the platoon leader nodded and turned to issue his own orders to his squad leaders did Dixon come up to her. "How bad is it, Nancy?"

Taking a moment to catch her breath, for the first time since dismounting her own humvee, she watched the platoon for a minute before turning to face Dixon. "Well," she managed between pants, "I've seen worse." Then as an afterthought she added, "But not tonight."

Her little stab at humor at a time like this told Scott that she had the situation well in hand. "You going to go with the flanking force, Nancy?"

She nodded. "Yes, of course. Need to get this circus moving. Dan Krammer is up front and will push you through as soon as the road is clear."

While her mind was too cluttered with details and her system too charged up from the rush of adrenaline, Dixon's was clear and quite reflective. She, and not he, despite his star and title, was in charge here. She was giving all the orders and for the first time he was little more than a spectator. It was, he realized, almost as if this were some kind of strange change-of-command ceremony, with him handing over the future of the Army to this young, hard-pressed infantry officer. Though Jan had on several occasions told him that it was time for him to start looking beyond his career as a soldier, this was the first moment that he finally realized that he was closer now to the end than to the beginning, or even the middle. The Army, his Army, now belonged to Kozak and others like her.

When she saw that the platoon leader was finished and the squad leaders were beginning to lead their people off, Nancy Kozak turned to Dixon. "You'll have to excuse me, sir. I need to go."

Recovered from her initial exertions, she spoke with confidence and determination. Dixon, facing her, did not know what else to say. He wanted to warn her, to tell her to keep their little talk earlier that evening in mind. But this was neither the time nor place for such talk. Instead he smiled. "Captain, take charge and move out."

Stepping back, Kozak rendered the sharpest hand salute she could manage and turned away. With the poise and confidence of the leader she was, Kozak moved to the front of the Second Platoon, raised her hand, then dropped it in a forward motion. The troopers of that platoon, arrayed in two files, followed her, weapons at the ready, into the darkness.

Though they were gone from view within a minute, Scott Dixon watched where he had seen them disappear, listening to the thud of their boots on pavement until that too had receded into the darkness. Finally, when the only sound he could hear was that of rifle fire coming from the roadblock, Dixon turned away and began to make his way back to his humvee.

Slowly making his way along the trucks halted in the middle of the street, he felt a pang of melancholy. This, he realized, would probably be his last battle. Even if they survived, and he had little doubt that he would, Dixon knew in his heart that he would never again be asked to put his life on the line. For just as Kozak knew that the charges brought against her by Lane would always mark her, no matter what she did, for the rest of her life, his career was as good as over too. No one, after all, remembers or promotes generals who lead retreats, no matter how brilliant those actions are. Just as well, he thought. I'm getting too old for this anyway.

That a second convoy would come popping out of the embassy and use the exact same route as the first pleased Julio Nariño. Now his fighters manning the barricade he had insisted be built would have a second chance against the troopers of the 11th Air Assault who were headed his way. His only regret was that he had delayed sending reinforcements, reinforcements, Nariño hoped, that would be sufficient to handle the Yankees.

Moving as rapidly as Kozak deemed prudent through the dark streets and alleys off to the left of the stalled convoy, the Second Platoon made good time. Guiding on the gunfire of the standoff between the Farcees at the roadblock and Dan Krammer's holding force, Kozak slowed as they neared a broad street that ran perpendicular to their front. While the troopers of the Second Platoon continued to move forward, hugging the buildings on either side of the street they had been moving along, Kozak stepped out of the file she was in, away from the buildings and into the open. As she slid her left arm through the sling of her rifle, she pulled the street map out of a pocket on her right thigh. Flipping on a small penlight, she stopped and looked down at the map in her hand to see if the street to their front ran into the rear of the Farcee position they were trying to outflank. Engrossed in her quick check of the map, Nancy Kozak didn't see the mass of figures running across their path on the street in question.

The troopers of the Second Platoon, however, did. Before

she knew what was happening, half a dozen rifles and squad assault weapons cut loose. In seconds the rest of the troopers of the Second Platoon joined in, just as the first volley of return fire, aimed blindly at their unexpected assailants, answered. It was a mad minute of wild and blinding fire, punctuated by an occasional hand grenade. Then, as quickly as it started, the sudden fury was over. Only a handful of Farcees who had been at the end of the relief column managed to escape the punishing fire that the Second Platoon had unleashed. Scampering back up the street they had just come down, the survivors threw themselves into open doorways or ran down alleys between buildings. As a fighting force and a factor in the battle in progress, they ceased to exist.

Shaken but still in control, the young lieutenant in command of the Second Platoon stood up, looked around, and marveled at the fact that he had somehow managed to survive his first firefight. Though he had made no decisions, issued no orders, and had won the short, violent engagement by the mere fact that his people saw the enemy first and reacted properly, he considered this a great personal achievement. He had, after all, faced fire and lived, without disgracing himself or his unit. Yelling out to his squad leaders to sound off with their reports, he listened as each one responded that they had negative casualties. As the smile on his face grew larger and larger, he looked to the left, then to the right, blinking his eyelids all the while in an effort to get rid of the spots that friendly and enemy muzzle flashes had burned into his eyes. He needed to find Captain Kozak and determine what she wanted him to do next.

It was at that moment, after calling out her name twice, that he realized that she was gone. It was his second squad leader, off to his left, that found her. "Hey, Lieutenant, over here. She's down. The captain's been hit." Panicked, the smile left the platoon leader's face as he raced over to where a medic and two soldiers were huddled over a prone figure. They were just about to roll her over onto her back when the platoon leader arrived. "Is she dead?"

The question brought no response, at least not from the soldiers gathered about Kozak. Instead Kozak provided the answer herself, though she didn't realize it. Hit twice, once in the right shoulder and a glancing blow on the side of her head, the image of another night attack carried out long ago in distant Mexico came to her raddled brain. When she spoke, her speech was slurred and her words barely audible to soldiers who still had ringing in their ears from their engagement with the Farcee reserve force. "Sergeant Maupin," she mumbled, "fix bayonets and forward at the double."

Looking over to the medic who was leaning over her checking her wounds, the platoon leader asked, "What did she say?"

Busy with his efforts to save Kozak, the medic simply repeated those words that he had understood. "She said, 'Fix bayonets, forward at the double,' or something like that."

"Are you sure?"

Anxious to be rid of the lieutenant so that he could find out where all the blood that was spilling onto the street was coming from, the medic shouted, "Yeah, I'm sure. She said fix bayonets and forward at the double. Now leave me be or I'll lose her for sure."

Standing up, the young officer looked down at Kozak for a moment, not realizing that the order that she had just issued had belonged to another battle fought in another time and place at a time when she had been as young as he was now. In the darkness that engulfed them, surrounded by enemies in a foreign city, and engaged in a life and death struggle as real as Nancy Kozak's, there was no time to reason or question everything, especially a clear order such as the one that he thought Kozak had just given them.

Looking over at his squad leaders as they and the troopers in their charge huddled behind any cover they could find, the platoon leader decided that he had no choice. He had to comply. Drawing in a deep breath, he yelled out. "You heard the order. Fix bayonets and forward at the double." By way of getting things going, the platoon leader jerked his own bayonet out of its scabbard, stuck it on the end of the warm rifle barrel, and called out to his platoon as he turned and began to race down the street they had just cleared of enemy soldiers, "Second Platoon, follow meeee!"

With the exception of the medics and two soldiers left by the nearest squad leader to provide security and assist in Kozak's recovery, the rest of the Second Platoon rose and madly rushed down the street behind their platoon leader. It wasn't a very brilliant maneuver. In fact, had anyone stopped and thought about it, they would have realized that they were in the process of doing exactly what the Farcee unit had been doing when they had all but annihilated it. But they were young soldiers, each and every one of them. Fired up with adrenaline and a blood lust that drove them beyond all human constraints, they could not be held back.

Nor, as they rounded the corner and fell on the rear of the Farcees covering the roadblock, would they be denied.

EPILOGUE

January 9

ITEM BY ITEM, SCOTT DIXON CLEARED EACH OBJECT AND FILE from the desk before him. As anxious as he was to get out of Washington, especially the Pentagon, he wanted to make sure that everything, including the borrowed desk he had used for the past two weeks, was in order. When he arrived at Fort Campbell, Kentucky, all he wanted to do was lose himself for a while in the task of rebuilding the division that he had led out of Colombia less than a month ago.

When he completed the sorting and filing, Scott stood up and looked down at the last item on the desk. Arranged neatly in a blue folder was his report on the combat operations of the 11th Air Assault Division in what was now being called the Colombian Affair. As with other past military adventures, especially those that had gone astray, there surfaced a need to call it everything but what it had been, which was a war. Though he knew that this one, like the other wars he had been in, would always be with him, right now all Scott wanted to do was put some distance between it and him.

Deep in thought as he stared down at the blue folder, Scott didn't notice General Fulk as he entered the room. "Ready to leave us for good, Scotty?"

Looking up, Scott made no effort to gather himself into the position of attention or in any way acknowledge the entrance of his superior. Instead he glanced down at the blue folder again and replied in a low faraway tone, "I've been ready to do that for months."

The smile that had been on Fulk's face when he entered slipped away. Walking over to a chair in front of the desk, the Chief of Staff of the Army sat down and let his arms drop over the side. "People told me before you came here last year that the Pentagon was no place for you. Seems it took a war to prove them right to me."

Scott ignored Fulk's comment. The losses they had just suffered were still too fresh in his mind to make light of them. Instead he walked around to the front of the desk and leaned against it. "I believe, sir, that this report," he said, indicating the blue folder behind him, "will serve you and the Army staff until my staff has an opportunity to settle in at Campbell."

Fulk raised his hand. "I'm sure it will do. You always deliver, no matter what."

"I was hoping," Scott countered, "to have it finished before the new division commander arrived and took over, but I don't think that's going to be possible."

Not knowing if he was complaining about the appointment of a major general to come in and take over the 11th, leaving him to drop back to the position of assistant division commander, or not, Fulk tried again to relieve the concerns Scott seemed to be having. "I talked to Bill yesterday. He isn't due to take charge until mid-February. By then, I'm sure, you'll have everything as squared away as that desktop you're leaning on."

"Talking about taking care of unfinished business, sir, I know that you have other concerns, and this issue is still rather touchy, but I would appreciate it if the recommendation for Nancy Kozak's award could be acted upon before I leave. I was hoping to make a personal trip out to Lawrence, Kansas, before reporting back to Fort Campbell. I wanted to deliver the medal to her in person while she is still convalescing at home."

Fulk nodded. "I'll take care of that right away. All that we lack is the Secretary's signature and that action is on his desk right now."

"I appreciate that, sir."

"Why," Fulk asked, "isn't she waiting until she returns to

duty to receive it? After all, it's not every day that a soldier is awarded a second Distinguished Service Cross for valor. I would have expected that you would have liked to make a big deal out of this whole affair, especially in light of what Lane had been trying to pull. It would in a very visible way complete her exoneration.''

"We discussed that, sir, the other day over the phone. She feels rather embarrassed, as it is, that she is receiving any award for her actions on the morning of December seventh. According to her, she doesn't even remember being hit, let alone ordering a bayonet charge." Then, dropping his voice, he added, "Besides, Nancy isn't the vengeful type, not really. All she wants to do is to get back to a unit and lose herself in her duties.''

"Just like you."

This last comment caused Dixon to smile. "Yes, sir. Just like me."

Standing up, Fulk offered Dixon his hand. "I'm headed out tonight on a trip to Europe for the NATO conference. That's why I came down here to say my good-byes. Is there anything else you need from me before we go our separate ways?''

For an instant the question intrigued Scott. Yes, he thought to himself, there were some things he needed from Fulk. Scott wanted to know why, for starters, Fulk had said nothing last spring when the administration had recommended sending the 11th Air Assault to Colombia despite the fact that everyone who had bothered to look at the situation knew that Colombia, like Yugoslavia, Somalia, Vietnam, and other such adventures, was a bottomless pit that defied quick, easy solutions. He wanted to know why people like C. B. Lane were allowed to build their careers over the broken bodies and careers of fellow officers. He wanted to know why good people like Hal Cerro and the men and women who had followed him into Colombia had been so casually thrown into a war simply because the polls showed that the American public favored, for the moment, such an action. There were many things that he wanted to know, so many questions.

But in the silence that followed Fulk's question, Scott asked none of them. Instead he looked down at his shoes and shook his head. "No, sir.''

Fulk smiled, reached out, and took Scott's hand. "Well, best of luck to you, Scotty. Say hello to Jan for me and take care of yourself." With that, Fulk turned and walked away, leaving Scott to pull his life together again and get on with the business of soldiering.

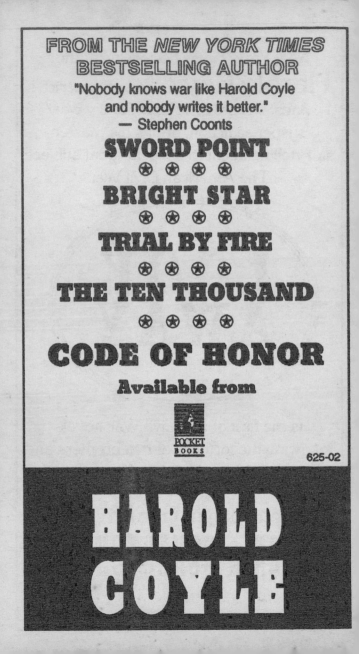